Next Door

A Neighbor's lie

Culdesac

(a chloe fine psychological suspense—books 1, 2 and 3)

NEXT DOOR

(a chloe fine psychological suspense—book 1)

BLAKE PIERCE

Blake Pierce

Blake Pierce is author of the bestselling RILEY PAGE mystery series, which includes thirteen books (and counting). Blake Pierce is also the author of the MACKENZIE WHITE mystery series, comprising nine books (and counting); of the AVERY BLACK mystery series, comprising six books; of the KERI LOCKE mystery series, comprising five books; of the MAKING OF RILEY PAIGE mystery series, comprising two books (and counting); of the KATE WISE mystery series, comprising two books (and counting); and of the CHLOE FINE psychological suspense mystery, comprising two books (and counting).

An avid reader and lifelong fan of the mystery and thriller genres, Blake loves to hear from you, so please feel free to visit www.blakepierceauthor.com to learn more and stay in touch.

BOOKS BY BLAKE PIERCE

CHLOE FINE PSYCHOLOGICAL SUSPENSE MYSTERY

NEXT DOOR (Book #1)

A NEIGHBOR'S LIE (Book #2)

CUL DE SAC (Book #3)

KATE WISE MYSTERY SERIES

IF SHE KNEW (Book #1)

IF SHE SAW (Book #2)

THE MAKING OF RILEY PAIGE SERIES

WATCHING (Book #1)

WAITING (Book #2)

RILEY PAIGE MYSTERY SERIES

ONCE GONE (Book #1)

ONCE TAKEN (Book #2)

ONCE CRAVED (Book #3)

ONCE LURED (Book #4)

ONCE HUNTED (Book #5)

ONCE PINED (Book #6)

ONCE FORSAKEN (Book #7)

ONCE COLD (Book #8)

ONCE STALKED (Book #9)

ONCE LOST (Book #10)

ONCE BURIED (Book #11)

ONCE BOUND (Book #12)

ONCE TRAPPED (Book #13)

ONCE DORMANT (book #14)

MACKENZIE WHITE MYSTERY SERIES

BEFORE HE KILLS (Book #1)

BEFORE HE SEES (Book #2)

BEFORE HE COVETS (Book #3)

BEFORE HE TAKES (Book #4)

BEFORE HE NEEDS (Book #5)

BEFORE HE FEELS (Book #6)

BEFORE HE SINS (Book #7)

BEFORE HE HUNTS (Book #8)

BEFORE HE PREYS (Book #9)

BEFORE HE LONGS (Book #10)

AVERY BLACK MYSTERY SERIES

CAUSE TO KILL (Book #1)

CAUSE TO RUN (Book #2)

CAUSE TO HIDE (Book #3)

CAUSE TO FEAR (Book #4)

CAUSE TO SAVE (Book #5)

CAUSE TO DREAD (Book #6)

KERI LOCKE MYSTERY SERIES

A TRACE OF DEATH (Book #1)

A TRACE OF MUDER (Book #2)

A TRACE OF VICE (Book #3)

A TRACE OF CRIME (Book #4)

A TRACE OF HOPE (Book #5)

Table of Contents

Prologue xi

Chapter One 1
Chapter Two 7
Chapter Three 13
Chapter Four 17
Chapter Five 27
Chapter Six 31
Chapter Seven 37
Chapter Eight 43
Chapter Nine 53
Chapter Ten 56
Chapter Eleven 60
Chapter Twelve 65
Chapter Thirteen 70
Chapter Fourteen 79
Chapter Fifteen 84
Chapter Sixteen 89
Chapter Seventeen 93
Chapter Eighteen 97
Chapter Nineteen 102
Chapter Twenty 106
Chapter Twenty One 113
Chapter Twenty Two 118
Chapter Twenty Three 126
Chapter Twenty Four 129

Chapter Twenty Five 134
Chapter Twenty Six 138
Chapter Twenty Seven 146
Chapter Twenty Eight 151
Chapter Twenty Nine 154
Chapter Thirty 159
Chapter Thirty One 163
Chapter Thirty Two 169
Chapter Thirty Three 172
Chapter Thirty Four 178
Chapter Thirty Five 184
Chapter Thirty Six 190
Chapter Thirty Seven 195

Epilogue 199

Prologue

Chloe sat on the front steps of her apartment building beside her twin sister, Danielle, watching as the police led their father down the front stoop, in handcuffs.

A large cop with a round belly stood in front of Chloe and Danielle. His black skin glistened with sweat as the summer night beamed down on them.

"You girls don't need to see this," he said.

Chloe thought it was a silly thing to say. Even at ten years old, she knew he was simply trying to block out the sight of their father being led into the back of a cop car.

That sight was the least of her problems. She'd already seen the blood at the bottom of the stairs. She'd seen how it was splattered on the bottom step and then soaked into the carpet that led into the living room. She'd seen the body, too. It had been facedown. Her father had tried very hard not to let her see it. But no matter what he did, the sight of all that blood had stuck itself to the walls of her head.

It was what she saw as the fat cop stood in front of her. It was all that she saw.

Chloe heard the door to the police car slam closed. She knew it was the sound of her father leaving them—she sensed, forever.

"You girls okay?" the cop asked.

Neither of them answered. Chloe was still seeing all of that blood at the bottom of the stairs, soaking into the blue carpet. She looked quickly over at Danielle and saw that her sister was staring at her feet. She wasn't blinking. Chloe was pretty sure something was wrong with her. Chloe thought Danielle had seen more of the body, maybe even the really dark spot where all of the blood seemed to have come from.

The fat cop looked up the front stoop stairs all of a sudden. Under his breath, he said in a hissing voice: "Christ, can't you wait? The girls are right here…"

Behind the cop, they brought a body bag out of the building and down the steps. It was the body. The one that had leaked all of that dark red blood on the carpet.

Their mother.

"Girls?" the cop asked. "One of you want to talk to me?"

But Chloe did not want to talk.

Sometime later, a familiar car pulled up behind one of the remaining cop cars. The fat cop had stopped trying to get them to talk and Chloe sensed that he was just there with them so they would not feel alone.

Beside Chloe, Danielle said her first word since they had been brought out to the front stoop.

"Grandma," Danielle said.

The familiar car that had showed up belonged to their grandmother. She got out of the car as quickly as her legs would allow. Chloe saw that she was crying.

She felt a tear sliding down her face but it was not like crying. It felt like something breaking.

"Your grandmother is here," the cop said. He sounded relieved, happy to be rid of them.

"Girls," was the only word her grandmother got out as she came up the stairs. After that, she started to sob and took both of her granddaughters in an awkward embrace.

Oddly enough, it was that embrace that Chloe would remember.

The sight of the blood would become faint. The fat cop faded after just a few weeks, as did the surreal sight of the cuffs.

But for her entire life, Chloe would remember that awkward hug.

And the feeling of something deep inside cracking, and then breaking.

Had her father truly killed her mother?

Chapter One

17 Years Later

Chloe Fine climbed up the stairs of her new home—the home that she and her fiancé had hunted for, for months—and she could hardly contain her excitement.

"That box too heavy?"

Steven dashed up the steps beside her, carrying a box labeled PILLOWS.

"Not at all," she said, hefting her own box, which read DISHES on the side.

Steven set his box down and took hers.

"Let's trade," he said with a smile.

He had been smiling a lot recently. Actually, there seemed to have been a permanent smile on his face ever since she had allowed him to slip an engagement ring on her finger eight months ago.

They marched together up the sidewalk. As they went, Chloe took in the sight of the yard. It wasn't the big sprawling yard she'd always envisioned. In her mind, her house had a big open yard with trees scattered along the back. Instead, she and Steven had settled on one in a quiet neighborhood. But she was only twenty-seven; she had time. Both she and Steven knew that this was not the house they'd grow old in. And something about that made it even more special. This was to be their starter home, the place they would learn the ins and outs of marriage—and maybe where they'd work at having a kid or two.

She could see their neighbor's house quite clearly. The lawns were separated only by a series of tall bushes. The picturesque white porch was almost identical to their own.

"I know I grew up here for the most part," Chloe said. "But it just doesn't feel the same. It feels like a different town."

"I assure you, it's exactly the same," Steven said. "Well, give or take a few new housing developments like the one we are currently homeowners in. Good old Pinecrest, Maryland. Small enough so you'll always run into people you don't want to but just large enough to not have to drive an hour to a grocery store."

"I miss Philly already."

"Not me," Steven said. "No more Eagles fans, no more Rocky jokes, no more traffic."

"All good points," Chloe agreed. "Still …"

"Give it some time," Steven said. "This will feel like home soon enough."

Chloe wished her grandmother was there in that moment to see this house. Chloe was pretty sure she'd be proud. She'd probably also waste no time in firing up the brand new oven in the kitchen in order to bake a celebratory dessert.

But she'd died two years ago, just ten months after Chloe's grandfather died in a car accident. It would have been poetic to think she'd died of a broken heart but that hadn't been the case; in the end, it was a heart attack that claimed her grandmother.

Chloe also thought of Danielle. Right after high school, Danielle had moved away to Boston for a few years. There had been a pregnancy scare, an arrest or two, and several failed jobs. All of that had eventually led her sister back here, to Pinecrest, a few years ago.

As for Chloe, she had gone to college in Philadelphia, met Steven, and started working toward her career of becoming an FBI agent. She had a few classes remaining, but the transition had been smooth. Baltimore was just a half hour drive to the west and all of her credits had transferred without a hitch.

The stars had seemed to align in some majestic way when Steven had managed to land a job in Pinecrest. As much as Chloe joked about not wanting to return to Pinecrest, something inside of her knew she'd always end up back there if even for just a few years. It was a dumb sentiment but she felt she owed it to her grandparents. Growing up, she couldn't get out of this place fast enough and she felt that her grandparents had always taken that a little personally.

And then the perfect house had come along and Chloe had started to love the idea of being back in a smaller town. Pinecrest wasn't tiny at all—a population of about thirty-five thousand made it a comfortable size as far as Chloe was concerned.

Also, she was excited to meet up with Danielle at some point.

But first, they had to finish moving in. The meager belongings she and Steven owned were packed into the back of the U-Haul that was currently parked askew in their small concrete driveway. They were now two hours into unloading the truck, in and out, back and forth, until they could finally see the back of the trailer through the last row of boxes and bins.

As Steven brought in the last of the boxes, Chloe began to unpack. It was surreal to realize that these were items from their separate apartments now being unboxed to share the same space they'd share as a couple. It was a warm feeling, one that made her glance at the ring on her finger with a confident smile.

As she was unpacking, she heard a knock on the front door—the first actual knock at their new home. This was followed by a woman's high-pitched voice saying: *"Hello?"*

Confused, Chloe stopped unpacking and walked to the front door. She wasn't sure what she was expecting to see but it certainly wasn't a face from her past. Strangely enough, that's exactly what she found waiting at the door.

"Chloe Fine?" the woman asked.

It had been eight years, but Chloe recognized the face of Kathleen Saunders easily enough. They'd gone to high school together. It was very dreamlike to see her here, standing at her front door. While not the best of friends in high school, they had been a bit more than casual acquaintances. Still, seeing a face from her past standing in the threshold of her future was so unexpected that it made Chloe feel dizzy for a moment.

"Kathleen?" she asked. "What the hell are you doing here?"

"Living here," Kathleen said with a smile. She had put on quite a bit of weight since high school but her smile was exactly the same.

"Here?" Chloe asked. "In this neighborhood?"

"Yes. Two houses over, to your right. I was coming in from walking my dog and I *thought* it was you. Well, you or your sister. So I came over and asked the man in the back of the U-Haul and he said to come on up and say hello. Is that your husband?"

"Fiancé," Chloe said.

"Well, how small of a world is this?" she asked. "Or… rather, how small of a *town*."

"Yes, I suppose it really is," Chloe said.

"I'd love to stay and chat, but I actually have to go meet with a client in about an hour," Kathleen said. "And besides, I don't want to keep you from unpacking. But listen… there's a block party this Saturday. I wanted to be the first to personally invite you."

"Well, thanks. I appreciate it."

"Hey, really quickly… how's Danielle? I know when she finished up high school she was going through some stuff. Rumor has it that she's living in Boston."

"She *was* in Boston," Chloe said. "But she's actually been back here in Pinecrest for a few years."

"That's so cool," Kathleen said. "Maybe invite her to the block party, too? I'd love to get to catch up with both of you!"

"Likewise," Chloe said.

She briefly looked over Kathleen's shoulder and saw Steven in the back of the U-Haul. He was shrugging his shoulders and giving a squinted up face that seemed to say: *I'm sorry!*

"Well, it was so good to see you," Kathleen said. "I hope to see you at the block party. And if not, you know where I live!"

"Yup! Two houses over, to the right."

Kathleen nodded and then surprised Chloe with a hug. Chloe returned it, pretty sure Kathleen had not been the hugging type back in high school. She watched her old (and new, she supposed) friend wave to Steven as she walked back down to the sidewalk along the street.

Steven came back up the porch steps, carrying the final two boxes. Chloe took the top one off for him and they carried them into the living room. The place was a maze of boxes, bins, and luggage.

"Sorry about that," Steven said. "I didn't know if that would be a welcome guest or not."

"No, it's fine. It was *weird,* but fine."

"She said she was a friend from high school?"

"Yeah. And here we are, living two houses apart. She seemed really sweet, though. She invited us to a block party this weekend."

"That's nice."

"She knew Danielle back in high school, too. I think I'm going to invite her to the party, too."

Steven started opening up one of the boxes, letting out a sigh. "Chloe, we haven't even been here an entire day. Can't we wait before inviting your sister into our lives?"

"We are," she said. "The party is three days away. So we're waiting three days."

"You know what I mean. Danielle has a tendency to make things difficult when they don't have to be."

Chloe *did* know what he meant. Steven had met Danielle four times and each of those occasions had been awkward—and neither of them had a problem saying as much. Danielle came with a particular set of issues, none of which were well suited for being around people she was unfamiliar with. So she supposed Steven was right. Why invite her to a block party where she wouldn't know anyone?

But the answer was easy: *Because she's my sister. She's been alone and hurting these last few years and as lame as it sounds, she needs me.*

A quick flash of the two of them sitting on those apartment stairs tore through her head like a desert wind.

"You knew I'd reach out to her eventually," Chloe said. "I can't very well be living in the same city and continue to shut her out of my life."

Steven nodded and came to her. "I know, I know," he said. "But a man can dream."

She knew there was a bit of barbed truth to the comment but she also recognized the joking tone. He was giving in, not wanting to let a discussion about her sister ruin moving day for them.

"It could be good for her," Chloe said. "Getting out and socializing ... I think I can bring it out of her if I can become something of a regular fixture in her life."

Steven knew the complex history between the two of them. And although he made no secrets about not being particularly fond of Danielle, he had always lovingly supported Chloe and understood her concern for her sister.

"Do what you think is best for her, then," he said. "And after you call her, come help me put the bed together in the master bedroom. I've got plans for it later."

"Oh, you do?"

"Yeah. All this moving has wiped me out. I'm exhausted, I'm going to sleep so hard ... and it's going to be so hot."

They both cracked up and found their way into each other's arms. They shared a lingering kiss that suggested maybe their first night in their new home *would* put the bed to good use. But for now, there were the mounds and mounds of boxes to unpack.

Plus, a potentially uncomfortable phone call to make to her sister.

It was a thought that filled her with equal amounts of joy and anxiousness.

Even as her twin sister, Chloe was never sure what to expect from Danielle. And something about being back in Pinecrest made her sadly certain that things with Danielle had likely only gotten worse.

Chapter Two

Danielle Fine popped a No-Doz, swallowed it down with a warm, flat Coke, then opened up her underwear drawer and dug down on the right side for the sluttiest thing she could find.

Danielle thought about Martin. They had been dating for about six weeks now. And while they had both decided that they were going to take it slow, Danielle had lost her patience. She had decided she was going to throw herself at him tonight; stopping at second base every time they saw one another was making her feel like a stupid teenager who didn't know what she was doing.

She knew what she was doing. And she was pretty sure Martin did, too. By the end of the night, she'd know for sure.

She ended up selecting a lacy black pair that barely covered the front and was practically nonexistent in the back. She thought about which bra to wear but decided on not wearing one at all. She and Martin weren't exactly dress-up types and besides, she knew she was very much lacking in the chest; there was no expensive bra in the world that was going to be of much help. Besides… Martin had told her he liked how her boobs looked when their shapes were visible through a T-shirt.

They were meeting early, catching an early dinner so they could make the 6:30 movie in time. The mere fact that they were doing dinner and a movie rather than cheap drinks and a trip back to his house for a painful make-out session was a point in her favor. She wondered if Martin was the kind who liked to feel that he was being a gentleman.

Six weeks with the guy… you should already know that kind of shit, she thought as she slid on the panties.

She got dressed in front of the full-length mirror on her bedroom wall. She tried on a few shirts before deciding to play it chill. She settled for a black, slightly tight T-shirt and a very basic pair of jeans. She was not the sort of girl who owned a bunch of dresses or skirts. She normally put on the first thing she grabbed in the morning. She knew she'd been blessed with her mother's good looks and, because she also managed to have immaculate skin, she usually went without much makeup, too. Her dyed black hair and intense brown eyes pulled the entire package together; in the blink of an eye she could make the transformation from innocent and sweet to aggressively sexy. It was one of the reasons she had never really cared about her small boobs.

With a quick look into the mirror, seeing the same figure, face, and T-shirt band logo that had all been there as a teen, Danielle was ready to head out to meet Martin. He was a greaseball of sorts, only not the kind that hung out in motor garages or racetracks. He'd toyed with amateur boxing at one point, or so he said. He had the body to make her believe it (another reason she was losing her patience) and currently worked as a freelance IT specialist. But, like her, he didn't take life too seriously and enjoyed drinking a lot. So far, they seemed like a perfect match.

But still. Six weeks without sex. She felt a lot of pressure. What if he refused? What if he really wanted to keep taking it slow and she just couldn't wait?

Sighing, she went to the fridge. To calm her nerves, she grabbed a Guinness from the fridge, popped the top, and took a swig. She realized she was putting alcohol on top of her No-Doz but shrugged it off. She'd certainly put her body through much worse.

Her phone rang. *If he's calling to cancel on me, I'll kill him, she thought.*

When she saw that it wasn't his name on the display, she relaxed. Yet when she saw it was her sister, she slumped her shoulders. She knew she might as well answer it. If she didn't Chloe would call her back fifteen minutes from now. Persistence was one of the few traits they had in common.

She answered the call, skipping hellos as she usually did. "Welcome back to Pinecrest," she said, as monotone as possible. "You officially a resident again?"

"Depends on if you're asking me or all of these unpacked boxes," Chloe replied.

"When did you get in?" Danielle asked.

"This morning. We finally got everything out of the U-Haul and are trying to get through the boxes and figure out where everything needs to go."

"Do you need some help?" Danielle asked.

The brief silence on the other end of the line suggested that Chloe had not been expecting this sort of generosity. Truth be told, Danielle had only asked because she knew Chloe would not take her up on it. Or, rather, Steven would not *want* Chloe to take her up on it.

"You know, I think we're good right now. I wish I would have thought to call you when we were unpacking all of the damned boxes."

"Maybe I wouldn't have offered then," Danielle said with dry sarcasm.

"Anyway, listen. Do you remember Kathleen Saunders from high school?"

"Vaguely," Danielle said, the name bringing to mind a bright and smiling teenaged face—the kind of face that always got a little too close when speaking.

"Turns out she lives in my neighborhood. Just two houses down. She came by a while ago and said hello. She also invited Steven and I to a block party this weekend."

"Wow, one day in and you already sound domesticated as hell. You buy a minivan yet?"

There was another brief silence; Danielle figured Chloe was trying to decide if the comment was a venomous barb or just a joke. "Not yet," she finally answered. "Need the babies first. But about that block party … I think you should come. Kathleen was asking about you."

"I'm flattered," Danielle said, not flattered at all.

"Look, we're going to end up hanging out anyway," Chloe said. "We may as well do it sooner rather than later to avoid all the phone tag. And I'd really like for you to see the house."

"I might have a date that day," Danielle said.

"Like a real date or just one of your poor one-night guys?"

"A real date. You'd like him, I think." That was bullshit. She was pretty sure Chloe wouldn't approve of Martin at all.

"You know how we can find out? Bring him, too."

"Ah Jesus, you're insufferable."

"Is that a yes?" Chloe asked.

"That's a *we'll see.*"

"I'll take it. How are you, Danielle? Everything going good?"

"Yeah, I suppose. Work is going well, and I'm about to go out on a date with the same guy for the twentieth time."

"Ooh, he *does* sound special," Chloe joked.

"Speaking of which, I need to get going," Danielle said.

"Sure. I'm going to text you our address. I hope you come to the block party. Three o'clock, this Saturday."

"No promises," Danielle said and then took a very long gulp from her Guinness. "Bye, Chloe."

She hung up without waiting for Chloe's goodbye. She had no idea why, but the conversation had been draining.

A block party, she thought with bitter sarcasm. *I know we don't talk all that often, but you'd think she'd know me better than that ...*

As this thought crept through her mind, she started to think about her mother. That's where her mind usually went whenever she was irritated with Chloe. As she thought of her mom, her hand went to her neck. Finding the area there bare, she hurried back through her small apartment and into the bedroom. She went to the jewelry box on her dresser and pulled out her mother's silver necklace—just about the only tangible thing she owned that had once belonged to Gale Fine. She placed it around her neck and tucked the simple little pendant beneath her shirt.

Feeling it against her skin, she wondered how often Chloe thought of their mother. She also tried to remember the last time they had both talked about what had happened that morning seventeen years ago. She knew they were both haunted by it, but really, did anyone ever enjoy talking about ghosts?

Now with only ten minutes left before she needed to leave to meet with Martin, she chugged down the rest of her beer. She figured she could just go and be a little early. She headed for the front door to do just that but then stopped in her tracks.

Directly beneath the front door, there was an envelope. It had not been there when she was speaking on the phone with Chloe.

She walked to it and carefully picked it up. It felt like watching herself in a movie because she had done this before. This was not the first note that had come.

The envelope was unmarked. No name, no address, no markings of any kind. She opened the flap, which had not been adhered to the rest of the envelope. She reached inside and found a simple square of cardstock paper, a little larger than a playing card.

She took the note out and read it. And then read it again.

She tucked it back into the envelope and carried the envelope to the desk along the far wall of the living room. She placed it there with the other four notes, all with similar messages.

She stared at them for a moment, fearful and confused.

Her palms grew sweaty and her heart started to beat harder.

Who's watching me? she wondered. *And why?*

She then did what she usually chose to do when something bothered her. She ignored it. She pushed this most recent note out of her mind, along with the simple message it carried, and headed out the door to meet Martin.

As she walked out of the building, the note's message flashed in her mind in little shocks, almost like a neon sign.

I KNOW WHAT REALLY HAPPENED.

It made no sense, but then again, it seemed to make all the sense in the world.

She looked down at her own shadow on the city sidewalk and couldn't help but walk a little faster. She knew she could not escape a problem by putting it in her personal rearview mirror, but it at least made her feel better.

I KNOW WHAT REALLY HAPPENED.

Her feet seemed to agree, wanting to stop walking, to run back and try to make sense of the letters—to call someone. Maybe the cops. Maybe even Chloe.

But Danielle only walked faster.

She'd managed to put her past behind her, for the most part.

Why would these letters be any different?

Chapter Three

"So you're still sticking with the chicken, huh?"

It was such an innocent question at its core, but it sent a flare of anger through Chloe. She lightly bit at the inside of her lip to keep any stray remarks from slipping out.

Sally Brennan, Steven's mother, was sitting across from her with an aged Stepford Wives sort of smile on her face.

"Yeah, Mom," Steven said. "It's food … food I probably won't even eat because of all the nerves. If someone wants to complain about the food at my wedding reception, then they can go home. Maybe grab some Taco Bell on the way."

Chloe squeezed Steven's hand under the table. He'd apparently picked up on her irritation. It was rare that Steven ever stood up to his mother, but when he did he came out looking like a hero.

"Well, that's not a very nice attitude to have," Sally said.

"He's right," Wayne Brennan, Steven's father, said from the other end of the table. The wine glass beside him was empty for the third time of tonight's dinner and he was reaching for the bottle of red sitting near the center of the table. "Honestly, no one gives a damn about the food at the reception. It's the booze they're looking forward to. And we'll have an open bar, so …"

They left the conversation hanging, the sour look on Sally's face making it clear that she still thought chicken was a bad choice.

But that was nothing new. She'd bitched and complained about nearly every decision Chloe and Steven had made. And she never failed to off-handedly remind them who was paying for the wedding.

As it turned out, Pinecrest was not only once again home to Chloe, but it was home to Steven's parents as well. They had moved there five years ago, technically just outside of Pinecrest in a smaller town called Elon. In addition to Steven's job, it had been one of the reasons Chloe and Steven had decided to move to Pinecrest. He worked as a software developer for a government contractor and had been offered a position that had been too good to turn down. As for Chloe, she was currently interning with the FBI while working on her master's in Criminal Justice. Because of the close proximity to FBI headquarters in Baltimore, it had all just made perfect sense

Chloe was already regretting living so close to Steven's parents, though. Wayne was all right most of the time. But Sally Brennan was, to put it mildly, an uppity bitch who loved to stick her nose in places it had no business being.

The Brennans as a couple were nice enough people, both retired, well-to-do and mostly happy. But they also coddled Steven. As an only child, Steven had admitted to Chloe numerous times that his parents had spoiled the hell out of him. Even now, when he was twenty-eight, they treated him far too much like a child. And part of that came across in an attitude of overprotectiveness. It was the main reason Chloe internally cringed whenever they wanted to go over the wedding plans.

Which, unfortunately, they apparently wanted to do over dinner. Sally had wasted no time in getting to the dinner choice for the reception.

"So how's the house?" Wayne asked, just as eager as Chloe to move away from the topic of the wedding.

"It's great," Chloe said. "We'll make it through the maze of boxes in a few days."

"Oh, and get this," Steven said. "A woman that Chloe went to high school with lives right down the street—like two houses down. Isn't that crazy?"

"Maybe not as crazy as it seems," Wayne said. "This city is just too damned small. You're bound to stumble over *someone* you know at some point."

"Especially in those neighborhoods where the houses are all on top of each other," Sally said with a smirk, making a not-so-subtle jab about their choice of location.

"Our houses aren't right on top of each other," Steven said.

"Yeah, we have a decent-sized yard," Chloe added.

Sally shrugged her shoulders and took another mouthful of wine. She then seemed to think about her next comment, maybe even almost deciding to keep it in, but letting it out anyway.

"Your high school friend isn't the only one in Pinecrest, right?" she asked. "Your sister lives around here too, if I remember correctly."

"Yes, she does."

She spoke the answer firmly but without being rude. Sally Brennan had never made any secrets about her distaste for Danielle—even though they had only ever crossed paths twice. Sally had the misfortune of being one of those clichéd bored housewives who lived for scandal and gossip. So when she found that Chloe had a sister with a rocky and dark past, she'd been both appalled and intrigued.

"Let's not dwell there, Mom," Steven said.

Chloe wished this made her feel defended but if anything, it made her feel slighted. Usually when the topic of Danielle came up, Steven ended up siding with his mother. He did have the good sense to know when to shut up but his mother usually did not.

"Will she be the maid of honor?" Sally asked.

"Yes."

Sally didn't roll her eyes at the comment, but her facial expression showed her feelings about it.

"She *is* my sister," Chloe said. "So yes, I have asked her to be my maid of honor."

"Yes, it makes sense," Sally said, "but I always thought the maid of honor should be chosen carefully. It's a big honor and responsibility."

Chloe had to grip the edge of the table to keep from coming back with a hard-edged reply. Noticing her tension, Steven did his best to salvage the situation. "Mom, give it a rest," he said. "Danielle will do fine. And even if something should go wrong, I'll make sure everything is covered. This is my wedding, Mom. I'm not going to let anything bad happen."

This time it was Chloe who nearly rolled her eyes. It was once again his way of standing up for her but of also not irritating his parents. Just once, Chloe would like for him to *truly* defend Danielle. She knew that

Steven had no real problems with her but that he was doing his best to pacify his mother's uneasiness of her. It was a little disgusting.

"Enough of this nonsense," Wayne said, reaching out for a second helping of the roasted potatoes. "Let's talk football. Now, Chloe . . . you're a Redskins fan, right?"

"God, no. Giants."

"Just as bad," Wayne said with a laugh.

And just like that, the uneasiness of the night was swept under the rug. Chloe had always valued Wayne's boldness in being able to ignore his wife's bitchiness, pushing along to some another benign topic whether she was done or not. It was a trait Chloe wished Steven had picked up from his father.

Still, as the night went on, Chloe couldn't help but wonder if Sally's worries were legitimate. Danielle was not the sort to dress up, stay quiet, and get in front of people. Danielle would be stepping out of her comfort zone at the wedding and Chloe herself had wondered how it might go over.

As those worries floated through her head, she thought of the little girls from so many years ago, sitting on the front stoop as the body bag was carried out of their apartment. She could easily recall the blank look in Danielle's face. She knew something had snapped in her at that moment. That, overnight, she had lost her sister.

And she suspected that, from that moment on, Danielle would never be the same again.

Chapter Four

It was raining when Chloe and her field work instructor arrived on the scene. She felt very minor league as she stepped out of the car into the drizzling rain. Because she was an intern having to go alongside her instructor in shifts with other interns, they were not given high-profile cases. This one, for instance, sounded as if it were a typical domestic abuse case. And while the details of the case did not sound very graphic or brutal, the very words *domestic abuse* made her cringe.

She had, after all, heard those words a lot after her mother had died. Her instructor must have been aware of her past—of what had happened with her parents—but had mentioned nothing of it this morning as they had headed out.

They were in the town of Willow Creek on that first day, a small town about fifteen miles outside of Baltimore. Chloe was interning with the FBI to eventually become part of the FBI's Evidence Response Team, and as they walked toward the simple two-story house, the instructor even let her take the lead. Her instructor was Kyle Greene, a forty-five-year-old agent who had been taken out of basic field work when he had torn his ACL while chasing down a suspect. He'd never healed properly from the injury and had been given the option to serve as an instructor and mentor of sorts for interns. He and Chloe had only spoken twice before this morning, having met via FaceTime a week ago to get to know one another and then two days ago, during her ride from Philly to Pinecrest.

"One thing before we go inside," Greene said. "I held this from you until now because I didn't want you dwelling on it all morning."

"Okay…"

"While this *is* a domestic abuse case, it is also a homicide case. When we get inside, there's going to be a body. A relatively fresh one."

"Oh…" she said, unable to contain her shock.

"I know it's more than you were expecting. But there was some discussion when you came in. Discussions to maybe let you peek behind the curtain right from the start. We've been toying with the idea of letting the interns have more responsibilities, letting them stretch out a bit more. And based on your dossier, we thought you'd be a prime candidate to test that out. I hope that's okay with you."

She was still taken aback, unable to form any real response. Yes, it was more responsibility. Yes, it meant more eyes would be on her. But she had never backed down from a challenge and she didn't intend to start now.

"I appreciate the opportunity."

"Good," Greene said, his tone indicating that he never had a doubt.

He waved her on to follow him as they walked to the porch and up the stairs. Inside, were two agents conversing with the coroner. Chloe did her best to ready herself for the scene and while she thought she'd done a pretty good job, she was still shaken when she saw a woman's legs sticking out from behind the kitchen island.

"So I need you to take a walk around the body," Greene said. "Tell me what you see—both in terms of the body and the surroundings. Walk me through your processing."

Chloe had seen a few dead bodies in the course of her interning; When she lived in Philadelphia, they had not been all that hard to come by. But this was different. This one felt a little too close to home—a little too familiar. She stepped behind the kitchen counter and looked down at the scene.

The victim was a woman who looked to be in her thirties. She had been hit in the head with a very solid object—most likely the toaster that lay shattered in pieces several feet from her. The brunt of the impact had been along the left side of her brow, hard enough to shatter the ocular cavity, making her eye look like it could very well slide out onto the floor at any moment. A pool of blood surrounded her head like a halo.

Perhaps the oddest thing about her was that her sweatpants were pulled down to her ankles and her underwear pulled down to her knees.

Chloe hunkered down closer to the body and looked for any other details. She saw what looked like two small scratch marks on the side of her neck. They looked to be fresh and in the shape of fingernails.

"Where's the husband?" she asked.

"In custody," Greene said. "He's admitted to it and already told the police what happened."

"But if it's a domestic dispute, why call the FBI in?" she asked.

"Because this guy was arrested three years ago for beating up his first wife so bad that she went to the ER. But she didn't press charges. And his home computer was flagged two weeks ago for potential snuff videos."

Chloe took all of that information and applied it to what she was seeing. She interlocked it all like a puzzle and spoke her theories out loud as they came to her.

"Given this man's history, he was prone to violence. Extreme violence, if the crushed toaster is any indication. The sweatpants pushed down and underwear not quite all the way down indicates that he was trying to have sex with her here in the kitchen. Maybe they *were* having sex and she wanted it to stop. Scratch marks on her neck indicate that the sex was rough and either consensual at first or entirely unwanted."

She paused here and studied the blood. "The blood looks to be relatively fresh. I'd estimate the murder to have occurred within the last six hours."

"And what would your next steps be?" Greene asked. "If we *didn't* have this guy in custody right now and there was an active search for him, how would you follow up?"

"I'd check for evidence of intercourse. We could get his DNA and get a match. While waiting for those results, though, I'd look for things like wallets upstairs in the bedroom, hoping for a driver's license. Of course, that's if it wasn't already suspected that it was the husband. If that were the case, we could get the name from the address."

Greene smiled at her, nodding. "That's right. You'd be surprised how many rookies miss the fact that it's sort of a trick question. You're in the guy's house, so you'd already know his name. But if it *wasn't* suspected that it was the husband, you're exactly right. Also … Fine, are you okay?"

The question took her by surprise—mainly because she *wasn't* okay. She had zoned out, staring at the blood on the kitchen tile. It pulled her all the way back into her past, staring at a pool of blood drying into the carpet at the bottom of the stairs.

Without warning, she started to grow faint. She braced herself against the kitchen island, afraid she was going to puke. It was alarming and embarrassing.

Is this what I can look forward to at any remotely gruesome crime scene? At any scenes that remotely resemble what happened to Mom?

She could hear Sally in the back of her head, one of the first things she'd ever said to Chloe: *I don't know how a woman would make an exceptional agent. Especially one with your traumatic background. I wonder if that sort of stress comes home with you ...*

"Sorry, excuse me," she mumbled. She pushed herself off the island and ran back to the front door. She nearly fell down the porch stairs on her way to the lawn, sure she was going to throw up.

Thankfully, the fates spared her that particular embarrassment. She took a series of deep breaths, concentrating so intently on them that she almost didn't notice when Greene came quietly down the porch steps.

"There are certain cases that get to me, too," he told her. He kept a respectable distance, letting her have her space. "There are going to be scenes that are much worse. Sadly, after a while, you sort of become desensitized to it."

She nodded, as she had heard all of that before. "I know. It's just ... this scene brought up something. A memory I don't like dealing with."

"The bureau has exceptional therapists to help agents process through things like this. So never think you're alone or that something like this makes you less of an agent."

"Thanks," Chloe said, finally managing to stand upright again.

She realized that she suddenly missed her sister very badly. As morbid as it seemed, fond thoughts of Danielle would flood through her whenever memories of the day their mother died surfaced in her head. It was no different now; Chloe could not help but think of her sister. Danielle had been through a lot over the years—a victim of circumstance as well as her own poor decisions. And now that Chloe lived so close, it seemed unthinkable that they should remain so distant.

Sure, she'd invited Danielle to the block part this weekend, but Chloe found herself unable to wait that long. And Chloe suspected that she wouldn't even come.

Suddenly, she knew: she had to see her now.

Chloe didn't know why she was so nervous when she knocked on Danielle's door. She knew Danielle was in; the same car she'd had as a teenager was parked in the apartment complex parking lot, still boasting the band stickers. Nine Inch Nails. KMFDM. Ministry. Seeing the car and those stickers brought a pang of nostalgia that was more sadness than anything else.

Has she really not grown up at all? Chloe wondered.

When Danielle answered the door, Chloe saw that she had not. Or, rather, it did not look like it in terms of appearance.

The sisters looked at one another for a period of two seconds before they finally moved in for a brief hug. Chloe saw that Danielle still dyed her hair black. She was also still sporting the lip ring, protruding from the left corner of her mouth. She was wearing a slight bit of black eyeliner and was decked out in a Bauhaus T-shirt and ripped jeans.

"Chloe," Danielle said, breaking into the faintest of smiles. "How have you been?"

It was as if they had seen one another just the day before. That was fine, though. Chloe had not exactly been expecting any sentiment from her sister.

Chloe stepped into the apartment and, not caring much how Danielle would receive it, gave her sister another hug. It had been a little over a year since they had seen one another—and about three since they had actually embraced one another like this. Something about the fact that they now lived in the same city seemed to have bonded something between them—it was something Chloe could feel, something she knew would not need to be vocalized.

Danielle returned the hug, albeit lazily. "So … you're … what?" Danielle teased.

"I'm good," Chloe said. "I know I should have called but … I don't know. I was afraid you'd find some excuse for me not to come by."

"I might have," Danielle admitted. "But now that you're here, come on in. Excuse the mess. Well, actually don't excuse it. You know I've always been messy."

Chloe laughed and when she entered the apartment she was surprised to find the place relatively tidy. The living area was sparsely furnished, just a couch, a TV and TV stand, a coffee table, and a lamp. Chloe knew the rest of the place would be the same. Danielle was the sort of person who lived on only the minimal amount of belongings. The exception, if she hadn't changed since her teen years (and it seemed she hadn't) was music and books. It made Chloe nearly feel guilty for the spacious and elaborate home she had recently purchased with Steven.

"Want me to put on some coffee?" Danielle asked.

"Yeah, that would be great."

They walked into the kitchen, again only boasting the necessities. The table was clearly something that had been scoured from a yard sale, given at least a bit of dignity with a ruffled tablecloth. Two lonely chairs sat at it, one on either side.

"Are you here to bully me about your block party?" Danielle asked.

"Not at all," Chloe said. "I was interning today and came to this crime scene that … well, it brought everything racing back."

"Ouch."

Silence hung between them as Danielle set the coffeemaker up. Chloe watched as her sister moved about the kitchen, a bit creeped out at how much it seemed she had not changed. She could very well be looking at the seventeen-year-old girl who had left home with the hopes of starting a band, despite their grandparents' wishes. Everything looked the same, right down to the sleepy expression.

"Have you heard anything about Dad lately?" Chloe asked.

Danielle only shook her head. "With your job, I thought you'd be the one to hear anything. If there was anything to hear."

"I stopped checking a while ago."

"Cheers to that," Danielle said, covering a small yawn with the back of her hand.

"You look tired," Chloe said.

"I am. Only, not like *sleepy* tired. The doctor had me on these mood stabilizers. It screwed with my sleep. And when you're a bartender who usually doesn't get home until after three in the morning, the last thing you need is a medicine that fucks with your sleep."

"You said the doc *had* you on them. Are you not taking them anymore?"

"No. They were fucking with my sleep, my appetite, and my libido. Ever since I stopped, I feel much better … just tired all the time."

"Why were they prescribed in the first place?" Chloe asked.

"To deal with my nosy sister," Danielle said, only half-joking. She waited a beat before giving an honest answer. "I was starting to get easily depressed. And it would come out of nowhere. I dealt with it in some … pretty dumb ways. Drinking. Sex. *Fixer Upper*."

"If it was for depression, you should probably get back on them," Chloe said, realizing as she said it just how intrusive she was being. "What do you need a libido for anyway?" she asked with a snicker.

"For those of us that *aren't* about to get married, they're pretty important. We can't just roll over in bed and get laid whenever we want."

"You never had problems getting guys before," Chloe pointed out.

"And I still don't," she said, bringing mugs of coffee to the table. "It's just too much work. Especially lately. This new one. A serious guy. We decided to take it slow … whatever."

"That's the only reason I'm marrying Steven, you know," Chloe said, trying to get into the joking mood right along with her. "I got tired of having to go out and work for sex."

They both had a laugh at this. It should have felt natural to laugh and smile together again but something about it felt forced.

"So what's up, sis?" Danielle asked. "It's not like you to drop by. Not that I'd know, as we haven't had that opportunity in almost two years."

Chloe nodded, remembering the one time they had actually spent together in the last handful of years. Danielle had been in Philly for some concert and had crashed at her apartment. They'd talked a bit, but not much. Danielle had been hammered and passed out on her couch. Their mom had come up in the conversation, as had their dad. It was the only time Chloe had ever heard Danielle openly speak about wanting to go visit him.

"That scene this morning," Chloe said. "It made me think of that morning outside of the apartment. I kept thinking about the blood at the bottom of the stairs and it got to me. I thought I was going to puke. And I'm *not* that kind of person, you know? The scene itself was pretty vanilla compared to some of the stuff I've seen. It just hit me hard. It made me think of you and I had to see you. Does that make sense?"

"Yeah. The mood stabilizers … I'm pretty sure all of the depression was coming from nightmares I was having about Mom and Dad. I'd have them and then be in a funk for days. Like, not wanting to get out of bed because I trusted no one else out in the world."

"Well, I was going to ask how you cope with it when you think of what happened, but I guess I know the answer, huh?"

Danielle nodded and looked away. "Meds."

"You okay?"

Danielle shrugged but she may as well have flipped Chloe her middle finger. "We're together for about ten minutes and you already go there. God, Chloe … haven't you learned to live your life without dragging that shit up? If you recall, when you called to tell me that you were moving to Pinecrest, we decided to not talk about it. Water under the bridge, remember?"

Chloe was taken aback. She'd just watched Danielle go from dry and sarcastic to absolute furious in the blink of an eye. Sure, the topic of their parents was a sore subject, but Danielle's reaction was bipolar in nature.

"How long have you been off the meds?" Chloe asked.

"Fuck you."

"How long?"

"Three weeks, give or take a few days. Why?"

"Because I've only been here for about fifteen minutes and I can already tell that you need them."

"Thanks, doc."

"Will you start taking them, please? I want you at my wedding. Maid of honor, remember? As selfish as it might seem, I'd like for you to actually enjoy it. So would you please just start taking them again?"

The mention of maid of honor did something to Danielle. She sighed and then relaxed her posture. She was able to look at Chloe again and while she was still angry, there was something warm there as well.

"Fine," she said.

She got up from the table and went to a little decorative wicker basket on the kitchen counter. She pulled out a prescription bottle, shook out a pill, and swallowed it down with her coffee.

"Thank you," Chloe said. She then pressed a bit more, sensing something else amiss. "Is everything else okay?"

Danielle thought about it for a moment and Chloe caught her casting a quick glance toward her apartment door. It was very brief but there was fear there—Chloe was sure of it.

"No, I'm good."

Chloe knew her sister well enough to know not to press it.

"So, what the hell is a block party, anyway?" Danielle asked.

Chloe laughed; she had nearly forgotten Danielle's ability to drop a subject and start another one with all the grace of an elephant in a china shop. And just like that, the subject was changed. Chloe watched her sister to see if she ever looked back to the door with that bit of fear in her eyes, but it never happened again.

Still, Chloe felt that there was something there. Maybe after some time together, Danielle would fess up.

But to what? Chloe wondered, casting a glance at the front door herself.

And it was then that she realized that she really didn't know her sister at all. There were parts of her that seemed very much like the gothed-out seventeen-year-old she'd last known so well. But there was something new to Danielle now… something darker. Something that needed meds to control her moods, to help her sleep and function.

It occurred to Chloe in that moment that she was scared for her sister and she wanted to help in any way she could.

Even if it meant digging into the past.

But not now. Maybe after the wedding. God only knew what sort of arguments and mood swings talking about the death of their mother and incarceration of their father would bring up. Still, Chloe felt the ghosts of her past stronger than ever while sitting there with Danielle and it made her wonder just how haunted Danielle had been by it all.

What kind of ghosts lurked around in Danielle's head? And what, exactly, were they telling her?

She sensed, the way she did a coming storm, that whatever Danielle was suppressing, it would all eventually involve her. Her new life. Her new fiancé, her new house. Her new life.

And it would all lead to nothing good.

Chapter Five

Danielle sat on her couch, reclining back against Martin, her leg draped over his, and she was very aware that she was not wearing underwear beneath her pajama shorts. Not that it would matter; somehow, he had refused her last night, despite no bra and the skimpy little panties. It seemed Martin was taking this whole taking-things-slow thing seriously.

She was also beginning to think that he was either just being a gentleman or was not sexually attracted to her. The latter was hard to believe, though, because she'd literally felt the proof of his attraction grinding against her legs and hips on the multiple occasions they'd made out.

She tried not to let it bother her. While she was indeed sexually frustrated, there was something to be said about finally finding a man who wanted more than just sex.

Tonight was a great example. They'd chosen to remain low-key, just sitting around her apartment and watching a movie. Beforehand, they had discussed Martin's day. Yet as an assistant manager at a print shop, there were only so many details to discuss. It was like listening to someone explain how paint dried. As for Danielle, she hated talking about her day. As a bartender at a local restaurant, her days were boring. She sat around and read most of the time. The nights were filled with stories to share but by the time she managed to get some sleep and woke up around one in the afternoon, she never wanted to go over them.

Once the niceties were over, they *had* kissed a bit, but it was all very PG. Again, Danielle found that she had no problem with that. Besides, ever since Chloe's visit, she had been bummed out. The mood stabilizers likely wouldn't even kick in until she took her second pill right before bedtime.

Thanks to Chloe's visit, Danielle had been thinking about her mother, her father, and the childhood that had passed her by like a warped flicker of film. Really, all she wanted was to be held by Martin—something it pained her to admit to herself.

They'd settled on one of her DVDs, popping in *The Shawshank Redemption* and curling up together on the couch like a couple of nervous and inexperienced middle school kids. On a few occasions, his hand would slip a little lower than her shoulder and she wondered if he was trying to make a move. But he remained respectable, which was both refreshing and infuriating all at once.

She also noticed that on a few occasions, his phone would ding. It was sitting on her coffee table right in front of them but he elected not to check it. At first, she assumed he was just being polite and not infringing on their date time. But after a while—what Danielle assumed had been at least seven or eight little dings—it started to get obnoxious.

Just as Tim Robbins locked himself in the warden's office and played some opera music over the PA for the prisoners of Shawshank Prison, it dinged one more time. Danielle looked to the phone and then to Martin.

"Are you going to check on that?" she asked. "Someone must really need you for something."

"Nah, it'll be okay," he said. He pulled her closer and stretched out. They were lying side by side. If she wanted, she could easily kiss his neck. She looked at the exposed space there and thought about it. She wondered how he might react if she kissed him there, maybe softly ran her tongue along the side of his neck.

The phone dinged again. Danielle let out a little chuckle and, without any kind of warning, sprang across Martin's chest. She grabbed the phone and pulled it to her chest. Stalled at his lock screen, she said, "What's your pass—"

Martin violently yanked the phone away from her. He looked more surprised than furious. "What was that about?" he asked.

"Nothing," she said. "Just playing around. You can check your phone while you're with me. I don't mind. If it's another girlfriend or something, though, I might have to go bitch-mode on her."

"I don't need you to oversee my phone usage," he snapped.

"Um, hold on. There's no need to get crazy about it. I was just playing around."

He sneered at her and shoved the phone in his pocket. He sighed and sat up, apparently no longer interested in cuddling with her.

"Ah, you're one of those guys, then," she said, still trying to find the line between joking around and being a little persistent. "Guard your phone like it was your dick or something."

"Leave it alone," he said. "Don't be weird about it."

"Me? Martin, I thought you were going to break my wrists getting it out of my hands."

"Well, it's not your phone now, is it? Don't you trust me?"

"I don't know," she said, raising her voice. "We haven't been going out all that long. God, there's no need to get so fucking defensive."

He rolled his eyes at her and looked at the TV. It was a dismissive gesture, one that pissed her off. She shook her head and, doing her best to keep her playful façade front and center, she quickly straddled him. She reached down as if going for his zipper but then angled for the pocket he had put the phone in. With her other hand, she started to tickle his right side.

He was taken aback, clearly unsure how to respond. Yet the moment her fingers found the edge of his phone, he seemed to flip a switch somewhere. He grabbed her arm and pulled it up in a vise-like grip. He then shoved her down on the couch, not yet letting go of her arm. It hurt like hell but she was not about to let him hear her scream out in pain. The speed and strength he showed reminded her that he had once trained to be an amateur boxer.

"Whoa, let go of my fucking arm!"

He did, looking down at her in surprise. The look on his face made her think he had not intended to get that rough with her. He had surprised even himself. But he was also angry; the furrowed brow and trembling shoulders were evidence of that.

"I'm going to go," he said.

"Yeah, good idea," Danielle said. "And don't even bother calling again unless it's going to start with an apology."

He shook his head—whether at himself and his actions or at her, Danielle wasn't sure. She watched him quickly walk for the door, closing it firmly behind him. Danielle sat on the couch, looking toward the door for several moments as she tried to figure out what exactly had happened.

No interest in screwing me and a surprise temper on him, she thought. That dude might be more trouble than he's worth.

Of course, she'd always been drawn to that kind of man.

She looked at her arm and saw red splotches where he had grabbed her and shoved her down. She was pretty sure they'd bruise. It wouldn't be the first time a guy had put bruises on her but she had really not seen it coming from Martin.

She toyed with the idea of chasing after him to see what had gotten into him. But instead, she stayed on the couch and watched the movie. If her past had taught her anything, it was that men simply weren't worth chasing after. Not even the ones who seemed too good to be true.

She finished the movie by herself and called it a night. As she shut off all the light, she felt like she was being watched—like she was not alone. She knew this was ridiculous, of course, but still could not help but look back to her front door, where the letter had appeared yesterday—and several times before—as if out of nowhere.

She remained on the couch and watched the door, almost expecting another letter to slide through the bottom. And twenty minutes later, when she got up and started getting ready for work, she did so with every light in the apartment on.

Slowly, a creeping paranoia churned within her. It was a familiar one, a feeling that had become something like a close friend over the years—a very close friend ever since those letters started arriving.

She thought of the pills and wondered for a moment if this were all in her head. Everything. Including the letters.

Was any of this real?

She couldn't help reaching back into her past, reminding herself of the darkness she thought she had escaped.

Was she losing her mind again?

Chapter Six

Chloe sat in the waiting room, looking at the sparse reading selection on the coffee table. She had visited two different therapists following her mother's death but had not really understood the purpose of those visits. Now, though, at the age of twenty-seven, she knew why she was here. She had taken Greene's advice and called the on-hand bureau therapist to talk out her reaction to yesterday's crime scene. Now she found herself trying to recall the offices she had visited as child.

"Ms. Fine?" a woman called from the other side of the room.

Chloe had been so deep in her own thoughts that she hadn't heard the door to the waiting room open. A pleasant-looking woman waved her back. Chloe got to her feet and tried her best not to feel like a failure as she followed the woman down a hallway and toward a large office space.

She thought back to what Greene had told her yesterday as they had shared coffee. It was still bright and shining in her mind because it had been the first bit of real advice a seasoned agent had ever given her during her very young career.

"I saw this therapist several times my first year. My fourth crime scene was a murder-suicide. Four bodies in all. One was a three-year old kid. Rattled the hell out of me. So I can tell you without hesitation ... therapy works. Especially if you start it at this stage of your career. I've seen agents think they're hot shit and don't need the help. Don't be one of those, Fine."

So no ... needing a therapist did not make her a failure. If anything, she hoped it might make her stronger.

She entered the office and saw an older gentleman of about sixty or so sitting behind a large desk. A window behind the desk revealed a small topiary outside, butterflies darting to and fro. His name was Donald Skinner, and he had been doing this for more than thirty years. She knew this because she had Googled him before deciding to make the appointment. Skinner was very prim and proper; he seemed to expand slightly, filling the room a bit more as he walked over to greet her.

He gestured toward a comfortable-looking armchair in the center of the room. "Please," he said. "Make yourself comfortable."

She sat down, clearly nervous. She knew she was probably trying a bit too hard to try to hide it.

"Ever done this before?" Skinner asked.

"When I was much younger," she said.

He nodded as he took a seat in an identical chair positioned in front of hers. When he sat, he hefted his right knee up on his right leg and folded his hands atop them.

"Ms. Fine, why don't you tell me about yourself… ending with why you are here today."

"How far back?" she asked, meaning it as a joke.

"For now, let's just focus on the crime scene yesterday," Skinner answered.

Chloe took a moment to think and then started. She held nothing back, even delving back into her past a bit to paint that picture for him as well. Skinner listened intently and now mulled over everything he had just been told.

"Tell me," Skinner said. "So far, out of the crime scenes you've visited, was this the grisliest?"

"No. But it was the grisliest thing I'd been allowed to actually *see.*"

"So you are willing to fully admit that it was this event from your past that caused you to react the way you did?"

"I suppose. I mean, it's never happened before. And even when it sort if *tries* to bother me, I can stomp it out pretty easily."

"I see. Now, are there any other factors that might have come into play? It's a new city. A new instructor, a new house. There's a lot of change."

"My twin sister," Chloe said. "She lives here in Pinecrest. I figured maybe the idea of seeing her again after a year or so… maybe that did it in addition to the scene being so similar."

"That could very well be the case," Skinner asked. "Please forgive me asking such a simple question, but did the murder of your mother lead you to a career with the FBI?"

"Yes. I knew by the time I was twelve, this is what I wanted to do."

"And what about your sister? What does she do?"

"She's a bartender. I think she enjoys it because she only has to be social for a few hours of the day and then she can go home and sleep until noon."

"And does she remember that day the same way you do? Have you spoken about it?"

"We have, but she won't go into great detail. When I try, she shuts me down pretty much right away."

"So go into those details with me right now," Skinner said. "It's clear you need to discuss it somehow. So why not with me… an impartial party?"

"Well, like I said earlier, it seemed like a pretty basic yet unfortunate accident."

"Yet your father was arrested for it," Skinner pointed out. "So to me, as someone not familiar with the case, I don't lean towards accident. It makes me curious how you can see it so clearly as such. So let's go over it. What happened that day? What do you remember?"

"Well, it was an accident *caused* by my father. That's why he was arrested. He didn't even lie about it. He was drunk, Mom made him mad, and he pushed her."

"I've given you the chance to go into greater detail and that's all I'm getting?" Skinner asked in a friendly tone.

"Well, some of it is blurry," Chloe admitted. "You know how past memories are sort of fogged over with rose-colored glasses?"

"Indeed. So… I want to try something with you. Because this is the first time we've met, I'm not going to try hypnosis. I *am* going to try a proven form of therapy, though. It's what some refer to as timeline therapy. For today, I hope it might help to dig further details from that day—details that are right there in your mind but have sort of been tucked away because you're afraid to see them. If you continue to see me, this sort of therapy will eventually help us to pluck the fear and anxiety that arise in you whenever you're faced with that day. Does that sound like something you'd be willing to undergo today?"

"Yes," she said without hesitation.

"Okay. Good. So... let's begin with where you were sitting. I want you to close your eyes and relax. Take a moment or two to clear your head and get comfortable. Give me a tiny nod when you are ready."

Chloe did as she was asked. She allowed herself to sink back into the chair. It was a very comfortable faux leather armchair. She felt that she was still tensing her shoulders, uncomfortable with being so vulnerable in front of someone she had never met. She sighed deeply and felt her shoulders go limp. She nestled into the chair and listened for the hum of the air conditioner. She found it, listened to its droning, and then gave a nod. She was ready.

"Okay," Skinner said. "Out on that stoop with your sister. Now, even if you can't remember the sort of shoes you were wearing that day, I want you to imagine that you are looking at your feet. Look down at your shoes. I want you to focus on them and nothing else—just the shoes you were wearing that day when you were ten years old. You and your sister out on the stoop. But keep your eyes only on those shoes. Describe them to me."

"Chuck Taylors," Chloe said. "Red. Scuffed up. Big floppy laces."

"Perfect. Now study the laces. Really zone in on them. Then I want your ten-year-old self to stand up without looking away from those laces. I want you to stand up and walk back to where you were before discovering the blood on the carpet at the bottom of the stairs. I need you to go back a few hours. But don't look away from those laces. Can you do that?"

Chloe knew she was not hypnotized but the instructions seemed so simple. So basic and easy. She stood up inside her mind and walked back into the apartment. When she did, she saw the blood, saw her mother.

"Mom is right there at the bottom of the stairs," she said. "Lots of blood. Danielle is somewhere, crying. Dad is pacing."

"Okay. But just look at your shoelaces," Skinner instructed. "And then see if you can go back farther. Can you do that?"

"Yeah. Easy. I'm with Beth... a friend of mine. We just got back from a movie. Her mom took us. She dropped me off and stayed there on the curb until I got inside. She always did that, not pulling away until she saw me go inside."

"Okay. So watch those shoelaces as you get out of the car and walk up the stairs. Then take me through the rest of the afternoon."

"I went inside the building and then up to the second floor, where our apartment was. When I walked to the door and pulled out the keys to unlock it, I hear Dad inside. So I just walked in. I closed the door and headed for the living room but saw Mom's body. It was at the bottom of the stairs. Her right arm was pinned beneath her. Her nose looked all smashed up and there was blood everywhere. Most of her face was covered with it. It was all over the carpet, right there at the bottom of the stairs. I think Dad might have tried to move the body…"

Chloe trailed off here. She was finding it hard to focus on those ratty old shoelaces. She knew the scene she was relaying far too well to ignore it.

"Danielle is standing right there, right over her. She has some blood on her hands and her clothes. Dad is talking really loudly into the phone, telling someone to come quickly, there's been an accident. When he gets off, he looks at me and starts crying. He threw the phone across the room and it shattered against the wall. He came over to us and hunkered down. He said he was sorry… he said there was an ambulance on the way. He then looked at Danielle and we could barely understand him through the tears. He said Danielle needed to go upstairs. She needed to change her clothes.

"She did, and I followed her. I asked her what had happened but she wouldn't talk to me. She wouldn't even cry. Eventually, we started to hear sirens. We sat there with Dad, waiting for him to tell us what would happen next. But he never did. The ambulance arrived, then the police. A friendly policeman took us outside on the stoop and stayed there with us until Dad was brought out in handcuffs. Until they brought Mom's body out…"

Suddenly, the vision of the busted up shoelaces was gone. She was back on the stoop, waiting for her grandmother to pick them up. The overweight cop was with her and although she didn't know him, he made her feel safe.

"You okay?" Skinner asked.

"Yeah," she said with a nervous smile. "The part about Dad throwing the phone ... I had totally forgotten about that."

"How's the remembered sight of it make you feel?"

It was a hard question to answer. Her father had always been quick to temper but seeing him do it in the wake of what had happened to her mother almost made him seem weak and vulnerable.

"It makes me feel sad for him."

"Have you blamed him for your mother's death ever since it happened?" Skinner asked.

"It honestly just depends on the day. Depends on my mood."

Skinner nodded and broke his statue-like posture. He got to his feet and looked down at her with a reassuring smile.

"I think we're good for today. Please call me if you experience this sort of reaction to a crime scene again. And I would like to see you again soon. Can we set up an appointment?"

Chloe thought about it and nodded. "We can, but I have a wedding coming up soon and we have all these meetings with florists and bakers ... it's a nightmare. Can I call you with a date?"

"Of course. And until then ... stick closely to Agent Greene. He's a good man. And he was right to direct you to me. Please know that this early in your career, having to come to someone like me to deal with your issues means nothing. It is not a reflection of your talents."

Chloe nodded. She knew this but it was still nice to hear Skinner say it. She got up and thanked him for his time. As she walked out the door and into the waiting room, she saw her father throwing the phone. But then there was a comment he'd made—one she had not forgotten but had become muddied until today.

He had looked at Danielle and, with something far too close to urgency in his voice, had said: "Danielle, honey ... go change your clothes. There's not much time before they get here."

That comment rolled through Chloe's head for most of the remainder of the afternoon, chilling her while also poking at a locked door she had managed to ignore for the last seventeen years.

Chapter Seven

Danielle woke up at eight o'clock, feeling as if she had not slept well at all. She'd gotten in from work at 2:45 and collapsed into bed at 3:10. She usually had no problem sleeping until well after eleven—sometimes even later—but when her eyes opened at 8:01 that morning, she could not go back to sleep. Truth be told, she really hadn't slept very well ever since she'd known that Chloe was coming back into town. It had felt like her past was slowly following her and it would not stop until it swallowed her whole.

Cranky and tired, Danielle showered and then ate breakfast. She did it all with Skinny Puppy's *Too Dark Park* album playing in the background. As she placed her breakfast dishes in the sink, she realized she'd have to go grocery shopping today. Most days, this did not bother her. But there was the occasional day where she felt like going out into public was a mistake... that people were watching her, waiting for her to fuck something up and point fingers.

She also feared that any time she went out allowed the letter writer a chance to follow her. One of these days, she figured the writer would stop playing around with her and just kill her.

Maybe today would be that day.

She drove to the grocery store, already knowing full well that this was going to be one of those days... one of those days where she was going to be afraid of everything. One of those days where she would constantly be looking over her shoulder. She drove quickly, even running a red light along the way, wanting to get the trip over.

Ever since Danielle started receiving the disturbing notes under her door, she found it anxiety-inducing to be in a public place for very long. It was far too easy to imagine the person who had been writing those letters to be following her. Even at work, she wondered if the writer was sitting at the bar, having just received a drink from her. When she picked up her Chinese food, was he following her, waiting to finally jump her as she walked back to her car?

Even after she had arrived safely at her destination, hurrying into the grocery store and practically racing a cart with a squeaky wheel down the aisle, the worry was there. The letter writer could be there with her, mirroring her steps on the next aisle over, maybe getting a good look at her across the produce section or across the cereal aisle.

It was a very real fear that flashed through her head the day following the surprising turn of events with Martin. The paranoia sank into her, causing her to lower her head and push up her shoulders. If someone wanted to see her face, they'd need to be very purposeful about it, to the point of stopping her and hunching down.

She hated that she was like this. She'd always faced these kinds of issues, which was why most of her dating relationships rarely lasted more than a month. She knew she'd developed a reputation for being a bit of a slut during her first tenure here in Pinecrest, but it hadn't been because she enjoyed sleeping around. It was just that by the time she was comfortable enough with a guy to sleep with him, she'd start to assume the worst about him. She'd end the relationship, take some time to recover, and then start again.

She'd gotten a bit better when she'd moved back to Pinecrest a few years ago. She'd left Boston and felt like she was retreating…but that was okay. She was at least retreating to somewhere familiar. The hardest thing to get used to was the stagnant dating scene. It had been okay at first, although she'd managed to ruin every single relationship she'd started. That's why the fight with Martin had struck her so hard.

Of course, there was the downside to Pinecrest. Far too many people remembered her and Chloe. They remembered how the poor little Fine girls had ended up living with their grandparents after their mother had died and their father had been taken to prison.

"Danielle, is that you?"

She turned toward the voice, startled. She'd been so lost in her thoughts that she'd managed to fully expose her face while reaching up for a box of Froot Loops. She found herself looking at a face from her past—a woman who looked terribly familiar but whom she couldn't quite place.

"Do you not remember me?" the woman asked, on the verge of entertained and offended. She was probably forty-five, maybe fifty. And no, Danielle did not remember this woman.

"I guess you *don't* remember me," the woman said. "I guess you were only thirteen or fourteen the last time I saw you. I'm Tammy Wyler. I was a friend of your mom's."

"Oh yeah, sure," Danielle said. She did not remember the woman at all but the name did sound familiar. Danielle assumed she was one of the family friends who had visited her grandparents in the year or two following the death of her mother.

"I almost didn't recognize you," Tammy said. "Your hair is … darker."

"Yeah," Danielle said unenthusiastically. She supposed the last time Tammy Wyler had seen her, she'd only just started her full rebellion mode. Back then, at thirteen or fourteen years of age, she'd usually opted for neon pink hair with black stripes. Now it was raven black, a style she realized was old and used up but seemed to still fit her perfectly.

"I always knew you came back around here but well … I don't know. I just never really got around to looking you up after you moved. You went to Boston or something for a while, right?"

"Right."

"Oh, so I hear Chloe is back in town, too. Bought a new house out near Lavender Hills, right?"

"Yeah, she's back," Danielle said, quickly approaching her tolerance limit for small talk and bullshit.

"I heard through the grapevine that she lives just a few houses away from a girl you guys went to high school with. I actually live about two streets over from her."

Poor Chloe, Danielle thought.

"Oh, and did she tell you about the block party?" Tammy asked, apparently unable to keep her mouth shut for any more than three seconds at a time.

"She did," Danielle said. She was hoping Tammy would take her short responses as a cue that she really wasn't the sort to just chat it up in the aisle of the grocery store.

There was a brief silence between the two of them where Tammy *did* seem to piece this together. She looked around awkwardly and bowed out with as much grace as she could. "Well, I hope you can make it. It was good running into you, Danielle."

"Yeah, you too," Danielle said.

She wasted no time in hunching her shoulders and casting her head down as she pushed her cart farther down the cereal aisle. Her need to get out of the store and back to her apartment was stronger than ever—now not just because of her usual paranoid feelings, but because of the awkward encounter with Tammy Wyler.

She rushed through the rest of her shopping, nearly colliding with an elderly lady in the dairy section. She went through the self-checkout (because why deal with chatty cashiers if you didn't have to) and hurried out to her car. When she was back out in the fresh air, she felt a little better. Of course, maybe the man sending the letters was sitting in one of the cars in the parking lot. Maybe he had been following her in the grocery store, listening to her speak awkwardly to Tammy.

She put her bags in the back seat and started the car. Before she had a chance to back out of her parking spot, her phone rang. She saw Martin's name on the display and didn't hesitate to answer. If he was calling to argue, she was game. If he was calling to apologize, she'd be open to that, too. Truth be told, she just liked the idea of being on the phone with someone she knew in that moment.

She answered with a simple, "Hey."

"Hey, Danielle," Martin said. "Look, I owe you one hell of an apology for last night. And not for just for getting rough. I shouldn't have been so weird about my phone. It's just that things are sort of going to hell at work. That's what the texts were. I knew it the moment they started coming in. I didn't want to face it last night. Does that make sense?"

"It does. But what doesn't make sense is why you didn't just tell me that last night."

"Because I'm stupid," he said. "I didn't want you to know that my job might very well be on the chopping block. And then when you got really playful about it, I just took it the wrong way. Danielle … I have never hurt a woman. Please believe me on that. And putting my hands on you like that last night … God, I'm so sorry." She said nothing. Her arms had bruised up a bit and she *had* felt a bit in danger. Still, she could hear what she thought was genuine sadness in his voice.

"Danielle?"

"I'm here," she said. "Just … I wish you would have told me all of this before it got to the point it did."

"I know. Please … can you forgive me?"

She knew she would. She was simply trying to think of what she could do to turn things in her favor. She smiled at the idea that came to her and couldn't help herself.

"Well, this PG relationship is coming to a stop. You're going to meet me at my apartment tonight and we're going to make out. I'm not going to sleep with you yet but … well, there's going to be touching."

"Um … okay. I can do that," he said, clearly confused yet appreciative.

"That's not it. My sister just moved into town. I told you that, right?"

"Yeah."

"Well, it's some swanky uptight neighborhood. The kind that has block parties. She's invited me to a block party this weekend. I want you to come with me."

"Oh. Okay. I can do that."

"Good," she said. "I'll see you tonight, then."

She ended the call just like that. She liked the idea that he had no idea how to respond to her. She also liked that she basically had control of him now—not in any sort of devious way, but just so that she could feel a little more comfortable around him.

Feeling a bit better, the paranoia now just a little seed of worry in the back of her head, she headed home. And she was delighted to find that she was excited for tonight. It had been a very long time since she'd actually *wanted* a man's hands on her.

That, plus the quickly fading paranoia, made her wonder if maybe Martin might be the right man for her after all. He seemed to be changing all sorts of things about her. Of course, he knew very little about those things and she'd keep it that way for as long as she could.

She continued home, starting to wonder just what in the hell you were supposed to wear to a block party.

It was almost enough to drive away the spike of paranoia that had firmly latched itself into her earlier that morning and had remained on her in the grocery store.

Almost.

She grabbed her phone and dialed up Chloe. She didn't even allow her sister time to say *Hello* before she started speaking.

"This block party… .can I bring a date?"

"… Yes, of course," Chloe said, clearly stunned.

"I'll see you tomorrow, then."

And with that, she hung up the phone, wondering what the hell she had just gotten herself into.

Chapter Eight

Chloe was pruning a head of broccoli when the doorbell rang. She knew right away that it was Danielle. She was quite nervous about this but, at the same time, happy to see something as stable as an actual boyfriend in her sister's life. Steven, meanwhile, was skeptical. He figured the boyfriend would be someone just like Danielle, creating an even tenser environment with two people to worry about.

Chloe had managed to shrug off Steven's attitude toward Danielle for most of their four years together but now that the wedding was getting closer, it was really starting to annoy her. But that was an argument for another day.

Chloe wiped her hands off on a dish towel and walked to the door. She took a steadying breath before she answered it. She hated to sway toward Steven's line of thinking but she was slightly worried about what Danielle would look like.

When she answered the door and found her sister somewhat made up and striking, she nearly did a double take. The black hair was put up into a cute little bun in the back. She was wearing a slight bit of makeup—just enough to help her cheeks glow—and had thankfully decided against band T-shirts or her standard pseudo-goth look. She *was* wearing black, but it was a semi-dressy tank top with delicate straps. Her tattoo showed along her upper back but that wasn't too distracting. The jeans she wore surprised Chloe the most; they were basic dark denim and quite tight, showing off her curves in a way Chloe had never seen before.

"Danielle, you look amazing," Chloe said.

"Yeah, don't get used to it." She stepped aside and nodded to the man who had come with her. "This is Martin."

"Pleased to meet you," Martin said, extending his hand.

Chloe shook it and noticed for the first time that he was dressed basically how she'd expected Danielle to show up. His T-shirt was wrinkled and his cargo shorts had a noticeable tear underneath one of the pockets. He wore a tattered pair of flip-flops with well-worn bands. His hair looked like it hadn't been washed in a few days. He looked tired and out of sorts. Chloe couldn't help but wonder if he was high. And if not high, almost certainly a user. She dreaded the moment when Steven met him.

"This house is enormous," Danielle said as she stepped through the foyer and into the living room.

"Yeah, it does feel big," Chloe said. "We're nearly unpacked. I think once all the crap is out of the boxes, it might not feel so big."

The sunlight was reflecting off of the polished hardwood floors as she led Danielle and Martin into the kitchen. Chloe bit back a tiny smile, enjoying the feeling of sort of showing off in front of Danielle. There was no malice in the feeling, but more of a basic sense of pride.

"Got kids?" Martin asked.

Wow, Danielle really doesn't talk about me, Chloe thought. "No," she answered. "Not yet and no time soon."

"Then why all the empty space?" Martin asked.

She was taken off guard by the nearly rude question but kept her cool. "Because you never know. We may have one someday, and we may have five."

"Whoa," Steven said as he came in through the door that connected the kitchen and the back deck. "Five?"

"You never know," Chloe said with a smirk.

"Oh, I'm pretty sure," Steven said. He then looked at Danielle and was genuinely taken off guard. "Danielle, you look great!"

"Thanks, Steven. Steven, this is Martin," she said, making introductions.

"Yeah, nice to meet you," Steven said. Chloe could tell that he had already judged Martin based on his appearance. And that was fine with her; she'd basically done the same thing, too.

"Based on what I know about Danielle," Martin said, "I didn't think her sister would be the block party type."

"Yeah, we were never really the same," Danielle said.

"Oh, that's for sure," Chloe said. "Different at just about every level you can think of."

"And what type did you think her sister would be?" Steven asked, taking an almost defensive stance beside Chloe.

"I don't know, man. Laid back, I guess?"

It was clear Steven had something else to say but had the good sense to bite it back. He nodded briskly to Danielle and said: "Good to see you, Danielle."

With that, he grabbed a beer from the fridge and headed back out onto the deck.

It would figure, Chloe thought. *The one time Danielle decides to be as civil as she knows how to be, her boyfriend turns out to be a prick. And the sad thing is, I don't think he even knows it. Maybe he's as socially awkward as Danielle. Maybe she finally met the right man, the perfect match.*

"So," Danielle said, doing her best to ease the tension, "Chloe, do you remember a really annoying woman named Tammy Wyler?"

Chloe thought about it for a moment and shrugged. She was still working the broccoli as she tried to pin the name. "Sounds familiar. One of Grandma's friends, maybe?"

"One of *Mom's* friends, or so she said. I ran into her in the grocery store today. She knew you had moved here. I think she lives a few streets over. She's coming to the block party, too."

Chloe shook her head with a smile. "Man… I forgot how quickly word travels around a place like this."

The sisters shared a knowing and slightly uncomfortable look, smiling at one another. Martin, meanwhile, looked a little uncomfortable and clearly out of his element. He was looking to the door that led to the back deck, as if wondering what he'd said to piss Steven off.

"So," Chloe said as she dumped the broccoli into a bowl with dressing and other ingredients. "You guys ready for the party?"

"I don't know," Danielle said. "I'm not really well-versed in uppity block parties."

"Just smiling, nodding, and getting drunk, right?" Martin asked.

Chloe forced out a chuckle, deciding that she did not like Martin at all. *Oh God,* she thought. *This was a mistake, wasn't it?*

Maybe it was. But it was too late to go back on it now. All she could do was mix up her broccoli salad and hope for the best.

As much as Chloe hated to admit it, she thought Danielle's lack of enthusiasm for the block party was on point. They walked together in a loose little group, Chloe and Steven in the lead with Danielle and Martin close behind. Chloe hadn't been quite sure what to expect, but it wasn't what she was walking through, that was for sure.

The women, for the most part, were dressed in gorgeous sundresses. Not only that, but there were women who were easily pushing fifty who were wearing tight and revealing outfits—nothing trashy, but enough to catch the eye of any man in the vicinity. There were glasses of wine everywhere, and trendy high-dollar craft beers, which Martin helped himself to right away.

Some people had set up lawn chairs and umbrellas at the foot of their driveway while others had opened up their entire garages for the party. Some people blared Bob Marley from their porches and decks while others opted for Jack Johnson. It was like a little fair right in the middle of the neighborhood.

Danielle quickly stepped up to Chloe, walking by her side. "So this is far too swanky for me. I'm going to take advantage of the free booze and then I think Martin and I are going to split."

"Stop it," Chloe said, hoping Danielle was just trying to be funny. "You haven't even been here for ten minutes."

When she saw Danielle smiling, she was relieved. Danielle was trying—she was *really* trying to not only appease her, but to have fun. Even when they were approached by two different women who recognized them from high school, Danielle did her best to seem social. She wasn't chatty with them—nor did Chloe expect her to be—but she did remain mostly civil.

As they walked through the party and made introductions, Chloe's agent-side took over a bit. Some of these people seemed to live the very definition of privileged upper-class Americans. The wives rolled their eyes at their husbands a lot. A few men and women who passed one another on the arm of someone else shared knowing looks. Chloe couldn't help but wonder how many affairs were actively taking place in Lavender Hills.

But at least it all looks good on the surface, she thought ironically. She sighed and looked over at her sister.

"Thanks for this," Chloe said as they stepped away from the second acquaintance from high school. "I know how difficult and boring it is for you."

"Well, just as long as you know … oh, and also … Tammy Wyler, dead ahead. Twelve o'clock."

Chloe looked ahead and was surprised to find that she *did* recognize the woman who had spotted them and was hurrying over. There were two other women with her, all of whom looked to be middle-aged.

"Beware," Danielle said from behind her. "This woman likes to *taaalk*."

"This is where I hop off the train," Steven whispered in her ear. "There's a lawyer friend of mine over there that I need to catch up with."

Before Chloe could make any kind of abandonment joke, Steven was gone. Danielle and Martin remained by her side. It made Chloe feel stranded while reminding her of just how antisocial Danielle typically was.

Keep it together for just a little while longer, sis. Please …

"Chloe Fine!" Tammy Wyler said as she approached. "My gosh, you've grown up."

"Hi, Mrs. Wyler," Chloe said.

Tammy waved the name away and shook her head. "Gosh, no! Just Tammy, please. So how are you liking the neighborhood?"

"It's nice. Very quiet, very quaint."

"Oh, it's so exciting to have you here. Now, where's this fiancé of yours?"

"He's mingling with some friends. Don't worry—you'll meet him soon enough."

Tammy looked back and forth between Chloe and Danielle, a beaming smile on her face. "Even though the hair is obviously different, you two look so eerily alike," she commented. "My goodness, you both look just like your mother."

"Yes, Grandma always made it a point to tell us that," Chloe said.

Something about Tammy's attitude was off-putting. She was cheerful in the same way Kathleen Saunders was cheerful—almost annoyingly so. But there was something very fake about it, too. She supposed it had to do with Danielle being there. People had never really known how to take Danielle and these older and seemingly snobby women would be no exception. To them, Danielle was likely nothing more than just a scar on the otherwise beautiful face of their generic little neighborhood.

"I was so sorry to hear about your grandmother's passing," Tammy said. "I regret not making it to the funeral but I was in France with my daughter when it happened."

"Oh, that's okay," Danielle said.

"Sort of lovely how it happened so shortly after your grandfather passed, though," Tammy said. "I guess they just couldn't stand to be apart."

"Yeah, it seemed fitting," Chloe said. But she was thinking: *Oh my God, I bet this is eating into Danielle like acid.*

"I thought you should both know that I think of Gale often. We weren't very close—not best friends or anything like that. But we knew each other well enough. She was beautiful and *so* smart. We were in a book club together and the way she pulled things apart… man, everyone rolled their eyes at her. She basically ruled over the Pinecrest Public Library Book Club."

"I remember her being a bit of a bookworm," Chloe said.

"Yeah," Danielle said. "Always had her nose stuck in a book. I used to steal her Danielle Steel books and look for the juicy parts."

Tammy placed an arm around the shoulders of one of the other women who had come over with her. "Girls, I don't know if you remember this lady, but this is Ruthanne Carwile. She and Gale were practically best friends when they were in school."

"Sure were," Ruthanne said. "I even babysat the two of you on more than a few occasions."

As with Tammy, there was something in Ruthanne's look that frustrated Chloe. She could not put her finger on it. It was like these women not only knew their past, but were still using it to form opinions of the Fine sisters. She also hated when people she barely knew talked to her about her mother by using her name. She had never understood why, though.

It was more than just poorly hiding their feelings now. Now it seemed almost mysterious … like they were hiding something. And Ruthanne even looked a little anxious.

"Holy shit!" Danielle exclaimed, out of nowhere. "I remember you! We used to watch cartoons at your house. You had all these videotapes with old cartoons."

"That's right," Ruthanne said, her anxious look replaced with delight. "And you loved Woody Woodpecker."

Martin had a laugh at this. Danielle elbowed him in the ribs and gave him a look that could have sliced through steel.

"I tell you," Ruthanne said. "I know your mother would love to see that the two of you ended up back in the same town. She loved you both so much. Man, I wish you could have seen that woman when she was younger. In her early twenties, she had men tripping over one another for a chance to date her. And *funny …"*

The smile on Chloe's face was genuine. She'd always loved to hear stories about her mother, even the exaggerated ones that their grandmother used to tell. She was about to respond when Steven's hand fell on her shoulder. Without even bothering to wait for a break in the conversation, he interjected himself.

"Hey, babe … come over here. There's someone I want you to meet."

"Hold on. These women knew my mom."

"Oh, this will only take a second."

Two things became abundantly clear to Chloe in that moment. One was something she had already learned somewhat—that whenever Steven wanted something, it was, to him, the most important thing on the planet at that time. The second was that Tammy and Ruthanne were giving Steven side-eyed glances and were embarrassed for her. Which, in turn, embarrassed Chloe.

So she could start a scene and argue or she could excuse herself from these ladies and go with Steven.

As it turned out, she didn't have to do either. There was another factor that she had not even expected, one that made her cringe when it presented itself.

Martin leaned in and whispered something to Danielle. Only Martin was not the best at whispering, apparently. Everyone heard it: Danielle, Chloe, Tammy, Ruthanne, and Steven.

"What, does he think he has her trained like a dog or something?"

Martin seemed to know at once that he had been too loud. Everyone looked at him awkwardly. Tammy and Ruthanne took a step back, looking at one another as if the other had a plan to get out of this awkward situation. Yet he didn't seem to care.

"What the hell did you say?" Steven asked, taking an aggressive step toward him.

Martin did not back up. He simply held his arms up in a show of surrender. A bottle of beer dangled in his left hand. Steven reached out and slapped it away. It shattered on the pavement. The sound of it caught the attention of others who were standing nearby.

When Chloe saw Steven rushing forward, her instinct was to reach out and take his arm. She could easily toss him to the ground. Some of the most basic of her physical training gave her about three different ways to take him down before things escalated. But she stopped when she thought of the embarrassment that would cause him. So instead, she let him go and was helpless for a moment as she watched

"Steven," Chloe hissed. "Stop it."

She'd only seen him this aggressive once before. It had been at an Eagles game in Philly when he nearly got into a fight with someone cursing loudly behind them. Seeing him like that had frightened her a bit but it had also showed her that he was passionate about certain things.

Martin moved so quickly that it took everyone by surprise. He threw a perfectly formed punch, clipping Steven's face, causing him to spin to the right.

Martin then grabbed Steven's arm, wrenched it forward, and then expertly applied a headlock. She was shocked when she saw the deadly pressure Martin was applying.

"Steven!" Chloe cried.

"Whoa, wait, Martin…" Danielle said.

Both women rushed to stop the squabble. A few other nearby men were rushing to assist as well. Seeing the fight getting worse and potentially out of hand, Chloe could no longer simply stand by. She had no idea what had gotten into Steven and while she was irritated with Martin, he was a stranger. She thought she knew Steven and, quite frankly, had no idea he was capable of such temper and violence. And right now, he was in a very dangerous situation. She wondered what kind of training Martin had because a random bum off the street would not be capable of moving so quickly and with such poise.

Chloe's training kicked in, and she, with the help of two middle-aged men, managed to haul Martin off of Steven.

The area below Steven's right eye was swelling and his head was flushed and red from the pressure of the headlock. Worse, though, was his look of humiliation.

She then looked at Martin, wanting to assess the damage that had been done. But he looked unharmed.

Embarrassed at Steven's actions, Chloe then looked at her sister. She was worried what this scene might do to their relationship, how it might push them even farther apart.

She saw the slight smile on Danielle's face and something about it jarred her. Had she actually enjoyed watching the fight happen? Had she *liked* watching Steven get bested in front of all of their new neighbors?

"Danielle?" she said softly.

Danielle blinked and looked away from Martin. She met Chloe's eyes and the smile disappeared. Instead, she looked around at the gathered crowd that had come to view the fight and then immediately looked to the ground. Her eyes went blank, her shoulders slumped.

"Come on, Danielle," Martin said as he got to his feet. "These fuckers have had enough of a show for today."

Martin started storming off. Danielle followed slowly behind. She gave Chloe only the slightest glance of acknowledgment as she left. Chloe saw a lot of the scared and shut-off ten-year-old sister she worried so much about when they were kids, after their mom had died. It was like looking directly into the face of a ghost.

And, like any worthwhile ghost, it frightened Chloe quite badly.

"Okay, that's enough," Steven said. "Show's over, everyone."

It then occurred to Chloe that more than fifty people were still watching the scene even as Danielle and Martin walked away. She looked down at the pavement and reached out for Steven's hand, ready to head back home. But he yanked his hand away and stormed off ahead of her.

Chloe did not lift her eyes. She followed after Steven and although she continued to look at the street beneath her feet, she could still feel people's stares on her. And although she hated to admit it, she hated Danielle in that moment… for bringing Martin, for associating with men like him.

But you invited her, she told herself. You wanted her here. What does that say about you?

She thought of that smile on Danielle's face. It carried some sort of secret… maybe one that Danielle wasn't even aware of.

And as far as Chloe was concerned, that was the scariest thing of all.

Chapter Nine

Chloe entered the front door less than twenty seconds after Steven. She felt tiny darts in her back all the way home from the stares of the people they would have as neighbors for the foreseeable future. When she closed the front door behind her, she saw Steven sitting on the couch, looking at the floor and clenching his fists. He was fuming.

"Talk to me, Steven," Chloe said.

"Who the hell acts like that when you've first met someone?" he asked. "Who acts like that, ever?" When it was clear that Chloe intended to give no answer, he kept going on. "The good news is that your sister found another outcast that's perfect for her. Neither one of them knows how to act when they're around other civilized people. What a joke."

"That's not quite fair," Chloe said. "Danielle at least tried to dress up a bit for today. And if you noticed, she was actually pretty civil."

"Yeah, compared to her usual weird antics and antisocial behavior, she was *charming*."

"Steven, I know you're pissed and maybe you even have a right to be. But Danielle had nothing to do with this."

"Of course she did! She brought him here, didn't she?"

"Yes, she did. But she did not whisper in his ear. She did not ask him to throw that punch, and also—you're the one who knocked the beer bottle out of Martin's hand. Sorry, but you can't blame either of those on her."

"Oh my God, Chloe. Please don't tell me you're taking her side on this."

"I'm taking no one's side. What I *do* need to know is where the hell this violent outburst of yours came from. I've never seen you so angry before. And I've *never* seen you throw a punch. It was scary, Steven."

"I know. I just… you know, as bad as it sounds, I don't care. They were embarrassing me. We have to live around these people, Chloe. This is our life now. And we're here less than a week and your oddball sister and her stupid boyfriend have essentially ruined that for us."

"That's a little overdramatic," Chloe said. "Even for you."

"Oh, is it? Well, while I'm being overdramatic, let me go ahead and tell you this: you need to find a new maid of honor because there's no way in hell I'm letting her anywhere *near* the wedding."

Chloe set her glass of water down and did her best to let her tremors of anger subside. They'd only ever had two serious arguments—a third one currently progressing before her very eyes—but on each of those occasions, she had to remind herself that she was not in a class or interning on a case. She could not grill him in the same way she had sometimes grilled people as part of her training.

"Steven, I'm afraid you have no say in that. She's my sister. She *will* be my maid of honor. You have no say in it. And neither do your overprotective parents."

"I think they *should*," he said. "They are, after all, footing the bill."

Chloe drew in a sharp breath, taking it in as an attempt to keep any harsh words from coming out of her mouth. In the end, she simply picked up the glass of water with her left hand and then showed Steven the middle finger of her right hand. She stormed out of the kitchen and to the back deck. She slammed the door behind her, almost hoping she might break something inside in the process.

She sat down in one of their deck chairs beneath the decorative patio umbrella. As she seethed, she could hear the commotion of the block party on all sides—the murmur of conversation and the occasional outburst of muffled laughter.

Probably talking about how crazy the new family in the neighborhood is, she thought. Probably laughing about the fight between Steven and Martin.

"Screw 'em," she said quietly to herself.

But even as she said that, trying to pretend that she did not care, there was one moment from the event that stuck out in her mind. It was that thin and nearly sinister little smile she had caught on Danielle's face.

It was somehow worse than the blank and distant expression she had gotten used to during their teenage years.

Something dark and a little evil seemed to be lurking behind that smile—as if she had enjoyed the fact that Steven and Martin were fighting. As if she had enjoyed the idea of causing chaos in the midst of such a perfect little suburban paradise.

Chloe tried to get the image out of her head but it went nowhere. Instead, she found herself picturing that smile looking out into a crowd from her position as a maid of honor in several weeks.

It was *not* a pretty picture.

She let out a deep sigh as she sank into the chair. She was going to have to talk to Danielle. She was going to have to find out what had been going on in the years since they had last actually spoken and hope the sister she had once known wasn't too far gone.

Chapter Ten

Danielle stared out the window of Martin's car, hating the fact that she felt like an angry child giving her parents the silent treatment. She wanted to ask Martin what had driven him to be so obnoxious at Chloe's house and during the block party. He'd always been a little irritating but never to that level. She also didn't ask him because she was pretty sure she knew. He'd acted that way for the same reason Danielle had found it difficult to look Chloe in the eye—for the same reason she always seemed to shrink inside of herself when she was around Steven.

It was because they had stepped into another world today. It was a world they told themselves they hated, a world they didn't need and did not care for. But truth be told, it was a world that Danielle had always dreamed for herself. She was making decent money as a bartender—it all came in the form of tips after eleven o'clock at night, really—and she spent very little money. She knew that one day, if she kept up with such practices, she would be able to afford her own house—maybe not in a neighborhood like Lavender Hills, but something much nicer than her one-bedroom apartment.

While Martin had never come out and said as much, she knew he had similar feelings. Yet today was the first time she'd ever actually seen him in such an environment. Needless to say, it had not gone well.

"That Steven guy is an asshole," Martin said as they neared her apartment. "A little pretentious, don't you think?"

"Yeah, I think that's safe to say." It wasn't a lie, as she had never really cared much for Steven anyway.

"He didn't like me, right from the start," Martin said. "It was obvious."

"That might be true," Danielle said. "But did you really have to make such smart-ass comments?"

"Hey, the one thing I said that set him off, I whispered to you. It's not my fault he heard. What was he doing? Eavesdropping? Just waiting for me to say one thing wrong so he could go off on me in front of all of his snotty new neighbors?"

"I don't know," Danielle said. "But I have to be honest with you. I didn't peg you as one of these guys who had to resort to name-calling and fist fights when something doesn't go your way. At the end of the day … you threw the first punch."

"So sorry to disappoint you," he said.

He slammed his hand down on the steering wheel.

"What is it?" she asked. She wasn't scared of his little mood swings. If anything, she found it entertaining. She could easily remember him getting upset with her the other night, so upset that he had pushed her down on the couch and bruised her arm. But if he did that sort of shit again, she'd be ready … and he'd be sorry.

"Nothing. The gas light is on. We're almost out of gas."

Danielle said nothing. She just looked out the window, wondering how it was that when Martin got angry about something, it fed into everything else about that day—even something as trivial as needing to put gas in the car.

He pulled the car into the next gas station they came to. He had a set expression on his face as he opened the door and stalked his way to the pumps, as if he thought the world was out to get him today. Danielle had never seen him in this sort of a funk and it made her feel like an idiot for thinking he might be this perfect man.

It brought to mind just how protective he had been about his phone the other night. Sure, he told her *later* that it had just been something concerning work. But why hadn't he said something then, when she was trying to be funny about it?

She looked down at the console and saw his phone. She'd spied him earlier putting his code in on the lock screen, so she knew how to get in.

She took a glance out the window and saw that he was zoned out, staring across the street while the gas pumped.

To hell with it, she thought.

She grabbed the phone and quickly punched in the four-digit code. The phone unlocked and she instantly went to his messages. She scrolled through, looking for texts from a couple of days ago. There were texts from her and there *were* texts from work. There were also messages from one of his weirdo friends but then, a few messages down, messages from a number he had not saved—the ID showed only a number and not a name.

She opened it and looked back to see if he was still zoned out. He was. She had a few seconds, at least until the *click* of the pump when the tank was filled.

Within the first two messages, she knew what she had found. And although she knew there was only venom ahead, she kept reading anyway. It was a simple back-and-forth between Martin and, Danielle assumed, a very needy and exploitive woman. The woman started the conversation.

Her: When you coming back by? It's been 3 days. Can't wait much longer. A girl has needs, you know…

Him: Oh I know. And I plan to meet them. Tomorrow, ok?

Her: You promise?

Him: Yes.

Her: Good. I'm already wet just thinking about it. You can't even imagine the things I'm going to do to you…

Him: Oh, I can imagine plenty. Feel free to send me your ideas and suggestions.

And boy, did she. Danielle would have blushed at some of what she was reading if she hadn't been so irate. *At least now I know why he's always so hesitant to be physical with me, she thought. It's because he's got some other woman's smell on him.*

Behind her, she heard the click of the pump. With shaking hands, she closed out of the message thread, pushed the button to put the phone to sleep, and placed it back in the console. She did it all with plenty of time to spare, as Martin didn't open the door for another five seconds.

She wanted to tell him right then and there. To tell him she knew about the other woman and about all of the very descriptive things she wanted to do to him—had probably already done to him, in fact.

But she stayed quiet. She wanted to see just how far he might take it. Maybe the ridiculous fight at the block party was going to uncover some part of him she had not seen yet.

She turned her head away from him as he pulled the car out of the gas station parking lot. As he started down the road, Danielle began to think long and hard about some things. Slowly, a smile crept to her lips and she wasn't even aware of it.

If Chloe had seen it, however, she would have recognized it right away.

But Chloe wouldn't have known what it meant… why the smile was there.

Think you're getting one over on me, do you? she thought, still refusing to look at him. *Let's just see how that works out for you.*

And then her mind wandered. It veered and stretched and eventually reached into a place she had not allowed herself to visit in a very long time.

A dark place.

A place she always thought she had left behind but which was always waiting there for her whenever there seemed to be no place else to go.

Chapter Eleven

As hard as she tried, Chloe could not get the image of Danielle's sinister little smile out of her mind. Something about it gnawed at her, an itch she could not scratch. She wrestled with it on Sunday and it occupied her mind while she and Steven sat around the house, avoiding one another. She could tell Steven was starting to feel ashamed of his actions at the block party but was not quite ready to own his part of it.

Still stumped by why Danielle's nearly passive smile continued to bother her, Chloe started to become aware that there was something there—something that smile seemed to be dragging up from the past. That's why Chloe wasted no time on Monday morning; she called Dr. Skinner's office as soon as she could. She was able to schedule an appointment for one o'clock that afternoon.

As the hour approached, Chloe started to wonder if she had somehow been lying to herself about her past—particularly about what had happened with her mother. She *had* been young and even the shrinks she had seen as a young girl had indicated that such a trauma might never truly be peeled all the way back. It was an idea that was heavy on her heart as she finally stepped into Skinner's office that afternoon.

"You told my receptionist that you had an eventful weekend," Skinner said. "Care to tell me about it?"

She did, with great embarrassment. But getting it out and speaking to someone other than Steven about it was quite helpful. She ended the summary with seeing the devious smile on Danielle's face and how it had seemed to trigger something within her.

"Do you think she simply enjoyed seeing Steven being confronted in front of your new neighbors?" Skinner suggested.

"I honestly don't know," she said. "But the more I thought about it over the weekend, the more I started to think about the day my mother died—about the very scene I walked you through last week. I was wondering if there might be something more there, some memory that might still be muddy."

"And you were hoping I could help to clear it up … if, that is, there is anything at all to be cleared up at all?"

"Yes, that's my hope."

"Well, we can certainly give it a try if you are willing," Skinner said. "The last time we attempted it, you seemed very flustered near the end. It's one of the reasons I stopped the session when I did. Are you sure you'd like to try it again?"

She almost said no. She felt like she was expecting some magic trick, for Skinner to reach inside of her head and pluck out the very thing she was looking for. It made her feel naïve and helpless. But before she could utter an answer either way, Skinner seemed to have made the decision for her.

"As you recall," he said, "I need you to make sure you are absolutely comfortable where you are sitting. And that means doing your best to rid your mind of any expectations … of any hopes or doubts. Can you do that?"

She pressed in against the chair, closed her eyes, and was reminded of just how comfortable it was. She also knew that he was going to ask her to concentrate on her breathing, to make sure that every part of her body was relaxed. She did all of that, hearing his voice but not paying much attention to it. She was trying to wipe her mind clear, to forget about the fight at the block party, about Danielle's smile …

"Do you remember the shoes?" Skinner asked. "The Chuck Taylors?"

"Yes."

"Can you still see those laces? The big looping ones?"

She could. And they were exceptionally clear. She could even see the dirt and grime on them.

"Are you back out there on the stoop to the apartment building?" Skinner asked.

She nodded. She was finding it hard to speak. She was intently focused on her shoelaces. Even before Skinner asked her to do so, she stood up, watching the loops on the tied laces shift. "I'm going back inside," she said.

"Good, good. Now this time, though, I need you to try to look beyond your mother's body and the blood. I know it will be hard, but I need you to try. Instead, I want you to give all of your attention to Danielle. Do you think you can do that for me?"

She nodded, understanding that she found speaking difficult because going back to that moment in time had happened incredibly fast this time. She felt dizzy, only in no way she had ever experienced before.

She watched her shoes move up the stairs, into the building, and then to their apartment. She heard her father inside, screaming—he was on the phone, she knew, speaking to someone with 911. But she ignored it as well as she could. As Skinner had asked, she even looked past the shape of her mother's body on the floor. Nope ... just the shoelaces, tied loosely and matted with dirt in places.

And then there was Danielle.

"Okay, I'm here," she told Skinner in a sleepy voice. "I see Danielle. She's standing over Mom's body."

"Do you see her as she was that day?" Skinner asked.

"Yes."

Blood on her clothes. A vacant look in her eyes as she stared down at their mother. Yes, this was a ten-year-old version of Danielle for sure.

"Okay, so now I want you to look away from those shoelaces and focus on her. Don't concentrate too hard. Just look at her and wait for it. See if something comes to you."

"It's ... no, it's not here. Not *now.* It's something later ... after the cops came. We were in the back of our grandmother's car."

"Can you see that car?" Skinner asked. "Can you see your sister in that c—"

The scene switched right away. She was no longer standing at the foot of the stairs by the motionless shape of her mother. She was sitting in the back seat of her grandmother's car. She and Danielle were huddled together. It was the first time Danielle had showed any real emotion. She was crying, but just barely.

Oh my God, I forgot about this, Chloe thought. How did I ....

"It wasn't him," Danielle said. "It wasn't Daddy. He didn't do this. I know it wasn't him."

From the front seat, their grandmother let out a little moan of sadness.

And it was that noise from the past that seemed to pull Chloe straight out of the memory. She opened her eyes and let out a short, jerky breath. She looked around the office, her eyes finally settling on Dr. Skinner.

"You okay?" Skinner asked.

"Yeah. I… I don't know how I forgot about that."

"Was it the answer you were looking for?"

She thought of Danielle's face in the back of their grandmother's car. There had been genuine sorrow there, real tears and a legitimate expression of grief. While it wasn't what she had been expecting, it seemed to open a few doors that had been closed for quite a while.

"I don't know," she answered honestly.

"Well, while we're here, why don't you tell me how your internship is going?" Skinner asked.

At first, she did it only because he'd asked—purely out of obligation and nothing more. But after a minute or so, she found that the distraction was a welcome one. She'd been so preoccupied with Steven and Danielle that she'd nearly forgotten the true center of her life—interning to become a field agent.

She spent the next half hour talking about the internship as well as what she planned to accomplish over the course of her career. And while it did indeed feel great to start looking into her future and seeing how it was coming into shape, she was also fully aware that it was her past that had helped to form the woman she was right now.

She got a text as she was walking out to her car. She checked it, assuming it would be Agent Greene, but did not recognize the number that popped up on her display. The message itself, though, clued her in.

Hey, it's Kathleen. Sorry I didn't get a chance to see you Saturday. Heard about what happened. Sorry to hear it. Hope all is well. Anywho… I'm going out with some ladies from the neighborhood

tonight for drinks. Ruthanne Carwile will be there, too. We'd love for you to come. Want you to see that one unfortunate event does not blacklist you! LOL.

At first, Chloe was a bit insulted by it. But she also knew just how easy it was to misread tone and voice in a text message. Based on what she had seen from Kathleen—the overenthusiasm and cheer—she didn't think her old high school friend would invite her out just to belittle her.

And besides, she sure could use a drink.

She thought of the way the crowd had gathered around Steven and Martin as they had fought. She easily recalled the expressions—some laughing, some hiding their heads as if they were too good to witness such a thing. And then, of course, there had been Danielle, detached and smiling.

Yes, she could use a drink. Hell… she could use a *few.*

Chapter Twelve

Danielle spent that night at work, going through her routines and doing her best to push Martin out of her mind. She mixed drinks, poured beers, flirted, even pretended to accidentally get a little water on her shirt from the seltzer hose to get a few great tips near the end of the night.

She had only ever taken two men home from her job at the restaurant bar. The ones who wanted her were easy to spot. They actually *weren't* the chatty ones trying to impress her. They tended to be the quiet ones, sitting at the edge of the bar watching her work. When she spoke to them, they'd respond confidently and make intense eye contact. As vain as it might seem, it was a nice feeling.

As she rounded out her shift that night, there were two of them. She could have had either of them. She knew that and tucked the idea away, taking it with her. Maybe after she was done with this whole Martin thing she'd allow herself another fling. She kept thinking about the texts, the pictures… and what she planned to do in response to them.

When she called last call, she nearly started flirting hard with one of them but decided not to. Too much trouble. Too much drama.

Still, driving home knowing that someone would want her—even if it was a partially drunk man who had been wearing a wedding band—made her feel good. It made her feel valued and wanted. She wondered if Martin thought he was the best thing out there for her… that her options were limited.

Little does he know, she thought as she parked her car in the lot in front of her building. Still on a high from the attention of the bar's patrons, she thought she might take a nice hot shower. She thought she might—

And then it came crashing down when she opened the door and entered her apartment.

There was another note on the floor.

She picked it up and read it. By the time she read it for the second time, her hands were sweating. She slowly walked into the kitchen, rereading it over and over again. It was a cryptic message but she was pretty sure she knew what it meant.

She set it on the kitchen table and read it yet again.

KILL HIM OR I WILL.

She crept over to her window and looked out over the rear parking lot of her building. She wasn't sure what she was looking for. Maybe someone lounging by their car, simply looking like they didn't belong. She wasn't sure. But all she saw was a darkened parking lot, partially aglow in yellow street lamps.

How long ago did they drop this letter off? she wondered. *Did I pass them in the hallway when I came inside the building? Did they drive behind me? Were they at the bar?*

Paranoia sank into her like a knife into her heart. She went to the kitchen counter and grabbed her meds. She popped the top off and looked inside the bottle.

No, she thought. *No. They make the paranoia worse. Ever since Chloe came by and demanded that you get back on them it's been worse, hasn't it?*

She was pretty sure it had been. She put the cap back on and slid the bottle into her junk drawer. She walked back to the note and picked it up, somehow feeling safer when it was in her hands.

KILL HIM OR I WILL.

It was the first letter that had given her an instruction—an order to be followed. And she knew what it meant. But did the letter writer actually *mean* it?

Suddenly, she couldn't stand to be in her apartment. She had to get out of there, had to make sure she was on the move and not staying stationary for the letter writer to come back and wait on her. She grabbed her keys and hurried outside. She did not feel safe again until she was in her car and the doors were locked. And even then she kept glancing into the back seat just in case.

She didn't know where she was going. She thought for a moment that she might drive to Lavender Hills. It was so late … surely Chloe would be home. But no. Then she'd have to tell Chloe about the letters. And God only knew how Steven would react to her dropping by at such a late hour.

She kept checking her rearview. Maybe the letter writer was tailing her, making sure he knew where she was at all times.

KILL HIM OR I WILL.

Martin … that was the *him*. She assumed this, anyway. It just seemed to fit. It felt right. Somehow the letter writer knew him. And maybe the letter writer even knew about the little skirmish at Chloe's block party somehow. Hell, maybe they even knew about Martin's other girlfriend.

As she thought this, the pictures and messages the bitch had sent went tearing through her head. She fumed, nearly gritting her teeth.

She'd tell him soon. Probably the next time she saw him. If he thought he could mess around on her like that and get away with it, he had another think coming. If he thought Steven had handed his ass to him, he wasn't going to be ready for the hell she would unleash on him.

KILL HIM OR I WILL.

Not a bad idea, she thought with a twinge of morbid humor.

But still, she continued to check her rearview, sure that someone was tailing her, watching her every move.

But she knew that was bullshit. There was no one on her tail. She was in the clear. She was free.

Free, she thought, as her mind wandered back to those messages on Martin's phone. *God, he had me. What a fucking idiot I am ...*

A flash of anger raced through her as something new came to her … an idea that was dangerous but seemed to have some merit to it. He'd known she was falling for him. She had not said it in words but she knew he had sensed it. And he had rewarded it by giving her a key to his apartment. She thought about that, about being able to enter his apartment.

And then she had another thought.

His car. It was an old clunker, a Chevy Cavalier that he'd somehow managed to keep running for ten years. It was a piece of shit, but man he loved that car.

With a smile on her face, she thought of where he kept the key—like an idiot, right under the passenger floor mat since the door locks were busted anyway.

Danielle turned around in the nearest parking lot she could find and headed in a different direction. With a devious plan in her mind, she headed for Martin's apartment.

Danielle was not running the headlights, so it was hard to see what was coming at her from down the gravel road ahead of her. Gravel pinged up against the bottom of the car in a series of dings. It sounded bad.

Not that she cared. She was behind the wheel of Martin's car now.

She knew this road well, as she had lost her virginity at the end of it at the age of fourteen. She'd come down here with many guys because it was so tucked away and isolated, an old cutaway road for state vehicles back when the water tower at the end of this road still serviced the town of Pinecrest.

But that tower had been condemned in the early nineties and the road was no longer used for anything other than promiscuous teens and defiant hunters when winter came. The road was bordered with pines and maples, blocking out most of the sky.

In the passenger seat, her cell phone rang… again. She ignored it when she saw Chloe's name on the display. It was the third time she'd called tonight.

She came to the end, to the edge of a lake. The lake, she knew, extended farther out into the surrounding woods. It eventually became a magnet for real estate as it filled in the expansive land behind one of Pinecrest's most notable snobby communities—snobbier, even, than Lavender Hills.

She made a U-turn and backed the car up to the edge of the water until she could feel the back tires sinking in the mud. She stopped, put the car into neutral, and waited to see how easily the back end would sink. She was surprised at just how quickly the drop off of the edge of the lake was taking the car, and she feared she might not make it out in time.

She quickly opened the door and scrambled out of the car. When she hit the ground and managed to get up running, she turned and saw that the car was already half submerged in the water.

There was a moment when she feared the front end would get caught in the roughage along the bank, but the weight of the back and the tug of the water freed it. She watched it sink, amazed at how fast it happened.

She did not stick around to reflect on what she had done. It was already eight thirty at night and she had at least a mile and a half to walk back to the main road. From there, she figured there was another mile or two before she would come to the first gas station—the first actual business that a cab would bother to come out and pick her up.

Back in her younger days, she'd simply hitchhike. She'd done it several times and had paid some men for those rides in ways she'd prefer to forget.

That's in the past, she thought as she made her way into the thickness of trees to hide herself away from anyone who might venture down the old state gravel road. *That's not who you are anymore.*

Of course, the question remained… *Who am I, then?*

She tried very hard not to think of the car she had just backed into the lake and how it might be a start to answering that question.

Chapter Thirteen

The one good thing about having an antisocial and moody sister was that it was usually a given that she would be home so long as she was not at the restaurant working. Chloe relied on this assumption as she approached Danielle's front door at six o'clock that afternoon. She knocked and waited in silence for several seconds. Just as she was about to knock again, she heard the slightest movement on the other side of the door.

"Who's there?" Danielle asked from the other side.

"It's Chloe."

She listened to the sound of the lock being unbolted from the inside and then the door opened quickly. Danielle ushered her inside and Chloe took note of how quickly she closed the door behind them. She almost commented on it but did not want to draw attention to the behavior; better to keep a check on it while she was here rather than give her the opportunity to deny it.

"What are you doing here?" Danielle asked.

"Steven and I have been at odds ever since the block party," she said. "We decided it might be best to take some time apart. Just a day or so."

"This isn't breakup territory, is it?" Danielle asked. "Although… no big loss. You can do much better."

"No, not breakup territory. And God, Danielle… I'm marrying him. You know that, right?"

Danielle shrugged, as if she was already bored with the conversation. "All the same," she said, "I'd hate to think you guys would end it over something my stupid boyfriend did."

"How are you guys?" Chloe asked.

"Same as you and Steven. Not talking. I'll probably break up with him. The more I get to know him, the more of an ass I see he is."

"I'm pretty sure that's the case with all men."

They sat down on the couch and Chloe could already feel an uncomfortable silence settling down around them.

"You had dinner yet?" Chloe asked.

"Yeah. Chinese. Orange chicken. There are some leftovers if you'd like some."

Chloe had actually had a quick dinner already but did not want to miss the opportunity to take Danielle up on free food. Something as simple and kind as offering leftovers was a big step for Danielle. It was frustrating because with every little baby step toward normalcy, there was something like her quickly shutting the door behind them to counterbalance it.

Or that creepy smile from the block party.

"Yes, please," she said.

Danielle walked into the kitchen, got the leftovers out of the fridge, and placed them in the microwave. Chloe watched her sister and almost felt bad for visiting. She had wanted to check in on Danielle, sure. But she was really there to see if she could see any further signs that might resemble that smile—or the vacant and ghostly look she had uncovered from her memories in Skinner's office.

"Danielle … are you okay?"

"Yeah. Why do you ask?" she said from the kitchen.

"You seem … antsy. When I came in, you couldn't close the door fast enough. Is it Martin? Are you worried he'll come by and start trouble?"

"No. He's an ass, but he's not stupid."

"Is it the medicine? Is it messing with your emotional state?"

"I wouldn't know," Danielle said. "I haven't taken it since you were here before."

"Jesus, Danielle. You apparently need it. If it was prescribed to you for mood swings, you need to take it. It's probably why you've been so …"

"So what, Chloe?"

The microwaved dinged. Danielle took the orange chicken out and brought it to the living room. She practically tossed it down on the coffee table in front of Chloe.

Chloe thought of that sinister smile from the block party. Of how she had been so chatty and happy one moment and then pulled into some dark corner of her mind a moment later.

"So all over the place," Chloe safely finished.

Danielle shrugged. She took a seat on the opposite side of the couch and looked toward the door. It was a very quick glance, but Chloe picked up on it. She was also fidgeting, nervously plucking at the fabric of her shirt and finding it hard to sit still.

"Danielle … if something was wrong, you'd tell me, right?"

"Probably not."

"I'm serious."

Danielle sighed and rolled her eyes. "I wish I could explain it to you. I really do. I'm just … I get paranoid sometimes. And maybe it's because I'm not taking the medicine. I don't know. I just … I'm always on the verge of feeling like something really bad is going to happen, you know? And it's been like that forever."

Even as she spoke, she looked toward the door. Maybe expecting someone she did not like to come knocking—maybe expecting an intruder. It was so hard to read Danielle when she was like this.

Chloe nodded. She *did* know. She'd been the same way up until she really started to devote her time and effort to therapy around the age of fifteen or so. She knew for a fact that Danielle had always just dialed it in. And the moment she could make her own decisions, she had stopped going to therapy altogether.

But now something was obviously bothering her. She looked to be on the verge of a panic attack, and Chloe found herself very worried for her.

"Maybe you need to go back to therapy," Chloe suggested. "There's all sorts of unresolved stuff going on, it sounds like. About Mom and Dad."

"Therapy? Yeah, no thanks."

"Then at least take the medicine," Chloe pleaded. "Don't be so stubborn."

Danielle nodded. "I will. I think I have to. I can't keep living this way."

"Do you think you're just very upset about what happened at the block party?" Chloe asked.

"Partly. But… it's beyond Martin. It's just… I don't know. I think I was hoping life would be better than this. Not needing meds to not be a paranoid bitch, you know?"

It broke Chloe's heart to hear her sister letting out these kinds of thoughts. With an awkward smile, she scooted over and put her arm out.

"What are you doing?" Danielle said.

"It's called a hug."

"Oh no."

But Danielle leaned into it and they snuggled together on the couch as if they were seven or eight years old again, back before their mother had been killed and life had beaten them over the head with misfortune. It was in that moment that Chloe realized that although life had driven a wedge between them, that gap was slowly closing. And if there was indeed something wrong with Danielle, be it mentally or emotionally, she was going to be right there by her side until the end.

Chloe stayed at Danielle's apartment until Danielle took one of the pills in front of her. They then remained on the couch, saying nothing at all, as they watched the first half of *Pretty Woman*—not because either of them particularity liked the movie but because it was a movie they had grown up on and, as odd as it seemed, was nostalgic for both of them.

An hour later, while Chloe was driving out to meet Kathleen and some of the other Lavender Hills women for drinks, the simple act of having watched that movie tonight helped Chloe to realize something.

She and Danielle were twenty-seven. Danielle was living in an apartment that, while not rundown, was far from luxurious. She also drove the same car she had driven when she had left home at seventeen. Meanwhile, she had roughly two hundred DVDs, God only knew how many CDs, and an overabundance of band T-shirts. It wasn't just that she was still blowing money on music and movies—it was that it was in the form of CDs and DVDs… physical components. While everything else had gone digital, Danielle had remained behind, still preferring to buy the physical items. Chloe had no idea why this struck her as sad but it did. Perhaps it was a characteristic of someone who was unwilling to move on. And if that was indeed the case with Danielle, surely the older familiar entertainment methods were not where inability to move on stopped.

Perhaps it reached all the way back to losing their mother and watching their father get carted off by the police.

It wasn't Daddy. He didn't do this.

She heard that ghost of a memory, spoken in her sister's voice, as she drove out to meet a group of women who could very well turn out to be her central group of friends. How that could still be possible after what had happened at the block party was beyond her, but she wasn't going to start questioning their motives just yet.

They'll never be my friends, though, Chloe thought as she neared her destination. *The looks on some of their faces at the party even before the fight… these people have already made up their minds about me. They probably only want to hang out with me just to get some juicy details about my past.*

She thought of Ruthanne Carwile and Tammy Wyler. She thought about how they had been a little too enthusiastic to meet her. And then, of course, there was the suspicious anxiousness she had seen in Ruthanne's eyes.

Maybe I'll dig that out of her tonight, Chloe thought.

But at the same time, this also made her feel left out. Even if she didn't want to admit it, she *wanted* to be friends with these women. And she was afraid that they had already pre-judged her—a fear that hurt more than she had expected.

They met at a little dive bar that Chloe had heard about while in high school but had never actually gotten the chance to visit. Once she was inside, she was rather surprised. It was more like a cocktail lounge than a small-town bar. When she entered, she found Kathleen and two other women sitting in a corner booth near the back, one of whom looked vaguely familiar.

"Glad you could make it," Kathleen said, scooting over in the booth.

Chloe sat down beside her and realized that the other face within the trio looked familiar. "Courtney Braxton?" she asked with a smile.

"The one and only," Courtney said, also with a smile. She had been one of the more popular girls in high school, graduating a few years ahead of Chloe. Her parents had been well-to-do but from what Chloe remembered, it was her willingness to do things with the boys behind the dugouts during PE that had truly made her so popular.

"And then this," Kathleen said, gesturing to the other woman, "as you know, is Jenny Foster. She's been back in Pinecrest for about ten years. She's a fifth-grade teacher at Pinecrest Elementary."

A friendly round of introductions filled the table as a waitress came by with refills and took Chloe's order. She ordered a mojito and did her best to fall into the rhythm of conversation. She quickly discovered that Courtney had been married for four years and that she and her husband had been trying to get pregnant for the last few months. She also discovered a lot of gossip about the neighborhood, none of which she paid much attention to.

"So I have to ask," Courtney said. "I heard about the scuffle between your husband and some other guy. Was it Danielle's boyfriend?"

"It was," Chloe said. "But we're honestly just all trying to look past that now."

"Sure, sure," Courtney said. "Is she okay? Your sister, I mean?"

"Yeah, she doesn't really let things like that affect her very much."

Kathleen chuckled, nodding her agreement. "I remember that about her from school. She just didn't give a damn what anyone thought about her."

"I don't remember her very well," Courtney said. "I remember the two of you looking identical but didn't she change her hair color like every month? And she always wore black, right?"

"Yeah, that was her," Chloe said, doing her best to inflect a tone that indicated she had no interest in discussing her sister.

"Well, I hope she dumps this guy," Kathleen said. "From what I hear, he was drunk or high or something."

"No, I don't think he was," Chloe said. "He and Steven just had a thing. They butted heads right away."

"Steven seems nice," Jenny said. "I met him for a bit just before it all happened."

"Yeah, looks like you got a good one," Kathleen said.

"So how about Danielle?" Courtney asked. "What is she up to these days?"

"She works as a bartender. Keeps a low profile, doesn't really get out much. She seems to like what she does, though."

She was simply speculating there. She honestly had no idea if Danielle liked what she did or not. She just wanted to move the conversation elsewhere without coming off as a bitch.

"Were either of your folks like that?" Jenny asked. It was an innocent question but still rubbed Chloe the wrong way.

"Yeah, a bit," she said. Although, honestly, her father *had* been very much a loner. He had been a friendly and fun man from what she remembered, but had never been very social.

"Maybe that's where Danielle gets it from," Courtney said.

The waitress brought Chloe her mojito, which Chloe started drinking right away to keep a confrontational comment from coming out of her mouth. Apparently, though, what she had planned to say was evident on her face.

"Forgive me for saying so," Kathleen said, "but I never understood her. She was always so pretty—you both were—but back in high school, she never really wanted much to do with anyone. Did she even ever go out and hang with friends or anything?"

"No," Chloe said, now no longer caring what sort of tone came out of her mouth.

"Is she still listening to that dark, angry music?" Courtney asked with a grin.

"I don't know. Are you still giving out hand jobs to any guy that gives you the time of day?"

At once, the trio of friends all looked simultaneously wounded. Apparently, they had not been expecting any sort of kick back. Honestly, Chloe had not either. But *damn,* it felt good.

"I'm sorry," Chloe said, not meaning it at all. "But did you guys want to talk about what's going on in your lives or did you just plan on attacking my sister?"

"Oh, Chloe, we weren't—" Kathleen started.

Chloe's phone buzzed in her pocket. She completely ignored whatever it was that Kathleen was saying to check it. She screamed a bit inside when she saw that it was Sally, her soon-to-be mother-in-law. Still, it gave her an excuse.

"Sorry, have to take this," she said. She took a large gulp of her drink and then walked out to the front of the bar, into a small waiting area.

She read the message, trying to remember a moment in the past year or so of her personal life where she had felt more frustrated. Gossipy neighbors and an overstepping future mother-in-law—it felt like far too much to bear all at once.

The text that had come through read: **What's the status of the wedding invitations? You guys agree on one yet? Clock is ticking if you want to get them out on time. Want to give your guests as much time to plan as possible.**

Why the woman insisted on texting her with these issues rather than Steven was beyond her. Probably because she didn't want to pester her precious little boy. She quickly fired off a text just so Sally wouldn't keep endlessly texting her.

Yup. Final decision in a few days.

She then pocketed her phone, dug a ten-dollar bill out of her purse, and stormed back to the table. She downed the rest of her drink as the other three women watched her. Chloe set her glass down, tossed the ten on the table, and gave a quick little wave.

"Sorry," she said. "Wedding stuff. But this was... well, not fun. But it was *something*."

Without letting Kathleen, Courtney, or Jenny say another word, Chloe turned and walked back out. It felt good to be a little cruel to women who apparently had nothing better to do than stick their noses in other people's business. Apparently, some things sincerely did not change from high school.

And once more, she was reminded of why she had been so happy to move away from this town when she graduated from high school. And yet her past still dug its claws in ... if not in haunting memories of her parents, then in the way people spoke of her family as if they were haunted.

It was just another way her past kept pulling back like an angry and relentless tide. She could only wonder how long she'd be able to fight it here in Pinecrest before she drowned.

CHAPTER FOURTEEN

The next morning, she met Agent Greene at HQ. He was on his phone sending a text when she crossed his path in the lobby. He looked up and smiled, instantly pocketing the phone.

"I was just texting you," he said. "We've got another crime scene to check out. You good taking a partial lead on it?"

"Yes," she said, handing him the coffee. "The other morning was just a fluke. You have my word on that."

"Did you take my recommendation to see Skinner?"

"I did. It was extremely helpful."

"Good. Now, why don't you drive this morning?"

It was a small gesture but meant quite a lot to Chloe. It was a show of trust—a way for Greene to show her that he wasn't afraid of letting her be in control for a while.

They drive out to a small suburban area ten minutes outside of Baltimore. The scene was located in a trailer park where the mobile homes were tightly packed in. As she pulled in behind several local police cars, she saw that many of the residents were swarming the small dirt thoroughfare that wound through the park.

Greene had told her only the basics on the way over, not wanting to affect her judgment too much. All she knew about the scene when she got out of the car was that they were walking into a drug deal gone bad. The FBI was involved because one of the men who had taken part in the deal was a highly wanted suspect in the Philly area for several counts of distributing.

As she and Greene walked up the shaky porch steps—made primarily of what looked like ancient wood and nails—the cops already on the scene seemed relieved. Chloe and Greene showed their IDs and were allowed inside.

Chloe noticed the smell right away. Blood. Garbage. The sticky sweet smell of marijuana—and here it was, just eight o'clock in the morning.

The scene was easy enough to piece together. Chloe stood a few feet inside the door, allowing Greene in as well. They both studied the place closely even though the crux of the story was plain to see directly in front of them.

A couch sat against the far wall of what served as the living room. There were two bodies on it, one of which was slumped nearly off of the couch. This body was missing the top left portion of its head. Blood had been splattered on the walls and was even now still spilling from the grisly wound onto the carpet.

The body beside it was just as dead, a large hole in the lower chest and upper abdomen area. It was gruesome, but she had properly prepared herself. While it was ghastly to see, it was not nearly as bad as what she had envisioned in her mind.

Still… there was a lot of blood. And it was very recent.

Shotgun, Chloe thought. *Close range. My God…*

The person with the wound to the chest had been holding a Glock. It lay discarded and useless by his feet. The Glock, it seemed, had been used to ward off the body that was currently lying in the center of the living room floor. The body was face down, the head turned to the side. From what Chloe could see, he had been shot high in the chest, just under the jaw, and directly under the right eye. Each shot had an exit wound, clearly visible from the back.

"I'll be damned," Greene said. He hunched down to the victim in the floor. He winced at the sight and then shrugged. "This is the guy on our list. Oscar Estevez. The feds have been after him for about three months."

A cop poked his head in the door behind them. "You might want to check the rear bedroom in the back," he said. "We've catalogued it but I'm sure you bureau guys might find it interesting.

Greene nodded and beckoned Chloe to follow him. She did, and they wound their way down the thin hallway to the back of the mobile home.

The entire place smelled of mildew and pot; it was so strong near the back of the trailer that it forced Chloe to start breathing through her mouth.

They came to a bedroom in the back of the trailer. The walls were adorned with pornographic posters. An old TV sat on top of a battered dresser. But what really attracted their attention was the fact that the mattress on the bed had been overturned, revealing the box springs. The cover from the box spring had been torn open, revealing several bundles of cocaine. It was all wrapped in plastic and taped up with black electrical tape. At first glance, there appeared to be at least twenty bundles.

"So what do you take away from this scene?" Greene asked

"Well, it looks like the criminals more or less did our work for us. Looks like some sort of drug deal gone wrong. Or a customer came in with a complaint and that went badly."

"Yes. At this point we can only speculate. It looks like a case-closed sort of ordeal but we'll still need to run an investigation. The bad news is that we're still going to be responsible for doing the paperwork and report. So let's go ahead and get a proper investigation of the place—maybe ask some of the locals scattered outside for some more details and—"

Greene's cell phone buzzed, cutting him off. He checked it and said, "One second."

He answered the call and stepped out into the hallway. Chloe was able to listen to his end of the conversation while also checking out the bedroom. She checked the drawers of the bureau and found a scattering of clothes, rolling papers, and several porn DVDs. She found no weapons of any kind, nor any proof that there was anything at play here other than a drug deal that had taken a very wrong turn.

Green came back into the room, his phone still in his hand. "So we need to make quick work of this scene," he said. "We've got another case to check in on. This one is right in your neck of the woods, I believe. Pinecrest, right?"

"Yeah. What's the case?"

"Possible missing persons case," he said. "Some guy named Martin Shields. Nothing too big. Probably just going to let the local PD handle it."

"You said Martin Shields?" Chloe asked, really hoping she'd heard wrong.

"Yeah. Why?"

Her thoughts instantly went to Danielle. Did she know yet? Or had she maybe even been the one to make the call?

"Shit. I know him. Well, sort of. My sister is sort of dating him."

"Really?" Greene asked, taken aback.

"Yeah. I don't think it's serious, but still…"

"Small world," Greene said.

"Exactly."

"If it's someone close to you, we can make it a priority over this, I think," Greene said. "And even if the local boys do want it, maybe I can keep you in the loop if you want."

"Yeah, I'd appreciate that," she said. But the wheels were still spinning in her head, as she wondered how Danielle played into all of it. It was also eerie, considering she had just seen Martin at the block party.

"Honestly, if your sister is dating him, maybe you should call her right now," Greene said. "We can start looking into it while still wrapping this mess up."

Chloe nodded and made her way back down the hall. She managed to not look at the gruesome sight in the living room as she stepped back outside. She pulled up Danielle's number and placed the call.

Danielle answered on the third ring with a sleepy-sounding: "Hello?"

"Hey, it's Chloe."

Danielle have an exaggerated sigh. "Yes, I took my medication today. Now, if you don't mind I'd like to get back to sleep."

"Danielle, when was the last time you saw Martin?"

"Um, the afternoon of the block party. He dropped me off, we were pissed at each other and haven't spoken since. Why?"

"I, um…I'm at work and we just got a call. Someone apparently reported him missing. And an adult has to be missing for at least a day before the report is taken seriously."

"Are you kidding me?" Danielle said. "Missing?"

"That's the repot right now. We're going to be looking into it in a bit. I was thinking maybe you knew something."

"Well, I sure as hell didn't make the call."

"Do you know who might have?"

"Well, he was apparently screwing someone while seeing me."

"Any idea who?" Chloe asked.

"I don't know her name, but I've seen her naked. There were pictures on Martin's phone. So wait…you mean this is for real? He's actually *missing*?"

"I'm hoping to find out for you as soon as I can."

"Well, keep me posted," Danielle said and then ended the call.

But as far as Chloe was concerned, there was absolutely nothing in Danielle's voice that expressed much concern.

Chapter Fifteen

It was a little maddening to be looking at wedding invitations while she could not get in touch with her sister. Chloe was really hoping that Danielle was only refusing to answer her phone because she was saddened by the news concerning Martin. Still, given the way Danielle had been acting, it was hard to assume the most innocent and safe scenario.

But she wanted to be a good wife, wanted to show Steven that she was just as involved with him and their upcoming wedding as she was about Danielle's well-being. Besides, it wasn't like Danielle hadn't behaved like this before, not answering calls and becoming distant. She was also discovering that she rather enjoyed the process of looking through the designs for the invitations. Given the way the last few days had gone, it was nice to be able to actually enjoy sitting down and trying to finish planning out the wedding.

Things were still tense since the fight but they were at least able to exist within the same room without getting angry. They scrolled through several selections on her iPad, looking at mock designs from the printer Steven's parents had recommended.Yet as they worked toward making a decision, Chloe started to realize that Steven was also distracted. He would give nods and *yeahs* or *sounds good*s whenever needed, but that was about it.

"You okay?" she asked.

"Yeah," he said, though he said it as if he were coming up from out of a deep sleep.

"You seem distracted. Everything okay?"

"Yeah," he said. "Just thinking about some things at work. Tomorrow is going to be a crazy day. Sorry…I guess I hadn't fully unplugged myself from work mode."

She swallowed down the comment that tried crawling its way out of her mouth. *You're distracted, huh? Let me tell you what distracted is. It's knowing that your sister's boyfriend has gone missing and now your sister won't answer her phone. That's distracting!*

"Anything you want to talk about?" Chloe asked.

Steven seemed to think about it for a while before shaking his head. "No. I don't want to make this any more miserable."

"Checking out invitations isn't your thing, huh?"

"Apparently not. Is that okay?"

Chloe shrugged. "Hey, I don't mind making this decision for us."

"Ah, and speaking of making decisions…Mom called today and asked if we wanted to come over for dinner again."

Although Chloe would rather have her fingernails plucked out one by one, she didn't want to cause any further tension. "That's fine," she said. "Just let me know when. If I were you, though, I'd wait a few days. You need to give that eye some time to clear up."

Steven reached up and gently touched the swollen and discolored area right below his eye—the result of the one single punch Martin had successfully landed. It looked much better already, but was still very noticeable.

"Have you even told your mother anything about what happened?" Chloe asked.

"No. No sense in embarrassing myself, I suppose. And I didn't want to have to tell her that it was Danielle's boyfriend."

He left it at that, the insinuation hanging in the air—the insinuation that his mother did not care for Danielle at all. Not that it was any secret.

"Speaking of which," Chloe said. "I was involved in a case today…a case about Martin. He's apparently turned up missing."

"Really? Who called it in?"

"Not sure yet," Chloe said.

"What a joke," Steven said. "That kind of guy, though ... you know. No real surprise that he flaked off. Missing ... probably not. Probably just jetted off to some other city because he's too unstable to stay anywhere long term."

Chloe let the topic die there. It was clear that he had no interest in her work; he was too preoccupied with trying to appease his mother with the wedding plans. More than that, Steven tearing into Martin would only result in him also tearing into Danielle. And she did *not* have the patience for that.

So they lapsed back into silence after that, once again looking at wedding invitations without any real excitement of the wedding to come.

Chloe woke up to the sound of her alarm the following morning. She was still tired from the night before, as thoughts and worries about Danielle had plagued her mind. She sat up in bed, Steven still asleep beside her, and checked her phone in the hopes that Danielle had at least texted during the course of the night.

But there was nothing from Danielle. She did have a text from Agent Greene, though. It read, **A woman named Sophie Arbogast reported Martin Shields missing. Looking into her ASAP.**

Good ... at least there was a sense of direction to the case already. She wondered if Danielle knew Sophie Arbogast.

She got out of bed, put on her running attire, and headed out right away. She preferred to run before eating or drinking anything, relying on the exercise to fully wake her up and clear her head. She'd only gone running in Lavender Hills once, and that had been at dusk on her first day as a resident.

She was pleased to find the neighborhood in absolute silence as she started her run at 5:45. The sun was just beginning to puncture the horizon, casting everything in an ethereal pre-morning purple. She had run two blocks before she saw another human being—an older lady sitting on her porch with a cup of coffee, reading from her Bible. At the end of that same block, she passed a man walking his dog but he was wearing headphones and didn't even take the time or courtesy to wave at Chloe.

The running app on her phone told her that she had run 1.79 miles when she saw a familiar face running toward her as she rounded the corner toward another street. She saw Tammy Wyler, their eyes locking at once, and Chloe knew there was no way to avoid her. Unless Tammy was one of those people who took their running *very* seriously, she wasn't going to be able to avoid having to stop and talk to her.

Which was fine, she supposed. But after the block party, it was easy to assume what the topic of conversation would be. She also wondered if Kathleen or one of the others had filled her in on their brief meeting over drinks.

As expected, Tammy slowed her pace significantly as the two women approached one another. While Tammy stopped altogether, Chloe continued to run in place, hoping it would clue Tammy in to the fact that she did not want to stop to chat long.

"I figured you for the running type," Tammy said. "No way someone can stay that slim and pretty without putting in the work."

"Thanks," Chloe said.

"I'm glad we've run into one another," Tammy said, unable to keep in a dumb little snicker at her lame wordplay. "You've been on my mind a lot since Saturday."

Oh, I bet I have, Chloe said.

"Everything is okay," Chloe said, still running in place. "It was just a misunderstanding. It's all smoothed over for now."

"How about Danielle?" Tammy asked. "How is she doing?"

It infuriated Chloe that everyone who had once known Danielle assumed they knew everything about her. When Tammy asked the question, she did it with a very sorrowful tone, indicating that poor Danielle likely needed all the help she could get.

"She's fine," Chloe said.

She tried to think of a happy medium—of a way to save face, spare her sister's fragile reputation, and also stay in the good graces of these women. If she planned to live in this neighborhood for the long term, she had to try to repair whatever damage had been done. She hated the social politics of it all but she knew it was a reality she was going to have to face.

"Well, tell her I asked about her, would you? You know ... I heard her boyfriend is missing. Is that true?"

The speed at which news traveled sometimes floored Chloe and now was no exception. She tried hiding her surprise, asking: "How did you hear about that?"

"Oh, news travels quickly around a place like this," Tammy answered, as if she had just read Chloe's thoughts.

"I'm finding that out," Chloe said, unable to hide her disdain.

"Well ... true or not, would you let Danielle know I'm thinking about her? She's in my prayers."

"Of course," Chloe said, forcing the words out. "Enjoy the rest of your run."

Without any clear signal that the conversation was over, Chloe resumed her run. She did not like that she was already irritated by the seemingly gossip-centered nature of the people in her neighborhood. It would make things very interesting as she advanced further and further into the bureau. Already, it was placing a strain on her personal life.

Chloe did her best to push that resentment aside for the time being. The mere mention of Danielle from Tammy Wyler had Chloe once again thinking about her sister. It wasn't unlike Danielle to not answer calls or texts, but something felt different this time—especially considering Martin's apparent disappearance.

Something's not right, she thought.

She thought of Danielle's meds. She thought about that eerie smile on her face when Martin had bested Steven in a headlock.

Before she knew it, Chloe was cutting her run short, heading back home. She was going to get an early start today. She was going to leave the house a little early and hope to catch Danielle by surprise.

She hated to be sneaky, but something inside of her—be it instinct or just a sister's nurturing tendencies—was really starting to worry about Danielle.

And with that inclination, the quiet of the morning seemed eerie rather than peaceful.

Chapter Sixteen

Chloe knew that she'd be waking Danielle up. It was 7:35 when she stopped by the Starbucks along the way, making sure she at least had a peace offering for waking her sister up so early. She knocked on her sister's door, chai latte with two shots of espresso in hand, waiting for the wrath that was sure to come.

Much to her surprise, Danielle looked very much awake when she answered the door. She gave Chloe a skeptical look and then allowed her to enter without saying a word. It wasn't until the door was closed behind them and Danielle had plopped down on the couch that she bothered to speak.

"It's early," she said. "Did you really miss me *that* much?"

"A bit," Chloe said.

She sat down, getting the lay of the land before proceeding. Danielle had clearly been awake for a while. Music was playing in the background and her laptop was opened on the coffee table. A cup of coffee sat adjacent to the laptop. The music was coming from the laptop's speaker, some type of industrial metal that sounded like nothing but humming and static through the little laptop speaker

"Why didn't you answer any of my calls or return any of my texts?" Chloe asked.

"Because I knew why you were calling. And I still don't have any answers for you."

"You've heard *nothing*? Did he maybe say something the day of the block party to make you think he was skipping town?"

"No. Nothing. He dropped me off, said he'd call when things blew over."

"You said you thought he was seeing someone else," Chloe said. "Did you actually read the text conversations?"

"Not all of them, no. I'd seen her boobs enough and read more than enough dirty texts. That's about all it was, anyway. Not going to get anything worthwhile out of that."

"Are you not worried about him?"

"No," Danielle said. "He's a grown man and he had at least two women that he was seeing. It doesn't seem so strange to me that he might just not be around. Maybe the pressure of two women got to be too much for him and he left town. God only knows how many other stupid women he has on the side."

"Well, we did get confirmation that it *was* a woman who made the call. Does the name Sophie Arbogast mean anything to you?"

Danielle shook her head. "No. Not that I know of." She took the chai latte without making sure it was hers and started drinking it, despite the fact that she still had a cup of coffee right in front of her.

"If I'm being honest," Chloe said, "you're probably right. Maybe he realized he overstepped his bounds at the block party. Even though he came out on top, he could still feel jaded about it all. Maybe he's embarrassed to be around you now and maybe the other woman failed him in some way, too. It's not uncommon for men with no real roots or reasons to stay in one place to just uproot and move at the drop of a dime. I just wanted to check in on you to make sure you're okay."

"I'm fine," Danielle said. "It's not like it's the first time a guy has pulled a fast one on me."

"And you aren't just pulling some rugged tough girl bullshit on me?" Chloe asked.

"No. We only went out for a little over a month. I *was* starting to think that he might be too good to be true, though. He was kind and gentle and I had to actually manipulate him into anything physical. And then ... well, then the block party happened and the phone texts and I saw what kind of guy he really was."

"And since then ... have you been—"

"Yes, I've been taking the meds."

Chloe got up, feeling that she was doing nothing but managing to get Danielle slowly upset. "Okay. I thought I'd just swing by. After the news I dropped on you yesterday, I just got concerned when you weren't answering your phone. Could you please give me a call if you hear from Martin?"

"Yes. But I honestly don't see him calling. I feel like he exposed himself Saturday; I think he never meant for me to see that side of him."

"Take care, Danielle."

She felt the need to say something else but before the words could come to her, she felt her phone vibrating in her pocket. She took it out and saw that it was Greene calling. She turned her back and walked into the kitchen to answer Greene's call.

"Good morning," she said. "I got your text about Sophie Arbogast. Do we need to visit her?"

"Eventually, maybe. For now, we've got something even better. We got a call this morning about someone spotting a car in a lake. I'm at the scene now and we've been able to confirm the plates. The car belonged to a Martin Shields."

"A body?"

"No. Not yet. We're going to get some folks out here to start dragging the lake in the next hour or so. For now, I'd like for you to meet me. How fast can you get to Monument Lake? The car was discovered off of an old state access road to the old water tower."

"Give me half an hour."

"Sounds good," Greene said. "And listen ... this really isn't a bureau matter as of right now. The local cops are running it. But I had asked to be pinged about any movement on the Shields case just because of your connection to it. It took some convincing, but I got Director Johnson to allow us to sort of work it from the sides. So just keep that in mind when you get here."

"Will do," she said. "Thanks for the help."

Chloe hung up and slowly placed her phone back into her pocket. She returned to the living room but did not sit back down. She had to deliver this news and then head to the scene. It was the first moment since she'd started her internship where a case was directly overlapping with her personal life.

And she did not care for it.

"Danielle … that was Agent Greene, my interim supervisor. They just found a car … Martin's car. It was pulled from Monument Lake."

A shock of fear trailed across Danielle's face, an expression that then seemed to morph into concern. For a moment, it seemed like her brain could not quite decide on which emotion to hone in on.

"Oh my God. Is he …?"

"We don't know. So far, there's no indication that there was a body inside."

"Like *just* now?" she asked. "They just now found it?"

"Yeah. I have to head out there. Are you … are you going to be okay?"

"I guess. It's just … well, that's a lot to process."

"This doesn't necessarily mean the worst, you know," Chloe said. "There's no body. Just the car."

"Yeah," she said dimly. "Okay …"

"Danielle … are you going to be okay?"

"Yeah. I'm okay. Just … keep me posted."

"I will," Chloe said. "And you make sure you call me if you start to feel overwhelmed with this, okay?"

Danielle only nodded and looked to her computer with a blank expression on her face. Chloe gave her one last glance and she once again got that feeling of something being off—of something being wrong.

Danielle did not look sad or worried.

Danielle looked *terrified.*

Chloe nearly said something about this but knew that Greene would be waiting for her. Besides, she also knew that Danielle would not talk about her emotional state—not until she'd had significant time to process it all.

So on that note, with an unsettled feeling in her heart, Chloe left her scared sister behind.

Chapter Seventeen

Chloe recognized the gravel road right away. While she had never ventured down it in her younger years, it had gained something of a mythical status when she'd been in high school. It had more or less been the Lover's Lane of Pinecrest. Now, it seemed the road had gone to ruin, weeds popping up along the center and the gravel almost nonexistent in places.

When she pulled her car in behind a series of police cars and another car she recognized as Greene's, a tow truck had started to pull the car out of the water. Two policemen were clambering out of the muck along the edge of the lake. She saw that they had attached some sort of cord to the tow truck's original haul, making it easier to pull the car from the water.

A small group of people—about ten in all—were huddled along the edge of the water, waiting for the car to be pulled fully out. She spotted Greene and joined him.

"You speak to your sister about this yet?" he asked her.

"Yes. I was with her when you called me. Question, though: if they are just now pulling the car out, how was anyone able to ID the car beforehand?"

"The back end struck an outcropping of rock about ten yards out. The front end was visible through the water, and you could just make out the license plate number. Now, tell me … what can you establish from the fact that the front end was sticking up?"

She answered as the tow truck pulled forward, pulling the car partially onto the ground. Mud and muck scraped against the underside as it hit the bank.

"It tells me that it was backed into the water. And if it was Martin's way of committing suicide, then that makes no sense. Why go through the precaution of doing that? If it was indeed backed into the lake, it means that whoever was driving wanted to make sure they had ample time to get out. That would lead me to suspect foul play."

Greene nodded his agreement. "So now let's see if the car itself has any answers."

Agent Greene was the only agent at the scene, giving him authority over the situation. Still, he allowed the local cops to have a look as they made notes for their own files. Once that was done, Agent Greene waved Chloe on to follow him as he looked the car over. He handed her a pair of latex gloves as they went to work.

"First thing I'm looking for," Greene told her, "is any sign that there was some sort of rigged setup behind the wheel or on the gas pedal. It's not unheard of for people to get really creative with this sort of thing. Maybe whoever was behind the wheel didn't even have to drive the car into the lake manually. But… as it stands, I don't see anything that suggests that."

Chloe, meanwhile, opened the glove compartment. A little cascade of water came spilling out as the flap dropped. She rummaged around inside and found nothing of interest: insurance documents, a pack of gum, a few discarded CDs. A few of the CDs were the exact sort of thing Danielle would listen to. Something about this made Chloe feel very protective of her sister—like she was suddenly too close to the scene for some reason.

"Anything good?" Greene asked.

"Nothing," she said, closing the glove compartment.

They then checked under the seats, looking for anything that might provide clues. It took less than two minutes to discover that there was nothing there.

As they closed the door, Greene looked to the trunk. It made sense to Chloe; she'd assumed they'd end up popping it open anyway. But based on what they had found in the car, she was fully expecting to find nothing more than a spare tire.

Greene looked back over to the huddled group of policemen, still eyeing the car. "Sheriff, you got the equipment to pop this trunk open?"

One of the men nodded and instantly walked over to one of the patrol cars. He rummaged around in the trunk and came back with a tool that Chloe had only seen once before. It looked like a modified screwdriver with a heavier head. She knew that there was no finessing to getting a trunk open so the tools used for the job seemed rather primitive.

The sheriff took his tool to the back of Martin's car and placed it roughly into the lock along the back of the trunk. Another policeman had gone to his car to get a short and stubby-looking pry bar, just in case. But as it turned out, the bar wasn't necessary. There was a clattering noise and then a very audible unlatching sound as the trunk popped open.

The sheriff looked inside for a moment and then directly at Greene.

"Bingo," he said.

Chloe and Greene peered into the trunk. Chloe felt as if she'd been slapped across the face when she spied the body in the trunk. It was unmistakably Martin. He looked up at them with featureless eyes, as if he didn't really care much one way or the other that he was dead. There were two large puncture wounds along his chest, one directly above his heart. They were both very obvious stab wounds.

As she looked down at the body, an alarming thought went through her head.

Has Danielle told anyone else about how she found out that he was cheating on her? If so ... shit ... she could end up being a suspect. And the meds she's been taking and skipping whenever she feels like it certainly isn't going to help matters.

"Well, at least now we know it certainly wasn't suicide," Greene said. He then looked over to Chloe, biting back a frown. "You going to be too close to this one to take part?"

She almost said yes. The idea that Danielle would likely have to eventually be questioned did not sit well with her. But at the same time, she knew she had to remain professional.

"No, I'm good."

"Okay," he said. "So here's the good news for this situation. The body is fresh and wet. If there were any sort of traces of the killer left on him, they'll be quite easy to pull. Especially hair ... like this one ..."

He trailed off and leaned closer to the trunk, nearly reaching inside. With a gloved hand, he pointed to a stray hair on Martin's right forearm. It wasn't much longer than the hair on Martin's head.

And while it was wet, it was still pretty clear to see that it was black. And short.

Like Danielle's.

Chapter Eighteen

Chloe felt the day blaze by her in the same way time seems to pass ridiculously fast in the moments following a car accident or some other traumatic event. She felt like the day was pushing her hard toward something that was going to crash down on her. She kept thinking of Martin and Steven fighting—and of that sharp little smile on Danielle's face as it had happened.

She had elected not to call Danielle. Not yet. She wanted to have that stray hair analyzed and studied, wanted to make sure all bases were covered before she contacted Danielle. She knew nothing could be done in a concrete manner without getting a DNA sample from Danielle, but she also knew there could soon be enough reason to arrest Danielle and then collect the sample.

Still, as she waited in the lab for the results of the hair and a partial fingerprint that had been discovered on the edge of the trunk, Chloe kept looking at her phone. And while she did, there was one thought that kept bouncing around in her head, a thought she hoped was just the result of an overreaction.

Oh God, Danielle, what did you do? What did you DO?

While she waited, she worked closely with Greene in one of the lab's empty offices as they tried to find anyone who would have seen Martin in the last day or so of his life. They used phone records and the people who were known to have seen him last. Because of the block party, Chloe was forced to offer up her own name, as well as Danielle's.

"I can question her for you if you'd like," he said.

"No, I'm okay with it."

"You sure? It's a hell of a lot to put on an intern."

When she only nodded, Greene looked away. "You know," he added, "if she'll submit to a DNA test, maybe we can rule her out anyway."

"The DNA test off of the hair takes what ... eight hours?" she asked.

"If the hair is in good condition and fresh—as this one is—it can be as quick as five hours."

Just as it seemed that Greene was going to offer some words of comfort, a knock sounded at the door. Another intern poked his head in, a guy Chloe had only met a few times who worked closely with another agent in the realm of information gathering.

"Two potential leads for you," he said. "We've got a friend of the woman who placed the missing person's call. Says Martin Shields hit on her all the time. Says they hooked up one time at a party a few months back. She doesn't seem at all surprised that he wound up dead in a lake."

"She available to talk?" Greene asked.

"Yes. She's waiting for a call."

"What's the second lead?" Chloe asked.

"We ran Martin Shields's credit card report. The last thing purchased on it was fifty-one dollars in gas. We checked with the station it was purchased at and they're cueing up the security footage from the parking lot. They think there's a chance we might be able to get a look inside the car."

"Thanks," Green said as the intern handed them his findings and took his leave. Agent Greene then seemed to think very hard about something before getting to his feet and sighing.

"Here's what we're going to do," he said. "I'll go check out this woman who claims to have slept with Martin. No sense in you getting your hands dirty in that social triangle of your sister's life. You check into the gas station."

"What about Danielle?"

"I'll send some of the cops down there in Pinecrest to speak with her."

"Any chance I can talk to her first? This is ... this is messed up."

"Sorry, I misspoke earlier; I can't let you do that. Personal ties and all. Surely you understand."

"I do. And surely you understand that I know my sister. She didn't do this … there's no way. Please … give me just a few minutes to let her know what's coming."

Greene thought about it for a moment and then lowered his voice, even though they were alone. "I get it. Family is family. It's a peculiar situation for sure. You talk to her, but know that if she leaves town or skips out on us, it falls on you. I trust you, Chloe. So I'm putting a lot of that trust on you right now. Do the gas station first and then talk to your sister. But if something does come out of it, I need you to contact me with details right away."

"Thank you," she said. "Will you get in any trouble for this?"

"No. Technically it's not *outside* the lines of protocol. Any humane agent would extend the same courtesy to a veteran partner. So yes … I'm sure. Just, get going *now*. Once these results come in …"

Chloe nodded, certain where he was taking the comment. She grabbed up the information on the gas station and Martin's credit card and headed out of the room. As she made her way to the front of the building, she passed by the door that contained the lab that was currently working with the hair and print found at the lake.

Her heart skipped a beat and she hurried by. And once again, as she headed out to her car, that same thought blazed through her head like a comet.

What did you do, Danielle?

The gas station in question was less than three miles from Danielle's apartment. She arrived at 11:25 and there was practically no one there. A few customers milled around inside looking at snacks and magazines but the cashier was very cooperative and happy to help her. He'd already been notified that Chloe would be coming so he had cued up the footage in question.

After getting another employee who had been stocking the shelves to cover the register, the cashier took her to the back of the store. There, a small supply room was tucked away, filled with boxes of snacks and impulse buy items. In the far right corner, there was a small setup for the security system. One large screen showed six different camera angles from out in the parking lot. Another screen showed two angles from within the store, and a third from directly behind the cash register.

"The car the cops were asking me about comes in right here," the cashier said, pointing to the center angle at the bottom of the screen.

After several seconds, Martin's car did indeed creep into view. It parked under the awning of one of the six pumps outside. Once it was under the awning, it was impossible to see who was in the car.

"Can you back the footage up and then slow it down?" she asked.

"Yeah. And I can pause it when you need me to. Just tell me when."

The cashier backed the footage up, causing Martin's car to speedily vanish backward out of the screen. He then played the footage forward, slowing it down significantly. The car came into frame and then, for a moment, nearly filled it.

"Pause it," Chloe said.

The cashier did as he was asked. The car's passenger side was facing the camera. She could easily the see the shape of a person on the inside. But from the distance between the camera and the car, as well as the distortion caused by the passenger side window, it was hard to see any details.

"Can you zoom in a bit?" Chloe asked.

"Yeah. But it'll be grainy."

The cashier typed in a command on a security system that Chloe was beginning to understand was a bit outdated. The footage zoomed in a bit, bringing the figure in the passenger seat into view. The cashier had been right; the footage was incredibly grainy.

But that didn't matter. Because Danielle's likeness was unmistakable. Her head was even partially turned in the direction of the camera, making it much easier to identify her.

Really, it came as no real surprise. After all, Danielle had left the block party with Martin. And according to the timestamp on the security footage, this occurred about half an hour after Martin and Danielle had taken their leave.

Still, this was proof. This was enough evidence for the FBI—aside from herself, of course—to eye her as a potential suspect.

"Thank you," Chloe said, her voice low and trembling.

She backed away from the footage slowly but by the time she was back out in the store, she was practically dashing for the door. She had to get to Danielle and speak to her one on one before the hammer came down on her.

And based on the evidence, she didn't think it was going to take too long.

Chapter Nineteen

Chloe was doing everything she could to not assume that Danielle was guilty or that she had any information pertaining to what had happened to Martin. Yet when she saw that her car was parked in front of her apartment building, she was relieved. That would at least show that she was not trying to evade any conversations about the topic. If she was guilty of anything, the chances would be good that she'd be moving around rather than sitting idly in her apartment.

Chloe knocked rapidly on Danielle's door. "Danielle, it's me. I need to speak to you right away!"

She heard a quick series of footfalls on the other side of the door as Danielle responded. She opened the door and looked almost like a different person. She couldn't quite figure out why at first but then she saw it as clear as day in Danielle's eyes.

She looked scared.

Chloe had seen her paranoid and out of sorts. It had been her state most of the time during the last few times they'd been together. But Chloe wasn't sure that she had ever seen her sister *scared.* And that, in turn, scared Chloe.

"What's wrong?" Danielle asked.

"It's Martin," Chloe said, realizing for the first time the weight of the news she was about to deliver. "His body was found in the trunk of his car. I'm sorry …"

Danielle nodded and bit at her bottom lip as it quivered. "My God. I just … how did this happen?"

Chloe walked in without being formally invited and turned to Danielle. "I'm only going to ask you this once and I'm going to believe your answer no matter what," she said. "Danielle, did you have *anything* to do with what happened to Martin?"

"No," she said, wiping a tear away from her left eye. "Nothing."

Chloe had expected Danielle to seem offended at the insinuation. But she was currently too frightened to be offended, or so it seemed.

"I know this is a shock and you need to process, but we don't have much time."

"Time?" Danielle asked, clearly not understanding.

"Danielle… there was a stray hair and a partial fingerprint discovered at the scene. They're both being analyzed right now. And based on what we know at the moment, you were the last person to see him alive. And the hair… it was black and short, like yours. There's footage of the two of you pulling into a gas station and that's the last recorded evidence of Martin's whereabouts."

"Okay, but what does that mean?" Danielle asked.

"It means that in the eyes of any respectable investigator, it's going to appear as if you had something to do with it. That if you didn't kill him, you at least know something about it. So Danielle… please. I need you to be honest with me. Tell *me* the truth before another agent has to speak with you."

Chloe watched as her sister's face went through several different emotions. For a moment, it looked like she was going to break into a sobbing fit. Then she looked almost angry. After another handful of seconds, she simply sat down on the couch and looked blankly at Chloe.

"He loved that stupid car," she said. "And when I found that he was cheating on me, something snapped. I know it's stupid but… I'm always the one to screw people over, you know? I'm not used to being the one getting fucked over. And then the thing at the block party… I felt like he had tried to fool me just to serve some purpose. So… I got his car and I backed it into the lake. Just to get back at him. Just to be a bitch."

"Jesus, Danielle… how'd you even end up with the car?"

"It's a piece of shit. All busted up. The locks don't work and he showed me a while back where the key was… it was one night when we were out drinking and he got hammered and couldn't drive. So I just waited around a bit… when I knew he'd be asleep. I parked my car a few blocks away and walked to his apartment building to take it. But I had no idea the body was in the trunk. Chloe … I swear it."

"God, Danielle. That was unbelievably stupid. What the hell?"

"I know … " she said, close to tears—a state Chloe had rarely seen her in.

"Danielle, if that's your hair on him … or if there's any evidence of you having driven the car, you're going to be in a lot of trouble. Do you understand that?"

"Yes, I do. But … Chloe, what if there's someone else?"

"What do you mean?"

"I think someone might be trying to frame me for this."

"That's a very strong accusation," Chloe said, already praying that it might somehow be true. "What makes you think that?"

For the second time in the last few days, Chloe could tell there was something on the verge of her tongue, something she wanted to say but could not bring herself to do so.

"Danielle, you have to tell me anything that might clear you of this."

"There's nothing," she said.

"Fine. Then I at least need to know what else happened that day after Martin stopped to put gas in his car."

"Nothing. There really wasn't even a *goodbye* between us."

Chloe sighed, feeling herself being pushed toward panic. She knew there was really nothing she could do for Danielle at this point. But she wondered if she could at least buy her sister some time.

It'll come down to the hair and the print, Chloe thought. *Maybe it'll come back inconclusive or maybe even with this other woman's hair on it …*

"Danielle, I need you to stay here," Chloe said. "Depending on what becomes of the prints and the hair, there's a good chance someone from the bureau will want to talk to you. And if you're not here and are hard to get in touch with, that's going to be a bad sign."

"I'm not going anywhere," she said. "Chloe … I know it was stupid. But I just got so fucking angry at him. I didn't know what to do … "

"Yes, it *was* stupid. And immature and … *fuck!* Danielle, I love you dearly but you need some serious help."

With that, she stormed toward the door. She hated to abandon Danielle in that moment but if she stayed there, she was going to lose her cool and really grill her. She stormed out and went back to her car. She felt tears welling up, tears for her sister and the incredibly awkward situation that would soon arise between them.

She was headed back to HQ, planning to visit the lab again. She made it about three miles into the trip when her phone rang. It was Greene, and from the very first word—a tired-sounding *hello*—she could tell that he did not have good news.

"Hey," he said. "I've got nothing but bad news. First, Sophie Arbogast claims that she hadn't seen Martin for three days. They were supposed to meet up two nights ago. She sent him some provocative messages, and she said they always made him return her texts or calls. I've got some guys looking into her story in terms of alibis and it seems like hers are going to check out."

"Is that all?" Chloe asked.

"No. Where are you right now?"

"Between Danielle's apartment and HQ."

"So you already spoke with her?" he asked.

"Yes." She wanted to go ahead and tell him about how Danielle had driven the car into the lake but could not bring herself to do it.

"Well, you might want to turn back around and go back to her place. They found a salvageable print on the key to Martin's car. A very fresh one. Chloe… I'm so sorry… but it's a match for Danielle."

That's when the tears *did* start coming and they came quickly and with force. Chloe excused herself from the phone and then turned the car around the next chance she got.

She was going to have to go back to Danielle's and somehow face the fact that her twin sister was the prime suspect in what was looking to be a pretty blatant murder.

Chapter Twenty

Chloe watched the whole thing happen and it was like having an out of body experience. She was both surprised and saddened to see that Danielle really didn't even fight it. She didn't protest too much and there were very few arguments. Greene stood with Chloe while another agent put handcuffs on Danielle and started leading her out of the apartment.

Danielle only looked at Chloe once, right in the middle of having her rights read to her. There was a heartbreaking stare between them in that moment—a moment in which Chloe realized just how broken and lost her sister was. It was also a look that made Chloe feel that maybe—just *maybe*—Danielle would have been capable of killing Martin. Even though Danielle had admitted to sinking the car—something that would surely come up in questioning—did that mean she could kill him, too?

Maybe … maybe she *did* do it.

She felt her heart breaking as she looked at her sister. *Maybe if I'd been a better sister over the years … reached out and tried to get to know her better. Maybe then I would have seen this coming …*

It started to sink in, a dark reality that she could feel on her like cobwebs. But still, it just made no sense. For one thing, how the hell would frail little Danielle have lifted the rather built body of Martin enough to get him into the trunk?

These thoughts whirled in Chloe's mind as she walked out behind the other agent who escorted Danielle through the doorway.

"Do you have a lawyer?" Chloe asked.

"No. And don't talk to me. You turned me in, didn't you? You didn't even give me a chance. You thought it was me right away."

"Danielle, I—"

"I said don't talk to me," Danielle snapped.

"I'll see that you get a good one. I'll—"

"Don't," Danielle said. "I don't want you involved in this."

Chloe did as her sister asked. She stopped talking as she walked along with the agent, who led her to a generic black sedan. Chloe watched helplessly as Danielle ducked down and got into the back seat. The agent closed the door and then shot Chloe an apologetic look before getting behind the wheel.

Chloe's thoughts flashed back to the morning she and Danielle had watched her father ushered into the back of a police car. For a moment, it felt like her life had come full circle.

"Will they take her to HQ?" Chloe asked Greene.

"Yeah, at the start. They'll interrogate her there. Depending on how that goes, they might move her. I imagine they'll angle for a DNA test, too. To try to match that stray hair they found on Martin's arm. I doubt they'll keep her long. Really, this doesn't have the weight of a bureau case. Pinecrest PD will likely wrap it up."

"I need to go," Chloe said. "I need to be with her."

"Give it some time," Greene said. "You know how the system works. You can be there right away but you won't get to speak with her for a while. Let the feds to their job. I'll make a call for you. I'll make sure you're allowed to speak with her as early as possible."

Chloe nodded and did her best to keep the tears from coming. She'd already almost puked in front of Agent Greene. Did she really want to *cry* in front of him?

"I want you to go home," Greene said. "Take the rest of the day. I'll cover with your supervisor."

"You'll call me when she's available to talk?"

"Absolutely. Do you need a ride? Are you going to be okay?"

"I don't know," she said.

And with that, she turned her back and headed for her car. The tears came right away now, and she did everything she could to not let Greene see them.

⚜ ⚜ ⚜

It was rare that Chloe allowed Steven to see her in a vulnerable state but that's exactly what he saw when she returned home. He was sitting on the couch, slipping a card into an envelope. She saw that it was a thank-you card for the tailor who had helped him with acquiring the perfect tuxedo for the wedding.

"You're home early," he said, uninterested. But then he saw her face, the clear signs that she had been crying, and got to his feet. "What is it?" he asked.

She told him everything. She told him about Martin's car… about Martin's body being found in the trunk and the stray hair and the fingerprint. She told him where Danielle currently was and how something just didn't seem to fit.

"Are you sure?" Steven asked. "I hate to mention it, but you *did* say that she was skipping some medicine to help with mood swings, right?"

"I did," Chloe said. "But even though I don't really know my sister, I know her well enough to know that she's not capable of killing someone."

Do you, though? she wondered, thinking of the sinister smile from the block party.

They sat down on the couch, Chloe feeling the weight of the day finally pressing down on her. She watched as Steven sealed the thank-you note. It actually made her feel a bit better to see that he was actually taking initiative in *anything* related to the wedding.

"What can I do for you?" Steven asked.

"Nothing," she said. "Just… just be here right now. I don't know how to handle this, Steven. And I just need you to be here for me. No snide comments about Danielle, okay? Can you do that?"

He put an arm around her, drew her close, and kissed her on the side of the mouth. "Of course I can," he said.

And he did. They sat together on the couch like that for a very long time. And while it was comforting, Chloe couldn't help but wonder what she had missed during those years she and Danielle had spent apart. What had Danielle been through? Had she encountered something that had shaped her in some unimaginable way—maybe even some way that would indeed make her capable of murder?

The scary part was that Chloe simply did not know the answer.

Scarier still was the fact that she'd likely find out within the next few days.

Chloe skipped her morning run the following day. She simply didn't have it in her. Her stomach was a knot of worry, nearly to the point of making her feel sick. She had a cup of coffee but was unable to eat much breakfast. She kept looking to her phone, waiting for Green to call or text.

He finally did, just after seven o'clock. "You're going to be mad at me," he said.

"Why's that?"

"We were given permission for you to talk to her around midnight. But I wanted you to get a good night's sleep. This isn't looking good for her, which means these next few days could be very long for you."

She *was* angry at first but was then able to see the care in his gesture. He was just trying to look out for her.

"Are you there right now?" Chloe asked.

"No, but I'm on the way."

"Then I'll see you in about half an hour."

She ended the call and took her uneaten breakfast of eggs and sausage links to the kitchen counter. Steven was sitting at the bar, scrolling through his newsfeed on his phone, slowly eating a bowl of oatmeal.

"You want this?" she asked, offering the plate.

"Sure," he said. "Who was on the phone?"

"Agent Greene. I've been cleared to go speak with Danielle."

"Oh," Steven said. "Do you think that's a good idea?"

"Why wouldn't it be?" Chloe asked.

"I don't know," he said. "It's evident that you feel certain she didn't do it. But if you go down there around people you're going to have to eventually work with and most of them think she *did* do it… that could cause some tension."

"You're absolutely right," she said. "But this is my sister. I have to be there for her."

When he nodded and sighed, his frustration was apparent. Chloe thought it might be something they'd need to discuss at some point. But for now, she was more interested in getting to her sister.

As she gathered up her things and headed for the door, Steven called out to her. "If you think you're going to be late getting home today, let me know. Don't forget, we're supposed to go to my folks' house for dinner tonight."

"Yeah," she snapped. Being around his parents was about the last thing she wanted to even think about considering everything that was happening. And the fact that Steven could even mention it right now was maddening.

She left the house without another word and made the drive to Baltimore. It was a tense ride as her mind pinballed back and forth between Danielle's situation and the growing turmoil between her and Steven. Deep down, she supposed this current situation with Danielle would really show Steven's true colors. Would he support her while Danielle went through this hell or would he continue to voice his disdain for her?

It was a selfish way to think, but she knew that in one way or another, her own life would be significantly different when all of this came to an end. She could beat herself up over not being an attentive sister all she liked, but it would change nothing. But if Danielle came out of this unscathed… well, things were going to have to change.

When she parked in the parking garage beside HQ, she did her best not to break into a sprint toward the building. When she entered, there were people looking at her with sympathy, some managing a nod of greeting while others quickly looked away.

As she made her way back to the interrogation rooms, Greene met her with a cup of coffee in hand. He gave it to her with a look of worry in his eyes.

"What's that look?" Chloe asked. "Is there something wrong?"

"No, not really. But we told her that you were coming to speak with her. We figured it might help to lift her spirits, you know? But she's refusing to see you."

"What?"

Greene led her into a nearby vacant conference room and closed the door. "She's in a bad state," he said. "I think she's afraid that she's disappointed you. She'd depressed and honestly just doesn't want to talk to anyone."

It broke Chloe's heart a little to hear these things, but she supposed she understood.

"She thinks I turned her in. She thinks I automatically assumed she's guilty."

"Yes, that too."

"Has she said anything that indicates she killed him?"

"No. But her alibis aren't strong at all. Being antisocial by nature, she doesn't really have much to offer. No one other than Martin would have seen her. She said she saw and spoke to you between the block party and the discovery of the car, but the time scale really doesn't even matter. It couldn't be used as a reliable alibi."

"You have to know… this is impossible for me to believe," Chloe said, almost pleading. "She has her issues, sure… but she's not a killer. At least I didn't think so. But… Jesus, I just don't know now. It doesn't seem like my sister, you know?"

Greene seemed hesitant to say anything. After a moment of thought, though, he finally said: "I think I believe you. But for now, we have to go with what the case gives us. You understand that, right?"

"I do," she said. "Thanks for the support. Look… there's this medicine she's on for her mood swings. I don't know which drug, honestly. Is there any way for you to check in to see if she's taking them?"

"She is," he said. "She requested them not too long after she got here. We had an agent go back to her apartment to get them."

"Good. Thanks."

"I can't imagine how tough this is for you. But keep a level head. I know you have to be a sister first, but this is a great time to prove that you can be an effective agent above all else. I know it might not be where your head is at right now, but this is an opportune time to prove yourself."

"That's a sobering thought," she said with a shaky laugh.

But the more the comment stuck with her, the more she could appreciate it—and the more determined she became to find some way to prove that Danielle was innocent.

CHAPTER TWENTY ONE

After the heartbreak of finding that Danielle was refusing to speak to her, Chloe decided to let it ride out for another day or so. While they had spent a great deal of time apart these last few years, Chloe felt like she knew her sister well. Danielle was going to clam up for a day or two, an adult version of the silent treatment. After that, she might allow some people in—hopefully her.

With an assurance from Greene that she'd still have access to Danielle tomorrow, Chloe headed out for the day. She went home and was once again anxious to see how Steven would react to all of this. She found herself wondering if he'd be supportive or relieved that his troublesome sister-in-law was out of the equation.

She rummaged around the house for an hour or so, trying to keep herself busy by cleaning, anything to keep her mind from obsessively latching onto Danielle. When she heard Steven pull up shortly after four o'clock, she felt like she was on the battle lines of some war no one knew was being waged. They had dinner with his parents tonight, and God only knew that was stressful enough. Adding all of this drama with Danielle was doing nothing more than firing the first shot.

Steven came in and seemed to be in a good mood. He usually was when he found her already home when he arrived home from work.

"Short day?" he asked.

"Yeah."

"Any movement on the thing with Danielle?"

She was a little surprised that he'd asked so blatantly. She was also surprised to find that there appeared to be genuine interest in his voice.

"No," she said. "Nothing yet."

He nodded and made a *hmm* sound of acknowledgment before heading off to the bedroom. Chloe had not realized until after they had been engaged just how tied down to his parents Steven was. Whenever they met with his family for dinner, he always made sure to get there on time. Even when they had visited them before they had moved back to town, even if it was out at a restaurant, Steven got stressed out about being on time. That was why she fully expected him to emerge from the bedroom ten minutes from now changed and completely ready for dinner—even though they weren't due to arrive for another hour and a half.

The fear that his parents might suffocate them a little had come to her before. But now that they were beginning to live out that reality, Chloe could feel it sinking in like a needle into her skin.

While Sally Brennan had more than enough of her faults, there was one positive to the woman: she could cook her ass off.

When Chloe sat down to Wayne and Sally Brennan's table that night with their baby boy, she had prepared a rack of lamb, seasoned asparagus, and a from-scratch salad that was accompanied by a homemade vinaigrette. The pleasantness of the food itself didn't last very long, though. Sally didn't seem to be able to go a whole five minutes without throwing out a barrage of questions.

"Steven, what's the bruise on the side of your head?" Sally asked.

Chloe winced a bit. She'd thought the bruising from the fight with Martin had faded enough so that Sally and Wayne wouldn't see it. Now the ball was in Steven's court. Would he gladly tell them that Danielle had brought a guy to their house that had made an ass of himself at a block party and started throwing punches? Or would he—God help us all—lie to his mother to help his soon-to-be-wife save some face?

"Oh my God, it was the stupidest thing," Martin said. "I left the medicine cabinet open the other night. I turned away for a moment and then turned around to walk back into the bedroom and ran right into the damned thing. The bruise was pretty nasty for the first day or two."

Wayne Brennan actually laughed heartily at this. "You always were sort of a klutz," he said, taking a large gulp of his glass of red wine.

"Still am, I guess," Steven said.

He reached under the table and gave her hand a little squeeze. *That was for you,* the gesture seemed to say.

There was silence at the table for a moment, broken only by the clinking of silverware against the plates. An uncomfortable feeling started taking root in Chloe's stomach as she noticed the thin and rather restrained look on Sally's face.

Then she spoke, and Chloe understood the uncharacteristic silence at the Brennan dinner table. She'd been holding back, trying to find the right time to drop her little bomb.

"Forgive me for asking," Sally said, looking directly at Chloe. "But I've heard from two different people that your sister was arrested on some absolutely ghastly chargers. Some are saying murder! That can't be right, can—"

"Mom…" Steven said, not only surprised but looking a little appalled as well.

"Well, I just wanted to know," Sally said, as if she was the one being attacked. "After all, if it's true and Danielle is going to be…preoccupied…it *does* affect the wedding."

"With all due respect," Chloe said, "my sister is being held for something she did not do. I haven't really been thinking too much about the wedding."

"Is there anyone else you can ask to take her place?" Sally asked.

The absolute nerve of this woman, Chloe thought. Sure, they were footing the bill for the vast majority of the wedding, but she was taking that responsibility like some sort of priesthood. To say she was using it as a control over Chloe was not overstating things. But now with this new development with Danielle, she apparently felt she had more leverage.

Fuck that, Chloe thought.

"No, not really," Chloe said. "And if it's bothering you that badly, Mrs. Brennan, maybe we should start talking about postponing the wedding."

The look on her face made it clear that she had not expected such a tactic from Chloe. She looked like someone had slapped her, being so dramatic as to even recoil from the comment.

"Oh, I hardly think so," she said. "I've already reserved the grounds at Elder Gardens! I don't see the need to make so many other people change their plans just because of your sister's misfortune."

"I didn't insinuate that," Chloe said. She had much more on the tip of her tongue but she bit it all back. Instead, she got to her feet and looked over at Steven. "Please… take your time in finishing. Enjoy your dinner with your parents. I'll be waiting in the car when you're ready."

"Chloe," Wayne said, using a rare authoritative tone. While he could be equally as annoying as Sally, he at least pretended to be a rational and kind human being most of the time. "This is a little rude of you."

"I'm so sorry," she said. "Maybe we should think of someone to replace *me* in the wedding, too, huh?"

"Chloe, please," Steven said.

"Oh, please," Sally said. "Are we going to pretend that this is really a surprise? We've always known Danielle was trouble. A rotten little girl from the start from what I hear."

"What you hear?" Chloe asked. "Do you always believe what you hear? Are you capable of thinking for yourself and forming your own opinions?"

Again, Sally's reaction was borderline comical in its drama. And Chloe was well aware that there might be something slightly wrong with her… because she loved seeing that look of faked pain on the woman's face.

But Chloe had heard enough. She walked away from the table, never looking back. She did just as she had said: she walked out to the car, got in the passenger seat, and closed the door. She sat there for a moment, staring at her phone. She wondered if it would do any good to call Greene and see if there was any way she could talk to Danielle. Even if she was refusing to speak to her, Chloe figured there had to be *some* way to get around that.

She went over the facts of the case in her head, mainly to obliterate her hatred for Steven's parents and this gossipy little community. It had been just two days. Two days and the grapevine had spread its sticky tendrils into the ears of Sally Brennan.

It was 7:47 when Steven came out to the car. That meant that he had stayed inside for another fifteen minutes after she walked out. Chloe could only imagine the sorts of vile things they had been saying about Danielle while she had been absent. Hell … they had probably gone so far as to convince Steven to call off the engagement.

He got behind the wheel, cranked the engine to life, and pulled out of the driveway. Three minutes passed before he said a word.

"That was a bit of an overreaction," he said.

"Was it? I think it was incredibly rude—and, might I add, calculated—to say something as stupid as that. She didn't wait for me to confirm or deny what people were saying. All she was worried about was who would fill my sister's slot on her little charts and guides she's making for the wedding. Which, by the way, is *absolutely* going to her head."

"Chloe, that's my mom. Want to watch your tone?"

"My *tone*? Are you even serious right now? She has no right to talk about my sister like that!"

"Chloe … you said it yourself the other day. The case against her is pretty solid. It looks like there's only one outcome. And Mom might be right."

"How so? Say whatever you're going to say, Steven."

"Fine. I don't think it's completely out of line for myself or for my mother to *not* want a murder suspect participating in the wedding."

Her first urge was to punch him. And she had never felt that way toward him before. Her second urge was to tell him to stop the car so she could get out. But she did neither. She swallowed it down and let it boil inside. The look on Steven's face—one that indicated he knew he had screwed up—was more than enough for her in that moment.

Chapter Twenty Two

Chloe wasted no time the following morning. Even though it was a Saturday, she sprang into action as if it were a typical workday. She even skipped out on her run again and managed to get ready for the day without uttering a word to Steven. He finally squeaked out a "Goodbye" from behind his cup of coffee as she walked out the front door, but she did not respond. She only closed the door hard and headed for her car, anxious to be away from him.

A small knot of dread started to form in her stomach as she finally made the decision: if Danielle wasn't going to speak to her, she'd get some information in other ways. She drove toward Danielle's apartment, that knot growing tighter and tighter with each mile. As she drove, she started to wonder at what point a case became too personal for an agent. Surely she was already over that line. She supposed Greene would have to sit her down at some point and tell her that she could no longer be active on the case.

But until then, she figured she'd do what she could.

As she approached Danielle's door, Chloe pulled out the small lock pick kit she had "borrowed" from her earlier days in the academy. It wasn't necessarily stealing, as it and various other resources were accessible to all agents in the skills labs. Without the proper guidance or instruction, though, what she was about to do would be heavily frowned upon.

It took her about ten seconds with the lock pick kit to get Danielle's door open. When she stepped inside, she closed the door quietly behind her, as if she knew she really shouldn't be there. She stood by the door and looked around. She wasn't even sure what she was looking for. She knew the bureau had already taken Danielle's laptop. They'd want to check her emails and all other digital communications with Martin.

She slowly walked a circuit around the apartment. She looked over her sister's belongings, realizing that she was in many ways the same young woman she had grown up with. The movie collection looked the same, the music collection looked the same, even the two shirts strewn on the couch with band names looked the same.

She walked into the kitchen, glad to see the prescription bottle gone and with Danielle. Feeling like a traitor, she started to snoop through her drawers and cabinets. She wasn't sure what she was looking for, exactly. When she found the kitchen not helpful, she walked into Danielle's bedroom. It was surprisingly neat. Then again, there was very little to be untidy; there was her bed (sloppily made), a single dresser, a bedside table, and a dirty clothes basket that was overflowing with mostly black clothes.

What the hell am I looking for?

She didn't know. She checked the bedroom closet and found nothing but a few boxes of old paperback books and a smattering of dressier clothes that probably never got worn. She also found nothing in the bathroom, though she did see an unopened pregnancy test kit which, she supposed, spoke volumes about Danielle's promiscuity.

When she walked back out into the living room, her eyes fell on the old roll-top desk that their grandmother had owned. It sat against the wall between the kitchen and the living room. When they had been much younger, Danielle had always been fixated on the roll top. She used it to play school, to do her homework, to sketch and doodle. It had seemed fitting that Danielle had taken it when their grandmother had passed away.

Chloe ran her hands along the curved portion that rolled up and down. She smiled at the memories it brought to the surface of her mind. Slowly, she lifted the roll-top to reveal the desk underneath. There, she saw scattered correspondence items: envelopes, stamps, loose-leaf paper, pens. There was nothing useful like an address book or a check register. Chloe frowned and started to roll the top back down.

But then she saw the few papers tucked in the back, behind a box of envelopes. They were very clearly hidden with some intention—the sort of thing you wanted to keep but not in plain sight. Chloe dug them out and found seven notes.

She read them and her heart seemed to stop beating for a moment. They were all short, most not even a sentence in length. They were also written in a very steady hand, all on what appeared to be sketchbook paper. They had apparently all come in envelopes that looked almost elegant. There were no addresses on the envelopes, neither of the sender nor the recipient. She read them one by one and, although they made her incredibly uneasy, they also instilled a hope that these might be the start of getting Danielle out of custody.

Reading over them, she tried to find some meaning or purpose behind them.

You'll never change, will you?

Tell anyone about these letters and I'll kill you. Stop looking into the past.

The guy you brought home last night is probably married. Slut.

Aren't you ashamed of what you've become? You should be dead, like your mother.

Does it hurt worse to be a whore or a failure?

YOU'RE ONLY GOING TO MAKE IT WORSE.

Kill him or I will.

The last one was clearly the most alarming. Was Martin the *him*? And if so, just who in the hell was delivering these letters? Chloe read them all again, returning each one to its envelope. When she was done with them, she held them closely to her side and carried them out of the apartment.

She felt like she'd discovered something important. Now the problem would be getting Danielle to speak with her. Chloe figured that if Danielle knew who was sending the letters, they might know who had really killed Martin.

It could have been her, some stubborn and logical part of her mind said as she returned to her car. But as she placed the letters on the seat, she knew better.

Knowing the messages those letters contained, she almost felt like the real killer was sitting right there beside her. And for some reason, they had something against Danielle.

But what? And why?

Chloe didn't know. But she sure as hell intended to find out.

She placed a call to Agent Greene before she was even out of the Lavender Hills subdivision. He answered right away, as he always did, and already sounded like the day had taken it out of him.

"You sound beat," she told him.

"No, I'm good. I've just been inundated with a shit-ton of information in the last half an hour. And you may find some of it extremely relevant, actually. Although I don't know if you would consider it good news or bad news."

"Is it about Danielle?"

"It is. She's fine... but they've transferred her. They've taken her to Riverside Correctional. As of about five o'clock this morning, she's officially being held in a prison."

"But she hasn't even been convicted yet!"

"True. But her alibis are so thin, Chloe. And the hair... that's the nail in the coffin. Her hair on the body... it was hers. She did submit to a DNA test and the hair came back as hers."

"Shit..."

"I think she'd probably speak with you now. I literally just got off the phone with one of the guys at Riverside. She's only been there for a little while, but she seems docile and cooperative from what he's telling me."

"I need to try..."

"I figured. I told them there was a good chance that I'd be sending an intern from the bureau to speak with her. I gave them your name and they obviously picked up on the last name matching. They're not thrilled with the idea, but they're going to allow it since she technically hasn't been convicted yet."

"Thanks, Agent Greene."

"Don't thank me yet. As an intern, this is going to be heavy. I honestly don't expect you to successfully separate the personal from the professional."

"It won't be a problem. I'll meet you at HQ after I've talked to her."

"Great," he said with a smile in his voice. "I'll see you then."

Chloe ended the call and increased her speed. Thinking of Danielle in prison was the equivalent of someone reaching into her past and breaking apart some of the better memories. She needed to speak to Danielle to learn *everything* she knew—to get to the bottom of the threatening letters she had found.

And then she was going to have to find who wrote them if she intended to clear her sister's name.

The officers greeted her warmly and wasted no time guiding her down the corridors of Riverside Correctional. At once, Chloe's alarms started going off. She heard someone screaming further off in the building. She could also hear another woman muttering something from somewhere close by, sounds of hatful gibberish.

And her sister was here. God help her.

The officers handed Chloe off to a guard who walked her down a final hall and then unlocked the door to a small room. It was decorated with only a small conference table and three chairs. Danielle was occupying one of the chairs. She looked up at Chloe as she entered and managed something that was supposed to be a smile.

Danielle didn't look as bad as Chloe had expected. She had been expecting to see a haggard woman, cried out and on the verge of losing her mind. Instead, Danielle simply looked tired. And because she always looked a little tired, it wasn't much of a difference in Chloe's eyes.

She also looked mad, though. Chloe supposed this was to be expected, given the way the last forty-eight hours of her life had gone.

"Danielle… I'm so sorry," Chloe said. "How are you doing?" Chloe had fully expected a hug at the very least. But Danielle remained seated and shook her head. She was clearly still very pissed off. When she spoke, her voice sounded rough and far away. "Not great, Chloe."

"I've been trying to figure out how—"

"I'm not expecting you to save the day," Danielle said. "I know there's only so much you can do. And you know what? When these men that have been interrogating me break down the way the case looks... I can understand why you thought it was me. It *does* sound bad. And I didn't help matters by sinking the damn car. I don't blame you for thinking it was me."

"You're right about me not being able to do much," Chloe said. "But the agent that is overseeing me is being very cooperative and understanding. He let me go look around your apartment for anything I could find. And I found the letters, Danielle... the threatening letters that came in the unaddressed envelopes."

Danielle said nothing; she looked at the surface of the table like a child being scolded by a concerned parent.

"Why didn't you tell me about them?" Chloe asked.

"Well, you read them. The one that said I'd be killed if I told anyone made me very hesitant to share that information. Besides... what the hell was I going to tell you? I don't know who is sending them and they come at random times. But this last one... they apparently knew I was dating Martin and... Chloe, do you really think they killed him?"

"It seems to point in that direction but it also seems a little too perfect. Like a setup."

"Chloe... I swear to you that I did not kill him. I understand how what I did to the car makes it look that way but you have to believe me."

"I do. But I have to tell you that the case against you is a strong one. The fingerprint and the hair basically nailed you. How did it get there if you didn't do it? The fingerprint makes sense, but not the hair."

"I just don't know," she said. "But I was in that car quite a few times. I don't think it's such a stretch to think that at some point, one of my loose hairs got caught on his clothes or his arm or something."

Chloe had considered the very same things but knew that it would all seem very flimsy in court. What made it harder was even this two-minute visit had confirmed Danielle's innocence in Chloe's mind. Again, though, the heart and gut instinct of a sister wasn't going to hold up in court, either.

"How is it here?" Chloe asked. "Do you feel safe, at least?"

"Well, they've got me in a holding cell at the end of the building away from gen pop. But they're refusing to even acknowledge my meds. I have no idea where they are ... probably with my personal belongings. I just feel trapped ... which I guess is the whole point of a prison, right?"

The little joke fell flat. Chloe tried to keep her own emotions in check. After all, what sense did it make for her to feel helpless when it was, in fact, Danielle who needed all of the help?

"I'll do what I can to make sure you get your meds. And I swear to you that I'll do everything I can to find out who really killed Martin. I don't know how long you'll be in holding until they actually charge you ..."

The door to the room opened behind them and a tall man with completely gray hair and an expensive suit stepped in.

"My lawyer," Danielle said. "State appointed."

"That's right," the man said, stepping forward and offering his hand. "Pete Jackson. I'll be working with Danielle and seeing what we can do to prevent this charge from sticking. I take it you're the sister she's mentioned?"

"I am. Agent Chloe Fine." Of course, she wasn't quite an agent yet, but this state-appointed lawyer didn't need to know that.

"Well, as the agent trying to free her, *and* the sister, I think it's important that you know this is not looking good. That fingerprint—"

"On the key, yes," Chloe said. "Are her prints anywhere on Martin's body?" she asked defensively.

"No, but the—"

"And has anyone found a murder weapon yet?"

"No," Jackson said, seeing where this was going.

"Then I'd kindly appreciate it if you wouldn't speak about your client as if the verdict has already been pinned on her. Maybe do your job a bit better."

"Of course I will try my best to reach an innocent verdict," Jackson said. "But you have to understand that based on what I'm working with, I have to look at where the evidence is pointing. And right now, it's pointing towards a lifetime sentence for second-degree murder. In the end, we may have to strike a plea bargain. I'm just trying to prepare Danielle for what she can potentially expect."

As if the words had placed some sort of spell on Danielle, she let out a gasping sort of moan the moment the sentence was over. Chloe had never heard such a sound come from Danielle, and it wrecked her. She cast a hateful look toward Jackson. He sighed and slowly backed out of the room, quietly closing the door behind him.

It was then that Danielle got out of her chair and rushed over to Chloe. The sisters embraced in a way they hadn't since childhood, in a way that brought back fun summer days as well as nights plagued with bad dreams. Chloe had to choke back her own little cry of sorrow as she wrapped Danielle in her arms.

"I want to tell you it's going to be okay, but I can't do that right now," Chloe said.

"I know," Danielle said into her ear. "And that's okay. It's not your job."

But Chloe disagreed. If she was going to pave her own way as an agent, what better way than breaking this case open—than rescuing her sister when it seemed there was an ironclad case against her?

If she was going to be an agent worth a damn, maybe it *was* her job.

Chapter Twenty Three

Of the two Fine sisters, Chloe was absolutely the more sentimental and emotional. But there comes a time when sentiment and emotion will only get you so far. It was very rare that they got results. It was this mindset that had Chloe leaving Riverside Correctional just fifteen minutes after she'd arrived. With tears still drying on the side of her face, she went back to HQ. She blasted right by her office and even neglected to check in with Greene. She went straight for the lab that was provided for the interns, just off of the primary lab for the field agents. Being a Saturday, it was very quiet in the lab, giving her the silence and space she needed to do her best thinking.

She took the letters from Danielle's apartment out of her laptop bag and started doing her best to come up with some sort of an answer. She used one of the basic evidence kits to study the letters and the envelopes closer. She had only ever done this once before in a real-life situation, helping to pull prints from a crowbar earlier in the year. Still, she'd gone through these motions more than a dozen times in the course of her training and was comfortable enough to be working it alone.

She started off by carefully dusting them for prints. She dusted the letters themselves first and then the envelopes. The powder revealed several fingerprints, all of which could easily belong to Danielle. She scanned the prints and ran them through the system. As she waited for results—which could take anywhere from ten minutes to two hours—she looked over the letters again. Was there some sort of symbolism in them, maybe even clues as to the identity of the writer?

She saw nothing that jumped out at her and decided it was just the deranged notes of someone with a very serious mental issue.

She then pulled out her laptop and pulled up the digital files that had been accumulated so far for the murder of Martin Shields. She found fairly detailed reports, including photographs of the car, the lake area, and the body. She found herself drawn to the pictures that showed the stab wounds, completely unable to imagine Danielle viciously ramming a knife into someone's chest.

It seemed absolutely impossible to her.

But she admitted to driving the car into the lake, she thought. *Really, how much more of a mental leap is it between doing something like that and seriously considering the act of putting a knife in someone's heart?*

"No," she said into the empty room.

Danielle didn't do this. We may feel like strangers sometimes, but I know her, dammit.

She handled the enveloped again, her hands secured in gloves. She checked the flaps and the sticker on the tapered edge of it. She looked at the underside of the flap, looking for any slight tears or gumming... any evidence that someone might have licked the envelope to close it. But she saw nothing of the sort. The writer had been careful there, too, using the sticker to close the envelope rather than providing a possible sample of their DNA by licking it.

As she tidied the letters up into a neat pile, the results from the fingerprints came back. She read over the results, not at all surprised by them.

The only prints on the envelopes and the letters were Danielle's. Of course she'd handled them. There was no way in hell she'd ever think her fingerprints would be lifted off of it in relation to a murder investigation one day.

Chloe let out a curse and slammed her hand down on the table. She was angry and frightened, two emotions that did not go well together. Not knowing what else to do and feeling very much like a kid who had gotten in over her head, she picked up her phone and placed a call to Greene.

"Hey, Fine," he said. "How's your sister?"

"Scared shitless," Chloe said. "And with good reason. Agent Greene... I know you don't know me very well at all but I need you to trust me. My sister did not do this. And I don't know how to explain it to you other than a sister's intuition. I *know* her. She didn't do this."

"Then you need to prove it. I want you to think like an agent… like you're no longer an intern but an actual field agent. If you wanted to prove her innocence, what's the most surefire way to do it?"

"I'd need to find something that links someone else to the scene," she said. She was vaguely aware that Greene was currently about as strict as he had ever been with her—but still helpful. She wondered if he had formed his own opinions about Danielle and the case.

"Good thinking. Now how would you do that?"

"Well, I'd need to revisit the scene. But the car's gone now. And by the time I get permission to look inside of it—assuming it's already at the scrap yard—Danielle would probably be convicted. So…"

She stopped, thinking. *So what? What would the next step be?*

It came to her slowly and it truly did make her feel like she was a huge step beyond an intern. "Agent Greene, where are you right now?"

"In town, about to interview a witness to a B and E. Why?"

"How soon can you meet me at the morgue?"

"And why would I want to do that?" Greene asked in a playfully mocking tone that let her know exactly why he'd want to do that.

"Because I need to get a look at the body."

"Good work, Fine. And yes… I can meet you there in an hour."

Chapter Twenty Four

Chloe had been required to undergo what the students had referred to as "morgue time" during her second year of classes, mostly to get used to the idea of having to look over dead bodies for evidence and clues. It had been an uncomfortable experience, but it hadn't really bothered her.

What she discovered when she met Greene at the morgue to look over Martin's body was that those classes were one thing—and being up close and personal with a freshly dead body—one she had recently met while still alive, at that—was a completely different situation. When she and Greene were granted access to the examination room, everything in the world seemed to go still and quiet. She looked over the body, completely nude and exposed to the halogen lights overhead.

The stab wounds had been slightly cleaned but not yet completely tidied up. Chloe could now see the marks quite clearly. She was surprised how almost *fake* they seemed. But it was all too real… and she was going to have to get used to it.

"Tell me what you're looking for," Greene said, clearly quizzing her.

"Any signs of a struggle other than the stab wounds," she said. "Bruising, abrasions, things like that."

"And why would those be of any interest to us?"

"They'd be a very good source for fingerprints."

"Indeed. Remember that we also have his clothes being scoured for prints and hairs as well. So far, nothing."

Greene stood back and let her examine the body. The only thing out of the ordinary she could find was a small bruise between the neck and the base of the shoulder. It was the kind that could have come from anything, small and light.

"Tell me what you're thinking as you process," Greene said. "Like if you were recording your notes."

"Nothing of interest right away," she said. "Though the fact that the wounds are from the front indicates a bigger chance of there being a struggle. That being said, I've looked at the wrists and the backs of the hands for any sign of a fight. Seeing that there are none leads me to believe that the murderer was right there with him when it happened. I doubt the killer took him by surprise. Therefore, the killer was likely someone he trusted."

Someone like Danielle, she thought.

She crossed her arms and gave it some more thought. "Of course, there could have still been a struggle, just a very bad one. But I've seen Martin move. He moves like someone with some training…perhaps a boxer or mixed martial artist. The headlock he put Steven into was a pro one. So perhaps he struck a defensive pose from his training to try to ward off an attack—but was just too late."

She leaned in and checked his hands again. She still saw nothing on them to indicate that he had been involved in a recent struggle. She did, however, find dirt beneath his fingernails. And it appeared to be fresh.

"I've got some dirt under the fingernails here," she said.

She leaned in closer as Greene selected a drawer to his right and fished around inside. "We technically aren't allowed to do this…" he said, but took something out of the drawer anyway. It was a simple scraping device, about the thickness of a sheet of thin cardboard but with the appearance of a scalpel.

Chloe used this to scrape some of the dirt out from beneath Martin's fingernails. It was tightly compacted but even from the few grains that fell onto the exam table, she could tell that there was also some blood mixed in with it.

"Looks to be some blood mixed in with the dirt," she said. "Could be his own, but if he tried to defend himself at all, it could also be the killer's."

"Good work," Greene said. "I'll head out and get someone to bag this up. I'll make it a priority and we should have results back from that blood within four to six hours."

The idea of it was exciting but she then realized that it could come back as Danielle's blood. And if that were the case, she would have been working this entire time to do nothing more than solidify Danielle's prison term.

Apparently, this realization showed on her face. Greene paused at the door and hesitated. "You sure you don't want to sit this one out?"

"I'm sure. Even if... well, even if the results come back with bad news, at least I'll know. And if it's her then I have to know why. I have to understand."

"With all due respect," Greene said, "that's something you need to let go of. Because in my experience, it's sometimes better that we don't understand why people kill."

He left the room, leaving Chloe to ruminate on that. And even as she did, one solid certainty floated through her mind.

It's not Danielle. It can't be ...

Chloe was back in the records room at HQ, going over the most recent report on the crime scene at the lake, when the door flew open. Two men walked inside, only one of whom she knew. Greene stood beside the other man, dwarfed by his size. The other man was tall and built like a pro wrestler, an attribute that was evident even beneath his suit. Chloe had seen him before and knew who he was, though she had never actually spoken with him.

Director L.J. Johnson took a seat directly across from Chloe, leaving Greene to stand. Johnson looked across the table at her with an expression that was hard to read. He looked from Chloe to the records, and then back to Chloe.

"I assume Agent Greene told you about our program to slowly allow some of our interns to get closer to the action, correct?" Johnson asked.

"Yes, sir."

"I stand by the decision but I will admit wholeheartedly that it irritated the eternal piss out of me when I discovered that you and Agent Greene had submitted another DNA test in this Martin Shields case. I called up Greene and chewed him out and fully planned to call you and ask who the hell you thought you were, too. After all, this isn't even a bureau case. The locals out there near Pinecrest are doing me a favor because of your connection to the thing. So I was pissed. But then the results came back and I'll be damned if I wasn't proven wrong."

"It's not Danielle Fine's blood, is it?" Chloe asked.

"No, it's not. The results came back for a man named Alan Short. And that is information that we are keeping to ourselves. When I leave this room, I'm dedicating two agents to tracking this man down. I am then going to personally push the paperwork that will lead to your sister's release. However … you have to be realistic about this. She is still a suspect until Alan Short is caught. She is still not to leave the state and must agree to further questioning."

"Of course," Chloe said. "Thank you."

"No, thank *you.* Impressive work, Fine. I look forward to working with you when you're no longer an intern. Agent Greene, keep up the good work on working with her."

With that, Johnson got to his feet and left the room. Greene gave Chloe a *can-you-believe-that* sort of look.

"One thing I noticed," Chloe said, "was that he's assigned other agents to bring this guy in. I feel like I've been demoted."

"Hey, you can't expect the entire world. Seriously … the fact that he came in to congratulate you is huge. So take that and your sister's presumed innocence as a victory. I'll keep you posted on progress in the Alan Short investigation. If he's a local, I imagine we'll have him in custody within forty-eight hours."

"That's great," Chloe said, feeling the weight come off of her chest right away.

"You know, she *will* probably be charged with *something.* Ditching his car like that seems highly suspect. She's off for now … but I fully expect that there will be an ongoing investigation."

"That makes sense," Chloe said, still simply relieved that Danielle was no longer the primary suspect. "So now what do we do?"

"For this case? Nothing. You've done everything you could. I think maybe you should call it a day and head home. When Danielle is released, I imagine your days will be rather hectic. Like Director Johnson said... we're sitting on this for right now. Which means the media won't know anything substantial until Alan Short is caught."

"Can I tell Danielle the news?"

"Not yet. We have to wait until the paperwork is done. But if Director Johnson is on it, that will be done very soon. Seriously, Chloe. Go home. Good work today."

She got up from the table and tidied up the records she had been looking through. She was visibly trembling as she tried to absorb everything that had happened during the course of the day—most notably the last five minutes or so.

She'd potentially freed Danielle.

She had Director Johnson—a man who would eventually be her supervisor—already thanking her and congratulating her.

It looked like the future was bright. It looked like the dark past that has pushed her toward these moments was finally releasing her from its clutches.

But as she'd soon discover, the past had a way of sticking around and not only surprising you, but shaking any future plans into dust. It was proven in the form of the letters that had been delivered to Danielle, hinting that the past was never too far away.

But who sent them? Chloe wondered, the questioning itching at her. *And perhaps more importantly, why?*

Chapter Twenty Five

Despite the tension that existed between them ever since the block party, Chloe and Steven had managed to remain civil. Chloe was still excited and pleased over the fact that her insights and work—with Greene's guidance—had helped to clear Danielle's name. She was so excited about it that when she found Steven on the couch, looking over his emails, she had every intention of jumping him. They'd not been physical for about a week—which seemed a shame since they had an entire house to break in.

That all came to a very cold stop when she arrived home and tried to share her news with him. She felt a little silly as she did it, beaming and feeling as if she was bragging. She started with finding the blood under Martin's fingernails and then the brief meeting with Director Johnson. But even before she told him the full details of Danielle's eventual release, it was clear that he wasn't going to be sharing in her joy.

"Hold on," Steven said. There appeared to be equal measures of fascination and disgust on his face. "You mean to tell me that you were right there, in the room with Martin's corpse?"

"Yes. I told you… I'm part of an experimental program that gives interns more freedom and responsibilities."

"Yes, I know that," he spat. "But you were right there with the body… and you had no problem still defending her?"

"No, I didn't," she said, instantly getting defensive. "No matter your feelings about Danielle, even your contempt can't overrule DNA evidence. Sorry her freedom is going to screw with your mom's perfect image for our wedding."

"I didn't say that."

"You didn't have to. It's been on your mind since the first time your mother complained about her."

"Chloe, that's not fair … or accurate."

"Well, that's good to know. Because when she is released tomorrow, she can't go back to her apartment. It's too risky and there will be media everywhere. So I want her to come back here for a few days."

"What?" Steven asked, incredulous. "Are you out of your mind?"

"No. What would be your problem with it?" She knew she had an argument on her hands now but she was digging her heels in. She wasn't worried about what Sally Brennan thought anymore. This was her sister's future on the line now. Sally could take her wedding money and shove it for all Chloe cared.

"There would be a convicted murderer in our house!"

"No … not convicted. Did you miss the part where I said she was being released?"

"And you think that matters?" Steven asked, yelling now. "Freed or not, this will stick with her. For years—maybe even her whole life."

"And how does that affect you, exactly?"

"Chloe … you're not thinking clearly. I get it. She's your sister. But she can't stay here."

"Well, she *is* staying here. I'm sorry but it's not open for discussion."

He looked at her as if he had no idea who he was speaking with. And what pissed her off more than anything was that she knew he was worried what his parents would think. That was the only reason he was being so stubborn.

"You said this new blood sample proves someone else was involved," he said quietly. "Until I hear otherwise, she could have still been responsible. She could still be a murderer."

"You want her to be, don't you? Then it'll get her out of your hair. And your mother's."

"You sound insane," he said, his voice still low and calm now. "And you know what? My folks have been trying to get me to see it for a while now."

"See what, Steven?"

"Your loyalty to your sister, no matter what. I know you two have been through some shit, but this is crazy. And Chloe… maybe this is a mistake. The engagement, the wedding. They were right, I think… we're not right for each other."

"Because I am loyal to my sister?" she asked. She wasn't hurt so much as she was confused and livid.

"Because there's just too much baggage there. And yes… partly because you'll constantly choose your delusional sister over me. And if that's the way it's going to be during our marriage, I want no part of it."

So it's finally come to this, Chloe thought. *He's essentially asking me to choose between him and Danielle.*

She loved him. She had no qualms with admitting that.

But there was an image of her sister, nearly catatonic while she sat on those apartment steps with a cop by their side. She remembered that day clearly and knew that no matter what life dealt them, she would always see her sister as that little girl. And she would do everything she could do protect her.

"I'm sorry, Steven," she said. "I'm not going to cut Danielle out of my life."

Without missing a beat, Steven said: "Then the wedding is off."

With that, he turned his back and headed for the door. There was no goodbye kiss, no hug, and barely even any eye contact. He went straight for the door and slammed it hard when he made his way out.

Chloe stood there, dumfounded. Her day had gone from the highest of highs to the lowest of lows in less than ten minutes. And all she was left with was this big house, now empty except for her. She looked slowly around the living room, taking in the absurdity of it all, before sinking to her knees and crying.

She was no stranger to weeping; she'd done plenty of it in the weeks following her mother's death and then again at the age of seventeen when the sense of not having a mother had really started to sink in as she ventured into the college years. But this weeping was some something new, something physically painful that seemed to grow inside of her stomach.

She wept on the couch, wanting to stop and get control but also knowing that it would be best to just let it all out. And when she thought of Danielle and the impossible situation *she* was in, she cried even harder—a sound that came back to her in small echoes that the large house sent right back to her.

Chapter Twenty Six

Sleep was incredibly fragmented that night. There were some moments where the knowledge that Danielle would be freed tomorrow had her excited and unable to sleep. Then another minute would pass and she would start to feel the weight of Steven leaving her all over again. It was a bold move and since Steven was not known for bold moves, she fully expected him to return at some point that night.

But he never showed up.

At some point, she managed to fall into something similar to a deep sleep but it did not last long. She received a text message at 5:35. She retrieved her phone from the bedside table without having much time to ruminate on the empty side of the bed behind her. With sleep-blurred eyes, she saw Greene's name on the display. The message read:

Paperwork will be approved by 8 this morning. We've already started getting things approved for you to be there to pick her up. Beware… the media will be there, too. I'll be there to assist.

With this news, any further sleep was out of the question. She got out of bed, put the coffee on, and took a shower while it percolated. After getting dressed and grabbing a quick breakfast of toast and oatmeal, she headed out. She figured she'd get there a little earlier than eight but she honestly wasn't too worried about that.

When she stepped out of her front door, there were several cars and two news vans parked on the side of the street. As she hurried to her car, the news crews also hurried forward. They came across the lawn as if they owned the place, their cameras and microphones at the ready.

"Are you absolutely certain your sister is innocent?" one reporter asked.

"Are you afraid of how this turn of events might hurt your career if it turns out Danielle was involved in any way?" another asked.

She cast her face toward the ground, refusing to even give them the privilege of filming her face. She got into her car and backed out quickly, nearly clipping a cameraman with the back end of her car.

If they're already at my house, she thought, *it's bound to be much worse at the jail.*

She drove quickly out of Lavender Hills, already spotting a few curious and nosy neighbors on their porches as the news vans gave chase. As she made it out of the neighborhood and onto the highway, she wondered if it was possible that any of her neighbors somehow already knew that Steven was gone.

These neighbors of hers—the women in particular—seemed to have a knack for knowing certain things. Why would her private argument with her fiancé yesterday afternoon be any different?

She couldn't help but feel a little sting of guilt. Maybe she *had* been too demanding. Maybe her absolute refusal to listen to his side when she'd told him that Danielle was going to be staying at the house had been out of line. It was, after all, partly his house.

But no... she refused to feel guilty. Steven and his parents had practically marked Danielle as a black sheep ever since she and Steven had started seriously dating. If that was the kind of people they were, maybe she really *didn't* need Steven and that sort of negativity in her life.

If she had to ride out this situation knowing that she had ultimately chosen her sister over a life with Steven, she was fine with that. It stung, but she could live with it and feel that she had made the right decision.

That, of course, led her to thinking of how Danielle had gotten into this mess in the first place. Her dating Martin wasn't all that peculiar, but the fact that someone had placed evidence pointing toward her on his body *was.*

She knew that she had basically been told to stay off of the pending case—that more seasoned agents were handling it now. But she couldn't help but wonder who Alan Short was and what his connection to Danielle might be. Perhaps Greene would stand true to his word and keep her updated. She had no reason to assume any different.

It took her half an hour to get to Riverside Correctional. She arrived twenty minutes early but she thought that was for the best. When she arrived, the parking lot and the street were swarming with television newscasters—some local and some on a national level. She realized that the death of Martin Shields itself was not newsworthy. But when you threw in a car backed into a lake and the possibility of planted evidence, it became even juicier. And if the news was running with the Alan Short story, it would be almost headline worthy while Short was searched for.

She toyed with the idea of simply sitting in her car and waiting for Greene to arrive but saw that it would do no good. Even before she had parked her car, reporters came rushing forward. Doing her best to outpace them, Chloe opened her car door and again walked with her head down.

More questions came hurling toward her and this time she did respond. She kept repeating *"No comment, no comment."* It was chilling and infuriating to hear so many people referring to her sister as a murderer. She had to make a great effort to not lash out at every misinformed question as the questions become more barbed the closer she got to the jail.

Apparently, a good Samaritan cop saw what was happening on his way into the building. He came rushing over and stood in front of her with his arms splayed and led her through the growing melee of reporters and cameramen.

"You will all back up and give Ms. Fine some room. Anyone even accidentally touches her, you'll be looking at fines. Got it?"

This pushed the tide of people back somewhat but not enough to make Chloe comfortable. She followed the cop to the building, where he ushered her in through the doors and into the front lobby. Once inside, she noticed that a few people were looking curiously at her—the receptionist, a few officers, a woman waiting in a chair in the lobby.

"Agent Fine," the cop said, "I'm Officer Wright. Sorry you had to deal with that."

"It is what it is," she said, barely noticing that he had referred to her as *Agent.* "They were outside of my home, too."

"Jesus," Wright said. "Anyway, I assume you're here for your sister?"

"I am."

"Let me see what I can do to get things rolling," Wright said.

Chloe spent the next ten minutes showing her badge to people and signing forms. As she was signing what she was told would be the last one while standing by a little kiosk that separated the central building from an expansive hallway, another officer came up beside her. Agent Greene was with him and he looked angry.

"Damned vultures are roosting outside," he said. "How did you make it in without cold-cocking one?"

"Oh, it took some effort."

The uniformed officer who had given Chloe the last form looked it over, stamped it, and then nodded. "You're good to go, Ms. Fine."

Chloe and Agent Greene were buzzed in through the door that led into the hallway. There was only one door along this hallway and as they stepped into the hall, it was opening. An armed guard walked out, ushering Danielle ahead of him.

Her arms were not cuffed and she was dressed in the same clothes she'd been wearing when she had been brought in. It had only been two days but something about this seemed barbaric to Chloe.

Danielle came quickly toward her and when she threw her arms around her, Chloe could hardly believe it. When she returned the embrace, Danielle felt as light as a feather. She was also trembling—maybe crying. Chloe wanted to know for sure but also did not want to embarrass Danielle, as she knew shows of emotion were not common for her.

So she let it go and, for the moment, simply held her sister in her arms.

And she knew in that moment that while she'd miss Steven for quite some time, she had absolutely made the right decision.

The bureau had not seen the sense in devoting agents to escorting Chloe and Danielle back to Pinecrest. Instead, two cops tailed them into Pinecrest where they were then handed off to two Pinecrest PD patrol cars. Those patrol cars followed them into Lavender Hills and then parked alongside the curb outside of Chloe's house. She pulled her own car into the driveway and parked, taking note of the news crews. There were more of them now—four from her count—but they seemed a little more hesitant to come after her with the cops' cars parked in front of the house.

The sisters hurried inside. Chloe could hear the clicking of phones and actual cameras as well as the murmurs of reporters as they made notes and spoke to television audiences.

"When I was a teenager," Danielle said, "I thought about learning to play the guitar. I figured I'd be a Liz Phair or Joan Jett or something. I thought it would be cool to have people with cameras following me around. I now realize what a stupid fucking dream that was."

Chloe couldn't help but laugh. They sat down on the couch together and it was clear that they didn't quite know how to behave around one another.

"So, Steven left," Chloe said as if she was commenting on the weather.

"What? When?"

"Last night. We had an argument and he left."

"Was it about me?"

"Partly," Chloe said.

"Chloe, I'm so sorry. It's my fault. You want me to call him and explain—"

"God, no! Honestly, it's a blessing, I think. His parents are insufferable and treat him like Jesus Christ."

Danielle shrugged and sank into the couch. "I'm sad for you but I'd be lying if I said I'm going to miss him. So … no wedding?"

"Doesn't look like it. Turns out you won't have to wear that bridesmaid dress after all."

"This day just keeps getting better and better," Danielle said with a wry smile.

Chloe got up and went into the kitchen to make them some lunch. As childish as it seemed, she used the mustard that Steven always claimed was *his* mustard on their sandwiches. As she put them together, Danielle turned the television on in the living room. She flipped through the channels, skimming the sorry excuse for early afternoon programming before settling on a local news program.

They both froze for a moment when they saw footage of them exiting Riverside Correctional. Their heads were down as they were ushered out by four policemen. She saw Agent Greene bringing up the rear, shooting scouring glances at the reporters that trailed them. Danielle turned it up and they both listened to the report.

"… .says that while the evidence is fairly solid, new findings in the case indicate that other parties were involved. These new findings aren't quite enough to exonerate Danielle Fine, but they are enough to apparently release her from custody. Officials are stating that the new findings are sensitive and not yet being fully revealed to the public due to the nature of the investigation. As for now, though, Danielle Fine remains the only suspect in the public's eye. When asked for comment, Baltimore City PD stated that Fine has agreed to remain cooperative in regards to questioning and other details of the investigation. Here, we see her leaving Riverside with her sister, up-and-coming FBI agent Chloe Fine. We've recently discovered that these two sisters have been through quite a lot, possibly even having witnessed the death of their mother at the hands of their father. We can't be—"

"And screw you, too," Danielle said, turning the television off. "I look like shit on TV."

"You haven't slept in nearly two days," Chloe pointed out. "Of course you're going to look tired."

"But not guilty, hopefully." She paused here as Chloe brought the sandwiches and some chips into the living room. "So what do you know about this Alan Short guy?"

"Nothing. You?"

"Same. And listen… I know you were just doing your job the whole time. And because of my idiot move of dropping that car in the lake, I know I looked guilty. It means a lot to me that you managed to look past that and not give up. It really does. No one has ever *not* given up on me, you know?"

Chloe didn't want to verbally confirm this, so she just nodded. "So, you don't know Alan Short. But can you think of anyone who might want you framed for Martin's death?"

Danielle sighed and looked at her sandwich—anything not to meet Chloe's eyes. "I don't know any one person," she replied. "But I should probably tell you about this one thing I've been keeping from you."

"What's that?" Chloe asked, a little spike of fear piercing her heart. Of course, she was pretty sure she knew what was coming. She was so sure that she went ahead and answered her own question. "Are you talking about those letters?"

"Yeah. And by the way, how did you say you found them?" Danielle asked.

"I went by your apartment after they arrested you. I wanted to see if I could find anything to free you. These letters ... if there's even a remote chance that Alan Short wrote them—hell, even if there isn't a chance he wrote them—I feel like we need to submit them as evidence."

"You saw them all, right?" Danielle asked. "One of them says that if I go to anyone about them, they'd kill me. And now, after Martin turns up dead, I believe it more than ever. That last one ... *Kill him or I will.* The 'him' was Martin, right?"

"We have no way of knowing that for sure."

"Seems a little wonky if it's not. The timing adds it all up as far as I'm concerned."

"When did you get the first one?" Chloe asked.

"About six months ago."

"And they'd just show up at random times?"

"Seemed like it," Danielle answered. "I've tried going back over my schedule for those six months to see if I could have done something to piss someone off. The worst I could come up with was turning men down at the bar."

"Well, what about less troublesome things? Have you gotten involved with new friends or people at work?"

"No. I don't have the patience for making friends, really. Although—funny enough, you'll love this—I did look into doing a book group."

"Did you join?"

"No. But it's pretty cool. I was looking through a few of things I had from Mom and found this book she had. *Different Seasons* by Stephen King. There was a little note inside of it with Mom's handwriting. They were reading it for a book club she was part of, right here in Pinecrest. I called the library and asked if they still did a book club and they said they did. So based on that, I almost joined. I even asked if there was any way to look into who might have been past members. I told them I was just doing some digging into my mother's history ... and that was the truth, as dumb as it sounds. Just to know there was a book club she once belonged to, you know? Remember how she loved to read?"

"I do."

"Anyway, they said they had records of sign-up sheets but nothing any farther back than 2002."

"But you've got notes that prove that Mom was part of this book club?" Chloe asked.

"Yeah. But then the threatening notes started coming and I got a little distracted. I just never even thought about joining again."

"Any idea how much time passed between the call to the library and the notes showing up?"

"I don't know for sure. Two weeks? Maybe three."

There was a lackluster tone in her voice that made Chloe want to cringe. Danielle looked tired and, despite being recently freed from prison, infinitely sad. Chloe recognized the signs of depression from Danielle's earlier years.

God, we can't go back to that, she thought.

"And what did you say about the timing adding it all up for you?" Chloe asked with a bit of sarcasm.

"Yeah, but a book club? You thinking some sinister librarian has it out for me because I didn't join?"

"No. But did you specifically mention Mom?"

"Yeah."

Chloe wasn't sure what it all meant—or of it meant anything at all.

But it was sure as hell worth looking into. Apparently, Danielle felt this, too. The living room fell into silence as both women turned their attention to the windows, keeping an eye on the media presence outside.

Chapter Twenty Seven

The news headlines didn't get any better. Reporters were now digging into the sordid history of their parents, painting Danielle as a victim of a childhood with no real parents. They had also uncovered a public intoxication charge from Danielle's past and were harping on that now as well.

Chloe was again alarmed that Danielle was starting to sink into some sort of vague depression. She was no longer trying to make light of things and the woman who had given her a hug at Riverside Correctional that morning seemed to have gone into hiding. That brooding little girl Chloe had grown up lurked right behind the surface, ready to slink out of hiding and take up residence.

They had sunk into silence after the talk about the book club, but it was a silence that Chloe broke after less than ten minutes. She thought she had picked up a very thin trail, one that might actually not even be there at all. But she had to try.

"Danielle, do you remember the day Mom died when we were in the back of Grandma's car? I remember you saying that you knew Dad didn't do it. Do you still feel that way?"

"I do," she said in that same sleepy tone. It wasn't that she didn't care about the discussion but it was almost as if it was taking immense mental willpower to take part in it—another signal of her depression looming.

"Any reason why?"

"I don't know. I just always had this sense that he wasn't capable of it. If you think back about it, he never hit Mom. Never even raised his hand to her from what I can remember. If he had *anything* to do with it, it was an accident. I mean, she fell down the stairs. There was no weapon, nothing malicious, you know?"

Chloe was still slightly hung up on the timing of it all—of Danielle inquiring about her mother being part of a book club just a few weeks before those threatening notes started. And while Danielle wasn't quite ready to make the jump to believing that the letter writer had something to do with Martin's death, the notes certainly did seem ominous.

But if she followed that trail, no matter how broken it might be, it all led back to one place: their mother. The book club was such a small thing and likely meant very little in the grand scheme of things. And Chloe knew that if she ventured down that trail, it would lead her toward looking into her mother's death and their father's incarceration—something she promised herself she would never do.

But now Danielle's name was being dragged through the mud. And if Chloe could make that stop by looking into their past, she figured it was necessary.

"Do you remember the cop that sat with us on the stoop?" Chloe asked, an idea suddenly springing to her mind.

Danielle smiled. "Yeah. Clarence Simmons, don't know why I remember his name. Big guy. Really nice. I remember that he looked almost as sad as we did the whole time he was there."

Chloe mulled over an idea for a moment. A slow anxiousness started to take shape in her stomach as the idea seemed more and more relevant. "Did he ever say anything to you that afternoon?" Chloe asked.

"Nothing in particular," Danielle said. "Just that it would be okay. He kept saying that over and over again. You know, it's funny … I didn't even piece it together until later … when I was going through that therapy nonsense right after it all happened. Did you know that he used to live next door to Amber Hayes?"

"Amber Hayes?" Chloe asked. She knew the name but wasn't sure why.

"Yeah. That girl that always had that stupid bike with the annoying bell, driving it everywhere and *ding ding ding.*"

"Oh God, yeah, I remember. Hold on … she lived like what … maybe three blocks away from the apartment, right?"

"Something like that," Danielle said.

"You have any idea where she lives now?"

"I do, actually. She tried chatting me up on Facebook Messenger a while back. She's living somewhere in New York, I think."

"You happen to have her number?"

Danielle rolled her eyes and pulled out her phone. "Well, I have the number of her business. She gave it to me, thinking for some reason I might need advertising services ... why, I have no idea."

Danielle found the number and gave it to Chloe. Chloe wasted no time calling the number. She knew she was working with a long shot, but it was one worth taking. The phone rang three times in her ear before it was answered.

"Helmsley Ad Services, this is Amber."

"Amber, hi. This is Chloe Fine. Do you remember me?"

There was a brief silence on the other end, broken by a response that was too theatrical to be sincere. "Yes! My God, how are you? I've seen the news ... how is Danielle?"

"She's scared, but good. She was just mentioning how you guys had chatted not too long ago."

"Yeah! I came to Pinecrest to see my folks about a month ago. I had been hoping to meet up with her."

"Look, Amber, I hate to be short with you, but I was hoping you could help me find an address. Do you remember the man you guys used to live next door to back here in Pinecrest? He was a policeman. Clarence Simmons."

Amber laughed and when she responded, there was legitimate joy in her voice. "Oh yes indeed. Mr. Simmons was so sweet. He and my father still talk. They met each other for a fishing trip last summer, I believe."

"Is he still in Pinecrest?" Chloe asked.

"No. He moved about eight years ago, I think. Maybe longer than that. He moved to New Jersey."

"Do you have an address? Maybe your dad?"

"You know, I *do* have an address. He still sends me Christmas cards. If you give me a few minutes, I can shoot it your way."

"That would be excellent," Chloe said. "Thanks so much, Amber."

She ended the call and found Danielle looking at her with something like awe. "Is it really that easy for you to get information?"

"Not always. I think this is what people at the bureau call *a lucky break*. She has an address but needs to look for it."

Danielle went to the window and looked out. Chloe looked over her shoulder and saw that one other news van had showed up. A petite woman was speaking in front of a camera, angled to capture the entire house in the shot. Two police cars were parked behind it all, one officer standing out by the hood. He smoked a cigarette and glared at the circus.

They remained in the house, Chloe feeling like a prisoner. She got updates on the hunt for Alan Short via texts from Greene. They also kept tabs on Danielle's story on news stations and the Internet but it was only infuriating them.

The monotony broke around 4:30, when Amber called back. Chloe made this call quick, too, but not without expressing her gratitude. She wrote the address down and ended the call, feeling that she might actually be getting somewhere.

"Trenton, New Jersey," she said.

"Lucky for us," Danielle said. "He could have moved to California or something. That would make this a little tough, huh?"

"You can't come with me," Chloe said. "Until you are absolutely one hundred percent cleared in Martin's death, you can't leave town. If you want, I can ask Greene to keep tabs on you."

Looking depressed, Danielle shook her head. "No. I'm fine with just the rent-a-cops outside. When are you going?"

"I'll leave in the morning. No sense in driving out there during rush hour only to catch him at night."

"So a girls' night in, I take it?" Danielle asked.

Chloe was irritated that she was trying to make a joke of it. But she also knew her sister well enough to know that joking was how she handled stress. It had always been the case, even from the age of five or so. Whenever she made such sweeping jokes, it was a sure sign of stress or worry.

And Chloe supposed there was still plenty to worry about as of right now.

"Looks like it," she said with a smile.

"Sounds good. You get the wine and I'll find something on TV."

It was good to hear Danielle in her devil-may-care attitude again, even if it was mostly staged. Like Chloe, Danielle was also sensing something being pieced together and wasn't sure how to feel about having to revisit their past to make sense of it.

Still, Chloe selected a bottle of red from the small wine rack in the kitchen and poured two glasses. When she walked into the living room to deliver one to Danielle, she noted that yet another news crew had arrived on the scene.

This either meant that something new in the story was developing or it was just a slow news day.

Chloe was fine not knowing. She looked away from the window and watched as Danielle scrolled through Netflix for something to watch.

She sipped from her wine and thought of the black cop who had been there with them as their lives had fallen apart. Clarence Simmons. She'd thought of him often over the years, giving him an almost mythic status. Knowing that she would be seeing him soon made her feel like she was taking a surreal step out of real life and into a place where dreams and nightmares never truly let go of you.

Chapter Twenty Eight

As the afternoon progressed, two things happened. First, Chloe and Danielle somehow made it through three episodes of *House of Cards*. Second, the news crews seemed to have scattered away outside. As night fell, they seemed to be almost like pesky insects, flying off in search of whatever the next source of light might be.

They turned the TV off around nine. Chloe went through some of the still-unpacked boxes and found a spare toothbrush and pajamas for Danielle. Danielle refused the pajamas, selecting instead one of Chloe's basic black running tank tops. She was asleep by 9:45, crashing hard in the guest bedroom on a mattress that had not yet been placed on the bedframe, which was still disassembled and pushed against the wall. It made Chloe realize that given Steven's departure from her life, this house may never be fully unpacked. She wasn't sure she'd be able to afford it.

Chloe's head was too filled with ideas and worries to even think about sleep. She enjoyed a glass of wine all alone, sitting at the dining room table. She thought about maybe going back through the case files one more time but saw no sense in it. Until Alan Short was apprehended, there would likely be no forward progress on the case.

By the time she had finished her glass of wine, she realized that she and Danielle had polished off an entire bottle. She wasn't nearly drunk but was moderately lightheaded. Maybe she'd be able to get to sleep after all.

She made her way through the house, going through a routine that she supposed wasn't old enough to be a routine yet; she and Steven had only been here for a week now. The routine consisted of locking the doors—the front, the back, and the side door that led to the patio. Because of the remaining news crews outside (they were down to just two now), she also made a point to close all of the blinds as well.

As she made her way into the kitchen and to the back door that led to the back porch, she reached for the cord on the blinds to close them. Her hand paused before she could grab them.

There was something on the porch. It was a small picnic basket.

She thought for a moment, wondering if she should collect it. Was it perhaps some sort of peace offering from a reporter who had a change of heart? Or maybe they were from one of the police crews who had been standing guard outside all day.

No, she thought. *The cops would have let us know they were bringing it. And a reporter wouldn't risk coming all the way across the yard while the police were stationed at the sidewalk.*

Then what was in the basket? And who had put it there?

Going against her better judgment, Chloe quickly opened the back door. She snatched up the basket, took a quick look around to make sure there was no one waiting to ambush her on the porch, and then quickly stepped back inside. She locked the doors, closed the blinds, and set the picnic basket on the counter.

No sense in waiting or trying to talk myself out of it, she thought.

Holding her breath, she threw open the snap-case lid of the picnic basket.

There were a dozen or so cookies inside. Chocolate chip. From the look and the smell, they looked to have been made from scratch rather recently.

Her first thought was that someone was trying to poison them. But that was both stupid and almost fantastical. She stared at the cookies for a moment as if they might present some sort of a riddle. That's when she saw the corner of a piece of paper sticking out from beneath the parchment paper that held the cookies.

She grabbed the corner of the paper and pulled it out. It wasn't paper, not really. It was an envelope. An envelope with a golden sticker seal, just like the ones that had been delivered to Danielle's apartment.

She opened it slowly, as if she thought the contents of the envelope might actually be able to harm her. She made certain to only touch the very corners of the envelope and the flap. Of course, there was nothing inside but a letter. Still, the letter itself spoke volumes despite its short length.

IT'S NOT OVER.

She stared at the letter for a moment, and the envelope. She had intentionally only touched it by the corners. She was aware that the other letters had not held any fingerprints, but she wanted to check this one as well. She ventured into her bedroom and took her old evidence kit out—the very same one she had used for evidence labs during her first few years at the academy.

She quickly set up a little station on her kitchen counter, dusting for prints. As she had suspected, there were none. She then did the same to the basket and even the parchment paper that held the cookies. But there was nothing.

She stood there and looked at the unexpected delivery for a very long time. She considered waking Danielle but decided against it. With everything she had been through the last few days, this was the last thing she needed to deal with.

IT'S NOT OVER.

That's for damned sure, Chloe thought. Someone had managed to sneak into her backyard and leave this on her porch. Someone had trespassed on her property, had come within about two feet of her back door during one of the most stressful times of her life and were basically taunting her with this note.

No, she thought with some anger. *No, this isn't over by a long shot.*

Chapter Twenty Nine

Even after several hours of sleep, Chloe decided not to tell Danielle about the basket of cookies and the letter. She'd disposed of the basket and cookies in the outside trashcan before retiring to bed, keeping only the letter. She read it once more as she woke up at six o'clock the following morning and then put it in the drawer of her bedside table.

When she went out to put the coffee on, she was not at all surprised to find that Danielle was apparently still asleep. As the coffee started to percolate, Chloe peeked into the guest bedroom and found her sister lightly snoring. *Good,* Chloe thought. *She needs her rest after all she's been through.*

Chloe picked at a small breakfast—a bowl of cereal and a banana—before finally getting dressed for the day. She thought she'd be more excited about potentially meeting with Clarence Simmons but she found that she was actually quite scared.

It's because you're digging up the past, she told herself. *And is that really any different than digging up a grave?* She thought of herself poised over her mother's grave with a shovel and something about the image nearly brought tears to her eyes.

She poured herself a thermos of coffee and then grabbed a Post-it from the kitchen bar. She scrawled a note on it for Danielle: *Gone to see Simmons. Will call when I'm on the way back. Make yourself at home and DO NOT LEAVE THE HOUSE.*

She headed outside and hurried to her car. There was only one news van and no one from it came rushing after her. She also saw the single police car parked adjacent to the news van. The officer watched her go to her car and even gave her a little wave. Chloe waved back, glad to see that the media circus had died down but, deep down in her guts, getting the feeling that this story was far from being over.

She made the drive from Pinecrest, Maryland, to Trenton, New Jersey, in just over two hours, speeding a bit most of the way. She pulled up in front of the Simmons residence at 9:42. She had not called in advance, not wanting to give him the opportunity to decline to speak with her. She had to hope that his retirement kept him at home, that he was more prone to kicking around the house than getting out and traveling.

Her hope was confirmed when she saw that the adjoining garage to the house was open. She saw a slightly overweight man petering around in the garage. He carried a screwdriver in his left hand and was studying a microwave oven that was sitting on a wooden table.

Chloe approached quietly but without stealth, not wanting to appear as if she was sneaking up on him. When it was clear that he had not yet heard her when she had closed in to just a few feet, she made her presence known.

"Mr. Simmons?"

He turned around to face her and it was like looking back into the past. The kind face that had remained with her and Danielle on that morning was very much the same. He now had a thin beard patched with gray and he had shaved his head at some point. But it was unmistakably him.

"That's me," he said. "But who's asking."

"I doubt you'd remember me," she said. "But we met briefly about seventeen years ago. My name is Chloe Fine."

His face went slack, though the start of a smile touched the corner of his mouth. He was in such shock that his fingers also went loose; the screwdriver fell from his grasp and clattered to the floor.

"Yeah, I remember," he said. "Good God, has it really been seventeen years?"

"It has," she said. "I was wondering if you wouldn't mind having a word with me."

Simmons still looked baffled but he nodded. "Yeah. Just trying to fix this microwave. Went on the fritz while I was heating up some sausage this morning." He scratched at his head and picked the screwdriver back up. "I assume this might be about what happened to your parents?"

"Yeah," she said. "And if it makes it any more pressing for you," she said, reaching into her pocket for her ID, "I'm interning at the FBI right now. On the way to becoming an agent."

He nodded as if he understood perfectly. "Lots of people that experience the sort of thing you did end up going into that line of work. My dad was shot and killed and then hung from a lamp post in North Carolina when I was seven years old. I knew by the time I was twelve that I wanted to be a policeman."

"So," she said, unsure how to handle his last comment. "Pinecrest didn't cut it for you after retirement?"

"No. My wife passed ten years ago and the rest of my family lives here in Jersey. Two sons and five grandkids."

"That sounds nice," she said.

"Yeah, it is," he said. "Anyway … what can I do for you, Ms. Fine?"

"Well, how well do you recall the case with my parents?"

"Clearly enough, I suppose. I remember that your father was just sort of sluggish when we took him in. Not much arguing and he didn't put up a fight. He went willingly. If you don't mind my saying so, it seemed like he had accepted what he had done and wanted to move on from it as quickly as possible."

"So there's no doubt in your mind that he did it?"

Simmons didn't answer right away. He tapped the screwdriver against the side of the microwave as he processed a few things.

"I never say there is no doubt," he said. "But from what I can remember, it was pretty clear that he was guilty. I'm sorry if that's not what you're wanting to hear but that's how I remember it. Now that you're older there are some aspects to the case you might want to know … maybe small things that were kept from you as a child. Are you okay hearing them?"

"Yes," she said, although she wasn't sure if this was true or not.

"Well, he was pretty much drunk when we took him in. Not wasted or hammered or anything, but he'd had a few. And keep in mind this was earlier in the day. I don't remember the time but it was well before lunch.

Aside from you and your sister, he was the only one there and he *did* have motive after all."

"Motive?" Chloe asked, almost offended. "What kind of motive?"

Simmons looked uncomfortable, though he now discarded the screwdriver. The course of the conversation had clearly distracted him. He, too, was having to go back into his past to do some digging. Chloe knew all too well how unpleasant that could be.

"When we checked up on any alibis—none of which he really pushed too hard, mind you—we found that he had probably been sleeping with other women. There was no hard, concrete evidence of this, but the writing was right there on the wall. When we asked him if this was the case, he didn't deny it but he also never gave names."

"Did you ever have any names? Women you were pretty sure he was seeing?"

"I don't remember. I'm sure if you pulled the files, some names might be there. But good luck finding them. Seventeen years ago for a case that appeared to be a slam dunk from the get-go …"

"So the theory was that he killed my mother in the hopes of freeing himself so he could be with one of these other women?"

"I believe so, yes."

"And you are certain he was guilty?" she asked again.

"Sitting there with you two girls on those porch steps, I wanted him to be innocent. Right up until he basically admitted to seeing women on the side, I hoped for that. But … I'm sorry, Ms. Fine. Everything pointed to him being guilty."

"Was there ever any question that maybe someone else was there with him when it happened?"

"You mean did he act alone? Yeah, pretty sure of it. I mean … based on what I remember. It *has* been seventeen years, after all. Forgive me for asking, but is there any specific reason for asking so long after it happened?"

Chloe was slightly surprised. "Have you not seen the news in the last few days?"

"Nope," Simmons said. "I don't think I've watched a single minute of news coverage ever since Sandy Hook happened. Not for elections, not for lotto numbers, nothing."

Chloe thought about divulging everything to him but didn't see the point. Like just about everyone else familiar with her father's case, Simmons thought he had been guilty. And she doubted there would be much to change his mind seventeen years removed outside of solid evidence—and there was none of that.

"Well, thanks for your time," Chloe said. She was a bit frustrated that her two-hour drive had culminated in a conversation that had lasted less than fifteen minutes.

"I take it I didn't tell you what you were hoping to hear?"

"I don't know *what* I was hoping to hear," Chloe admitted.

He smiled at her and pointed toward the house. "Why don't you come inside and get a glass of tea or lemonade or something. Maybe we can go over the case in detail... maybe figure out how to get you the names of those women that might have known your father."

She nearly took him up on it. But then she thought about Danielle, sitting alone in her house with news crews outside, and knew she couldn't.

"Thanks for the invite, but I really need to get going."

Simmons nodded, as if he had expected as much. "Well, I hope you find whatever it is you're looking for."

You and me both, she thought as she headed back to her car.

She felt a bit like a spoiled brat, but hearing tales of how her father was sleeping around on her deceased mother was not how she wanted to spend her morning. And with that thought in her head, she headed back for Pinecrest with more questions than answers.

Chapter Thirty

Chloe was a little over halfway home when she received a call from Greene. For a moment she worried that it would be about Danielle—that she had gone rogue and left her house, perhaps even trying to leave town. Or maybe the Alan Short thing had fallen through and all signs were pointing back to Danielle again.

She answered the call before these speculations could get the better of her. "Good news?" she asked hopefully.

"Depends on how you look at it," Greene said. "Pinecrest PD had a few officers go by the residence of Alan Short. He wasn't home. Turns out he hasn't been to work in the past two days, either."

"That would be *bad* news, then," Chloe said. "He's apparently making a run for it."

"That's true. But some might also see it as a sign of guilt—of a sign of needing to get away from something. What about you? Did you meet with your retired cop?" Chloe had informed Greene of her mission before leaving that morning.

"I did. But I don't think it really did much. In an odd way, I guess it *did* help to have some closure from that morning. Simmons seemed absolutely sure my dad was guilty. Said there were a few affairs around town that basically proved it."

"Well, at least you tried, right?"

"Right. Thanks for the update. You sure there's nothing I can do?"

"You can get back home to your sister as quick as you can. Once news gets out that there is a search for a second suspect, the reporters might come out of the woodwork for Danielle again, wanting to know how it feels to be free. Consider this your first lesson in media relations:

they won't stop until after the story is done, run into the ground, and retread about one hundred times."

"Thanks for the tip," Chloe said.

Though honestly, if a few more irritating reporters was going to be the worst of what she'd have to put up with before this was all over, she thought that might be okay with her.

But then her thoughts went back to the basket of cookies and the note.

IT'S NOT OVER.

And for reasons she could not explain, that damned note was starting to seem like some dark prophecy.

After she got back home, Chloe was relieved to find that Danielle had indeed stayed put. Her rebellious side seemed to even have the most foundational laws of safety and good sense down. When she got home, Chloe found Danielle looking around on the Internet. The current article she had up was telling what sort of man Martin Shields was.

"I had no idea the asshole had two DUIs on his record," Danielle exclaimed. "No wonder he always looked tense and nervous whenever he got behind the wheel."

"Well, I suppose today is the day to learn new things about people we thought we knew," Chloe said.

"What do you mean? What did Simmons know?"

"Well, he stands by the ruling that dad was guilty. Said Dad confessed to the murder. Said he confessed to a lot more, too. Namely at least one affair. He was apparently seeing a few other women while he was married to Mom."

"Bullshit."

Chloe shrugged helplessly. "I'd like to think so. But Simmons had a straight head on his shoulders and he seemed so sure."

"Aren't there records and files for this kind of shit?" Danielle asked.

"Yes, but he said they'd take some digging to find. And if it comes to that, I think I'm prepared to do that digging. But I don't know that we'd really need to. I was thinking about something the whole ride back here.

Let's say Dad *was* cheating. In a town like this, someone would know about it. Word gets around. And I think a good place to start would be with the book club. *Someone* there knew Mom or Dad, even if it *was* just Tammy Wyler."

"Oh yeah! She wouldn't shut up about the fucking book club at the block party! How did I miss that?"

"Don't feel bad. I almost did, too. The fight between Steven and Martin basically dwarfed anything else that happened that day."

"So you want to what? Join a book club?"

"Sure," Chloe said, already taking out her phone. "Why not?"

She typed in *Pinecrest Public Library* and then *book club*. She was directed to the Pinecrest Public Library website. There, she found the current book the club was reading (*Sharp Objects* by Gillian Flynn) and when the club typically met (Tuesdays and Thursdays, at six o'clock in the evening). She also found the phone number and extension for the woman who managed the book club, a lady by the name of Mary Elder.

She pressed the number on her screen and the phone placed the call. She listened to it ring in her ear until it was answered on the third ring.

"Pinecrest Public Library," a woman said.

"Yes, hi," Chloe said, doing her best to shrug off the nerves and exhaustion the last few days had set upon her. It was hard to sound cheerful, but she did her best. "I was wondering if there was any process for joining the book club. Any paperwork or anything?"

"No ma'am," the equally cheerful voice replied. "Just a contact form where we ask about reading preferences and things like that. Are you interested in joining? We meet on Tuesdays and Thursdays, so you'd be welcome to come to the meeting tonight. The club is about one hundred pages into the current book, but that's okay."

"You know, I think I might just do that," Chloe said. "Six o' clock, right?"

"That's right. Can I get your name so we can go ahead and be expecting you?"

Chloe gave her name and felt like she had tossed a grenade at the poor lady. "Chloe Fine."

"Oh, okay," Mary Elder said, clearly taken off guard. "We'll be happy to have you." There was something like sympathy in her voice. Chloe leaped at it like a fish to bait.

"I know, I know," she said. "Seems weird. And I don't want to cause any distraction at the club. I just need to get away from all of the drama, you know? And I heard someone in my neighborhood say that my mother used to be in a book club … maybe the same one, I don't know. I thought it might help."

"Oh, of course," Mary Elder said. "I remember your mother a bit, actually. And it would be lovely to have to join us. I'll put an extra seat out tonight."

Chloe smiled. She was a better actress than she'd thought. "I look forward to it," she said.

Chloe ended the call and found Danielle grinning at her. "Well, you're just a filthy little liar, aren't you?"

"Hey, I like to read."

"I do, too," Danielle said. "Can I tag along?"

"I don't think that would be the best idea. Even though the headlines have started to indicate that you might not be guilty, you know how this town is. You'd be shunned."

Danielle sighed and got to her feet. She went into the kitchen and popped the top off of another bottle of wine, regardless that it was only two in the afternoon.

"Well, if I'm staying here by myself again, you might need to go out and get more wine."

They shared a laugh—a sound that was alien to both of them. It seemed out of place in the quiet house with the remaining news crew and police car buzzing around outside. But it was the first time since she had returned to Pinecrest that Chloe thought things might turn out all right between them.

Of course, all they had to do now was completely clear Danielle's name.

Chapter Thirty One

The Pinecrest Public Library was surprisingly large for the size of the town it accommodated. It was two stories tall, the bottom portion mostly dedicated to children's and middle grade books. When Chloe entered at 5:57 to join the book club, she was directed to the back of the bottom level by a series of signs adorned with arrows and the heading of BOOK CLUB.

She followed the signs to a cozy-looking conference room where several folding chairs had been set up in a semicircle. A small table was set up in the back with bottles of water and light snacks. A few women had already arrived, sitting in some of the chairs and in the midst of conversation. A woman who had been standing by the table in the back came up to her with a smile on her face.

"Hello there," this woman said. "I'm Mary Elder. I organize the book club."

"Oh, nice to meet you," Chloe said.

Mary Elder looked to be pushing sixty. If she had been here twenty years ago, the idea that she had interacted with her mother in the midst of this very book club was not too farfetched.

"I'm so glad you could join us. If you need a copy of the book, we have a few extras."

Chloe did not have the book, nor did she intend to start reading it. "Oh, that's okay. I have it at home and forgot to bring it. I'm about halfway through it."

"Great! Well, have a seat or help yourself to some snacks. We'll begin soon."

But Chloe barely heard the end of this comment. Instead, her attention was on the door. A familiar face walked through and when that face turned in Chloe's direction, it was filled with shock.

Ruthanne Carwile stood there, frozen for a moment, as if she had looked directly into the eyes of a ghost. She entered the room slowly, finally giving Chloe a little nod of recognition before taking a seat next to a group of three women.

Chloe ventured to the back table, giving the room and its participants some room to breathe—to operate the way it usually did when there wasn't a stranger around. She watched as small groups of friends joined together while Mary Elder took a seat at the end of the semicircle. By Mary taking her seat, it appeared that the other eleven women in the room took this to mean that it was time for the meeting to begin.

Chloe took a water and then found a seat. She took one across the semicircle from Ruthanne, wanting to keep an eye on her. The way Ruthanne had looked at her made her a little wary. There had been a split second where Chloe had seen pure disdain; it was clear that Ruthanne was not happy that Chloe was there.

"Before we get into the book tonight," Mary said, "I wanted to introduce our new member. And Chloe, this isn't calling you out… we do this to all new members. So everyone, please welcome a Pinecrest local who has just recently come back into town, Chloe Fine."

There were a few strange faces around the room. No one knew how to react to her presence. They'd obviously all seen the news headlines and, even if that were not the case, would likely all know about her history. She was the youngest person in the room, with the closest runner-up being about thirty or so, she guessed.

Mary seemed to sense the tension and did her best to tame it. But by the time two words had come out of her mouth, Chloe realized that the librarian was unintentionally helping her out.

"I remember when Chloe's mother used to be in this club," she said. "She was always so insightful and just a ton of fun to be around. Chloe, I'm very glad to have you join us and hope you can bring that same level of insight your mother did."

"I'll try my best," Chloe said. She then looked around the room and tried to put on her best sympathetic look—not quite saddened, but somewhere closer to reflective. "If you don't mind my asking, was anyone else in the room a member when Mom was here?"

She knew that if anyone in the room was sentimental, they'd speak up. She hated to play on people's emotions but she had to bet that recent news headlines would cause them to assume that she was here mainly to escape the drama of her sister and to perhaps find some old memories of her mother for peace.

As she expected, it worked.

Two women raised their hands, neither of whom was Ruthanne Carwile.

"I was part of the club when Gale was a member," one of the women said. "And Mary is right... she was so into reading. Always had some insights into the books that I could never even dream of. And she sometimes brought this cheese dip she made herself. It was delicious."

"My goodness," the other woman said. "I nearly forgot about Gale Fine's cheese dip."

"You know," Mary said, "I believe she also volunteered a few hours a week to help tutor kids that had problems reading. I'd have to go back into the records to look into that, but I think—"

"She did," Ruthanne said. Her voice had very little cheer to it and when she spoke, she did not look at Chloe.

What the hell is her deal? Chloe wondered.

"I thought so," Mary said.

Silence filled the room again. That awkward tension fell upon them once more and this time, it caused Ruthanne to stand up. She looked around the room apologetically, only glancing in Chloe's direction for a split second.

"I'm sorry," she said. "Excuse me for a moment." Ruthanne then exited the semicircle, leaving her book behind, and quickly left the room.

"Forgive me for asking, dear," the older woman who had mentioned the cheese dip said. "How well do you remember her?" She nodded toward the door as she asked, indicating the question was regarding Ruthanne.

"A bit. I ran into her at a Lavender Hills block party and some things came back to me. She would hang out with Mom every now and then, I think. Danielle and I would watch cartoons in her living room. And I think she used to make us grilled cheeses for lunch some afternoons when she and Mom were hanging out."

"Ruthanne took it hard when your mother died," Mary said. "She stopped coming to the book club for about six months. It was odd because no one realized they were so close." Mary then paused and looked around the room. "Dear, I'm so sorry. I don't know how this became all about you and your mother. I feel like we sort of ambushed you there."

"No, no, not at all. I actually appreciate it. Actually, if you don't mind, I do have one more question I was hoping someone might be able to answer."

No one gave a nod yes, but no one shut it down, either. So Chloe asked her question.

"Near the end of Mom's life, was there anything she said or did to make someone think she might be scared or in trouble?"

It was clear that the question was too much for some in the room. A few people were flipping through their books, even studying the notes they had taken. Really, it was just Mary Elder and the woman Chloe now thought of as Cheese Dip Lady that looked engaged.

"No, not really," Mary said. She then looked to the door where Ruthanne had just made her exit. "I… well, I don't know that this would be the appropriate time or place to talk about these things."

"I understand," Chloe said, sensing her window of opportunity closing. "If I could—"

"There were rumors," Cheese Dip Lady said. "About your father. With all due respect, aren't you working for the FBI? I assume anything we have to say about him, you've probably already discovered on your own. That being said… yes, there were rumors. Rumors that your father was having an affair."

"Yes, I know those rumors."

Cheese Dip Lady then also looked toward the door. She said nothing but that gesture was more than enough to get her point across.

There were rumors that your father was having an affair with Ruthanne Carwile.

It was then Chloe's turn to stand up and excuse herself. She looked to Mary Elder with sincere apology in her eyes. Any idea that she had come here tonight to actually enjoy a book club had been dashed.

"I'm so sorry," she said. "I think I need to be excused, too."

"Chloe," Mary said. "Maybe wait awhile."

Oh, I plan to, she thought as she exited the semicircle. As she headed for the door, a thought occurred to her— one that was so simple and outrageous at the same time that it might just lead somewhere.

Before leaving, she walked behind the semicircle to the place where Ruthanne had been sitting. Chloe picked up the copy of *Sharp Objects* Ruthanne had left behind. Her eyes briefly studied the small slip of paper that was barely sticking out between the pages.

"I'll make sure she gets this," Chloe said.

Very few of the women met her gaze and those who did looked worried and very awkward. With that, Chloe took her leave and rushed out to her car. She didn't even bother looking for any signs of Ruthanne in the parking lot. She got behind the wheel of her car and opened up the book. In the waning light of the afternoon, she flipped through the pages, working on a hunch.

She found what she was looking for at the very back of the book. It was a single sheet of notebook paper with a few notes about the book scrawled across it. The print was pretty and quite legible.

With her heart beating a little faster, Chloe set the book in the passenger seat and started the car. She headed for work, feeling confident she'd have plenty of space to work in the practice lab at this hour.

Leaving the library, she called Greene. She felt that at this stage, with such a huge hunch taking form, she might need a bit more experience on her side. Greene answered right away, sounding hopeful but also a little distant.

"Have a productive day?" he asked.

"I think maybe I did," she said. "Are you available right now?"

"Well, I just finished dinner with the family. What do you need?"

"Is there any way you can meet me down at the lab sometime soon? I have something I think might be worth looking into."

"Give me an hour. And please don't take this the wrong way, but distance yourself from the case. Pretend your sister isn't involved. Would it still be worth looking into?"

Chloe was thinking about the basket of cookies that had been delivered to her porch, hiding a very simple note inside.

A note with very precise penmanship.

"Absolutely," she answered.

Chapter Thirty Two

When Chloe arrived at the lab, Greene was not there yet. The hour he'd requested still had another fifteen minutes attached to it. Still, Chloe found a workspace at the lab (there was only one other intern working in the entire lab, doing something with an old glove) and set up. She took Ruthanne Carwile's notes of out of the copy of *Sharp Objects* and set it out beside the envelope that contained the letter that had come with the box of cookies.

As Chloe took the letter out of the envelope, she felt like she was stepping through a door—and that door might close behind her and trap her in this new place. And that was fine with her. Because that new place was a world where her studying of handwriting analysis and her subsequent excelling at it was no longer something she did for practice; she was putting it to use now and it could very well free Danielle for good.

She scanned in both handwriting examples, first the letter and then the notes. She then uploaded them to the cloud and powered up her iPad. She opened up a side-by-side comparison of the samples and within five seconds was pretty sure she had a match. Of course, as an intern who had already been given a rather long leash, she needed Green to confirm it.

While she waited, she tried to imagine why Ruthanne Carwile would be sending Danielle threatening letters. Such an act might make sense if it was someone younger, someone like Kathleen Saunders who had gone to high school with them. But Ruthanne was much older, pushing fifty—the age their mother would have been if she were still alive.

So maybe there's something to that, she thought. *Ruthanne knew my mother well enough to have her over for drinks while Danielle and I watched cartoons in her living room. With that sort of familiarity, how well did she know Dad?*

The thought raced across her mind that perhaps it had indeed been Ruthanne that her father had been having an affair with. It would explain why Ruthanne had so quickly exited the book club when the conversation turned to Chloe's parents.

She tried to think of how to find out if there was any merit to this aside from contacting Ruthanne personally. She was about to call Danielle with this theory—perhaps asking if she'd ever had any odd moments with Ruthanne either in their youth or after she came back to Pinecrest—when Agent Greene stepped into the lab.

"So where are we at?" he asked, taking a seat beside her at the exam table.

She quickly ran through the course of her day, filling him in on her nearly fruitless conversation with Clarence Simmons and ending with finding the notes in Ruthanne's copy of *Sharp Objects*. She then told him about finding the basket of cookies with the hidden note on her back porch last night.

"They must have been staking the place hard," Greene said, a bit disappointed. "They'd have to have been watching the shift changes with the officers outside of your house in order to get into your backyard. I'll have to take that up with the Pinecrest PD. That's inexcusable."

"It is, but that's okay for now. Look…I scanned in Ruthanne Carwile's notes and placed them alongside a scan from the letter that came last night."

She showed him her iPad screen where the two scans still sat side by side. "In my estimation," she said, "there are at least four similarities to the handwriting that make this a match. But I think the most telling one can be found on the way she ends her unconnected Rs."

She then zoomed in to the R in the letter: *IT'S NOT OVER*.

It was capitalized, as was the heading on the notes from the book that read: *GROWTH VS. FEAR*.

She caught Greene smiling a bit as he gave her a nod. "And what would you say the second most striking resemblance is?" he asked, quizzing her.

Even in the excitement of a moment such as this, she did not mind him quizzing her. It kept her focused and made her distance herself from the personal nature of the case.

"I'd say either the slanted elongated shape of her capital O or the straight, unbent shape of her apostrophe." She pointed to the apostrophe on *IT'S* from the letter and several apostrophes within the notes.

"I'm happy to say," Greene said, "that while it would still be subject to scrutiny, this is more than enough to pursue Ruthanne Carwile as the person who has been delivering the notes to your sister. But I'm afraid it will do basically nothing in furthering the case for Danielle's innocence. Still... a great find."

"So how quickly can we move on this?" she asked.

"Always so eager," Greene said with a chuckle. "I'll call Johnson and fill him in on this detail. The fact that this most recent letter was sent while your sister was the subject of a murder investigation makes it extremely bad for Ms. Carwile. And while I call, you drive."

"Drive where?"

"To wherever this woman lives. Your neighborhood, right? Based on this handwriting analysis, we've got enough to bring her in for questioning at the very least. If we wanted to *really* push, we could charge her with interfering in a federal murder investigation. Seriously, Fine... this is some great work."

Chloe took the compliment but tucked it away for later. In her mind's eye, she saw her house and then the streets that connected all of Lavender Hills. Danielle would be at her house, alone and waiting for an update. Meanwhile, one street over and half a block down, Ruthanne Carwile was sitting in her own home, maybe pondering the next threatening letter she'd write for Danielle.

It was frightening in a way she could not explain. And it also pissed her off.

"Yeah," she said, shutting down her iPad and getting to her feet. "Let's go get her."

Chapter Thirty Three

Chloe looked at Ruthanne through the one-way glass. The woman looked like a dog that had been scolded, tossed into a cage, and wasn't sure who to trust. There was a rather humane moment where Chloe felt bad for her. It was clear that Ruthanne Carwile had never expected to spend a second of her privileged life in an interrogation room. She was looking around the room as if she had stepped through a doorway into another world.

There were two men in the room with her—a cop who stood by the door with his arms folded over his chest, and a Pinecrest detective named Peterson. Their presence seemed to jolt her. It had been Chloe and Greene who had come to her house, after all. She had likely been expecting to see a familiar face while she was being questioned.

"Will I get to speak with her?" Chloe asked.

"Not unless it's absolutely necessary," Greene said. "Think about it… she'd try to use the fact that she knew your mother against you. She may even get defensive enough to try making you feel small—making you feel like that little girl that used to sit on her living room floor watching TV."

Chloe nodded. She had figured as much. She was nervous but not as much as she thought she'd be. She had interrogated two suspects before, as part of her training. To this day, she was pretty sure one of them had been fake, just a stand-in for the purpose of her coursework. So if she *did* get to speak with her, she felt confident that she could be effective.

She and Green watched as Peterson did a fine job with his own interrogation. It wasn't in-your-face or hostile but there was a sense of urgency to every word that came out of his mouth.

He slid a printout of the scans Chloe had created across the table to her. Ruthanne looked at them and revealed that she had perhaps the world's worst poker face.

"We know for a fact that one of these is yours," Peterson said. "And after scanning them and placing them side by side, it looks like they're *both* yours. Would you like to take a guess as to which is which?"

Ruthanne pointed to the paper, tapping the right side. "These are my notes from my book club. They were in my book."

"Yes, that's right," Peterson said. "And what about this other one? What about this one little sentence? *It's not over.* What's that mean?"

Ruthanne shook her head. "I don't know. That's not from my notes."

"Oh, I know that," Peterson said. "See, this note was delivered to Danielle Fine last night, while she was staying with her sister. And the reason we're asking you about it is because even you can surely see how similar the penmanship is."

"I see that, yes. But I did not write that."

Peterson nodded and then gave her another sheet of paper. It was murky through the glass but Peterson saw that it was a picture of Martin Shields. "Does this man look familiar to you?" Peterson asked.

Ruthanne nodded and said: "Yes. He was at the block party in Lavender Hills last weekend. He got into a fight with Chloe Fine's fiancé."

"And did you know that he turned up dead just several days later?"

"I did know that. One of my friends heard about it and told me."

"Had you ever spoken with or seen Mr. Shields at any time before the block party?" Peterson asked.

"No, sir."

Chloe was studying her closely. Watching Ruthanne's face was like a case study of recognizing facial tics. When she told the truth—when she denied something and actually *meant* it—the relief was evident on her face. But when she lied, her responses were quick and her face would tense up as if she had smelled something unpleasant.

"And did you speak with him during the block party?"

"I don't think so. And if I did, it was nothing more than a *hello* or a *nice to meet you.*"

Peterson leaned back in his chair and nodded sympathetically. Chloe thought he was very good at what he did. He was making it seem as if he thought it was a little silly that they had pulled this poor innocent woman out of her home to answer such dumb questions.

"Now, I understand that you knew Chloe Fine and her sister back when they were kids … that you and their mother were friends."

"We were for a while, yes. Not very close, but we'd enjoy a drink together every now and then."

"The girls would sometimes watch cartoons in your living room while you and their mother hung out on the porch, correct?"

"Correct," Ruthanne said. The expression on her face made it clear that she was not comfortable with where the conversation was headed.

"Do you recall what sort of conversations you had with her?"

Ruthanne squirmed a bit in her chair and took a moment to gather her answer. "Not really. Probably just work stuff. Complaining about work, marriages, and so on."

"Was Mrs. Fine not happy in her marriage?"

Ruthanne actually cringed at the question. "There were times when she wasn't."

"And were you there for her during those times? Did she come to your house to seek some of that talking time on the porch?"

"No."

"Do you know why not?"

"I'm sorry," Ruthanne said. "What does this have to do with anything?"

It was Peterson who bristled this time, not liking that he had been interrupted. He again pushed the handwriting analysis over to her. "Well, I'm trying to figure out why someone would send such mean letters to Danielle Fine. You see … this letter is not the first. And what that means is that we have at least five more letters that we can scan and compare to your book club notes. And I have to tell you, Ms. Carwile … based on just this one comparison right here, I think we're going to find quite a lot."

"I didn't write this note," she said. But she was close to tears and could no longer look at the paper.

"Are you sure?" Peterson asked. "Because here's the deal… whoever dropped this note off on Chloe Fine's back porch did so while Danielle was part of a murder investigation. That makes this more than just a threatening note. It makes it interference in a federal case. And that's a hefty fine… maybe even some jail time. So I want this cleared up as soon as possible. If whoever wrote this can fess up now and issue an apology to Danielle Fine, I think the matter can be settled without any fuss. So let me ask you again before this gets out of hand… did you write this note and the others that came before it?"

Ruthanne answered in a sob that seemed to surprise her as it came out of her throat. She slapped the two papers Peterson had showed her off of the table.

"Yes," she said. "I sent the notes."

Peterson gave her a moment before he pressed on. "Can you tell me why?"

She shook her head. "It was a bitch thing to do. I never liked that girl. And her being in Pinecrest, coming back after failing elsewhere, it reminded me…"

Something then seemed to snap into place for Ruthanne. She sat up and looked to the glass. "Is Chloe back there?" she asked Peterson. "Chloe, I'm sorry. And you can tell Danielle, too. I'm sorry about the notes. It was stupid and immature…"

"Okay, so now please try to follow me," Peterson said. "You sent Danielle those letters for what you say are stupid reasons. Jealousy, maybe? Or maybe you just straight up don't like her. Honestly, I don't care. And now that you've admitted it, it's not an issue. However… part of my job is to try to find threads in things. And if you knew Chloe and Danielle Fine's mother—Gale Fine—and sent these messages to Danielle seventeen years later, it makes me wonder why.

"You see, we've now discovered that it's a well-trod theory that Aiden Fine was having at least one affair. And while no one ever came forward with one, someone that maybe spent routine time with his wife, learning about him and his schedule…"

"Absolutely not," Ruthanne said. She said it quickly but with a bit of shock, but still Chloe wasn't sure she was telling the truth.

"Okay, I believe you," he said, though Chloe wasn't sure he did. "Do you happen to remember where you were on the day Gale Fine was killed?"

"I was at home. I remember getting the call, but I don't remember who it was. I heard that she had been killed, that he was on his way to prison, and the girls were sent off to their grandparents."

"Let me ask you *this,* then," Peterson said. "All of this happened in Pinecrest. Their deaths, the girls being carted off to the grandparents' ... and your friendship with their mother. How long have you lived in Pinecrest?"

"I've been here for years," she said. "I moved from Boston to Pinecrest with my first husband. When we divorced, I nearly moved to Baltimore. But I met a man during my hunt for a house and he lived in Pinecrest. We got married and bought a house in Pinecrest so I stayed put."

"But you and your husband ... your second husband, that is, are no longer together, correct?"

"Right. We divorced last year. He moved to Texas and left me the house."

"Is that when you started sending the notes to Danielle Fine?"

Ruthanne shook her head. "This was about six months ago when I started doing that."

"And you still don't have a good reason?"

"No."

She's lying, Chloe thought.

On the other side of the glass, Peterson got up and looked down at her. "Let me check on a few things," he said. "I think I can get you away from all of this with just a slap on the wrist in terms of the letters. Hang tight, okay? I'll have you out of here as soon as I can."

The relief in her face was so clear that it was jarring. *She's hiding something,* Chloe thought.

Peterson left the interrogation room and came into the little observation area. He joined Chloe and Greene, staring at Ruthanne through the glass.

"So," he said. "She's lying her ass off. I just can't tell about what."

"She knows more than she's letting on," Chloe said.

“She does,” Peterson said.

“It also makes me think that maybe she knew your father better than she’s letting on,” Green said. “That or your grandparents.”

“What if she really knows what happened to my mother?” Chloe asked. “She could have the answers to the whole thing ...”

Greene made a startled motion as his cell phone buzzed inside of his pocket. He took it out and read the text message that had just come through.

“Maybe she does,” Greene said. “We can start looking for ourselves if you want. I just got a notice that we’ve got a search warrant for her house approved.”

Chloe looked at the harmless-looking woman on the other side of the glass. She barely remembered the woman from her childhood, but she *could* remember sitting in front of her TV with Danielle.

Had Ruthanne been keeping secrets even then?

Chloe felt a little sneer come to her face as she started for the door. Green quickly thanked Peterson for his hard work and then followed her out. Chloe wasn’t sure but she thought he seemed as if he was now just as anxious to get to the bottom of it all as she was.

Chapter Thirty Four

They walked up Ruthanne's porch steps under the cover of night as the late summer evening chewed through its last bit of evening light. It glowed like an angry strip of red along the horizon. Chloe watched as Greene expertly picked both the key lock and the dead bolt. It took him less than twenty seconds and then they were stepping inside Ruthanne's house.

The place was meticulously cleaned and smelled like a mixture of lemon and vanilla. It was one of the smaller houses on the street but the inside was still quite beautiful. The front door opened into a small foyer with high ceilings. This took them into an alcove where a right-hand turn would take them into the kitchen and a left-hand turn would lead into the living room.

Chloe stayed with Greene, not quite sure what they were looking for just yet. *If she knows the truth about Mom, what form would that truth take? If it's something more than just firsthand knowledge, what else would she have?*

"Can you think of anything your mother might have given this woman while they were friends?" Greene asked.

"No. I really barely even remember her at all."

"So based on what we know and what we *anticipate,* what do you think we should be looking for?"

"If we want immediate answers, I don't know," she said. "If we can find a laptop, I think we need to take it. Maybe there are documents or receipts or… I don't know. Something. Or maybe we could get into her emails. Her phone would be the best bet, but she had that on her at the station."

"I'm going to give you ten minutes to look the place over," Greene said. With that, he took out his phone and started scrolling through his contacts. "In the meantime, I'm going to call Peterson and see what they can do to get her phone from her. We'd basically have to charge her with something at that point, though. And at this stage, that will be tough."

Chloe again found herself appreciating the lengths Greene was going to allow her to learn unhindered. But at the same time, she was very aware of each and every step she made through Ruthanne's house as she started her search. She scanned the living room and did see a laptop sitting on the edge of a walnut coffee table. She figured it was worth a try, so she opened it up but was presented with a password screen. Frowning, Chloe left it and headed further into the living room.

She came to a small hallway that contained only a coat closet, a bathroom, and the staircase to the second floor. The stairway brought her to another hallway. This one contained another bathroom and two bedrooms. The first bedroom was rather small and was filled with boxes. Chloe checked the boxes and found an assortment of things that made her wonder if Ruthanne had considered moving away from Pinecrest recently. There were books, a spare coffeemaker, unopened packs of toilet paper, tampons, Q-tips, and other toiletries. There were also several boxes of clothes that had been packed up.

Chloe left this makeshift storage room and walked into the other bedroom. This was the master, as immaculately cleaned as the rest of the house. A queen-sized bed sat in the center of the room, against the far wall. Pushed into the right corner of the room was a small desk. An iPad and a few books sat on the top of it. Off to the side, there was a small organization cube, the type that helped to sort letters, paper, correspondence, and so forth.

Chloe found the exact same kind of envelopes and little golden seals that had been used to deliver the notes to Danielle. She thumbed through them, wondering if maybe she pre-wrote the letters. But all she found were blank pages.

A small ornate filing cabinet sat beneath the desk. It was the kind of thing that looked like it was more for decoration than serving an actual purpose, made of wicker and frilly bronze knobs. It was no larger than two feet high, fitting perfectly beneath the desk. Chloe dropped to her knees and pulled out the first of the two drawers. There were a few scattered pictures, some showing Ruthanne with a man whom Chloe assumed was one of her husbands. Judging by the clothes, she supposed they were no older than ten years old.

In the back of the drawer, she found a battered-looking photo album, the collectible kind that only held one or two a page.

She opened it up and nearly dropped it.

There was a picture of her parents in the first sleeve. Her mother was grinning widely while her father gave her a kiss on the cheek. With trembling fingers, Chloe turned the page. This time the picture was just her father. He was looking away from the camera, his gaze following that of a young girl…

That's either me or Danielle, she thought. She'd seen enough of their childhood pictures to recognize the frizzy blonde hair.

"What the hell?" she said.

She kept turning and saw three more pictures of her family. Her mother was only in one more of them. The focal point of the pictures was undoubtedly her father.

She turned yet another page and it was like jumping forward in time. She saw her father again, but he was older. His hair was graying and his eyes looked tired. More than that, this one appeared to be a selfie. There was a concrete wall behind him, scarred and cracked, likely the inside of a cell or some sort of resource room at his prison.

He's got to be at least forty in this picture, Chloe thought. *Oh my God… this is recent. Very recent, maybe.*

There were two more recent pictures of her father. Each one was more jarring than the one before it. Chloe hated to admit it, but she had the intense urge to cry. Yes, she and Danielle had willingly made the decision to just pretend he no longer existed—but that had been *after* he had started to ignore them. To see him in the present, sending pictures of himself to someone they barely knew… it felt obscene.

She came to the end of the album and instantly went to the bottom drawer. The only thing in it was an old cardboard keepsake box. It had a flimsy little decorative latch keeping it closed. She broke it off in her hurry to open the box.

Inside, she found several folded sheets of paper. But sitting on top of them all was a phone. It was an iPhone, about two models behind the most recent. Taking a chance, she tried to power it on. She waited until the Apple logo came on, the loading bar starting to fill beneath it.

While she waited, she took one of the folded pieces of paper at random. She unfolded it and found a right-leaning script that had made up a letter that occupied about half a page. She barely even scanned the letter itself. She went straight to the salutation.

A little cry of sadness rose out of her throat when she saw her father's name.

"Agent Greene!"

She called his name, not giving a damn that her voice was thick with emotion and that she was on the verge of crying.

"Coming!" he said. He sounded concerned, as did his footfalls as she listened to them coming up the stairs.

While she waited for him, she looked at another of the letters. Without counting, she supposed there were at least twenty in all. She scanned this letter a little more closely before coming to her father's name again. Some of the words she saw included: *never loved her, soulmate, anything for you, be together again soon* and *deepest love.*

She wanted to tear the letter to shreds. She might have done just that if Greene had not come into the room in that moment.

"What is it?" he asked, his hand hovering over his sidearm. She supposed her voice *had* been rather alarming.

"She *was* having an affair with him. It's here … in these letters. I don't know how far it goes back, but some of this paper looks old and worn. And then there's this," she said, sliding the photo album his way. "There are pictures of our family in here and … and recent pictures of my dad."

"What about this?" Greene asked, picking up the old iPhone.

"I don't know yet."

The phone had fully booted up, allowing Greene to look it over. He went to Pictures and found the gallery empty. He then checked for texts but found not a single one. But when he checked the call history, he found pay dirt. He showed the screen to Chloe. She observed the six listings, noting that they were all made to the same number.

"You recognize this number?" Greene asked.

"No. But they're all made on the same day… on Tuesday of this week."

"The day Martin Shields was killed," Greene said, finishing her thought for her.

Without another word, Greene instantly pulled out his phone and made a call. Chloe only half listened as she picked up another letter and read it. This time, she read it word for word.

Ruthie,

It was good seeing you last week, even it if was through the dirty glass. I can't tell you how much it means to me that you still come all the way out here to see me. But just think ... another year or two and there will be no more waiting. No more long trips. I'll be with you all the time.

I think of you all the time. It makes the nights longer, but that's okay. You're the only reason I have to even look forward to getting out. Two years ... two measly years. You can wait that long for me, right? I hope so.

Write me back when you can. And if it's not asking too much, could you send another of your "special" pictures? Maybe something with black lace this time?

Yours,
Aiden

There was too much in the letter to process. For starters… two years. What about two years? She was pretty sure she knew what it meant but… *how?*

Greene had gotten off the phone. Distantly, Chloe was aware that he had called someone at the bureau to trace down the owner of the number they had found on the stow-away phone.

"Find something?" he asked.

She nodded and handed him the letter she had just read. "Can you make a call and find out what my father's status is? I haven't cared for so long… I just figured he'd rot in prison. Was that naïve of me?"

"I don't know enough about the case to say for sure," Greene said as he scanned through the letter. "Jesus, Chloe… this is rough. I'm sorry you're uncovering all of this."

"I'm not," she said, meaning it. She was, however, finding it very hard to imagine telling Danielle everything she had discovered during the course of this day.

When Greene's phone rang, it startled them both. He looked at the display and said, "They must have a name for that number already."

He answered it and Chloe waited patiently, listening to only Greene's side of the conversation.

"That was quick… yeah." A pause and then, very slowly, Greene added: "Can you please repeat that?… Yeah, okay. Thanks."

He killed the call and looked gravely at Chloe. "Pick up those letters and anything else you found. We're taking them to her as proof. This thing just blew up on her."

"Why?" Chloe asked. "Greene… whose number is that in the phone?"

He smiled, as if he couldn't believe their luck. "It appears that Ruthanne Carwile has been using that old phone to call Alan Short."

It took a full second for the name to register. Alan Short—the man who had somehow gotten some of his blood under Martin's fingernails.

"Holy shit," she said.

"It's enough for a conspiracy charge," Greene said. "And if we push hard enough, probably enough to free your sister."

Danielle, Chloe thought, again sickened by the fact that she was going to have to relay all of this information to her.

But first there was Ruthanne to deal with. And truth be told, Chloe couldn't wait to see the look on that bitch's face when she plopped these letters and pictures down in front of her.

Chapter Thirty Five

Earlier, Chloe thought Ruthanne had looked like a scared dog inside the interrogation room. But now, as she was forced to watch things unfold from the other side of the glass again, it was *Chloe* who felt like a dog. Only she imagined this might be what a dog felt like when it was chained to a post and *really* wanted to get after the maimed rabbit at the edge of the yard, wanting to tear its throat out.

It was made worse by the fact that she was in the observation room alone. Greene had joined Peterson in the interrogation room. As she watched, both men stood on the opposite side of the table from Ruthanne. Greene held a manila envelope under his arm. Ruthanne had noticed it and couldn't seem to take her eyes away from it.

Peterson wasted no time with pleasantries this time. He leaned over the table, closing the space between them significantly.

"I'm going to ask you this last time… and I want you to think long and hard about your answer," he said. "Were you at any point in the last twenty years or so involved in an affair with Aiden Fine?"

Ruthanne was not able to answer. Her lips were trembling and she kept staring at the envelope. Seeing it, Chloe was pretty sure Ruthanne knew what they had found. Slowly, she nodded her head.

Greene opened the folder and pulled the contents out. He spread the letters out on the table. He even pulled the small photo album out of the folder and placed that in front of her as well.

"These are all addressed to a woman named Ruthie," Greene said. "I assume that is a nickname for Ruthanne. If I am wrong, please correct me."

Again, Ruthanne shook her head. "They're written to me."

"How long have you been keeping in touch with him?" Greene asked.

"Ten years or so," Ruthanne said. She took a moment and managed to stave off the emotional breakdown that she had seemed to be on the brink of having. She was finally able to look at Greene and Peterson. Now that she had been found out, she looked almost relieved. She sank into the chair and looked at them both with a sleepy sort of interest.

"How about the affair? When was that taking place?"

"For about eight months before . . ."

"Before what?" Peterson asked. "Before Gale Fine was murdered?"

"Yes," Ruthanne said, the word coming out of her mouth like venom.

"So we've learned that you were indeed involved with Aiden Fine," Peterson said. "Is there anything else you want to admit to?"

Ruthanne thought about this for about five seconds—long enough to make Chloe feel certain that she was trying to decide just *how much* the men in front of her knew. In the end, she decided to stay silent.

"We're going to note your silence," Peterson said, clearly irritated. "And I'm going to ask you a simple question: were you in any way involved with the death of Gale Fine seventeen years ago?"

"No."

"Are you sure? Maybe you started to have strong feelings for Aiden . . . maybe you wanted more than an affair and getting rid of Gale was the best way to get what you wanted."

In the observation room, Chloe was starting to cringe at the line of questioning. The impact of the questions was proof that she had no business being in that room. She was glad that Greene had put his foot down and insisted that she stay out of there.

"No, *no*!" Ruthanne said. But even through the glass, Chloe could see that something in Ruthanne was about to break.

Apparently, Greene took notice of this, too. He used a highly effective tactic and took the questioning elsewhere . . . for the moment.

"Okay, so we have one more item for you. Do you know a man named Alan Short?"

This question seemed to rock her. The emotion she was showing drained from her face for a moment. Again, she had showed her hand. She could deny it all she wanted but the reaction to the question gave them the real answer.

"No."

"You seemed shocked when the name came out of Agent Greene's mouth," Peterson told her. He then turned to Greene and added: "Want to show her the last item in your folder, Agent Greene?"

Greene reached into the folder and even before his hand came out, Ruthanne started talking again.

"Yes, I know him. We dated for a while and he—"

She stopped, uncertain of how to continue. Whatever it was inside of her that had been on the brink of collapsing or breaking was only seconds away from going nuclear.

"He what?" Greene asked. "Did he know Martin Shields? For that matter, did *you* know Martin Shields? Before the block party, I mean. I only ask because Alan Short's blood was found under Martin's fingernails. You do the math, Ms. Carwile. You do the math and—"

The sound that came out of Ruthanne's mouth was the wildest sound, the most guttural noise from a human throat, that Chloe had ever heard. And when she started talking again, it was a mix of shouting and weeping. She stood up from her chair so fast that Peterson's hand went to his service weapon at his hip.

"I had to get her out of the way! And we figured framing her for a murder would do it!"

"Had to get who out of the way?" Peterson asked.

Even before she answered, Chloe knew where this was going. She started to unwrap the entire thing in her head as each detail was revealed, and it took every ounce of strength within her not to rush into the interrogation room and break Ruthanne Carwile's fucking neck.

"Danielle! When he came back, she couldn't be here. So I had to have her removed…"

"When he came back?" Peterson asked. "I'm not following."

"When Aiden got out. He's up for parole in two years. I needed everything set up and ready when he got out. He wanted it that way, too. We planned this, you know? Get all of the distractions out of the way. No remnants of his old life… including Danielle. Because when she started digging into her mom's past… and calling the library… I got paranoid. I started sending the letters, trying to scare her off."

"Did you hire Alan Short to kill Martin Shields?" Greene asked.

"No. He just volunteered. I had to talk him into it near the end, but he was happy to do it."

"Jesus," Peterson murmured. "So you're telling me the man you're dating right now killed Martin Shields?"

Ruthanne opened her mouth to respond, but more wailing came out. She sank into the chair again and nodded. "Yes. And Martin scratched him in the fight. Right across the cheek."

"Where is he now?" Peterson asked, already reaching for his phone.

But then something dawned on Peterson—the very same thing that had come across Chloe's mind about thirty seconds earlier. He approached the table again, no longer worried about the location of Alan Short for the moment.

"Seventeen years ago ... you were having an affair with Aiden Fine. *You* did it, didn't you? You killed Gale Fine. Pushed her down the stairs. And now, seventeen years later, you couldn't bring yourself to kill again. So you tried threatening letters to drive Danielle away. And when that didn't work, you found some idiot to do it for you ..."

Ruthanne looked pitiful as she fought with an admission. Seeing her in a saddened state, as if she were the victim, enraged Chloe. She couldn't stand still any longer. In tears, she exited the observation room. She stormed the few steps to the interrogation room and threw the door open. She made a direct course for Ruthanne but was stopped instantly by Greene.

"Think about what you're doing," Greene said.

Chloe heard him, but just barely.

"Say it," Chloe said, her voice surprisingly calm. "Tell us what you did. Admit to it, you twisted bitch!"

Ruthanne looked Chloe in the eyes. Seeing genuine sorrow and regret there turned Chloe's stomach. "You had gone to the movies with a friend and Danielle was at the park with some kids, playing soccer. Your mom was at work. He called me over. Your mom came back home early with a headache, one of those migraines she used to get all the time. She walked in on us and there was an argument. I pushed her down the stairs ... and to this day I don't know if I meant to—"

Chloe surged against Greene but he held her in place. *Get control, Chloe thought. Get control of yourself or you won't be able to see how this ends ...*

"We decided to say he had done it, that it had been an accident. Involuntary manslaughter, saving me from jail, or so we thought. But it turned out to be second degree—a longer sentence. Still, he promised that when it was all over that he'd come for me, that we could be together. He wrote me letters after he was in jail ... you only have some of them here," she said, slapping at the table.

Chloe gave one final surge, having to bite her lips to keep from screaming at her. Greene gently pushed her back and looked at Peterson.

"That's an admission of guilt," he said. "Can you handle it from here?"

"Yeah," Peterson said, still looking a little shocked.

Greene led Chloe back out into the hallway and quickly into the observation room before anyone could see the state she was in. She wiped tears away from her eyes and did her best to quickly regain control. Through the glass, she could hear Peterson reading Ruthanne her rights.

"Sorry," Chloe said. "God, I'm so sorry. I just couldn't stand here and ..."

"It's okay," Greene said. "It might be on me a bit for even letting you this close to it. But I need you to tell me right now—are you okay? Can you finish this out with me?"

"Finish it?"

"Yes," Greene said. "If you're up to it, I think you should ride along and be there when we get Alan Short for the murder of Martin Shields."

The mere thought of this seemed to re-center her. It reminded her that she had not been asked to be a part of this investigation because of her history or her personal ties with it. Even after the shattering revelations she had just heard spilling for the mouth of Ruthanne Carwile, there was still a case to wrap up.

"Yes," she said, meaning it. "I'm good. When do we go?"

"As soon as she gives us a location," Greene said, hitching a thumb back toward the glass.

They both looked through it as Peterson finished reading the Miranda rights to the woman who, seventeen years later, had finally admitted to the murder of Chloe's mother.

Chapter Thirty Six

In the passenger seat of Greene's car, Chloe took a moment to text Danielle. She would have rather called, as texting seemed too impersonal, but she wasn't sure she could keep it together emotionally. And considering they were currently on the way to apprehend the man who had killed Martin, she thought it best that Agent Greene not see her lose her cool for the second time in less than an hour.

Ruthanne had given up Alan's location pretty much right away once she had been charged with the murder of Gale Fine. She'd given up much more than that, actually, letting them in on every little detail of their plan.

Since the night of the murder, Alan had been staying at a Super 8 motel in the small town of Maysville, a splat on the map between Pinecrest and Baltimore. He'd signed in under a fake name and had been paying cash. The plan, according to Ruthanne, was for them to split town and head to Alan's hometown of Charlottesville, Virginia, as soon as Danielle had been properly charged with Martin's murder.

Chloe did not relay all of that to Danielle, though. She kept it brief and to the point: **I know it's getting late. Found lots of answers and about to wrap up the last one, I think. I'll tell you everything when I get home. Just know this: it's looking very good for you.**

She received a response fairly quickly, just as the faint light of the Super 8 sign crept into view up ahead. There were two patrol cars ahead of them, compliments of the Pinecrest PD, with Detective Peterson in one of them. No one was running their flashers and they were keeping their speed to just slightly above the posted speed limit. They did not want to tip Alan Short off at all.

In fact, when they reached the parking lot, Agent Greene pulled in along the side, parking beside the front office. The two patrol cars went to the opposite end, one parking behind a large economy van and basically out of sight.

"I can't have you coming in," Greene said. "Johnson would have my head. But I want you to be part of it." He pulled out his phone and dialed up her number. "Answer this call and listen along. I'll have it in the interior pocket of my jacket. Sorry… not very high tech, so it's the best we have."

With that, he pressed CALL and Chloe answered it right away. Greene then stepped out of the car and ran into the front office. She listened closely as Greene spoke with a woman at the front desk, letting her know what was about to go down. Without any fuss or trouble at all, she provided a key to the room Short was staying in.

As all of this went down, Chloe watched the other end of the lot. Peterson was out of the car, walking slowly to the open walkway that connected all of the rooms. When he was under the shadow of the awning covering the walkway, the three other officers followed behind. When they fell in line, one behind the other, they all placed their hands on the stock of their holstered sidearms.

Greene came out of the office, walking as if he belonged there. Anyone seeing him from the street might assume that he had simply rented a room for the night. He headed in the direction of Peterson and the waiting cops. As he moved toward them, they started moving forward. They met slightly off-center of the walkway with the door and window of Room 206 between them.

Through the phone, Chloe could hear Greene counting: *"One … two … three."*

Their entrance was not as dramatic as the busting down of the door. Instead, Green quickly stalked forward and inserted the key into the lock. As he did, Peterson and the officers fell in behind him, breaking into a flanked position with two on either side of him. Greene turned the lock and entered the room.

After that, Chloe could only listen, as the men entered the room and her phone was suddenly flooded with noise.

"On the ground, Mr. Short!" someone yelled.

"What the hell is this…?" came another voice, apparently that of Short.

"You're under arrest for the murder of—"

"Hands where I can fucking see them!"

"On the ground, *now*!"

There was a silence that felt uncomfortable even through the phone. It was broken by a single word shouted by Peterson.

"Gun!"

And then Chloe heard three gunshots through the phone. Someone screamed and then there was a sound like thunder.

Someone fell, Chloe thought. *Or a door was slammed.*

"I'm hit," someone said. "Just a graze though."

"Shit. Did we get him?"

"Don't know," said another voice, this one unmistakably Greene's.

Chloe sat up, sensing the situation getting out of control. Someone was shot, she thought. But Short was apparently still lively enough to escape into the bathroom. What other door would there be to shut?

Chloe felt a stir of instinct. She set her phone to the side and quietly got out of the car. She looked to the right, to the office and then the edge of the motel. It was barely illuminated in the glow of the Super 8 sign.

She walked quickly to the edge of the office and peered into the darkness behind the motel. She could see nothing, but she *did* hear a slight commotion. She went further into the dark alley beside the motel and started to make out movement farther down. And as she saw the movement, she heard a muted voice.

"Get out of there *now,* Mr. Short, or we *will* break the door down. You've shot a cop. Anything you do from this point out makes it that much worse for you."

Understanding what she was seeing further along in the darkened space behind the motel, Chloe hurried toward the movement. As she drew closer, she saw that her hunch was right. Alan Short was escaping through the small bathroom window. He was barely able to fit through, but he was already halfway out, his head dangling down as his left arm reached for the ground.

Chloe was unarmed, so when she saw the gun in Short's right hand, she hesitated. But only for a moment. She moved quickly, sticking to the side of the building. By the time she was close enough for Short to hear her footfalls, she was less than ten feet away from him.

He tried raising the gun but then started slipping through the window. Behind him, they both heard the sound of the bathroom door crashing down.

Chloe delivered a hard right-handed haymaker that took Alan Short hard in the side of his head. He slipped the rest of the way out of the window and fell to the pavement. Chloe acted right away, stomping down on his right wrist. As Short released the gun, she dropped down on his back. She planted a knee in the center of his back and drew his arms back hard.

He cried out in pain as she pulled backward. He wrestled against her but she had him pinned in a way where every movement applied more pressure to her hold.

She heard commotion from the edge of the motel, from where she had slunk toward the window. She was relieved to see Greene and Peterson running toward her. When they came to her side, she saw a grin of satisfaction on Greene's face.

"I'll yell at you about getting out of the car later," Greene said as he took over. "But for now, job well done."

Chloe stepped back as Greene applied handcuffs to Alan Short. And as Peterson read Short his rights, Chloe leaned against the wall. For a moment, she thought she might faint.

In the end, she had to fight back tears. It was a fight she was still having with herself even as she and Greene escorted Alan Short to Peterson's patrol car.

She did not realize just how large Alan Short was until she watched him bend down to fit into the back seat. Alan Short was a large man and the idea that she had pinned him to the ground sent a flood of accomplishment through her.

"It was her, wasn't it?" Short asked before Peterson closed the door. "She turned me over."

"If you're referring to Ruthanne Carwile, yes, she did. But only after we busted her for a murder seventeen years ago. Did you know about that?"

"Yeah, she told me. She has nightmares about it."

Good, Chloe thought.

"So she's been arrested, too?" Short asked.

"In the process," Peterson said. "Maybe we can find you two a cell together."

"To hell with that," Short said. "She's a wildcat in the sack, which is why I stuck with her for so long, but that bitch is straight up crazy."

"But yet you killed for her," Greene said. "Makes me wonder who's the *truly* crazy one."

With that, Peterson closed the door to end the conversation.

And as the door shut in Alan Short's face, Chloe couldn't help but feel as if it might even be the sound of a door closing within her own life—a door that she had often opened up in order to obsess over the past.

But she knew that before she could truly hope to have that door closed, she had to fill Danielle in on everything first.

It would be difficult and they'd probably both cry a lot.

She just hoped Danielle hadn't gone through all of the wine in the house while she had been alone. God knew they'd need some to get through the entire story.

Chapter Thirty Seven

Two days later, as they sat in Chloe's car following Martin's funeral, Chloe handed her phone to Danielle. There was a news article up, from a link Agent Greene had sent her.

"Looks like it's official now," Chloe said.

Danielle took the phone and read over the article Chloe had just read. Chloe read it for a second time as well, just to experience it again. The headline read **Ex-girlfriend Cleared in Murder Case as Larger Conspiracy is Revealed**.

The article told most of the story that had been uncovered by Chloe and confessed by Ruthanne Carwile. Seventeen years ago, Ruthanne Carwile had killed Gale Fine when she came home to find Ruthanne and Aiden Fine in bed together. The murder was easily passed off as involuntary manslaughter—a simple push of aggression that caused Gale Fine to fall down the stairs. But in her guilt Ruthanne had confessed that she had done it on purpose. In court, though, a sentencing of second degree murder had been passed down.

Per her confession, Aiden had been horrified, and yet he had silently taken the blame for Ruthanne. She visited him once in prison, and he told her he did so because he felt guilty about their affair, and guilty that the affair had led to his wife's death, even if he had no hand in it. She had tried to make plans with Aiden, that when he got out of prison, they'd be together, but he refused until several years later, when he admitted he still loved Ruthanne and agreed she could start visiting him again.

Chloe wasn't able to read the entire thing again, though. Danielle seemed to tire of it before she came to the end. She closed the window out and handed the phone back to Chloe.

"If it ends with how Ruthanne kept tabs on Aiden Fine's rogue and troubled daughter—those words from Fox News this morning, by the way—I don't want to hear it. It creeps me out."

Chloe understood that. Truth be told, it creeped her out, too.

She caught Danielle looking back out at Martin's graveside. The service had been brief and the crowd turnout had been thin. Chloe still wasn't quite sure why Danielle had insisted on coming. Maybe because, despite all of the drama that had come with him in the end, the fake façade Martin Shields had showed her had been the closest Danielle had come to finding a man she trusted.

This might set that search back, Chloe thought.

"You know, I'm going to look for a new place to live starting tomorrow," Danielle said, still looking at the grave. "I can't go back to that apartment. I need to… *grow up,* I guess."

"You're welcome to come back to my house," Chloe said. "You can stay as long as you like. It's not like Steven is coming back anytime soon."

"You know that for sure?" Danielle asked.

"Yeah. He sent me a series of dates this morning, wanting to know when I'd be available to meet him. He wants the engagement ring back."

"Classy," Danielle said.

"But understandable."

Danielle sighed. "Do you feel any better now knowing that Dad was *basically* innocent in Mom's death?" she asked.

"No. If anything, I hate him more."

"You know what I hate?" Danielle said. "That the asshole has been cleared of his charges. He's going to be freed, isn't he?"

"I don't know," Chloe said. It was a true answer, though Peterson and Greene seemed to think it would only be a matter of time now that Ruthanne had confessed to everything.

"Let's get out of here," Danielle said.

Chloe started the car and pulled out of the lot. They'd been sitting there for fifteen minutes now, the service long since over.

Five minutes down the road, Danielle pressed the side of her head against the passenger window and started to cry. She cried openly and she cried hard.

Chloe had never seen this before, not in such a raw way. She had no idea what to do so she did what every sister-instinct in her demanded: she reached out and took her sister's hand.

Danielle took it and gave it a squeeze. Chloe drove on like that, with Danielle's hand in hers. She couldn't help but think of the two of them in the back of their grandmother's car seventeen years ago, holding hands while somewhere behind them their mother's body was taken to a morgue and their father was taken to prison.

For a moment, she felt trapped in a loop—the same loop that had brought her back to trying to understand why her mother had been killed. Now that they had answers, though, she hoped the loop would break and allow them both to, finally, escape.

Epilogue

5 months later…

She should have been excited about graduating. She should have been thrilled that she would no longer be an intern and would actually be carrying a badge and an ID that didn't need to come with an instructor or a special set of restrictions.

But what Chloe was most excited about was that she could see Danielle from her seat. She was tucked away in the nearly three thousand spectators in attendance but, as was usually the case with Danielle, somehow managed to stand out. She had started to grow her hair out. And even though it was still raven black, hiding their genetically similar blonde hair, Danielle looked just like their mother. Danielle caught her looking and gave a little wave. Chloe waved back and tried to remember a time in the past when she had ever felt such an outpouring of love and support from her sister.

From up on the stage, the commencement speaker stepped down. A smattering of applause filled the open yard, but not too much. The entire graduation ceremony had been much stuffier than Chloe had been expecting. Still, when the emcee stepped up and said, "And now for those graduating from the School of Evidence Response…" she felt like an excited high schooler, anxious to step out and experience the world.

The list of graduates for the Evidence Response Team was rather short. Chloe's name was the sixteenth called. As she got to her feet and headed for the stage, she thought back not to the sound of Peterson's door closing on Alan Short and not even of the numerous compliments Greene had given her after the case had been wrapped.

Instead, she thought of Danielle, crying against the passenger side window. That crying had come *after* the case had been wrapped—after they had gotten all of the answers to all of their questions about their mother's death. It was an example of how when things came to an end, it was not necessarily a *finality* to things.

Sometimes, things just kept going on and on. It was something she and Danielle had both come to terms with over the last five months.

Yet as she stepped down from the stage, diploma in hand, she also knew that sometimes the best way to bring an end to things was to focus on a new beginning. She did not believe in fresh slates to start over from, but she *did* believe that with enough drive, people could escape the chains of the demons of their past.

As she walked back to her seat, she spotted Agent Greene. He was sitting close to the stage with other agents who had served as instructors. The look of pride she saw on his face when their eyes met was beyond compare. She thought it might be what it felt like to have a parent so obviously proud of you.

She'd never know, of course. And that was fine with her, for the most part.

After all, she had a new beginning. She had lost her parents and her fiancé, and she had nearly lost her sister.

But that new beginning sat just ahead, easily within her grasp. Maybe whatever came next would shape her into something new, something better. Maybe it could shape her in a way that she had never dared to dream of while mired to her heartbreaking past.

She looked back at Danielle, still smiling and waving, and that future seemed as bright and as real as ever.

A Neighbor's Lie

(a chloe fine psychological suspense—book 2)

Blake Pierce

Table of Contents

Prologue 205

Chapter One 209
Chapter Two 215
Chapter Three 222
Chapter Four 232
Chapter Five 237
Chapter Six 242
Chapter Seven 253
Chapter Eight 262
Chapter Nine 268
Chapter Ten 274
Chapter Eleven 280
Chapter Twelve 284
Chapter Thirteen 288
Chapter Fourteen 295
Chapter Fifteen 298
Chapter Sixteen 304
Chapter Seventeen 308
Chapter Eighteen 318
Chapter Nineteen 323
Chapter Twenty 329
Chapter Twenty One 335
Chapter Twenty Two 341
Chapter Twenty Three 346
Chapter Twenty Four 353

Chapter Twenty Five 357
Chapter Twenty Six 363
Chapter Twenty Seven 366
Chapter Twenty Eight 371
Chapter Twenty Nine 376
Chapter Thirty 380
Chapter Thirty One 387

Prologue

Working as a nanny was not the life that Kim Wielding had envisioned for herself, but it was actually quite enjoyable. Which was a little surprising, considering in her early twenties she'd had a career she wanted to pursue in Washington, DC, firing along the campaign trails and writing speeches for underdog candidates. And she'd almost landed it.

Almost.

Life just worked out in funny ways sometimes.

Now, at the age of thirty-six, those dreams of working in DC were long gone. She'd replaced them with another dream: of writing the great American novel in her downtime as a nanny. She'd sort of fallen into the job after a promising candidate she had worked for had been miserably defeated. That was all it had taken for her to sit on the sidelines for a while. And while on those sidelines, a very easy means of employment had landed in her lap. She hadn't even considered watching kids in any capacity, but it had fit.

Kim reflected back on her first job as a nanny as she sat at the kitchen island inside the home of Bill and Sandra Carver. It was hard to believe it had been a little over ten years ago. It was a stretch of time that had somehow blurred those memories of working in DC, of writing speeches with hope and just a smidge on untruth.

Her laptop sat in front of her. She had hit the forty-thousand-word mark on her book. She figured she was about halfway through it. Maybe she'd finish it up in another six months or so. It all depended on the direction the lives of the three Carver children took. The oldest child, Zack, was in ninth grade this year and seriously eyeing football as a pastime. The middle child, Declan, played soccer. And if the youngest, Madeline, stuck with gymnastics, Kim was going to be running around in a frenzy for the next few months.

She closed the lid of her laptop and looked around the kitchen. She was thawing chicken for dinner. The counters had already been wiped down, the dishes were done, and the fourth load of laundry was currently churning away in the washing machine. Until the kids got home, her day was done. It was how she'd been able to work on her book for the last forty-five minutes.

She glanced at the clock and saw that the day had managed to sneak away from her—something that she was starting to understand happened to nannies quite a bit. She'd need to leave to pick the kids up from school in fifteen minutes ... and that was no small feat, seeing as how the Carver kids were aged in crude stairstep fashion, the youngest in elementary school, the middle child in middle school, and the oldest in high school. All told, it was just over an hour's worth of travel and traffic time to pick them all up from school and return home with them. It sounded worse than it was, though, as Kim had recently discovered how wonderful audiobooks could be to kill time in the car.

She got up and checked the chicken, nearly defrosted in the sink. She then swapped the laundry into the dryer and got all of the spices out that she would need to complete dinner. As she was setting the paprika down on the counter, someone knocked on the front door.

It was a fairly common occurrence in the Carver household. Sandra Carver was an Amazon junkie and Bill Carver always had schematics and blueprints being FedEx'd to their home. Kim grabbed her purse, figuring she'd go ahead and leave for school pick-ups after bringing the packages inside.

She opened the door, her eyes instantly going to the floor of the porch in search of an Amazon box. That's why it took her brain a full second to understand that there was the shape of a person standing in front of her. When she looked up to see their face, her line of sight was blocked by—something.

Whatever it was, it smashed into her head. It connected right between her eyes, along the top of the bridge of her nose. The cracking noise inside of her head was deafening but she barely had time to register it before the sensation of falling overruled everything.

When she hit the Carvers' hardwood floors, the back of her head struck hard. She felt blood rushing out of her nose as she tried scrambling backward.

The person from the porch came inside. They shut the door causally behind them. Kim tried to scream but there was too much blood in her nose, cascading down into her throat and mouth. She coughed, almost gagging, as the person took one large step forward.

They lifted that blunt object again—a pipe, Kim thought vaguely as pain swept through her mind like a hurricane—and that was the last thing she saw.

Before that final blow, her mind went to a strange place indeed. Kim Wielding died wondering what would happen to that chicken, still defrosting in the Carvers' sink.

Chapter One

Because of the way her life had started—a dead mother, an incarcerated father, and grandparents who were always hovering over her—Chloe Fine often preferred to do things on her own. People sometimes referred to her as a severe introvert and as far as she was concerned, that was fine with her. It was this personality that had driven her toward getting exceptional grades in school and had helped her to blast through her studies and training at the FBI academy.

But it was also that personality that had caused her to end up moving into her new apartment without a single person to help her. Sure, she could have hired a moving company, but her grandparents had taught her the value of a dollar. And since she had strong arms, a strong back, and a stubborn mindset, she'd elected to move in by herself. After all, she only had two heavy pieces of furniture. Everything else should be a cakewalk.

This was proven to not be the case when she finally managed to lug her dresser up the stairs—with the assistance of a dolly, several ratchet straps, and a thankfully wide stairwell leading to her second-floor apartment. Yes, she'd managed to do it but she was pretty sure she had pulled a thing or two in her back along the way.

She'd saved the dresser for last, knowing it would be the hardest part of the move. She'd intentionally packed the boxes light, knowing it would be a one-woman job. She supposed she could have called Danielle and she would have helped but Chloe had never been the type to ask family for favors.

Chloe sidestepped a few boxes of her books and notebooks and collapsed in the recliner she'd had since her sophomore year of college. The thought of Danielle being here with her to sort through all of her stuff and start to set the place up was appealing. Things had been not quite as strained between the two of them since Chloe had uncovered the truth about what had occurred between their parents when they'd been young girls, but there was definitely something different. They were both very aware of the weight of their father hanging over their heads—the truth of what he had done and the secrets he had been keeping. Chloe felt that they were both dealing with those secrets in their own ways and they knew their opinions differed in some nearly psychic way that only close sibling are capable of.

What she had never dared express to Danielle was just how much she missed their father. Danielle had pretty much always resented him after he had been taken to jail. But Chloe had been the one who had missed that father figure in her life. She had been the one who had always dared to hope that maybe the cops had gotten it wrong—that there was no way her father had killed their mother.

And it had been that hope and belief that had resulted in the little adventure they'd taken together that had culminated in the arrest of Ruthanne Carwile and an entirely new viewpoint on the case of Aiden Fine. The thing that had sort of backfired on Chloe, though, was that in uncovering those little secrets, she had started to miss him even more. And she knew that Danielle would find this horrifying and maybe even masochistic in a way.

Still, despite all that, she wanted to call Danielle over to celebrate the small albeit hard-earned victory of moving into her new place. It was just a small two-bedroom apartment in the Mount Pleasant neighborhood of Washington, DC—small, barely affordable, but exactly what she had been looking for. It had been about two months since they'd hung out—which seemed odd, given everything they had gone through the last time they'd been together. They'd spoken on the phone a few times and while it had been pleasant enough, it had also been very surface level. And Chloe wasn't good at doing surface level.

Screw it, she thought, reaching for her phone. *What could it hurt?*

As she pulled up Danielle's number, the reality of the situation sank in. Sure, it had only been two months since everything had happened, but they were different people now. Danielle had started to pick up the pieces of her life. She had a job that could potentially start paying quite well—a bartender and assistant manager at an upscale bar in Reston, Virginia. As for Chloe, she was still figuring out how to go from having been recently engaged to now being single and apparently not able to remember how to go about finding a date.

You can't force something like this, she thought. *Especially not with Danielle.*

With her heart churning over it, Chloe sent the call. She fully expected it to go to voicemail. So when it was answered on the second ring by a chipper-sounding Danielle, it took Chloe a moment to respond.

"Hey, Danielle."

"Chloe, how are you?" she asked. It was so odd to hear Danielle's voice with an edge of cheer to it.

"Pretty good. I moved into the apartment today. I thought about how nice it would be to celebrate it by having you come visit and have a bottle of wine and some really unhealthy food. But then I remembered your new job."

"Yeah, grinding away," Danielle said with a laugh.

"Are you liking it?"

"Chloe, I'm *loving* it. I mean, sure, it's only been three weeks but it's like I was born for this job. I know it's only bartending but…"

"Well, you're assistant manager, too, right?"

"Yeah. A title that still scares me."

"I'm glad you're liking it."

"Well, how about you? How's the apartment? How was the move?"

She didn't want Danielle knowing she had moved it all in by herself, so she kept the answer generic—which she hated to do. "Not too bad. I still have to unpack, but I'm just glad to be in, you know?"

"I'll absolutely come have that wine and greasy food with you soon, though. How is everything else?"

"Honestly?"

Danielle was quiet for a moment before she responded with: "Uh-oh."

"I've been thinking about Dad. I've been thinking about going to see him."

"And why in God's name would you do that?"

"I wish I had a good answer for you," Chloe said. "After everything that happened, I just feel like I need to. I have to make sense of it all."

"My God, Chloe. Leave it alone. Isn't this new job of yours supposed to keep you busy solving *other* crimes? Man … I thought I was the one who spent all of her time living in the past."

"Why does it upset you so much?" Chloe asked. "Me going to see him …"

"Because I feel like we've both given him enough of our lives. And I know if you see him, my name is going to come out of one of your mouths and I'd rather not have that happen. I'm done with him, Chloe. I wish you could be, too."

Yeah, I wish the same thing, Chloe said but kept the comment to herself.

"Chloe, I love you, but if you plan on the rest of this conversation being about him I'm going to say goodbye now."

"When are you working again?" Chloe asked.

"Every night this week, except Saturday."

"Maybe I'll come by and see you Friday afternoon. I expect you to serve me whatever drink you consider your specialty."

"Better not plan on driving home, then," Danielle said.

"Noted."

"How about you? When does your new job start?"

"Tomorrow morning, actually."

"In the middle of the week?" Danielle asked.

"It's sort of an orientation thing. Mostly meetings and all of that for the first day or so."

"I'm excited for you," Danielle said. "I know how much you've wanted this."

It was nice to hear Danielle speaking highly of her work. Not only that, but even pretending to take an interest in it.

There was a heavy silence between them, one that mercifully ended with Danielle saying something that was rather out of character for her. "Be safe, Chloe. With the job … with Dad … with all of it."

"I will," Chloe said, the comment taking her off guard.

Danielle ended the call, leaving Chloe to look around the central area of her apartment. It was hard to see the totality of the place because of all of her clutter but she already felt that the place was home.

Nothing like an awkward conversation with Danielle to make a place feel like home, she thought idly.

Slowly, stretching her back, Chloe got out of the recliner and went to the box closest to her. She started to unpack it, getting a sense of what her life would be like if she didn't figure out how to reconcile relationships. Whether it was with her sister, her father, or her ex-fiancé, she didn't have the best track record of keeping people close.

At the thought of her ex-fiancé, she came across several framed pictures sitting at the bottom of the first box. There were three pictures in all, photos of her and Steven; two were from their earlier days, when dating had been the only thing on their radar. But the third was a picture of them after he had proposed... after she had said yes and nearly started crying.

She gathered the pictures up out of the box and placed them on the kitchen counter. She rummaged around and found her trashcan sitting on the other side of the room, next to her mattress. She took the pictures to it and dropped them into the trashcan. The sound of the glass breaking in the frames was a little too delightful.

Easy enough, she thought. *Can't wait to move on from that debacle. Now, why can't you move on from this nonsense with your father just as easily?*

She had no answer for that. And the thing that scared her was that she felt the answer might be hiding in a conversation with him.

With that thought, the apartment seemed emptier than before and Chloe felt very much alone. The mere thought of it made her go to the refrigerator and start on the six-pack she'd purchased earlier in the day. She opened the bottle, a little alarmed at just how good that first swallow was.

She did her best to occupy herself that afternoon and well into the night, not by unpacking but by slowly going through the boxes one by one and trying to decide if she needed each and every item. The trophy she'd won for the debate team in high school went the way of the trashcan. The

Fiona Apple CD she had been listening to when she lost her virginity as a sophomore in high school, she kept.

Any pictures of her father went into the trash. It hurt to do it at first but by the time she was on the fourth bottle of beer, it was easier.

She made it through two boxes... and would have probably gone through at least one more if she had not gone to the fridge only to find that she had somehow gone through the entire six-pack. She looked at the clock on the stove and let out a little gasp at what she saw.

It was 12:45 at night. *So much for getting a good night's sleep before my first day, she thought.*

But what was even more alarming was the fact that she was more upset about the empty six-pack than having a potentially groggy morning on her first day with the bureau. She fell into bed after brushing her teeth, the room spinning a bit, as she realized that what she had really been trying to do that night was make herself not give a care about trying to erase memories of her father.

Chapter Two

Chloe hadn't been sure what to expect when she stepped into the FBI headquarters the next morning. But what she absolutely had not been expecting was to be met by an older agent in the lobby. She saw him as he spotted her and wasn't quite sure what to do when she noticed that he was walking directly toward her. For a moment, she thought it was Agent Greene, the man who had served as her instructor and partner on her sort-of case that had led to uncovering the truth about her father.

But when she got a better look at his face, she saw that this agent was another man entirely. He looked hardened and made of stone, his mouth drawn in a tight line across his jaw.

"Chloe Fine?" the agent asked.

"Yes?"

"Director Johnson would like to speak with you before orientation."

This both excited her and scared her. Director Johnson had made exceptions for her when she had been partnered with Greene. Was he perhaps having second thoughts? Had her actions in that last case perhaps gotten him into some hot water? Had she come this far only to have her dreams crushed on the first day?

"What for?" Chloe asked.

The agent shrugged, as if he really didn't care. "This way, please," he said.

He led her to the elevators and for a moment, Chloe felt as if she had stepped back in time. She could see herself stepping into these same elevators a little over two months ago with this exact same knot of worry in her stomach, knowing that she was going to meet with Director Johnson.

And just like last time, that knot of worry began to grow tendrils into the rest of her body as the elevator started sliding upward.

The stone-faced agent led her off of the elevator when it came to a stop on the second floor. They passed several offices and rooms before the agent came to a stop outside of Johnson's wing. The secretary at her desk gave her a polite little nod and said, "You can go on in. He's waiting for you."

The stone-faced agent gave her a similar nod—only not nearly as polite—and gestured toward the office door. It was clear that he was not going in.

Doing her best to stay calm and reserved, Chloe walked to Director Johnson's door. *What am I so afraid of?* she wondered. *The last time I was called to his office, I was granted responsibilities and duties most new agents in my shoes don't get.* This was true, but it did nothing to settle her nerves.

Director Johnson was sitting at his desk, intently reading something on his laptop when she entered. When he looked up, all of his attention was on her; he even closed the lid on the laptop.

"Agent Fine," he said. "Thanks for coming. This will only take a second. I don't want you to miss any of the orientation—which, I'll go ahead and let you know—is fairly quick and painless."

Hearing *Agent Fine* was still something of a head trip for her, but she tried not to let it show. She sat down in the chair in front of his desk and smiled as evenly as she could. "No problem," she said. "Am I… well, is something wrong?"

"No, no, nothing like that," he said. "I wanted to present you with an option concerning your duties. I understand that you're heading into a career with the Evidence Response Team. Is that something you've always had your eye on?"

"Yes sir. I have a pretty strong eye for detail."

"Yes, that's what I hear. Agent Greene spoke very highly of you. And despite a few hiccups in the events from two months ago, I have to admit—I was very impressed as well. You carry yourself with a confidence and unwavering certainty that is rare in newer agents. And it's because of that and the feedback I got from Agent Greene and a few of your instructors from the academy that I want to ask you to reconsider your department of interest."

"Is there a particular department you had in mind?" Chloe asked.

"Are you familiar with the ViCAP program?"

"The Violent Criminal Apprehension Program? Yes, I know a bit about it."

"The title is fairly self-explanatory, but I think it also lends itself to your knack for evidence. Plus, if I'm being quite frank, the Evidence Response Team has a quite large group of first-year agents this time around. Rather than you getting lost in the crowd there, I think you might fit well within ViCAP. Is that something that might interest you?"

"If I'm being honest, I don't know. I'd never really thought about it."

Johnson nodded but Chloe was pretty sure his mind had already been made up. "If you're up for it, I'd like for you to just give it a try. If you find after a few days that it's not a good fit, I will personally see to it that you are seamlessly placed back into your current slot with Evidence Response."

She honestly wasn't sure what to say or what to do. What she *did* know, though, was that it made her feel rather accomplished and proud to feel that her director felt so strongly about placing her in a department solely based on her skills and positive feedback from her peers.

"Yes, I can work with that," she finally answered.

"Fantastic. There's already a case I want to place you on. You'd start on it tomorrow morning. Maryland State PD has been running it, but as of this morning, placed a call for assistance. I'll be placing you alongside another agent that finds herself without a partner. The one she had been assigned folded under the pressure and called to resign yesterday."

"Can I ask why?"

"With the Violent Criminal Apprehension Program, some of the crimes tend to be a little gruesome. It happens to some new recruits... they make it through training, seeing the sample cases and even the real-life scenarios. But in the end, realizing they'll be *living* in it... it's too much for some."

Chloe said nothing. She tried to fathom having to make such a decision and it was beyond her. She'd been wanting a job like this for as long as she could remember—for as long as she knew the difference between right and wrong.

"Will I need any additional training?"

"I'd recommend more firearms training," Johnson said. "I'll make sure that's all set up for you. Your previous scores from Evidence Response enrollment in terms of firearms look quite good, but you may want a few extra skills in that area once you really get into the thick of ViCAP—should you decide to stay on."

"I understand."

"Well, unless you have any questions, I guess you can go ahead and get started with orientation downstairs. You've still got three minutes before it starts."

"No more questions at the moment. And thanks for the opportunity. And the trust."

"Of course. I'll handle all of the paperwork and someone will call you about your assignment by the end of the day. And Agent Fine…I have a good feeling about this. I think you'll be a remarkable asset to ViCAP."

It was then, as she stood up to leave his office, that she realized that she had never been very good at accepting compliments. Perhaps it was because she had never received very many of them throughout her younger years. Now she simply smiled awkwardly and made her exit. The knot of nervousness that had been in the pit of her stomach was gone now, replaced by a flying sensation that made it feel as if her feet weren't even touching the ground as she made her way to the elevators.

Orientation was about what she had expected. It consisted of a list of dos and don'ts that came from a collection of seasoned agents. There were examples of cases gone wrong, of cases so bad that past agents had quit over them or even committed suicide. The instructors told miserable tales of murdered children and serial rapists who had not, to this very day, been apprehended.

As these stories were passed along, Chloe could hear little murmurs of uneasy conversation in the crowd. Two seats to her left, she heard a woman whispering to the man beside her.

"Apparently, my partner heard these stories before us. Maybe that's why he bailed." She said it in a bitchy way, a mean-girl sort of way that instantly annoyed Chloe.

With my luck, that's the partner-without-a-partner Johnson wants me paired up with, Chloe thought.

The session eventually ended for lunch. When it did, the instructors on stage broke the crowd up into the specific departments. When Chloe heard *Evidence Response Team* called, she felt a small pang of sorrow. She watched as about twenty recruits walked down to the stage and collected on the right side. Knowing that she was supposed to be among their numbers less than three hours ago made her feel a little isolated, especially when she saw that some of the agents seemed to have already formed friendships.

When the agents in the Violent Criminal Apprehension Program were called, she got up and headed for the floor. The crowd she walked with was smaller than the Evidence Response Team. Including herself, she counted only nine. And one of them was indeed the woman who had made the comment about her partner quitting.

She was so focused on this woman that she didn't notice the man stepping up beside her as they made their way to the floor.

"I don't know about you," he said, "but I feel like I need to be hiding my face. Being part of a program with the word *violent* in it… makes me think people are judging me."

"I don't think I've ever thought of it that way," Chloe said.

"Well, do you have a tendency towards violence?"

He asked it with a smirk and it was that smirk that somehow helped her to realize that the man was extremely good-looking. Of course, the comment about a tendency toward violence skewed it a bit.

"Not that I know of," she answered awkwardly as they reached the floor where their group was gathered.

"Okay," the instructor, an older gentleman dressed in jeans and a black T-shirt, said. "Lunch first, then we'll meet up in Conference Room Three to go over some details and run through a Q and A. Before all of that, though…" He paused here and looked at a sheet of paper, scrolling through it using his finger. "Is there a Chloe Fine here?"

"That's me," Chloe said, nearly breaking into a sweat from having been singled out in this group of people she did not know.

"I need to speak with you for a moment, please."

Chloe walked toward the instructor and saw that the gentleman was also beckoning another agent forward.

"Agent Fine, I see here that you are a new addition to ViCAP, directly from the recommendation of Director Johnson."

"That's correct."

"Good to have you. Now, I'd like to you meet your partner, Agent Nikki Rhodes."

He motioned to the other agent that he had beckoned toward him. Sure enough, it was the bitchy woman from earlier. Nikki Rhodes smiled at Chloe in a way that made it clear that she knew she was beautiful. And even Chloe had to admit it. Tall, perfectly tanned skin, sparkling blue eyes, sickeningly straight blonde hair.

"Nice to meet you," Rhodes said.

"Likewise," Chloe said.

"Now, you two go enjoy lunch," the instructor said. "From what I understand, you'll be working a case early tomorrow. You were both at the top of your class, so I expect to hear some very big things about the two of you."

Rhodes gave her a smile and Chloe could feel the fakeness of it. She hated to automatically assume someone was not a genuine or authentic person, but her gut had always been spot on with things like this. The instructor had turned to join the rest of the group, leaving the two women alone. Noticing that the eyes of a superior were no longer on them, Rhodes turned and walked away without saying anything at all.

Chloe kept back from the rest of the group for a moment, trying to get her head straight. She'd woken up this morning excited to start her career as a member of the Evidence Response Team. Everything for the foreseeable future had essentially been planned out. And now here she was, placed into a department she was not very familiar with, assigned to a partner with a stick up her ass.

"She doesn't exactly seem like a people person, does she?" someone said from behind her.

She turned and saw the man who had walked with her down to the floor—the handsome one who had asked if she had any violent tendencies.

"No, she doesn't."

"Imagine having most of your courses with her at the academy," he said. "It was miserable. Speaking of which… I don't remember you being in any of my courses or modules."

"Yeah… I'm sort of new. I was placed in this department this morning."

A look of mild shock came over his face. "Oh, okay. Well, welcome to ViCAP. I'm Kyle Moulton and if your new partner doesn't want to have lunch with you, I'd like to take her place."

"Help yourself," Chloe said, finally falling in behind with the rest of the group. "It's fitting of my day to say the least."

"How so?"

"Because nothing else has really gone as planned, either."

Moulton only nodded as they left the auditorium. Even though Moulton was a stranger (albeit a handsome one), it was nice to have him by her side as they walked to the catered lunch waiting for them elsewhere in the building. She was afraid that if she had to step into this uncertain future completely alone, it might make her rethink everything.

"Plans are overrated anyway," Moulton said.

"Not to me. Plans mean structure. Plans mean predictability."

"I don't think *predictability* was in the job description for our positions," Moulton joked.

Chloe smiled and nodded but had never quite looked at it that way. Quite frankly, it frightened her a bit. Which made no sense, really. Her life had never been anything more than an unpredictable pile of utter crap, so why would her career be any different?

Luckily, she had learned to roll with the punches. And if snotty bitches like Nikki Rhodes happened to obscure her path along the way, then Rhodes could either adapt or get the hell out of her way.

Chapter Three

The following morning, Chloe got a rude awakening to how the remainder of her career would be structured. Her phone rang at 5:45, the call coming from one of the assistant directors who worked under Director Johnson. She had barely managed to croak out a raspy "Hello?" before the man on the other end started to speak.

"This is Assistant Director Garcia. Is this Agent Chloe Fine?"

"It is." She sat up in bed, her heart hammering as a surge of adrenaline flooded through her, kicking out the remnants of sleep.

"You're to meet Agent Rhodes in Bethesda at seven a.m. You'll be working together on what we believe is a pretty open and closed case of gang violence, likely from MS-13. Any questions should come directly to me, at this number. Agent Rhodes will be given the exact same information. Following this call, the address will be texted to your phone. Do you have any questions, Agent Fine?"

Chloe was sure she had some questions, but they were hiding in the wake of her first actual assignment.

"No, sir."

"Good. Be safe and smart out there, Agent Fine."

And that was it. That was how she got her first assignment. She knew that they would not come like this in the future; they'd been told this much at orientation yesterday. Still, it was quite an effective way to kick off her first day on the job.

She'd already laid her clothes out and showered the night before, doing everything she could to make sure she would not be late for whatever awaited her on the first day. She dressed, grabbed a bagel with some cream cheese, and poured a thermos of coffee that she had set to brew at

5 a.m. last night. During all of this, the text from Director Garcia came through, giving her the address in Bethesda. When Chloe got to her car, only fifteen minutes had passed since the call had come in.

She'd been to Bethesda, Maryland, several times so she knew it was a quick drive—a little less than half an hour, especially leaving this early and getting in front of the miserable morning commuter traffic. Once she was out of the grind of DC's streets and onto more open lanes, she plugged the address into her GPS and saw that she was only twenty-two minutes away.

She found herself wanting to call Danielle. She felt herself driving toward one of the more memorable and meaningful moments in her life and felt the need to share it with someone. But she knew Danielle would still be sleeping and that she would also probably not understand the excitement of it. And that was fine with Chloe. They had different interests and passions, and neither one had ever been particularly great at faking their enthusiasm.

She arrived at the address two minutes ahead of the time her GPS had given her. It was a rundown one-story apartment building, the kind that was usually visited by the police at least a dozen times over the weekend for violence, drugs, sexual assault, and just about anything else imaginable.

She'd fully expected to be there ahead of Rhodes but was a bit dejected to see the other agent not only already there, but walking up the porch steps toward the crime scene.

Annoyed, she parked along the side of the street and hurried up the sidewalk. She made it up to the porch just as Rhodes opened the door to head inside.

"Good morning," Rhodes said, clearly not meaning it.

"Good morning. What did you do ... fly here?"

Rhodes only shrugged. "It doesn't take me very long to get ready in the mornings. It's okay, Agent Fine. This isn't a race."

As they stepped inside, they saw a man standing in the center of a small cluttered living room. He turned toward them and his eyes seemed to hang on Agent Rhodes for a moment. She was wearing very modest black slacks and a conservative white top. Her hair had been straightened and although she'd claimed she took very little time to get ready, it was obvious that there had been some makeup work done that morning.

"You with the bureau?" the man asked.

"Yes," Chloe said quickly, as if making sure the man knew there were two agents present, not just the tall pretty blonde one.

"Agents Rhodes and Fine," Rhodes said. "And you are?"

"Detective Ralph Palace, Maryland Homicide. I'm just taking a few final notes, as I understand this is your case now."

"What can you tell us to get us started?" Chloe asked.

"It's pretty basic. Gang-related murder. MS-13 is a big one in this area, so that's what we're going with. The bodies of a husband, wife, and thirteen-year-old son were removed yesterday afternoon, about seven hours after the call was placed. Reports of shots fired, and this place ended up looking like *this*." He waved his arms all around, indicating the mess of the apartment. "Some pretty simply police work revealed that the father once had ties with a rival gang, the Binzos."

"If MS-13 is involved how is ICE not on this?" Chloe asked.

"Because it hasn't been proven yet," Palace said. "With immigrant-related gang crimes, we have to be pretty certain. Otherwise, we can expect lawsuits and grievances about the unfair treatment of ethnic groups." He gave a shake of his head and sighed. "So if you guys could prove this one way or the other, that would be great."

He made his way to the front door, taking a business card from his wallet as he did. It was no surprise at all when he handed it directly to Rhodes. "Call me if you need anything else."

Rhodes didn't bother with a response as she pocketed the card. Chloe assumed she had been the kind of girl in high school and college who had gotten acclimated to having guys ogle her all the time. This encounter with Detective Palace had no doubt been just another one of those tiresome moments.

Chloe took a moment to look around the place. The coffee table in front of the couch had been overturned. Something—a dark soda from the looks of it—had been spilled from the table during the melee. The dark fluid had mixed with what was clearly drying blood on the pale shag carpet that covered the entire living room up until the adjoining kitchen. There was more blood splattered on the walls. There was also some smeared on the linoleum floor in the kitchen.

"How do you want to split this up?" Rhodes asked.

"I don't know. If shots were fired, there's a good chance one went into a wall or the floor. And from the messy look of the place, it wasn't a simple shootout. There was a struggle. And that tells me there's probably fingerprints somewhere as well."

Rhodes nodded. "We also need to figure out how the killer got in. Did you get a look at the front door? No signs of forced entry. So that means one of the family members let the guy in—maybe someone they knew well and trusted."

Chloe agreed with all of this and found herself impressed with Rhodes and the way she had already checked the door before even stepping inside.

"Why don't you look around outside for signs of forced entry?" Rhodes suggested. "I'll see if there are any signs of what type of weapons were used in here … see if there are any bullet fragments or anything like that."

Chloe nodded in agreement but was already sensing that Rhodes was doing her best to angle herself as the lead in the investigation. Chloe took it in stride, though. Based on what Palace had told them—and the fact that this had been assigned to two brand new agents with the oversight of an assistant director—she knew it was considered a small-time task in the grand scheme of things. So if Rhodes was going for some sort of power play already, it wasn't anything to get bent out of shape over. Not yet, anyway.

Chloe headed back outside, running the scenario through her head. If the killer was someone the family knew, why the struggle? If the killer had used a gun, three shots one right behind the other would not have allowed much time for any sort of struggle at all. But the door had indeed showed no signs of being forced open. So really, some sort of forced entry was more likely than the killer simply being allowed inside. But if not at the front door, then where?

She walked slowly around the building, realizing that calling it an apartment building was a bit of a stretch. She became more and more certain that it was some sort of urban housing, perhaps offered as some form of government aid. It was at the very edge of a collection of four identical buildings, separated by a strip of mostly dead grass between each one.

The left side offered nothing. It was mostly featureless with the exception of a small gas tank and a busted spigot where a water hose was coiled uselessly on the ground. But when she got around back, she saw several opportunities. First, there were three windows. One looked into the kitchen and the other two looked into bedrooms. There was also a set of concrete stairs that led up to a back door. She checked this door and found it unlocked. It opened up into a very small area that looked to have served as a mudroom. A few pair of dirty shoes were on the floor and a tattered dirty coat hung from a hook on the wall. She checked the door and the frame and found that it was all sound. From her point of view, she could not see where it had been forced open at any time in the recent past.

She went back to each window, looking for anything suspicious, and was not disappointed. On the third window, looking into what she assumed was the master bedroom, there were two small chunks of wood removed from the frame. They had been crudely removed, as if chipped away. One was along the bottom edge, where the frame sat against the edge of the pane. The other was along the top of the bottom portion of the frame. Whatever had happened to chip the wood had also caused a crack to form in the glass, though nothing hard enough to break it.

She did not want to touch anything out of fear of damaging any prints that had been left behind. But by standing on her tiptoes, she could see that this particular chip in the wood would have allowed someone from the outside to push down to disengage the window lock.

She went back inside through the back door and made her way into the master bedroom. There was no clear indication that anyone had entered through the window. But she also knew that a thorough dusting might tell a different story.

"What are you doing?"

She turned and saw Rhodes standing in the doorway to the bedroom. She had a skeptical look on her face as she studied Chloe.

"This window has been tampered with from the outside," Chloe said. "We need to collect prints."

"You got evidence gloves?" Rhodes asked.

"No," Chloe said. She found this ironic; had she started her day as a member of the Evidence Response Team as she had originally planned, she'd have them on her. But after Johnson had switched her department yesterday, she hadn't thought to bring any evidence-based equipment along.

"I've got some in my car," she said. She then tossed Chloe a set of keys with a look of annoyance. "In the glove box. And please lock it when you're done."

Chloe muttered a subdued "Thanks" as she passed by Rhodes while leaving the room. She wondered why Rhodes would keep evidence gloves in her car. As she, Chloe, understood it, each agent would be supplied with the appropriate equipment and materials for any given case from the bureau. Had Rhodes been given the correct supplies? Had her late addition to the ViCAP program already come back to bite her in the ass?

She went outside and found a box of latex gloves in Rhodes's glove compartment. There was also an evidence kit, which she took out as well. It was a small emergency kit but better than nothing. And while it showed that Rhodes was prepared, it also indicated that she wasn't going to go out of her way to help Chloe. Why keep it a secret that she had gloves and an emergency evidence kit in the glove box unless she had planned on keeping them for herself?

Determined not to get too bogged down by such details, Chloe slapped the gloves on as she walked back into the house. As she passed by Rhodes again, Chloe handed her the evidence kit. "Thought we might need this, too."

Rhodes gave her a biting look as Chloe headed back for the window. She checked the area that has been chipped and found that her hunch was correct. It would allow someone from the outside to apply just enough force to the lock to get it to pop open.

"Agent Fine?" Rhodes said.

"Yeah?"

"I know we don't know one another, so I'm going to say this as polite as I can: Can you please watch what the hell you're doing?"

Chloe turned back toward Rhodes and gave her a defiant look. "Excuse me?"

"Look at the carpet under your feet for God's sake!"

Chloe looked down and her heart sank. There was a footprint there, just a partial one but clearly the top half of a footprint. It was made of what looked like dust and mud.

And she had stepped on it.

Shit …

She stepped back quickly. Rhodes took her place by the window, kneeling down to look at the print. "Hopefully you didn't ruin it enough to make it unusable," Rhodes spat.

Chloe bit back the retort that jumped up on her tongue. After all, Rhodes was right. She'd somehow overlooked something as glaringly obvious as a footprint. *It's because I'm just in my head too much,* she thought. *Maybe Johnson switching departments on me is affecting me more than I thought.*

But she knew that was a lame excuse. After all, so far this crime scene had essentially been nothing more than evidence collecting—which was what she had been wanting to do all along in the first place.

Feeling embarrassed and enraged, Chloe walked out of the room to collect her breath and her thoughts.

"Jesus," Rhodes said as she observed the print. "Fine … why don't you see what you can find out there that might of some use? There are bullet holes in the kitchen wall I didn't get a chance to look at while you were outside. I'll wrap this up … if it's even possible."

Again, Chloe had to bite back quite a few vile comments. She was in the wrong here and that meant she had to overlook Rhodes being a bitch. So she kept quiet and headed back out into the central area of the apartment, hoping to find some way to redeem herself.

She went into the kitchen and saw the bullet holes Rhodes had mentioned. She saw the casings in each hole, several inches deep into the plaster. She was sure they'd be able to find out what kind of gun had been used based solely on that. So as far as Chloe was concerned, the bullet holes were a gimme—an easy clue that would give them just enough information to keep the case chugging along.

Maybe there's something else, though, she thought.

She walked back toward the hallway and stopped where it connected with the living area. If the killer had indeed come in through the window in the master bedroom, this would likely be where the shooting had started. The lack of blood or chaos in the bedroom indicated that nothing violent had happened back there.

She looked to the couch and saw the spray of blood on the floor in front of it. *Probably the first shot,* she thought. She observed the layout of the place and could see it all in her head. The first shot had killed someone on the couch. That would have caused anyone else on the couch to jump up quickly, perhaps knocking over the coffee table. Maybe they tripped over it or tried jumping over it. Regardless, the blood and spilled soda on the other side of the overturned coffee table indicated that this person did not make it out.

Still, it made her wonder. She slowly walked into the living room, following the path she assumed the bullets had gone. The amount of dried gore on the back of the couch gave her enough evidence that the person sitting there had died right away. She could see no entry on the couch where the bullet had torn into it, meaning it had lodged somewhere in the victim's head.

She could easily see two bullet holes in the kitchen wall, about three inches apart. She could see them from the couch. But if there were two stray shots there, maybe there were more elsewhere. If there were, it might give them a more precise chain of events throughout the scene.

She went to the coffee table and hunkered down. If someone had stumbled here before being shot, the killer would have aimed low. She looked around for any other stray shots and saw none. The killer had apparently hit his target.

However, she did see something else that she had not even been looking for. There was a small desk pushed against the wall to her right. It held a decorative bowl and a framed picture. Stuffed between the legs of the table was a tattered wicker basket with old mail and books. Between that basket and the back legs of the table was a cell phone.

She picked it up and saw that it was an iPhone. She pressed the power-up button and the screen lit up. The lock screen was a picture of Black Panther. She pressed the home button, expecting the passcode screen to pop up. When it didn't, she was surprised. Instead, it opened without an issue.

Must have been the son's phone, she thought. *And maybe the parents rigged it so there was no passcode so they'd have access at all times.*

It took her a moment to understand what she was looking at. She saw a young boy's face with some weird zombie-like features cartooned over it. She checked the edges of the screen and then saw the telltale signs of Snapchat. She was looking at a video (or a "snap") that had not yet been sent.

"Holy shit," she whispered.

She then realized how warm the phone felt. She looked to the battery indicator in the upper right corner and saw that it was in the red.

She ran toward the hallway, gripping the phone. "Rhodes, do you see a phone charger in there?" she yelled.

There was a pause before Rhodes answered. "Yeah. On the bedside table."

By the time the full answer was out of her mouth, Chloe was already entering the room again. She saw the charger Rhodes had mentioned and instantly ran to it.

"What is it?" Rhodes asked.

Chloe couldn't help thinking: *Wouldn't you like to know, you bitch?* But she kept it quiet as she plugged the charger into the phone.

"I think the son was on Snapchat when the killer came in. And I think he was sending a snap to a friend. Only he never got a chance to send it."

She played the video that had been on the screen when she found the phone. It was of a young boy, maybe twelve or thirteen. He was sticking his tongue out, his face highlighted with the zombie-like animation. Within two seconds, the first gunshot sounded out. The phone was jostled and then a second gunshot sounded out. The boy appeared to fall to the floor, the phone was jostled again, and then the screen went black—apparently coming to a stop in its resting place beneath the little desk.

That's where the snap ended. The entire thing lasted about five seconds.

"Play it again," Rhodes said.

Chloe replayed the video, this time paying attention to the jostled moments. For about a quarter of a second, there was the shape of a figure standing in the hallway, coming into the living room. It was brief, but it was there. And because the phone was a newer one, even in its hectic movements, the image was fairly clear. Chloe couldn't make out a face with her untrained eye, but she knew the bureau would have no problem running a frame-by-frame analysis and enhancing the footage.

"This is literally the smoking gun," Rhodes said. "Where did you find the phone?"

"Under the desk pushed against the wall in the living room."

Chloe could tell that Rhodes was excited by the find but did not want to give her too much credit. Instead, she nodded her approval and went back to her work, dusting for prints underneath the window.

They both sensed that, thanks to the Snapchat video, their work here was just about done. They had the perfect piece of evidence and anything they did afterward was just going to be out of methodology and routine.

Chloe figured she might as well play along and not cause any further tension between them. She took the phone with her back into the living room. She walked across the kitchen and set about digging the bullets out of the wall. But she knew the key to the case was in the phone she carried, waiting to bring the killer of this family to justice. And in the back of her mind, she couldn't help but feel that this was too easy. She was sure that Rhodes might also be thinking the same thing—as well as a way to somehow make it backfire in Chloe's face.

Chapter Four

They returned to FBI headquarters two hours later with what Chloe felt was more than enough evidence to have a suspect in custody by the end of the day. The Snapchat video was the most powerful thing they had found, but they had also managed to come across two solid fingerprints, the footprint on the bedroom carpet, and two hairs clinging to the bottom of the bedroom window.

They presented their findings to Assistant Director Garcia, huddled around a tiny conference room table in the back of his office. When Chloe showed him what she had found on the phone, she saw him trying to bite back a smile of satisfaction. He also seemed pleased with how professionally and by-the-book Rhodes had bagged and catalogued all of the evidence they had found.

Maybe she should switch departments, too, Chloe thought with a bit of venom.

"This is some incredible work," Garcia said, standing up from the table and regarding them as if they were prized students. "You worked quickly, thoroughly, and I don't see why we won't be able to get a solid arrest off of this."

Both agents gave their thanks. It made Chloe feel a little bit better to see that Rhodes was just as uneasy with accepting compliments as she was.

"Now, Agent Fine, I got a call from Director Johnson just before you came in here. He wants to meet with you in about fifteen minutes. Agent Rhodes, why don't you head down to the lab to see what happens to all of the evidence when it's brought in?"

Rhodes nodded, still playing the part of the good student. As for Chloe, she felt herself panicking again. When she'd visited Johnson yesterday, he'd thrown her one hell of a curveball. What did he have planned now?

Keeping her questions to herself, she walked down the hall toward his office. When she entered the small reception area, she saw that his door was closed. His secretary gestured to one of the chairs along the wall while she spoke to someone on the phone. Chloe took the chair and finally took a moment to reflect back on what today had meant to her and for her career.

On the one hand, she had discovered a significant piece of evidence that would likely lead to the arrest of a gang member who had killed an entire family. But at the same time, she'd made a very rookie mistake by potentially damaging what had been a fairly decent print. She figured in the long run, the print would not matter thanks to the Snapchat evidence. Still, she was embarrassed as hell by being called out by Rhodes in such a way. She figured the best she could hope for was to come out even—her amazing find balancing out her bone-headed mistake.

When the door to Johnson's office opened, her thoughts broke apart. She looked to the door and saw Johnson poke his head out. He saw her and didn't even say anything. He just beckoned her toward him, into his office. It was impossible to tell if this was a show of simple hurriedness or anger.

She entered his office and when he closed the door behind her, he gestured to the chair on the other side of his desk—a spot that was becoming more and more familiar to Chloe. When he sat down behind his desk, Chloe thought she could finally read his expression. She was pretty sure he was irritated about something.

"You should know," he said, "that I just got off the phone with Agent Rhodes. She told me about how you basically trampled a footprint at the crime scene."

"That's accurate."

He nodded, disappointed. "I'm torn, because on the one hand, she's just as new as you are. And by her calling to essentially tattle on you pisses me off. But at the same time, I'm glad she told me. Because even though this *is* your first day, it's important to keep tabs on this sort of thing. You understand, of course, that I don't call every agent that makes a mistake into my office to ask them about it. But for you, I thought I should check in with you since I did sort of throw you a curve ball at the last minute. Do you feel it threw you off your game?"

"No. I simply overlooked it. I was hyper-focused on looking at the window and didn't even see the print."

"That's understandable, if not a little clumsy. But Assistant Director Garcia tells me you found evidence that should lead directly to an arrest—a cellphone with a Snapchat window open. Correct?"

"Yes sir." And for reasons she did not understand, she felt herself wanting to add: *But anyone could have found it, really. It was sort of just dumb luck.*

"I consider myself to be a fairly forgiving man," he said. "But do know that many more mistakes like the one with the footprint might result in some fairly serious consequences. For now, though, I want you and Rhodes on another case. Do you see a problem working with her?"

The word *yes* was on her lips but she did not want to seem petty. "No, I think I can manage it."

"I had a look at her files. Her instructors say she's incredibly sharp but has a tendency to try doing things on her own. So my advice to you would be not to let her take full control over a case."

Yeah, I've already seen some of that, Chloe thought.

"And to be fair, I have warned her against this," he went on. "I also told her I didn't appreciate it when brand new agents tried to throw others under the bus. So I expect her to shape up on the next case. Director Johnson and I will be overseeing it from here on out, just to make sure everything is done by the book."

"Okay. I appreciate that."

"Other than potentially ruining a print, I think you did a great job today. I'd like for you to spend the rest of the day writing up a report on the scene and your interactions with Agent Rhodes."

"Yes sir. Anything else?"

"That's all for now. Just… as I said… if you start to feel that my last-minute change to your plans is affecting you work, let me know."

She nodded as she got up. As she exited the office, she felt like she had just dodged a bullet—like a kid who had been called to the principal's office but had been let off with only a small slap on the wrist. Still, having Johnson commend most of the work she'd done earlier in the day set her mind at ease.

She headed back down to her little workspace—a glorified cubicle was really all it was—with her mind reeling. She wondered if there had ever been a new agent who had been called into the Director's office twice in less than forty-eight hours. It made her feel both elated and somehow closely scrutinized all at the same time.

As she waited for the elevator, she saw another agent coming around the corner. Chloe vaguely recognized his face from the small group of agents who had been included in the ViCAP group the day before.

"You're Agent Fine, right?" he said with a smile.

"I am," she answered, unclear of where the conversation was headed.

"I'm Michael Riggins. I just heard about the case you and Rhodes were assigned to. Gang-related family murder. Word has it that there's an arrest in progress already. That's got to be some kind of record, right?"

"I have no idea," she said, though she did feel that it had all happened very fast.

"Hey, you know, not all first-day agents got to go out into the field today," Riggins said. "Some were mired in research or paperwork. There's already murmurs of a few of us heading out to grab a drink after work today. You should come by. It's the place two blocks over, Reed's Bar. We could use a legit success story to lift our spirits. But maybe don't invite Rhodes. Everyone… well, no one seems to really care for her."

Chloe knew it was mean-spirited but she couldn't help but smile at the comment. "I might show up," she said. It was the best answer she could give… much better than explaining that she was very much an introvert and wasn't the type to just hang out at a bar with people she didn't know.

The elevator arrived, its doors sliding open. Chloe stepped on and Riggins waved goodbye to her. It was bizarre to have someone envious of her situation, especially after the conversation she'd just had with Johnson. It was a feeling that sort of *made* her want to go out to the bar, even if it was only for a single drink and a half an hour of her time. The alternative was heading back to her apartment and continuing to unpack. And that was not something that particularly lifted her spirits.

The elevator took her up to the third floor, where her workspace sat alongside similar spaces shared by other agents. As she made her way down the hall, she passed Rhodes in the hallway. She thought about saying *hello* or to sarcastically thank her for the out-of-nowhere meeting with Johnson. But in the end, she decided to take the high road. She wasn't going to fall for Rhodes's little games.

Still, even passing the woman in the hall and exchanging nasty stares was enough to make the decision for Chloe: yes, she would go to the bar tonight. And unless her day drastically changed, she'd likely have much more than just one drink.

That seems to be happening a lot lately, she told herself.

It was a thought that haunted her throughout the rest of the day, but, much like recurring thoughts of her father, she managed to push it back into the darker corners of her mind.

Chapter Five

When she arrived at the bar at 6:45, it was about what she had expected. She saw several faces that were familiar, but none that she knew well. And that was because she did not know any of them well at all. Another downside of having her department switched by Johnson at the last minute was that there were very few people in the ViCAP group who had taken the same courses or training modules as she did.

The two faces she recognized the most were both male. First, there was Riggins. He was sitting with another male agent, talking animatedly about something. And then there was Kyle Moulton, the good-looking agent who had offered to take her to lunch after the first stage of orientation—the man who had somehow stuck out to her because he had asked her if she'd ever had any violent tendencies. She was a bit discouraged to see that he was speaking with two other women. No surprise there, though. Moulton was drop-dead gorgeous. He looked a bit like Brad Pitt from his earlier years.

She elected not to interrupt him and instead to go sit with Riggins. As conceited as it might seem, she liked the idea of hanging out with someone who had seen her accomplishment from the morning as something to marvel at.

"This stool taken?" she asked as she plopped down on the seat beside him.

"Not at all," Riggins said. He seemed genuinely happy to see her, his slightly chubby cheeks widening with his smile. "I'm glad you decided to come. Can I buy you a drink?"

"Sure. Just a beer. For now."

Riggins waved the bartender over and had him add Chloe's first drink to his tab. Riggins himself was drinking rum and Coke, of which he ordered a second when he ordered Chloe's drink.

"How was your first day?" Chloe asked.

"It was okay. Most of my day was research for a case involving an interstate drug runner. It sounds boring but I actually enjoyed it a lot. So how was a full day with Rhodes by your side?" Riggins asked. "Sure, wrapping that case must have been great but she already has a reputation for being hard to handle."

"It was pretty tense. She's a great agent but…"

"Say it," Riggins said. "I can't call her a bitch because I don't like calling a woman a bitch in front of another woman."

"She's not a bitch," Chloe said. "She's just very direct and thorough."

Their conversation went on for a bit longer and it was all very casual. Chloe snuck a few peeks over in the direction of Agent Moulton. One of the women had left, leaving him to speak with only one. He was leaning in close and smiling. Chloe tended to be a little naive when it came to relationships, but she was pretty sure Moulton was enamored with the woman.

This disappointed her in a way she had not been expecting. It had only been two months since she and Steven had called things off. She assumed she was only interested in Moulton because he'd been the first friendly face that had bothered speaking to her after Johnson had pulled the rug out from under her feet. That, plus the idea of heading back to her new apartment all alone was not appealing. The fact that he was incredibly good-looking also played a part as well.

Yeah, it was a mistake to come out. I can drink for much cheaper at home.

"You okay?" Riggins asked.

"Yeah, I think so. It's just been a long day. And tomorrow is shaping up to be just as long."

"You driving or walking home?"

"Driving."

"Eh… I better not offer to buy you another drink, huh?"

Chloe smiled in spite of herself. "That's very responsible of you."

She stole a glance back over toward Moulton and the woman he had been speaking to. They were currently both getting to their feet. As they made their way toward the door, Moulton gently placed his hand along the woman's lower back.

"Can I ask what got you started down a road that led to a career like this?" Riggins asked.

She smiled nervously and finished off her beer. "Family issues," she answered. "Thanks for inviting me out, Riggins. But I need to get back home."

He nodded as if he understood. She also noted that he slowly looked around the bar and saw that he was the only one that would be remaining. It made her think that maybe Riggins had some ghosts of his own that he was wrestling with.

"Take care, Agent Fine. May tomorrow be as successful as today."

She made her exit, already making plans for how to finish out her night. She still had boxes to unpack, a bedframe to put together, and an assortment of laundry and kitchen odds and ends to put away.

Not quite the exciting life I was expecting, she thought with a bit of sarcasm.

As she made her way to her car, still parked in the parking garage beneath FBI headquarters, her phone rang. When she saw the name on the display, rage flushed through her and she almost ignored it completely.

Steven. She had no idea why he would even be calling. And that's why she decided to answer. She knew that if she didn't, the mystery of it all would drive her crazy.

She answered the call, not liking how nervous she instantly felt. "Hello, Steven."

"Chloe. Hey."

She waited, hoping he'd just dive into whatever he had called for. But it had never been like Steven to get right to the point.

"Is everything okay?" she asked.

"Yeah, everything is fine. Sorry … I didn't even think about how me calling you might make you think …"

He trailed off here, reminding Chloe of one of the many little annoying traits he had never realized about himself.

"What do you need, Steven?"

"I want to get together to talk," he said. "Just to sort of reconnect and check in on each other, you know?"

"I don't think so. That wouldn't be the best idea."

"There's no ulterior motives here," he said. "I promise. I just… I feel like there are things I need to apologize for. And I need… well, I think *we* need closure, you know?"

"Speak for yourself. Things are pretty much closed for me. No closure needed."

"Fine. Then consider it a favor. I just want like half an hour. There are some things I'd like to get off my chest. And if I'm being honest… I'd just like to see you one more time."

"Steven… I'm busy. My life is crazy right now, and…"

She stopped, not even sure where to go from there. And really, it wasn't like she had this massive social calendar that would prevent her from seeing him. She knew that for Steven to make such a call was huge. He was having to humble himself, which was not something he had ever done well.

"Chloe…"

"Fine. Half an hour. But I'm not coming to you. If you want to see me, you'll have to come to DC. Things are crazy here right now and I can't—"

"I can do that. When's a good time for you?"

"Saturday. Lunchtime. I'll text you a place for lunch."

"Sounds good. Thanks so much, Chloe."

"You're welcome." She felt that there was more she should say, anything to ease the tension. But in the end, all she said was "Bye, Steven."

She ended the call and pocketed her phone. She couldn't help but wonder if she'd only caved because she was in a rather lonely position. She thought of Agent Moulton and wondered where he and his lady friend had gone off to. More than that, she wondered why she was so hung up on it.

She reached her car and drove home as the streets of DC began to darken toward night. It was a remarkable city; despite the congestion and weird blend of history and commerce, it was somehow beautiful all the same. It set her into a melancholy state as she headed to her apartment—an empty new apartment in a location she had felt fortunate to find but that now felt like some isolated island calling her home.

When her phone stirred her awake the following morning, it pulled her out of the haze of a dream. She tried snatching at the tendrils of it as it escaped but then stopped, wondering if it was even worth it. The only dreams she'd had as of late involved her father, stranded and alone in prison.

She thought she could even hear his voice humming some old Johnny Cash tune he'd often sung around their apartment when she'd been a little girl. "A Boy Named Sue," she thought. Or maybe not. All of those songs started to sound the same.

Still, "A Boy Named Sue" was in her head when she slapped at her nightstand for her phone. As she yanked her phone from its charger, she saw that her clock read 6:05—just twenty-five minutes before she had set her alarm to go off.

"This is Agent Fine," she answered.

"Agent Fine, it's Assistant Director Garcia. I need you in my office right away. Shoot for within the hour. I've got a case I need you and Agent Rhodes on as soon as possible this morning."

"Yes, sir," she said, sitting up. "I'll be there right away."

In the moment, she didn't care that it was another day with Rhodes. All she cared about was that so far, she was 1-0 as far as cases went and she was eager to improve upon that record.

Chapter Six

Chloe arrived in Assistant Director Garcia's office three minutes later. He was sitting at the small conference table in the back, looking through a few papers. She saw that he had already set out two cups of coffee for them, steaming and black, on either side of the table.

"Good morning, Agent Fine," he said as she entered. "Have you seen or spoken with Agent Rhodes?"

"She was pulling in just as I got on the elevator."

Garcia seemed to think about this for a moment, maybe confused as to why she had not simply waited at the elevator if she'd seen Rhodes. She then wondered just how much Johnson had told him about the little power struggle that was at play in their partnership.

Having finished her own coffee in her car on the way, Chloe sat down in front of one of the cups and sipped from it. She preferred a splash of cream and some sugar but didn't want to appear high maintenance. Just as she started sipping, Rhodes entered the room. The first thing she did was shoot Chloe a look of annoyance. She then took the seat in front of the other cup of coffee.

Garcia eyed them both, apparently sensing the tension, but then shrugged. "We've got a murder in Landover, Maryland. It's a case that appeared pretty normal at first. Maryland PD is running it right now but they've asked for our help. It's also worth mentioning that Jacob Ketterman of White House Public Affairs knows the victim. He used to work with her back in the day. He has requested we look into it as well, as a favor. And when it comes from the White House, we try to keep it quiet. That should be simple with this case. It's a pretty simple homicide from the looks of it. It's one of the reasons we're putting new agents on it.

It'll be a good test and there seems to be so pressing time table, although of course we'd like it solved as soon as possible."

He then slid two copies of his report over to them. The details were brief and to the point. As Chloe read over them, Garcia recited what he had learned.

"The victim is thirty-six-year-old Kim Wielding. She was working as a nanny for the Carver family when she was killed. From the best we can tell, someone entered the home and killed her. She was hit in the head twice with something very hard and then strangled. There were two rather nasty blows to the head. It has yet to be determined which of those things killed her. We need the two of you to find out who did it."

"Was the murder the sole reason for the killer to visit the home?" Chloe asked.

"Seems that way. Nothing was reported stolen. The house seemed exactly the way the Carvers last saw it… with the exception of their dead nanny. The address is right there in the files," Garcia continued. "I just got off the phone with the sheriff in Landover. Both of the Carvers and their three children have been staying at a motel since the murder occurred two days ago. But they'll be meeting with you at the house this morning to answer any questions. And that's it, Agents. Get out there and get another win for us. Head down to HR and check out a car between the two of you. You familiar with the process?"

Chloe was not, but nodded anyway. She assumed Rhodes already knew the ins and outs. Given the way yesterday had gone, Chloe assumed Rhodes knew just about every single piece of information on how the bureau was run.

Both Chloe and Rhodes got up from the table. Chloe took one last gulp of her coffee before heading out of Garcia's office. They walked down the hallway toward the elevator without a word shared between them.

This is going to be a long day if she and I don't get past this stupid rivalry nonsense, Chloe thought.

As Chloe pushed the Down arrow, she turned to Rhodes and did her best to not just break the ice—but to obliterate it.

"Agent Rhodes, let's just get it out in the open. Do you have a problem with me?"

Rhodes smirked and took a moment to think about her answer. "No," she said finally. "I don't have a problem with you, Agent Fine. But I am a bit hesitant to work with someone that was placed into ViCAP at the very last minute. It makes me wonder if someone is doing you favors—favors that are unfair to other agents that busted their asses to be part of this program."

"Not that it's any of your business, but I was *asked* to join this program. I was perfectly content to stay my course with the Evidence Response Team."

Rhodes shrugged as the elevator doors opened up. "I'm not so sure the ERT would have been so thrilled with how you muddled that footprint yesterday."

To that, Chloe remained silent. She could keep having this little war of words with Rhodes, but it would do nothing but make the working relationship even worse than it already was. If she was going to bring it to a stop, she was simply going to have to prove herself to Rhodes.

Besides, she *had* screwed up yesterday. And the only way to fix that was to prove herself with this new case.

When Rhodes elected to drive without any sort of conversation about it, Chloe let it ride. It wasn't worth getting upset about. On the way to Landover, Chloe started to wonder if something had happened at some point during Rhodes's path to get to where she was—something that caused her to be bossy and to overcompensate. She had plenty of time to ponder this during the half-hour drive to Landover because Rhodes was still not making any real effort to talk.

They arrived at the Carver residence at 8:05. It was a gorgeous house in a well-to-do neighborhood, the type where all of the lawns were perfectly edged to show the perfect lines of the sidewalks. There was a newer minivan in the driveway, parked in front of the garage. Rhodes pulled in behind it and killed the engine. She then looked over to Chloe and asked: "We good?"

"I don't think so, but that doesn't matter. Let's just focus on the case."

"That's what I meant," Rhodes spat as she opened the door and got out.

Chloe joined her and as they did, a man and a woman got out of the minivan—the Carvers, Chloe presumed. A quick round of introduction reveled that these were indeed the Carvers, Bill and Sandra. Bill looked like the type who never really got much sleep but thrived off of it. Sandra was rather pretty, the type of woman who probably didn't have to put much effort into it. But she also looked tired, especially as she looked toward the house.

"I understand you've been staying in a motel?" Chloe asked.

"Yes," Sandra said. "When it happened, Bill was away on business. The cops were coming in and out of the house and there was... well, there was just so much blood. So I picked the kids up from school, took them to dinner, and then took them to a motel. I told them what had happened and it just seemed morbid to come back right away."

"I got back home yesterday morning," Bill said. "Around noon or so yesterday, the police gave us the okay to get back into the house. But the kids and Sandra were just too creeped out by it."

"That might be for the best," Rhodes said. "We'd like to get a look at the scene, if that's okay."

"Yes, the sheriff told us you were coming," Sandra said. "He instructed us to tell you that there's a file with all of their information on the kitchen counter."

"Before we head inside," Chloe said, "I was wondering if you'd like to tell us a bit about Kim?"

"She was so kind-hearted," Sandra said.

"And great with the kids," Bill said. As he said it, there was a waver in his voice. It was as if the full weight of what had happened was only now starting to catch up with him.

"Do you know if she had any bad blood with anyone?" Chloe asked

"Not that we know of," Sandra said. "We've been asking ourselves that for the past two days. It just... it makes absolutely no sense."

"Any failed relationships?" Rhodes asked. "Maybe an estranged ex-boyfriend or something?"

"She has an ex, sure," Bill said. "But she rarely mentioned him."

"But she *did* mention him?" Chloe asked.

Something akin to understanding flashed in Sandra's eyes. "You know, she did say how it was something she had to *escape*. And I don't think it was a joke. I mean … she never really talked about him."

"Do you have a name?" Rhodes asked.

"No," Sandra said. She then looked to Bill for the answer but he only shook his head.

"Did Kim ever stay here?" Rhodes asked.

"Yes. If Bill and I ever went on little mini-vacations, she'd stay. We have a guest bedroom that we always joked was Kim's. She'd also sometimes just stay overnight on days where the kids had really been struggling with homework or school stuff."

"Which bedroom is that?" Rhodes asked.

"Upstairs, first one on the left," Bill said.

"Would you mind just hanging out for a while in case we need to speak with you after we have a look around inside?" Chloe asked.

"We don't have to come in, do we?" Sandra asked.

"No," Rhodes said. "You're welcome to just stay out here."

Sandra seemed relieved at this. But she still looked at the house as if she were expecting an axe murderer to come barreling out of the front door at any moment.

Both of the Carvers remained in the driveway while Chloe and Rhodes headed for the porch. It was a wraparound porch, complete with a porch swing and two rockers. Chloe opened the front door and they stepped inside.

The local and State PD had done the cleanup, according to Garcia's reports. And from what Chloe could tell, they'd done a great job of it. Of course, it would have been much easier to get a read on the scene if the evidence was still there—including any blood that had been spilled. Whoever had tasked the bureau with taking on this case apparently had no clue as to how forensics or evidence collection was carried out.

Chloe saw a folder sitting on the kitchen counter—the report and files from the sheriff, she supposed. She walked across the foyer and through the living room to retrieve it. She opened it up, flipping through the basic report and skipping to the crime scene photos. She walked back to the front door to show Rhodes and they both studied the five pictures, comparing it to the now immaculately cleaned scene.

In the pictures, there was blood on the foyer floor, right up to the doorframe. The body of Kim Wielding lay sprawled on the floor, her left foot no more than six inches from the front door. In the second picture, it was very evident that she had been struck in the face with a blunt instrument. Her nose had been partially caved in and the lower half of her face was nothing more than a sheet of blood.

"Safe bet she was answering the door," Rhodes said.

"Which means she knew the person," Chloe added. "Or that she had been expecting someone."

Rhodes took the pictures from the folder, not necessarily snatching them away, but not being polite about it either. "This pisses me off."

"What does?" Chloe asked.

"This case. A single murder in an upscale neighborhood. With a cleaned murder scene and no direct help from local PD, what the hell can we do?"

"I say we skip the scene. I mean, we have the pictures. That's enough. What would we learn if the body and the blood were still here?"

"Plenty. We'd also have the chance to search for our own evidence."

Chloe didn't press the issue any further. Truth be told, the entire situation irritated her as well. But there was no sense in dwelling on it.

"I'm heading to the upstairs bedroom," Chloe said. She figured if there was no crime scene to give them answers, they'd have to look elsewhere. And if there was an ex-boyfriend in the picture, it seemed that any place she lived might have some clues.

She headed upstairs while Rhodes remained downstairs, studying the living area. Chloe entered the room Sandra Carver had mentioned and found it very tidy. A small desk sat against the far wall. A single bedside table sat between the doorframe and a queen-sized bed, adorned with a lamp and a Nicholas Sparks paperback.

She checked the closet and found only a few changes of clothes and spare linens. There was also a small backpack, the kind worn around the chest as a satchel of sorts. She checked it and found lipstick, lip balm, six dollars, and a library card.

Chloe sighed as she took a final look around the room. There was nothing of note here; anything worth finding had apparently already been picked up by the local PD. There was likely to be a bit of paperwork to claim any evidence from the PD in her future.

She headed back downstairs, where Rhodes was hunkered down on the floor, closely inspecting the area where Kim had been killed. She glanced up to Chloe, still irritated, and said: "We're going to have to pay a visit to the State PD. The report here says they took a laptop that was sitting on the kitchen bar. A Lenovo with a lock screen blocking access. I'd like to know if they found anything on it."

"We need to find out if the police located her car, too. If she was killed here, that meant she likely had her car here. So where the hell is it?"

"I looked for that information in the report," Rhodes said, nodding back over to the file on the kitchen counter. "It says her car wasn't here when they arrived on the scene."

"We got the license plate number?"

"Yeah. It's all in there."

As Chloe came to the bottom of the stairs, Sandra Carver came rushing through the front door. She held something in her hands, holding it out toward them in a way that reminded Chloe of that scene from *The Lion King.*

"I just remembered this," she said, excited and maybe a little embarrassed.

It was clearly an iPad, but why it had Sandra so excited remained to be seen.

"It's Kim's iPad," Sandra explained. "Madeline would use it a lot to do these interactive games for school. Bill and I have our own tablet, but Madeline thought she was something special because Kim let her use hers. It's been in our van for the last two days, tucked into the little pocket behind the passenger seat."

Chloe took it and pressed the Power button. She was presented with a lock screen. Apparently, she'd used up all of her luck with such things yesterday with the Snapchat video.

"You said your daughter used it," Chloe said. "So I assume you know the passcode?"

"Yes! It's five-three-oh-nine."

Chloe typed in the code and the iPad unlocked. She was greeted to a home screen filled with the smiling faces of three children—the Carver kids, she assumed.

There weren't many icons on the home screen—just Spotify, Facebook, Instagram, and the built-in Apple apps like Messaging, Calendar, and FaceTime. She ignored all of the social media apps for now and tapped the Messages icon. There weren't many threads, and one of them was between Kim and Sandra Carver.

"Find anything?" Bill asked.

"I don't know yet," Chloe said as she started opening threads involving any male name. She was hoping to stumble across threads from the ex-boyfriend. She sat down at the bar, looking through all of them. Within a minute or so, she thought she had found what she'd been looking for.

"I think I might have found the ex," Chloe said, showing Rhodes the iPad.

Rhodes came over, her expression making it clear that she doubted the authenticity of Chloe's claim. But Chloe felt that she had stumbled upon something—potentially their first true led into the murder of Kim Wielding.

The text thread that Chloe had found consisted of a few broken conversations, scattered out over the course of several days.

The most recent, from five days ago, was quite telling. And Chloe knew that by the time Rhodes reached the end of it, she'd be just as certain as Chloe was. The thread was between Kim and a man named Mike, and it was not pretty.

You babysitting again?

It's not babysitting. I'm a nanny. This is my job.

Want to take a break and come see me?

You know I'm not going to do that. Stop asking. Stop bothering me.

No need to be a bitch. I'm not gonna wait around for you, you know.

Good. Don't wait.

Fuck you.

Beneath that conversation were a few attempts by Mike to start a conversation. But Kim had apparently never responded. The next actual conversation between them occurred a little over two weeks ago. Again, it was Mike who had initiated the conversation.

Why'd you stop calling?

Because I have nothing to say to you.

I know you're still upset. I'm sorry. I said it like 100 times already. I was dumb and frustrated and things got out of hand.

All true. Especially the dumb part.

Give me another chance. Please.

No. You were a mistake. I wish I'd never met you.

Seems pretty fucking harsh.

It does. But the truth hurts. Please stop contacting me.

You want that?

No. But I NEED it. Please stop. Leave me alone.

You know you miss me.

The conversation stopped there, and there were no more messages. It made Chloe think that at some point, Kim really had managed to break away from Mike. Maybe she had temporarily blocked him or simply deleted all of the messages between them. She wondered why Kim hadn't deleted the thread, especially if she knew one of the Carver kids was using it.

Maybe for evidence if it ever got out of hand, Chloe thought.

Chloe knew that if it came down to it, they could have the bureau get a warrant to uncover the deleted messages, but she didn't think it would come to that.

She tapped on Mike's name, bringing up his contact information within Kim's phone. He was listed as Mike Dillinger. His phone number was right there for the taking. But even being her first official case, Chloe knew that calling a man like Mike Dillinger would only clue him in to the fact that he was in trouble, causing him to run.

"I'll make the call," Rhodes said.

Of course you will, Chloe thought.

As Rhodes called in an information request on Mike Dillinger, Chloe looked through the rest of the text messages. There was nothing else alarming, nothing to indicate that Kim Wielding had any real enemies. If anything, they showed that Kim had been very loved—by the Carver kids, her mother, and her sister.

She listened as Rhodes was placed on hold, understanding that with the iPad, she was essentially holding a dead woman's last few memories. Again, though, she wondered what they might find on the laptop. She looked through the records the State PD had left for them and found the contact number of the officer in charge. She made a call, which was fielded by a receptionist, and she left a message to be notified when a final report of all findings on Kim Wielding's computer was completed.

She ended her call just moments before Rhodes concluded her own call. "We've got a home address and a work address," Rhodes said. "We also have confirmation that Mike Dillinger has a police record. A single B and E charge from when he was eighteen, and a slap on the wrist for being involved in a bar brawl a few years back."

"Seems like a strange fit for a respected nanny working in an area like this one," Chloe said.

"I was thinking the same thing. But… well, we don't always choose the best men, do we?"

"That's for sure," she said, thinking of Steven. "How far away is Dillinger's work?"

"Right here in Landover, somewhere downtown."

And that was all that needed to be said. They both left the Carver home, Chloe carrying the iPad. She showed it to the Carvers again when they made their way to the car. "We'll need to hang on to this. Thanks again for giving it to us."

They both nodded, but seemed not to really care. "Can we…" Bill Carver started to say. He collected his thoughts and, from the looks of it, his emotions, and managed to finish: "Can we go back inside?"

"Yes. You can live in your house again," Chloe said. "It looked to me like the State PD did a good job making sure the place was clean. And if you do think of anything else that might help with the investigation, please give us a call."

She handed Sandra Carver one of her cards—the first business card she had ever handed out as an agent. In the back of her head, she filed it away as a meaningless milestone.

"One last thing," Chloe said. "Where did Kim live when she wasn't here?"

"She has an apartment over on Lyndon Street," Bill said. "It's not even ten minutes from here."

"Do you happen to have a key?"

"No," Sandra said. "But she gave us access to her hide-a-key. It's hidden under the topsoil in a flowerpot by her door. There's a lock on it and the combination is two-two-five."

"Thank you," Chloe said, turning away toward the car.

With the Carvers slowly making their way to their front porch, Chloe and Rhodes backed out of the driveway. Because Rhodes was back behind the wheel, Chloe was able to see the look of fear and uneasiness on Bill Carver's face as he and his wife cautiously stepped through their front door.

Chapter Seven

Kim's apartment was a cute little townhouse mockup that was clustered tightly between two identical apartments. She lived in a quaint little apartment complex that looked like just about any of the other hundreds of similar complexes between Landover and the maelstrom of DC.

Before heading into her apartment, they cruised around the parking lot looking for a car with the license plate number the State PD had provided. After ten minutes, and two full circuits of the parking lot, they were unable to find any matches.

They parked and found Kim's apartment. Chloe found the key exactly where Sandra Carver had indicated, digging under a layer of topsoil to get it. She rolled in the combination on the silver ridges on the underside of the hide-a-key box and opened it up. With the key in hand, she unlocked Kim's apartment and stepped inside.

Right away, she felt like she was trespassing. Not only had this poor woman been savagely killed, but now two women she had never met, much less *known*, were about to snoop through her apartment.

"Cute place," Rhodes said as she stepped in front of Chloe to take the lead.

It *was* a cute place. And it only reminded Chloe that she still needed to unpack all of her boxes at her own apartment. Maybe one day it would be this cute. There were twin built-in bookshelves in the living room, one on either side of an entertainment center that held a small flat-screen television. The kitchen was attached but separated by a decorative room separator. The entire place was immaculately clean and organized. It looked barely lived in at all.

They looked the place over with a rookie's level of care, making sure every nook and cranny was checked so as to not miss any potential clues. Once the living room and kitchen were thoroughly combed over, they ventured into the rest of the apartment, which was only a bedroom, a small office space, and a bathroom.

The found nothing in the bedroom. It, like the rest of the apartment, was well organized and uncluttered. It made searching the place very easy. They found a MacBook that they could not get into due to the unlock-by-touch ID feature, but nothing else. There was a journal of sorts in the nightstand drawer but it contained only what looked like old to-do lists, inspirational quotes, and what appeared to be attempts at original poetry.

The bathroom turned up nothing of interest, with the exception of a bottle of Oxycodone that had been prescribed about a year ago. The same was true of the office. The space was essentially empty, occupied by only a desk that held several books, and some out of season clothes that had been tucked away in the closet.

Chloe and Rhodes spoke very little while they looked around. Things felt tense between them, though Chloe wasn't exactly sure why. She supposed most new agents, freshly partnered up with one another, experienced something similar. And if she was being honest, she assumed it was even worse among competitive females who were paired up.

They spent nearly forty-five minutes looking through the apartment. When Chloe was done scouring the bedroom, she went into the living room, where Rhodes was looking at the titles on the built-in bookshelves.

"Thoughts?" Rhodes asked without turning to look at Chloe.

"I think she might stay at the Carvers' more than she stays here. The place is ridiculously clean and well kept."

"That's for sure," Rhodes said. She pointed to one of the books on the shelf on the right side of the television. "*Speech Writing Essentials*," she said with a chuckle.

"Makes you wonder how her life might have turned out to be if she'd remained in DC and kept pursuing politics," Chloe said.

"It also makes me wonder what changed to make her abandon it," Rhodes said, turning away from the bookshelf. She seemed to actually ponder this for a moment before heading for the door. "Ready to go look into Mike Dillinger?" she asked, flipping the topic of conversation in a nearly mechanical manner.

"Yeah," Chloe said.

She took one final look around the apartment, finding it hard to believe they'd found nothing. She knew that if the case got out of hand, they'd confiscate the laptop and someone at the bureau could hack into it for any helpful material that might be saved on it. But for now, that seemed like a very extreme measure to a case that, so far, was very boring and uneventful.

Mike Dillinger's place of employment had been listed as Duke's Service Center, located in downtown Landover. However, when Chloe and Rhodes pulled up in front of the place, it was clear that it was closed—and not just as a result of business hours but from an apparent lack of business. There was a neglected and crooked sign in the garage's central window of the front office that read: FOR RENT OR SALE.

"This doesn't really strike me as the kind of neighborhood where a garage like this would have really prospered," Rhodes said.

Chloe nodded her agreement. She'd seen much worse, but the neighborhood was the sort where old men sat on their filthy stoops, sipping from brown paper bags—the sort where teens huddled around street corners during the afternoon and cop cars routinely canvassed late at night.

"Well, it's still early," Chloe said. "Maybe we can catch him at home before he starts his day."

Rhodes had apparently been thinking the same thing because she wasted no time pulling away from the garage and heading further into the downtown district. It was just now beginning to creep toward nine in the morning, so most businesses were just now starting to turn on their lights and unlock their doors. Chloe saw a few people gathered at a derelict public bus stop and one woman pushing an old shopping cart, walking as if it hurt her bones to do so.

As an agent, she knew that it was stereotyping to label a place as the "bad part of town" but that's exactly where they were. And while she knew that poverty did not automatically equate to "bad," the gang markings on some of the buildings she passed certainly did. She was again stuck on the question of how a woman like Kim Wielding had ended up dating a man from this side of town.

Ten minutes later, Rhodes pulled onto a one-way street and parked at the end of the block. She pointed to the apartment building to their right and said, "This is it. Apartment Twenty-eight."

They got out of the car and walked inside. The lobby wasn't so much a lobby as it was an empty space with a single bench bolted into the floor against the far wall. There was an elevator to the right but it was blocked off with an old sawhorse, a hand-lettered sign stating that it was out of order.

They bypassed the elevator and headed for the stairs, which were just as grimy as the lobby. A few stairs up, there was something sticky on one of the steps—coffee or soda that had been there for quite some time. It was clear to see that this building was not high on the maintenance list of the city council.

When they reached the second floor, they found it empty. A single window at the far end of the hallway shone musty morning light into the hall. It did a much better job of illuminating the hallway than the series of overhead lights—many of which were burned out. The start of the hallway was home to Apartment 21. Apartment 22 sat adjacent on the other side of the hall. Chloe and Rhodes walked down the hallway toward Apartment 28, listening to the muted sounds coming from within the building: the drone of a morning television news program, a woman coughing, someone slamming a door shut.

They came to Apartment 28 and Rhodes wasted no time in knocking. She rapped firmly, not bothering with any attempt to try to seem passive.

"I don't get how a woman who seemed to have been as high-profile as Kim Wielding would have ended up with someone who lives here," Rhodes said, echoing Chloe's earlier thoughts. "It makes me think there's a longer story tied to them."

"Or that my assumption that he's the ex the Carvers mentioned is wrong," Chloe admitted.

Rhodes knocked again, a bit harder this time. Chloe was pretty certain Mike Dillinger wasn't home. It would be inconvenient to leave here empty-handed, but it wouldn't be the end of the world. They had evidence that he had been involved with Kim and they even had a phone number to pin to him.

"I doubt this creep has a social life," Rhodes said, hammering at the door again. "If he's not home, where the hell is he?"

While Rhodes hammered on the door, Chloe just happened to turn around to peer back down the hallway. A man had come to the top of the stairs and paused in mid-stride as he started down the hall. His eyes were locked on them and the only part of his body that was moving was his right arm. It was slowly moving inward, as if he intended to hold his stomach.

"Rhodes," Chloe whispered. "Company."

Rhodes turned in that direction. By the time she did, the man's hand was now touching his hip, as if tugging at the waist if his pants.

"Don't move," Chloe said, going for her sidearm. "We're federal agents. Keep your hands where I—"

The man pulled a gun from the waist of his pants just as Chloe freed her own. He wasted no time in moving, firing off two shots as he fled back down the stairway. Chloe was too shocked to fire her own. She was also too busy falling to the floor, fairly certain she'd actually heard one of the rounds pass by her head. She slid against the opposite wall, pressing herself to it and aiming her sidearm down the hall. It was a Sig Sauer .09 millimeter, the only gun she'd ever truly been comfortable with.

"Rhodes, did you…"

But Rhodes, also on the floor, wasn't moving. She was moaning, however, and there was a growing pool of blood starting to gather around her waist.

"Shit," Chloe said. With her gun still aimed down the hallway, she slid over to Rhodes. She'd been hit low in the stomach on the right side. She was holding her sidearm with her right hand and cupping the wound with her left.

"Rhodes, can you—"

"Go after him," Rhodes interrupted. Her voice was soft and clearly pained. "I'll be fine. Get my phone. Call nine-one-one."

Chloe was shaking but managed to look past it as she fished Rhodes's phone out of her partner's pocket. She dialed 911 but Rhodes snatched the phone from her hand. "Go!" she hissed through a sigh of pain.

"Yeah," she said, really just as a confirmation to herself.

She tried to remain as calm as she could as she sped back down the hallway. But as she strode ahead with stealth that surprised even her, a flood of curse words ran through her head like some meditative chant.

Day Two on the job and I'm going to die. Right now, right here in this shitty building ...

She came to the edge of the wall where the stairway started. She collected her breath, putting a plan together in her head. If he was there, waiting for her, she'd have to shoot him. But if he wasn't there, she was going to have to give chase. And who was to say he had gone down to the lobby, toward the street? Maybe he had run up the stairs to the third or fourth floor in an attempt to throw her off.

She gathered up her nerves and pivoted out into the open air at the top of the stairs. Her finger was pressed against the trigger, ready to fire off a shot or two or God only knew how many. Her nerves were on fire, her muscles drenched in adrenaline.

But the man was not there.

Working on gut instinct, she ran down the stairs. It would just make more sense for him to have run for the streets, opening up innumerable methods of escape. She ran down the stairs, not even sure if she'd have it in her to shoot a man—at all, much less on just her second day on the job.

She came to the bottom of the stairs and tuned right, back toward the lobby.

Something moved to her right, something big and fast. She barely saw it at all but managed to get her arm up into a defensive posture in time. That was how she was able to block a clubbing blow with the butt of a Glock that would have knocked her back on her ass.

She did stumble at the attack, but moved quickly and folded her blocking arm over the man's attacking arm. This pointed the gun away from her while also forcing him to take a hard step to the left to prevent his arm from being wrenched from its socket. As he took this step, Chloe twisted his arm hard and then swept his moving left leg out from under him. When he fell backward as a result, she fell on top of him, throwing a hard forearm into his neck.

As he coughed and gagged, she kicked his weapon away and then rolled him over. He tried to fight against her as she did it, but he was weak from the blow to the throat. She threw an elbow into his ribs to make it even easier. She then grabbed his right arm and pulled it back behind him., She did the same with his second and applied the first set of handcuffs in her career.

Holy shit, I just did that, she thought. There was pride in it, but a pungent sense of terror as well. This was real now. It was all real—more than just some dream.

What now?

She honestly wasn't sure. So she did what seemed smartest to her. She couldn't leave Rhodes to bleed out upstairs but she also couldn't leave this asshole down here alone to escape on foot.

She stood a few feet behind him and leveled her Sig at him. "On your knees and then to your feet," she said.

"Go to hell."

"Now, asshole. If you do it now, I may be able to make it upstairs and help my partner. If you don't and she bleeds out, you'll be convicted of murdering a federal agent. So I suggest you get to your fucking feet. *Now!*"

He considered this for a moment but then managed to get to his knees with Chloe's hesitant assistance. He then got to his feet and when he was standing, Chloe gave him a push toward the stairs.

"Second floor," she said. "Try anything stupid and I *will* take out your knee."

He walked faster than she expected. She wondered if the gravity of what was happening to him had finally sunken in. As they made their way up the stairs, she tried to imagine this man texting Kim Wielding.

"Is your name Mike Dillinger?" she asked.

He said nothing. He only turned his head slightly in her direction.

"I suggest you answer me. You'll only make it harder on yourself."

"Yes. I'm Mike Dillinger."

"Why did you find it appropriate to fire at federal agents, Mr. Dillinger?"

He shrugged and looked to the ground.

When they reached the top of the stairs, Chloe nudged him forward with the barrel of her gun. It was probably irresponsible and frowned upon at the bureau, but she didn't care. She'd nearly died, Rhodes *might* die, and this man seemed to not care about any of it.

Rhodes had managed to push herself up into a seated position, leaning back against the wall beside Apartment 28. She was still bleeding, a crimson trickle spilling over her bloodstained left hand, still covering the wound. Her eyes were narrowed and her breathing was labored.

Chloe nudged Mike Dillinger with her gun and gave him a little shove downward. "On your knees, head against the wall."

He moved slowly—so slowly that when he did hit his knees, Chloe gave him a nudge forward from behind to help him place his head against the wall. She then knelt by Rhodes and surveyed the situation.

"Let me see," she said.

"No," Rhodes said. "I'm good. Ambulance should be on the way."

"Should be, yes. Now let me see it."

Rhodes moaned and gave in. When she moved her hand, a little gush of blood spilled out over her stomach and pooled in her lap where there was already an alarming amount gathered. Chloe knew that she needed to apply pressure but she was also pretty sure that might not be enough in this situation.

She looked around in a panic as an idea occurred to her. It was a little crazy but she didn't know what else to do. She got to her feet and closed in on Mike Dillinger. "Lift your arms."

He did so slowly, his entwined fists pressed against the wall just like his forehead. When his arms were up, Chloe reached down and grabbed the hem of his T-shirt. She lifted it up over his head and then slid it up his arms where it got caught on the chain of the cuffs. She then reached into one of the sleeves and grabbed the shirt, pulling and tearing with the other. The T-shirt tore right down the seam of the sleeve and beyond.

"What the hell are you doing?" Dillinger asked.

Chloe ignored him, tearing the shirt until she had torn it all the way down. She now had a length of cloth in her hand, fairly durable and thick cotton. She wadded it up, folding it three times over, and then pressed it firmly to Rhodes's wound. Rhodes hissed in pain but then relaxed. Chloe looked into her face and saw that she was growing pale and that her eyes were slipping closed.

"Stay with me, Rhodes," she said. "Can you do that?"

"Mmm-hmmm..."

But as Chloe looked at her, she wasn't so sure. Even now, less than ten seconds after applying her makeshift little tourniquet, the cloth was beginning to soak through with blood.

"Hold on," she said urgently. "Come on, Rhodes. Hang in there...."

But Rhodes's eyes were closing and her breathing was becoming more and more labored. She focused on that noise until another noise broke her concentration. This was a much more welcome noise, the blaring of an approaching ambulance siren.

And while the sound did bring some relief, Chloe wasn't sure that it was going to reach them in time.

Chapter Eight

Everything happened so quickly that Chloe honestly had a hard time keeping up with it all. The paramedics rushed in, making a fuss about the building's elevator being broken. When they rolled Rhodes down the hall and toward the stairs, her pulse was weak and flickering. Several police officers came in behind the ambulance, also responding to Rhodes's call. There was some conversation between Chloe and the cops, most of which she could barely follow. All she knew, five minutes after Rhodes had been cleared from the hallway, was that Mike Dillinger had been removed from the building by the Maryland State PD. Two officers were currently delivering him to the nearest police station for holding and interrogation.

Meanwhile, Rhodes was being hurried to the hospital. As Chloe made her exit from the building, she tried to read the faces of the paramedics to see if they were filled with hope or defeat. She saw a bit of both, and that did not make her feel any better.

She got into her car and placed a call to Agent Garcia before starting the engine. She filled him in on what had happened, ending by letting him know that she was heading to the PD to question Mike Dillinger. Garcia had sounded rather flustered, but let her know that he would be there with her within an hour.

She started the car and pulled out into traffic, not aware that she was shaking until she came to a red light. Up ahead, she could see the lights and flashers of the police cars, taking Dillinger into custody.

How the hell did all of this happen? she asked herself. *It was all way too fast. It doesn't feel real ... and I don't know if I'm going to be able to question that man without losing my cool.*

She suddenly found herself wondering how the people she had gone through Evidence Response training with were doing today. She wondered if any of them had been shot at this morning or had their partner's blood drying on their hands.

The light turned green and she continued on, following the cop cars ahead to what she felt was going to be her first true test as a ViCAP agent.

She looked through the double-sided glass at Mike Dillinger. He was sitting in a steel folding chair behind a long metal table. A policeman sat on the other side, filling out paperwork and asking Dillinger a series of questions. He'd been in there for a little over half an hour. Chloe was rather relieved that the whole process was taking so long. She had no problem going in to question Dillinger, but she'd feel much better if someone like Assistant Director Garcia or Director Johnson were here.

Hell, she'd even feel a little better if Rhodes was here. But she was currently fighting for her life, probably in an operating room by now. As she waited for her time to head into the interrogation room, she glanced down at her hands. She'd washed them three times already but she could still see faint traces of Rhodes's blood.

As she stood there, arms folded and thoughts all over the place, the door opened. She was surprised to see not Garcia, but Director Johnson enter the room. He closed the door behind him and took a moment to study Chloe's composure.

"How are you?" he asked.

"Good."

"I heard the report from the police. Can you give me your rundown?"

She nodded and spent the next three minutes giving Johnson her version of events. She did her best to downplay the fact that she was well aware that if Dillinger's aim had been a bit better, she could very well be dead right now.

"I called the hospital about two minutes before I stepped in here," Johnson said. "Rhodes is in surgery right now and it's too early to tell if she's going to make it or not. The nurse I spoke with did let me know that your quick thinking and poise under pressure might have saved her life. Without you there, she would have died in the ambulance."

Chloe wasn't sure what to say to that. She just waited patiently as Johnson looked through the glass.

"Police searched Dillinger's place. We have some agents there, too. The guy is a piece of work, that's for sure. We might have found why he'd be so brazen as to shoot at two FBI agents. There are encrypted files on his computer and some USB drives—the sort of encryptions we've seen hundreds of times before. Our experts are pretty sure it's all dark web stuff. Rape movies, snuff films, things of that nature. We aren't sure yet, but it's likely headed that way." Johnson paused here and stared at Chloe, almost like a concerned parent. "You know, you don't have to interrogate him. You've done more than enough already."

"No, I think I'll be okay."

"Would you like me to come in with you?"

Chloe thought about it and shrugged. The next comment out of her mouth felt as if it had slipped out… not the sort of thing she should say to someone so high above her.

"With all due respect, sir, do you coddle all new agents like this?"

"No. Just the ones I convince to switch departments only to have them shot at and save the life of another agent. Just so happens, you're the first."

"Then yes, I'd like you in there with me."

"Then what are we waiting for? Come on."

Johnson opened the door and led them a few yards down the hallway. He knocked on the door to the interrogation room and it was answered by the officer ten seconds later. Johnson showed the officer his badge and more or less bullied his way into the room.

"You done here?" Johnson asked.

"Nearly."

"Give us the room for ten minutes. After that, he's all yours again."

It was clear the officer did not appreciate being shoved around like this, but he conceded. He took one glance back to Dillinger—still shirtless from Chloe's quick-thinking first aid measures—and left the room, closing the door behind him. Johnson folded his arms and stood against the far wall, eyeing Dillinger. It did two things: intimidate the hell out of Dillinger, and let Chloe know that that floor was now hers.

She stepped towards the table, doing her best to appear that she had done this hundreds of time in the past.

"I'm Agent Chloe Fine," she said. "You might recognize me from when you took a shot at me—at the same time you seriously injured my partner. Mr. Dillinger, I'm going to skip the niceties here and ask why you'd so blindly fire at someone that happened to be knocking at your door."

"Two women that looked like they didn't belong there were in my hallway, fucking with my door," Dillinger said in a shaky voice. "I didn't believe you when you said you were federal agents." Dillinger looked slightly frightened but there was also a sort of boredom to his posture in the chair and the way he spoke. He knew he was in trouble and apparently didn't see the point in either begging to being defiant.

"Apparently not. But still … do you make a habit of shooting at people that come knocking on your door?"

"I'm not stupid," Dillinger said. "I saw you going for your side—figured you had a gun. I thought you might have been sent by someone that might have it in for me."

"And who would have it in for you?" Chloe asked.

"A few people."

"Understandably so," Chloe said. "Mr. Dillinger, there are FBI agents and State policemen currently working to decrypt certain files they found on your laptop and several USBs. It might take a little time, but they *will* get through. Why don't you go ahead and tell me what we're going to find?"

Dillinger folded his hands and set them on the table, perhaps trying to seem aloof. But the nervousness on his face betrayed it.

"Fine then," Chloe said. "Why don't you tell me how you know Kim Wielding?"

The mention of the name seemed to rattle him for the slightest of moments. But he then chuckled and said, "What about that uppity bitch?"

"Why don't you tell me?" Chloe asked. "She is, after all, dead. And I'm starting to think you killed her."

Dillinger's reaction confused her. He stared at her as if she had pulled a gun out and shot him. But it passed after a quick moment when he then shook his head and looked down to his still-folded hands.

"I'm not saying anything else until I speak to a lawyer."

"At least tell me how she knew you."

He grinned and cocked his head at her. "Why? The two of us together don't make sense to you? She too good for me? I get it. You wouldn't be the first to think such a thing."

"How long did you know her?"

Dillinger glared up at her as if she was stupid, like an adult flummoxed by a child. "No more conversation until I speak to a lawyer."

Chloe turned back to look at Johnson. He nodded and then reached for the door. When he opened it, Chloe wasted no time in heading out, not even lured back into the room when she heard Dillinger chuckling at her. Chloe and Johnson went directly back to the viewing room, Johnson giving the officer who had previously been with Dillinger a little nod, as if to say: *Carry on.*

"What are your initial thoughts?" Johnson asked when they were back behind a closed door.

Chloe took a moment before answering. She felt as if she was being tested, that Johnson was looking for some very specific answer. "He's guilty of *something*, but I don't see enough to instantly pin Kim Wielding's murder on him."

"I'll work with the State boys to make sure they get what they need from the bureau. Fine… you've done remarkable work today and I've been in your shoes before. Being shot at, watching a partner's life hang in the balance. It's hard. So I want you to take the rest of the day. Don't go back to the office. Go home. If you decide you need someone to speak with, I'll make sure you get directly through to a bureau psychologist."

His concern for her was unexpected and touching. And since she knew better than to argue with him, she only said: "Thank you, sir."

"I would still like a report on my desk within two days about what happened."

"No problem," Chloe said, opening the door and heading out.

As she walked down the hallway and toward the front doors, she felt a wave of emotion crashing over her. It was one she had felt twice that morning, trying to claim her. She'd managed to fight it off both times but now her defenses were down. By the time she made it to her car, she was weeping so hard she had to take a moment to crank her car. And when she did finally turn the key in the ignition, the sight of Rhodes's faint bloodstains on her hands set it off all over again.

And as was usually the case when she grew emotional, she thought of her father. Only this time when she thought of him, it caused the crying to stop.

She had the rest of the day at her disposal. And she knew where he was.

She considered her options for a moment and then pulled out of the parking lot with a terrifying plan hatching in her head.

Chapter Nine

When she came to her apartment, she already knew that she was not going to stop. When that wave of emotion had crashed against her heart and finally broke her in the police station parking lot, it had brought something with it. Just like an ocean wave bringing shells and kelp and other detritus from the ocean floor to the shore, her wave had brought something else as well.

It had brought an unsettled feeling about her father. And it was that feeling that had her coasting by her apartment building and toward the ramp for the interstate. It was nearly a two-and-a-half-hour drive to the Somerset Correctional Facility in Pennsylvania, the prison that her father had been held in for nearly twenty years now. But she figured that would give her plenty of time to clear her head and to think long and hard about what she might finally say to her father, Aiden Fine.

Roughly halfway along her trip, her cell phone rang. While she had not yet saved the contact, she recognized Director Garcia's number. She answered it with her heart in her throat, fearing that this would be news about Rhodes's condition and that it would not be good.

"This is Agent Fine."

"This is Assistant Director Garcia. I thought you'd want an update on Rhodes. The surgery is not over, but they have her stabilized. Barring some unseen problems during the remainder of the procedure, she's going to pull through. And the doctors are saying you saved her life by applying that compress. She would have bled out if not for you."

"That's great news," Chloe said. "Thanks."

"Director Johnson tells me you're taking the remainder of the day for yourself. If I might be so bold, let me suggest just relaxing at home. Take some time to process all of this and let us know how we can help."

She smiled nervously, looking ahead to the open interstate in front of her. "Yeah," she said. "Maybe I'll do that."

She'd been expecting to have to show her ID and badge to see her father but she was surprised that she simply had to undergo a check-in process—not as a federal agent, but as Aiden Fine's daughter. She was then ushered into a room that looked very much like every visitation scene she'd ever watched on a television drama. There was a long row of booths, all joined together to look almost like a single long, yet partitioned desk. The booths were two-sided, the front and back separated by bulletproof glass. One side was for visitors; the other side fed into the prison, allowing prisoners to come for face-to-face visits.

There were no other visitors when Chloe took her seat at the center booth. Her TV-based version of these booths was broken apart when she saw that the booths did not have traditional phone-based communication sets bolted to the walls. Instead, each side had a small microphone that was hooked to a send and receive button—basically a high-tech CB radio.

She sat there in the quiet with a single guard standing several feet away, as she waited for someone to usher her father in. Idly, she wondered if he'd even recognize her. It had, after all, been seventeen years since he'd last seen her.

It took five minutes for a door to buzz on the other side of the glass. A guard walked alongside her father. Aiden Fine looked rail thin and wore a beard that was in need of a shave. His eyes looked rather wild as he was ushered to the seat in front of Chloe. With the glass between them, they stared at one another before her father finally said something.

"Chloe." Her name came out of his mouth in a dry little sob.

"Hey," was all she could find to say. After some courage, she also managed: "I'm surprised you recognize me."

"You don't look all that different."

"You do," she said. "But I had this picture of you in my head that I wasn't even sure was accurate or not."

He nodded, as if he understood perfectly. "It's nice to see you," he said, clearly fighting back a wave of tears. "What made you decide to visit?"

She knew she could go one of two ways. She could play the part of the grown woman who had lived a childhood without a mother or a father, and with a haunted memory of the day her father had been arrested. Or she could be true to herself. She could behave the way she felt, use the words that came naturally to her rather than filtering them.

And that's what she chose to do.

She lifted her hands and showed them to him. "I'm an FBI agent now. Part of the ViCAP program. The blood you see on my hands is my partner's. It's just stain … it'll come off if I scrub really hard, I guess …"

"Chloe … how did you … ?"

Her father was starting to lose the battle with his emotions … which seemed fitting because a small part of Chloe's mind felt like it was coming unhinged. She had thought about this moment forever and now that it was here, she realized that she was not ready for it. She had not properly prepared herself. Coming directly off of the heels of her first arrest and watching her partner nearly die had certainly not helped, either.

"I'm so proud of you," he said through the tears.

"I don't care, Dad. I know that sounds bad but … I didn't come here for encouragement or some sappy moment between us. I don't know why I came."

Yes, you do, she thought. *Seeing Rhodes like that ... all that blood and her life literally in your hands there for a moment ... it made you think of him. It made you think of the day you saw your mother dead at the foot of the stairs and your father being taken away in handcuffs.*

"Do you know … that it wasn't me? Someone did. My sentence was reduced and …"

"I know it wasn't you that killed Mom," she said. "We know Ruthanne Carwile did it. I found that out several months ago. But … that doesn't change too much for me. You were in on it … You were … You wanted it to happen. Enough so that you're still in prison for conspiracy to murder."

"I know," he said. "And no … I didn't *want* it to happen. I'm so sorry. Chloe … please believe me. I'm a changed man now. I'm so different now and I hope you can forgive me. I hope to be out of here soon and I didn't even know how I'd go about getting back into life. If I had you and Danielle there to help me …"

"Why didn't you just tell the truth?" Chloe asked. "Ruthanne's name never came out of your mouth during the trial. I looked back over the old records just to be sure. And you never mentioned her. Not once."

"I was … I was in love."

"Just not with my mother?"

"We fell out of love a long time before that. She'd tell you the same."

"But I can't ask her because she's fucking dead," Chloe spat.

Aiden recoiled at the comment, as if someone had thrown a punch at him.

"Even with Ruthanne taking the charge of murder, you're still on the hook, too," Chloe said. "Not with the prison system. That's already been taken care of, I guess. I mean with Danielle and I."

"Did Ruthanne tell you everything?" he asked.

"She told me enough."

"I doubt she told it all. If she chose to do so, she could tell her complete side of things and free me completely."

Chloe sighed and looked away, not liking the sight of him in tears. "I didn't come here to talk about Mom or Ruthanne."

"Then why did you?"

"Because I was so close to someone that nearly died today. I had them under my hands as they bled out. And for the longest time, whenever I have thought of death, I think of you."

He wiped tears away from the corners of his eyes and did his best to regain his composure. Part of Chloe felt miserable; she was not intending to be so venomous toward him. It was simply coming naturally.

"I thought about you the other day," he said, almost randomly. "Someone was talking about amusement parks and roller coasters. It made me think of that time we went to Virginia and we took you girls to King's Dominion. Remember how you threw a fit because you were too small to get on that one ride that had all the loops, but Danielle was like two inches taller and was able to go on?"

She felt something go loose in her chest and her own tears came now. She lowered her head, refusing to let him see her cry.

"Stop," she said. "You can't do that. You aren't allowed to do that."

"Chloe, I just—"

Before she realized what she was doing, Chloe got to her feet. "I have to go," she said. "This was a mistake. A huge mistake."

"Chloe, just please think about it. I don't know when I'll be released, but it could be soon. And I want a life with my daughters."

"I thought the plans were for you and Ruthanne to reunite," she said. "Sorry if me arresting her fucked that up for you."

"I'm so sorry, Chloe! I was in love and wasn't thinking straight. It was all messed up! I can't help that I was so messed up in the head over Ruthanne! I'm sorry!"

She stopped at these last few comments and turned back around to him. She wanted to hurt him and the next thing out of her mouth felt appropriate.

"I wish I could forget you like Danielle has. I wish I could hate you, Dad. But…I can't and I don't know why. Even after finding out you didn't actually kill Mom… that it was just that bitch Ruthanne…"

"Chloe…"

"I have to sever everything with you or I'll go crazy with all of the wondering. And I know how to do it. I have to know."

"Know what, Chloe?"

"Did you love Mom? Did you ever *really* love her?"

"Of course I did. I always did, I think. I wish I could explain to you how wrecked I was in the months—hell, the *years* that passed after her death."

"That's bullshit, Dad."

"Chloe, I—"

"What, asshole?"

But he could only shake his head. When she saw a tear spill down his cheek, she sneered at him and walked back toward the exit. She nodded at the guard and he walked out ahead of her, opening the door.

The walk from the visitation room to the parking lot felt even longer and harder than the one she had taken from the interrogation room with Mike Dillinger and back to her car. Knowing that her father—the man she had wondered, dreamed, and reflected upon for most of her life—was right behind her made her feel like a little girl running away from a disappointed parent. And for all she knew, that's exactly what was happening.

But even through that, the logical part of her mind had latched on to something he had said—some bit at the end when she had been leaving. *I was in love and wasn't thinking straight. It was all messed up! I can't help that I was so messed up in the head over Ruthanne!*

It made her think of the seemingly bizarre relationship between Kim Wielding and Mike Dillinger. It made her wonder if there was something she had missed. She had instantly started assuming that Dillinger would lead them to whatever dark answers there might be. She had been so fixated on that, she had almost overlooked Kim. Maybe she had some secrets she was hiding. Maybe Kim, like Ruthanne, had been living with secrets that had come dangerously close to breaking the surface.

With that concept taking shape in her head, Chloe headed back the way she had come, beginning to round off an almost six-hour drive that had resulted in a visit that had lasted less than fifteen minutes.

But as far as Chloe was concerned, that had been far more than enough.

As far as she was concerned, she was fine if she never saw him again.

Chapter Ten

She supposed it was emotional exhaustion that allowed her to fall asleep so quickly that night. She lay down at 10:30 and fell asleep almost right away. When she woke up the following morning, she was amazed to see that it was 7:50. She checked her phone and saw that there were no missed calls or texts, though she did have several emails. One of them was from Assistant Director Garcia and had been sent to her and several others—people, she realized after checking the email addresses of them all, who were agents with the ViCAP program.

She read the email as she sat up in bed, feeling incredibly well rested.

As many of you know, Agent Rhodes was shot in the line of duty yesterday. After surgery, doctors were calling her case stable. As of 11:30 tonight, doctors have indicated that she is out of the woods and on a road of recovery that should last just a few weeks.

The email went on to give the address of the hospital in Landover, as well as Rhodes's room number. Chloe was glad that her name had not been mentioned in the mail. Simply hearing Garcia and Johnson tell her how doctors had claimed she had essentially saved her partner's life had made her feel uneasy.

Chloe got ready for the day casually, smiling at the remembrance of how she had rushed through getting ready the day before in an attempt to beat Rhodes. She was at work just before nine o' clock. She got a few smiles and nods as she made her way to her cubicle on the third floor. She thought of checking in with Garcia or Johnson but decided not to. She just wanted to get to her desk without having to think about anything that had happened yesterday.

She went onto the bureau's network and saw that the file on Kim Wielding had been updated. There was more information on Mike Dillinger and the crime scene at the Carvers' home. She printed off all of the new files and gathered them up, adding them to her files. She then spent the next several minutes at her desk, drinking coffee and reading up on the case.

Dillinger had still not admitted to the murder of Kim Wielding. In fact, he was now flat-out denying it. While he had been denying the murder or any sort of physical involvement with Kim, the feds had managed to crack his decrypted files. They had all been homemade sex movies of a graphic nature—some borderline rape—though there was nothing inherently criminal on them. There was an investigation into two of the women on the films, with the suspicion that they were possibly under eighteen years of age.

Agents had also uncovered deleted history on his laptop, indicating that Dillinger spent a lot of time on the dark web. He had ordered DMT and heroin from a supplier in the last three weeks but it was later on in the history—as well as additional proof in his bank statements—that would nail him even if he did turn out to be innocent in Kim Wielding's murder. He was selling the movies he was making at home on the dark web. There were deposits in his bank account for small amounts from these deals and, from what agents had discovered, Kim Wielding had even been featured in one of the more recent films he'd sold.

Feeling a little sick to her stomach at this news, she then tried to focus on Kim Wielding's information. She didn't learn anything new. Kim had gone to a great college, had once worked in Washington for a few political organizations, and had then quit without any real reason. And somehow, she'd become a nanny.

That doesn't seem right, she thought. *To go from a promising career in DC to a nanny ... something had to have happened.*

As she started to consider this path, someone knocked on her cubicle wall. She turned around in her chair and saw Garcia standing there. He grinned at her and took a look at the newly printed pages and her growing file.

"I wasn't sure if you'd come in today or not," he said.

"I'm fine. I figure some desk work, reading through these files on Wielding and Dillinger would at least keep me busy."

"I take it you heard the good news about Rhodes?"

"I did."

"You might want to visit her. Johnson visited her and said she asked about you. I think she'd like to see you."

"I may do that," she said. "Hey … do you know what happened with Kim Wielding? What caused her to stop chasing a career in DC to start working as a nanny?"

"I'm not sure. I think she just got burned out. Political crap isn't for everyone, you know? But we actually have an agent assigned to look into that. Maybe the two of you can work together on that if you want. So you don't think Dillinger killed her?"

"I'm starting not to. All of his movies and interests … they point to sex and nothing else. Gratification. Exploitation. The only reason I can find for him to kill someone that he made one of these sick movies with is because they knew about it and were thinking of turning him in."

Garcia nodded. "Sounds reasonable. Maybe I *will* hook you up with this other agent. You interested?"

"Sure."

"Be honest, Fine. Don't push yourself."

She thought about meeting her father yesterday and of the blood she had finally gotten off of her hands when she had returned home late yesterday afternoon.

"Yeah, I'm sure. Research and digging is easy. I think I can manage to avoid shootouts in my cubicle or back in suburbia."

"I'll let Director Johnson know. For now, is there anything you need from me?"

"No thanks."

Garcia gave her a wave goodbye and left her to the files on Kim Wielding and Mike Dillinger. And while all of the information was easy to follow and even seemed to lead down paths of reason that were intriguing, her mind wandered over and over back to her father and what he'd said to her about Ruthanne Carwile: *"I doubt she told it all. If she chose to do so, she could tell her complete side of things and free me completely."*

She started to wonder what exactly Ruthanne's "side of things" was. And then in the back of her mind, she wondered if Danielle might know something about it. She'd always been a big secret keeper and always seemed to either clam up or get defensive whenever their father was mentioned.

When the thought wouldn't leave her mind by lunchtime, Chloe made a decision that made her feel a little guilty. She phoned up Garcia as she gathered up the Wielding files.

"I think maybe I did push it a little," she said. "You mind if I head home? I'm going to take the Wielding files with me just to keep my brain active."

"That's fine. Just go enjoy the weekend. We'll see you back on Monday. And I talked with Johnson about getting you back on the Wielding case with this other agent. I'm pretty sure you'll start on that come Monday."

"Thanks again," she said, ending the call and wasting no time in getting to her feet. She gathered up her files and headed for the elevators, feeling like she was playing hooky right before a big test.

She sat on one of the chairs at her small kitchen table, her feet kicked up on a box of books that had still not been unpacked. She looked hard at Danielle's number before actually placing the call. Even after what they had gone through in uncovering most of the truth about the murder of their mother, it was still awkward to speak with Danielle. And knowing that she was going to be bringing up their father this time … that made it even more of a harrowing thought.

She finally pressed Call, doing so as if she was hitting the detonator on a bomb.

"Hello?" Danielle's voice answered seconds later.

"Hey. How are you?"

"I'm good. You?"

"Fine."

God, this is awkward, she thought.

"Good," Danielle said. "Now that we have that totally banal introduction out of the way, what's wrong?"

"I'm not going to make it tonight like I had planned."

"It's okay. I figured you'd back out. You really never were the late-night drinking type."

"It's not that. The last twenty-four hours have been…"

"Have been what?" Concern bloomed in Danielle's voice and the kindness of it made tears sting at Chloe's eyes.

Chloe opened her mouth and for the next ten minutes, she told Danielle about hunting down Mike Dillinger and the shooting. She didn't stop until she recounted her leaving the police station in Landover and having a miniature breakdown in her car.

"Chloe… my God. I'm so sorry. What do you need? Do you need me to come down there and be with you for the weekend?"

"No," Chloe said, moved beyond words at the gesture. "But thank you. There *is* something else I should tell you, though."

"Chloe… are you okay? What is it?"

"I went to see Dad yesterday."

The silence on the other end of the line spoke louder than any actual words Danielle had said so far. When she did finally respond, her words sounded barbed and thick.

"Why in God's name would you do that?"

"I honestly don't know," Chloe said. "The adrenaline and the feelings that were running though me… my mind went to him. And I've been wanting to talk to him ever since we found out the truth… about Ruthanne and Mom…"

"Chloe, he's toxic. You know that, right? If you let him haunt you, it's going to do nothing but pull you down."

"He says Ruthanne knows details about the story that would prove he had nothing to do with the murder. Enough to maybe free him completely… to end his even already shortened sentence."

"Oh, bullshit. He's a loser, Chloe. He always has been. How can you not see that? Of course he says there are details to free him. He wants to stay in your head. It's his way of controlling you. Damn, aren't *you* supposed to be the FBI agent here? It doesn't take a genius to figure out what he's trying to do."

"Maybe. But … Jesus, Danielle … why are you going off like this?"

"Because he's a miserable son of a bitch and he doesn't deserve any more of my thoughts or time."

"I think you and I should talk," Chloe said. "Sort through all of this."

"I'd love to meet with you and talk. But not about him."

"Danielle …"

"Dammit, Chloe. Can't you see that I'm *finally* starting to get my life together? Why do you have to bring the past back up like this?"

"Because I have to let it go. *We* have to let it go."

"Oh, I have!"

"Have you? Then why do you get so angry and defensive about him?"

Danielle sighed heavily through the phone. "Chloe, I'm going to get off of this phone before I say something I shouldn't. When you get things back to normal, I'd love to see you. And my offer stands … if you need help getting over what happened to you yesterday, call me and I'll do my best to come down there to see you. But I can't go through this right now."

And with that, Danielle ended the call. Chloe remained seated, staring around the apartment. Boxes still needed to be unpacked, the TV still needed to be plugged in and hooked up. The place was chaotic and messy. Chloe couldn't help but wonder if she was putting it all off on purpose. If it did not *feel* like home, she'd not be able to *think* of it as home.

And right now, she felt a very long way away from any true sense of home.

Chapter Eleven

She'd forgotten all about her meeting with Steven until her phone dinged at her with a calendar notification the following day. The meeting was in two hours and the note of **Choose A Place** on her calendar made her realize that she had never texted Steven back to tell him where to meet her. Badly in need of a drink, she chose a bar about half a mile away, a place with a reputation for amazing burgers and daily drink specials. She texted the location and a time to meet—12:30—feeling like she was poking at a beehive.

She got ready in a hurry, honestly not giving a damn what she looked like. As she headed out, she thought about what Danielle had said yesterday about leaving the past behind them. It was difficult to do with her father but she was looking forward to the day when she could put all of this Steven nonsense behind her.

It was a notion that seemed to grow stronger when she saw him sitting at one of the high-rise tables at the back of the bar. His boyish smile and the squared angle of his shoulders, the *aren't-I-a-good-boy* look on his face—God, how had she ever convinced herself that marrying him would be a good idea?

And then she saw who was sitting beside him. Part of her wanted to scream. The other part of her wanted to turn around and walk back out.

It was his mother.

Sally Brennan sat on the other side of the table like a statue someone had gotten tired of lugging around. She sat prim and proper, her nose turned up at just the right angle as Chloe walked toward them.

Chloe took one of the high-backed chairs at the table and decided in an instant that she wasn't going to fake this. She was not going to pretend to be polite. It was bad enough that he had somehow swindled her into meeting with him, but he'd even brought his mother along.

"I wasn't aware we were going to have company," Chloe said.

"It's nice to see you, too," Sally said.

Chloe ignored her completely. It was the sort of thing she had never had the courage to do when she and Steven had been engaged. But now Chloe found that she *wanted* to piss this woman off.

"Thanks for coming," Steven said. "Can we keep things civil, please?"

"Yes. What can I do for you, Steven? Why did you want to meet?"

"Closure."

"What kind of closure? I gave you back the ring."

"No... that's not what I mean. Not closure to the relationship. I mean closure towards us."

"I don't follow."

"Maybe closure isn't the right word. I feel like maybe we just gave up too quickly," he said. "I think with some time and conversation, we can work things out."

Chloe had to bite back a laugh. And once she had it down, she started to wonder if Steven and his bitch of a mother were playing some cruel joke on her. But no... from what she could tell, Steven was being serious.

"Did it ever occur to you—to either one of you—that I don't want to work things out? Did either of you ever even consider that maybe I was relieved when things fell apart?"

"Are you serious?" Sally said. "Steven was the best thing that ever happened to you or your family."

Chloe slowly turned to Sally and smiled politely. "As of earlier this week, I'm a federal agent with the United States government. If it weren't for that, I'd slap you right across your Botox-laced face. Kindly shut up and let your son handle his own conversations."

Sally's eyes grew wide and she leaned back in her chair. Steven, meanwhile, hunkered down. "Don't talk to my mother like that."

"Well, maybe you shouldn't bring her to situations like this, Steven. I know you well enough. I damn near married you. You're a smart enough guy. Why did you bring her? Is she supposed to be your muscle?"

"Chloe... what's happened to you?" He asked it as if he was genuinely concerned about her.

She thought about entertaining him with the story of what had happened to her and Rhodes. But she knew it would be useless. Steven and his mother would somehow try to twist that into a lesson about how her work was too dangerous and that she needed Steven in her life to protect her.

"What happened to me is that I'm finally starting to live for myself. To live my own life. And I find it insulting and pretty fucking funny to think that you assumed I'd just nod and cry and welcome you back."

"But Chloe, you can't—"

"Was there anything else?" she snapped.

"Chloe..."

"Sorry you drove all the way out here," she said. "But this conversation is not going to happen." She then turned to look at Sally and said: "If you get on the road in the next hour or so, you can be back home before dark. Maybe tuck him in nice and tight and read him a bedtime story."

Sally opened her mouth to say something but no words came out. Chloe turned on her heel and left, feeling their stares on her back. She fully expected Steven to call after her in some masculine and demanding way, but he didn't.

Back out on the street, a smile came to Chloe's face. She hadn't expected it to feel so good to tell Sally Brennan off in such a way but the feeling that flushed through her was pretty close to a good orgasm. She quickly walked to the end of the street and retreated into a different bar. This one was a smaller sports bar, slowly starting to fill with the college football crowd. Chloe disappeared into the crowd, pulled herself up to the bar, and ordered a rum and Coke.

She stayed there for quite a while, oblivious to the football games on the multiple screens around her. Instead, she did her best to think of why she had been so unable to detach herself from her father while Danielle had moved on rather easily.

Around her third drink, she figured it shouldn't be all that hard to step away from the past. And if she could make her separation from the memory of her father as enjoyable as she had her meeting with Steven and his mother, why *couldn't* she leave her father in the past?

Because even though you now know he didn't kill her (though he did have a hand in the planning, no matter what he says), she thought, there are still unanswered questions. And by your nature, you can't stand unanswered questions.

She wasn't sure if this was a positive character trait or a negative one. But in the thrum and bustle of the noisy crowd and with her fourth drink appearing like magic in front of her, she decided that it wasn't worth the worry. The past was the past… and as long as she could keep her eyes on the future, that's exactly where it would stay.

CHAPTER TWELVE

Chloe went back to work on Monday morning with a stunted kind of guilt—the feeling of returning to work after nursing a hangover for most of Sunday. She sat down behind her desk, placing the Wielding file back on her desk. She was setting up her workspace and about to check her email when she noticed the flashing red light on the landline phone at her desk. She'd only ever used this phone once and that was only to get accustomed to the voicemail system. It was no secret that about ninety-eight percent of all calls and messaging in the bureau were now done through cell phones. So the blinking red light struck her as very interesting.

She dialed into the system, punched in her passcode, and found that she did indeed have one message. She smiled and felt a bit of warmth spread through her when she recognized the voice.

"Hey, Fine. It's Rhodes. I realized I didn't have your cell number saved. I guess I wasn't the best partner, huh? Didn't even ask for your number. Anyway… it's Sunday, around two in the afternoon. It's the first time I've been coherent enough to pick up the phone. I wanted to say thank you and… I don't know. Thank you doesn't seem like enough. Let's just say that when I get out of here, I'm taking you out to dinner and drinks and pretty much whatever the hell else you want. I hope this finds you well."

Near the end, there was a waver of emotion in Rhodes's voice. It got to Chloe and she was glad when the message was over. She placed the receiver back on the cradle with a little click.

"Everything okay?"

She turned and saw Garcia approaching her cubicle. He was carrying a cup of coffee and looked far too chipper for eight in the morning on a Monday.

"Yeah," she said. "I had a message from Rhodes. Seems she's doing well."

"That's what I hear, too," Garcia said. "So Johnson wants you in his office in about fifteen minutes. He's going to reassign you with another partner and set you guys on figuring out who killed Kim Wielding. Because the more we discover about Dillinger, it appears less and less likely it was him."

"I figured. Are the Carvers back in their home?"

"Yes, but they are also being very cooperative in regards to helping with the case. Between just the two of us, I think it's going to end up being a simpler case that we're thinking. It's suburbia. Well-to-do families concerned with money and appearance. I guarantee you, sex or an affair or both is somehow at the center of the entire thing."

"I'd take that bet," Chloe said.

"Fifteen minutes," Garcia said, pointing at her in a little gun motion. "Johnson's office. Don't forget."

She spent those next fifteen minutes clearing out her inbox and taking one final glance at the Wielding files to have it fresh in her mind while speaking with Johnson. She then made the walk to his office, wondering if it was normal for an agent this new to the game having been in her director's office so many times in her first week on the job.

She entered the waiting room just in time to see someone else walking into Johnson's office. She looked to the receptionist and was waved inside. "Yes, it's okay," she told Chloe. "He's expecting you."

Chloe walked in behind the other person. As she closed the door behind her, she realized that she recognized the person who had entered the office ahead of her. It was Kyle Moulton. He gave her a quick look of surprise that seemed to say: *Funny meeting you here.*

Johnson gave them a quick nod of acknowledgment and then gestured to the two seats on the opposite side of his desk. "Good to see you both," he said. "Please, have a seat."

Chloe did as she was asked, slowly starting to put the pieces of this all together. With her luck, Moulton would be her new partner—the agent that Garcia had told her was keeping up with the Wielding case.

"I'll keep this short and to the point," Johnson said. "Agent Fine, this is Agent Kyle Moulton. Did you two ever cross paths during the academy?"

"Only recently," Moulton said.

"Shortly after orientation," Chloe said.

"Good, good. Agent Fine, Agent Moulton has been working on the investigation into the murder of Kim Wielding. Based on your familiarity with the case, I'd like for the two of you to work together on this. And as I've said from the start, the sooner we can get it resolved, the better."

He said this with an air of conspiracy, as if he knew damned good and well that both Chloe and Moulton knew that there was only interest in this single murder because someone higher up the chain in DC wanted it looked into.

"Is ... is that it?" Moulton asked.

"Yes. Agent Moulton, run this like you had originally planned. Are there any leads you're after today?"

"Yes, sir. I've got a possible lead at a Yacht Club right here in town. The Carvers were members, the father quite involved. But it was Kim that took the kids to the children's programs. Phone records indicate she might have had a good friend that worked there."

Johnson nodded his approval and then gave a little clap. "Okay, great. Get us some answers and let's get this over with. I think the two of you can work well together based on what I've seen so far."

"Thanks, sir," Chloe said as she got to her feet.

She made her way for the door with Moulton behind her. They passed awkwardly through the lobby and out into the hallway.

"I heard about how you saved your partner," Moulton said. "That was pretty badass."

"It was luck," she said. "I was nervous as hell. Just thinking with my gut."

"Whatever it was, it makes me feel safe to know you're with me now. For however long."

She recalled how she had felt a pang of jealousy when she had seen Moulton at the bar the other night, sitting with two women and leaving with one of them. Standing next to him, she still found him handsome and a little mysterious, but she was confused by his overall aloofness. He had a sort of goofy charm to him but the sort of stature that made it seem that he could ditch the goofiness without warning and become something else.

"So we're headed to a yacht club?" she asked as they came to the elevators.

"Yeah. And if I'm being honest, I don't know if it's going to amount to much. But there are no leads at all on this thing."

"There has to be something," Chloe said. "Something in her life led her to a scumbag like Mike Dillinger. There's got to be a story there."

"Did you hear the latest on Dillinger?"

"No."

"This morning, he was formally arrested for two counts of sex with a minor as well as sexual abuse and profiteering from it. Add shooting a federal agent and he's going to be looking at about twenty-five years."

The elevator arrived and they stepped on. "Good," Chloe said, though she almost wished Dillinger *had* killed Wielding. Not just because it would mean this case would be closed, but because the asshole deserved a life sentence as far as Chloe was concerned.

"So, day one as my partner and you're headed to a yacht club," Moulton said. "Really, could you ask for anything better?"

"Maybe being *on* a yacht?"

"Yes, that would be better. With a margarita or two." He smiled and then added, "Yes, I think we're going to work together just fine."

She couldn't help but smile. If she could get over this stupid little crush, she thought he was exactly right.

Chapter Thirteen

They arrived at the Angler Head Yacht Club half an hour later. It was situated facing East Potomac Park. From the parking lot, they could see another yacht club, thrown up against the Potomac River the same way houses were built seemingly overnight in growing subdivisions. It was a pretty enough morning—seventy-three degrees and partly cloudy—but because of the early hour, the place was mostly empty.

"So here's what we know about Kim Wielding's link to this place," he said. "This is really the only public place she was ever seen with the Carver kids outside of the car rider line at their school. She has a friend that works at the restaurant and bar here, an older lady named Madeline Duplin. We know this because they have spoken on the phone at least three times and because Ms. Duplin had sent Kim a birthday card over the last two years."

"Have you spoken to her yet? Does she know we're coming?"

"I spoke with her last night on the phone. She asked that I not bother her after hours, as her husband is ill. But she was more than happy to see me here this morning."

Impressed with his ability to boil the facts down to just the basics, Chloe followed him across a large lawn that bordered the Potomac. A restaurant stretched out over the water, held up with enormous planks and steel struts that dived down into the water.

They entered the restaurant and found only two tables occupied. "Thin breakfast crowd," Moulton said.

As they stood at the door behind the **Please Wait To Be Seated** sign, a woman came out of the kitchen area. She spotted them, smiled, and walked forward.

"Agent Moulton, I assume?" she asked.

"That's me," he said. "The suit gives it away, huh? Ms. Duplin, this is my partner, Agent Fine. She'd also familiar with Kim's case."

"Good to meet you both," she said. "I've brewed up a pot of coffee just for the three of us if you like."

"That would be great," Chloe said.

Madeline Duplin led them through the small restaurant, choosing a table at the back. As she had said, there was a carafe of coffee and three mugs, along with sugar packets and a creamer jar.

As they sat down, Madeline poured the coffee for them. "I'm still a little shocked that Kim is gone," she said. "And I guess I should start off by saying that I didn't know her all that well. But she was one of those people that seemed just… too perfect, you know?"

"Her phone records show where you spoke with her a few times," Moulton said. "Can you tell me what those calls were about?"

"Sure, sure. I spoke with her twice because I was working behind the scenes, trying to get her on the waiting list for the little fishing tour we put on for the kids a few times a year. She forgot to sign up and felt awful. I spoke with her here a few times and told her I'd see what I could do. The third time was because she was helping to organize a fundraiser we had here last year."

"But you knew her well enough to send her a birthday card on two occasions?" Chloe asked.

"Oh, I have a list of people about a hundred deep that I send birthday cards to. Mostly parents or nannies that bring their kids to the little events for kids that the club puts on. If you don't mind my asking, how did you know about that?"

"We found the cards in a folder of some Kim's things at the Carver home," Moulton said.

"Speaking of which," Chloe said, "did you ever see Kim with Bill and Sandra?"

"I saw her out with Bill a few times. Bill helps out with fundraisers here and there as well."

"And how would you describe their interactions?"

Madeline frowned as she started sipping from her coffee. "At first, I thought nothing of it. I thought it was healthy that a father would be so casual and friendly with the nanny of his children. But there was one time—at the banquet last Christmas—that it seemed almost weird to me."

"How so?" Moulton asked.

"I happened to walk out of the main hall and saw them standing really closely off in a corner, like they were trying to sneak away from everyone for a while. They weren't doing anything, mind you, but standing *very* close. There were also a few times that night that I caught small things: Bill placing his hand on the small of her back as he passed her, staring at her off and on. It was just off-putting."

"Do you think anyone else noticed?" Chloe asked.

"I have no idea."

"Let's just get to the core of it for a second," Moulton said. "Did you leave that banquet with even the slightest wonder in your head that there might be something going on between them?"

"It crossed my mind. But then again, I felt like I knew Kim well enough. I didn't think she'd have it in her to mess around with a married man—especially not the father of the kids she was taking care of."

"Any idea where Sandra might have been when you spotted these situations?" Chloe asked.

"Probably somewhere else on the grounds helping with the Secret Santa games."

Chloe and Moulton remained quiet for a moment, both drinking their coffee. Chloe obviously could not read Moulton's mind, but she had a pretty good idea that they would be speaking to Bill Carver next. She knew he had been questioned by the police mainly because there had been an attractive woman in his house most of the time and the news media couldn't help but cause most people to automatically assume the worst. But then again, she could recall the little bit of time she had seen him while she and Rhodes had been at their house. He had seemed in shock, sure. But had there been some other underlying emotion, something that had made him seem uneasy?

The more she thought about it, the more she thought there might have been.

"Is there anything else you can tell us about Kim?" Moulton asked.

"Nothing that I haven't already said. She really was a fine young woman. I think the fact that she left her potential political job in this miserable town in order to take care of kids speaks volumes about her. She was always smiling, always willing to help."

"Did she ever mention any boyfriends?" Chloe asked.

"Not to me, no. But again, we never had any truly deep conversations."

Chloe and Moulton shared a glance, to which Moulton nodded. He sipped from his coffee once more before slowly getting to his feet. "Thank you so much for the coffee and the time, Ms. Duplin," he said.

"Of course. Not a problem. I hope I was of some help."

"All information is some sort of help," Moulton said.

Chloe gave Madeline a smile as she also took a final sip of coffee. She and Moulton headed for the exit as one of the two tables that had been occupied started to clear out. They didn't speak until they were back outside.

"You think Bill Carver and Kim were sleeping together?" Moulton asked.

"I think it's dangerous to assume such a thing. But then again, a woman that would be involved in something like that… it might not take too much more of a leap to end up being involved with someone like Mike Dillinger."

"Both of the Carvers are still at home. They're keeping their kids home from school for a few more days to make sure they're adapting well. Kim's funeral was supposed to be this afternoon, but the lack of evidence to help find her killer has the coroner wanting to delay it."

"Seems like bad timing to talk to him now."

Moulton shrugged. "Or perfect timing. At the risk of seeming like an ass, he'd be vulnerable."

"That *is* an ass-like thing to say," she said. "But it's true. I say we go."

"I'm glad you said it first," he said with a sly smile.

And when he turned away to get into the car, Chloe let out a heavy sigh. That smile and the way he carried himself—if she didn't get a grip on her little crush soon, she might be in a world of trouble.

⚜ ⚜ ⚜

Chloe wasn't sure what she had been expecting when they arrived at the Carver house, but it certainly wasn't what she saw when Bill Carver answered the door. He looked positively haunted. There were dark circles around his eyes and he looked as if he had not slept in quite some time. He looked back and forth between Chloe and Moulton, taking a while to realize that he did indeed know these two people.

"Agent Fine," he said distantly. "And ... Milton, right?"

"Moulton," Agent Moulton corrected. "Mr. Carver, do you have a moment to speak with us?"

He nodded and invited them in. The house was quiet and somber. Chloe could hear the soft thudding of footsteps somewhere upstairs as Bill led them into the living room.

"Is everyone home right now?" Moulton asked.

"Yes," Bill said. "Sandra is upstairs with the kids. They've never been to a funeral before and she's trying to prep them. They heard us talking about how it is still going to be a few more days and were curious."

"That might be for the best," Chloe said. "Mr. Carver, we need to ask you some very frank questions. Some that might make you quite angry."

His shoulders slumped and he looked back and forth between them again. Chloe could read it in his eyes; he knew this would come eventually.

"We have it on good authority," Moulton said, "that there have been moments in the recent past where you and Kim were seen together, alone. Most notably at the yacht club. Mr. Carver, I need you to be straight with me. Even if it was just one single time in a moment of weakness, I need to know if there was ever a physical relationship between you and Kim Wielding."

What came next was so anticlimactic that Chloe thought she'd heard Bill Carver wrong at first.

"Twice. About three weeks apart."

"Was one of those instances sometime around the Christmas banquet at the yacht club?" Chloe asked.

Bill nodded.

"Does your wife now?"

His mouth turned down, not into a frown but into a look of annoyance. "I think she maybe has a suspicion. She's never asked and I certainly never told her. I don't think Kim ever did, either. But ever since she was killed… I think maybe she has an even stronger suspicion."

"What was the relationship between the two of you like?" Moulton asked.

"We were always very friendly. She was working for us for more than a year and a half before anything ever happened. We had a drunken kiss during the Fourth of July last year, which we both profusely apologized for the following week. The first time we slept together was the night of the banquet you mentioned. It was quick and spontaneous—nothing planned. It happened in the employee bathroom at the yacht club's dance hall. The second time was in February. Here, in the house. In the kitchen."

"You seem to be taking it hard for just an occasional sexual relationship," Chloe said. "Did you care for her in other ways as well?"

"Yeah. For a while, I really did. She was such a good person, you know. So good that it makes me wish those things had never happened—that we'd never had sex …"

"On the day she was murdered, you were away on business, correct?" Chloe said. She knew this was correct but wanted to be sure he wasn't altering his story in any way.

"Yes. In Chicago. I originally had two more days left but obviously came home early."

"And what about a man named Mike Dillinger? Does that name sound familiar? Maybe you heard Kim mention the name in passing?"

"Not that I can remember."

"Mr. Carver," Moulton said, "do you happen to know if Kim did any drugs?"

The question seemed to shock him, almost enough to make him seem partially awake. "I don't think so. If she did, she hid it very well. Of course, I'd be the last person she'd tell since we'd employed her as a nanny."

Moulton looked at Chloe and raised an eyebrow. It was yet another way that she could tell that, if given the chance, they'd work well together.

They could communicate with all these little non-verbal cues. That raised eyebrow seemed to say: *Anything else?*

She answered his eyebrow by saying, "Well, thank you for your time, Mr. Carver. You have my card from before, so I just ask that if you think of anything at all, please contact me."

"I will."

"And please let your wife know that we'd like to speak with her in the next few days. Maybe sometime after the funeral, though."

A voice from the entryway to the living room spoke up, freezing Chloe's heart for a moment. "Oh, no need to wait," Sandra Carver said. "We can talk now."

There was a look of disgust on her face, touched with hurt. Her eyes were brimming with tears and her arms were folded. Her eyes looked as if they might literally leap from her face and burrow into Bill Carver's heart.

That poor woman just heard everything, Chloe thought.

"Sandra…" Bill said.

She just shook her head. "We can talk in the kitchen," Sandra said, still looking at Bill but speaking to Chloe and Moulton.

And without waiting to see if either of the agents were following her, Sandra Carver turned her back and walked toward the kitchen. When Chloe and Moulton followed behind her, Chloe could hear the soft but powerful sobs as Bill Carver broke down.

Chapter Fourteen

Sandra waited a moment before saying anything. She stood at the kitchen bar, looking at both of the agents as a tired and annoyed look slowly filled her face.

"Don't look at me like I'm supposed to be all broken-hearted," Sandra said. "I never knew *for sure* until now. But he's right. I always suspected it. It was the way he looked at her every now and then when he thought I wasn't paying attention. And I just didn't question it."

"Can I ask why not?" Chloe asked.

She and Moulton were standing at the kitchen bar while Sandra sat at the table. She shrugged and started to nervously rub her hands together. "Because I don't think I've been all in on this marriage in a few years. He's a good enough guy—infidelity aside—but we just lost it. I almost don't blame him for screwing Kim. She was kind, loving, and gorgeous. I knew if I asked him about it, it would cause a fight. And a fight that big might lead to a divorce. And… I don't know. It's too messy. Not worth it."

"Would you say you two had a hostile relationship after you hired Kim?"

"No, not really. We just… I don't know. He slowly threw himself completely into work. He was a good enough dad to the kids and all but he wasn't really *here* even when he wasn't away on work. I lost respect for him after a while. And… Jesus, he even sort of stopped working in bed. He was diagnosed with some sort of erectile dysfunction two years ago. So I lost my desire for him along with my respect. But I guess Kim did it for him. Fixed his ED, I guess."

"Did you hear the entire conversation?" Moulton asked.

"I heard enough."

"Can you answer the same questions for us then?"

"You mean about the drugs? I can't see Kim doing drugs. I mean, I know everyone had secrets and all that, but Kim and drugs just wouldn't make sense to me."

"And what about Mike Dillinger?"

"No idea. Never heard that name. But you know, after Agent Fine and her other partner were here, I did start thinking about where you could maybe get some more information. I mean, I'm not thrilled that she fucked my husband behind my back but she still didn't deserve to die."

"And did you come up with something else?" Chloe asked.

"Maybe. There's another woman in the neighborhood that works as a part-time nanny. She's a younger woman. Mid-to-late twenties, I think. She works for the Damiani family. One of the Damiani kids is friends with our middle child, Declan. She and Kim would arrange playdates sometimes. Especially during the summer. They probably spoke at least twice a week. Kim spoke highly of her."

"What's this woman's name?" Chloe asked.

"Courtney Vedas. I'm pretty sure she's working for the Damianis today, actually. I imagine she might even attend Kim's funeral, though I'm not sure."

Chloe nodded as she took all of this in but in the back of her head, there was another track starting to pave itself out. *If she suspected that Kim and her husband were messing around, would* she *be capable of killing?*

It was a long shot, but not one that Chloe was willing to dismiss just yet. She made a mental note to check back in with Sandra Carver in the next day or so. With that, though, she ended their discussion.

"Mrs. Carver, I'm sorry you had to find out about your husband in such a way," she said. "Please let us know if you think of anything else. As for now, could we get the Damianis' address?"

Without saying anything, Sandra took a small stack of Post-its from a well-organized little basket at the edge of the kitchen counter. She scrawled an address on the top one and handed it to Chloe.

Sandra walked them to the door, not bothering to look in on her still-sobbing husband in the living room. When Chloe stepped out of the house, she felt as if someone had lifted a huge weight from her shoulders. Not only was she glad to be away from what was sure to be a very tense exchange between Bill and Sandra Carver, but another thought dawned on her.

Their day had started with a single lead at the yacht club—a lead that had turned into a promising conversation with Bill Carver. And while neither of those had really netted anything substantial other than Bill and Kim's affair, they had both resulted in a third lead. And considering it was barely past lunch yet, Chloe couldn't help but feel that they'd manage to wrap this case quickly, just like Director Johnson had been hoping.

CHAPTER FIFTEEN

When Courtney Vedas answered the door at the Damiani residence, she was carrying a baby in one arm and hoisting a laundry basket on her hip with the other. She looked out at Chloe and Moulton with a confused look. It was clear that she had not been expecting company, but the appearance of two complete strangers had thrown her off. She was very pretty and toned, her flat stomach showing slightly thanks to the high-cut T-shirt she was wearing.

"Can I help you?" Courtney asked.

"We're Agents Fine and Moulton," Chloe said. "We just spoke with the Carvers, trying to get some answers regarding the death of Kim Wielding. She suggested we speak with you, as you apparently had a few playdates between these kids," she said, nodding toward the baby with a smile, "and her own."

"Oh… sure, um, come on in," Courtney said. "But the place is a mess. It usually is on laundry day."

"How many kids do you keep?" Chloe asked.

"There are three of them. This is Amelia," she said, kissing the baby on the head. "The other two are upstairs, playing Fortnite."

She led them into a living room that was clearly the epicenter of laundry day. There were piles of clothes and towels on the sofa and the room's two recliners.

"Well, it's clear that you have your hands full," Moulton said. "So we'll make it quick. We know that there were playdates between the older kids where both you and Kim were sort of forced into interacting. How would you describe the relationship?"

"Friendly, I guess. Kim was never rude or anything, but when she didn't want to talk or be social, it was always clear on her face, you know?"

"How many times would you say the two of you spent any significant time together?" Moulton asked.

Courtney thought about it as she placed baby Amelia into a Pack 'n' Play against the living room wall. "Ten. Maybe twelve."

"Did she ever talk about boyfriends?"

"Not that I can remember. We did have one conversation about how finding a good man is next to impossible. We used to refer to it as a fairytale."

"Did you ever get the feeling that maybe she was in some toxic relationship?" Chloe asked. "Or maybe she was being abused?"

"No. If any of that is true, she never mentioned it around me."

"Do you know if she did drugs?" Chloe asked.

"Again … it never really came up. The most I know for a fact she ever did was drink wine. She told me a story one time about smoking pot for the first time in high school but that's it."

"Do you know if she had any close friendships with the other neighbors?"

"I don't think so. She was really only ever in the neighborhood when she was watching after the Carver kids. Which was a lot."

"Well, let's say Kim was the type to keep secrets," Chloe said. "If you thought she might have some secret life, is there anyone in the neighborhood or even just good friends with the Carvers that might have been a part of it?"

"Well, there's Mr. Hall two streets over—he's a bachelor at the age of fifty and doesn't make a secret of having a different woman living with him almost every month. Kim and I joked about how skeevy and gross he is all the time. There's also the hottie soccer coach from the middle Carver kid's soccer team but he …"

"What is it?" Moulton asked.

"Sorry. Random thought," Courtney said. "You know … Kim spent a lot of time at the library. She took the kids to this reading group. And one of the Carver kids—I'm not sure which one—was in some Lego group that held meetings there. She went to the library a *lot*. She'd tell me about conversations she had with one of the librarians."

"Do you know which one?"

"Shelby something… not sure about the last name. I got the sense that they were pretty close. I bet she'd be the person you need to talk to. As I understand it, the women at the library are pretty bad gossips, too."

"That's a huge help," Chloe said.

"Is there anything else you can think of?" Moulton asked.

"I don't think so," Courtney said. She started folding a pair of jeans and then looked over to Amelia again. "I have to say, though… this neighborhood. This community. It's the same as anywhere else just like it. Pretty houses, well-to-do people. It all looks good on the outside, but there's just… *crap* under it. Affairs and spousal abuse and tax-cheating. A bunch of fakes, you know?"

Chloe nodded and said, "Do you think that would include Kim?"

Courtney seemed to think hard about this for a moment. Chloe was nearly convinced that she was choosing not to answer the question before she responded with: "I'd like to think not… but who the hell can even tell anymore?"

The library in question was just a fifteen-minute drive outside of the Carvers' subdivision. It was a small but beautiful building, complete with a back lawn filled with trees, chairs, and picnic tables. When Chloe and Moulton got out of the car and walked toward the doors, there was a small reading group of toddlers sitting on a blanket, listening to an older woman read.

They walked in through the front sliding doors and for a moment, Chloe was transported back to her middle school years—specifically during the summers, when she'd opted not to spend time with friends or family, instead retreating to the public library and losing herself in old Sherlock Holmes novels. The smell of books and overworked printers brought it all back to her.

They approached the check-out desk, where two women were stationed behind computers. The woman on the right looked up to them as they approached, giving a tired smile. "Can I help you?"

"We were hoping to speak with a librarian named Shelby," Chloe said. "Not sure of a last name."

The other woman at the second computer spoke up, her voice a little uncertain. "I'm Shelby Wickline. The only librarian here with that first name."

Chloe approached her side of the check-out desk and kept her voice low. "We're Agents Fine and Moulton with the FBI," she said quietly. "We were told you'd spoken with Kim Wielding a few times during her tenure as a nanny for the Carver family."

"That's correct," she said, a small little frown touching the corners of her mouth. Chloe guessed the woman to be in her forties but the frown made her look much older.

"Could we speak to you in private?" Moulton asked.

Shelby gave the other librarian a perplexed look, to which the other librarian nodded. "Sure," Shelby said. "We can speak in the conference room in the back."

Shelby came out from behind the desk and led the agents to the back of the library where three doors sat along the back wall. She opened the door to the middle one, taking them into a small room that was mostly occupied by a table and several chairs.

The moment Chloe had closed the door behind them, Shelby asked, "Do you know who did it yet?"

"We don't," Chloe said. "That's why we're here. We were hoping some of the conversations you'd had with her might lead us closer to a suspect."

"Oh," Shelby said, clearly deflated. "Well, she really wasn't the type to share too much personal information."

"Did she ever mention a man named Mike Dillinger?"

Shelby thought about it for a moment and then nodded slowly. "I think at one time she *did* mention seeing a man named Mike. I'm pretty sure it was nothing serious, though."

"No details on him at all?" Moulton asked.

"Not that I can remember."

"Do you know if she had any other romantic relationships while she was working for the Carvers?" Chloe asked.

"If she did, she never mentioned them."

"What about Bill Carver? Did you ever suspect anything between the two of them?"

"I personally never did. But…well, you know these sorts of neighborhoods."

"Could you elaborate on that?" Chloe asked, thinking instantly about how Courtney Vedas had made a similar comment.

"Well, the Carvers lived in that really well-to-do subdivision. And it's like something out of a really bad soap opera if the rumors and gossip are to be believed."

"Did you ever hear any gossip about Kim?" Moulton asked.

"No. Which is odd. She was a bit older—mid- to late thirties, I believe—but incredibly pretty. And single. That would have made her ripe for the picking when it came to the grapevine. But I never heard anything about her."

"What about the Carvers?"

"Well, rumor had it that Bill Carver was clearly sleeping with other women while he was traveling for work. He was always known to be something of a flirt. But I know the Carvers. I don't see Bill as being the type to cheat on his wife."

You apparently aren't a very good judge of character, then, Chloe thought.

"Is the library generally a place where gossip is shared?" Moulton asked.

Shelby chuckled and nodded. "Absolutely. You have a bunch of stay-at-home moms that have their kids involved in all kinds of activities. Throw in a retired grandmother or two and it can get pretty toxic."

"Can you think of anything you've heard in the last year or so that might have directly affected the Carvers or Kim Wielding?" Chloe asked.

"Not right off the top of my head, no. I suppose of there *was* any truth to the rumors of Bill having an affair, there's a chance that Kim might have known about it."

Chloe slid one of her business cards across the table to Shelby. "In the following days, if you think of any other information, please let us know," she said.

"I will." She plucked up the card and considered something for a moment. "You know, I may be reaching here, but something seemed a little off with Kim the last time I spoke to her."

"How long ago was this?" Moulton asked.

"Three weeks or so. She seemed sort of moody. Depressed, even. And that was not something I had ever seen out of Kim. She was usually always full of smiles and laughter. I remembered thinking she seemed sad about something that last time…"

Maybe that was when she was starting to realize her mistake of being involved with Mike Dillinger, Chloe thought.

"Any feeling as to what it might have been that was bothering her?" Chloe asked.

"No. And… well, shame on me, but I never even bothered to ask her."

And with that, Shelby looked down to the table as a tear trickled out of her eye, thinking about things she should have said, perhaps.

A shift in mood three weeks before she was murdered, Chloe thought. Either something had happened in her personal life or something in her life had been starting to change. Had she been developing feelings for Bill Carver that went beyond their two romps? Or was she perhaps starting to regret giving up a career in DC for a life in suburbia with kids that weren't even her own?

Suddenly, based solely on the dead-end conversation with Shelby Wickline, there were many new unanswered questions. And with the trail growing colder and colder, Chloe started to feel that if some of them weren't answered very soon, the trail would come to an end, with no killer at the end of it.

Chapter Sixteen

The day came to an end with no leads and no real hope. Thinking back on it later, Chloe supposed that was why she wasted very little time when she and Moulton arrived back in DC. Chloe didn't even bother grabbing anything to eat for dinner before getting in her car and making the drive to Reston, Virginia.

She'd obviously not liked the way the last conversation with Danielle had ended. And she knew if she stayed in her apartment by herself with no leads on the Wielding case and no resolution with Danielle, she'd overthink everything. Never one to leave things lying dormant, Chloe made the drive with little hesitancy. Besides… she wanted to see her sister thriving in her new position with responsibilities and the stress that came with them.

When she parked in front of the bar—a place called Vexes—she noticed right away that it was a trendy place. Even before she opened the door to go inside, she saw the lighting was very dark. Odd electronic pop music was playing at a low volume, a mixture of melody and glitchy beats.

There was a large lounge area that was sparsely populated, connected to a more traditional restaurant setting. An elaborate bar separated the two areas, lined with light blue ambient lighting. There were only a few people sitting at the bar and there, behind it with her back to Chloe, was Danielle. She was fitting a spout on a keg of beer beneath the bar.

Chloe approached the bar and sat down like any other patron would. When Danielle was done fixing the spout, she looked up and laid eyes on her new patron. She smirked as she walked over to her sister.

"What'll it be?" she asked.

"Whatever you feel you make the best," Chloe said.

"I make a mean mojito."

"I'll have one of those, then. And a few minutes of your time, if you can manage it."

Danielle grabbed a glass and a few bottles from the rack at the center of the bar. "There's a little table in the back of the lounge area," she said. "I'm pretty sure it's open. Go grab it for us and I'll be there in five minutes."

Chloe did as she was asked, a little disappointed at the lack of excitement Danielle had showed at her appearance. Sure, there had been some shock in her smirk, but that had been about it. Chloe had thought that after working together to uncover what had truly happened to their parents, things might finally be mended between them. But now Chloe had to face the fact that it might have only served as a temporary solution—a solution that was already falling apart.

She found the table in the back of the dimly lit lounge area and sat down. She looked around the place and decided the darkened atmosphere, peculiar music, and borderline modern appearance of the place fit Danielle rather well. She knew why she was here and knew where the conversation would eventually end up. The trick, of course, was to approach that topic without pissing Danielle off before anything was resolved.

Danielle appeared in the darkened lounge a few minutes later, Chloe's mojito in one hand and a beer in the other. She sat down at the other side of the table, sliding the drink over to Chloe.

"It's good to see you," Danielle said. "Sorry if I bitched you out on the phone the last time we spoke."

Chloe shrugged and took a sip of the drink. It was very good—the sort of alcoholic drink with enough bite to make sure you drank it slow but smooth enough to make you want to savor it.

"It is what it is," Chloe said. "This is a nice place. How does the assistant manager role suit you?"

"Not too shabby. So long as I stay behind the bar, I don't get tasked with too many of the manger shit. The owner and manager is a pretty cool guy. I think he has a crush on me, which works in my favor."

"He won't slap your wrist for having a drink with your sister while you're on the clock?"

Danielle shrugged. "I'm on break. And he's not here tonight. But I should tell you, I can't chat long. I do need to get back to work soon. The other tender on the schedule tonight is an idiot. But we keep her on because she's insanely hot, knows how to work cleavage like a fucking savant, and keeps men at the bar well into the night."

"Danielle... look, I hate to do it but—"

"But you're going to ask questions about Dad. And keep bringing him up. Right? I figured that's why you'd show up unannounced."

"It's not as simple as all of that," Chloe said.

"I know. It never is. It never *was.* I just thought you were always the stronger of the two of us, you know? It pisses me off that he still has such a hold on you."

"I don't exactly like it, either."

Danielle shrugged as if she honestly couldn't care less and took a very large gulp from her beer.

"I keep trying to pull memories out of my head," Chloe said. "But no matter how hard I try, I can't remember any time when Dad was abusive to Mom. Can you?"

Danielle looked at Chloe as if she were stupid. "Are you for real? I saw him get rough with her at least three times. One of them was an out and out right-handed punch to her stomach."

This was all news to Chloe. It felt like *she* had been punched in the stomach. She'd never seen anything like that from her father. Yes, she'd seen their father get angry from time to time—especially at their mother—but never any form of physical abuse.

"It doesn't surprise me that he would make sure to never do such a thing in front of you," Danielle said. "You were something special to him for some reason. He liked you better than me... I don't think that's some big secret. Maybe he made sure that you never saw it. But I sure as hell did."

"So why are you telling me now? Why not months ago when we were uncovering the truth?"

"Because you had this fake view of him. I didn't see the need to pile more shit on the pile. But now... Jesus, Chloe. If this is what it takes for you to let it go, I can keep going if you want. The man was a monster as far as I'm concerned ... even if he *didn't* kill our mother."

It then occurred to Chloe that perhaps Danielle's anger at the mere mention of their father didn't come out of some sort of entitled anger, but a protective love for her older sister.

"Is that why you flipped out when I told you I went to see him?" Chloe asked. "Because you want *all* ties to your life cut off from him? Including me?"

"Partially. That and I hate the fact that you never quite saw the monster I saw. You were always more forgiving. I worried that the longer you stayed around him, the better the chance was that you'd have your heart broken. And that's why it irritates me even now that you won't just cut the bastard from your life."

"He says there's evidence that could get him out of prison sooner."

"Of course he's saying that! Anything to thread you along—anything to make him seem like the victim. Chloe ... I hope you're not this blind in your work. If you are, you don't have much of a career ahead of you."

Chloe winced at the low blow but couldn't help but wonder if Danielle was right.

"Danielle ... did he ..."

"What?"

"Did he hurt *you*?"

Danielle said nothing. She just sipped from her beer and looked at her sister as if she was learning how to speak to her all over again.

"Would it matter?" Danielle asked, getting up. She then did something that took Chloe by surprise. Danielle hugged her and kissed her cheek. It was the most affection she had seen from her sister since she had walked back into her life about a year ago.

"Drive safely back home, sis," Danielle said. "The drink is on me."

And then she headed back to the bar, ending their brief visit almost as soon as it had begun. Chloe watched her go, noting that Danielle had not really answered her question.

Did he hurt you?

But maybe, Chloe thought, no answer was the strongest answer of all.

Chapter Seventeen

The next morning, Chloe was behind the wheel of a bureau car, once again headed back into Bill and Sandra Carver's neighborhood. Most people were headed out to work with coffee cups and packed lunches at their side as they headed out to their cars. The morning was pretty enough, a thin layer of mist blanketing the yards as the air grew warmer.

"Places like this always creep me out," Moulton said from his place in the passenger seat.

"Why is that?" Chloe asked.

"I think Courtney Vedas summed it up perfectly. Nice houses, nice lawns, but people with such messed up secrets and ambitions. It's like peeling back the pretty wallpaper of a bedroom and finding cockroaches and mold."

"Cheerful," she said.

He smiled thinly. "I grew up in a place like this. I never really liked it."

"Clearly."

She didn't like that any conversation that didn't directly involve work seemed to be forced or strained between them. It made her feel as if he could sense the crush she had on him—a crush she honestly wished she could just ignore. It made her feel immature and a little unprofessional.

She ignored the tension and pulled past the Carvers' house. The plan of the morning was to meet with the Carvers' neighbors. It felt like a stretch yet as she parked the car in front of the neighboring home, she saw a man sitting on the porch; it almost seemed as if he had been waiting for them to come. As Chloe and Moulton stepped out of the car and started up the sidewalk, she took note of the name on the mailbox: Schwartz.

As they neared the porch steps, the man on the porch stood up from the rocking chair he had been sitting in and looked at them with concern. "Can I help you?" he asked.

Moulton showed his badge, taking the lead. "Agents Moulton and Fine, FBI," he said. "We're looking into the death of Kim Wielding. Being that you live next door to the family she worked as a nanny for, we thought you might have some information to help us along."

The man offered his hand, though he looked uneasy. Moulton shook it, as did Chloe. "David Schwartz," he said. "And unfortunately, I don't know how much help I'll be."

He took his seat again. A small table sat by the rocking chair, holding a cup of coffee, a Bible, and a notebook.

"Well, we're honestly just looking for anything you can share with us about Kim or the Carvers," Chloe said. "Did you know Kim?"

"I knew who she was. We were on a waving basis."

"Do you have a wife?" Moulton asked.

"Yes. She left for work about ten minutes ago. But she was on the same waving basis as I was. We know the Carvers, of course, but we aren't exactly friends. We'll both borrow small things from time to time like most neighbors do, but that's about the extent of it."

"Can I get your honest opinion about your neighbors?" Moulton asked.

"They're fine, I suppose. If I'm being one hundred percent honest, I never really fully trusted any man that can spend so much time away from home because of work, though. And from what I gather, Bill is gone quite a bit. Which I suppose is why they needed the help of a nanny."

"How about Kim?" Chloe asked. "You say you barely knew her, but did you ever see her speaking with anyone else in the neighborhood?"

"Yes, a few times. There's a gay couple that lives a few streets over. She would chat with them if they happened to walk by. This gay couple... they're really big into fitness. Always running or walking."

Whenever he said *gay*, it seemed to pain him. Chloe looked at the Bible and wondered if there was a direct correlation.

"Do you know their names?"

"Andrew and Collin Dorsett. They live in the third house from the end of the block over on Hyde Street. I'm pretty sure they both work from home, so you could probably speak to them this morning."

Chloe had to bite back the words that came to mind, instead leaving them as nothing more than a thought. *Keeping your watchful eye over the gay couple, I see.*

"Would you say that the Carvers seemed like a happy family?" Chloe asked.

"From a distance, sure. They have some really good-looking kids. Polite, too. Just like any other family in this neighborhood, they seemed well put-together. Like they had the world right there at their fingertips. But again, I didn't know them well. They could have been hiding things, you know. Most people do."

Chloe and Moulton nodded. Moulton then gestured to Schwartz's coffee and Bible. "We'll let you get back to your quiet time," he said. "Thanks for your time, Mr. Schwartz."

"No problem," he said, resuming his seat in the rocking chair. "God bless."

Chloe and Moulton returned to their car. When Chloe was back behind the wheel, she looked back up at Mr. Schwartz, already back to his Bible.

"You look like you don't trust him," Moulton said.

"Oh, I think he's telling us the truth. I don't doubt anything he said. But the way he had to force the word *gay* seemed a little off-putting."

"Well, you saw the Bible, right?"

"I did. But I was trying not to assume one thing equated to the other."

"I grew up in rural North Carolina," Moulton said. "Trust me … the majority of the time, those two things *do* go hand in hand. Now … let's go visit Mr. Schwartz's gay friends."

They smirked at one another, the tension now gone, as Chloe headed to the end of the street and took a right onto Hyde Street.

⚜ ⚜ ⚜

Andrew and Collin Dorsett did indeed both work from home. When Chloe knocked on the front door of their home, it was answered within ten seconds by a tall handsome man carrying a small laptop in his opened palm. Somewhere in the house behind him, another man was speaking to someone else, an empty space here and there indicating that he was on a phone call.

"Hello?" the man with the laptop said as he stood in the doorway.

"Are you Andrew or Collin Dorsett?" Chloe asked.

"I'm Collin. Can I ask who you might be?"

"We're Agents Fine and Moulton with the FBI," Chloe said. "We're looking into the death of Kim Wielding and are trying to talk to anyone that night have spoken with her in the past few weeks or so."

Collin frowned as he stepped to the side to allow them inside. "God, that was terrible what happened to her."

"So you knew her well?" Moulton asked.

"Pretty well, sure."

"She ever talk about any ex-boyfriends?" Chloe asked.

Collin led them into the kitchen. He set down his laptop and poured himself a cup of coffee from a very expensive-looking coffeemaker.

"Not that I can remember. Coffee?"

Moulton shook his head, but Chloe accepted a cup. As Collin poured it, Andrew entered the kitchen. He was shorter than Collin but just as equally handsome. He was in a T-shirt and joggers, looking inquisitively at their visitors.

"These are FBI agents," Collin explained as he handed Chloe her coffee. "They're asking about Kim. You don't ever remember her talking about boyfriends, do you?"

"I don't think so. She was fairly talkative but I don't ever recall her talking about men."

"Do you know what her relationship with the Carvers was like?" Chloe asked.

"She talked highly of them," Andrew said.

"And she loved those kids," Collin said. "She was crazy protective over them. So I guess that means she liked Bill and Sandra well enough, too."

"Did either of you pick up on any vibes that there might have been something going on between Kim and Bill?"

"It's funny that you say that," Andrew said. "I said it as a sort of dirty joke one day … about how it had to be tempting for a married man to have someone as pretty as Kim around. And she got pretty uncomfortable."

"Did she ever reveal anything at all personal to either one of you?" Moulton asked.

"Not much. She told us some old stories about her time in DC. About how she once had dreams of being a speech writer or something like that."

"Did she ever provide any names of the people she worked with?" Chloe asked.

"If she did, I didn't pay attention," Andrew said.

"Same here."

Chloe was growing frustrated with the lack of progress. She hated to ask vague or directionless questions, but she was quickly running out of ideas. "The last few times you spoke with her, was there *anything* that stuck out to you?" she asked.

"I don't think so," Andrew said.

"I don't know how specific you're going for," Collin said, "but I do remember her saying she didn't feel too well the last time we spoke with her. It was just in passing, like it usually was."

"Oh yes, I remember that," Collin said. "She said she was feeling very tired. She had made a doctor's appointment because of it."

"She was pretty sure she had a urinary tract infection or something, too," Andrew said. "She said she had woken up several times the night before to go to the bathroom."

"She didn't elaborate on that?" Moulton asked.

"No. I suppose it's not the sort of thing that makes for great casual conversation."

"Let me ask you something," Chloe said. "A gay couple in a neighborhood like this. You guys ever get any hostility from anyone?"

The two men looked at one another and shrugged, almost perfectly in sync. "I wouldn't say we've ever experienced anything hostile," Collin said. "But we do get the occasional looks of muted disgust when we're out walking and holding hands."

"And we did find a flier on the windshield of our car about how homosexuality is a sin," Andrew added. "But we found that funny, not threatening."

"How about the Carvers? Did you know them well?" Moulton asked.

"Not very well," Andrew said. "There was one day where we were walking by their house and one of their kids asked us to toss the football around for a bit. We did and when Sandra came out, we had the talk with her—that yes, we were a gay couple and not just roommates. She was cool with it. A really nice lady, actually."

"One more question," Moulton asked. "And it might sound a little obscene, but we're just trying to narrow our focus. If there was anyone in the neighborhood that you could see Kim being involved with—maybe a secret affair or just a friendship she might want to keep hidden—who would you single out?"

Collin smiled as a thought came to him. "I'd probably say CJ Jackowski. He lives back on Whitehurst Street. A thirty-something bachelor. I think he's been married before. He's a doctor at one of those doc-in-a-box places in town. But he also volunteers as a soccer coach for two youth leagues. And I don't mind saying in front of my beloved husband that the man is extremely hot. And he knows it."

"No offense taken," Andrew said, nudging Collin. "I'd consider leaving you for him."

Chloe remembered that Courtney Vedas had mentioned a hottie soccer coach but had never elaborated on it.

"Does he have a reputation in the neighborhood or something?" Moulton asked.

"No. It's just that damn near every woman—married or not—can't help but do a second-take whenever they pass by him. Kim mentioned once or twice that she thought he was good-looking in this shy sort of flirty way."

"One of the Carver boys was on one of his teams, right?" Chloe asked.

"I think so," Collin said.

"Thanks, guys," she said, taking a long gulp of her coffee. "For the info and the coffee."

"No leads, huh?" Andrew said.

"Nothing strong, no," Moulton said. "So if you think of anything else," he said, handing out one of his business cards, "please call us."

"Sure thing," Andrew said. "And I hope you find the bastard that did this. Kim was a sweetie. This is something I don't think anyone in the neighborhood saw coming."

"And honestly, I can pretty much tell you she didn't have any sort of connection to CJ Jackowski. But he knows everyone in this little subdivision. Mainly because everyone wants to know him. He's probably be your best source of information."

"Thanks," Chloe said as she and Moulton headed for the door. "I don't suppose you know whether or not Jackowski is working today, do you?"

"He is," Collin said. "He did his morning run early this morning. We passed by one another. He only does his run early on the days he works."

"Stalker," Andrew said.

Collin only shrugged. "Clinic Express," he said. "Out on Hightower Road."

"See?" Andrew said. "Stalker."

The two laughed at one another as Chloe and Moulton walked out to their car. And it was then, as Chloe looked out to the right, at the rows and rows of houses with green lawns and cute porches, that she realized just how like a maze it all was. It all looked the same, broken up by roads and turns, as if it had all been set up to trap you, to make you wonder if you had made the right turn in an effort to get out.

Chloe sat in the waiting room at Clinic Express, looking at the posters urging patients to get their flu shot right away. Moulton sat next to her, looking a bit uncomfortable. The receptionist had seen them and told them that she would send Dr. Jackowski out to see them as soon as he was free. That had been five minutes ago and Moulton had looked uneasy ever since.

"Don't like doctors?" she asked.

"I don't mind doctors. I just hate being in hospitals and doctors' offices when I don't have to be. Doctors are fine. It's the germs I hate."

"You're the type that has like three bottles of hand sanitizer in your glove compartment, aren't you?"

"No. Just one."

"Do you want me to see if I can get one of those masks for you before we speak to Dr. Jackowski?" Chloe joked. "Or maybe some sterile gloves?"

"Is that supposed to funny?" Moulton asked, though he himself was smiling.

About a minute later, the room leading back to the exam rooms opened up. A nurse poked her head out and said, as quietly as she could without drawing attention: "Agents?" And then she waved them toward the door.

She led them down a small hallway where three offices were located. She led them into the last one, where a man was jotting down notes into a pad. Chloe knew this was Dr. CJ Jackowski not only because the nurse had led them to him but because Andrew and Collin Dorsett had been right; the man was gorgeous. His face was perfectly chiseled and his hair was simple yet well kept. His blue eyes were like gentle pools staring up at them, his lips made for kissing.

He looked up from his notepad and shoved it to the side of the desk. There were no chairs in the office so Chloe and Moulton were forced to stand. Jackowski stood as well, leaning back against the edge of the desk.

"I've got to say," he said, "I've never had FBI agents come in here. My receptionist said you had some questions about a case?"

"Somewhat," Moulton said. "We're looking into the murder of Kim Wielding and were hoping you might be able to tell us something about her."

"She worked for the Carvers," Jackowski asked. "A nice woman from what I could tell."

"Yes," Chloe said.

"I didn't really know her. I only spoke to her a few times and it was always in passing. The longest conversation I had with her was at a party out at the yacht club and that wasn't very long at all."

"You were the soccer coach for at least one of the Carver kids, right?" Moulton asked.

"Yes. Declan. A pretty good soccer player, as a matter of fact."

"Did ever speak to Kim during practices?"

"No. She was always in a hurry to leave. It was sort of sad, really. She was the one that always brought him to practice. I don't know that Declan's dad ever made it to a single practice. Games, either. I would see Sandra—the mom—at a few games, but never the father. But Kim was always there with him."

"We were told by some people in your neighborhood that you'd be the person to come to if there was anything to be learned about anyone else in the neighborhood," Chloe said.

Jackowski sighed and shook his head. "I'm not sure how I ever got labeled as such. There was this thing a year or so ago where a woman in the neighborhood showed up drunk at my house. Sort of hit on me. I called the police on her when she wouldn't leave my porch. She's a single mom, so there was no angry husband or anything, but I guess she just labeled me as a gossip when word got out. But I never told anyone. When I learned that people thought I made it my business to know everyone else's business, I never really struck out to prove them wrong. No sense in starting more unnecessary drama, you know? Especially not in a small little subdivision like ours."

"The few times you *did* speak with Kim, did she share anything that might indicate that she was in some sort of trouble?"

"No. It was mostly just in-passing sort of things. Hi, how are you. Some weather we're having. That sort of thing." His mind seemed to wander for a moment and then he added: "But there was this one time …"

"What time?" Moulton asked.

Jackowski took a moment to draw up a memory. As it came to him, it seemed to alarm him a bit. "There was this one morning when I was out for a run…probably around seven or seven thirty. I passed by the

Carvers' house and saw Kim sitting in her car, parked in front of the Carvers' house. She was speaking really animatedly to someone on the phone. Not yelling or screaming but clearly upset about something. I didn't want to seem nosy, so I just ran on by instead of waving or stopping to say hello like I usually would have. I do remember thinking that it was hard to picture Kim being upset about *anything*."

"I take it she had something of a good reputation around the neighborhood?" Chloe asked.

"For sure. She was so good with those kids. And everyone seemed to like her. Which is why I was so shocked when I heard that she had been killed."

"And because you didn't know her all that well," Moulton said, "can we assume you wouldn't have any idea who might have killed her?"

"Sorry, but no."

"Did she ever visit you here, as a doctor?" Chloe asked.

"No. I can check the records to see if she ever came in and saw someone else. But I'd assume she probably saw some other doctor. Most patients that come into a place like this have little to no insurance."

"Well, thank you for your time," Chloe said.

"Sure. Let me know if there is anything else I can do to help."

When they exited his office, she felt like they were closing a door behind them. They had come across no solid leads, no clues, *nothing* that was bringing them even remotely close to finding Kim Wielding's killer.

Not the result I want on my first case, Chloe thought. *There has to be something we're not seeing. Something we're missing.*

It made her think of her father and how they'd thought that case had been so simple from the beginning but then, years later, they'd found that her father had *not* been guilty of murder—that there had been another woman involved all along. It had felt like there had been some added part to the story, years later.

So what part of Kim Wielding's story isn't being told?

It was a good question, and she thought the answers they were looking for could be found there. The trick, of course, was knowing where to look.

Chapter Eighteen

With no clear leads and no avenues to pursue, Chloe and Moulton headed back to FBI headquarters. They arrived shortly after lunch and when they went their separate ways—each to their own office—Chloe found that she did not want to work solo for the rest of the day. Sure, maybe it was the crush working on her, but she found that her mind tended to be sharper when she was with Moulton. Also, the back and forth—which was, on occasion, a bit flirtatious—helped to stir conversation.

Instead, she found herself at her desk, pulling up every file the bureau had on the Kim Wielding case, most of which had come directly from the Maryland PD. There was nothing new, all details she had already read and started to commit to memory. Even when she viewed it through this new lens of trying to find nooks and crannies that might lead them to other parts of Kim's life that weren't apparent and obvious, Chloe could find nothing.

She was beginning to understand that Kim Wielding wasn't as prim and proper as she seemed on paper. What sort of connection did she have to Washington? Presumably, she'd been important enough to someone to warrant an investigation into the sort of murder case the bureau would usually not waste their time on.

She did somehow end up with a man like Mike Dillinger, she thought. *She can't be as squeaky clean as she seems.*

But no matter how much she pored over the files and her own case notes, she could not seem to become unstuck on the case. Just as she started to feel useless, she remembered something she had learned from one of her instructors while she had been attending the academy: *If you feel stuck on a case, start to dive into another one—even if it is one that has already been solved. You'd be surprised how well this works to push your lines of logic forward to anything else your mind might be occupied with.*

And as it just so happened, there *was* another case on her mind.

She pulled up the recent documents she had submitted in regards to her father's case. While the original files concerning her mother's death and her father's arrest had not yet gotten the digital treatment, she did have easy access to all of the notes she had gathered in finding that Ruthanne Carwile had had more to do with her mother's death than her father. But now, even with these notes painting a clear picture, there was the newest revelation that her father had provided—that there was a piece of evidence somewhere out there that could potentially free him of everything. A piece of evidence that could get him out of prison after all of these years.

Looking over the case files, Chloe suddenly couldn't stand to be sitting still at her cubicle. She went to the elevators and took a trip down to the basement level, where records spanning back as far as 1937 were tucked away in folders and old filing cabinets. As she walked along the aisles, there was something comforting about it all. Sure, having everything digital was convenient and foolproof, but there was something simple and beautiful about having hard copies of so many files and records neatly tucked away in tangible form.

She knew where the original files from her father's arrest were because she'd been down here months before as she and Danielle had holed up and pulled Ruthanne Carwile out into the light. She found the filing cabinet she needed within three minutes and pulled it open. The smell of old papers and neglect wafted up at her, as warm and familiar as an old library.

She pulled out the single folder on her father's arrest and the murder of her mother. She knew the only reason the file was even in the hands of the bureau was because of the child endangerment aspects the case had brought up. Although a federal agent had not touched the case until a week or so after her mother's funeral, even that slight involvement had been enough for a file to be created for the case.

She took the file with her back to the elevator and took it to her cubicle. Protocol told her than she needed to sign the file out but she didn't see the need. She'd only look at it for a while and return it. Besides, she didn't want to create an actual paper trail that would back up the fact that she could still not let go of the case—of her mother's death her father's seemingly wrongful arrest.

It wasn't exactly wrongful now, was it? she thought to herself. He willingly went to jail so that Ruthanne would not be convicted. Seems pretty fucking thought out and willing to me.

Of course, there was nothing in the file that surprised her. She knew it all by heart, the original report doing everything but saying that her father was out-and-out guilty. The picture had painted itself, even before Ruthanne Carwile had really come into the picture at all.

So there was one version of the story accepted as truth before Danielle and I uncovered he truth—about Ruthanne and the affair with Dad. That had been a little twist to the story ... a story that looked cut and dried from the start.

So where was that twist in Kim Wielding's story? There had to be one. The link to Mike Dillinger just made no sense. Not unless Kim had a dark side, no more immune to the lures and secrets of suburban life than anyone else in the Carvers' neighborhood.

She then remembered Collin and Andrew Dorsett mentioning that Kim had complained about a possible UTI. She wondered how much manpower would have to go into checking with doctors within a twenty-mile radius of the Carver residence for any doctors that Kim might have gone to. She pulled up an email and fired off the request to Assistant Director Garcia. It felt like a Hail Mary, but it was better than nothing.

As she returned her attention to the Kim Wielding case, the day rolled by slowly. She got confirmation from Garcia that he'd set someone to the task of checking with doctors in the Bethesda, Maryland area to see if Kim Wielding had set up any appointments within the past six weeks. It felt like very slow progress but it also made Chloe feel that she was doing her job with at least some degree of success.

As the day came to an end, Chloe started to dread going home to her apartment. She knew she'd have to buckle down and unpack everything else—to actually get her life started and in order. But feeling so stuck at a dead end on the Wielding case made the mere thought of unpacking and setting up unbearable.

She thought of Rhodes, stuck in a hospital bed and probably salivating over a chance like the one Chloe currently had. It made Chloe feel guilty, like she was not fully appreciating the fact that she was currently living her dream. It just so happened that this dream of hers had started with a case that seemed to have no leads or clues at all.

While thinking of Rhodes, Chloe's phone rang. She saw that it was Moulton and answered it quickly.

"Hey."

"Hey yourself," Moulton said. "I saw where you made a request to see if Kim ever made a doctor's appointment."

"Yeah. It's a shot in the dark, but one worth taking."

"You think if it *was* a urinary tract infection, it might have been caused by having sex? Maybe with someone *other* than Bill Carver?"

"I'm starting to wonder about that exact thing, although UTIs have several different causes," she admitted. "The fact that she was involved with Mike Dillinger in any sort of capacity is just mind-boggling. Makes me think she might have had some secrets we need to uncover."

"You want to see if we can start uncovering them over a drink or two this evening?"

The idea was certainly tempting, but Chloe knew that drinks with Moulton would only cloud her mind.

"Thanks for the invite, but I'm going to pass. I think I'm going to swing by the hospital and check in on Rhodes."

"A much more noble cause than getting buzzed over a case handing us our collective asses," Moulton joked. "Let her know I said hello."

"Will do. See you tomorrow."

She gathered up her things, sticking her files and laptop into her bag, and headed out. She had been working there long enough to know most of the faces, making very brief chitchat with some of the people she passed as others also made the five-o'clock journey to the parking garage. As she took the elevator down, she felt like she was forgetting something. It was a little itch at the back of her head, not too dissimilar to the feeling one gets when they think they might have left a light on at home before leaving for the day.

It was so fleeting that she had managed to ignore it completely by the time she got to her car. She spotted Moulton getting into his car and she couldn't help but wonder if he had decided to simply go on home once she had turned down his invite for a drink. The thought made her smile; it actually made her feel like a crush-stricken school girl. And she hated that.

She pulled out of her parking spot and headed to the hospital. Her thoughts were so preoccupied with Moulton and visiting Rhodes that the little itch of forgetfulness she had felt moments before was obliterated, not even a blip on her radar.

Chapter Nineteen

When Chloe entered Rhodes's hospital room, her old agent looked cranky and irritated. Yet when she set her eyes on Chloe, the thinnest of smiles spread across her face. She used the bedside remote to cut off the television, which had been showing an afternoon talk show.

"I heard Mike Dillinger was booked on sex crimes," Rhodes said, skipping the niceties.

"He was," Chloe said. She sat down in the visitor's chair against the wall, surprised at how natural it felt to be here with Rhodes. "He has nothing to do with the death of Kim Wielding, but he apparently had an ongoing list of deviant behaviors that he's managed to keep mostly hidden for several years."

"So we can count that as a success then," Rhodes said. "No killer, but we did bust a scumbag anyway."

Chloe smiled, surprised that she had not yet seen that silver lining among her feelings of failure. "What's the latest from the doctors?"

"Barring an unforeseen complication, I should be able to get out of here within two days. I'm getting headaches, but they say that's common for the amount of blood that I lost." She looked down to her hands, folded in her lap, and cleared her throat. "Which leads me to once again thanking you for saving my life."

"No need to thank me. I was acting on pure adrenaline. I think about using Dillinger's shirt as a tourniquet and I can't even recall when I got the idea. I was thinking without thinking, if that makes sense."

"Perfect sense. How about the case? Any breaks?"

"None. Which is ridiculous because in a neighborhood like that, a woman who messed around with someone like Dillinger should have tons of rumors circulating about her, right?"

"Maybe she just hid her secrets really well," Rhodes said. "Some women are pretty good at that."

"And it's so much easier to keep those secrets when you're dead," Chloe said.

"Have you started looking at the case with the assumption that Kim Wielding *was* keeping secrets?"

"No."

"Not to poke fun at you, but that's the Evidence Response Team in you. You're too concerned with looking for evidence that's probably not even there. For Violent Crimes, you have to assume the worst about people—sometimes even the victims. More often than not, there's a reason for violent crimes against people, no matter how skewed it might be."

"Yeah, but when the darkest thing in a woman's life is a relationship with someone like Mike Dillinger…"

"Then it seems like that would be a damned good place to start."

"We started there," Chloe pointed out. "His alibi on the night she was killed is airtight."

"But maybe he knows some of her secrets."

Chloe had considered it before but it was an idea that had lost its traction after Mike Dillinger had been arrested for other crimes following his interrogation about Kim Wielding.

She spent the next few minutes filling Rhodes in, right down to how Garcia had tasked someone with looking into potential doctors' visits in the weeks leading up to her death concerning a possible urinary tract infection.

"You ever had a UTI?" Rhodes asked.

"Once. It was miserable."

"You know how ladies tend to get them, right?"

"Sex."

"Exactly. Not always, but often. And really, is it so hard to believe that if a woman like Kim Wielding would sleep with the father of the family she worked for as well as a douchebag like Mike Dillinger, she might be venturing elsewhere for sex?"

It seemed so simple, like such an easy connection to make. Especially when she applied Rhodes's filter to it: assume people are not good from the start. Assume everyone is keeping secrets. But even if they did discover the doctor who treated Kim's UTI, where would that lead them? Probably nowhere.

"Let me tell you," Rhodes said. "If this case is not wrapped up by the time I get out of here and get back to work, you're never going to hear the end of it from me."

"Oh, I'm sure," Chloe said.

"They teamed you up with Moulton, didn't they?"

"Yeah. He's pretty sharp but there's this sort of relaxed quality to him that I think keeps him from being too attached to the cases."

"He's also fun to look at," Rhodes added. "Any tension there?"

"Um, no," Chloe said, hoping the red wasn't showing in her cheeks.

Rhodes cast her a look that indicated she wasn't so sure. "So... a potential UTI. That's the only lead?"

"For right now, yeah."

But Chloe's mind was starting to adapt to what Rhodes had suggested. What if Kim's darker secrets spread beyond Mike Dillinger and a few heated and spur-of-the-moment romps with Bill Carver? What else could she have been hiding?

And where might she have hidden those secrets?

Again, her thoughts went back to Mike Dillinger. At the start of the case, he seemed to stick out like a sore thumb, something that did not quite fit with Kim's life.

But as the case wore on, he didn't seem so out of place at all.

She wondered who else might have known about her relationship with Dillinger. The killer, perhaps?

And if so, how might they work toward ensuring Dillinger was eyed for the crime?

"You just had a thought, didn't you?" Rhodes asked with a smile.

"I did. A good one, I think."

"Care to share?"

Chloe got to her feet, throwing on her jacket. "I think I know where to look for Kim Wielding's car."

On the way to Mike Dillinger's apartment building, Chloe called up Bill Carver. When he answered and she identified herself, he did not sound very pleased.

"Can I help you?" he asked with just an edge of irritation.

"I have a hunch about where to find Kim's car. Would you happen to have a spare key?"

"No. Why would I?"

She decided to keep the crude comments to herself and instead asked: "Is Sandra there? Maybe she has a key?"

"No. She's spending some time with her sister in Alexandria in light of all that has happened."

Chloe shrugged to herself as she drove. Really, it was no big deal. She could request to have a police unit come by to pop the locks if need be. She thanked Bill for his time and then continued on to Dillinger's place.

She quickly ran a circuit of the block around the apartment building but did not find a license plate matching Kim Wielding's. She checked the two surrounding blocks and found nothing as well.

On the third street over from Dillinger's apartment, Chloe found it. Kim's car was parked in a public lot, out in plain sight. It was the kind of discovery that made her feel stupid for not having been able to find it before now. But she had not been alone. Two full days had passed without anyone else having located the car, either.

With no available parking spots, Chloe parked on the side of the street and walked through the lot to Kim's car. She was not at all surprised when she found it locked. She also noticed one of the tires was flat and wondered if that was the reason she hadn't driven to the Carvers' on the day she was killed. She spent the next half hour living through one of the few monotonous parts of her job. She placed a call to the local PD for police assistance to unlock the car. While she waited, she called Garcia to fill him on her discovery. She also called Moulton, who seemed a little too excited.

"How the hell did no one see it?" he asked.

"It's literally out in plain sight," she said. "Easily overlooked, I guess."

"What's it look like inside?"

"Just about as clean as her room at the Carvers' and her apartment. I'm honestly not expecting to find too much."

"So no need for me to come out?"

"I don't think so. I'll call if anything changes."

She ended the call just as a police cruiser pulled up behind her car. She watched as the policeman popped the lock and smiled at her. It was the sort of smile that seemed to say, *"See how easy that was?"*

She thanked him as she opened up the driver's side door. The policeman stayed there but hung back, as was protocol, to make sure everything was okay.

In the floorboard of the passenger side there was a long-sleeved hoodie. In the back, there were two paperback books and a pen on the seat. Feeling that this had been a waste of time—for both her and the policeman who was still watching—she popped open the glove compartment. She found an old iPhone charger, a few loose coins, and miscellaneous odds and ends such as paper clips, the vehicle's registration, and a drawing of what looked like a dog that had been signed by Madeline Carver.

Yet as Chloe dug through all of this, she saw something in the back of the glove compartment. Tucked away in the corner, partially hidden behind an old Chick-fil-A ranch packet, was a small plastic bag that had been balled up. Chloe pulled it out and found it folded into several sections, tied down with a rubber band. She pried the band off, unfolded the plastic bag, and found a very small amount of cocaine. It wasn't a lot at all, maybe just enough for Kim to grab a quick hit at the end of the day—or at the start of the day, for that matter.

She had no evidence bags on her (she was sure Rhodes would have, though, she thought with a smile) so she pocketed the bag. She then searched the rest of the glove compartment but found nothing else of interest.

The last places she checked were the little catch-all compartments along the bottoms of the doors. The driver's side was the only one that had caught anything. There wasn't much in it, just a few scattered things along the bottom. There were two balled up tissues, a crumpled Post-it note, and a few scraps of paper. She sifted the papers out onto the floor and straightened them out.

The Post-it read: **New PTA Time: 7:30. Tuesdays.**

Chloe put it back in the little catch-all compartment and went to the other scraps of paper. One of them was just as innocent. It read: **Fieldtrip to Apple Orchard, $7 due next Wednesday.**

But it was the last little scrap of paper that caught Chloe's attention. It wasn't a scrap of paper at all, but a receipt. It had come from Walgreens nine days ago. Three items had been purchased, paid for with cash: an Almond Joy candy bar, a box of Benadryl gel caps, and a First Response pregnancy test.

Chloe stared at the receipt in shock for a moment, as if it had practically handed her an answer and she wasn't quite sure what to do with it just yet.

It wasn't a urinary tract infection causing her to run to the bathroom so much, Chloe realized. She was pregnant. Or at least thought she was. And with even the threat of an unwanted pregnancy ...

Well, that created motive for a father who wanted to keep an affair secret.

Chloe grabbed the receipt and closed the car door.

"All good?" the policeman said.

"Yes, thanks."

But she was barely aware of saying anything at all. She was thinking of Bill Carver. And while it was an obvious jump to make, she had to remind herself of his alibi. There was ample proof that he had not been in Maryland when Kim had been killed.

So who then?

Chloe tucked the Walgreens receipt into her pocket and headed quickly for her car, thinking that if luck was on her side, there might be a way that she could find out.

Chapter Twenty

She dialed up Agent Moulton as she sped her car toward the coroner's office. The fact that they were holding on to the body because of lack of any leads was going to turn out to be extremely helpful. Of course, she had no idea how much longer they could hold the body. No more than another day or so, surely.

Maybe that would be all the time she needed, though.

Moulton answered on the second ring. "Find anything worth mentioning?" he asked.

"Yes. Did you go out for drinks?"

"Yes indeed."

"How many have you had?"

"I'm on my second."

"I need you to stop and meet me at the coroner's office."

"You get a break?" he asked.

"I don't know for sure." She filled him in on finding the receipt and making the somewhat educated leap that connected it to the conversation Kim Wielding had shared with Collin and Andrew Dorsett.

"Sounds like a safe bet to me," Moulton said. "I can be there in twenty minutes."

Chloe felt a stirring of excitement as those twenty minutes passed. She finally felt as if the case was getting somewhere, that she was finally getting a break. It also baffled her that something as basic as an old Walgreens receipt was all it had taken to get her feeling hopeful about the case again.

But even with this revelation, the fact remained that there was a very good chance that she had hindered the case herself by assuming things about Kim Wielding's personality. Now, realizing that Kim might very well have had more than one skeleton in her closet, Chloe felt they were almost starting over from scratch. She felt that if Kim had in fact been pregnant when she had been killed, they could not assume it was just from some well-to-do (yet cheating) man living in the Carvers' neighborhood. They had to assume she was just as likely to sleep with someone like Mike Dillinger as she was someone like Bill Carver.

She was thinking of Mike Dillinger and how a seemingly respectable woman like Kim Wielding might end up involved with him when she pulled into a parking spot in front of the coroner's office. She saw that Moulton had already arrived, locking up his car three spaces over. Chloe joined him and was taken aback at how happy she was to see him. She tried to convince herself he was just someone who could be present while she used this lead to crack the case, but she knew the truth. Try as she might, she just could not ignore how she really felt about him.

"You think this might be it?" he asked her.

"I don't know," she said. But it *felt* like movement. It felt like a catapult, actually. But she did not want to admit it.

"If it is, I'm *making* you come out for a drink."

"Sounds good. It's a date."

The smile he gave her pinged at her heart in a way that made her uneasy. It was almost enough to take away from the ball of excitement for the case that continued to roll downhill, gathering into a huge snowball that, she feared, might eventually engulf her.

Being that it was getting on past seven in the afternoon, it took a while for Chloe and Moulton to get a moment with the pathologist who had performed the autopsy on Kim Wielding. She was a tired-looking woman, rather mousy and irritated. After Chloe filled her in on the reason for their visit, the pathologist—Dr. Nancy Moreno, according to the receptionist who had gone back to find her—sighed deeply and looked at both Chloe and Moulton as if they were stupid. She stood several feet from them as they sat in chairs in the lobby. From her posture alone,

Chloe was quite sure that Moreno would not be inviting them back to where she worked.

"The autopsy was quite brief and to the point," Moreno said. "They usually are when they cause of death is so obvious. If a man gets brought in with a gunshot wound to the face, we don't spend too much time, for instance, looking into his bowel health at the time of his death."

"Yes, but we're not looking for something else that might have led to her death," Chloe said. "We need to see if she was pregnant at the time of her death. Is that possible at this stage?"

"It is."

"Is that not something that is regularly checked in the autopsies of women who are at optimal child-bearing age?" Moulton asked.

"No," Moreno said. "Not unless there is a reason to do so—perhaps if bloodwork showed signs of symptoms related to pregnancies."

"How soon can you check into this for us?" Chloe asked.

Again, Moreno looked irritated. "You say it could help crack a homicide case?"

"It could lead towards that, yes," Chloe said.

"Give me two hours. And please know that if she *was* pregnant but conception was less than three weeks ago, it may not be instantly traceable."

"Given that she was suspicious enough to go out and buy a pregnancy test, I'd say it was well beyond three weeks," Chloe said.

Moreno only nodded, still not inviting them beyond the lobby. "I'll let you know as soon as I have the results."

With that, Moreno turned and headed back the way she had come, through a set of double doors at the back of the lobby. Chloe and Moulton exchanged a sour look as the doors closed shut behind her.

"You ever dealt with a pathologist before?" Moulton asked.

"No. I hope they don't all have this disposition."

"So … I really wish I hadn't started drinking. Having to wait for two hours, it makes me want to go ahead and finish it off—to at least get a good buzz going."

"Maybe instead we come up with a list of potential fathers," she said with a teasing smile. "My bet is on Bill Carver."

"Not Mike Dillinger?"

"Probably not. Remember, I found that cocaine in her car. I don't think she'd mix business with pleasure. Of course ... who knows? I made the mistake of assuming she was too high-scale to get mixed up with people like Dillinger."

"Well, the good news is that if it *is* Dillinger, he's in prison now and we have easy access."

"And if she *is* pregnant, it may not necessarily mean much of anything," Chloe said, though she hoped it wasn't true. "If she lived the promiscuous lifestyle that it's starting to seem she did, there are far too many X factors ..."

This seemed to be the comment that set them both to delving into their own thoughts. Chloe hated to just sit there waiting for Moreno to come back with results but she also knew there was nothing else to do. Not until they had a definitive answer from Moreno.

Her thoughts wandered slowly from the Kim Wielding case to the file she had taken from Records earlier in the day. She tried to envision the naive little girl she had been when those reports had been filed away—when her father had been sentenced a lengthy prison stint that, it turns out, he was not solely responsible for. Her father's arrest had been what had set her dreams of one day working with law enforcement in motion but now it seemed like such a strange and jilted dream that she had nearly distanced herself from it.

"I doubt she told it all. If she chose to do so, she could tell her complete side of things and free me completely."

That comment about Ruthanne Carwile swam through her head, one of the things her father had said to her when she had visited him a few days ago. It made her wonder—much like Kim Wielding's case—what other branches of her father's story had not yet been revealed. What other skeletons did he have shoved deep into his closet?

"Fine?"

She snapped out of it when she heard her name. It was Moulton, still sitting beside her. "Yeah?" she asked.

"You looked zoned out there for a minute. You okay?"

"Yeah. My mind was just wandering. This case has me thinking of something else. Another case ..."

"Was it the one about your father?" he asked.

Her look of shock was apparently not hidden very well. Moulton cringed a bit and shook his head. "Sorry. But… well, I heard about how you helped to bust a woman a few months back—a woman that ended up being part of your father's case."

"You know about my father's case?"

"Just the basics," he said sheepishly. "Just the few things I've heard. Mostly about how you kept digging and managed to uncover the fact that the crimes your father was convicted of were not committed alone. It's pretty impressive, if you ask me."

The words *but I didn't ask* were on her lips but she swallowed them down. He was trying to pay her a compliment. The last thing he deserved was a shitty attitude from her just because she could not let go of her father's past.

"It was necessary for me to move on, I think," she said, surprised at her own truthfulness. "But I still can't completely move on."

"Yeah… family drama can be like that. I don't have it to those extremes, but I've had my fair share."

Before she could say anything else, the double doors swung open at the end of the lobby. Sure that there was no way two hours had passed, Chloe checked her watch. It had only been an hour and fifteen minutes since they had arrived and spoken to Moreno. She was either in a hurry to get rid of them or the results had been more apparent than she had suspected.

"You were right," Moreno said. "She was pregnant. About eight to ten weeks from the looks of it."

"Can you get a blood sample from the embryo for DNA testing?" Chloe asked.

"I already took a sample. We should have the result in about twelve hours. But… I assume you know that a DNA test won't do much good unless you have a DNA sample from the father to compare it to."

"Yes, I know," Chloe said. Still, she was sure that any refusal to take such a test—particularly on Bill Carver's part—would basically indicate his guilt. Or Mike Dillinger, for that matter.

"Thanks for your understanding and promptness in getting this done," Moulton said.

She nodded and replied, "I hope it helps."

Chloe and Moulton made their way to the exit, the parking lot having gone dark outside since they'd entered.

"Do you think it will make any difference?" Moulton asked her.

"I do. If the father knew she was pregnant, and he was very much afraid of this fact… that might give us motive. Especially in a neighborhood where people will do just about anything to keep a secret from being brought to light."

Chapter Twenty One

Director Johnson had gone home for the day, so it was Assistant Director Garcia who fielded Chloe's call. He sounded friendly enough when he answered the phone, a trait about the assistant director that Chloe was quickly getting used to. However, when she filled him in on their discoveries over the past few hours, he did not seem quite as pleased.

"Fine… you can't just go around ordering DNA tests without someone's approval. Namely mine or Director Johnson's. More than that… Jesus… Agent Fine, can you just come in first thing in the morning? We'll meet in Director Johnson's office. Bring Agent Moulton with you as well."

"I'm not sure I understand," she said. She was on the phone, still sitting in the coroner's parking lot with Moulton in her passenger seat. "If I crossed some sort of a line…"

"Just show up tomorrow morning. Director Johnson's office. Eight o'clock."

Garcia ended the call there, leaving Chloe to stare at her phone. She looked away from it and then to Moulton, a look of worry and disbelief on her face.

"What line did you cross?" Moulton asked.

"That's just it. I don't even know. The DNA test, I think. Or maybe coming to the coroner without getting permission first?"

"That doesn't seem right."

"Well, whatever it is, Garcia is asking that you also show up to an eight 'o clock meeting with me in Director Johnson's office tomorrow morning."

"Dragging me down with you, I see. Damn, Fine. You'll be the end of me."

He was doing his best to soften the situation but she could see his nerves showing in the thing smile he flashed her. And even in the shadow of that joke, Chloe wondered just how close to the truth he was.

Had she somehow managed to put not only her own career in jeopardy, but Agent Moulton's as well?

When she woke up at six the following morning, Chloe checked her email right away. Through half-blurry eyes, she saw that she had an email from the coroner's office, straight from Nancy Moreno. The mail was brief and to the point: *DNA sample taken from Wielding embryo. Results ready when there are parental samples available for comparison.*

Given Garcia's reaction on the phone last night, Chloe wasn't sure if this would even be worth getting excited about—much less worth mentioning.

She went through her typical morning rush, surprised with how calm she felt. She figured the meeting would go one of two ways: she was going to get heavily scolded, or she was going to be released. She honestly didn't think she would be released. In the back of her mind, she knew that she was only working in ViCAP because Director Johnson had seen something in her that made him want to move her from her original goal of the Evidence Response Team. She figured the worst he might do was to admit his mistake and move her back to the ERT.

Of course, it did no good to speculate. That was something she was starting to learn with each new twist and turn of her career. So she remained as calm as possible as she drove to headquarters, wondering how different her life might be—and Moulton's as well—within the next hour or so.

When she arrived at Johnson's office, his door was open. She wasn't sure why, but Chloe thought this might be a good sign. Apparently, he had not spent the morning with it closed, brooding and angry behind it. When she entered, she found Garcia and Johnson sitting on opposite sides of the small conference table in the back of the office. There were a few sheets of paper in a thin stack sitting in front of Johnson.

"Thanks for coming, Agent Fine," Johnson said. She could not tell from his tone or expression what kind of mood he was in.

As she took a seat at the table, Moulton came in behind her. He looked a little tense as he took the seat next to her.

"I'll make this as brief as possible," Johnson said. "Agent Fine, I understand that you moved on the Kim Wielding case last night, paying a visit to the coroner's office. Can you please explain the logic and thought behind this?"

"Yes, sir. One of the very few leads we were able to establish was that one witness had been in conversation with Ms. Wielding recently and she had divulged that she was having to use the restroom very frequently. This led us to think that she may have had a urinary tract infection. And since those are often spread through sex, we thought it might be worth looking into any sexual partners other than the ones we already knew about—Bill Carver and Mike Dillinger. So I placed an information request yesterday for any doctor's appointments Kim Wielding might have made in the weeks before her death, thinking maybe she would have mentioned the sex partner to the doctor.

"When I found Kim Wielding's car, I searched it and discovered a receipt from a drugstore, showing that Kim had purchased a pregnancy test before her death. That led me to the obvious conclusion that she could have very well been pregnant when she died. And if she was, that could potentially be used as motive if the father knew and did not want the secret out."

Johnson and Garcia shared a look that Chloe could not quite decipher. After a few seconds, Garcia spoke. "The pathologist reached out last night... not to turn you in, but just to give us a heads-up. Fine... for anything related to additional exams on a body that has already been turned over to the coroner, you need Director Johnson or myself to sign off on that. You can't just go in to whatever lead you think might be worth pursuing with guns blazing. Dr. Moreno should have known not to go through with the exam. We told her that much when she called."

"I'm confused," Moulton said. "If she didn't know that we needed your sign-off on it, why did she call at all?"

"She realized her mistake. And by the time she realized that Wielding had indeed been pregnant, she admitted that her anger got the best of her and she went ahead and ran all of the necessary tests."

"There's also the fact that even though we know she was pregnant," Johnson said, "there is no way to discern who the father is. Not unless any suspects submit to a blood test."

"Yes, sir. But I was thinking any man's adamant refusal at such a test might indicate guilt."

"That's a pretty sweeping assumption," Johnson said. "Tell me … now that you know she was pregnant, what is your next course of action?"

"I'd like to speak with Sandra Carver," she said, the idea coming to her out of the blue. "I can't help but wonder if she might have some thoughts on her former nanny now that she knows that her husband was occasionally sleeping with her. It only makes sense that a woman working as a nanny that would sleep with the father of the kids she was caring for, as well as a man with the habits of Mike Dillinger, was likely involved in some other secrets."

"That's a suitable place to start," Garcia said.

Johnson nodded in agreement and then looked at Moulton. "Agent Moulton, are you in agreement with this approach?"

"Yes, sir. There really haven't been many leads. We can't exactly be picky."

Johnson again nodded. "Agent Moulton, you're excused. Please wait outside for a moment."

Looking confused, Agent Moulton got to his feet and left Johnson's office. He closed the door behind him; it was the first time Chloe had felt at all uneasy or scared about the meeting.

"Agent Fine," Johnson said, "it appears that there are quite a few areas of protocol that you are apparently forgetting about."

"I'm sorry about the coroner," she said. "I will not let—"

"I'm beyond that. It was a necessary step that needed to be taken and I am willing to look past that so long as you follow protocol from now on. No, now I am talking about you taking files out of the archives and treating them as your own."

A shot of heat spiked through Chloe's body. *I forgot to put the file back, she thought, mortified. That was what the itching feeling of forgetfulness was all about yesterday.*

"Oh my God," she said, meaning every bit of the dramatic flair that went into her voice. "I forgot. I have it with me right now, in my computer bag. I didn't mean—"

Johnson waved the comment away, leaning forward in his chair. "Agent Fine, you are of course allowed to use any records within our archives, so long as it is for pertinent case work. As I understand it, the files you took yesterday were regarding your father's case. A case that has been closed for a while, despite recent discoveries made by you and your sister."

Before Garcia also chimed in, a single thought went through Chloe's mind.

How did they find out? Not only do they know I forgot to return the files, but they knew they were about my father.

Before she had time to even speculate, Garcia said: "We just want to be sure you are of a sound mind. We know your father's case is very close to you—especially since you came across all of that new information several months ago. But if it's something that is still haunting you, we can't have you working on active cases out in the field."

"I know. And I'm sorry. But I made the mistake of visiting him the other day and—"

"With all due respect, I don't need to hear about all of that," Johnson said. "I just need some reassurance that you aren't going to use your time as an agent to try to dig up the ghosts of your past."

It hurt Chloe to hear this, but she knew that he was right. And honestly, she had not even realized that this was what she was doing.

"Lastly," Johnson said, "I'm going to give you another forty-eight hours to wrap the Kim Wielding case. If there is no suspect by then, we may just remove the bureau from it, despite the favor that has been asked by Jacob Ketterman."

The look of dissatisfaction on his face at this made Chloe feel a little better. She nodded and opened up her laptop bag. She took out the file about her father and slid it across the table to Director Johnson.

"I am truly very sorry about this," she said. "And the coroner visit and test requests… I don't know. I honestly just didn't even think about it."

"Was it perhaps because you were too preoccupied with your father?"

"No," she said, perhaps a bit too sharply. Garcia seemed to flinch at it.

Johnson sighed and got to his feet. "I'll take your word for it," he said. "So please just prove it to me. That's all, Agent Fine. You're excused."

Chloe left right away, not wanting to give Garcia or Johnson another second to come up with anything else they did not find fitting about her performance. She closed the office door behind her and looked at Moulton, still sitting on the chair in the little waiting area outside the office.

"Are we fired?" he asked.

"No. But we now have two days to close this Wielding case or they're going to take the bureau off of it."

"I think your idea about reaching out to Sandra Carver is a good one. I think she might see it as a little too soon—you know, after discovering that her husband was cheating on her—but I don't see that we have any other choice. Just try not to get me into any more trouble."

"I promise nothing," Chloe said with a sly smile.

Her comedic attempt and the smile itself felt fake. Because now that she was on a timer, the case suddenly felt more elusive and impossible than ever.

Chapter Twenty Two

They drove out to Alexandria, having gotten the address for Sandra's sister from Bill. He did not seem too thrilled with the fact that Chloe and Moulton would be paying his wife a visit without him by her side, but Chloe was beyond caring what he thought. Truth be told, she was getting pretty damn tired of people and their secrets.

They arrived at the sister's house at 9:10. It was a very nice house, probably somewhere near a million dollars or so if the neighborhood was any indication. As they walked up the porch steps, Chloe couldn't help but wonder if this neighborhood held the same secrets and scandals as the Carvers' little subdivision.

She knocked on the door and was greeted with silence. She knew that Sandra Carver's job as a proposal coordinator for a military telecom company allowed her to work from home; the only times she needed to report to the offices in DC were for board meetings or when her company was wining and dining potential buyers. She also knew that, according to Sandra's schedule, she was not due for any such meeting for another two weeks. All that to say, she had nowhere to be. Which was good, given the blow her life had just taken.

Chloe nearly knocked again after twenty seconds of silence. But the door was finally answered. It cracked open a bit and a single tired-looking eye peered out.

"Haven't you assholes done enough?" Sandra Carver asked from behind the mostly closed door.

Chloe let the comment bounce right off of her. She also managed to say nothing about the fact that neither she nor Moulton had anything to do with her husband's unfaithfulness.

"We're sorry to bother you again," Moulton said, apparently picking up on Chloe's irritation. "But we've had some other news come to our attention and, if we're being totally honest, thought you might be the best and most brutally honest source of information."

Sandra thought this over for a moment before stepping out onto the porch. "It's not my house so I'm not inviting you in. What kind of news are you talking about?"

"We discovered yesterday from the coroner's office that Kim was pregnant when she was killed. A little over two months."

"It wasn't Bill," she snapped. "And by the way, he's broken down and told me everything about what happened between them."

"And you believed him, just like that?" Moulton asked.

"Yes. Also, I know for a fact he had a vasectomy three years ago."

"That certainly does help then," Chloe said, a little disappointed that that particular possibility had been so easily squashed. "But I want you to please think very hard about any other men you think Kim might have been involved with. Even if it was nothing more than assumptions or gossip. We're slowly finding that your neighborhood isn't exactly the most forthcoming."

"I've been wondering that same thing myself," she said. "I still find it hard to believe that she managed to seem so clean and pristine while fucking my husband and getting mixed up with that Dillinger character. And I just can't come up with anything. The only thing that I'd even bother considering is the man that recommended her to us as a nanny."

"Did they have a history?"

"Just a professional one, I think. But whenever I would mention his name around Kim, she seemed to get a little uneasy. I always assumed it was because she didn't like the compliments and flattery. But now ... yeah, I'd be willing to start speculating on them."

"Who was this man and how did he end up referring her to you?"

"His name is Gerald Denning. She used to work for him as a nanny out in DC."

"Does Denning live in your neighborhood now?"

"No. He's lives in Vista Acres, about ten miles closer to DC."

"Do you know what he does for a job?" Moulton asked. "That name sounds pretty familiar."

"I don't know what he's doing *now* but he used to work for the Department of Health and Human Services. He was released two years ago."

"Any idea why?" Chloe asked.

"No. But you know, even if the two of them weren't messing around, he'd be a good place to ask questions. The way I understand it, he knew her pretty well in DC before she gave up her career on the trail."

"Thank you, Mrs. Carver."

"Sure." She walked back toward the door, indicating that she was done with the conversation. "Have you talked to my husband?" she asked.

"Briefly yesterday," Chloe said.

"Like I said . . . the vasectomy rules him out. But still, but I'd consider it a favor if you went by and asked him about it. Scare the shit out of him."

Neither of them said anything about this as Sandra opened her sister's front door and went back into the house. She didn't bother looking back at them when she closed the door behind her.

"I won't lie," Moulton said as they headed for the car. "Scaring Bill Carver over this does sound like fun. But I bet a simple phone call to Garcia will get us the information we need on Gerald Denning."

"I was thinking the same thing. And if he had given us a glimpse into the woman Kim used to be, I think we may be able to get some answers before our two days is up."

"You still think she had a dark side?"

"Exhibit A would be any involvement with Mike Dillinger. Exhibit B would be the fact that a woman with high career ambitions in Washington decided to give it all up to become an overpriced nanny."

"I'm glad you brought that up. I've been wondering the same thing but it's not really a man's place to question a woman's career motives. Political correctness and all."

"I'll make the call to Garcia," she said.

"And I'll listen in, hoping you don't get us in trouble again."

She gave him a playful frown as she pulled out her phone. It occurred to her as she placed the call that Moulton was openly flirting with her for the first time. The timing was terrible but it seemed to fit the tone of the day; where there was progress in the case, there seemed to also be progress toward finding out if there was anything worth mining out of a relationship with Moulton.

Priorities, she scolded herself as the phone started ringing in her ear. Yet until Garcia answered, she and Moulton locked eyes, their gaze thick with expectancy and something else that she wouldn't dare put a name to just yet.

Chloe could hear in Garcia's voice that he didn't like giving out information about a man who had once worked for the federal government. But the history of Gerald Denning was apparently known to most within the bureau, but kept secret—almost like some sort of sick inside joke.

Gerald Denning had been released from his position within the Department of Health and Human Services a little over two years ago. He was fifty years old when he was released, and he had been serving with the agency since the age of twenty-nine. By the time of his release, Denning had managed to make a modest name for himself, making a very respectable living without having to become any sort of public figure.

For the last five years of his stretch with the Department of Health and Human Services, Gerald Denning had served as second in command with the Office of Health Reform. This came to an end due to a scandal that made some headlines but stayed mostly quiet. His wife began to have severe panic attacks—so severe that she had to be hospitalized. Shortly after her first stay, she attempted suicide and spent a few weeks in and out of psychiatric clinics. During this time, Denning was filmed by an anonymous source hiring a prostitute, parking with her in an alleyway three blocks from his home, and apparently receiving oral sex from her (these details were hidden by the grainy footage as well as the closed car door).

The footage went public and though it was a hot topic around DC for a day or so, the media decided to keep it quiet out of respect for his ailing wife. Denning was of course relieved of his position and had been living quietly with his wife in a Maryland town not too far away from DC ever since.

Chloe and Moulton received all of this information from Garcia over the phone. It was a little heartbreaking but also quite revealing all at the same time.

"Can I ask why Denning's name came up?"

"It's looking like Kim Wielding was his nanny when she was living in DC. Any chance we can find out the dates she was hired by him?"

"It would be easier for you, I'd think. Gerald Denning isn't going to willfully answer a call from the bureau. But listen…I ask that you remain discreet. And if he gets really shitty with you, drop it. If it's something you feel warrants further investigation, we'll handle it with someone higher up the ladder."

"Any chance Denning is the one who asked Jacob Ketterman to have the bureau look into her death?"

"Doubtful. Denning has done everything in his power to stay away from anyone working for the federal government. Which is why I'm not the biggest fan of you approaching him."

"But you'll allow it?" Chloe asked.

There was a moment's hesitation before Garcia said, "I'll have his address to you within the next fifteen minutes."

Chapter Twenty Three

Vista Acres looked like the kind of neighborhood that usually sat close to hospitals, expensive houses occupied by doctors and surgeons. She supposed there were several neighborhoods like this all around southern Maryland and northern Virginia, populated by people who had once worked in DC and lived very well. The houses were gorgeous, and the landscaping was quite frankly ridiculous in some cases.

Vista Acres sat ten minutes off of the hectic mayhem of the Beltway and about fifteen minutes from the Carvers' neighborhood. It was almost like some hidden idyllic village for people who had ventured through careers in Washington and just hadn't been able to handle it.

They parked in front of the house, along the curb even though the driveway leading to the garage could easily hold eight cars. Moulton took the lead, something Chloe appreciated in a chivalrous sort of way. They both knew that Gerald Denning could potentially be rather volatile, and Moulton wasn't going to allow Chloe to step into such a situation.

Moulton knocked on the door as they looked around the nearly cavernous front porch. It was decorated in a strange design that Chloe thought looked like a strange mish-mash of traditional Greek and modern. She figured the porch itself was worth more than half a year of rent for her apartment.

The door was answered by a tall and slender man. His hair was mostly gray but well kept. Had it been colored, Gerald Denning could have passed for a man in his late thirties rather than his early fifties.

"Can I help you?" Denning asked, clearly annoyed. Chloe assumed this was not the sort of neighborhood where people got unexpected visitors very often.

Moulton showed his ID, and Chloe followed suit.

"Agents Moulton and Fine," Moulton said. "We're here to see if you—"

"Yeah, I don't think so," Denning said, closing the door.

Moulton stepped forward, blocking the door with his foot. "We have no interest in your old scandals," he said. "We're working a murder case and think you might be able to help us find the killer."

A look of confusion clouded Denning's face—a look that quickly morphed into surprise. "A murder? Who's been killed?"

"A woman that we are told once worked for you," Chloe said. "Kim Wielding."

The confusion transformed into shock. Denning stepped back from the door and then looked around as if he needed to collapse in a chair.

He did not invite them in but Moulton took advantage of the situation and stepped inside slowly. Chloe followed behind him, leaving the door open as to not make Denning feel like he was trapped.

"When did this happen?" Denning asked.

"Five days ago," Chloe said. "She was murdered at the Carver residence. Sandra Carver tells me that it was you who recommended her for the job."

Denning had resigned himself to the fact that the agents were here to stay. He slowly waked through the foyer and into a comfy-looking den where he sat down heavily on a small reading chair.

"Yes, I did. Kim worked as a nanny for my wife and I for nearly two years when we were still living in DC."

"What was that working relationship like?" Chloe asked, watching his face closely for any telltale indicators.

"Good. She was great with the kids and became almost like family to Cecily and I."

"Cecily is your wife?"

"Yes."

"Is she here, too?" Moulton asked.

"I am," came a voice from behind them. They turned to look as a waifish woman stepped into the room. She looked sickly yet pretty. "Gerald, who are these people?"

"FBI agents," he said. "They … they just told me some very bad news. Kim Wielding was killed several days ago."

It seemed as if it took Cecily Denning a while to process this information. A dawning look of shock slowly came to her face and she began to shake her head. "Oh my God. Do you know who did it?"

"No," Moulton said. "Not yet. We've come to—"

"Agents," Denning said, getting to his feet and taking his wife's hand. "Please give me a moment, would you?"

Without waiting for an answer, he led his wife out of the den and into the hallway. Chloe could hear their footsteps slowly retreating as Denning started to speak to his wife. While they waited, Chloe and Moulton looked around the den. A built-in bookcase was filled with books that looked to be mostly biographies and books about governing law. All of the furniture looked very fancy, like a strong wind could very well tear it all apart.

Denning came back into the room three minutes later. He looked stressed and tired as he returned to his seat. "Sorry about that," he said. "If you know about my idiotic behavior in the past, you likely also know about Cecily's breakdowns and hospitalization. When we get news like this, we have to handle it with kid gloves. Her brother passed away last year and I swear I thought she was going to try killing herself again …"

"That's fine," Chloe said. "And given the nature of her condition, we can try to make this as quick as possible."

"Okay … but … you say she was killed at the Carvers' residence?"

"Yes. And while we're on that topic, do you mind me asking how you and Sandra Carver crossed paths?"

"She had to come to the Department of Health and Human Services a few times over the course of several months when she was working up a proposal background. I worked fairly closely with her for a while."

"And how did you meet Kim Wielding?" Moulton asked.

"It was probably about ten or twelve years ago. She was trying to help get this grassroots campaign started for a young man running for congress. God help my poor brain, but I don't even recall who that young man was anymore."

"Do you know why she quit working in DC?" Moulton asked.

"I think she got tired of all of the backstabbing and toxic environments. Some people… some are just too kind to cut it in Washington. I think Kim Wielding was one of those people."

"Did you ever see her after she stopped working as your nanny?"

"Oh sure. We'd have lunch here and there. When things got really bad with Cecily, Kim was there to just listen to her, you know? She was a huge help."

"So you remained friends for a while?" Moulton asked.

"That's right."

Chloe caught a flinch in his expression, as if Denning might be getting uncomfortable with where the conversation was heading.

"When was the last time you saw her, Mr. Denning?" Chloe asked.

"Oh, I don't know. Maybe four months ago. She came by to visit. Stayed for lunch, if I recall."

Moulton leaned forward in his seat and lowered his voice. "Forgive me for asking, Mr. Denning. But were you and Kim Wielding ever romantically involved?"

Denning smiled lazily and his eyes legitimately started to water. "Cecily doesn't know, but we had dinner a few times and I admit I hoped something more would come of it, but it was evident that there was no connection there. I was thirteen years older than her and although she used to joke about having a thing for older men, I guess I was just never good enough."

"So no sexual encounters with her?" Chloe asked.

"No." Denning snapped the response. It came out almost like a defensive dog's bark.

"Are you confident enough in that answer to provide evidence that could back that up?" Moulton asked.

"What the hell is that supposed to mean?" Denning asked.

"Kim Wielding was a little over two months pregnant when she was murdered," Chloe said. "We believe if we can find out who the father is, we could potentially start a trail towards motive."

"You think someone killed Kim Wielding because she was pregnant?"

"I think if someone wanted to keep something a secret bad enough, they'd do just about anything," Chloe said.

"Would you be willing to undergo a DNA test to ensure you have not been physically intimate with Kim Wielding anytime in the recent past?"

Chloe could practically see the gears turning in Denning's head. She was pretty sure he had already lied about something and was now doing his best not to stumble over that lie.

"Absolutely not. This accusation is absolutely ridiculous."

"One last opportunity here," Moulton said. "Let's face it. You aren't some vast shining figure in DC. I can ask around and probably get someone to find out certain information if I really wanted to. So this is your last chance … honestly, did you and Kim ever have a sexual relationship?"

The sneer on Denning's face was answer enough. And when he spoke, he did so with a tremble of anger in his voice. He leaned in very close, nearly falling from his chair so he could speak quietly to them, that anger pushing every single word.

"Early last year, after she had been working for the Carvers for about a year or so, she came to visit. Cecily was in Baltimore, visiting a specialist. She came over because she was scared of this guy she had been seeing, some lowlife piece of shit that was threatening her. I don't know if you knew this about Kim or not … but she was into drugs for a while. I think she kicked the habit—coke, mostly, I believe—but found it hard to separate herself from this man. She came over asking for advice, of any legal ramifications to getting a restraining order. She was very emotional and one thing led to another."

"So you did sleep with her?" Chloe asked.

"Yes."

"Just the one time?"

"No. We made a thing of it for several months. Noting emotional, tough. Just sex. I think she was seeing other men, too. But, well, in the moment those sorts of things didn't really matter to me. I think she was using sex as a way to kick the drug habit. I don't know." A tear escaped his eyes and he wiped it away so fast that, for a moment, Chloe thought he was slapping at himself in frustration.

"Mr. Denning?" Chloe said, concerned.

"Cecily can't find out," he said. "At the risk of sounding conceited, I just have no idea what this might do to her."

"Is there any chance she already knows?" Chloe asked. "And maybe in order to keep it from making things worse for her, she's keeping it to herself rather than confronting you with it?"

"No. She'd tell me."

"When is the last time you slept with Kim Wielding?" Chloe asked.

"I don't know. Four months? Maybe five?"

The words *I don't believe you* were on Chloe's lips but she kept them to herself. In the back of her mind, she had an idea. And if she got mouthy or really pushed at Denning, it might make things more difficult for them in the long run.

"Can you think of anyone else she might have been sleeping with?" Chloe asked.

"I don't know. I always suspected maybe there was something with Bill Carver, but of course I never came out and asked her."

"Do you know anything about her life that might help us find her potential killer?" Chloe asked. But really, this was all filler—ways to make Denning feel at ease while she continued to formulate her plan in the back of her head.

"Just that man that threatened her all the time."

"We've looked into the man we believe you're talking about," Chloe said. "His alibi checks out. But we may have to revisit him and interrogate him further."

"Thank you for your time," Moulton said. "And we are indeed sorry to drop this on you with your wife here in the house."

Denning nodded as he got to his feet. Chloe felt a little sick to her stomach when she saw that he was wiping another tear away. He said nothing else to them as he ushered them to the door. As he led them out, Chloe looked back through the large foyer and the extended hallway, where she saw the slim figure of Cecily Denning.

A woman on the verge of nervous breakdowns at any moment with a history of needing treatment for such a condition, Chloe thought. There's no way she doesn't at least suspect something between her husband and a younger, prettier woman who seems to show up at random times.

Even when Chloe was getting into the car and preparing to verbalize her plan to Moulton, she felt like she could still sense the presence of Cecily's looming figure in the hallway. It was almost as if the woman were trying to follow her—to haunt her until this case was closed.

Chapter Twenty Four

"How well do you remember your physical exam prior to joining the academy?" Chloe asked.

She had driven the car just two blocks over, parked in front of a house that was for sale. It was a bit nicer than Denning's and it hurt her head to try to figure out how much that house might sell for. She and Moulton sat in the car, watching a series of gray clouds scatter in from the east.

"All too well," Moulton said. "It involved my first prostate exam."

"Too much information. Anyway, they took blood samples, right?"

"Yeah. You, too, I assume?"

"That's right. Which makes sense. They have to check for a myriad of things. I want to say there were two or three different tests where they had to take my blood."

"Sounds about right," Moulton said. "Why do you ask?"

"Because I'm pretty certain that anyone with a job within the federal government has to take those some kinds of tests. I might be wrong about this, but I don't think I am."

Moulton smiled and nodded at her. "And you're thinking this means that somewhere in Washington, there's a medical report with some of Gerald Denning's information."

"Yes. I am honestly not even sure if they'd still have him on file after what happened but I certainly think it's worth a shot."

"Agreed. I anxiously await being able to witness you calling Garcia and requesting that information."

"You saw Denning's face when you kept pressing him on the issue. He's hiding *something*."

"I agree with that as well. All joking aside . . . do you want me to make the call?"

"No. I think I should."

"And what about Bill Carver? Shouldn't we verify his vasectomy? I'd say the chances are pretty good that he might be the father, too, if Sandra is lying about that."

"If so, that still doesn't make him capable of being in two places at once. Remember, he was out of town when Kim was killed. Several states away, in fact."

"You're right. So if Garcia allows this and nothing comes out it . . . we're back to square one?"

He was right, but she wasn't about to let that defeat her. After all, they now knew that Kim Wielding had a darker side than they had imagined. She had been sleeping with at least three different men in the course of six months or so and they had all likely overlapped.

Before Moulton could argue any further, she pulled out her phone and placed a call to Garcia.

He answered on the third ring and sounded hopeful. Chloe frowned when she realized that she was likely going to end up pissing him off yet again. She told him about her hunch, about how she suspected that the DNA test that had been conducted on Kim Wielding's unborn baby might very well line up with DNA results in Gerald Denning's medical records.

"Fine, are you fucking kidding me?" Garcia asked.

"No sir. In speaking with him this morning, both Agent Moulton and I believe it's worth looking into. He admitted to a sexual relationship with Wielding that was active, according to him, up until about four months ago."

"Director Johnson will have to sign off on this. And Fine . . . if nothing comes of it, it might mean your ass. This is dangerous territory. No one much likes Denning, sure. But this could be seen as antagonizing an already tiresome and dead situation."

"I understand, sir. I'm willing to take the risk."

"Have it your way. I'll pass the request to Director Johnson. But don't be surprised if he calls you right away to chew you out."

Garcia ended the call there, leaving Chloe to grimace at the silence on the other end of the line.

"What did he say?" Moulton asked.

"He thought it was a grand idea. I should be getting a call from Director Johnson any moment now to congratulate me on my keen thinking."

Moulton laughed out loud at this as Chloe cranked the car and pulled away from the gorgeous house. At the end of the block, she looked in the direction of Denning's house but turned in the opposite direction instead, heading back out toward DC. She waited for her phone to ring, bringing with it the angry and demanding voice of Director Johnson.

But it did not ring. And with every second that passed, she thought more and more that her hunch might just be right.

She did not get a call from Johnson for the remainder of the day. Back at headquarters, she checked the records to make sure a DNA test had also been conducted on Mike Dillinger during his arrest. She was pleased to find that a swab test had indeed been done. Just to cover all of her bases, she sent those results to the coroner for comparison with Wielding's baby—making sure to get Garcia's permission first.

She was well aware that it might be tomorrow morning before she got results from her request to match Denning's DNA with that of the Wielding baby. And still, every minute that passed without Johnson calling her seemed like a small victory.

When there was no movement by four o'clock that afternoon, she called it a day and headed home. She fully intended to head home without any convenient roadblocks this time; she was going to head back to her apartment. Maybe she'd even manage to unpack a few things before she went to sleep. She had no idea why, but being around so many upscale neighborhoods during the last few days had motivated her to finally get started on her own place. While she had no delusions that she would ever be able to live in a house quite as nice as the Carver residence (and surely not like the one Sandra's sister or Gerald Denning lived in), it was still nice to know that she had a place that was hers—a place that, no matter how cluttered and unorganized—she could call home.

She thought about picking up Japanese takeout on the way home for an early dinner, but when she picked up her phone to call it in, another thought went through her head.

Her father's voice: *"Did Ruthanne tell you everything?"*

And with that thought, she uttered a curse. Her heart hammered in her chest and no matter how hard she tried to ignore it, those words would not leave her head, nor would the image of her father starting to cry before she had last left him.

She cursed again, pulled a U-turn as soon as she was able, and headed northeast on the interstate toward Philadelphia.

Chapter Twenty Five

It was rather alarming how easy it was. She made the drive to Philadelphia, making a call to Riverside Correctional Facility to request some time with one of their inmates. After giving her name and badge number, she was told she could meet with the inmate within the next hour, but it had to be before lockdown.

And just like that, she was given a meeting with the woman who had killed her mother.

She arrived at the prison just after six. Because it was after business hours, there was not much activity within the prison. She was able to be checked in, scanned, and escorted back to the visiting area in less than ten minutes. It was very similar to the setup she had gone through while visiting her father: an escort, a guard at the door, and then the inmate. Only at Riverside, there were no glass partitions and old phones. She was led to a what looked to have perhaps once been a small conference room of sorts. When she stepped into the room and the guard closed the door behind her, she hesitated for a moment.

Ruthanne Carwile was sitting right there, directly in front of her. She sat at a small table, her hands folded on top of it, her eyes wandering toward Chloe.

The guard whispered through the door before closing it all the way. "Let me know if you need anything."

Chloe only nodded. When the door was closed completely, an unexpected surge of rage flashed through her. She recalled the last time she had seen Ruthanne; it had been in an interrogation room and her first partner—Agent Greene—had to restrain her when she had rushed at Ruthanne.

"Chloe," Ruthanne said.

Her voice sent a chill down Chloe's spine. She slowly walked to the table. As she did, she subtly placed her hand into her jacket pocket and felt for her phone, as if to make sure it was there.

"Hi, Ruthanne."

Ruthanne eyed her suspiciously. "Why are you here? I figured you'd stay as far away from me as possible."

"I'm here because it occurred to me that even though we found out about what you did, I don't know the whole story. My father won't tell me everything because he's afraid of disappointing me. Ironic, isn't it? He worries about that *now*."

"I can understand that. He was always crazy about the two of you. We talked about running away together—him leaving your mother and we'd just start a life together in a different state. But he never would. He was always worried about leaving the two of you. I daresay he loved you girls more than your mother."

It wasn't surprising to hear, given how he had treated her mother. Still, Chloe found herself clenching her fists and her jaw, doing everything she could to keep herself from leaping across the table to strike Ruthanne.

"You know that your admission to the murder shortened his sentence, right?"

"Yes, I heard that in court somewhere along the way."

"How does it feel to have traded places with him? To know that you're likely to spend the rest of your life in jail while he's back out in the world?"

"Oh, I was angry as hell at first. Thought it was unfair. But your father took the fall for me. I figure it's my turn to pay it forward, even if it means we won't end up together. He loved me so much that he sacrificed his time and his life so I wouldn't have to go to jail."

"Yet here you are," Chloe said, unable to contain the evil smile that rose to her lips.

"Chloe, did you come here to just rub this all in my face—that you found out the truth and now I'm behind bars?"

"No. I came here because I want the truth that my father won't give me."

"I don't know that I'm comfortable with that. The last time you saw me, you came barreling across the room for me."

"That was stupid. I'm a federal agent. I lay a hand on you, it means my ass. What do you have to lose? The way I hear it, you're in here for twenty-to-life, right? Have you told the whole truth to anyone in the court system? Judges, psychiatrists?"

"No. Because it wouldn't matter. I'm here, probably for life. I can keep a few of my demons in. No point in making me out to sound worse than it already is."

"I need to know. For my own sake, I need to know what really happened. I hate to go so low, but considering you killed my mother, I think you owe me that at least."

Ruthanne seemed to consider it for a moment, looking at her still-folded hands. She then slowly began to talk. Not once through the entire thing did she look up at Chloe. Chloe didn't know if it was because she was concentrating or if she found it impossible to look at the daughter of the woman she had murdered. She hoped it was the latter.

"That morning... your father and I had planned to meet up at the apartment—your home. Your mother was to be out most of the morning for work. You were going to a movie with a friend. Danielle was also with a friend, though I don't remember what she was doing. I was supposed to meet your dad there at one in the afternoon. Only... I was tired of hiding it. We did it all the time and I wanted him for myself. I was done sharing. So I made a bold move—I called your mom. I told her I needed to talk to her and if she could meet me at her house at twelve thirty. I pretended to cry and that's what did it. I was going to tell her about your father and I. And just in case she didn't believe me, I wanted her to be there when he showed up, expecting only me in his bed."

She paused here and when she did, Chloe found that it was getting hard to breathe. She hated this woman with every nerve in her body and sitting through this was torture.

"She showed up and I told her. And she got mad, obviously. She believed me right away but told me she'd fight for her marriage, that she was not just going to roll over and give up. I thought that was sort of pathetic. What self-respecting woman would stay with a man that is so sexually active with another woman—a man that does stuff with that other woman that his wife doesn't do…"

"Please watch yourself," Chloe said through clenched teeth.

Ruthanne nodded, still not looking up. "I knew then that the only way to get rid of her was to kill her. And I had thought about it before, though I had never told your dad. I mean, I mentioned here and there but he thought I was joking—just saying things to make him feel like he was very important to me, which he was. But I had never done anything like that before. I couldn't shoot someone. Couldn't stab someone. I thought about poison, maybe. I considered that one for a while.

"But right then and there, as we were arguing, I saw how close she was to those stairs that led downstairs. And I thought to myself: *Just one push. One hard push and down she goes.* I figured there was a chance she'd break her neck and die. And even if she didn't, she'd likely break *something.* And even if that happened, it would bring everything out into the open. She'd still be there when your father got home and he would have to choose. It was a win-win for me.

"But then your mother slapped me. Hard. Right across the face. It just about knocked me on my ass. And that's what it took. I punched her in the face. I think I broke her nose and that's where the blood came from. She reeled a bit and then I shoved her. She went down the stairs backwards and landed on her head, rolling over right on top of it when she bounced. I heard something snap. I also heard her let out this strangled gasp at the bottom, wet from the bloody nose and blood in her throat, I guess."

It was then that Chloe realized that Ruthanne was enjoying this. She was doing everything she could to get under Chloe's skin. Hoping she might lash out at her. Chloe was shaking, trying to hide it but failing miserably.

"Why are you shaking?" Ruthanne asked defiantly. She finally looked up at her and when she did, Chloe saw a malevolent glee in the woman's eyes. "You wanted to hear it. You wanted the truth."

"So you're telling me my father had no idea about any of it?" she managed to ask.

"That's right. He was simply expecting to come to his apartment and find me in his bed, waiting for him. Like we'd done so many times before.

Instead, he came home to a dead wife. And for a minute, I thought he was going to hurt me. He was upset, Chloe. He did cry for her. But in the end, he chose me. *Me*. Not your mother, not you or your sister. *Me*."

Chloe nodded. She felt tears welling up in her eyes and she'd be damned if she would let Ruthanne see them. She got up and turned away, heading quickly for the door.

"Guard!"

"Is that all?" Ruthanne asked. "Really? You don't want to know anything else? Maybe about how he spent a weekend with me at your mother's favorite little lake house up on Union Lake?"

Chloe realized she was leaving with Ruthanne feeling as if she had the upper hand. And while that hurt, it was worth it.

The guard opened the door and Chloe quickly went out. Ruthanne was still talking but it was muted by the closed door.

"You okay?" the guard asked when they were out in the hallway.

"Yeah," Chloe said. She reached back into her jacket pocket again, this time removing the phone. She woke it up and smiled in spite of her tears.

She'd had her voice recorder app running the entire time. When she pressed STOP in the hallway, it read 6:17.

She'd recorded every single word Ruthanne had said.

"You sure you're okay?" the guard asked. "You look a little shook."

"I am," she said, pocketing the phone. "But it was well worth it."

Sitting in the parking lot, she seriously considered heading to yet another prison—to Somerset Correctional, the prison her father had been calling home for the last eighteen years. From Riverside, it would be about a three-hour drive—maybe just two and a half if she sped the entire way—and she would get there around nine. She pulled up the number on Google through her phone and was about to call to check on the protocol. But before she could make the call, her phone rang in her hand. She saw that it was Garcia calling, took a moment to compose herself, and answered.

"This is Agent Fine."

"Fine, it's Garcia. Look…the test results came back, and you were right. There's a match between Kim Wielding's unborn baby and Gerald Denning. We got the call five minutes ago."

"So what do we do now? Is that enough to arrest him?"

"It gets tricky. It depends on how he responds. Listen…his past makes this a very touchy situation. I want you and Moulton to hang back for a while. We're going to send two men to his home and explain the situation. It's too late to do much of anything right now without causing a scene, so we will wait until tomorrow. If Denning is smart, he'll at least comply and come in for questioning. When he gets here, I want you and Moulton on it. I wouldn't risk placing you on the team to bring him in, but this is your case. This was your call. And you deserve first crack at interrogating him."

"Thank you, sir."

"I'll call tomorrow. Could be eight in the morning, could be noon. No clue right now."

"I understand."

"Call Moulton and fill him in."

With that, Garcia ended the call. Chloe took a moment to sort out everything she had just learned in the past fifteen minutes and then pulled up Moulton's number.

As it rang, she heard Ruthanne Carwile's voice in her head and it sparked a furious anger within her.

He was simply expecting to come to his apartment and find me in his bed, waiting for him. Like we'd done so many times before. Instead, he came home to a dead wife.

She wasn't certain it was enough to free her father, but it was certainly a step in that direction.

The question was whether or not her father would even want her to take that step.

There was only one way to find out.

She quickly pulled out of the Riverside parking lot and placed a call to Somerset Correctional to see if it would be possible for her to meet with her father one more time.

Chapter Twenty Six

It took a little pushing, but she was able to arrange to speak with her father. It took a series of calls to get it done, all of which made the drive pass by even faster. She found that she was not nearly as nervous this time, that she was almost excited to talk to him—not because she had a strong desire to do so, but because she now knew that she had something over him. That she had the opportunity to catch him in a lie and to prove that he was just as monstrous and worthless as Danielle claimed he was.

As she parked in the Somerset visitors' lot, she could understand Danielle's point of view. After all, even to Chloe his memory felt like some demonic entity rattling its chains in her head and demanding attention. And if she wanted to be free of it, she knew what she had to do. She just didn't know which direction to take the conversation she was about to have. Hell, she wasn't even sure she'd be able to speak coherently when she saw him, despite the power she felt she'd be going into the conversation with.

She decided then and there, as she walked into the Somerset lobby, that she was not going to tell her father about the conversation she'd had with Ruthanne. She was not going to let him know that she had a recording that could potentially free him overnight.

The next several minutes passed by as if she were in a dream. She was escorted back to that row of dirty glass partitions and the CB-type phones. Her father was already sitting at one of them, under the watchful eye of a guard who stood against the wall behind him.

Chloe sat down slowly, realizing that she was starting to feel very tired—both physically and emotionally.

Her father picked up his receiver and spoke her name. "Chloe?"

"Hey," she answered, still not sure what she would say.

"I wasn't expecting to see you again after last time. Is everything okay?"

She let out a strained chuckle. "No. No, things are never okay when they involve you."

"So why are you here? What can I do for you?"

"I wish I could forget you," she said. "I wish I could forget you like Danielle has. I wish I could hate you, Dad."

"Chloe…"

"Please shut up, Dad. I told you last time that I have to sever everything with you or I'll go crazy. Tell me the truth."

"About what, Chloe?"

"Did you love Mom? Did you ever *really* love her?"

"Of course I did."

"That's bullshit, Dad."

"Chloe, I—"

"Just tell me," she interrupted. "Just tell me the truth so that I can get it done and be done with you."

"Tell you what? Sweetheart, I don't know what you want to hear."

"If you loved us, how could you throw your life with us away? What was so fucking special about Ruthanne?"

"I don't know," he said without reservation. "I could have given you hundreds of answers in the few years after it all went down. But now…now I barely remember. I loved her, too. I know you don't want to hear it, but I did."

Oh, I know, she thought. I know all of this.

And for just a moment, she nearly pulled out her cell phone. But she decided not to at the last moment. *He doesn't deserve the relief,* she thought. *And I don't want him thinking I went to see Ruthanne just because he suggested it.*

"Chloe, you don't have to do this if you don't want to."

"Do what?"

"Torture yourself over me and my mistakes."

"The sad thing is that you're wrong. I have to or you're going to haunt me forever. I need these answers in order to let you go. And quite frankly, you're not worth it… all of this stress and sorrow."

"So what did you come here to tell me?"

"That I'm through with you, Dad. Danielle had the right approach. When we found out the truth about Ruthanne, I was so happy. I thought things could be okay with us when you got out. But the more I learn and the more time passes, I know that just won't happen."

Her father could only nod to this.

Chloe got to her feet, not wanting to see him crying again. It would either break her or piss her off—and she didn't want to find out which.

"Bye, Dad," she said.

And just as easily as she had come into the room in a dreamlike state, she left in exactly the same way.

On her way back to her car, she took out her phone. Then she sat behind the wheel for a moment, listening to the recorded confession from Ruthanne. When it was done and she placed it back into her pocket, it felt like a bomb. And it was both horrifying and comforting to know that she was the only one with the detonator.

Chapter Twenty Seven

Chloe got the call from Garcia at eleven o'clock the following morning. When she and Moulton arrived at headquarters just after noon, one of the first things Chloe saw as they headed for Denning's interrogation room was Cecily Denning. She was holding a cup of coffee and sitting on a bench by herself just outside of the lobby, near the hall that led to the interrogation rooms. She was shaking, had clearly been weeping, and looked absolutely lost.

So much for trying to keep this all from her, she thought.

She could not bring herself to simply ignore the poor woman. She stopped at her side, not sitting down but staying close. "Mrs. Denning, has anyone bothered speaking to you yet? Maybe offered to get you some help?"

"Oh yes," she said. "There's someone on the way right now, I believe."

"Are you okay?"

"I am," she said. "I needed… needed this, I think. To break away from him. I just… my God, I had no idea. What a bastard."

Hearing those last three words made Chloe think that Cecily would indeed be okay within a few days. Maybe she had been waiting for something like this to happen so she could finally break away from the man who had already committed so many sins against her.

Not knowing what else to say, Chloe gave the woman an apologetic little nod and headed down the hallway. Moulton pulled up beside her and whispered, "You think she really had no idea?"

"I think with what Denning put that poor woman through, she was probably pretty oblivious—consciously or not—to just about anything he did."

They came to an intersection in the hallway and took a right. A few doors down, she saw Garcia and several agents gathered around. They stood by an open door which, Chloe saw as she approached, was the observation room. She and Moulton stepped inside with Garcia and looked out through the double-sided glass. Gerald Denning was sitting in the room, nervously tapping his foot at the table. He was not handcuffed, holding a cup of coffee with one hand and looking through a small stack of papers with the other.

"Has he said anything at all incriminating yet?" Chloe asked.

"He hasn't really said much of anything," Garcia said. "The men that went for him told him they needed his cooperation with a case. When they told him what case, he got a little defensive. When the threat of leading him out of his lovely home in handcuffs for all of his neighbors to see came up, he was a little more willing to play ball."

"I passed by his wife on the way in," Chloe said. "I take it she knows he was sleeping with Kim Wielding?"

"Oh yeah. When you get in there, have a look at the red splotch on the left side of his face. That came compliments of his wife."

Chloe did her best to hide her nervousness. It was not the interrogation itself that she feared, but the feeling that this moment could be vitally important to her career. The man she was about to interrogate was not any normal suspect. His history and scandal made it a loose-wire sort of situation. She could feel Garcia's eyes on her as she opened up the door to the interrogation room. Moulton followed behind her and she was a little relieved to see the obvious unease on his face.

Once inside the room, Moulton leaned against the back wall with his arms folded. He looked intimidating not because of his size—he was, after all, of average build and size—but because of his expression. He looked cold and calculated. Chloe knew this was really just an act, but Denning would not.

Noting Moulton's posture, she also knew this was a sign that she was to do most of—if not all of—the talking. She slowly approached the table and sat down in the chair on the other side.

"You lied to me, Mr. Denning. And we have DNA tests to prove it."

"I was trying to protect my wife." He was close to tears and his voice was ragged.

"It seems to me that you were trying to protect yourself. If you were trying to protect your wife, you wouldn't have had sex with Kim Wielding."

"Don't you dare judge me."

"Oh, I'm not judging. I'm just stating facts. But you know … I'll even give you that. I can see you not saying anything to us while we were there. You revealed a bit but not the pregnancy bombshell. I understand you not wanting your wife to know about that part especially."

"So let me guess," Denning said, his tone mocking and sad at the same time. "You think that she told me about the pregnancy and I just couldn't have that get out. So you think I killed her. Is that right?"

"Based on your history of trying to keep secrets, yes, my mind went there. The minds of several others as well. Which is why you and I are currently meeting in this interrogation room."

"I had no idea she was pregnant, by the way. The first I heard of that was when the agents came by to pick me up this afternoon."

"You'll forgive me for not believing you, I hope."

He shrugged and slapped the table in frustration.

"So please … tell me," Chloe said. "For real. When was the last time you slept with Kim Wielding?"

"A little over two weeks ago."

"And how regular were your encounters?"

"There was no schedule. She'd text me and ask if I was free."

"Was she always the one to initiate these meetings?"

"No. Sometimes it would be me."

"Are there text conversations on your phone to back this up?"

"Not my personal phone. We used a few of those cheap burner phones that you can get at any drugstore. I paid for them in cash so nothing would show up on the credit card bills or checking account."

She nodded. "Really doing your best to protect your wife."

He looked at her with pure fury, but she also watched a tear trickle out of the corner of his eye.

"I'm not proud of the things I've done. But when Cecily started going through her mess, she was not at all responsive to my needs. She had absolutely zero desire for me and I got desperate. That's where the scandal with the prostitute came from. That's why I jumped at the chanced to be with Kim when the opportunity arose."

"Is this supposed to make me feel sorry for you?"

"With all due respect, Agent, I don't give a shit how you feel about me. But I did not kill Kim Wielding. And there are text messages on my burner phone that will back that up."

"And where is this burner phone?"

"It's in my car, between the seat and the center console. It's hidden by a folded up scarf that is also tucked into that space. The code to unlock it is 1905."

"And what about Kim's? Do you know where she kept hers? Did she hide hers as well?"

"I honestly don't know."

Chloe stood up from her seat and looked back at Moulton. He nodded and exited the room. Chloe turned back to Denning and gave him a cursory look. "We're going to check your phone and see what we can do about finding Kim's. For now, is there anything else you lied about earlier that you'd like to fess up to?"

He shook his head. "I swear to you, I had no idea she was pregnant. She never told me."

Perhaps it was the pleading and desperate look in his eyes, but something within Chloe nearly believed him.

"Hang tight, Mr. Denning."

With that, she followed Moulton out of the room. In the hallway, the room to the observation room opened. Garcia came out, nodding. "You did good, Fine. I didn't think he'd give up that much information."

"It's still not enough," she said. "If he's right about the text messages…"

"Well, why don't you go figure that out and get back here as soon as you can?"

That was all the prodding she needed. She had been given two days to wrap this case up and here she was, barely at the end of the first one, finally feeling as if she was moving forward. With Moulton at her side, she rushed to the elevators. And when she once again passed by Cecily Denning, still sitting alone on that bench near the front of the building, her fragile-looking shape only pushed Chloe on even harder

Chapter Twenty Eight

One thing Gerald Denning had not lied about was where he kept his burner phone hidden. After Moulton had used an old-school electronic lock disabling device to pop the lock of the brand new Mercedes in the Denning's garage, Chloe found the phone easily enough. She tossed the decoy scarf to the side and pulled the phone out of its hiding place between the seat and the center console.

She punched in the code Denning had given them—1905—and the home screen popped up. Chloe had never used one of these cheap burner phone before but it was incredibly easy to learn her way around. There were no contacts stored in the phone. When she went to Call History, there was only one number, several calls coming in from the number and just as many going out.

From there, she discovered the only text thread on the phone. She didn't bother starting at the top. She simply scrolled up a bit and read enough to confirm that the messages were indeed between Kim Wielding and Gerald Denning. Because there were no contacts, it took her a while to make out which messages were coming from Denning. But once she figured it out, the conversations made far too much sense.

For instance, one from about six weeks ago read:

Alone tonight. You?
Where?
My apartment. Carvers don't need me for a few days.
Not sure. C is in a mood. Depressed.
Oh. Maybe some other time?
Maybe. Tomorrow?

Sure. Can you be here in the morning? Find some interesting way to wake me up?

Ha! Yes. I'm sure I'll think of something.

See you then.

Chloe felt a stirring of anger within her. She couldn't help but think of Cecily—mentioned as "C" in Denning's texts. What sort of mental anguish was the woman going through as her husband texted back and forth with a younger woman? She thought of the lame excuses Denning had used about not getting his needs met and it only angered her more.

"You okay?" Moulton asked. He had been reading the thread over her shoulder and he looked just as enraged as she was.

"Getting a little pissed off," she answered.

She scrolled back down, looking for the conversations that might actually prove that Gerald was not guilty of murdering this woman he was sleeping with behind his ailing wife's back.

C will be at her specialist in Baltimore for 2 days next week. Want to come over?

We can't…not in your bed. I have SOME morals, you know.

You do?

Shut up!

Doesn't have to be the bed. There's the shower. The guest bedroom.

That's true. The loveseat in the den has always looked comfy.

We can give it a try.

How soon can I come over?

Friday afternoon. I'll pick you up at your apartment.

"My God, this guy is a legitimate creep," Moulton said.

Chloe nodded, forcing herself to keep scrolling. The thread went on and on forever. She caught glimpses of more provocative conversations and purposefully passed them by as quickly as she could. Finally, she came to a section of the text thread that seemed to give what they had been looking for. It was a text from Denning that got no answer. And there were several after that, a series of empty texts with no responses.

Got some free time this evening. You at home or with the Carvers?
You playing hard to get?
Some other time, then. Let me know.

Two days passed and he tried again.

You mad at me or something? Everything okay?
Did the Carvers find out about us? You still working for them?
Starting to worry. Text back please. Or call or just come by. Miss you.
Okay. I guess this means we're done?

"That last one was from one day after her murder," Moulton said indicating the date above the message. "Doubtful he'd send a message about trying to hook up if he knew she was dead."

"Unless he's just trying to make it look that way," Chloe pointed out.

She took the phone and pocketed it. She then closed the car door and walked out of the Dennings' garage, out into the afternoon.

"We need to find Kim's phone," Moulton said.

"Yeah. And I think it would probably be at her apartment. If it was at the Carvers' house, I'd think at least one of those last texts to her would have been responded to."

"Didn't you and Rhodes already check her place?"

"We did. But that was before we knew just how messed up Kim Wielding was. If she was serious about keeping something like this hidden, she might have gone to great lengths."

They walked quickly back to their car, Moulton taking the driver's seat. As he pulled away from the curb and started out toward Kim Wielding's apartment, Chloe couldn't resist; she looked back through the text threads between Kim and Denning. It was quite bad in some parts, getting nearly pornographic. She wondered how a seemingly upstanding woman who was a loving and kind nanny could so easily morph into the woman who was sending these texts.

It was sad and, as far as she was concerned, a little scary. But if she had learned anything within the last year—particularly with Ruthanne Carwile and her father—it was that when people felt they *had* to keep a secret, they would go to just about any lengths to keep it protected.

It was 2:15 when they arrived at Kim's apartment. Chloe retrieved the hide-a-key box from the hiding spot inside the decorative flower pot. She locked in the combination the Carvers had given her several days ago, popped the little box open, and got the key. When she unlocked the door this time, Chloe did not feel the sense of trespassing she had felt on their first visit to the apartment. Instead, she felt like they had walked into a tomb—a place that was going to reveal secrets about a woman's hidden life after her death.

It even seemed foreboding once Moulton cut the lights on. Now that she knew the kinds of things Kim Wielding had been capable of, Chloe felt nearly trapped in the house. She felt that if they didn't come away with *something,* the case could very well be lost.

Fortunately, they had a very easy way to start looking. She took Denning's burner phone out of her pocket and called up the only number that had ever sent a text to the phone. Four seconds passed before the sound of a ringing phone could be heard from elsewhere in the apartment. From their place by the tiny foyer, the ringing seemed to be coming from directly ahead of them, very soft.

They entered the living room and for a moment, Chloe thought the ringing was coming from the television. But as she neared the TV and the built-in bookshelves, she realized that the ringing—the phone now on its fourth ring—was coming from somewhere slightly to the right of the TV. Moulton had located it first, though; he was already walking toward the bookshelf. When he started pulling books away from the shelf, she had a moment of déjà vu as she recalled Agent Rhodes pointing out the *Speech Writing Essentials* book.

"Bingo," he said, reaching to the back of the shelf where the phone had been hidden by several books. As he grabbed it, he added: "I wonder why she hid it when this is her own apartment."

"Maybe she had the Carver kids over here from time to time. Remember, she did let them use her iPad. Or maybe Denning had her paranoid. Someone that had messed up as bad as he had in his past would probably be doing just about anything to cover his ass in the midst of an affair."

Moulton sat down on the couch and found his way to the text threads. Unlike Denning, Chloe had saved a contact to her phone, though it was only labeled Jerry—which was, of course, a form of Gerald. Still, it would be enough to perhaps deter anyone nosy enough to actually look for and eventually find the phone.

There were two separate threads on Kim's phone. Moulton instantly opened up the one from "Jerry." Right away, they saw the same conversations they had seen on Denning's phone. Right down to his final text asking if she was okay or if they had been found out, it was exactly the same.

"What was the other text thread?" Chloe asked.

Moulton went to the second thread. This contact had not been saved. It was just as well because it wasn't much of a conversation at all. It was two separate messages, sent back to back eight days ago. Kim had wisely not responded to them. The messages read:

If you tell ANYONE, I'll fucking kill you. ESPECIALLY Gerald.

You made it easy for him didn't you? Just call him up and open your legs you whore. You should be ashamed of yourself. You should kill yourself and spare your bastard child of having to live its life with a mother like you.

"Well, it's not Gerald Denning, that's for sure," Moulton said.

"But it's sure as hell motive. And I think if we can find out who owns this number, we'll find the killer … or, at the very least, someone that can lead us to the killer."

"The question I have, though," Moulton said, "is this: does Denning know about these texts?"

It was a good question—one that helped Chloe feel the case was a coming to a close with even more assuredness.

She smiled at him and said: "Let's go ask him."

Chapter Twenty Nine

When they arrived back at headquarters, Chloe found Gerald Denning a nearly broken man. It was clear that he had been crying and his head was resting on the surface of the table, his eyes nearly closed completely. Chloe and Moulton watched him through the glass as Garcia filled them in on everything that had happened while they had been away.

"His wife asked to speak to him. She asked for a divorce. It got pretty heated. He begged her to not give up on him but she left. Said she was going to go home and pack some bags."

"Did someone accompany her?" Chloe asked. "The poor woman has been through so much. And it's on record that she tried to kill herself because of either panic attacks or having a lousy husband. Or both."

"No. But she called her mother," Garcia said. "I watched her do it. Listened to the conversation. She'll have a support system with her."

"What about their kids?" Chloe asked.

"She didn't go into great detail. The mother bitched about it, I think. From what I gather, they have two kids, both grown. One lives out West somewhere. The other, I don't know where they live but I think they more or less removed themselves from the family when the scandal hit a few years back."

"Poor woman," Moulton said, looking awkwardly to Denning on the other side of the glass.

"What did the two of you find?" Garcia asked.

Chloe handed him both of the phones. "He was right," she said. "According to the texts we found, he either had no idea she had been killed or he staged the last few texts after her death. But we found two texts on Kim Wielding's phone that indicate *someone* knew about the pregnancy."

"And," Moulton added, "it was someone protective of Denning."

"Another mistress?" Garcia asked.

"No idea," Chloe said. "How long will it take us to track the number down?"

"If the texts warrant it, I can know within five minutes."

Moulton pulled up the two threatening texts and showed them to Garcia. "I'd say these warrant it."

"Holy shit," Garcia said. "Let me make a call. I'll have it for you as quickly as I can."

"In the meantime, are we okay to go back in and speak with him?" Chloe asked.

"If you think it's necessary."

Chloe thought about it for a moment before nodding and heading back out into the hallway. Moulton followed her and stopped her before she opened the interrogation room door.

"You okay?" he asked.

"Yes. Why?"

"I think we can leave him alone until we find out who this other text is from. Unless it's just a matter of rubbing his nose in it. And while I'm all for that, just remember that Garcia is watching."

There was part of Chloe that knew he was right. But a larger part of her knew that Moulton wasn't haunted by the mistakes of a father who had ruined lives with the same sort of selfish actions. She supposed she could try to explain it to him, but he wouldn't understand. And really, did she want to open up that box on him so soon in their partnership?

"I'll be good," she said, trying to speak lightly to lighten the situation a bit.

She went into the room, taking a small amount of pleasure in just how startled Denning seemed. She walked straight to the table as Moulton closed the door behind them. Denning looked up to them with hope in his bloodshot eyes.

"Did you find the phone?" he asked.

"We did."

"Thank God. Can I go home now? Cecily has it in her head that she wants to leave me."

"Of course you realize that any killer that could think at least one step ahead would keep sending texts after the murder. Just to try to throw off police."

"Oh my God," Denning nearly screamed. "No... that's not who I am. I *did not do this!*"

"Mr. Denning, were you sleeping with anyone else?"

"No, I—"

"Maybe someone that even knew Kim Wielding. More than that... someone that might have known she was pregnant?"

"No. Just Kim. I swear on my life."

"See, you've already lied to me once in the past, so I don't know if I can believe that."

"Damn you! You found the phone! You know it wasn't me! So what sort of sick pleasure are you getting out of this?"

"The phone proves nothing," she said.

Chloe honestly didn't know how to answer his question. And in that moment, she knew why she was doing this—why she was wanting so badly for the killer to be Denning. What she could not realistically take out on her father, she was trying to take out on Gerald Denning. In the back of her head, she could still hear Moulton's warning: ... *Just remember that Garcia is watching.*

Chloe had to look away from Denning. She felt cheap. She also felt like she was exploiting this man's weaknesses—and she was doing it to try to make herself feel better because she could not escape her own demons.

She turned away from the table and headed back for the door. She briefly caught a glimpse of Moulton's face as she reached for the door. He looked sad and a little uncomfortable, like he wasn't quite sure how to respond.

She left the interrogation room and stood in the hallway for a few seconds before Moulton came out behind her. Before she heard his voice, though, a thought occurred to her. Something she had seen today had chilled her and it came back in that moment like a strong wind, trying to push her in a certain direction. But before she could latch onto it, Moulton was there. He placed a hand on her shoulder and spoke softly. And God help her, as if she wasn't dealing with enough, the desire to kiss him in that moment was like some physical weight pushing against the back of her head.

"What's going on, Fine?"

The last name, she thought. *Ouch.*

She felt the explanation coming to the tip of her tongue—everything about her father and how his sins and desires had ended her mother's life and deeply affected her own. Hell, she'd even venture into Danielle territory, telling him about her weird relationship with her sister.

But before any of it came out, another voice interrupted them. It was Garcia, rushing toward them as he came out of the observation room door.

"We can't get a match on the number that sent those texts," he said. "It was apparently also a burner phone. My money is on Denning in there, trying to throw us off."

Chloe again recalled that image from earlier in the day … the image that had made her feel haunted in an odd way. And even before Garcia told them what he had discovered, Chloe knew.

She saw the fragile figure standing in the distance, down a hallway shrouded in shadows. A figure like a ghost. Like someone who had forgotten what life was supposed to be.

I have to talk to Cecily Denning, she thought. I think she knows more than she's letting on. If Denning did indeed do this, she has to know. But she's so used to her husband failing her … she probably knows that any other mistakes from him could ruin him—could ruin them.

And besides, that poor woman could use someone to talk to right now.

"I'd like to go speak with Cecily," Chloe said. "Now that this is all out of the bag, I wonder if she might be a bit more forthcoming."

Garcia nodded, rubbing at his head. "Good idea. But guys … if it's not Denning, then I don't know that we have a case at all. That forty-eight hours will be gone before you know it."

Chloe was well aware of that as she headed back down the hall. She could literally feel every second slipping away from her and she'd be damned if she was going to let her time run out before wrapping this damned case.

CHAPTER THIRTY

It was nearly 6:30 by the time Chloe and Moulton arrived at the Denning residence yet again. As they got out of the car, Chloe felt her nerves start to build. She was going to be questioning this poor lady about her cheating husband again—about how he had been unfaithful to her in so many different ways.

She knocked on the front door and within seconds could hear heavy footfalls coming toward the door. It was then opened just a crack. Slowly, Cecily Denning peered out with eyes that had clearly seen its share of weeping that night.

"I know you're trying to help," she said through the door, "but I'm sort of tired of seeing both of you."

"I can understand that," Chloe said. "But we have just a few more questions. And then maybe we can lay this case to rest and leave you and your husband alone."

Cecily sighed and then opened the door a bit more. "Yeah, you can come in. Just don't refer to him as my husband again. If you do, I might snap."

Chloe winced at her choice of words, given her history. Wanting to keep the visit as brief as possible, Chloe started her line of questioning as soon as Cecily closed the door behind them.

"I'm back in the bedroom, packing," she said. "Make it quick, because I plan on being out of here just as soon as possible."

"Our director said you had called your mother to be with you," Moulton said. "Is that right?"

"Yes. But she's useless. I'm driving to her place. She lives in DC. Doesn't *everyone* live in DC these days?"

"And your kids are no help?" Chloe asked

"None. Just as useless as my mother."

"Mrs. De—I'm sorry... can I just call you Cecily?" Chloe asked.

"Yes, please."

"Did you know that your husband was involved in a relationship with Kim Wielding?"

"Of course I did," she said in a half-yell. "I pretended not to just so I wouldn't have to deal with it all but yes, I did. And I wouldn't call it a relationship. It was just sex."

"How long did you know?"

"A few months," she said. She never looked at them as she spoke. They were in the bedroom now, an enormous room with a closet that was nearly as big as the living room in Kim Wielding's apartment. Cecily went into this closet, retrieved a few shirts, and brought them back into the bedroom where she had s suitcase on the bed, already stuff with a few odds and ends.

"And did you know she was pr—"

"Pregnant?" she interrupted with a shrieking laugh. It sent a chill down Chloe's spine and she wondered just how close Cecily Denning was to another panic attack—or something much worse.

"Yes, pregnant."

"Yes," Cecily said. There was a strange gleam in her eyes, as if she were enjoying some grand joke. "I knew because the little bitch came by here almost two weeks ago to speak with Gerald. Thankfully, Gerald was away. In fucking DC, of course. Tying to mend bridges and get some sort of a job back. She came to talk to him and when I told her he wasn't here, she asked to come in to speak with me. She told me everything... all about the *affair*." She said the word "affair" as if it were the punchline to a very bad joke.

"She told you... just like that?" Moulton asked.

"Yes. Said she felt guilty. That things had gotten out of hand. And then she told me she was pregnant. She cried the entire time. Real tears, no faking. I almost felt sorry for the little whore."

"And you knew about the affair before then?"

"Yeah. For a few months."

She went into the closet again, this time coming back out with two pairs of shoes. She shoved one into the suitcase and left the other pair—a nice pair of heels—sitting by the suitcase.

"Did you let her know you knew?" Chloe asked.

"No. Look… I'm not stupid. I haven't been sexually active with Gerald in a while. I loved him and all but when I had my… my *episode* a few years ago, I lost all interest in any form of a sex life. Gerald had to get his kicks elsewhere. And while it hurt… I understood."

"Do you know how they kept in touch?" Moulton asked.

"Those cheap drugstore phones," she said. "I knew. I found Gerald's a few months ago. I used to read their texts. It was funny. It hurt, but it was still funny… trying to imagine Gerald trying to talk to a woman like that."

Chloe could sense the desperation and, she hated to think it, the edge of something very wrong with Cecily in that moment. Chloe did not think it was a panic attack that was coming on, but there was certainly something *off* about the woman.

She then replayed the last few seconds in her head. A slow knot of worry started to churn in her stomach.

I knew because the little bitch came by here…

I almost felt sorry for the little whore.

"Cecily, have you ever used one of those phones?"

"Oh yeah. Pretty recently."

The woman was now speaking as if she was just passing time with a dear old friend. Moulton gave Chloe a strange look but she very faintly nodded her head.

Oh my God, she thought.

Slowly and deliberately, she started to reposition herself. She wanted to make sure her firearm was close to her hands.

"Did you have Kim's number?" Chloe asked.

"No. But I did get it off of Gerald's phone." She had a thoughtful but worried look on her face. It seemed as if she realized that she had just said something she shouldn't have.

"And did you ever text her?" Moulton asked, the same realization now dawning on him as well.

Cecily finally turned to face them. There was a smile on her face that looked a little maniacal. "Yes! I got that junk phone and I texted her the day after she came by here to tell Gerald that she was pregnant. Maybe said some rough stuff. Just to scare her, you know? But what choice did I have?"

"So you convinced her not to tell him about the baby?" Chloe asked.

"That's right. When she was here, I begged her not to tell Gerald and she agreed, at least at first. We both agreed that there was no way he would ever get his life back if people found out and the news went public. The conversation didn't end on the best terms, though. She was still undecided. Said she had to think about it. Stupid bitch…"

Chloe saw something in Cecily's eyes that alarmed her but also seemed to ease her into the next few moments. She saw something in Cecily Denning's eyes that she could only describe as *unhinged.* Perhaps the panic attacks and other issues had led to some sort of mental instability. And if that was the case, Chloe felt that she was watching that instability slip in behind the controls of Cecily's logic and reason.

"Did you see Kim at all after that?" Chloe asked.

Cecily slowly sat down on the bed, nodding. Chloe thought this was it. This was the moment Cecily would break. Chloe felt rather bad for being responsible for pushing her to whatever edge she was about to fall from.

"I would drive by the Carvers' residence almost every day after that," she said. "If Kim's car was there, I'd circle the block a few times, just thinking."

"Thinking about what?" Moulton asked. Chloe noticed that he had very slowly started to close the distance between himself and Cecily.

"How my life would be if Gerald found out about Kim's pregnancy. If the media found out. Everyone thinks I'm crazy, you know. Something like this would not only bury Gerald, but it would also add to that version of me."

"Mrs. Denning," Chloe said. "Did you ever contact Kim after the confrontation here at your house?"

Cecily smiled. It was as if she knew they were on to her and she was simply having a bit of fun now. "I did. Like I said, I contacted her on that secret little phone. She and Gerald had these throwaway phones they'd use to contact one another. They thought they were being so sneaky…"

"We saw those texts," Chloe said, realizing that Cecily was now repeating herself. She had already confirmed buying the junk phone and sending the texts. She wondered what, exactly, was going on in the woman's head.

"Mrs. Denning, there are some things you said on those texts that don't look good."

"I know. I wanted to scare her. Wanted her to think straight about it."

"But in the end, you took it into your own hands, didn't you?" Moulton asked. He had managed to make it a few steps closer without being noticed. Chloe was impressed with how stealthy he was but also a little unnerved at how casually he had dropped the question.

"My own hands," Cecily said with a chuckle as she placed her high heels into her suitcase.

In a flash, she was no longer shoving one of those heels into her suitcase. It was instead coming straight across in a hard arc through the air, gripped tightly in her right hand. By the time Moulton registered this—it was, after all, a rather ridiculous-looking sight—it was far too late. He let out a surprised little yelp and took a staggering step backward.

The point of the heel struck him just below the temple. It drew blood right away, the shock of it forcing Moulton to his knees.

Chloe rushed forward, her hand hovering over her sidearm but not drawing yet. After all, if she could not take down a woman as frail as Cecily Denning, she did not deserve to be an agent.

As Chloe decided on the best hold to put Cecily in, Cecily reached back into her suitcase. As her hand landed on something, Chloe wrapped her right arm underneath Cecily's left. As she pulled the woman's meager weight toward her, she hooked her left arm around Cecily's stomach. Chloe's goal was to wrench her down in one hard jerking motion, hopefully onto the bed; going to the floor in this hold with any real force would likely dislocate Cecily's shoulder or break her jaw.

But Chloe never got the chance. Apparently, Cecily's hand had landed on exactly what she had been looking for in her suitcase. Chloe's vantage point did not allow her to see what sort of handgun Cecily had stowed away in the suitcase. All she saw was the gun in Cecily's grip, blindly turned upside down and toward her face.

Chloe ducked down, losing her grip, as the gun went off. Had she been a single second slower, the round would have torn directly into her forehead.

She still had a slight grip on Cecily's left arm. She tugged it hard, making the woman buckle and bend downward. Chloe then drove her shoulder hard into the back of Cecily's knees. Cecily buckled hard and went sprawling forward with a cry. The gun went off again, this time pointed high and to the right. Glass shattered as Cecily rebounded from the edge of the bed.

Chloe fought for a suitable hold as Cecily did her best to turn herself over, angling for another shot. Before she could manage to level the gun, though, Moulton was there. He had dived toward her, throwing a shoulder hard and high into her chest. As they went tumbling to the ground, he slid on the floor and managed to wrap Cecily's head in a front headlock with his left arm while twisting her right arm with his own.

Cecily cried out, dropping the gun as Moulton held her down on the ground. Chloe quickly kicked the gun away, slipped her handcuffs from her belt, and applied them as if she had done it hundreds of times. When she heard the click of the cuffs, she felt the adrenaline spiking through her. She was dizzy for a moment as the world swam, everything catching up to her at once. She shared a crazed glance with Moulton as he got to his feet, leaving Cecily on the floor. She wasn't writhing or scrambling or trying to get to her feet anymore. She had accepted her defeat and just lay there, looking at Chloe.

"I had to," she said through a soft sob. "If she told anyone, it would be over. For me, for Gerald… for our life together. I couldn't…"

And then Cecily Denning broke. It was as if something inside of her literally shattered as she tried to get out her skewed justification in murdering Kim Wielding.

The adrenaline quickly faded as Chloe heard the woman letting out gut-wrenching sobs. Maybe she was realizing for the first time exactly what she had done—not only killing a pregnant woman, but also firing a shot at an FBI agent.

Chloe looked behind her and saw where the bullet had torn into the wall—the same bullet that had been about one second shy of tearing through her skull and into her brain. But the wails of Cecily Denning broke her attention and she felt that she had to look at the woman… not out of any sort of respect, but because even though she was a murderer, Chloe could not deny that the woman had been through a lot.

"You okay?" Moulton asked quietly over Cecily's sobs.

Chloe only nodded, mainly because she did not trust herself to talk.

In fact, she was trembling so badly that she wondered if she might be having some sort of panic attack of her own.

Chapter Thirty One

Chloe was speaking with the bureau shrink when Cecily Denning spilled every single detail of the murder of Kim Wielding. The psychologist was asking how she had responded to the gunshot that had nearly taken her life. She was then asked if she had felt prepared for the assignment given that such a frail and unstable woman had nearly gotten the best of her.

After being approved to return to the closing of the case, she was sent out of the little office and was asked to send Agent Moulton in next. She found him sitting in a small conference room across the hall from the interrogation room Cecily Denning was sitting in—the very same room her husband had sat in less than two hours before. Garcia and one of the agents who had taken in Gerald Denning were sitting with him, both drinking coffee.

"You're next," Chloe told Moulton. "Be ready to feel totally inferior."

"Already there," Moulton said sheepishly as he got to his feet.

When he was gone, Chloe sat down and looked at Garcia. The coffee smelled good and even though it was nearing 8:00 in the morning, she found herself craving a strong cup.

"Cecily Denning spent fifteen minutes telling us how she killed Kim Wielding," Garcia said. "She waited for a time during the day where she knew the Carver kids would be in school. She walked right up to the porch, rang the doorbell, and hit her with a lead pipe that she'd found in her garage a few weeks ago. She said she thought about a gun—the same gun she had hiding in that suitcase—but wasn't sure she'd be able to do it. She said the pipe felt more natural, like it was no big deal."

"Did she get to speak to Gerald?" Chloe asked.

"God no. We'll keep the two of them away from one another for as long as possible."

Chloe nodded, deciding that she was going to get some coffee anyway. "Where's the coffee?" she asked.

"Break room at the end of the hallway," Garcia said. "But listen, Agent Fine… I want you to know that you did a great job. Moulton went through the scene detail by detail, and even Cecily Denning's accounts made you seem like a superstar. I spoke with Director Johnson shortly after she confessed and he's a very happy man. Fantastic work, Fine."

"Thanks." She headed for the door but paused when a certain thought struck her. "When I was speaking to her in her house, there was a moment where it seemed like she wasn't there anymore. She seemed unhinged. You could see it in her eyes. She wasn't faking it; it was legitimate."

"Yeah," Garcia said with a sigh. "I sensed some of that when we were talking to her."

"She'll probably cop a plea based on some mental state or another, won't she?"

"That's anyone's guess," Garcia said. "And certainly not anything for you to worry about. You did your job and you did it well."

Chloe left the room with a frown and started down the hallway to grab her cup of coffee. She gave the interrogation room door a fleeting glance as she passed by it.

As she came to the break room, she was surprised to see Moulton there. He was placing a lid on a Styrofoam cup of coffee. He smiled at her guiltily and said, "Going to need this to deal with a shrink at this hour."

"Yeah, I'm going to need it just to process it all. Have fun in there."

"Oh, sure." He passed her and started out of the room, but paused and turned back to her. "Fine… there was something I wanted to ask you."

"What's that?"

"Can we do something outside of this? The job, I mean? Dinner, maybe?"

Her first instinct was to say yes, but something held her back. "I don't know," she said. "Can I think about it?"

Smiling, he nodded and headed out. It was as if he had been fully expecting this answer. And honestly, she had no idea why she had not simply said yes. Maybe it was because his timing was terrible. She smiled at this as she watched him go.

Chloe let out a little chuckle of disbelief as she went to the coffeepot. As she poured a cup, she tried to ignore the trembling in her hands and the slight ringing in her ears from Cecily's gunshot, but they were both too strong to be ignored.

They were almost as strong as the other thought that was finally able to surface to the back of her head now that this case was wrapped.

She thought of what she had on her cell phone—the voice recording of Ruthanne's entire confession.

She had enough evidence to clear her father… to probably have him released within a month or so, barring paperwork and bureaucracy. But there was still one last thing she needed to do. And it scared the hell out of her.

After taking a huge gulp of the coffee, she took out her cell phone and texted Danielle: **We need to talk.**

She got home at ten that night, after filling out all of the appropriate paperwork. She had seen Moulton only once after he had met with the psychiatrist, but they had not gotten a chance to talk. Thankfully, it was Moulton's invitation to dinner that was on her mind as she drifted to sleep rather than the brief yet deadly struggle with Cecily.

She didn't sleep well (maybe because of the late caffeine intake or maybe because her mind simply refused to shut off completely), so when her phone dinged at her early in the morning, she gave it an irritated snarl.

She glanced at her phone, assuming it would be Garcia to tell her there was one last thing she had forgotten to do in wrapping the case. But it was another name, a name she had not been expecting at all.

Danielle.

As she also looked at the time with blurry eyes, she saw that it was 6:15 in the morning. She sat up in bed and took the call, assuming that any call from Danielle at such an hour could only bring bad news.

"Hello?" she said.

"You said we needed to talk?" Danielle asked.

"Yeah. Look... I had to do it, Danielle. I had to talk to her. To at least see."

"What? You mean you visited Ruthanne?"

"Yeah."

"You're pathetic, Chloe."

Chloe let the comment ride for a moment. She had to remind herself that as far as they knew, their father had attempted to work with Ruthanne Carwile to frame her for murder less than six months ago.

"I had to know, Danielle."

"Was there anything to the story? Was he for real?"

"Yeah. She told me the whole thing. And she had no idea, but I was recording it all on my phone. It's probably enough to get him out right away. To clear his name, maybe."

"Congratulations," Danielle said sarcastically. "What will you do with it?"

"I don't know," Chloe said. "It's too much... too much responsibility. Too much control. I think I have to turn it in."

"Don't you dare. That asshole deserves to be where he is. He's just as twisted and screwed up as Ruthanne Carwile is even if he didn't kill Mom."

"Maybe. But... Danielle... he's our dad."

"Chloe... I go back to what I told you at the bar. You dig any deeper into this and you and I are done. I mean that."

"Please don't be like that."

"I'm sorry. The fact you went and spoke to the woman that killed our mother is bad enough. But if you use it to free Dad—playing the part of his little puppet..."

She didn't bother finishing her statement.

"Danielle..."

"Do what you want," Danielle said. "But I have to go. Maybe I'll talk to you soon."

With that, Danielle hung up. Chloe looked at the phone as if it were a snake that had just bitten her and then threw it across the room. She sat in bed for several minutes, staring at the phone and, though it pained her to even think it, starting to really resent her sister's intense hatred of their father.

Ten minutes later, she walked to her phone and picked it up from the floor. She placed a call and waited for the person on the other end to pick up.

"Good morning, Director Johnson," she said, each word feeling very heavy coming out of her mouth. "I have a question about what I might need to do in order to submit new evidence regarding my father's old murder case."

CULDESAC

(a chloe fine psychological suspense—book 3)

BLAKE PIERCE

Table of Contents

Prologue 397

Chapter One 399
Chapter Two 404
Chapter Three 408
Chapter Four 418
Chapter Five 424
Chapter Six 429
Chapter Seven 437
Chapter Eight 445
Chapter Nine 450
Chapter Ten 457
Chapter Eleven 461
Chapter Twelve 466
Chapter Thirteen 471
Chapter Fourteen 480
Chapter Fifteen 487
Chapter Sixteen 490
Chapter Seventeen 501
Chapter Eighteen 507
Chapter Nineteen 511
Chapter Twenty 520
Chapter Twenty One 525
Chapter Twenty Two 529
Chapter Twenty Three 540
Chapter Twenty Four 544

Chapter Twenty Five 548
Chapter Twenty Six. 556
Chapter Twenty Seven 562
Chapter Twenty Eight 570

Prologue

Jerry Hilyard pulled his Mercedes Benz into his driveway just after one o'clock on a Monday afternoon and smiled wide. There was nothing better than owning your own business and being rich enough to call it a day whenever you wanted.

Jerry looked forward to the look of surprise on his wife's face when he told her he was taking her out for a surprise lunch. He wanted to make it a brunch, but he knew Lauren would still be nursing a hangover from the night before. She had stayed out way too late, going, for reasons he still did not understand, to her twenty-year high school reunion. By lunchtime, she should be less cranky—and maybe even up for joining him for a Bloody Mary or two.

He smiled when he thought of the good news that he would be sharing with her: he was planning a two-week getaway to Greece. Just him and her, without the kids. They'd be leaving next month.

Jerry walked to the door, briefcase in hand, excited about how the afternoon might turn out. He found the door locked, which wasn't unusual. She had never been a trusting sort of woman, even in a neighborhood as well-to-do as theirs.

As he unlocked the door and made his way into the kitchen to pour himself a glass of wine, he realized that he could not hear the bedroom television. The house was just as quiet as when he had left. Maybe the hangover had not yet run its course.

He wondered how the reunion had gone last night. She hadn't really spoken about it that morning. He had been in her same graduating class but he *loathed* sentimental nonsense like high school reunions. All it was at its core was an excuse for classmates to get together ten or twenty years later to see who was doing better than everyone else. But once Lauren's friends had convinced her to go, she'd gotten almost excited about seeing some of her old classmates. Or so it had seemed. The intake of alcohol last night indicated that it might have been a rough night all around.

These thoughts were parading through Jerry's head as he made his way through the upstairs hallway toward their bedroom. But as he neared the doorway, he stopped.

It was very quiet.

Sure, this was to be expected if Lauren was indeed taking a nap and had not put on Netflix to finish binging whichever show had been her fancy for the week. But this was a different kind of quiet… a total lack of movement or motion that seemed out of place. It was like a silence he could hear—a silence he could literally *feel.*

Something's wrong, he thought.

It was a frightening thought but still, he moved toward the door quickly. He had to know, had to make sure…

Make sure what?

All he saw at first was red. On the bedsheets, on the walls, a dark red so thick and dark that it was almost black in places.

A scream pushed itself up through his lungs and out of his mouth. He didn't know if he should go running to her or downstairs to the phone.

In the end, he did neither. His legs gave out and the weight of his gut-wrenching screams took him to the floor, where he pounded his fists, where he tried to make sense of the horrific sight in front of him.

Chapter One

Chloe focused, narrowed her vision down the sight of the gun, and fired.

The recoil was gentle, the blast light and almost peaceful to her. She breathed deeply and fired again. It was easy; it came naturally to her now.

She could not see the target at the other end of the indoor range, but she knew she'd made two good shots. She was able to get a sense about these things lately. It was one of the ways she knew she was growing into the position as an agent. She was more comfortable with the sidearm, the stock and the trigger as familiar as her own hands when she could really get into the zone. In the past, she'd gone to the range only as a study of sorts, a way to improve and get better. But now, she enjoyed it. There was freedom to it, a weird release from firing at even just a paper target.

God knew she needed to feel that way as of late.

It had been a lackluster two weeks at work, leaving Chloe with nothing much to do but assisting others with data and research work. She'd nearly been pulled in to help a team with a small-time hacking sting and she'd been far too excited about it. It made her realize just how slow things had been for her as of late.

That's how she ended up at the range. It wasn't necessarily her ideal way to pass the time, but she knew she needed some practice. While she had been among the best in her class on her way through the academy, being transitioned from the Evidence Response Team to the Violent Crimes Program had made her realize that she could never be too sharp, too on top of her game.

As she fired off several more rounds into a target fifty yards away, she understood how people were drawn to it. You were absolutely alone, just you and your firearm and a target in the sights. There was something very Zen about it, the focus and the intent behind it. And then there was the *pop* of the gunshot in the open space. The one thing Chloe had always taken away from her time at the range was just how fluid the relationship between the human body and a sidearm could be. When focused, her Glock felt like a simple extension of her arm, something else she could control with her mind in the same way she controlled the movements of her fingers or arms. It was a cautionary example of how her gun should only be used when absolutely necessary because when you are trained to use it, it can start to feel almost *too* natural to squeeze the trigger.

When her session was over, she collected her targets and took stock. She had a surprising number of direct hits to the center of the target but a few stragglers to the outside, right along the edges of the paper.

She took a few pictures of the targets with her phone and made a few notes, ensuring that she would improve next time. She then tossed the paper targets and made her way out of the facility. As she did, she felt yet another thing that she assumed was so appealing to those who spent a great deal of time at the range. The feeling of numerous recoils thrumming through her hands and wrists felt peculiar, yet at the same time, pleasant in a way she could not quite describe.

As she made her way out through the lobby, she saw a familiar face coming through the door. It was Kyle Moulton, the man who had been assigned as her partner but also a man she had not seen much of over the last few weeks due to the slow caseload. She had a moment of school-girl panic when Moulton flashed a smile at her as the doors closed behind her.

"Agent Fine," he said, with an almost sarcastic tone. They knew each other well enough to drop the *Agent* and just use first names. In fact, Chloe was certain there was some romantic tension brewing between them. She'd felt it on her end almost right away, from the moment she had seen him to the moment they had wrapped their first case three months ago.

"Agent Moulton," she responded in kind.

"Blowing off steam or just passing the time?" he asked.

"A bit of both," she said. "I'm just feeling restless lately, you know?"

"I do. Riding a desk doesn't seem to do it for me, either. But… well, I didn't know you frequented the gun range."

"Just trying to stay sharp."

"I see," he said, smiling.

The silence that fell on them was the typical one that Chloe was getting used to. She hated to feel so conceited, but she was fairly certain he was feeling the same thing she was feeling. It was evident in every little glance they gave one another and the way Moulton could not look at her in the eyes for more than three seconds—like right now, in that moment, as they stood at the doorway of the shooting range.

"So look," Moulton said. "This may sound stupid and it might even be a little reckless, but I was wondering if you'd like to have dinner with me tonight. Like, not as partners."

Chloe was unable to keep the smile from jumping up on her face. She wanted to say something a little biting and sarcastic in response. Maybe a cliché *"Well, it's about time,"* or something like that.

Instead, she settled for a much safer and genuine: "Yeah, I think I'd really like that."

"If I'm being honest, I've wanted to ask you for a while now but… well, it was always so busy. And these last few weeks have been pretty much the opposite."

"I'm glad you finally decided to ask me."

That silence wrapped around them again and this time, he was able to meet her gaze without looking away. For a moment, she was pretty sure he was going to kiss her. But the moment passed and he nodded toward the doors.

"I'd better get to it," he said. "Call me later to let me know where you'd like to eat."

"I will."

She stood there for a moment, watching him enter the range. As far as the start of some sort of relationship, it had been awkward. It was the equivalent of a nervous pre-teen standing around at a dance when she'd heard that some cute boy had his eye on her. It made her feel incredibly naïve and juvenile, so she walked away as quickly as possible.

It was nearing five o'clock and since she had nothing on her schedule, she simply decided to head home. There was no use in going back to her little cubicle only to watch the last fifteen minutes or so tick away. Thinking of the time, she then realized that she didn't have much time to prepare for dinner with Moulton. She had no idea what time he preferred to have dinner but she assumed it would be sometime around seven—which gave her just a little more than two hours to figure out where to eat and what she was going to wear.

She hurried to the parking garage and got into her car. Here, she again fell into high-school-girl mode. What if they ended up in her car for some reason? It was pretty gross, considering she hadn't bothered cleaning it since she and Steven had split up. And as she thought of Steven, she realized *that* was why she felt so awkward easing her feet back into the dating pool. She had only had one serious relationship before Steven, and then she and Steven had dated for four years before getting engaged. She wasn't at all used to the dating scene and the idea of it seemed antiquated and, if she was being honest, a little scary.

She did her best to calm herself on her fifteen-minute commute to her apartment. She had no idea what Kyle Moulton's dating history was like. He could be just as out of the loop and rusty as she was. Of course, judging from his looks, she doubted this was the case. Honestly, if she was basing it all on just his looks, she had no idea why he was interested in her.

Maybe he's into girls with broken pasts and a tendency to throw themselves far too hard into their work, she thought. Guys find that sexy these days, right?

By the time she reached her street, her nerves had calmed quite a bit. The anxiety was slowly turning into excitement. It had been seven months since she had called it off with Steven. That was seven months without kissing a man, without having sex, without…

Let's not jump the gun, she told herself as she fit her car into a parking spot at the end of her block.

She got out of the car, mentally running through what she had in her closet that would look nice but not *too* nice. She had a few ideas of what to wear, as well as a few ideas of where they could go for dinner, as she had been craving Japanese as of late. Some sushi would really hit the spot, actually, and—

As she walked to her front stoop, she saw a man sitting on the top step. He looked rather bored, his head propped up in one hand while he scrolled through his phone with the other.

Chloe slowed a bit and then came a complete stop. She knew this man. But there was no way he could be here, sitting on the steps to her apartment building.

There's no way ...

She took another slow step forward. The man finally noticed her and looked up. Their eyes met and when they did, Chloe felt her heart shudder.

The man on the steps was Aiden Fine—her father.

Chapter Two

"Hey, Chloe."

He was trying to sound normal. He was trying to make it sound as if it were a perfectly normal thing to have him show up on her step. Never mind the fact that he had been in prison for nearly twenty-three years, serving time for playing a hand in the murder of her mother. Sure, recent events that she herself had uncovered showed that he was likely innocent of those charges, but to Chloe the man would always be guilty.

But at the same time, she had a small yearning to go to him. Maybe to even hug him. There was no denying that seeing him here, out in the open and free, stirred up a huge range of emotions within her.

She didn't dare move a step closer, though. She didn't trust him and, worse than that, she did not fully trust herself.

"What are you doing here?" she asked.

"Just wanted to come by and visit," he said, getting to his feet.

A million questions swirled through her head. Chief among them was how he had found out where she lived. But she knew that anyone with an internet connection and stubborn determination could figure that out. Instead, she tried to be civil without being warm and inviting.

"How long have you been out?" she asked.

"A week and a half. I had to work up the nerve to come see you."

She recalled the phone call she had made to Director Johnson when she had found that last piece of evidence two months ago—evidence that had apparently been more than enough to free her father. And now here he was. Because of her efforts. She wondered if he even knew what she had done for him.

"And this is exactly why I waited," he said. "This ... this silence between us. It's awkward and unfair and ..."

"Unfair? Dad, you've been in prison for most of my life ... for a crime I now know you weren't guilty of but didn't seem to mind taking the fall for. Yes, it's going to be awkward. And given the reason for your incarceration and the last few conversations we've had, I hope you understand if I don't come to you, dancing and tossing flowers your way."

"I absolutely get that. But ... there's so much time we've missed. You might be unable to feel that yet, being so young. But those years I wasted in prison, knowing what I sacrificed ... time with you and Danielle ... my own life ..."

"You sacrificed those things for Ruthanne Carwile," Chloe spat. "That was your choice."

"It was. And it's a regret I've had to live with for nearly twenty-five years."

"So what do you want?" she asked.

She moved toward him and then past him, toward her door. It took more willpower than she thought to pass by him, to be that close to him.

"I was hoping we could grab dinner."

"Just like that?"

"We have to start somewhere, Chloe."

"No, actually we don't." She opened her door and turned back to him, looking him in the eyes for the first time. Her stomach was in knots and she was doing everything she could not to get emotional in front of him. "I need you to leave. And please don't ever come back."

He looked genuinely hurt but his eyes never left hers. "Do you really mean that?"

She wanted to say yes, but what came out of her mouth was "I don't know."

"Let me know if you change your mind. I have a place in—"

"I don't want to know," she interrupted. "If I want to get in touch, I'll find you."

He gave her a thin smile, but there was still some pain there. "Ah, that's right. Working with the FBI now."

And what happened with you and Mom is what led me down that path, she thought.

"Bye, Dad," she said, and stepped through the door.

When it closed behind her, she did not bother looking back. Instead, she made it to the elevator as quickly as she could without appearing as if she were in a hurry. When the doors slid closed behind her and the elevator started going up, Chloe pressed her hands to her face and started to cry.

She stared into her closet, thinking very hard about calling Moulton and letting him know that she couldn't make it tonight after all. She wouldn't tell him the real reason why—that her father had gotten out of prison after spending twenty-three years there and had suddenly showed up on her doorstep. Certainly he'd understand the trauma of that, right?

But she decided that she was not going to let her father ruin her life. His shadow had hovered over far too much of her life already. And even something as small as canceling a date because of his presence was giving him too much power over her.

She called Moulton's number and when it went to voicemail, she left her suggestion for a dinner spot. With that done, she took a quick shower and got dressed. As she was slipping into a pair of pants, her cell phone rang. She saw Moulton's name on the display and her mind went to the worst scenarios first.

He's changed his mind. He's calling to cancel.

She actually believed this until the moment she answered the phone. "Hello?"

"So yeah, Japanese sounds good," Moulton said. "Now, maybe you can tell because of the extreme lack of detail and follow-through, but I don't do this much. So I don't know if I come pick you up or if we just meet there …?"

"Pick me up, if you don't mind," she said, again thinking of the ragged state of her car. "There's a pretty good place not too far from here."

"Sounds good," he said. "See you then."

...I don't do this much. Even though he'd admitted such a thing, Chloe still found it hard to believe.

She finished getting dressed, fussed with her hair a bit, and waited for a knock on the door.

Maybe it'll be your father again, she told herself. Although really, if she was being honest, it wasn't her own voice that was speaking to her. It was Danielle's voice, condescending and confident.

I wonder if she knows he's out yet, Chloe thought. My God, she'll be absolutely furious.

She didn't have time to dwell on this, though. Before she could, there was a knock at the door. For one paralyzing moment, she was sure it was her father. It made her freeze for a second, unwilling to answer it. But then she recalled how Moulton had been just as uncomfortable as she had been outside of the shooting range and she realized just how badly she wanted to see him—especially after the way the last few hours of her life had gone.

She answered the door, putting on her best smile. Moulton had one of his own. Maybe it was because they rarely saw one another outside of work, but Chloe found his smile sexy as hell. It also helped that while he had dressed rather plain—a button-down shirt and a pair of nice jeans—he looked incredibly handsome.

"Ready?" he said.

"Absolutely," she said.

She closed the door behind her and they headed out into the hallway. Once again, there was that perfectly still silence between them, one that made her wish they were a bit further along. Even something as simple and innocent as him reaching out to hold her hand... she needed something.

And it was that simple need for human contact that showed her just how much she had been rocked by her father showing up.

It's only going to get worse now that he's out of prison, she thought as she and Moulton took the elevator down to the lobby.

But she was not going to let him ruin this date.

She pushed all thoughts of her father out of her mind as she and Moulton stepped out into a warm evening. And to her surprise, it actually worked.

For a while.

CHAPTER THREE

The Japanese restaurant she had selected was a hibachi grill–type place, with the big open stovetops to allow large groups to sit around and watch the cooks perform their artistry. Chloe and Moulton opted for a table in the quiet, more private area of the restaurant. When they were both seated, she was pleased to find that it felt natural to be in a setting like this with him. Physical attraction aside, she had liked Moulton from the first moment she had met him. He had been the one shining light in a day where she had been switched from the Evidence Response Team to the Violent Crimes Program. And here he was, still making awkward moments in her life more bearable.

She didn't want to ruin the night with such conversation, but she also knew that if she didn't get it off her chest, it would be a needless distraction.

"So," Moulton said, picking at the corners of his menu as he opened it. "It wasn't odd that I asked you out?"

"I'm sure it depends on who you ask," she answered. "Director Johnson might not think it's the best idea. However, in keeping with honesty," she said, "I've kind of been hoping you'd ask."

"Ah, so you're a traditionalist? You wouldn't have asked me out? You would have waited for me to ask?"

"It's not so much being a traditionalist as it is being scarred from a past relationship. Which I supposed I may as well let you in on. Up until about seven months ago, I was engaged."

The shock on his face was only momentary. Fortunately, she saw no fear or awkwardness there. Before he could comment on this, the waitress came by to take their drink orders. They both ordered a Sapporo, placing the orders quickly, as not to let the momentum of their conversation stall out.

"Can I ask why it fell apart?" Moulton asked.

"It's a long story. The condensed version of it is that the guy was overbearing and couldn't separate himself from the shadow of his family—his mother in particular. And when I suddenly had a career with the FBI sitting right there in front of me, he wasn't very supportive. He also wasn't at all supportive of my own family issues..."

It then occurred to her that he probably knew about some of her family history. When she had gone digging it up near the end of her training, she was well aware that it had made the rounds of the academy grapevine.

"Yeah, I heard bits and pieces about that..."

He let the comment hang. Chloe took that to mean that if she wanted to tell him about it, he would listen. But if she'd rather not go there, he was fine with that, too. And at the moment, with everything that was on her mind, she figured it was now or never. *No sense in waiting,* she thought.

"While I'll spare you the details for some later day, I guess I should let you know that I saw my father today."

"So he's out now?"

"Yes. And I think it's mostly because of discoveries I made about my mother's death over the last several months."

It took Moulton a while to figure out where to go from there. He, too, used sipping from his beer as a method of taking his time. When he had a large gulp of it down, he replied with the best answer he could have.

"Are you okay?"

"I think so. It was just very unexpected."

"Chloe, we didn't have to go out tonight. I would have understood if you called it off."

"I almost did. But I didn't see the point in giving him control over yet another part of my life."

He nodded and they both took the silence that followed as a time to look over their menus. The silence remained between them until the same waitress came back to take their orders. When she was gone, Moulton leaned across the table a bit and asked: "Do you want to talk about it, or are we ignoring it?"

"You know, I think I'd rather just ignore it for now. Just be aware that there might be times tonight where I might be distracted."

He smiled and slowly got up from his chair. "That's fair. But let me try something, if that's okay."

"What? ..."

He took a large step toward her, bent down a bit, and kissed her. She jerked back at first, unsure of what he was doing. But when she realized his intent, she let it happen. Not only that, but she kissed him back. It was soft but with just enough urgency to give her the idea that he had been thinking about this probably as long as she had.

He broke the kiss before it started to get uncomfortable; they were, after all, sitting in a restaurant surrounded by other people. And Chloe had never been one for public displays of affection.

"Not that I'm complaining," she said, "but what was that for?"

"Two things. It was me being brave ... something I am rarely able to do with a woman. And it was also me giving you another distraction ... hopefully one that can outweigh the distraction of your father."

With her head swimming a bit and warmth radiating through her entire body, she sighed. "Yeah, I think that might just have done it."

"Good," he said. "Also, I suppose it negates the whole *are we supposed to kiss at the end of this date* nonsense that I always screw up."

"Oh, after that one, we better," she said.

And, as Moulton had hoped, thoughts of her father's sudden appearance seemed very distant.

Dinner went much better than she could have hoped. Once they wrestled around the topic of her father showing up and then continued onward after Moulton's unexpected kiss, it went very smoothly. They talked about learning the ins and outs of the bureau, music, movies, acquaintances and stories from their time at the academy, their interests and hobbies. It felt natural in a way she had not been expecting.

Sadly, it made her wish she'd gotten rid of Steven sooner. If this was what she had missed out on by taking herself off of the dating scene for him, she had missed out on a lot.

They'd finished eating but stuck around for a few more drinks. It was another opportunity for Moulton to display his care and affection as he stopped at two drinks while Chloe had a third. He even asked if she'd feel more comfortable taking a cab if she was uncomfortable with him getting behind the wheel.

He took her back to her apartment, pulling up to the curb a little after ten o'clock. She was far from drunk but had a nice enough buzz going to wonder about things she might not otherwise entertain.

"I had a great time," Moulton said. "I'd like to do it again very soon if you don't think it will get in the way of work."

"Me, too. Thanks for finally asking me."

"Thanks for saying yes."

Never one to claim she was a master at the art of seduction, she responded to that comment by leaning in and kissing him. Like the kiss in the restaurant, it started slow but then started to build. His hand was suddenly on the side of her face, slipping down to the back of her neck to pull her closer. The armrest was between them and she found herself tilting her body to allow her hand to find his chest.

She wasn't sure how long the kiss went on. It was slow and wildly romantic. When they parted, Chloe found herself slightly out of breath.

"So, we've already covered the fact that I never really got to date," she said. "So if I do this next part wrong, you'll have to forgive me."

"What part?"

She hesitated a moment but the three drinks urged her on. "I want to invite you in. I'd make the claim that it's for coffee or another drink, but that would be a lie."

Moulton looked genuinely surprised. It was a look that made her wonder if he had misread her. "Are you sure?" he asked.

"That sounded bad," she said, embarrassed. "What I meant was … I'd like to do this without an armrest between us. But I'm not … I'm not going to sleep with you."

Even in the dim light, she could see his face redden at this comment. "I never would have expected you to."

She nodded, a little embarrassed herself. "So … do you want to come in?"

"I really, really do."

With that, he kissed her. This time, it was a bit more playful. In the midst of it, he elbowed the armrest in jest.

She broke away from him and opened her door. As they walked to the stoop of her building, she could not remember the last time she'd felt herself so … so *floaty.*

Floaty, she thought with a smile. It was a word Danielle had once used in explaining what it felt like to come down off of the physical high of an orgasm. The memory suddenly had Chloe feeling warm all over, reaching out and taking Moulton's hand as they entered the building.

They took the elevator and when the doors closed, Chloe surprised herself by pressing him against the elevator wall and kissing him. Now able to properly place her hands on him, she grabbed him by his waist and pulled him to her. This kiss was a bit more passionate, hinting at so much more she wanted to do to him in that moment.

He was just as eager, his hands finding the small of her back. When he pressed her closer to him and their bodies met, she let out the tiniest of gasps. It was a little embarrassing.

The elevator came to a stop and she pulled away. She could only imagine the looks on the faces of the people she shared the building with if they caught her making out in an elevator. She was relieved to find that Moulton looked a little out of sorts and was breathing a little heavily.

She led him down the hallway, four doors down to her apartment. It then occurred to her that other than Danielle, Moulton would be the only person to have visited her apartment.

It's a shame I don't plan on wasting time with a tour, she thought.

It was yet another thought that made her feel a little embarrassed. She had never felt quite this physically needy when it came to a man. After a while, sex had become this formulaic, expected thing with Steven. And if she was being honest with herself, the times she had been left satisfied had been few and far between. And because of that, she hadn't really had much of a desire for any sort of intimacy with him.

Chloe unlocked the door and they stepped inside. She flipped on the kitchen light and hung her purse on one of the barstools.

"How long have you been here?" Moulton asked.

"Six months or so, I guess. I don't really have much company."

Moulton stepped to her and placed a hand at her waist. When they leaned in and kissed, it was slow and purposeful. It only took a few moments before he gently pressed her against the bar and their kiss deepened. Chloe felt herself growing breathless again, feeling a level of desire she had not felt since becoming intimate with a boy for the first time in high school.

She broke the kiss long enough to lead him to the couch, where they sat next to one another and immediately continued. It felt good to simply be with a man in such a way, especially one who made her feel like this. If she included the portion of her relationship with Steven where physical intimacy had practically gone cold, she had not been kissed and touched by a man like this in about a year and a half.

Eventually, after what felt like mere seconds but was in reality more like five minutes, she was leaning into him and he had no choice but to lie down. Chloe lay on top of him and when she did, one of his hands found its way up the back of her shirt. That small skin-on-skin touch pushed Chloe to an edge she did not see coming. She sighed against him and he responded by slipping his hand further up her back and running it along the side of her bra.

She sat up, straddling him, and smiled down at him. Her head felt like it was swimming and every muscle in her body was begging for more.

"I meant what I said," she said almost apologetically. "I can't sleep with you. Not so soon. I know it might seem old-fashioned..."

"Chloe, it's fine. You tell me when it's enough and we're good. Tell me when I've worn out my welcome."

She smiled down at him. The response was almost enough to make her change her mind. But she felt strongly that they should not be rushing this. Sitting on top of him on her couch was already pushing her limits.

"The welcome won't be worn out," she said. "Would I sound like too much of a headcase if I asked you to stay? No sex, but like…actually *sleeping* together?"

The offer seemed to surprise him. She supposed it *was* rather strange.

And do you know why you're asking such a thing? It was Danielle's voice in her head, always mocking but also helpful at the same time. *It's because Dad showed up today and screwed your world up. You want Moulton here so you won't be alone tonight.*

"I'm sorry," she said. "That seems conflicting and dumb and—"

"No, it's okay," Moulton said. "That sounds nice. I do have one thing to ask, though."

"What's that?"

"More kissing, please," he said with a smile.

She returned the smile and happily obliged.

She stirred awake some time later to Moulton getting off of the couch. She lifted herself up on one elbow. Her shirt had come off during their make-out session but that had been it. It had been weird to fall asleep on her couch with her pants on but she was oddly proud of their restraint. She glanced at the clock on the wall and saw that it was 5:10 in the morning.

"You okay?" she asked.

"Yeah," he said. "I just…I felt weird sleeping over. I didn't want it to be weird in the morning. I thought it might be best if I left. But at least there's not the added awkwardness of sex."

"Maybe that was my plan all along," she joked.

"Should I rush out and we pretend this didn't happen?" Moulton asked.

"I think I'd like you to stay. I'll put some coffee on."

"Yeah?"

"Yeah. I think I'd really like that, actually."

She slipped her shirt back on and made her way into the kitchen. She went about setting the coffee up while Moulton slid his own shirt back on.

"So it's Thursday," he said. "I don't know why, but it feels like Saturday."

"Is it because what we did last night is usually reserved for Friday nights? A way to kick off the weekend?"

"I don't know," he said. "I haven't done something like that for a while."

"Get out of here," she said as she set the coffee maker to brew.

"Seriously. Junior year of high school, I think. That was good year for me in terms of make-out sessions without the sex."

"Well, you apparently didn't miss a beat. Last night was... well, it was much more than I was expecting when you picked me up."

"Same here."

"But I'm glad it happened," she added quickly. "All of it."

"Good. Maybe we can do it again. This weekend, maybe?"

"Maybe," she said. "But my restraint is already feeling weakened."

"Maybe that was *my* plan after all," he said with a sultry smile.

She blushed and looked away quickly. She was a little taken aback by how much she enjoyed seeing him in such a flirty state.

"Look," she said. "I need to grab a shower. You're welcome to anything in the fridge if you want breakfast. There's not much there, though."

"Thanks," he said, seemingly unable to take his eyes away from her.

She left him in the kitchen and went into the bedroom, which the larger bathroom was connected to. She stripped down, turned on the water, and stepped into the shower. She almost felt like giggling over how the night had gone. It had made her feel like a teenager, enjoying the feeling of him there with her and feeling comfortable enough with him to know that he wasn't going to pester her for sex. It had been romantic in an odd way and there had been two moments where she had nearly gone back on her claim of not sleeping with him. With a glee she was not used to, she secretly hoped he might decide to summon up the nerve to come join her under the water.

If he does, all restraint is going out the window, she thought.

She was just about done with her shower when she did indeed hear him enter the bathroom.

Better late than never, she thought. Her entire body tensed up with excitement and she found herself instantly eager for him to join her.

"Hey, Chloe?"

"Yes?" she asked, a bit provocatively.

"Your phone just rang. Maybe I was being nosy ... but I looked. It was from the bureau line."

"Really? I wonder if something has come up ..."

She then heard the ringing of another cell phone. This one was closer, presumably in Moulton's hand. Chloe peeked out of the shower, pulling the curtain slightly to the side. They exchanged a look before Moulton answered his phone.

"This is Moulton," he answered. He stepped back out of the bathroom and into her bedroom. Realizing why, Chloe turned off the water. She grabbed a towel from the rack and stepped out, grinning at him when he stared while she quickly wrapped the towel around her. Just because they had made out for about an hour and a half last night did not instantly mean she was okay with him seeing her completely naked.

There wasn't much of a conversation to eavesdrop on. It was mainly just Moulton listening and saying, "Okay ... yes, sir ..." a few times.

The call lasted about a minute and when he was done, he comically poked his head into the bathroom.

"Is it okay for me to come in?"

Wrapped in a towel that covered all of her private spots, she nodded. "Yes. Who was that?"

"That was Assistant Director Garcia. He said he tried to call you but you must have slept through it." He smiled at her and then went on. "He said I should call you or come by and wake you up. There's a case they want us on."

She chuckled as she stepped out of the bathroom and into the bedroom. "You think last night will affect the way we work together?"

"It might cause me to sneak into your motel room after hours. Other than that ... I don't know. We'll see."

"Would you pour me a cup of coffee? I need to get dressed."

"I was sort of hoping I could use your shower."

"Of course. Though it would have been nicer if you'd asked ten minutes ago when I was still in there."

"I'll know better next time," he said.

As he went to the shower and Chloe started to get dressed, she realized that she was happy. *Quite* happy, in fact. Throwing a new case on top of all that had happened last night … it seemed as if her day had not been devastated by the sudden appearance of her father at all.

But if living with such an estranged family history had taught her anything, it was that you never truly escaped it. One way or the other, it always seemed to catch up with you.

Chapter Four

At roughly the same moment Chloe was being reminded what it felt like to lose herself in a man, her sister was in the middle of a nightmare.

Danielle Fine was dreaming about her mother again. It was a recurring dream she'd been having since the age of twelve or so—one that seemed to take on a different meaning with each stage of life Danielle entered into. The dream was always the same, never changing in detail or plot.

In the dream, her mother was chasing her down a long hallway. Only, it was the version of her mother that she and Chloe had discovered that day as young girls. Bleeding, wide-eyed, and lifeless. For some reason, the dream had always assumed she'd broken a leg in the fall (even though there were no official reports of any kind that had ever suggested such a thing) so the dream version of her mother dragged herself across the floor in pursuit of her daughter.

Despite the injury, her dead mother was always right on her heels, just a few fingertips away from grabbing her little ankle and pulling her down to the floor. Danielle ran away from the grisly vision in terror, her eyes cast to the end of the hallway. And there, standing in a doorway that seemed a universe away, was her father.

He would always be kneeling, opening his arms to her with a huge smile on his face. But there was blood dripping from his hands and in a moment of dream-panic that always woke her up, Danielle would stop running, stuck between her dead mother and her maniacal father, unsure of which direction was the safest.

It was no different now. The dream came to a crashing conclusion, jarring Danielle awake. She sat up in bed slowly, so accustomed to the dream now that she knew what it was even before she was fully awake. Groggily, she looked over to the clock and saw that it was only 11:30. She'd only been asleep for about an hour this time before the dream had come sneaking in.

She lay back down, knowing that it would take a while before she'd be able to go back to sleep. She shook the dream away, having learned many years ago how to shut it out by reminding herself that there was nothing she could have done to keep her mother from dying. Even if she had come clean with all of her little secrets about things she had seen and heard and experienced in regards to her father's toxic personality, there was nothing she could have said or done that would have kept her mother alive.

She turned over and looked toward the bedside table. She almost reached for the phone to call Chloe. It had been three weeks since they'd last spoken. It had been tense and awkward and it had been her fault. She knew she had been projecting a lot of negativity toward Chloe, primarily because Chloe didn't hate their father with the venom and angst that she did. It had been Danielle who had made the call three weeks ago, realizing that Chloe was waiting for her to make the next move since the last conversation they'd had before that had not gone so well—with Danielle practically telling her sister not to reach out.

But she didn't know Chloe's schedule. She had no idea if 11:30 was too late. Truth be told, Danielle had been having trouble falling asleep before two in the morning as of late. Tonight was one of her rare nights off from the lounge and also a night where she was not needed for any sort of sign-offs or approvals for the renovation of the bar her boyfriend bought for her.

She quickly pushed all thoughts of work out of her head as she searched for sleep. If she started thinking about work and everything on her plate, she would never get back to sleep.

Once again, she thought of Chloe. She wondered what sorts of dreams and nightmares her sister had about their parents. She wondered if she was still hung up on the idea of freeing their father and, if so, whether she had decided to keep it to herself.

Eventually, sleep caught back up to her. When it did, Danielle's last thought was of her sister. She thought of Chloe and wondered if it was finally time to forgive and forget—to let the memories of their father stop roadblocking her from a meaningful relationship with Chloe.

She was surprised at how happy the thought made her... so happy that when she did fall asleep again, there were the thinnest little traces of a smile on her face.

The young bartender who had been hired as her replacement had caught on quickly. She was twenty years old, drop-dead gorgeous, and was like some sort of savant at reading drunk men. Because she was doing so well, Danielle was able to meet with her boyfriend and the contractors at the building that would be her own pub and restaurant in about a month and a half.

Today, there was HVAC work being done, as well as some last-minute paneling in a back room that would serve as a reserved room for larger parties. When she arrived at the scene, her boyfriend was looking over a contract with an electrician. They were sitting at one of the tables that had recently been unpacked—one of three set-ups Danielle was supposed to choose from in terms of the types of tables she'd have in the restaurant.

Her boyfriend saw her as she entered. He quickly said something to the electrician and then came over to meet her. His name was Sam Dekker and while he wasn't necessarily the most honest or intelligent man, he made up for it in rugged good looks and a shrewd yet refined business acumen. He was about eight inches taller than she was so when he gave her a quick kiss, he had to lean down to do so.

"Reporting for duty," she said. "What can I do today?"

Sam shrugged, looking around the place in an almost theatrical fashion. "Honestly, I don't think there's too much you can do. It's all starting to fall into place. I know it might seem silly, but you might want to start looking through the ABC catalogue and figure out which brands of liquor you prefer to serve. Go ahead and figure out where you want the little overhead speakers for music and things like that. Those are the sorts of things that get lost in the shuffle and suddenly pop up as last-minute nuisances near the end of the project."

"I guess I can do that," she said, a little disappointed.

There were days when she stepped onto the renovation site and felt as if Sam was really just entertaining her—giving her menial tasks to do so he could handle the important things. It felt degrading in a sense but she also had to remind herself that Sam knew what he was doing. He had opened three bars that were doing incredibly well, one of which he sold to some big national company last year for more than ten million dollars.

And now he was choosing to back her in her own little endeavor. It was an endeavor that he'd had to talk her into. He insisted that she had the smarts to run a place like this, but only after all of the moving parts had been set into place.

Most girls that date semi-wealthy guys get jewelry and cars, she thought as she walked to the soon-to-be lounge area. *Me ... I got a bar. Not a bad deal, I guess.*

She did feel a little out of her depth most of the time when she thought about the road ahead. She'd actually be in charge of a place. She'd be running things and making decisions. There was also a degree of guilt to it as well. She felt the opportunity had been handed to her for no real reason other than she had happened to end up in a relationship with a guy that knew how to get businesses started. As a result, she was aware that there were many things she had to sacrifice and things she simply allowed Sam to get away with. She never questioned his late nights out, always buying the stories that he was in meetings or with contractors, wining and dining them. She'd been a part of some of those meetings, so she knew it was true—most of the time.

She also felt that she had to show her appreciation as often as she could. That meant not nagging when she didn't see him for several days. It meant not getting too up in arms when he expected certain things in the bedroom. It meant not getting pissy because despite buying her a bar and trusting her to run it, the whole idea of marriage had not been mentioned a single time. Danielle was pretty sure Sam had no intentions of getting married. And for now, she was fine with that, so she saw no reason to argue about it.

Besides … what did she have to complain about? She'd finally met a guy who treated her like royalty—when he was around—and she seemed to be on a path to easily earned success.

It's because most things that seem too good to be true usually are, she thought.

When she reached the room that was going to be the lounge area, she pulled the digital blueprints up on her phone. She made indications where the speakers could go and also made a note about potentially adding some sort of tinted window along the back wall. It was in doing things like this that she felt the dream of it all becoming a reality. Somehow, this was all really happening to her.

"Hey …"

She turned and saw Sam standing in the framed doorway. He was smiling at her and looking at her with the hungry expression he often shot her way when he was feeling frisky.

"Hey yourself," she said.

"I know it seems like I just brushed you off," he said. "But really … these next few weeks, all I'm really going to need from you are a few signatures."

"You're working me too hard," she joked.

"I fully intended for your training with the newbie at the bar to take longer. It's not my fault we ended up hiring a bartending genius." He approached her and wrapped his arms around her waist. She had to look up into his eyes but it always made her feel safe for some odd reason; it made her feel like this man would always *literally* watch over her.

"Let's grab lunch later today," Sam said. "Something simple. Pizza and beer."

"Sounds good."

"And tomorrow … what do you say we go somewhere. A beach … South Carolina or somewhere like that."

"Really? That seems spontaneous and very much like a burden to all of this work around us. In other words … it sounds nothing like you."

"I know. But I've been getting so wrapped up in this project and... I realize I've been neglecting you. So I want to make it up to you."

"Sam, you're giving me my own business. That's more than enough."

"Fine. I'll be selfish about it then. I want to get away from all of this and be naked and alone with you near the ocean. That sound better?"

"It does, actually."

"Good. So go to the bar, check in on the newbie. I'll pick you up for lunch around noon."

She kissed him and although he was clearly rushing it, the sentiment of everything he had just said did not escape her. She knew it was hard for him to be emotional and sincere. She rarely saw that side of him so when she did, she dared not question it.

Danielle walked back through the mostly open spaces of the old brick building that would soon be her bar-slash-lounge. It was hard to think of it as hers, but that was very much the case.

When she stepped outside, the sun seemed brighter than it had when she had gone in. She smiled, still trying to make sense of everything her life had become. She thought of Chloe again and made the decision to call her in the next few days. Everything else in her life was going so well, she may as well try repairing the tense relationship between her and Chloe, too.

She got into her car and headed back to Sam's other bar—the bar he had hired her to work in six months ago. She was so distracted by the thought of going away with him for the weekend that she didn't notice the car parked on the side of the street as it inched out into traffic behind her.

If she *had* noticed it, she might have recognized the driver, though she hadn't seen him in a very long time.

Still, did a daughter ever truly forget what the face of her father looked like?

CHAPTER FIVE

When Chloe and Moulton arrived at Garcia's office, Director Johnson was already there, waiting for them. It appeared that he and Garcia had been looking through case files; Garcia had a few pulled up on his desktop screen while Johnson had a small pile of printouts in front of him.

"Thanks for coming so quickly," Johnson said. "We've got a case out in Virginia—a small town on the other side of Fredericksburg, in an upscale neighborhood. And I should probably start with saying that the victim's family has some very powerful political friends. That's why we've been called in. Well, that and the gruesome nature of the death."

As Chloe took a seat at the small table in the back of Garcia's office, she did her best not to seem too obvious that she was trying to create some distance between herself and Moulton. She knew that she was probably glowing, beaming from the way the night and the morning had gone. She wasn't sure how Johnson might react to any kind of relationship between them and she honestly didn't want to test it.

"What are we looking at?" Chloe asked.

"Four days ago, a husband came home from work to find his wife dead," Garcia said. "But it was more than that. She had not only been murdered, but brutally so. There were multiple stab wounds—sixteen by the coroner's count. The crime scene was a mess… blood everywhere. It's unlike anything the local PD has ever seen."

He slid a folder over to Chloe with a look of warning on his face. Chloe took it and opened it slowly. She peered inside, saw just a flash of the crime scene photo, and then closed it just as quickly. Based on her one glimpse alone, it looked more like a slaughterhouse than a murder scene.

"Who is the victim's family friends with?" Moulton asked. "You said someone in politics, right?"

"I'd really rather not give out that information," Johnson said. "We don't want it to seem as if the bureau plays favorites when it comes to bipartisan matters."

"What's the level of local police involvement?" Chloe asked.

"They've kicked off a county-wide manhunt and have the State PD involved," Garcia said. "But they're being asked to keep it quiet. The local PD is understandably upset because they feel like we're hindering a case that is already a bit outside of their comfort zone. So I need you to get down there as soon as you possibly can. Also… and please listen closely: I thought of you two for this case because of how well you've worked together in the past. And Agent Fine, you seem to have a knack for this small-town, isolated community sort of crime. However, if the case itself and those crime scene photos make you feel uneasy—like it might be a little too much for you to handle at this stage of your career—let me know now. I won't judge and it won't count as any sort of mark against you."

Chloe and Moulton exchanged a look and she could see that he was just as eager as she was to take the case. Still, unable to help himself, Moulton took a look at what was inside the folder. He grimaced a bit as he flipped past the few crime scene photos and scanned the very brief report in the back. He then looked back over to Chloe and gave a nod.

"We're good as far as I'm concerned," Chloe said.

"Same here," Moulton said. "And I appreciate the opportunity."

"Glad to hear it," Johnson said, getting to his feet. "I'm excited to see what you two can do. Now… get moving. You've got some driving to do."

Moulton was behind the wheel of the bureau car, heading off of the beltway and heading toward Virginia. Barnes Point was only an hour and twenty minutes away, but the Beltway made just about *anywhere* feel like it was on the other side of the planet.

"You sure about this?" he asked.

"About which part?"

"Working together on a case like this. I mean … we were making out like two horny teenagers about ten hours ago. Will you be able to keep your hands off of me while we're working?"

"Don't take this the wrong way," Chloe said, "but after what I saw in that folder, doing that with you again is the farthest thing from my mind."

Moulton nodded his understanding. He veered off onto the next ramp, hit a straight stretch, and stepped on the gas. "All jokes aside, though … I enjoyed last night. Even before the part back at your place. And I'd like to do it again. But with work …"

"We should remain strictly professional," she finished for him.

"Exactly. And, to that end," he said, sliding his iPad out of the hollowed center of the console, "I downloaded the case files while you were packing."

"Did you *not* pack?"

"You saw my bag. Yes, I packed. But I'm quick about it." He shot her a cute little sly grin as he said this, indicating that she had perhaps taken a bit longer than he had expected. "I didn't get a chance to look it over, though."

"Ah, some light reading material," Chloe said.

They both chuckled and when Moulton rested his hand on her knee while she started to read the file, Chloe wasn't sure they *would* be able to keep it professional.

She perused the case files, reading the important parts out loud for Moulton. They found that Garcia and Johnson had done a fine job of summing it up. The police report was quite detailed, as well as the pictures. They were still no easier to look at and Chloe didn't blame the local PD. She figured *any* small-town police force might be out of their element on something this violent and bloody.

They shared thoughts and theories and by the time they passed a sign telling them that Barnes Point was fifteen miles away, Chloe had changed her mind. She thought they *would* be capable of working professionally together. She had spent the last few weeks so wrapped up in her physical attraction to him that she had nearly forgotten how sharp and intuitive he could be when it came to casework.

The idea then occurred to her that if they could truly make this work, she might have what just about every woman on the planet desired: a man who respected her as an equal in career and intellect but also in the bedroom.

You're not even a day into this, a voice said in her head. Danielle's voice again. *Are you really getting all dreamy and ga-ga about it already? Jesus, you made out with him for a few hours and didn't even sleep together. You barely know him and—*

But Chloe chose to shut those thoughts away.

She then turned her attention to the coroner's report. It told the same story Johnson had told them, but in more detail. And it was these details that she focused on. The blood, the violence, the potential political motive. She read them over, studying with intense focus.

"I'm thinking this isn't politically motivated," she said. "I don't think the killer was too concerned with the powerful political friends that the Hilyards might have had."

"I heard confidence in that statement," Moulton said. "Please explain."

"Lauren Hilyard was stabbed sixteen times. And every single wound was centered in the abdomen area, with only a single stray one slicing into her left breast. The coroner reports that the wounds were ragged and almost on top of one another, indicating someone made stabbing motions one right behind the other. The note here in the reports says: *as if in a blind rage or frenzy.* If this was the act of someone with political motivation, there would likely be some sort of message or other indicator."

"Okay, then," Moulton said. "I'm on board. It's not politically motivated."

"That was easy."

He shrugged and said, "I'm coming to understand that people in DC think *everything* has political motivations. So what if the Hilyards maybe sort of kind of know someone higher up in a political office. Not everyone is going to care."

"I like the way you think," she said. "But I don't know that we rule it out one hundred percent just yet."

They were closing in on Barnes Point, and the fact that they had been entrusted to round up a case with potential political ties was not lost on her. It was an amazing opportunity for both of them and she had to make sure that was where her focus was for the time being. For now, nothing was more important than that—not suddenly reappearing estranged fathers, not the voice of her stubborn and joy-dead sister…not even a potentially perfect romance with the man sitting next to her.

For now, there was the case and only the case. And that was more than enough for her.

Chapter Six

Barnes Point was a quiet yet cute city, with a population right at nine thousand. The Hilyard residence sat just outside the city limits, in a little subdivision called Farmington Acres. The victim's husband, Jerry Hilyard, had not yet been able to bring himself to return to his home since discovering his wife's body; with no immediate family living nearby, he had been invited to say elsewhere in the neighborhood, with close friends.

"I think I might have needed to get farther away than just a few houses down," Moulton said. "I mean, can you imagine what this poor guy is going through?"

"But he might also need to be close to his home," Chloe suggested. "To the place where he and his wife had shared a life together."

Moulton seemed to consider this as he drove their rental car further into the subdivision, toward the address the State Police had forwarded them while they'd been en route. It was yet another example of how Chloe was beginning to both understand and respect the fluidity of the way the bureau worked. It was hard to imagine that just about any information she needed—addresses, phone numbers, work histories, criminal records—was readily available, just a call or email away. She assumed agents eventually got used to this, but for now, she still felt quite privileged to be part of such a system.

They arrived at the address and walked to the door. The mailbox read *Lovingston* and the house itself was a carbon copy of just about all of the other homes in the neighborhood. It was the sort of neighborhood where the houses were right on top of one another but the environment was quiet—a good place for kids to learn to ride their bikes and probably a lot of fun during Halloween and Christmas.

Chloe knocked on the door and it was answered right away by a woman with a baby in her arms.

"Are you Mrs. Lovingston?" Chloe asked.

"I am. And you must be the FBI agents. We got a call from the police a while ago saying you'd be on your way."

"Is Jerry Hilyard still staying here?" Moulton asked.

A man appeared behind the woman, coming from the open room to the left. "Yeah, I'm still here," he said. He joined Mrs. Lovingston at the door and leaned against the door frame. He looked absolutely exhausted, apparently not having slept well ever since he had lost his wife in such a brutal fashion.

Mrs. Lovingston turned to him and gave him a glare that made Chloe think the baby in her arms might be in for some nasty looks in the future. "You sure you're up to this?" the woman asked him.

"I'm fine, Claire," he said. "Thanks."

She nodded, held her baby tighter to her chest, and headed back elsewhere in the house.

"Come on in, I guess," Jerry said.

He led them into the same room he had come in from. It looked to be a small den of sorts, mostly decorated with books and two elegant-looking chairs. Jerry fell into one of the chairs as if his bones were starting to give out on him.

"I know Claire might seem a little hesitant about you being here," Jerry said. "But… she and Lauren were good friends. She thinks I need to be grieving… which I am. It's just…"

He stopped here and Chloe could see him wrestling with a flood of emotion, trying to make it through this conversation without crumbling in front of them.

"Mr. Hilyard, I'm Agent Fine and this is my partner, Agent Moulton. I was wondering if you might be able to tell us about any political ties your family might have."

"Jesus," he breathed. "It's overblown. The local PD made a huge fuss about it and got all freaked out. I'm pretty sure that's why you were called in, right?"

"*Are* there political ties?" Moulton asked, sidestepping the question.

"Lauren's father used to be really good golf buddies with the Secretary of Defense. They grew up together, played football together, all that. They still hang out on occasion—duck hunting, fishing, things like that."

"Did Lauren ever speak with the Secretary?" Chloe asked.

"Not since we've been married. He came to our wedding. We get a Christmas card from his family. But that's about it."

"So do you think what happened might be due to that relationship?" Moulton asked.

"If it is, I have no idea why. Lauren was not into politics at all. I think it's just her father's way of making himself seem important. Someone killed his little girl so it *must* be because he knows important people. He's kind of an ass like that."

"So what can you tell us about the last few days of Lauren's life?" Chloe asked.

"I've already told the police everything I could."

"We understand that," Moulton said. "And we have copies of all of their reports. But for us to properly get a foothold here, we may be asking you some questions that have you repeating a few things."

"Fine, that's good," Jerry said.

Chloe thought the man might not quite be aware of what was happening, exactly. He looked incredibly detached. If she didn't already know the traumatic situation he was going through, she might have assumed he was on drugs.

"The first question may seem silly in light of what has happened," Chloe said, "but can you think of anyone who might have had a reason to be upset with your wife?"

He sneered and shook his head. When he spoke, his voice trembled in a sort of eternal yawn. "No. Lauren stayed to herself these days. An introvert. It had gotten even worse as of late ... drawing into herself, you know?"

"Any idea why?"

"She had a rough past. Messed up parents and all that. She was sort of a bully in high school. I guess that's what she'd be classified as these days. Or maybe a mean girl. She'd been coming to terms with those mistakes as of late. I think it got worse when she got that damned high school reunion invitation in the mail."

"She was anxious about going?" Chloe asked.

"I'm not sure. It made her sad, I think ... to think about the people she had maybe been mean to."

"Did the two of you graduate together?" Moulton asked.

"We did."

"And did you go with her to the reunion?"

"God no. I hate that sort of stuff. Posturing and pretending to like people you mostly hated in high school. No. I sat it out."

"You say she was an introvert," Chloe said. "Did she not have many friends?"

"Oh, she had a few. Claire was one of them. And the friends she did have were like family to her. They were extremely close."

"Have you spoken with them since this happened?" Moulton asked.

"Just one. She called shortly after she found out to see if I needed anything."

"Are these friends that perhaps went to the reunion with her?"

"Yeah. Claire went, too. But she's also sort of an introvert. I think she went just out of curiosity."

"Do you and Lauren have any children?" Chloe asked. "A neighborhood like this, I figured there would be at least one kid in every house."

"We have two. Our oldest, Victoria, is eighteen; she just started college this year. She ... well, she chose to spend this very difficult time with her grandparents. And because she went with them, our youngest—Carter—wanted to go, too. I've never had the best relationship with my in-laws but my kids being with them right now is a godsend. I feel like a terrible father, but if my kids were here, I'd crumple up and just break, I think."

"Is there any animosity about your children being with their grandparents right now?" Moulton asked.

"I want them here with me ... just to see them. But I'm a mess. And until the house is in better shape ... that's where they need to be."

"You said your oldest *chose* to be with them during this time," Moulton said. "Why is that?"

"She couldn't wait to get out of our house. She had a strained relationship with Lauren for the last few years. Some toxic mother-daughter stuff. Our daughter ... she was having boys over, sneaking in the house at night. She was doing this as young as thirteen. Had her first pregnancy scare at fifteen. And if you do the math in your head ... Lauren was thirty-seven. We had our daughter when Lauren and I were both nineteen."

Chloe thought the tumultuous family situation could not be making this any easier on Jerry Hilyard. She didn't think there was anything there worth digging into, though it might do some good to eventually speak with the daughter.

"Mr. Hilyard, would you have any objection to us taking a look around your house?" she asked.

"That's fine. The sheriff and a few of his men have been in and out a few times. The code to get in is two-two-two-eight."

"Thank you, Mr. Hilyard," Moulton said. "Please contact us if you think of anything else. For now, I think we'll speak with Mrs. Lovingston to see if she has any details to share."

"She's told the police everything she knows. She's starting to get irritated, I think."

"What about her husband? Did he know your wife well? Did the four of you frequently hang out together?"

"No. Claire's husband works out of town quite a bit. I did FaceTime him to make sure he was okay with me staying here. And anyway, it was mainly just Claire and Lauren. They had a weekly thing where they'd drink wine on the front porch, switching houses every week."

Claire stepped into the room slowly, apparently having put the baby she had been carrying down for a nap.

"And we'd do the predictable things that women do. Talk about our husbands, reminisce about the past. I'd tell her about the highs and lows of having a baby. And, more recently, we'd talk about what she was going through with her daughter."

"What can you tell us about Lauren and what might have led someone to do such a thing to her?" Chloe asked.

"Lauren made some decisions during high school that her parents did not particularly agree about," Claire replied. "Once Lauren graduated high school and had her daughter … well, college was out of the picture."

"They were embarrassed," Jerry added. "They got pissed and moved to New Hampshire. They feed our daughter these brutal lies about Lauren whenever they can."

"Trying to make up for the mistakes and neglect from raising Lauren," Claire said. "A couple of real assholes."

Sensing the conversation headed to a bashing session, Chloe spoke up. "Mrs. Lovingston, would *you* happen to be able to think of any enemies or even strained relationships Lauren might have had?" Chloe asked.

"Not outside of her family. And while they are a couple of jerks, they certainly wouldn't do this. This is … this is deplorable."

Moulton reached into his inner pocket and pulled out a business card. He placed it on the coffee table and stepped back. "Please … if either of you think of anything else, please don't hesitate to contact us."

Both Claire and Jerry gave only curt nods. The conversation had been brief but it had taken its toll on them. Chloe and Moulton made their exit in an awkward silence.

When they were outside, heading for the car, Chloe paused for a moment on the sidewalk. She looked down the street, in the direction of the Hilyard house, and saw that it was just out of sight. Still, she was starting to agree with Moulton. Maybe it was a little too close. And if the bedroom still looked anything like what she had seen in the photographs Johnson had showed them, it seemed almost morbid that Jerry was staying so close.

"Ready to go check out the house?" Chloe asked.

"Not really," Moulton said, the images he'd seen from that case file still clearly in his mind. "But I guess we've got to start somewhere."

They got back into the car and headed back the way they had come. Right away, Chloe kept telling herself that it couldn't be as bad as it had appeared in the pictures—all of that crimson red among the crisp white sheets.

⚜ ⚜ ⚜

It took all of twenty seconds to get to the Hilyard house. The fact that it closely resembled the Lovingston house—and most every other house on the block—was creepy as hell as far as Chloe was concerned. They entered through the front door with the code Jerry Hilyard had given them and stepped into an absolutely still and silent house.

Knowing exactly why they were there, they wasted no time and went directly upstairs. The master bedroom was easy to find, the room all the way at the end of the hallway. Through the opened door, Chloe could already see streaks of red on the carpet and the sheets.

She was relieved, however, to find that the scene truly didn't look as bad as it had appeared in the pictures Director Johnson had showed them. First and foremost, the body had been removed. Secondly, the bloodstains had been sitting longer, making them paler in color.

They walked to the bed, careful to step over any blood splashes left on the carpet. She could see areas in the blood splatter where the coroner and initial investigators had accidentally stepped in it. Chloe looked to the other side of the room, toward a dresser and where a small flat-screen TV was mounted to the wall. *She was probably watching TV when it happened, maybe purging her head of high school reunion memories ...*

Chloe then went downstairs and had a look around. She could see no signs of forced entry and no clear indications that anything had been stolen. She looked around the living room, the kitchen, and the guest bedroom. She evens stepped out on the back deck and had a look around. There was a small patio table in the corner. An ashtray sat in the center of it, under the shade umbrella.

Chloe made a *hmm* sound as she saw the ashtray's contents. There were no cigarette butts in the tray, but some other kind of ash and paper. She leaned down to it and took a light whiff. The scent of marijuana was unmistakable. She sorted through some things in her head, trying to figure out if this could be relevant in any way.

Chloe jumped a bit when her phone rang. Moulton, stepping out onto the back porch to join her, caught her look of momentary shock and smiled. She rolled her eyes and answered the call, not recognizing the number.

"This is Agent Fine," she answered.

"This is Claire Lovingston. I thought you might want to know that I just got a call from one of my friends, Tabby North. She was one of the close friends that Jerry was telling you about. She asked if anyone else from the police had come to speak with me. I told them the FBI had just visited and she'd like to speak with you."

"Does she have information for us?"

"Honestly… I don't know. Probably not. But this is a rather small community. I think they just want to get to the bottom of it. I'm sure you'll find them incredibly helpful."

"Great. Text me her number after this call."

Chloe killed the call and filled Moulton in. "That was Claire. She said one of Lauren's other friends called her to see if anything new had developed. She'd like to speak with us."

"Good. I won't lie… I'm pretty much done here. That bedroom is giving me the creeps."

It was a good way to explain it. Chloe could still see the pictures in her head, so seeing the scene without the body was like looking into some old abandoned place she was not meant to see.

Still, they went back to the bedroom and took some time to check the place over, looking in the bathroom, the walk-in closet, even under the bed. After finding nothing of interest, they left the house and, moments later, the Farmington Acres neighborhood. Chloe again thought that it was incredibly quaint—a perfect neighborhood to grow a family and shape a future.

So long as you were okay knowing that, from time to time, there might be a murder to contend with.

Chapter Seven

Tabby North was a redhead who had the kind of body that Chloe assumed saw the gym at least four days a week; it was also a body that, in Chloe's humble opinion, could use a few more meals. She was gorgeous in a very obvious way, but she looked as if a strong wind might blow her away.

Chloe and Moulton met Tabby at her house and found that she had invited another close friend, a woman who apparently went to that very same gym with Tabby. This woman was Kaitlin St. John, who was crying when Chloe and Moulton showed up. They gathered together on Tabby's screened-in back porch, where Tabby treated them to a pitcher of lavender lemonade. Chloe could not help the thoughts that blew through her head—of how pretentious it all seemed, these women quickly approaching forty, with their tiny waists and trendy health-nut drinks.

These thoughts are certainly not why Johnson stated he thought you had a knack for these small neighborhood-based cases, she thought to herself.

To be polite, she sipped from the lemonade. Despite her negative thoughts, it was actually delicious.

"I assume you ladies have already spoken to the police?" Chloe asked.

"Yes," Tabby said. "And while I fully understand that they are doing their best, it was quite clear that they had no idea what they were doing."

"They're spooked, too," Kaitlin said.

"Spooked by what?" Moulton asked.

"By the idea that it might have some sort of political reasoning. I guess you know about Lauren's dad being all buddy-buddy with the Secretary of Defense. I'm sure the local police would rather avoid a media circus if they can help it."

"So, *is it* politically connected?" Tabby asked.

"It's far too early to know for sure," Chloe said. Already, she was getting an uncomfortable vibe from these two. She did not doubt their grief; it was apparent in their expressions and the fact that Kaitlin had been openly crying since they'd showed up. But she also had no real problem picturing these two sitting around—perhaps with Lauren Hilyard and Claire Lovingston—gossiping about everyone in town. She wondered how much of what they might discuss right here and now would end up hitting the Barnes Point grapevine.

"Can you tell us when you last saw Lauren?" Moulton asked.

"It was the night before she died," Tabby said. "We all met up at our high school reunion."

"We practically had to drag Lauren to it," Kaitlin said. "She always hated that kind of thing."

"Well, she hated that sort of thing *after* school was over," Tabby corrected. "She always wanted to try to leave the high school years in the past."

"Did she seem any different that night?" Chloe asked.

"Nothing that I noticed," Tabby said.

"Same here," Kaitlin said. "I daresay she ended up having some fun later on in the night. Lauren…well, she was the heartthrob of our high school. All the guys wanted her and when Jerry Hilyard just happened to knock her up during senior year…man, it was like the place had exploded. She lost some of that allure, you know. But the way everyone treated her that night at the reunion…I think everyone forgot about that. And it was like she was the queen bee all over again. I think she needed that."

"Was there a big crowd?" Moulton asked.

"Pretty big," Tabby said. "This is sort of a strange part of town. Lots of people that went to our high school either graduated or ended up coming back this way after college. It's not exactly a wealthy city, but this side of town is known for being the wealthy side, you know? Anyway, for a few moments, Lauren actually looked happy."

"We understand that Lauren was among those that graduated and stayed around," Chloe said. "Were you all friends in high school?"

"Yes. Hell… Lauren and Claire were friends from kindergarten."

"So would you say they were the closest out of the four of you?"

"Probably," Kaitlin said. "They've always been besties. We know they had their little private porch sessions. It's sweet… but yeah, from time to time, I felt a little left out. How about you, Tab?"

Tabby shrugged. "Not really. I always knew they were super close."

"Was there anyone at the reunion that maybe crossed Lauren the wrong way?" Moulton asked.

"Not that I remember," Tabby said.

"Same here," Kaitlin said. "But you know… you live in a place like this where a lot of the people you grew up with stick around for the long haul and things can get tense sometimes. It was obvious between *some* people at the reunion. But not with Lauren. I don't think she really had many people that disliked her in high school. Jealous for sure… but not *dislike*."

"Did you maybe meet up with anyone else at the reunion that Lauren was friendly with in high school but sort of drifted away from afterwards?"

"We did, actually," Tabby said. "A woman named Brandie Scott. She lives in town, too. Just on the other side… so we never really see her. It was nice to reunite with her, though. I wouldn't say we were all that friendly with her, just maybe talked to her a few times in school, but never hung out."

"Did she and Lauren hang out at the reunion?"

"For a while. I actually specifically remember them laughing about something over by the bar. I remember because Lauren hadn't really laughed a lot recently. I think she had something going on at home. Maybe with her stupid parents again."

"Would you happen to have Ms. Scott's phone number?" Moulton asked.

"I do," Tabby said, taking out her phone and starting to scroll. "I actually got it from her the night of the reunion."

"What about ex-boyfriends?" Chloe asked as Tabby found the number. "Were there any of Lauren's exes in attendance?"

"No," Kaitlin said, smiling for the first time during the conversation. "Lauren only ever dated one guy before Jerry. And the only reason they broke up was because he moved. To Alabama, I think."

"Well, I think that's all we need for now," Chloe said. She slid Tabby one of her business cards and said: "Please send Ms. Scott's information to this number. And don't hesitate to contact me if either of you think of anything else that may be helpful."

Tabby texted Brandie Scott's number right away. She looked a little disappointed that the conversation was over. But, as Chloe had suspected from the start, a group of best friends that were caught up in memories of the friend they had just lost was not going to be the best source of information. If there was any dirt to uncover, she and Moulton were not going to find it here.

She took one last sip from her lemonade and got to her feet. Both of the women escorted them back through the lovely house and through the front door. They both stood on the porch and watched as Chloe and Moulton left.

"Initial thoughts?" Moulton asked.

"I think they're both very sad about the loss of their friend," Chloe said. "But I also think that just about every word of the conversation we just had with them will be public knowledge in Barnes Point by the end of the day."

"I got that same feeling, too. And tell me … maybe it's just me. Is there something sort of weird about these older women hanging out in the same city, in the same circles they were in during high school?"

"I for one would never do it," Chloe said. "But I don't think it's as uncommon as you might think. Especially in smaller towns."

Moulton started the car and pulled away from Tabby North's house. "Want to check out this other sort-of friend?" he asked. "Brandie something-or-another?"

"Already on it," she said, saving the number Tabby had sent her to her contacts list. She then placed the call, already hoping that the woman on the other end would turn out to be at least somewhat different from the thin and almost cliché housewives she'd met so far today.

As Tabby had said, Brandie Scott lived on the other side of Barnes Point. It was only a fifteen-minute drive between the houses, but Brandie Scott may as well have been living on the other side of the world. Where the carbon copy two-story homes in the expensive plots within Farmington Acres and surrounding areas painted a picture of wealth and well-to-do homeowners, the other side of town was quite different. There were mobile home parks and one-story homes that looked nearly abandoned, many with sings that either read FOR SALE or CONDEMNED on them. There were old shops that had been closed for quite some time. This side of town looked like something the better part of town had perhaps vomited up and tried to cover up hastily in its tracks.

Brandie Scott had agreed to meet them at a little coffee shop on a street that showed some of the signs of neglect as the rest of the area but was still somehow alive and thriving. When Chloe and Moulton entered the place, all eyes were on them—which weren't many, seeing as how it was 4:15 on a Thursday afternoon.

A slightly overweight woman waved to them from the third table to the right. She did so as quickly and subtly as she could, as to not draw more attention to herself. Chloe and Moulton walked over to her and the woman visibly grew tense.

"Brandie Scott?" Moulton asked.

"That's me," she said. "Have a seat, I guess."

The agents did so and once they were seated, Brandie seemed to relax her posture just a bit. "I hate to be a nag," she said, "but I don't have much time. I had to ask for an hour off of work to come here to meet you."

"Oh, I'm sorry," Chloe said. "You work here in town?"

"I do. I have two jobs, actually. I work nights as a janitor out at the hospital in Farmville. And I also squeeze in about twenty hours a week at Dollar General here in town … which is what I'm doing now."

"You sound like a busy lady," Chloe said. "We'll make it as quick as possible. We assume you know about what happened to Lauren Hilyard?"

"Yeah, I heard. Tabby North told me two days ago."

"Since it happened, have you spoken to the police?"

"No. They haven't reached out."

"Well, as I told you on the phone, we just came from Tabby North's house where we spoke with her and Kaitlin St. John. They mentioned that you and Lauren weren't ever particularly close, but that you talked quite a bit at the high school reunion over the weekend."

"Yeah, we did. They're right … Lauren and I were never really close. But unlike a lot of those women, Lauren at least made a point to try to be polite when she saw me."

"What do you mean by *those women*?" Moulton asked.

"Women like Tabby North. Claire Lovingston and that whole bunch. Some of them think the rules of high school still apply—that they're required to continue to oust the girls that weren't popular in school."

"But you say Lauren wasn't like that?" Chloe asked.

"It depends on who you ask. If I'm being honest, she was one of those mean girls in high school, you know? She was never really mean to me but went out of her way to ignore me. I'd like to think that changed with her after high school … but I don't know her well enough to be sure. The few times I ran into her, she seemed a little different … not quite as mean-spirited."

"Do you recall her having a lot of enemies in high school?"

"There were plenty of people that were jealous of her. But I think hate might be a strong word. People like me, if I'm being honest, were very jealous of her. She was beautiful and had the attention of all of the guys. But it was mostly jealousy, you know? She was that unattainable girl … the girl all the dudes wanted and all the girls wanted to be. You know the type? So while there were plenty of people that surely didn't like her, I think it would be a stretch to call those people enemies."

"So when you spoke with her at the reunion, was it cordial or sort of forced?" Chloe asked.

"It was a very friendly conversation. She had come into Dollar General a few days before to get some sort of weed killer for her flower beds. We chatted a bit then and when I saw her at the reunion, I was just being polite—asked her how her flowers were doing. It got us on a tangent about some stupid project we'd had to do for biology in high school."

"Even though she was polite to you on occasion after high school, do you know if there were any people she was *not* polite to?"

"Oh, I'm sure there are several. One person that instantly comes to mind is the woman that used to work as a nanny for the Hilyards."

"What's the story there?"

"Well, years ago, Lauren was working as a hairdresser in the better part of town. And Jerry had the same job he has now—some sort of marketing or copywriting job for the only ad firm here in Barnes Point. So there were a lot of late hours. This was years ago, when Victoria still needed a babysitter and wasn't old enough to watch Carter herself. They hired a nanny and from the way the story goes, it didn't last very long. Some sort of altercation took place between Lauren and the nanny. There are about a hundred versions of the story floating around town but the way I understand it, Lauren ended up slapping this woman and pushing her off of the front porch, screaming at her. There was some talk of the nanny pressing charges but it never came to anything."

"If that story is true, does it jive with how you remember Lauren in high school?" Moulton asked.

"Maybe not to that extreme, but yes … it reminded me a lot of the Lauren I knew back then. *If* the whole story is true."

"Can you think of any other stories like that since after graduation?" Chloe asked.

Brandie thought about it for a moment and then shook her head. "No. That's the only one that sticks out."

"Do you happen to have a name for that nanny?" she asked.

"Yvonne Dixon. She's still here in town. Lives right up the street in one of the Gladstone Apartments, in fact."

"Are you close with her?" Chloe asked.

"No. But on this side of town, you tend to start to know where everyone lives. I'm pretty sure she'd be open to talking to you. And I don't know what it is … but it always seems that babysitters and nannies always have the best gossip. The most truthful gossip … if there's such a thing."

During the course of her brief career, Chloe knew that this did tend to be the case. She assumed it was especially true in a smaller community like this. Having a nanny who once worked for the Hilyards as a potential lead made the case feel like it had some wheels to it—like they might wrap this thing before barely even got started.

CHAPTER EIGHT

Chloe did her best to keep her feelings in check, but being an active agent was still so new to her that it made her want to break out into a grin whenever she had the chance to flash her ID and badge. She found herself doing just that as she and Moulton spoke with the owner/landlord of the Gladstone Apartments complex.

"FBI?" the owner asked, genuinely shocked. "What on earth do you need to speak with Ms. Dixon for?" He was an aging man, pushing sixty, hiding his stark white hair beneath a John Deere hat.

"We're not at liberty to say," Chloe said. "Although, for your peace of mind, I can assure you it's not in regards to anything she's done."

"It's about that Lauren Hilyard murder, isn't it?" the owner asked.

"I'm sorry sir, we really can't say," Moulton echoed.

"Can we please just get her apartment number and contact information?" Chloe asked.

The owner nodded and went to a tattered filing cabinet behind his desk. He flipped through a few papers and brought one back over to them. It had her apartment number listed, as well as her phone number and last known residence before becoming a resident of Gladstone Apartments.

Chloe snapped a picture of the document with her phone and nodded her thanks to the owner.

"Do you know if she's currently working anywhere?" Chloe asked.

"Working as a babysitter for some family out on the other side of town in one of those subdivisions."

"Farmington Acres?" Moulton asked.

"Nah, some other one. I don't know the names of all of them. But if you're looking to talk to her, I'm pretty sure she's home. I saw her car out there in the parking lot when I came back inside from cleaning out the gutters about half an hour ago."

"Thank you very much," Chloe said.

She and Moulton stepped back outside, Chloe looking to the picture she had snapped. "Apartment number seven," she said.

The apartment complex was two stories, each story holding eight apartments. It was the type of apartment building where the stairs were all outside and the entire place looked like one big house rather than an apartment building. They followed the order of the numbers on the door and found number seven at the very bottom corner of the first floor.

Moulton knocked on the door and they heard an immediate, "One second," called out from inside.

Yvonne Dixon answered the door about twenty seconds later. She was sweating a bit and the apartment behind her smelled like Lysol or Mop and Glo, or some similar cleaning product. She gave them a skeptical look, not opening the door all the way.

"Can I help you?"

Again, Chloe was delighted to flash her badge and ID. "We were hoping you might have some time to speak with us about your history with Lauren Hilyard."

Yvonne frowned slightly as she glanced back and forth between the agents. "I heard about that," she said. "It's … well, it's sad."

"We understand you used to work for her," Chloe said.

"Yeah, I did." She paused a moment, apparently seeing where this trail was going to eventually lead. She opened her door up and waved them inside. "Come on in. But excuse the mess. You caught me in the middle of cleaning."

They walked inside and Chloe found that while the apartment itself was small and rather dingy, Yvonne kept it tidy and clean.

"The landlord told us that you have a job out on the other side of town," Moulton said. "Did you have the day off?"

"No. I work for the Nelson family. The father is usually on the road, traveling for business. The mother works a dispatch position for the sheriff's department in town. She has some odd hours, usually forcing me to wake up around four in the morning. But it gives me the afternoons off; she's usually off of work by three or so."

"How long have you worked for this family?" Chloe asked.

"A little over three years."

"Well, according to the story around town, things didn't particularly end well with you and Lauren Hilyard."

"That's putting it mildly," Yvonne said. "I'm sure there are many versions of the story floating around town, but here's what *really* happened. Carter, their son, was five at the time. He was preschool age and Lauren had me going through this really simple and quick tutorial sort of thing to help prepare him for kindergarten. She much preferred that over sending him to one of the preschools in town. The kid was bright as all get out and whenever he did exceptionally well, I'd give him a Blow Pop as a reward—a reward, mind you, that Lauren approved of.

"Well, this one day . . . I still don't know how it happened, but Carter got the gum from the Blow Pop in his hair. And he didn't bother telling me. He was playing in his room then comes down and tells me it's been there for like fifteen minutes. I did my best to get it out with some weird methods I found online—dish soap, peanut butter, all that. But nothing worked. I tried calling Lauren but she never answered her phone. So I made a judgment call and I cut it out. It didn't *butcher* his hair or anything, but it was noticeable. When Lauren got home and saw it, she went right the hell off. She had lost her temper with me several times before, but this was *bad.* This was nuclear."

"We heard she slapped you," Moulton said.

"Yeah, she did. She asked me to step out on the porch to talk. I assumed it was so her kids wouldn't hear us arguing. The moment I stepped out there, she started screaming at me. The moment I tried to get a word in, she slapped me. Busted my lip and took me by such surprise that I damn near fell down her porch steps."

"I assume she fired you that day?" Chloe asked.

"That's just the thing. When I didn't show up the following day, she called to see where I was . . . like she fully expected me to come in. It was like she was pretending nothing had happened. She eventually apologized for slapping me. But of course, I never went back to work for her."

"Did you speak to her at all after that? Like maybe whenever you might have happened to pass by one another in town?"

"No. It was always just dead silence. Jerry did try to approach me one day in the grocery store to make amends but I told him I wasn't interested."

"Do you remember what she was like in high school?" Moulton asked.

"I didn't go to school around here. I moved to Barnes Point for a guy. A guy that ended up beating on me and moving away. But then I was sort of stuck …"

"How are you typically treated by the little groups of women around town?" Chloe asked. "I know this place can be a bit clique-y."

"I'm never *mis*treated, but it's clear that if you haven't *always* been part of the group, you aren't welcome in."

"So it's safe to say that you have an unbiased opinion of the friend groups around here?"

"I suppose so. I will say that most of the women around here come off as being stuck up. Like they're better than you. Which is dumb. Because if they were all that, why the hell did they stick around a place like Barnes Point after high school or college?"

"Well, given your rather neutral position on the town and its people," Chloe said, "can you tell us of anyone else you think might have been rubbed the wrong way by Lauren Hilyard?"

"As a matter of fact, yes. Just last week, I heard that she had fired the guy they had coming in to rework her flower beds."

"Did things get out of hand?" Moulton asked.

"From the way I hear it, it did. A little screaming match and everything. It wasn't until later that I found out the guy she had hired was sort of a creep. And I think that's why Lauren fired him."

"What do you mean?"

"The guy is a Hispanic dude that doesn't live around here, but used to do a lot of work for the wealthier families. A jack-of-all-trades sort of guy. Landscaping, light carpentry, that sort of thing. Then word got out that he got caught peeking into windows and … um, well, pleasuring himself while he peeked."

"Do you have a name for this guy?"

"Sorry, no. But he drives a blue truck with one of those ladder and utility racks on the back. The sticker on the side of the truck says First Choice Handyman."

"How reliable would you say this story is?" Chloe asked.

"Pretty reliable. I heard it from a woman that lives a few houses down from the Hilyards. She works at the bank and those ladies are *always* gossiping. She said she and her husband were out for a walk when Lauren had her little shouting match with him."

"Thank you very much for your time," Chloe said.

"Sure," Yvonne said. "But... there are people talking. Saying that Lauren's death is related to some sort of political stuff. Is that true?"

"It's really just too early to say," Chloe said. "But hopefully the information you just gave us can help us find out."

Yvonne seemed pleased with this, giving them the faintest of smiles as they walked toward the door. She opened it for them and saw them out, giving them a wave as they got into the car.

"First Choice Handyman," Moulton said as he typed it into his phone. He found the number on Google and called it right away. "Let's find out if he was doing anything more that working the flower beds when he was at the Hilyards' residence."

Chapter Nine

When calling First Choice Handyman, Moulton was met with a voice message. The recorded message told him that business hours were from eight to five and that if he left a message, someone would call him back soon. Moulton did not leave a message. Instead, he went back to the Google search results and found out more about the business. It was owned by a man named Oscar Alvarez. The business had several reviews on Google and Yelp. The ones that specifically mentioned the man's level of work were all great. But many of them seemed to be bemoaning the fact that he had been caught masturbating while looking through windows. One even suggested that Oscar Alverez peddled child pornography.

"Damn, the internet can be a mean place," he said. "I wonder how soon we can get this guy's records from the bureau."

"I think we'd be better off just heading to the local police department to see what they have."

"And that's why you're considered the lead on this case," Moulton said with a smile.

They located the Barnes Point police station thirteen minutes later. It was located at the end of a rather long Main Street stretch that seemed to be situated right in the zone that separated the wealthier side of town from the other side of the tracks.

When they walked inside, the woman at the reception desk gave them a smile. Chloe wondered if Ms. Nelson—the mother of the family that Yvonne Dixon currently worked for—had been sitting there earlier in the day.

"Can I help you?" the woman asked.

"We're the FBI agents that were sent out to look into Lauren Hilyard's murder," Chloe said. "We were hoping to get some information about a man that we believe might be a suspect."

"Oh, you'll want to speak with Sheriff Jenkins," she said. "And boy, will he be glad to speak with you. I'll buzz him and let him know you're here. But go ahead and go on back. He's the last door on the left at the end of the hall."

They walked beyond the counter and through a door that the receptionist buzzed them through. They found the sheriff's office at the end of the hall, the door already open.

"Sheriff Jenkins?" Chloe asked.

The middle-aged man behind the desk looked up from a stack of papers he had been sorting through. Behind him, a map of the state was on the wall, marked up and labeled with various Post-its.

"Yeah?" he asked. But he seemed to understand who they were within another second or two … perhaps by the way they were dressed. "You with the bureau?"

"We are," Chloe said. They both showed their identification and introduced themselves. At once, Jenkins seemed relieved.

"Well, I don't have much on the Hilyard case," he said. "But what I do have, you're welcome to."

"We actually think we might have a lead," Chloe said. "We were wondering what you might be able to tell us about a guy named Oscar Alverez."

"Ah hell," Jenkins said, reclining back in his chair, looking as if it was the first bit of rest he had gotten all day. "How'd his name come up?"

"We spoke with a few people and discovered that Lauren Hilyard fired Alvarez last week, the day before the high school reunion."

Jenkins shook his head slowly. "See … I hadn't heard that yet. I've talked with everyone I could think of that was close to that family and didn't hear that a single time. I didn't even know they had hired Alvarez for anything."

"From what we gathered, he was leveling out the ground for the flower beds. There was apparently some huge fight, seen by one of the Hilyards' neighbors and then passed around the town grapevine."

"Well, *that* I can believe." He rolled his chair over to a filing cabinet and thumbed through some of the documents. Chloe wasn't sure why, but she always felt a certain charm whenever she watched someone use a filing cabinet. It was something reliable, something tangible and not encoded on some network or electronic filing system.

"Oscar Alvarez," Jenkins said, pulling out a folder and sliding it over to them. Moulton picked the folder up but didn't look through it yet. He seemed to be perfectly happy listening to Jenkins as he gave a play-by-play. "He was arrested for lewd conduct two years ago while building a back porch for the Harper family. According to Mrs. Harper, she saw him fondling himself one time but figured maybe he was… well, *adjusting* or scratching. But then she caught him trying to peer through her bedroom window while she was changing, again fondling himself. Forgive me for being so crude, but he left some… *evidence* behind, right there on the side of the house."

"Did he do time for that?"

"Three days here in the cell and a three-thousand-dollar fine. He stayed away from Barnes Point for a while after that. He came in here about eight months ago, spoke to me directly, and swore that he was a changed man. Said he wanted me to be the first to know because he was going to try to drum up more business here in Barnes Point. I told him good luck because no one would hire him again based on what everyone knew of him. To my surprise, a few did hire him. Small stuff, mostly. He's cheaper than the well-known handymen and construction companies around here and, if I'm being honest, he does much better work."

"Where does he live?" Moulton asked.

"The town of Winston, about ten miles south of here. Lives in a double-wide off the road a bit."

"Has there been any more trouble with him?"

"No. Nothing serious. Sure, stories still circulate, but there's nothing to them. As far as I was concerned, he was true to his word: he was a different, improved man."

"You said as far as you *were* concerned?" Chloe asked.

"Yeah. I decided to look around… do some digging on him when he came back. It seemed like nothing serious at first. I'm not one to judge a man, you know? We all make mistakes."

After hearing this, Moulton opened the folder. There were only three sheets inside of it. He scanned them and read the juicer parts out loud. "Assault in 2003, spousal abuse in 2006, arrested for public indecency in Roanoke in 2009." Moulton raised his eyebrows. "And you never suspected a thing after he came to you?"

"I did, of course," Jenkins said, a little offended. And for a while, I continuously checked up on him. Drove by the job sites, called the people that hired him. And I never got a single complaint. However… the timing with his being fired by Hilyard and then her showing up murdered… yeah, that's hard to look past."

"Do you have an address for him?" Chloe asked.

"It's there in the folder. You want me to come along?"

"I don't think so. For now, let's just play it safe and pay him a visit… see what comes from it. But be ready to move in the event we need assistance. And if you have a cell or interrogation room, can you make sure it's ready to go?"

"Oh yeah, I can handle that."

Moulton was already typing Alvarez's address into his GPS app. When he had it plugged in, he nodded to Chloe. "Thanks, Sheriff," he said.

Chloe nodded to him as she exited the office. She saw that the aging sheriff looked a little relieved not to be headed out. She wondered if it was so he could place the blame solely on the FBI if this murder did indeed have ties to something political.

Best not to give him anything to place blame about, then, Chloe thought as they headed back through the station and out toward the car where night had started to fall.

The town of Winston made the lesser part of Barnes Point look classy by comparison. The little town consisted of a convenience store that doubled as a fried chicken restaurant and a post office. Anything else the town might have was hiding down the winding back roads that snaked into the rural Virginia woodland.

Because of the town's small size, they were able to find Oscar Alverez's address quickly. His double-wide trailer sat about a quarter of a mile off the road, visible only because of the rather well-maintained driveway. When they parked behind the truck that read First Choice Handyman on the side, Chloe noted the shed that was being built on the backside of the property. She recalled Jenkins saying the work Alverez did was better than anyone else in Barnes Point. If the foundation for shed was any indication, he was exactly right.

As they walked across the yard toward the porch, the porch light came on and the front door opened. A Hispanic man looked out at them, his dark hair and beard seeming to stretch out into the night.

"Who's there?" he asked.

Quick to come to the door when he saw headlights, Chloe thought. *Seems a little suspicious to me ...*

She noticed Moulton stepping up ahead of her, taking a protective position. She couldn't help but smile as he slowly pulled his ID from his jacket pocket. "Agents Moulton and Fine, FBI," he said.

"FBI? What the hell for?"

His accent was not very thick. He sounded just like any other suspicious American. It made Chloe wonder just how long Alvarez had been in the country. She also wondered—perhaps a bit stereotypically—if he'd have anything to worry about in terms of legal standing as a US citizen.

"We'd just like to ask you some questions," Moulton said.

"No," Alvarez said, clear panic in his voice. "I've done nothing wrong."

"No one is saying you have," Chloe said. They had reached the porch by then but stopped at the bottom of the stairs. They wanted to give Alverez every indication that they were not here to be intrusive. "We're only here to ask about a woman you recently worked for."

Alvarez considered this for a minute and then stepped out onto the porch. He closed the door behind him and leaned a hip against the porch railing.

"Are you not going to invite us in?" Chloe asked.

"No. What woman are you talking about?"

"Lauren Hilyard. We were told you were working on flower beds for her and she fired you."

"Yeah, that lady is crazy. *Loco*."

"Can you tell us why she fired you?" Moulton asked.

"I don't even know why, man. She said I was getting too much dirt in her yard. Said I was being too rough with the grass. And then she called me a pervert because of things I did in the past. That bitch started screaming at me, right in the front yard."

"Did you leave right away?"

Alvarez nodded, but stayed quiet.

"Yes or no, Mr. Alvarez?"

"I don't know what else you want to know. I left when she told me I was fired. She didn't even pay me. And I haven't bothered trying to get it out of her because I don't want to deal with her crazy ass again."

"Would it surprise you to know that Lauren Hilyard was killed several days ago?" Chloe asked.

She looked for some sign of shock on Alvarez's face, but there was none. If there had been, it would have been quite visible in the glow of the porch light.

"No, I did not know that."

"It's believed she was killed just a day or two after she fired you."

"Oh, and you think I did it?"

"I said no such thing," Chloe said. "You just happen to be the last person that she was in a verbal confrontation with."

"That makes me guilty?"

"Stop doing this," Moulton asked. "Look ... you're refusing to allow us inside your house. You're being a little difficult with our questions. All of that *does* make you suspicious. Especially when you consider the criminal record you have."

"That's in the past. And I'm done with this. Goodnight, Agents."

"No, we aren't done," Chloe said. "Mr. Alvarez, can you give us proof of your whereabouts Saturday night and Sunday of last week?"

He nodded and said, "I could."

And then he opened his door and headed back inside.

"Mr. Alvarez, if I have to, I *will* arrest you. We can question you here or at the station."

"This is discrimination," Alvarez said. He gave a slight smile, as if he knew exactly what he was doing. "Prejudice."

"No, this is you being difficult to work with," Chloe said.

"And this," Moulton said, stepping up onto the porch, "is me arresting you."

He moved with a speed Chloe had not been expecting. It was almost like a dance in a way. He managed to spin Alvarez around and bring each arm behind his back without being too rough. By the time the cuffs were on Alvarez, he looked as if he wasn't quite sure what had just happened.

"Go," Moulton said. "To the car. *Now*, Mr. Alvarez."

The smile was no longer on Alvarez's face. He had tried to play the prejudice card and it had backfired. Besides…Chloe figured that this was not the kind of community that was going to toss him too much sympathy just because of his ethnicity. He had a criminal record and most of the people in Barnes Point already had negative views of him.

Guilty or not, she doubted anyone was going to have much sympathy for him in Barnes Point. She figured they'd find out soon enough as they escorted him in cuffs to the back of their car. He didn't say a word the entire time and came along easily enough. It made Chloe feel uneasy—a feeling that had still not let up by the time they reached the precinct.

Chapter Ten

Chloe and Moulton both sat on the opposite side of the small table, facing Oscar Alvarez. "I'm not exactly sure why you chose to do things this way," Chloe said. "If you are innocent, why not answer our questions?"

"Because I am tired of everyone doubting me. I am tired of everyone thinking that I did not change. I did very dumb things. But that was in the past. That is not me anymore."

"So where were you all day Sunday? That was when Lauren Hilyard was murdered. Can you give your whereabouts?"

"I was at home. Listening to the preacher from Lynchburg on my TV. After that, I went out for a while."

"Where?"

"To the grocery store. Then to a friend's house."

"Who is the friend?"

Alvarez shook his head. "They are not involved."

"We're not saying they are. But if we can get a picture of where you were around the time Mrs. Hilyard was killed, we can let you go. It's rather silly we had to bring you in the way we did."

"I agree," Alvarez said. "Am I being charged with her murder? Do you have evidence?"

"No, not at this time," Moulton said.

"So you will let me go. I know the laws."

Something occurred to Chloe, something that had gnawed at her a bit while they had been standing out on Alvarez's porch steps. "Excuse me for a moment," she said, mostly to Moulton, but loud enough so they could both hear her.

She stepped out of the small interrogation room. The viewing room was the next door down. She found Sheriff Jenkins there with two other officers, watching the interrogation on a small flat-screen television.

"I think we need to get someone over to Oscar Alverez's house," she said. "He's hiding something. And he was adamant about not letting us into his trailer."

"I'd need a warrant for that," Jenkins said.

"Go over and just check the place out. Don't go inside or anything like that. Take a look around. See if you can find some sort of justification for going inside."

"You think he's the killer?" one of the officers asked.

"No idea. But he *is* hiding something. And I think whatever it is will answer your questions."

"Let's hop to it then," Jenkins said. "You good here?" he asked Chloe.

"Yes. And thanks for your help."

As Jenkins and the officers left the room, Chloe walked back into the interrogation room. Moulton was in the middle of asking Alvarez if he'd had any shouting matches with other clients.

"I've had disagreements in the past, but nothing like that."

"Were you aware that a woman on the other side of the street, just a few houses down, saw the altercation?"

"No. I didn't know that."

Chloe took a breath and leaned forward, doing her best to appear sympathetic. "Level with us, Mr. Alvarez. We know you're trying to hide something—maybe some secret. And when we have you here trying to get answers in the midst of a murder investigation, that looks incredibly bad."

"No, I'm hiding nothing." But even as he said it, he looked away and stirred uncomfortably in his seat.

"The sooner you can tell us, the easier it will be on you. If you try to ride this out and we find out that you were lying… it's going to be bad. Even if whatever secret you have has nothing to do with Lauren Hilyard."

Alvarez looked to the table, to his interlaced fingers. He looked back at Chloe and Moulton, and then back to his hands—back and forth like a metronome as he wrestled with something.

"If I tell ... there could be trouble. For me, maybe. But it's not me I am worried about."

"If you're honest with us, perhaps we can help," Chloe said.

He then chose to look at them directly. Chloe was shocked to see the glistening of tears in the corners of his eyes. "It is ... my cousin."

"What about him?" Moulton asked.

"He is staying with me for right now. He hopes to find carpentry work somewhere. I wish I could hire him, but I can't. I am letting him stay with me until we find work for him somewhere."

"Why would you keep that a secret?" Chloe asked. But before the question was fully out of her mouth, she thought she knew. As an American, you couldn't turn on the news these days without hearing some story about it—no matter what side of the argument you fell on.

"How long has he been with you?" Moulton asked.

"Two days. I spent Saturday driving to Georgia to pick him up. We stayed overnight and came home Sunday. He came in somewhere by Eagle Pass, Texas, several days ago and has been hitchhiking ever since. He is not supposed to be here, according to the government. Please ... he can't go back. Let me keep him here, for a better life."

Well, what a little mess we've stumbled into, Chloe thought.

"Is he at your trailer right now?" Moulton asked. "Is that why you would not let us come in?"

"Yes," Alvarez said.

"But he can confirm that you were on the road, coming back from Georgia, on Sunday?" Chloe asked.

"Yes, he can."

"And he's here illegally?" Moulton asked.

Alvarez nodded curtly and said: "Yes, whatever the hell that means."

"We honestly care nothing about that," Chloe said. "How that is handled will come down to Sheriff Jenkins. We are more concerned with the murder case. And if your cousin can clear you, then you are free to go."

She stood up again and mouthed *"One second"* to Moulton. She then stepped outside of the room and called Jenkins to give him a heads-up of what he was about to step into. She found herself legitimately concerned for Alvarez and the outcome of his situation—particularly while living in a rural town in the South.

Jenkins answered and Chloe filled him in. When she was done, she was met with a heavy silence that was broken only by Jenkins uttering a curse. He thanked her and then hung up, leaving Chloe to listen to a dead line.

Chapter Eleven

Danielle had gotten a lot accomplished in the past twelve hours but she still felt as if she had done no real work. She'd gone back to the bar and made sure the new bartender was still as good as always (she was) and then spent most of the rest of the afternoon talking to ABC vendors and audio installation experts.

Now she was relaxing at home—home being Sam's huge apartment—with a glass of wine and a book. It was 9:30, a full hour and a half after Sam was scheduled to be back home. It was nothing new, as he came and went all the time, his schedule keeping him consistently busy.

But as the clock ticked to 9:31, Danielle's suspicion grew too heavy to ignore. She walked to the bedroom and found his secondary iPad charging on the bedside table. She unlocked it (the code was the score of the Patriots vs. Falcons Super Bowl) and opened up his calendar. Under today's date, he had nothing scheduled for after 7 p.m.

She then went to his text messages. Her suspicion arose again when she found that there were only two text threads on it: one between him and her that went back several months, and another between him and the lumber provider he was using for the new bar and lounge remodel. But she had seen the countless text threads on his phone. Why had this iPad been cleaned out?

Stop pretending like you know anything about how technology works, she told herself. *Maybe most of the other messages go directly to his phone. What the hell are you looking for anyway?*

She set the iPad down and went back into the living room. No sooner had she picked up her glass of wine than she heard the familiar sound of his key in the lock. She quickly sat back down, wanting to assume the position of a woman who had lazily been lounging around, waiting for him to get home.

He came through the door carrying his briefcase in one hand and his more rugged and beaten up bookbag over his shoulder. There were also little flakes of sawdust in his hair. She sometimes made fun of the different roles he had to assume in the course of a day: one minute a bartender, the next, a carpenter; after that, a businessman.

"I know, I know," he said. "I'm late."

"And you have sawdust in your hair," she pointed out.

"Yeah, I know. I was playing with the skill saw down at the lounge. But hey … the stage is coming along great. Did you get those speakers we were talking about?"

"I did. They ship out tomorrow."

He set his bags down by the door and looked apologetically at her. "I know it's late. Did you have anything planned?"

"No. It's okay. We can do dinner or something tomorrow."

"You sure?"

"Sam … it's fine."

"Okay. Well … why don't you find something for us to watch? This sawdust is itching my neck and scalp. I need to hop in the shower."

"Yes, please do."

He stuck his tongue out at her and dashed from the kitchen to the large master bedroom. She listened to him rummaging around for a moment as she considered sneaking up on him in the shower. While the sex between them was still amazing, it had waned a bit as he had gotten heavily involved in the lounge project—*her* lounge project. It had been a little over a week; not only did she want it, but he'd appreciate a little spontaneous shower sex.

She got to her feet and tiptoed to the bedroom door. As she waited to be sure he was in the shower, a thought occurred to her, an itching doubt like an insect buzzing around her head.

"I was playing with the skill saw down at the lounge … the stage is coming along great."

This was a lie. She knew that the last of the cuts for the stage had been done yesterday. She'd called the contractor early this morning to make sure she had the right measurements for the speakers. But why would he lie about that?

She heard the closet in the bathroom open as Sam got a clean towel. Danielle dipped into the bedroom and stealthily made her way to the bathroom door just as Sam turned the shower heads on. He paused for a moment and walked back toward the mirror over the sink. Danielle ducked backward, nearly getting caught.

She watched from around the door frame as he looked at himself in the mirror. He was looking at something between his neck and shoulder. He sighed and said, "Damn."

The mirror was along the side wall, so she was able to spy on him without showing up in the mirrors. It also gave her a clear view of what he was so interested in on his neck.

Slight bite marks. A small and light bruise in the perfect shape of a mouth.

A hickey.

And I haven't kissed him like that in over a week, she thought.

Her anger got the better of her, flashing across her mind before any form of reason even had a chance. She stepped into the bathroom just as he backed away from the mirror.

"Something wrong?" she asked.

He wheeled around, clearly caught in guilt. But he tried to play it off as a cool sort of surprise. "Jeez, you scared the hell out of me!"

"Did the hickey come from the skill saw, too?" she asked.

"It's not a hickey," he said, though he subtly started to shift his head so that the area wasn't as obvious. "I think one of the boards I was carrying today must have rubbed me on the shoulder—"

"You're good at lots of things, Sam. But lying isn't one of them."

She then watched something take place within his expression that alarmed her. In the space of about two seconds, his countenance changed from concern to indifference.

"Really?" he asked, stepping toward her. It was only then that she realized he was completely naked, as he had been just about to step into the shower. "Because I've been doing it for about a month now and you're only now finding out."

"Who is it?" she asked. She wanted to cry, but she was just too mad.

"You don't know her. And it's none of your business."

"You're a bastard," she said. She turned away from him and stormed into the bedroom.

"We can talk about it when I'm out of the shower," he said.

"Going to get her smell off of you?" she screamed.

"Oh, shut up. What do you care, anyway? I'm giving you a life you would have never had if you hadn't met me. So don't even pretend like you're too good for this."

"For *this*?" she asked. "For what?"

"A man that gets some on the side."

"Go to hell," she said. "Take your shower. I'll be gone by the time you get out."

Sam laughed at this. He walked to the bedroom door, seemingly unaware that he was still nude or simply not caring. "That's hilarious. You're going to leave me?"

"I've left better men for much less," she said.

"Oh, I'm sure you have," he said, storming into the room. And then, as if he were doing nothing more casual than swatting at a fly, he reached out and slapped her. It hit hard, spinning her in a half circle, nearly making her go to the ground.

"I know about your past," he said. "Don't think I don't know how much you used to get around. I saved your sorry ass. And you're really going to leave me?"

The anger came flaring up again and she went barreling at him, throwing a wild left-handed blow. Had she been more focused and not so consumed with hatred, it might have done some real damage. Instead, it bounced off of his right arm. He responded in kind, slapping her again. The right side of her face felt like it had exploded. When she stumbled backward, he kept coming at her. He used both hands to shove her hard against the wall. The back of her head struck it and for a moment, she saw little black stars in her line of sight.

"You can't leave me, you silly little girl," he said. "Where will you go? What will you do? You've got a huge opportunity lined up for you.

A business that could make you incredibly wealthy. And you're going to leave it because I like to get a stray piece every now and then?"

"Shut up," she said, afraid she might cry in front of him.

He came to her and pressed her against the wall in a way that was somewhere between threatening and sexual.

"You're not stupid," he said, leaning in and gently biting her lip just hard enough to hurt. "You aren't going anywhere."

She screamed in his face and he jolted a bit, smiling at her. It was exactly what she wanted. In his distraction, she brought her knee up hard and fast. Since he had no pants or boxers on, she was able to feel the connection and knew her aim had been dead on. He howled and dropped to the ground. He reached out for her leg but she was already out the bedroom door.

As he hurled insult after insult her way, calling her names she'd already heard many times before from many different men, Danielle ran straight for the front door. As she did, she was fully aware that she was not only running out on Sam, but on a bright future—a future that was right there in front of her, dangling like a poisoned carrot.

Chapter Twelve

Chloe's phone rang just as she stepped into the main office of Barnes Point Motel 6. When she saw Danielle's name on the caller ID, she was conflicted. Conversations with Danielle had not exactly gone the best as of late. But as it was currently coming up on 10:30 at night, she followed her instincts. Danielle calling this late was probably going to result in bad news of some kind or another.

"I need to take this," she told Moulton as they approached the desk. "Can you handle getting the rooms?"

"Plural?" he asked, a playfully disappointed smile on his face.

She returned it and said: "Well, Johnson will get suspicious if there is only one room listed on the expense report. As for how you and I handle that later... I'll let you choose."

She stepped back out into the parking lot and answered Danielle's call. "Hey, Danielle. What's up?"

She heard a muffled sniffle followed by what sounded like a contained sob. Danielle was crying. It didn't happen often but when it did, it never failed to break Chloe's heart.

"I didn't know who else to call..." Danielle finally managed.

"Is everything okay? Danielle... what is it? What's wrong?"

"Sam... he hit me. Hard. Pushed me. He was cheating on me... and I..."

"Are you hurt?" Chloe asked.

"No... I. Ah Jesus, give me a second."

Chloe did just that. She listened as Danielle took several moments to get herself together. Heavy breaths, stifled sobs, and finally, a strained and tired voice finally speaking. "He faked putting sawdust in his hair and said he needed a shower. He had a hickey. Not from me. He put the sawdust in his hair just to have an excuse ... to wash the smell of another woman off of him."

"And he hit you?"

"Twice. And then slammed me into the wall. I had to leave. I had to. I did the right thing, right?"

"Of course you did. Danielle ... you should file a report. That's abuse."

"No. I don't want it dragged out."

"Where are you right now?" Chloe asked.

"My apartment. About twelve miles away from his place."

"Will he come for you?"

There was silence for a moment as Danielle thought about this. "Shit, I don't know. I don't know ... Chloe, this is a mess."

"It'll be okay. Do you have some place else to go?"

"It's all gone," Danielle said. "The business he was building for me. The bright future, the escape from this miserable life ... it's all gone." She sounded more angry than hurt now. In terms of Danielle, that was probably a good thing.

"Danielle, listen to me. Do you have anywhere to go?"

"I can just say here."

"Don't take that chance. He might come for you ... and if you aren't going to call the police on him, that could be dangerous. You need to get out of there."

"And go where, Chloe? I have nowhere to go."

"Do you remember where my apartment is?"

"I can't stay with you," Danielle said, nervously laughing off the thought.

"It's fine. I'm in Virginia, on a case. There's a spare key in my mailbox down in the lobby. The combination to the mailbox is seven-one-seven. You're welcome to stay there for as long as you need."

"Are you sure?" Danielle asked.

"I'm positive. Pack a bag and get to DC. I don't know how much longer it will be before I come back, but make yourself at home until then."

"Chloe… thank you."

"If you really want to thank me, you'll report the bastard."

"It's not worth it."

Chloe was pretty sure what she meant was it wasn't worth the trouble she'd have to go through in order to follow through on it. But they could discuss that later.

"Fine. Just give me a call when you're settled in my place, okay?"

"I will. Thanks, Chloe."

"Of course. Call me if you need anything else."

She hung up just as Moulton came walking over to her. He showed her his hand, which held two room keys. He then realized that she looked flustered and said, "Everything okay?"

"Yeah. Just… some stuff with my family."

"Anything bad?"

"I don't think so," she said. "Now come on… if it gets much later, we'll miss out on the tension of whether or not we're going to break our pact to keep things professional."

She followed him to the rooms, already rather certain the pact would be broken fairly quickly. With the case still looming over their heads and their one lead having been freed once his alibi had been verified, and now these issues with Danielle, she thought it might be exactly what she needed to refocus her mind.

Immediately afterward—no more than twenty seconds after Chloe had started toward the bathroom door to take a shower—she heard her phone ring. Still in her underwear, with her dirty clothes in hand, she walked over to the bedside table where her phone sat. She saw Assistant Director Garcia's name and answered it right away, feeling a little odd to do it wearing nothing but her bra and panties.

"This is Agent Fine," she said. She then mouthed to Moulton, still lying in bed and catching his breath as well, *"Garcia."*

"Agent Fine, have there been any significant breaks in the last couple of hours?" he asked.

"No. We had a potential suspect but that turned into a dead end. It actually turned into something of a small criminal matter here in town, actually. But the sheriff is handling it."

"Okay. Well, this is going to seem like it's coming out of left field and I do apologize for that. But I need you and Moulton to come back to DC. Specifically, Johnson wants to see Moulton in his office tomorrow morning."

"Has there been a break in the case?" she asked.

"No, nothing like that. I can't really address the reasons with you over the phone."

"Does Director Johnson need to see me as well?"

"Maybe later in the day. But no, you are not to attend the meeting between him and Moulton in the morning. He's to be there at eight o'clock sharp."

"Okay," Chloe said. She had tons of questions but could tell from Garcia's voice that he would not be answering any of them.

She ended the call and looked back over to Moulton. He was sitting on the edge of the bed now, a sheet covering the lower half of his body. He looked concerned. "Garcia, huh?" he said.

"Yeah. Calling for Johnson. They want us back in DC in the morning. Johnson wants to meet with you in his office at eight."

"Did he say why?"

"No. But he did say that I shouldn't come. Not until later in the day." She paused here and then suggested: "Do you think he knows about… us?"

Moulton shrugged. "Doubtful. Even if he did, I don't think that would be any reason to pull us off of this case."

Chloe wasn't positive, but she thought he looked incredibly troubled. His face was set in stone and his eyes seemed to dart everywhere, never staying focused on her.

"What is it?" she asked. "Is something wrong, Moulton?"

"No. I'm good."

She was pretty sure he was lying. He knew something… he was just choosing not to say anything about it. She decided not to pry, figuring that if there was anything serious, he'd tell her.

"Well, I'm going to grab a shower," she said. Then, almost as a test, she added: "I might need some help, if you're interested."

The smile he gave her was thin and forced. "I might sneak in later. But don't wait."

It was also clear that he *knew* she was on to him—that she had noticed that something was troubling him. Now, it was up to her to decide if she would leave it unspoken. For now, she figured it would be best left alone. If there was something he needed to tell her, they had a whole ride back to DC for him to do so.

She went to the bathroom and stepped into the shower. She wondered what Moulton could be hiding from her as she waited to see if he would join her or not. But as it turned out, she finished her shower alone, beginning to wonder what secrets her new lover was hiding from her.

CHAPTER THIRTEEN

"Are you sure you don't need to tell me anything?" Chloe asked.

They'd been driving for a while, a little less than halfway back to DC. Moulton was behind the wheel, staring out at the night-shrouded road with a set look of determination on his face.

"Let me ask you something," he said. "And it's going to sound confrontational but please know that I don't mean for it to be."

"Okay ... what?"

"Do I know everything about you?"

The question took her by surprise. It also made her think of all the drama she'd been having as of late with her father and Danielle. "Of course not," she said.

"And even if we were closer ... even if we'd been seeing one another for maybe a few months more, are there things about your life you still might not want me to know?"

"I'm not sure. Why do you ask? Moulton ... what the hell is going on?"

He thought about it for a while and for a moment, Chloe thought he was going to come clean. But in the end, he shook his head. "I'll tell you tomorrow, after I meet with Johnson. You have my word on that."

"Fine," Chloe said, using a tone that indicated it was anything *but* fine. "Just let me know ... I mean, is everything okay? Are you in some kind of danger?"

"No, nothing like that."

She did not like the cold edge he had to him; he was speaking to her as though she was annoying him, like he honestly didn't want to speak to her. So that's exactly what she gave him as they continued on toward DC—Moulton remaining quiet while Chloe tried to figure out whether or not she could fully trust the man behind the wheel.

⚜ ⚜ ⚜

It was well after midnight when Moulton dropped her off in front her apartment. She found herself wanting to kiss him goodbye but he was too preoccupied with his thoughts. He still seemed distant and cold, so she gave him only a quick "goodbye" as she got out of the car. He returned it, waved in a lazy and forced way, and then pulled away from the curb. She watched the car as it turned off onto another street, wondering what was going on in Moulton's head.

She then remembered that there was even more drama waiting for her in her apartment… if Danielle had truly taken her up on her offer. She hurried inside and went to the row of occupant mailboxes in the lobby. She opened hers and found it empty—mail, spare key, all of it.

Her heart started racing as she rode the elevator up to her floor. Danielle had never handled the harder things in life particularly well. That meant that Chloe could be in for a very long night of listening to her sister rage on and on about how her life had not turned out the way she wanted it to, how all men were devious pigs and how her life had started its downfall the moment their deplorable father had gone to prison.

Needless to say, when she unlocked the door to her apartment and heard '80s music playing, she was surprised. INXS was currently playing and when she entered the kitchen, she saw Danielle swaying back and forth as she cleaned off the kitchen counter. When she heard the door close as Chloe entered, Danielle wheeled around in shock. When she saw Chloe standing there, she raced to her right away and wrapped her up in a hug.

"I wasn't expecting you so soon," Danielle said.

"And I wasn't expecting you to clean my apartment," Chloe countered.

"I had to find something to do. I have all of this nervous energy to get out and let's face it… your counters are nasty."

"Sorry. I don't really have much time to clean." She reached in the fridge, grabbed a beer, and popped it open. She took a long gulp, as if the swallow itself would wash the tension of the last few hours away. "So, how are you?"

"Pissed off more than anything," she said.

Chloe noticed the red marks on Danielle's face. At least one of the slaps she taken earlier in the night had caused a slight welt.

"Did he come for you?" Chloe asked. "To your apartment, I mean?"

"Hell if I know. I got out of there about two minutes after I got off the phone with you. I just … I feel so stupid. The signs were there the whole time. And the more I think about it, the more I think he was giving me this business as some sort of front. He has money going around so many places and …"

"What?"

"Nothing. I don't even want to waste my time talking about the bastard. Let's talk about you for once. How have *you* been?"

There was the obvious secret she was keeping from Danielle: the fact that their father had come to her front door just two days ago. It was news that would hit Danielle with as much force as the slaps she'd endured earlier, but Chloe didn't see the point in keeping it a secret. Given what was going on with Moulton—whatever it may be—she felt like there were too many secrets in her life at the moment.

"I was doing great until yesterday. I came home and there was a visitor waiting for me. Danielle … Dad is out. He was sitting on my steps, waiting for me."

"Are you kidding me?" Danielle asked.

"No. For real. He was right there, just waiting for me. Asked if I wanted to grab lunch or dinner."

"Oh my God. What did you tell him?"

"I told him I wasn't interested. I told him if I ever wanted to see him or speak with him, I'd find his information and get back to him."

Danielle uttered a curse and nodded to Chloe's beer. "You got another one of those?"

Chloe retrieved another beer from the fridge, popped the top, and handed it to her sister. She noticed that Danielle was shaking slightly, the sort of tremors that run through a body when nerves take over. Danielle walked into the living room and sat down on the couch. Chloe followed closely behind, trying to be conscious of the fact that Danielle was going through a lot. Having been abused by a man she thought she loved and then finding out her father—a man she had spent most of her life hating—was now out of prison and free … that could be a lot.

"Talk to me, Danielle," Chloe said. "What are you thinking?"

"I'm thinking that it sucks that once the world starts to look good from a higher vantage point, that same world makes sure to buck you right off and remind you of your place. Chloe … I woke up this morning with my future looking better than I could have ever imagined it. And now … now all of *this*."

"I don't think it means much of anything that Dad is out," Chloe said. "I think he'll realize we want nothing to do with him and he'll move on with the rest of his life."

"If you want nothing to do with him, then why did you work so hard to set him free?"

It was a fair question and one that, on its face, was rather simple. "I knew there was something wrong with the way it all went down," Chloe explained. "I couldn't just let that rest. And when I started to dig, I slowly found out about Ruthanne … how Dad wasn't Mom's killer."

"He came to you, Chloe. He did that for a reason."

"Danielle … he *wasn't* the killer. And he *is* my father. I can't write him off like you did. But I also don't like the idea of just letting him back into my life either."

"I hope you know that I'm not hating him just because it's easier to hate him than to forgive him," Danielle said. "There are things you don't know … things I can't …"

Chloe reached out and took Danielle's hand. She could feel the shaking, light but definitely there. "You can tell me," she said. "Quite frankly, in our own family life and my personal life right now as well, I'm done with secrets."

Danielle shook her head. "No. I can't. I'm not ready."

"Danielle … you can tell me. He's out now. If there's a reason you're scared of him, you have to let me know."

She looked at Chloe, tears in her eyes, and let out a chuckle that was drowned out by the thickness of her tears. "Let's just say that the marks on my face right now are nothing new. And that my inability to trust men came from somewhere."

"What about your vagueness?" Chloe asked. "Where did *that* come from?"

The laughter was real this time, and Danielle wiped the fallen tears away. "Maybe someday soon, I'll tell you everything. But I can't right now."

"Please don't take this the wrong way," Chloe said. "But you being vague like this, it's make me assume certain things. And they're pretty bad."

"Assume away," Danielle said. "Whatever it is you're assuming, it's probably pretty close to the truth."

Chloe had nothing to say to that. She could only sit there with her sister, reflecting on how they had grown up with two different pictures of their father.

And wondering if he had been showing them two different faces.

Chloe woke up at 5:35 the following morning. Danielle was still asleep on the couch, insisting that she was not going to share a bed with her sister when she had no idea what her sister's sex life looked like. Although she hadn't had sex with Moulton in her own bed, Chloe was still afraid she'd blush, so she had not argued.

She thought of Moulton as she quietly made her way out of the apartment, not wanting to wake Danielle up. She considered texting him but recalled that cold distance he'd been giving off the night before. She figured she'd at least wait until after his meeting with Johnson to reach out to him. If he wanted her support, he'd ask for it.

She walked up the street to her favorite coffee shop, ordered a dirty chai, and then sat in the back of the shop. She Googled the number of the correctional facility her father had been released from, waited through the automated system, and then pressed zero to get an operator. Chloe asked for information regarding a recently released prisoner, only to be told that office hours didn't begin until 8:30. Chloe then explained it was for FBI business and gave her badge identification number. The woman was apologetic and told her that she'd do what she could to push it through as soon as possible.

"What exactly are you looking for?" the woman asked.

"I need to know the exact date Aiden Fine was released. And then I'd like to know the number of his parole officer."

"I'll do what I can to get that for you as quickly as possible, but it might not be until well after business hours."

"I understand," Chloe said, ending the call.

She sipped on her drink in the back of the shop, watching people come in and out. She again had to fight the urge to contact Moulton. She left the shop and walked around the block, listening and watching as DC started to wake up to a foggy Friday morning.

She was headed back to her apartment when her phone rang. She was fully prepared to be impressed, assuming it would be the woman from the correctional facility, having already gotten her the information she was looking for. Instead, she saw Moulton's name on the display. She answered it right away, trying not to sound too excited.

"Hey," was all she said when she answered it.

"Hey, Chloe," he said. She would never admit it to his face, but she loved to hear him call her by her first name rather than her last—as most agents tended to do with one another. "Look, I'm sorry I was such a dick last night. This meeting… it could be bad."

"But you said you're not in any kind of trouble."

"Well, nothing life or death, no. But with less than two hours before the meeting, I feel like I need to tell you what's going on. I don't know for sure what the meeting is about, but I have a pretty good idea. I got an email from Johnson last night that all but confirmed it."

"So tell me," she said. "I'm not the judgmental type. I'd hope you know that by now."

"I do. But… how about over coffee? Somewhere close, because I don't have much time."

She smiled and looked back down the street where she had just come from. "I know just the place," she said.

It was clear just from looking at Moulton that he had not gotten much sleep last night. He'd apparently been kept awake by the stress of whatever his meeting with Director Johnson was about. He was dressed nicely, though, and had done his best to look presentable. When he sat down at the table with his cup of coffee, he looked like a man who was about to set out on a long journey.

"Thanks for agreeing to meet with me," he said. "After the way I behaved last night, I don't know if I would have if the roles were reversed."

"You *were* a little cold," she said, "and coming right after sex, it makes a girl wonder." She'd meant for it to sound almost comical but she knew it had fallen flat. "Besides… the moment I said we had been called back to DC, I knew something was wrong. Your attitude and mood completely changed."

He nodded, sipping from his coffee in an obvious attempt to delay the conversation. When he set the cup down, he had no choice but to go on. "Look… these past five weeks or so, when it's been sort of slow at the bureau, Garcia had me working with this small group that was tracking down this money laundering scheme… some set-up between a drug dealer out of Boston, a real estate agent in New York, and a bank here in DC. To tell you the truth, to this day, I'm still not quite sure how the operation was being run. But what I do know is that the group I was working with somehow got intel about where a shipment was being dropped." He used air quotes when he said *shipment*. "Now, these guys dealt in cash because it's ultimately harder to trace. And when they talked about shipments, it was basically drops… places where the money would exchange hands."

He stopped here, but Chloe had a good idea she knew where it was going. She had never pegged Moulton as a dishonest man, but still… all men had their faults and no one is perfect.

"We made three arrests outside of this drop. One was a pretty big one, a guy that had been wanted for electronic bank fraud for almost a year. But even more than that… we had the shipment in question. Right there in front of us, tucked away in these storage totes, in a warehouse in the middle of nowhere just outside of Boston. Including myself, there were four of us. And I can see by the look on your face, you see where this is going."

"How much was in the shipment?" Chloe asked. She wasn't sure how she felt about this. She wasn't even sure she should be hearing it; she felt like she was associating with a criminal.

"Six and a half million dollars."

She dropped her head and leaned closer to him. "How much did you take?"

"Each of us took one hundred grand. We thought it would be just small enough to go unnoticed. After all, no one had tracked the shipment. We were the first to find it."

"Then how do you think Director Johnson found out?"

"I have no idea. I haven't deposited anything. I've got it hidden… and I've been using that cash to pay for everything in the last few weeks, trying to slowly get rid of it, you know? I know it was stupid… but it was so easy. It was *right there* and no one knew about it."

"Some of the bills could have been marked or tagged in some way, I suppose," Chloe suggested.

"Yeah, that's what I'm thinking, too."

"Kyle… if this is what the meeting is about, and he has proof… this could be *very* bad."

"I know. But… I wanted you to know about it before the meeting. If it *is* what the meeting is about, then I don't know what happens after that. I didn't want to take the chance of not seeing you one more time before I get whatever punishment is coming to me. I had to tell you."

While she was indeed seeing him in a new light now, she also felt sorry for him. She had never seen him frightened before. She reached across the table and took his hand. "I get why you didn't want to tell me," she said. "And who knows… if there were four of you involved, maybe the disciplinary action won't be as bad as you're thinking."

"An agent of twelve years got caught stealing just seventeen thousand dollars from a Russian money train three years ago," Moulton said. "He lost his job and spent eighteen months in federal prison. So that's the standard I'm looking at."

"Jesus, Kyle…"

He nodded and tapped nervously at the table. "Anyway, I need to get going. I just had to see you before I go. And I know it sounds selfish, but I hope you can forgive me for this. I think what you and I started here… I think it might have been pretty good. Pretty powerful. But if today goes the way I'm expecting it to go…"

He left the comment hanging there, as if speaking it out loud might make it a reality. "Wish me luck," he said as he passed by her. He leaned down and kissed her softly on the side of the mouth.

"Do you want me to ride with you to headquarters?" she asked.

"No. It'll just make it harder. Bye for now, Chloe."

And just like that, he was gone. She watched him walk through the door and back out onto the street, leaving Chloe alone in the back of the coffee shop for the second time that morning.

CHAPTER FOURTEEN

Chloe's nerves were shot by the time she got behind the wheel of her car and started to work. Her heart was breaking for Moulton, despite the obvious crime he had committed, and she also wished she could be there for Danielle while she hid out at her apartment with nothing to do. She recalled what Danielle had said about her own life the night before, about how one moment you were standing on top of it all only to have the world knock you on your ass and remind you who was really in charge.

She felt some of that as she parked in the garage and walked into the FBI building. She had woken up yesterday morning with Moulton still there, both of them feeling the beginnings of a potential relationship stirring between them. They'd then been called in on a case together, giving her an active and interesting case for the first time in almost six weeks. Her life had been on an upward trajectory, despite the jarring surprise of having her father show up unexpected on her doorstep.

And now look where you are, she thought as she nestled into her cubicle. She looked down the hallway toward Garcia's office, wondering if she might catch a glimpse of Moulton. She checked her watch and saw that it was 8:10. His meeting had already started by now, on the floor above hers in Johnson's office.

She tried answering emails as well as she could. She jotted down notes on the Lauren Hilyard case, thinking she might call Sheriff Jenkins later in the day to see if there had been any developments with Oscar Alvarez and his cousin. It made her wonder what would become of that case. Would Johnson send her back down there on her own or perhaps with another partner?

She tried to focus on all of these things, but it was too hard; her thoughts were solely on Moulton and what his future might look like.

When her phone rang at 8:37, she couldn't help but jump a bit. She grabbed her phone, hoping to see a familiar number: Garcia's, Moulton's, or even Johnson's. Someone to let her know what was going to happen to Moulton.

But the number was unfamiliar, though she *did* recognize the area code.

It was the correctional center—the place her father had been a resident of until recently.

"This is Agent Fine."

"Hi, Agent Fine. This is Tammy over at Somerset Correctional. I spoke with you earlier this morning. I have the information you were looking for."

"Thanks for being so fast," Chloe said.

"Sure, sure. Now, the inmate Aiden Fine was released two weeks ago. Apparently, some new evidence arose in his case and he was paroled out. As for his parole officer, it's a man by the name of Benjamin Nettles. Do you need his number?"

"Yes, please."

Tammy gave her the number and that was the end of the call. Chloe didn't even wait to consider her next step. She thought of Danielle last night, how she had started trembling when she'd heard that their father had been released from prison. How she had hinted at the fact that there were some secrets about him that Chloe might not even guess at.

She called the parole officer and he answered on the third ring. "Benjamin Nettles here," he answered.

"Mr. Nettles, this is Agent Chloe Fine with the FBI. I need the contact information for a man who was recently paroled. A man by the name of Aiden Fine."

Nettles obliged and as Chloe wrote down her father's phone number she realized that she, just like Danielle, was starting to tremble.

⚜ ⚜ ⚜

By eleven o'clock, Chloe's nerves were in such a state of disarray that she started to feel ill. She was worried about Moulton, still not having heard from anyone about the meeting. On top of that, she was currently pulling into the parking lot of a small Italian restaurant, where she had agreed to meet her father for lunch. The awkward conversation had taken place nearly an hour and a half ago but Chloe could still hear every single word of it in her head.

She walked into the restaurant, mostly dead from the early hour, and spotted her father right away. He was sitting in a corner booth, eating a breadstick and looking out the window. Chloe stood there and simply watched him for a moment. It had been years since she had seen him without bars or bulletproof glass between them—other than two days ago when he had showed up at her door. Looking at him like this, he looked like a normal man. Not a home wrecker, not a potential murderer, not the monster Danielle painted him to be.

Just a man. Just her broken father.

She walked over to the booth and slid in. He looked up and smiled when he saw her. The smile was genuine and filled with enough joy to make Chloe uncomfortable.

"Thanks so much for calling," he said. "I was really worried you were going to keep your distance."

"I was, too," she said. "And I can't help but wonder if I have reason to."

He sighed and tossed his breadstick back down in the basket. "Even after it was proven that I wasn't the one who killed her, you still hate me?"

"I never hated you, Dad. Not even when I thought you did it. Not even when I found that you were technically innocent but were sleeping with the woman that *did*." She smirked and then, unable to help herself, added: "How *is* Ruthanne, by the way?"

"Well, that's something at least," he said.

They paused for a moment as a waitress came by and took their orders. Aiden ordered lasagna; Chloe got an Italian hoagie. They sat in silence for a moment, Chloe taking one of the breadsticks from the basket in the center of the table. She wondered if Moulton's fate had been decided yet. She wondered if Danielle's boyfriend had tried getting in touch with her.

It was odd how easily these thoughts came to her while her father sat across the table from her. She'd expected to be tense and always on edge in his presence. But there was something about his posture, even the way he looked longingly at her, hoping for some sort of conversation, that made her realize once again that he was not some monster. He was still her father despite it all, and she guessed things might always feel natural around him. She just wished reuniting with him could have been a little more meaningful—maybe even a little more emotional.

"How's Danielle?" he asked.

"She's doing okay," Chloe said, not even considering the idea of telling him the truth.

"I thought about going to see her…"

"That would be a very bad idea," Chloe said. "How would you even know where she is?"

"Do you?"

"Yes, I do."

"She living with a guy?" It sounded like an accusation rather than a question.

"Leave her alone, okay? She's not nearly as forgiving as I am."

Aiden looked as if he wanted to say something, but bit it back at the last moment. The waitress came by with their food, making Chloe realize that the silence they had originally been sitting in had lasted longer than she'd thought.

"Dad…"

It sounded weird to call him that as he sat directly across from her. While it still felt natural, she had to get used to the sound of it. "When we were kids, was there ever something that happened to Danielle? Maybe something between her and Mom or her and you that I never knew about?"

He thought about it for a moment as he dug into his lasagna. "Not that I know of."

It took everything within her not to tell him how Danielle had started to tremble and shake when she'd learned that he was out of prison—tried not to tell him how Danielle had insinuated that he had treated her in a way that was just as bad as anything Chloe could imagine.

"Why did you always prefer me?" Chloe asked.

He looked at her as if she had just fired a gun at him. "I never showed more affection to one of you more than the other."

"You did, Dad. I never understood it until later in life, but you did. You never really *avoided* Danielle, but you were distant from her."

Even as she said this, something started to present itself in her mind. It was a thought, murky and slow, like something dead in the water, slowly rolling over to reveal its pale belly.

"I don't remember ever being that way towards her. But then again … I wasn't the best father, now was I?"

"I didn't say that," she said. But she was only halfway present. She was trying to figure out the thought that would not quite come to her. There was something there … a repressed memory perhaps? Something about him treating Danielle differently. Something about privacy, maybe? That felt right but made no immediate sense.

"So tell me how you ended up working for the FBI," he said.

She tried a bit longer to get that memory to surface but it seemed stuck. So she did her best to appease him just enough to make it through this meal. Of course, she didn't want to tell him that it was her mother's murder and his arrest that had eventually led her to this career. So she gave a generic answer. Every question he asked her for the next fifteen minutes, she gave him generic answers. She told him nothing intimate or deep about her life. When he asked if she was seeing someone, she told him, "Not right now." Which, as far as she knew, might very well be true now.

"Chloe … I need to ask you something," he said as he slid his empty plate to the side. "I'm not proud of it and it shames me to ask it."

"What?"

"I need to borrow some money. Not a lot, just enough to get me through the next few weeks. Unlocking bank accounts from almost twenty years ago is pretty tough. I have a tiny nest egg waiting for me at the bank, but it's harder to access than I thought... especially because your mother's name is on all of the paperwork."

Serves you right, she thought, a little guiltily. She did not want to give him the money. She didn't think he was lying to her, but it was the principle of the thing. Everything this man had put her and Danielle through... everything he had done all those years ago that had led to the death of her mother...

It also revealed the true purpose of him trying to tie things up with her. He cared nothing about reuniting or working on their relationship. He was only after a loan, plain and simple. She hated how much this hurt her—how betrayed she felt.

"How much?" she asked. Despite the hurt, she was fine giving anything to him. Maybe it would keep him away and she could finally move on.

"Maybe fifteen hundred? Just enough to pay the rent and get some groceries. As soon as I get that money freed up, I'll pay you back."

"Well, I don't have that kind of money on me. But my checkbook is in the car. I can write you a check if you like."

"That should be fine," he said. He truly did look embarrassed. "Thanks, Chloe."

She didn't bother with a *you're welcome.* In fact, she was too busy trying to think of a way to end the little daddy-daughter date without seeming like an utter bitch.

But as it turned out, she didn't have to think too hard. Her cell phone, sitting on the edge of the table, rang. She reached for it immediately when she saw Garcia's name on it.

"I have to take this," she said.

Aiden gave her a nod of understanding and started to look at his own phone.

"This is Agent Fine," she answered.

"Fine, it's Garcia. I came by your cubicle but you weren't there."

"Yeah, I'm out to lunch. What's up? Is the meeting with Johnson and Moulton over?"

"It is. And we'll fill you in just as soon as you get here. Meet us in Johnson's office as soon as you can. How far away are you?"

"I can be there in twenty minutes."

"See you then."

She ended the call and started to get up. "Sorry. I have to head back to work right away."

He smiled, also getting up. "Look… you're giving me a loan. Let me settle up the bill here."

Gee, thanks, she thought. She hurried out of the restaurant and got into her car, grabbing her checkbook. As she wrote the check for her father, every muscle in her hand screamed that she was being a fool. She was pressing so hard on the check that a black blot of ink came out as she finished signing her name to it.

She saw him coming out of the restaurant just as she placed the checkbook into her purse. She got out and handed him the check in an almost thrusting sort of motion—like the check was a dagger of some kind.

"Thanks," he said. "I really will pay you back. You just have to answer my calls when I reach out."

"We'll work on it," she said, wanting to make no such commitment. "Sorry again… but I really have to go."

She didn't wait for a response and didn't give him another glance. She got into the car, backed out, and headed out onto the street. As she headed to headquarters, she realized that she had the steering wheel in a death grip. Her knuckles were white and her jaw was clenched. She tried to decide if she was tense and angry over the lunch with her father, or because she was still clueless as to what had become of Agent Moulton.

Or maybe it was that memory from her past that had tried to present itself, only to sink away into the depths of her mind.

In the end, she decided it was all of it. And she did not relax or allow herself to breathe easy until she was parking her car in the bureau parking garage. But even then, it was sheer tension that pushed her forward.

Chapter Fifteen

When she entered Johnson's office, she saw that Garcia wasn't there. Johnson, however, seemed to be specifically waiting for her, standing behind his desk and looking out the window to the streets below. When he turned to her as she walked in, he had the same look she imagined someone might have when they had to break the news that a loved one has died. It made her heart sink.

"Chloe, I'm going to cut to the chase," he said.

"Okay." She did not sit down. Johnson was standing, so she would stand, too. Besides, there was too much nervous energy cascading through her to sit still.

"Agent Moulton got himself into a hell of a lot of trouble. As of ten thirty this morning he has been indefinitely suspended. He'll go to trial in a few weeks and if he's found guilty, he's looking at jail time. I doubt it will be anything more than a few months, but his career with the FBI will be destroyed."

She did her best not to seem devastated. She became angry with Moulton in that moment, wondering how he could have been so stupid. She could remember him saying *"It was right there ..."* and explaining how easy it had seemed.

"Is he in the building?" she asked.

"No. he was escorted out of the building. He'll be allowed to return tomorrow with another escort so he can get his personal belongings." He sighed here and placed his hands on his hips. "Agent Fine, I need to you be honest with me here: did you know anything about what he was up to?"

"No, sir. He told me this morning, just before the meeting."

"Why would he do that?"

"Despite what he's being charged with might suggest, it's because he's an honest man at heart. He felt he needed to tell me because … I don't know. Maybe because he felt he owed it to me, as my partner."

Dodged that one, she thought. *Although, would it be the worst thing if Johnson knew the two of you were sleeping together? Hell, Moulton probably told him during the meeting. He probably had to come clean with anything unethical he's done while working for the bureau.*

"I thought he was honest, too," Johnson said. "And a damned good agent. This whole thing shocked the hell out of me."

"Same here," Chloe said, unable to keep all of her emotions in check.

"But despite what has happened with Moulton, I'd still like for you to take this Barnes Point case back up. I got a call from Sheriff Jenkins this morning. I had to call him back directly after the meeting with Moulton, actually. He says he has a potential witness … someone that claims they know who killed Lauren Hilyard. He's looking into the witness's story, but a lot of people in that town are still assuming it had something to do with Lauren's father and his friendships with higher-ups in Washington. I tried explaining to him that we feel that's not the case, but they are too scared and won't listen. Look, I'd brush him off if we were slammed with cases. But he seemed pleased that you and Moulton were there in the first place. He asked if you'd been pulled, but I assured him we'd send you back down there."

"Okay," she said. "When do I leave?"

"Soon. In the next hour, if possible. I'm going to send Agent Rhodes down there with you. She's just now really getting back on her feet and I think it would be a good exercise for her. Assistant Director Garcia is briefing her on the case right now. And honestly … with Moulton gone, she may be your long-term partner, anyway."

"Yes, sir."

"Jenkins speaks highly of you, Fine. Keep up the good work."

"Thank you."

With that, Chloe went back to her cubicle. She thought of Moulton and where he might be at that very moment. She wished she could have at least said goodbye to him. It was stupid thing he had done and she wanted to be mad at him. After all, his idiocy was ending the spark of a relationship they had started.

He's probably much more concerned about other things, Chloe, she thought to herself. *Let's not be selfish.*

She had to focus very hard to gather up her notes when she got back to her cubicle. Once or twice, she was sure she was going to start crying. Everything was piling up, pushing against her: Danielle's problems, her father showing up and asking for money, and now Moulton being pulled away from her and likely kicked out of the bureau. It felt cliché to be thinking such a thing, but she felt like everything was falling apart.

Just as the second wave of nearly crying passed, she heard a heavy knock at the edge of her cubicle wall. She turned in her chair and saw a familiar face there.

Rhodes was smiling at her, dressed in the suit she often wore into the field rather than the office attire she had been wearing for the last few weeks as she had gotten her feet wet with paperwork following her shooting. She looked confident. She looked ready to *really* get back to work.

"Hey, Fine," she said. "We ready to rock this thing or what?"

Chloe managed an honest smile. She fondly thought of how she and Rhodes had butted heads at first—small differences that had come to a screeching halt after Rhodes had nearly bled out in her arms after being shot.

"You know what?" Chloe said with stern determination. "I think I am."

Chapter Sixteen

The ride back into Barnes Point was uncomfortable for Chloe, but she did her best to hide it. She was genuinely interested in getting back up to speed with Agent Rhodes, but her mind was fixated on Moulton. She knew more information would come day by day in regards to what would happen to him. Until the trial, though, she knew there was nothing to do but wait and assume the worst.

The little bit she learned about Rhodes on the way back through Virginia was eye-opening. She had been tasked with research jobs, helping other teams locate information to push their cases along. She had also been assigned several jobs where she had listened in on wiretapped conversations regarding a sex trafficking operation that was suspected to have its central hub in Louisiana.

"It's disgusting what these perverts do," Rhodes said as she talked excitedly about the position. "Trading girls for a gram of coke, auctioning them off to the highest bidder for the night and then ultimately selling them for life to someone that will take them to some deplorable place in another country where they'll be rented out for the equivalent of three American dollars."

"Sounds like you're pretty passionate about it," Chloe said.

"I am. Which is odd because it was nothing more than a blip on my radar when I started with the bureau. I've been talking to Director Johnson about permanently assigning me to the task force that is working towards bringing that ring—and several other like it—down for good."

The closer they got to Barnes Point, the more natural it felt to be talking to Rhodes. As cheesy as it seemed, she wondered if there might be some sort of unspoken link between them, given the trauma they had shared just a few months ago. It had been a hell of way to start her first case—watching her partner get shot and nearly die on the way to the hospital—but Chloe understood that it had shaped her in some way. And as morbid as it may seem, she had Rhodes to thank for it.

"By the way," Rhodes said, "I'd be a total jerk to not say it… but I'm sorry about Moulton. It was out of nowhere, huh?"

"Yeah. It makes no sense. But… it is what it is. He regrets it and maybe he'll take some lesson away from it."

"For what it's worth, I'm sorry. Seems like you're on some deranged carousel of getting new partners."

Chloe gave her a smile, slightly forced. "Hey, I think I ended up with a good one."

Rhodes seemed content with that response. Chloe was pretty sure Rhodes was feeling some of the unease between them and this single comment seemed to dissolve it.

"So," Rhodes said, "Garcia filled me in, but would you mind giving me your perspective of the case?"

"Sure."

Chloe spent the remainder of the trip going over the case step by step. It actually did her some good, too. It helped her to step away from the drama she had been dealing with back home and to reorient herself toward the case. And as she talked it out with Rhodes, she started to get a better feel for the turn of events. She wasn't quite sure why; it was nothing that was absolutely concrete, nothing she could quite put her finger on.

And with that growing certainty in mind, she actually grew excited when she saw the Barnes Point welcome sign up ahead.

Sheriff Jenkins was out on a call when Chloe and Rhodes reached the precinct. However, the lady at the dispatch desk told them that he had been expecting them and had made things as easy as possible for them.

"He called my supervisor and said there was a witness in the Hilyard case," Chloe said.

"That's right. And she just happens to be in the back, speaking to a few of our officers to officially file the report."

"Fantastic. Can you point us in that direction?"

The woman got up from her desk and led them down the hallway. As they passed by the little room she and Moulton had interrogated Oscar Alvarez in the day before, a tiny flare of guilt shot through her. The receptionist brought them to the last office at the end of the hallway. She knocked on the closed door and it was answered at once by a slightly overweight cop with a handlebar moustache. He saw and apparently recognized Chloe, excitedly stepping to the side.

"Come on in," he said. "It's Agent Fine, right?"

"Yes, and this is my partner, Agent Rhodes." She looked to the table in the center of the room, giving a polite smile and nod to the woman sitting there. She looked to be in her late fifties, was perfectly tanned, and had her hair straightened to perfection. It was clear that she was from the Farmington Acres side of town. "Is this the witness?"

"Yes," the officer said. "This is Sheree Goodman. She came in this morning to tell us what she saw but is only now able to provide the time to fill out the report."

"Sorry," she said. "I had a work meeting this morning and this was the only time I had."

"Do you mind if we speak to her?" Chloe asked.

"Of course not. Help yourself. If you need me, I'll be up front."

The officer left the room, closing the door behind him. Chloe took one of the remaining seats at the table. She glanced at the report form in front of Ms. Goodman and saw that she was doing a very thorough job.

"Ms. Goodman, can you tell me exactly what it is that you witnessed? And then tell me why you waited so long to come forward with it?"

"Well, at first I figured it was none of my business, and I should keep my nose out of it. But then I heard there still hadn't been an arrest or even real suspects in Lauren's murder, so I thought I had better come forward."

"Okay, I can appreciate that," Chloe said. "So what exactly did you see?"

"Well, it was Sunday and I knew that Lauren was there by herself. Jerry goes in to his office most Sundays, trying to get things set up for the employees on Monday. He's co-owner of the print company, you know?

Anyway... I just happened to be out on the back porch, firing up the grill while my husband was inside making burger patties. I just happened to look to the left, towards the street, and saw someone that looked familiar walking down the sidewalk on the other side of the street."

"And where, exactly do you live?" Rhodes asked.

"Farmington Acres. Four houses down from the Hilyards."

"And based on your knowledge of Jerry Hilyard's schedule, can I assume you know them relatively well?"

"Fairly well. Jerry would come over every now and then to watch Redskins games with my husband. But Lauren and I were never very close. The age difference and all..."

"Okay, so you saw this familiar person," Chloe said. "Who was it?"

"This young man has something of a reputation. He's a local guy named Sebastian Fallen. A younger guy... maybe in his mid-twenties, I'd think. Sometimes during the summer, he'd cut the grass and tend the ground at Farmington Acres pool, always with his shirt off. The teenage girls make such a fuss over him."

"So, it's not unusual for him to be in the neighborhood then?"

"He rides through from time to time. But it's rare to see him around on a weekend. I'll admit... I was curious. He looked like he was in a hurry and had his head down, like he didn't want anyone to see him. So I walked down the porch steps and went to the front yard, pretending like I was checking the mail from the day before. I barely saw him because he was moving so fast, but I saw him dart between the Hilyard house and the one to the right of it—the Andersons. And he was staying very close to the Hilyard house."

"You're certain?" Chloe asked.

"Yes. I even remember that he was wearing a black T-shirt with some band name on it. Rush, I think."

"What was your initial thought?" Rhodes asked.

"Honestly, I thought Lauren might be cheating on her husband. But I *did* know Lauren well enough to know that she's not the cheating type. She and Jerry were overly adorable together."

"You said this Fallen fellow has a reputation," Chloe said. "What sort of reputation do you mean?"

"Well, he's very sneaky about it and has never been caught or arrested, but there's many rumors that he's the go-to guy in town for drugs. I don't think it's anything serious … none of the bad drugs, you know? I've heard he sells marijuana and that sex drug, whatever it's called."

"Ecstasy?" Rhodes asked.

"Yes, that's the one."

"So do you think he was selling Lauren drugs?" Chloe asked.

"It's the only other thing I can figure. It makes more sense than an affair, but I don't even think Lauren was the type to do drugs."

"Do you know about what time of day this was?" Chloe asked.

"About noon or so. Surely no later than one o'clock."

Chloe thought all of this information over before getting out of the chair and heading for the door. "Thank you for your time, Ms. Goodman. Looks like you're doing a great job on that report."

Ms. Goodman picked up the pen she had been using and turned her attention back to the form. It was clear that she was filled to the brim with questions but was restraining herself. When Chloe and Rhodes were back in the hallway, they saw the officer who had greeted them coming down the hall toward them.

"That was fast," he said.

"What can you tell us about this man she saw … this Sebastian Fallen?"

"He's like a ghost," the officer said with a smirk. "We pretty much know he's selling drugs around town. Mostly pot. But we can never manage to catch him and no one will rat him out."

"Other than the drugs, do you think he's bad news?" Chloe asked.

"Hard to say. I don't know … a town like this, if he's busy selling pot and we can't catch him, I find it hard to believe he's into other things. Between me and you, he *does* sort of creep me out. We've had him in here twice for driving under the influence. He has this general attitude of not seeming to give a damn about anything."

"Has anyone gone looking for him since Ms. Goodman's story?"

"Not yet. Not enough hard evidence. Honestly, it might seem a little shady, but Sheriff Jenkins was planning to put a road check up about a mile away from Nelly's tonight, hoping to catch him. We figured we'd try to bring him in and then ask about what he's been up to this last week or so."

"What's Nelly's?" Rhodes asked.

"That would be one of the two bars in Barnes Point. Nelly's is on the other side of the tracks—the bar you go to, to play pool and hook up with people from high school that you used to hate."

"And Fallen frequents this place?" Chloe asked.

"Every weekend, he's a regular." The officer then looked at his watch and smiled. "Hell, it's almost five thirty on a Friday afternoon. He's probably already been there for an hour or so."

"Agent Rhodes and I will pay him a visit, then." *After the day I've had, God knows I could use a drink,* she thought.

"Need some backup?"

"I think we're good. But thanks all the same. Please let Sheriff Jenkins know we came by and what we're up to."

The officer nodded, watching them head back down the hall toward the front of the building.

As they stepped outside and headed for the car, Rhodes asked: "Is everyone in this town as nosy as Ms. Goodman seemed?"

"I wish that was the extent of it," Chloe answered. "There are weird friendships all through this town. People that were friends in high school together are still friends well into their thirties and forties. The women especially … some weird little cliques."

"That sounds terrible," Rhodes said. "You know what doesn't though?"

"What's that?"

"The idea of heading to a bar on a Friday afternoon with the woman that saved my life. I think the least I could do is buy you a drink."

"Seems fair to me," Chloe said as she pulled out of the parking lot and headed out into Barnes Point in search of a sleazy bar.

Nelly's looked like any other run-of-the-mill tacky bars. A little hole in the wall place that advertised drink specials in the window with a simple letterboard. The Friday night drink specials were highballs for two dollars and pitchers of Bud Light for five. Dusk hadn't quite fallen in Barnes Point yet but the parking lot in front of Nelly's was filling pretty fast. One single look at the place before they even stepped inside, and Chloe felt certain that Jenkins and his men ended up out here at least a few times each weekend.

The interior didn't do much to improve Chloe's initial gauge of the place from outside. While there were "no smoking" signs everywhere, the place still held the stinking remnants of cigarette smoke from years past. The paint on the walls was tinged with it and the odor hung in the air like a ghost.

The bar was nearly filled, though there were only a dozen or so seats positioned along it. Roughly twenty tables—including four scarred booths—filled the rest of the area. In the back, three men were engaged in a game of darts while two younger couples were playing pool at an ancient-looking table. Currently, a pretty blonde was leaning over the table in an exaggerated fashion, her breasts practically falling out of her top. She was getting the attention she wanted as just about every pair of male eyes in the place were turned her way.

Chloe knew that it was irresponsible to drink while on the job but she also knew that she and Rhodes were clearly sticking out like sore thumbs. Besides, if things went well, they'd be out of here before they even finished their first drink.

"Grab a table," Rhodes said. "I'll get our drinks and ask the bartender which of these charming gentlemen is Sebastian Fallen. What's your poison?"

"A Guinness for me."

Rhodes nodded and headed to the bar. Chloe sat down at one of the booths, not wanting to be at a table in the middle of the place to draw more attention. She scanned each person and saw what you might expect to see at a small-town bar on a Friday evening. Mostly men, sitting at the bar and looking to the TVs behind the counter or to the drinks in front of them as if they were crystal balls. Other men, looking out of the bar's one window, perhaps pretending that the streets out there were streets in other cities—nicer cities they might never see. As for the women, they were all pretty much clichés, too. Pretty little girls, probably between twenty-one and her own age, clinging to those last remnants of being young. Trying to have fun and attract attention with their bodies. The one exception was a woman sitting at the far edge of the bar. She was a little overweight and looked sad—like life had been beating her relentlessly. She drank some kind of fruity drink and gave the liquor bottles behind the bar a deadpan stare.

Rhodes joined her in the booth with their drinks. Rhodes had also gotten a Guinness—another sign that maybe they were supposed to be partners, Chloe joked to herself. It made the pain of not knowing Moulton's fate that much more bearable.

"Did the bartender point out Fallen?" Chloe asked.

"No. But he said he had never seen us around here before. He also said we were both very pretty. And because of that, he guaranteed that Fallen would come to us in a very short matter of time... and holy shit, it looks like he was right."

She gave a slight nod to her left. Chloe looked that way and saw a man walking toward them, carrying a glass of what looked like rum or whiskey in one hand and a small tray with three shot glasses balanced on his other. If this *was* Sebastian Fallen, Ms. Sheree Goodman had been right. The young man was incredibly good-looking; his hair was disheveled in a good way and the five-o'clock shadow outlining his face made his dark eyes seem radiant somehow. She supposed when you looked like that, you probably had no problem being confident enough to approach two strange women with drinks.

"Hey, ladies," he said. "You mind if I join you?"

Rhodes bit back a smile. Chloe could tell that she was trying to decide whether or not to play the part of the bashful woman or keep her composure. Chloe, on the other hand, had no intention of pretending to gush over him. She wanted to get out of here as soon as possible.

"That would be fine," Chloe said.

Rhodes scooted over closer to the wall to give him some room. He then took two of the shot glasses off of the tray and gave Chloe and Rhodes each one.

"What's this for?" Chloe asked.

"You're not from around here. So I guess you're visiting. Consider this a welcome present."

"That's nice," Chloe said, taking the shot glass. She sniffed it and winced at the acrid aroma of straight tequila. "But I don't take shots from strangers. What's your name?"

"Sebastian."

"Well, thanks, Sebastian." She downed the shot and fought back a grimace. God, she hated tequila.

She saw Rhodes give her a shocked look which she then hid right away. She straightened up and pretended to psych herself up. She then took her shot as well, slid the glass over to Sebastian, and said, "Thanks."

"I mean this in the nicest way possible," Sebastian said, "but you two look too nice to be in a place like this. What made you choose to come to Nelly's? There's a much nicer bar on the other side of town . . . a lounge area and dinners and cocktails and everything like that."

"Those places are boring," Rhodes said.

"They are," Chloe said, sipping from her Guinness. It was much better than the tequila but she simply didn't have the taste for it in that moment. There was too much going on and she was hesitant to put anything in her body that might slow her down. "But those places don't tend to have people like you."

"People like me?" he asked, sitting forward and giving her a smile. It was a charming smile—a sweltering, sexy one, if she was being honest. Chloe felt confident that Sebastian Fallen went home with a different girl every weekend . . . probably a girl from this very bar.

"Yes," Chloe said. "You're Sebastian Fallen, right?"

"Yeah," he said, giving her a curious look. He was still so locked in his confident swagger that he didn't think to be alarmed that she knew his last name.

Very slowly, Chloe reached into her interior jacket pocket and took out her ID. She laid it on the table and opened it up. "We need to ask you a few questions, Mr. Fallen."

"Is this for real?" he asked. His eyes were wide and he was clearly alarmed, but the traces of that smile were still on his face.

"It's very real," Chloe said.

"What do you need to speak with me for?" he asked. He was suddenly very unconfident. He sat up straight and started sliding toward the edge of the seat.

"Just to ask you some questions," Rhodes said.

"Yeah, about what? The FBI in Barnes Point… seriously? What the hell is going on?"

"We just need to know where you were and what you were doing last Sunday."

Sebastian thought about it for a moment and then his eyes narrowed. He knew what they were looking for and his continued rigid posture made it clear that he wasn't going to give up the information easily.

"What is this about?" he asked. "Am I being accused of something?"

"We don't know yet," Chloe said. "That's why we're hoping you'll just answer our questions and make this as easy as possible on everyone."

"Last Sunday?" he said. "I was here and there and everywhere. I stay busy on the weekends, you know."

"Do you recall paying a visit to Farmington Acres?"

That narrowed look came over his eyes again. He looked back and forth between them, not quite in a panic, but heading toward it.

"Yeah, I was over there for a little while."

"Were you visiting someone?"

"Yeah. Well, no. Not really. I was over looking at the old push mower in the maintenance shed at the pool. I cut the grass over there during the summer, you know?"

"Well, it's coming up on fall now," Rhodes said. "Why the need to see the mower?"

"The blade needs to be replaced. And really, I'm trying to talk the cheapskate property owners into getting a new one."

"Was that the only place you visited?" Rhodes asked.

The panic was in his expression now. He slid out of the booth and stood by the table, trying to regain his swagger. "Look, if I'm not being charged with nothing, you can't question me like this."

"We can actually," Chloe said. She then leaned forward and lowered her voice into a conspiratorial whisper. "Sebastian, we know what everyone says about you. We know what the police even know but can't seem to get you tagged down for. And honestly, I don't care about that. If you're selling weed, I have to tell you that's against the law. I'd be a shitty agent if that weren't the case. But that's not why we're here."

He shook his head. "Tell me what it's about and maybe I can tell you."

She wanted to grab his well-toned neck and wring it. But she kept her cool, not wanting this to turn into a scene.

"We suspect that you paid a visit to the Hilyard house on Sunday afternoon. Right around noon. Is that correct?"

Again, just a shake of the head. "Nah. Wasn't me. I don't even know the Hilyards."

"Who *do* you know in the Farmington Acres area?" Chloe asked.

"Nah, I'm done," he said. That swagger was back but it was forced—just an act now.

He started to walk away and when he did, Chloe felt her cool not only slip away, but plummet. She was on her feet before she was fully aware of what she was doing. She grabbed his right arm, spun him around, and pinned it behind his back. She then pushed him against the table, the edge of it slamming into his stomach. He let out a whoosh of air and then bent over, gasping for breath.

Rhodes came in behind Chloe and applied a pair of handcuffs. Chloe looked around and was not surprised that every eye in the place was no longer on the scantily clad girl playing pool; everyone was looking at them.

"You made me make a scene," Chloe said. "And now, instead of answering questions at a table, over drinks, you can answer them from the interrogation room at the Barnes Point Police Department."

"Go to hell," he said loudly. "Both of you." He even chuckled as he said it. He was trying to gain face, trying to show everyone here at the bar—people he saw every week—that he wasn't fazed by this.

It took everything within Chloe not to shove an elbow into his defenseless ribs. Instead, she grabbed his shoulder and pushed him toward the door. Behind them, as the door to Nelly's drew closed, she could hear laughter and the murmurs of gossip. She wondered idly just how long it might take for the entire town to know that their primary supposed drug dealer had been taken into custody by the FBI. And, perhaps, even how long it would take before people started to wonder if it was about Lauren Hilyard's murder.

Chapter Seventeen

Any lies or defenses that Sebastian Fallen had for himself fell apart the moment his pockets were emptied at the station. There were two ecstasy pills in a clear baggie and a rather unique-looking short pipe that reeked of pot. When these items were taken from him, there was no hint of that confidence and swag as he was led to the back of the station. Jenkins was back from his earlier call and when he saw Chloe and Moulton escorting Sebastian to the back of the station, a thin smile touched his lips.

"You mind if I join in?" Jenkins asked as they escorted Sebastian into the same room Chloe had led Oscar Alvarez into two days ago.

No ... not two days ago, she thought. *That was only yesterday. Good God, the last twenty-four hours have been crazy.*

"Of course," Chloe said.

Jenkins sidled up beside her and whispered into her ear. "I've been trying to land something on this kid for two years now," he said. "You might have just done me a huge favor."

They entered the room, where Rhodes roughly guided Sebastian to the single chair behind the desk. Chloe wasted no time, standing on the other side of the desk and leering down at him.

"When people refuse to answer questions like rational human beings, it makes me think they've got something to hide," she said. "I told you: I don't care about you selling drugs. Right now, I'm more interested in why you were seen lurking around the side of the Hilyard residence last Sunday... the same afternoon her husband discovered her murdered."

Sebastian looked like a scared animal, backed into a corner. "You know, I heard someone killed her. Heard it was bad. But … there's no way I did it. You don't think it was me, do you?"

"I don't know right now," Chloe said. "Mainly because of the way you tried to get away from us at the bar. I need you to tell us right now what you were doing in Farmington Acres last Sunday … specifically why you were seen running behind the Hilyard house."

He looked to Jenkins, almost like he was looking for someone to back him up. He then looked down to the table, his eyes darting back and forth.

"Sebastian," Jenkins said. "I know you sell marijuana. Maybe other stuff, too. And we can deal with all of that later. I'll tell you this, though: the level of cooperation you give these agents might go a long way to how you're charged with the drug stuff. You understand me?"

"For real?" Sebastian asked hopefully.

"Yeah. I give you my word."

Sebastian sighed and then looked up at the agents. He looked frightened and a little ashamed as well. "I was telling the truth about the lawn mower stuff," he said. "I have proof of that, because I called the owner and tried convincing him to get a new mower again."

"But that's not the only reason you were in Farmington Acres?" Chloe asked.

"No. I went to the Hilyards' house because Jerry Hilyard had called me the night before. He asked if the rumors about me were true … if I was still selling."

"He was looking to buy from you?" Rhodes asked.

"Yeah. But it was clear he wasn't the type that had ever done something like that. I asked what he needed and he didn't know how to answer. He said he wanted something mellow, but strong enough that it would sort of serve as a relaxer. Something for pain."

"So why did you not go by there Saturday night?" Chloe asked.

"I wasn't in town. I was up in Farmville with this girl. So I told him I would get it to him sometime the next day. He said he'd probably be at work but I could leave the stuff on his back porch."

"And is that how it went down?" Chloe asked.

"Yeah. On their back porch, there's this ceramic frog, holding a flower pot. He left a little roll of cash there for me, and I left the weed."

"You never saw Lauren Hilyard while you were there?" Cloe asked.

"No. I assumed she wasn't home since Jerry had me leaving the shit on the back porch."

Chloe believed him, but it still left a lot of unanswered questions. His story placed him at the Hilyard residence sometime within a five-hour period when Lauren had been killed. But she also knew that it might be difficult to prove that he had left there directly after getting his money.

"Which did you do first? Drop the drugs or check the mower over at the pool?"

"I went to the Hilyards' first."

"How long would you say it took?"

"I don't know. Jerry asked me not to park right in front of his house... said he didn't want people making assumptions, you know? So I parked a few houses down and walked. Between the walking, getting to their backyard and then back to my car, it was maybe three minutes. Five at most. I don't know for sure."

"And did you go straight to the pool from there?" Rhodes asked.

"Yeah. You can check my call history. I call Mr. Hamlet after checking the mower out."

"How long do you think transpired between delivering the drugs and making the call?"

"I don't know. I looked the mower over pretty good. Maybe twenty or thirty minutes."

"What did you do after you left the pool maintenance shed?" Jenkins asked.

Sebastian froze here and started to shake his head. He gave Jenkins and both agents that hopeful look again. "Can this just stay in here?" he asked. "Like, does anyone need to know?"

"The only reason anything you tell us would need to leave this room is if we need to check your alibi," Chloe said.

Sebastian let out a little curse.

"What is it, Mr. Fallen?" Rhodes asked.

Sebastian looked at Jenkins with worry in his eyes. "You know the Shanks family that lives out there in Farmington Acres?"

"Yeah, what about them?"

"I went to their house after that."

"What for?" Jenkins asked.

"Me and Rebecca sort of have this thing… I go see her once or twice a week."

"You and Rebecca Shanks?" Jenkins asked, incredulous. He then turned to Chloe and Rhodes, a look of disbelief on his face. "Rebecca Shanks is married… has been for probably fifteen or twenty years. She's at least forty years old." He then turned back to Sebastian and added: "Where the hell was her husband?"

"He works out of town all the time. He's been in Europe for the last two weeks. We've been doing this for almost a year."

"Ah, Christ," Jenkins said.

"Sebastian," Chloe said. "How long were you there?"

"I stayed until about seven o'clock. I remember that for sure because that's what time her husband FaceTimes her every night."

Chloe looked back to Jenkins. "You know her well?"

"Well enough, I guess."

"You think she'll admit to this?"

Jenkins shrugged and started to pace the room. While Chloe could not put herself in his shoes, she could imagine what it must be like for one crime to dig up the dark secrets and sins of the town he called home.

"I can text her and let her know what's up," Sebastian said. "But… look, her husband doesn't have to know, right?"

"Not technically," Jenkins said, sounding disgusted.

"You know the locals much better than we do," Chloe said. "Sheriff, do you mind looking into that? And maybe following up on this call to the pool's property owner?"

"Yeah, I can do that."

Chloe had another question on her tongue but it was interrupted by the buzzing of her phone. She took it out and glanced at it. A surge of hope flashed through her when she saw that she had received a text from Moulton.

"Agent Rhodes, I need to take this," she said, gesturing to her phone. "Can you wrap up here and meet me out front?" Before waiting for an answer, she looked at Jenkins. "Is there somewhere private I can take this?"

"You're welcome to my office. Straight across the hall."

She left the room, already reading Moulton's text. It was simple and to the point: *Sorry about how it all went down. Doubt I'll get to see you anytime soon. Call when you get this if you can.*

She stepped into Jenkins's office and pulled up Moulton's number. She hated that she was so nervous, so angry and yet so desperate for him to somehow go free. She wished she could convince herself that she wasn't falling for him, but the jarring of her heart as the phone started to ring in her ear said otherwise.

"Thanks for calling," he said. His voice sounded softer than she had been expecting. She could not imagine the stress that he was under.

"Of course," she said. "How are you?"

"Scared out of my mind," he said. "I just wish there wasn't even a trial. If I'm going to be punished, I'd rather know right away what was going to happen. This waiting is punishment enough."

"Johnson was vague on the details," she said. "What are you looking at, exactly?"

"I'm suspended until the trial at the very least. And even if by some miracle the court goes easy on me, I'm still looking at some jail time. I have no idea how much. And I'm doing everything I can to not compare this to cases like this I've heard about from the past."

"I hear you're being escorted to the building tomorrow to get your stuff."

"Yeah. Escorted. Like I'm some massive danger to the people in that building. I understand what I did was a crime, but they're treating me like I'm a psychopath. I don't know for certain, but I'm fairly certain they've got someone parked outside of my building. But hey… that won't last too long. I may be placed into custody as early as tomorrow and held in a federal remand facility until the trial. Again … I won't know any of this for sure until tomorrow."

"Do you need anything?"

"No. I just wanted to make sure I got to speak to you. I feel like tomorrow is going to start this massive snowball going downhill effect. I have several meetings and all of these reports to fill out." He paused here, perhaps sensing that he was letting his despair run wild with his words.

"Anyway, how's the case?"

"It's moving, but a little too slowly. I've been partnered with Rhodes again and she seems excited about it."

"Good. I guess I should let you get back to it, then."

"Yeah … but Kyle … I mean it. Please let me know if you need anything."

"I will. And again … I'm really sorry. I was badly wanting things to work between the two of us. But I guess I made sure that won't be happening."

She didn't know what to say, so she let her silence speak for her.

"Anyway, thanks for calling," he said. "It was good to hear from you."

The line clicked in her ear, which was fine because she had no idea how to respond.

What had just occurred was much worse than a breakup. It was saying goodbye to someone, not knowing if she would ever see him again.

Chapter Eighteen

It was 9:15 when Chloe drove back into Farmington Acres. Rhodes had asked if they should check out the Hilyard residence again just to validify Sebastian's story. With nothing else to do—other than go back home and obsess over what was happening with Moulton—Chloe agreed.

When she pulled up in front of the house, she saw that a few of the lights were on. She wondered if Jerry had finally found the courage to move back in and if the bedroom had been cleaned. Curious, she walked up the steps with Rhodes behind her. When she knocked on the door, she did so lightly, trying to keep in mind that there was likely a grieving man inside, trying to learn how to live in this house without his wife.

Jerry Hilyard did indeed answer the door. He looked as if he had just stepped out of the shower. He was dressed in a plain white T-shirt and a pair of gym shorts. He looked better than he had the day before but was still clearly not in a good frame of mind.

"Mr. Hilyard, it's good to see you," Chloe said. "I wasn't expecting you'd be here."

"I wasn't either," he said grimly, inviting them into the house. "But I figured I had to start sometime. It's only been a week and they are only just now releasing Lauren's body... but still. I felt stagnant over at the Lovingston house."

He led them into the kitchen where something was baking in the oven. It smelled like pizza.

"Has the room been cleaned?" Chloe asked.

He shook his head. "No. Someone is coming tomorrow to do it."

"Are you sleeping here?"

"I don't know. I might try the couch. But already … just showering and trying to scrounge up something to eat … it's weird."

"Well, we're actually glad you're here," Chloe said. "We've been working on the case and so far the only two potential leads have turned out to be dead ends. Just to verify the latest one, I do have a question for you: did you contact Sebastian Fallen last Saturday night?"

"Yeah," he said. "I did. Am I in trouble for that?"

"No. But … can we assume it was to arrange for the purchase of marijuana?"

He looked a little embarrassed, but nodded all the same. "Yeah. Lauren and I would use it from time to time. Nothing habitual or anything. We'd sit out on the back porch and have a joint on occasion."

"Can you tell me how you arranged the sale?"

"I asked Sebastian how much it would cost and I got that amount of cash and wrapped it up. Put it in the flowerpot out back, the one held by this ugly ceramic frog."

"And he delivered?"

"I think so. I mean … it was the following day, after the call, that I found Lauren. It wasn't until the next day, when the police were here, that I noticed the old ashtray out on the back patio table. The ashes were in there and the room had a very light smell of it. If the police noticed, they didn't say anything."

"Did Lauren ask you to make the call to Sebastian?" Rhodes asked.

"No. She only ever indulged when I did. I figured she'd be all stressed out from the reunion and it might help her mellow out."

"In the past, has Sebastian always been your resource?"

"Twice before. Before him, it was someone else in town … and I'd really rather not go down that road and rat someone out."

"How long ago would you say it's been since you used that seller?" Rhodes asked.

"About two years, I'd say."

"Do you know Sebastian Fallen well at all?" Chloe asked.

"No. I'd seen him here and there but that's about it. Seems like a good enough guy, I guess. A bit of a ladies' man from what I understand."

"Were the doors locked all day on Sunday?" Rhodes asked.

"I can't say for certain. They were when I got home. I remember having to unlock the front door. And the back door is almost always locked. But I guess Lauren could have forgotten to lock it back when she went out to get the pot."

"Do you mind if we take a quick look around?" Chloe asked.

"Help yourself. When you're done, there will be pizza in here if you want it. I just made it to have something to do. I'm not even hungry . . . haven't been since last Sunday."

They went to the back door and checked it out. Chloe had checked the doors the first time they had been here but she double-checked now; from both the inside and the outside, there was no evidence of someone forcing the lock. Outside, Chloe swept her flashlight around the back porch and spotted the ceramic frog. She checked the flower pot in its faded green hand but saw nothing.

"Sebastian's not our guy," Chloe said, looking down into the yard.

"I was thinking the same thing," Rhodes said. "Just waiting for the sheriff to give us a call to confirm." She then nodded toward the back door, to where they could still see Jerry in the kitchen. He was sipping from a beer and looking at something on his phone. "You think he might remember something in the coming days? Maybe some detail he forgot about in the midst of losing his wife?"

"Hard to say. I just—"

The ringing of her phone interrupted her. She dared to hope it would be Moulton with some good news, but when she answered it, she was greeted with Sheriff Jenkins's voice on the other line.

"I just left the Shanks residence," he said. "It took some prodding, but Rebecca admitted to the affair. And the reaction I got out of her makes me think it might be over now."

"Did she confirm the amount of time Sebastian was there?"

"She did. She said he came over around one thirty or so and left around six forty-five."

"How about the pool owner? Did he confirm the call from Sebastian?"

"He did. So does Sebastian's call log on his phone. He made the call at twelve fifty-one and it lasted four minutes."

That still leaves about half an hour for Sebastian to have gone back to the Hilyard residence if he wanted to, Chloe thought. But honestly, she knew this wasn't the case. After all … he'd had an entire afternoon of sex with a woman almost twice his age on his mind. It was very doubtful he'd have committed the gruesome murder of another woman before heading over to the Shanks' house.

"Thanks, Sheriff. We're heading back to DC, but we'll be back to follow up." She ended the call and pocketed the phone.

"Back to DC?" Rhodes asked. "Why not just stay here for the night?"

"Honestly, I've got a family situation back home I need to check on. It's only an hour and fifteen minutes. Do you mind?"

"Not at all," she said. "So long as Johnson doesn't care. Is everything okay?"

How would I even begin to explain everything going on with my family right now? she wondered.

"Yeah," she said. "Everything's fine. Just…you know. Family drama."

She opened the back door and headed back inside the Hilyard kitchen. She was well aware that Rhodes was giving her a questioning look, but she chose to ignore it. For right now, a skeptical partner was the least of her concerns.

Chapter Nineteen

When Chloe got off of the elevator and started walking toward her apartment two hours later, she heard the yelling right away. Someone was arguing quite loudly, raising their voice and using choice words. Chloe frowned, wondering how long it would go on. She just wanted to collapse in bed and forget about this day.

But then she realized that she recognized the woman's voice.

Danielle.

She ran to the apartment and unlocked the door. As she swung it open, she heard the voice Danielle was arguing with for the first time. It made her stop in her tracks for a moment, paused at the door.

"Dad, what the hell are you doing here?" Chloe asked as she closed the door behind her.

He was standing between the kitchen and the living room. Danielle was in the living room, nearly backed against the wall. She looked absolutely enraged, but at the same time, frightened out of her mind. Chloe had never seen such fear in her sister's eyes before.

"Chloe, I…"

"That's a great question, Chloe," Danielle said. "What the hell *is* he doing here? He said he had lunch with you…"

"Dad… you can't just come by unannounced," Chloe said, ignoring Danielle. "Especially when it's almost midnight. Why are you here?"

She took a few steps closer toward him, hoping to defuse the situation, when she got her answer. She could smell alcohol on him—something very strong, a smell that reminded her of the cheap bourbon he used to drink.

"I wanted to see you, that's all," he said. "But then I got here and Danielle was here, so…"

"I need you to leave, Dad."

"But I—"

"Oh my God, why can't you just listen?" Danielle asked, her voice still in that near-scream.

Aiden looked like he had something to say but swallowed it down at the last minute. He turned away from Danielle and then took one lurching step toward Chloe. The reek of bourbon was unmistakable now, as was the glossed over look of exhaustion in his eyes. He was very drunk and riding on a wave of emotion that had been pent up for almost twenty years.

"Dad … what's wrong with you?"

"I'm good," he said. "Paid the deposit on my apartment thanks to you. It's nice to be cared for and—"

"Not now, Dad. Please … Danielle and I need you to leave for right now."

"Yeah," Danielle shouted. "You can't just jump into our lives when you feel like it! I thought you'd be more comfortable on your own by now, you fucking jailbird."

Aiden frowned and looked at the floor. It was an expression that actually made Chloe hate him a little rather than pity him. "I messed everything up," he said. "Everyone I love just ends up hurting."

"Dad, you—"

"I'll call later," he said. He looked over his shoulder at Danielle one last time. Danielle turned away from him so he wouldn't see her crying.

He walked to the door, the only sound in the apartment his shuffling feet. He closed the door slowly behind him and when Chloe heard the soft click, she was glad he was gone. It was perhaps the first time in her life when she legitimately hoped she would never see him again. It broke her heart but it was also freeing in an odd way; it felt like finally being able to let go of her past.

"Chloe, what were you thinking?" Danielle asked, walking quickly toward the living room. For a moment, Chloe thought Danielle was going to hug her but she stopped short in the end and asked: "How could you have lunch with him?"

"Because I'm a sentimental sap," she said. "He showed up on my doorstep a few days ago and I sent him away. I felt bad about it so I offered to have lunch with him."

"How … how could you do it so easily?"

"It wasn't easy. But I thought about him being locked up for almost twenty years, maybe wishing he knew how our lives were going. Wishing he could see us. And I felt bad for him."

"You *are* overly sentimental." The tone she used indicated that this was not meant as a compliment. Not at all. "And he said you helped him pay his bills or something. His rent? Chloe, did you actually lend him money?"

"Danielle … I love you. But this is none of your business. It was my money and—"

"He helped kill our mother, Chloe! Of course it's my business!"

"Danielle …"

Danielle shook her head and marched to the far corner of the living room, where she had been keeping the single bag she had packed. She grabbed it up, shoved a few of her things in it, and then started walking toward Chloe—looking through her and at the door.

"Where are you going?" Chloe asked.

"Back home."

"Danielle, you can't. What if Sam comes looking for you?"

"He's easier to face than my father. And if he thinks he can just come by here whenever he wants, then your apartment isn't safe for me."

"Danielle, don't be stupid."

Danielle wheeled around and the look she gave her made Chloe's fists clench, going into defensive mode.

"I know you were his favorite," Danielle said. "And honestly, I prefer it that way. But in this scenario, you're the stupid one, Chloe."

Before Chloe could say anything else, Danielle was opening the door and storming out. Chloe instantly started to go after her but put on the brakes. She had seen Danielle like this more times that she could count: when she couldn't get a toy she wanted as a child, when their grandparents had not approved of the boys she had started to date at the age of fifteen, when they had first started looking into the finer details of their mother's death together.

She knew better than to go after her. And even if she did go back to Sam, Chloe had no doubt that Danielle could handle herself. She was not the kind of woman who would take shit from a man twice.

Still, as Chloe slunk into her apartment, she could not help but feel that she was letting everyone down. Danielle was disappointed in her, her father had unrealistic expectations of her, and she felt like she was absolutely nowhere on the Lauren Hilyard case. And while she had no hand at all in what had happened to Moulton, she couldn't help but feel like she was abandoning him.

Chloe crashed on the couch and simply stared into space. She looked to the corner of her apartment, where Danielle's bag had been until about two minutes ago, and wondered how it was possible for life to so quickly turn on a dime. It sent her thoughts toward Lauren Hilyard—a woman who seemed to have everything, a woman who had been enjoying her high school reunion one night and was then brutally murdered about twelve hours later.

If this job was teaching her anything, it was that life could be both beautiful and brutal. Sometimes it managed to be both at the same time. The trick, apparently, was to be able to accept them both in equal measure.

Around the time she and Danielle had started to unlock the secrets of their parents' past—at the same time news crews had started to park outside of her house—someone on Garcia's staff had sent her an email with information about the bureau's onsite therapist. It was something she had easily dismissed at first but had surfaced in her mind while she had tried to get to sleep following Danielle's departure.

She slept terribly that night. She spent a lot of that time wondering if all young agents just getting their start had to find ways to separate their personal lives from their jobs. Of course, she knew that her father's case had made her career something of a special case, but still… she knew she could not be an effective agent if she was constantly bogged down by her past.

Sometime between three and four in the morning, she finally managed to get to sleep. She jerked awake at six in the morning, though, as her alarm went off. She sat up right away because she knew the longer she lay in bed, the less motivated she would be to seek the help she felt she needed.

She ate a quick breakfast while she checked her email. She fought the temptation to call Moulton. She also fought the urge to call Danielle. It would do nothing but cause trouble and make things even stranger between them. She slowly got dressed for the day and as she drove in to work, she called the front desk and asked to be transferred to the bureau therapist, a woman named Mary Ziggler. She spoke with Ziggler's secretary and was able to nail down an appointment at ten o'clock. As soon as Chloe set the phone down, she found herself trying to think of a logical reason to call and cancel it. Of course, there was the need to get back to Barnes Point sometime soon. But all she'd managed to do there was to bust someone for potential illegal immigration and bring in a small-town drug dealer. Not exactly a case-solving performance.

As she was looking over the forensic files on Lauren Hilyard's murder, a familiar voice spoke up from behind her. "Barnes Point today?"

Rhodes was standing at the corner of her cubicle, poking her head in. She had a cup of coffee in one hand and her phone in the other. She looked about as tired as Chloe felt, making Chloe wonder what sort of night she'd had.

"Probably at some point," Chloe answered. "I'd really rather wait until we *know* we have something before we head back down there. The next time we visit Barnes Point, I'd like to come back to DC having wrapped the case."

"I get that," Rhodes said. "Sorry. I've been buried in paperwork for the last few months, recovering. The idea of getting out there and even just snooping around for leads is exciting to me."

Chloe nodded, not sure what to say. As an awkward silence fell around them, she noted that it was 9:55. "Can we get back to this later?" she asked. "I've got something I need to do at ten."

"Sure. You open for lunch?"

"I don't know yet. I'll text you."

Rhodes took this as a clear sign that Chloe was not interested in chitchat at the moment. Chloe hated to seem so dismissive but her mind was in a hundred different places. She and Rhodes gave one another a polite smile as they parted ways. Chloe went to the elevators and headed directly for Mary Ziggler's office.

She wasn't quite sure what to expect but it certainly wasn't what she walked into. Ziggler's office was really just like any other office. It was a bit larger than Garcia's office but smaller than Johnson's. There were two plush chairs against the wall, facing Ziggler's desk. When Chloe walked into the office, Mary Ziggler looked up with bright eyes behind small reading glasses and smiled warmly.

"Agent Fine," she said. "Come on in."

Chloe sat down in one of the plush chairs, taken a bit off guard by just how soft and inviting they were.

"I seem to recall," Ziggler said, "that I was given your name several months ago when your father's case was at your fingertips. I think some of your superiors were fully expecting you to pay me a visit. Can I ask why you decided not to?"

"I never really thought about it," she said. "I'm not one that really gushes her feelings out, you know?"

"Most people in your field aren't," Ziggler said. "So what's changed? Why have you come in today?"

"Oh…so it's just like that?" Chloe asked with a nervous laugh. "Right to the point?"

Ziggler reclined in her chair and returned the laugh. "That's another thing I know about the majority of agents—particularly ones in the ViCAP program: they aren't big fans of small talk. Though I can fabricate some if you like."

"God, no. No, right to the point is fine."

"So I ask you again," Ziggler said politely. "What brings you here today?"

Chloe started speaking slowly, starting with her father on her steps. She also mentioned starting a relationship with someone though never named the person. She knew there was a confidentiality agreement between the two of them but she still did not want to divulge the information about her and Moulton. She ended with the stagnant case in Barnes Point and the explosive scene between Danielle, their father, and herself the night before.

She looked at the clock on the wall and saw that getting it all out had taken exactly sixteen minutes. She was rather surprised; it had felt like no more than five.

"So it seems like you're being pushed to these great impressive mountaintops and then pushed down into dark valleys," Ziggler said. "Would that be fair to say?"

"Yes. Riding a high one minute and then struggling to even give a damn about anything the next."

"Given the way your childhood was, would you say it seems to be a pattern?"

"I don't know. I've thought about that. But once I got used to the fact that my mother was dead and my father was in prison, things were mostly okay. Aside from those two things, childhood was okay."

"The loss of parents to a child your age is sometimes an almost vague thing," Ziggler said. "Too young to grasp the totality of it but just old enough to feel the loss. It makes sense that you'd still be a little undecided about your father after all this time. You were never sure how to feel about his absence as a child and even now as an adult, with a better understanding of what happened on that day, it's still polarizing."

"That makes sense. But I need to know how to move past it. I need to know how to keep my feet on the ground I've found for myself. My career, my hopes and dreams… and not focusing so much on everyone else."

"There's no reason you can't do both," Ziggler said. "You're dealing with more baggage that most agents your age, you know. What *you* need to start to understand is that when your mother passed away, it did not automatically make *you* her fill-in."

Chloe felt like she'd been punched in the stomach. She sat up, a little offended but also a little dumbfounded. "I don't follow you."

"Tell me… why do you care so much that your father and your sister find some way to co-exist?"

"Because they're family. The relationship they have now is toxic."

"And that affects you, yes?"

"Of course."

"How does that affect you, exactly?"

"Well it… I can't… shit, I don't know. I hate that Danielle can't stand him. She talks about him like he's a monster. I sometimes think she might know something about him that she's not telling me."

"Replay all of that. Yes, they could be the sentimental worries of a stressed out sister—or any family member, in fact. But the need for preservation of one's family often comes down to a maternal instinct. Not that this is a bad thing. But I wonder if you have subconsciously been trying to play the role of mother in this family… maybe even while you were living with your grandparents."

I'll be damned, Chloe thought. *She's right.*

A million memories of living with their grandparents flashed through her head: her helping Danielle with her homework, helping Danielle clean her room, making sure any disagreements between Danielle and their grandparents were resolved.

"That's a good point," Danielle said. "I can even—"

Her cell phone buzzed in her pocket. She gave Ziggler an apologetic look as she took it out. "Sorry. I'm in the middle of a case and like I said, I'm not sure where my sister is right now."

"It's fine," Ziggler said, waving the apology away.

Chloe checked her phone and saw that the call was from Danielle. The fact that she was calling so soon after having walked out made Chloe think that there was nothing but bad news on the other end.

She answered it quickly, a little uncomfortable that Ziggler was sitting only a few feet away. "Hey, Danielle."

"Chloe, I'm sorry. I'm so sorry. But I need your help."

"What is it? What's wrong?"

"He's at the door. It's locked, but he's hammering on it."

"Danielle, call the police."

"I can't. Too much mess… he'll turn it to look like I'm the bad guy and…"

"Jesus, Danielle. Are you at your apartment?"

"Yes, and he—"

"Lock yourself in the bathroom. I'll be there as soon as I can."

As she killed the call, she noticed that Ziggler had straightened up in her seat. She eyed Chloe with a bit of concern. "Is everything okay?"

"I don't know," she said. And then, with a smile, she added: "This is one of those cases where the maternal instinct is just going to have to take over."

And with that, she sprinted out of Ziggler's office and headed for the parking garage.

CHAPTER TWENTY

Danielle's apartment in Reston was only a thirty-one minute drive from the bureau's parking garage—forty-five when traffic was bad. Because Chloe drove in a way where speed limits were only a vague suggestion, she made it to Reston in just over twenty-five minutes, pulling up in front of Danielle's apartment exactly twenty-seven minutes after she had left Mary Ziggler's office.

She ran into the building and up the first flight of stairs to the second floor. A small part of her wished that Sam would still be there but she found the hallway empty. Apparently, he had given up.

Or maybe he got inside, she thought grimly.

She had to fight instinct and not instantly reach for her sidearm. Even having her hand on her hip right now was not the wisest move. But she continued on, undaunted, to Danielle's door. It could have just been her imagination, but she thought she could smell the light scent of sweat and some sort of workplace smell like dirt or sawdust.

Chloe tried the door and was grateful to find it locked and in full working order. Apparently, Sam had been smart enough not to force himself inside. She knocked on the door, speaking right away to let Danielle know she was safe.

"It's me, Danielle. Open up."

She heard hurried footsteps right away, coming toward the door. The lock was undone from the other side and the door opened right away. Danielle wasted no time in coming to Chloe, giving her an awkward yet tight hug.

"Are you okay?" Chloe asked.

"Yeah. He just scared me. I thought he was going to knock the door down or something."

"How'd you get him to leave?" Chloe asked.

Danielle broke the hug and ushered Chloe inside. "I told him I called the police. He laughed for a while but he must have believed me. He left about ten minutes ago."

"Why was he here?"

"He told me through the door that he had been driving by, keeping a check. He said he saw me coming in the building last night. He wanted me back… wanted me to come home with him."

"How long was he banging on your door?"

"I don't know. Maybe fifteen minutes. I have never heard him that angry before, Chloe. That's the only reason I called you. He was… he was telling me about his other women. There are apparently two of them. He was telling me what they did for him and why—"

"Quiet," she said. "Don't even think about it. Don't give him the pleasure of it."

Chloe thought about what Ziggler had told her, about how she tended to lean toward some maternal need to take care of Danielle in a way their mother was no longer able to.

"You're coming back to my place," Chloe said. "And you're staying there until he gets tired of coming after you."

"I can't, Chloe. I treated you like crap last night. And if Dad knows where you are and—"

"Stop it, Danielle. Get your bag and come with me."

Danielle looked to be holding back tears. She actually looked like some fragile thing perched on a shelf, close to falling and shattering. Something started to boil up inside of Chloe and whatever maternal stuff Ziggler had been talking about started to morph into something else—something a little more prehistoric in nature.

"Where did he go from here?" Chloe asked.

"The new place… the one he's building for me. He's meeting with another contractor over there later today."

"What's the address?"

"Chloe ... we can't call the cops on him. He'll tie me up in his legal mumbo-jumbo and that'll be a nightmare."

"What's the address?" Chloe asked again.

"One seventeen Nelson Street."

"Pack a bag. I'll be back in a while."

"Chloe ... no. Don't go over there. He's mean and psychotic and just nothing but trouble."

She smiled thinly at her sister and said, "And things *didn't* work out for the two of you?"

"Funny," Danielle said. "But seriously, Chloe ..."

"Give me half an hour. I'll be right back."

Danielle said something else, but Chloe barely heard it. She was already hurrying down the hallway, her blood boiling. She thought she had found an answer to the question that had been plaguing her for the last day or so.

How do you separate your past problems from the present?

You take action and you shut your problems down in your own way, one by one.

The front windows of the place Sam had been remodeling for Danielle were covered in plastic tarp. Still, she could see the figures of a few people moving around behind it. She parked behind a large work truck and stepped out. She walked into the place as if she had every right to be there. She caught a large whiff of the scent she'd smelled outside of Danielle's door: grime, dirt, dust, and sweat. The place was big, even with the stacks of lumber and unpacked furniture pressed tightly against the walls.

She had never met Sam before, so she had no idea who she was looking for. She approached two men standing by a sawhorse, a few boards, and a skill saw. "Excuse me," she said. "Would either of you happen to know where Sam is?"

"Back behind the stage," one of the men said, making very little effort to hide the fact that he was looking at her rear end.

"Thanks."

She walked toward the stage area at the back of the room, finding a doorway to the right side. This led her through a small hallway which emptied into a back room where a small table had been set up. There, she saw three men standing by the makeshift table—nothing but three large barrels and a sheet of plywood. All three men looked up at her as she entered. Two of them were dressed in work clothes. The other wore a casual white dress shirt and a pair of jeans.

"I'm looking for Sam," Chloe said.

"That's me," said the man in the white shirt and jeans. "Can I help you?"

Chloe approached him slowly, feeling all of her rage coming to the surface like lava. "Yes, there was something I needed to discuss with you in regards to Danielle Fine."

"What about her?" he asked.

Chloe threw out a quick right-handed jab that connected squarely with his throat. When his hands went up to his neck, she delivered a swift blow to his stomach. When he doubled over for this blow, she grabbed him by the back of the neck and pushed him hard against the wall.

The two men who were with him stood back in stunned silence. One of them was biting back a grin. Truth be told, so was Chloe.

She was so pleased with herself that it almost cost her.

He came springing off of the wall, clearly still shocked but trying to save some face. He threw a haymaker of a punch that nearly collided with her jaw. She blocked it, wrenched his arm backward, and then threw another punch that took him in the side of the face. As he stumbled backward, one of the men behind them had apparently seen enough.

"Hey," he said. "Wait just a damned minute."

He made the mistake of laying his hands on her. He grabbed her by the shoulders and pulled her away from Sam. There was some force to his grip but it was clear that he was not accustomed to fighting. He left his entire torso open, allowing Chloe to pivot, turn, and send her opened palm into his chest. He let out a comical *whooof* as he stumbled back and fell to the floor.

She turned back to Sam in time to see him coming at her again. He, too, was apparently not used to having to defend himself. He was coming at her in a hunched over football tackle, fueled by embarrassment and rage. There were about three counters she could easily dish out but she knew she could not hurt him too badly; he certainly wasn't worth losing her job over.

She sidestepped the attack while making a sweeping motion with her left foot. He went sprawling to the floor in a heap. Chloe walked over to him and placed her foot hard against his lower back.

"If you go to her apartment looking for Danielle again and I find out about it, I'll come back for you on an official basis," she said, showing him her badge. "And if you raise your hand to her again, I'll come back in n a very *un*official basis. Do you understand?"

Sam made a hacking noise through his hurt throat and responded by raising his middle finger.

Chloe drew her foot back and delivered a blow directly between his splayed legs. He let out a groaning sound as he slowly tilted over and fell to the floor.

"Hey now," the one remaining man said. "I think that's enough."

"It's not," Chloe said, turning away and walking back toward the door. "For men like him, it's never enough." She then looked back at Sam. He was wincing from the blow to his nether region and there was legitimate fear in his eyes. Chloe enjoyed the sight of it far too much. "Am I understood?" she asked.

"Yes."

"Say it then. I have two witnesses here. Tell me."

"I won't bother her again. You have my word."

He was trying to inflict some anger into his voice but it was quickly overridden by the pain and the fear. She nodded to him, looked at the other two men for a moment, and took her leave.

By the time she got back to her car, she started to understand that she could get into quite a bit of trouble if Sam reported this. But she doubted he would. A man like Sam would never want to admit that a woman had gotten the better of him—even if that women *was* an FBI agent. Therefore, Chloe wasn't too concerned. The only regret she had about the whole thing was that she had not invited Danielle to come along to watch.

Chapter Twenty One

"So, are you not going to tell me what you did?" Danielle asked.

She had been quiet ever since she and Chloe had left Danielle's apartment fifteen minutes ago. She had never seen Chloe in such a mood before. She looked angry and very much in charge. For perhaps the first time in Danielle's life, she truly hoped that anger wasn't focused on her.

"I just let him know, in no uncertain terms, that you were off limits."

"With your mouth or with your fists?"

Chloe couldn't help but smile. "Maybe my feet, too."

"Thank you, Chloe. I hate to say it since it meant you having to beat the hell out of someone, but it means a lot to me. More than you know. But… you didn't have to do that. I can take care of myself."

"Oh, I know that. But I can help from time to time. I think maybe that's why things have always been a little strained between us. We never really want the other to help. But we have to get over that."

"Does that include coming to terms with how screwed up our recently freed father is?"

"I think it does, actually. But I don't want to talk about that right now."

This irritated Danielle but she didn't say anything else about it. She looked out the window to a sky that was looking slightly gray with rain clouds.

"Okay," Danielle said. "On to other things then. Have you given any more thought to the reunion?"

"Honestly, no. Danielle … this case I'm currently working on involves these bitchy women that just had their high school reunion. It's been a stark reminder of just how much I hated high school."

"All of it?" Danielle asked. "Even Jacob Koontz?"

"How dare you speak that name?" Chloe said with a smile. She hadn't thought of Jacob Koontz—the first boy she'd kissed and fought with her grandparents over—in a very long time.

"What's so bad about these women you're talking about?" Danielle asked.

"I can't give you details, of course. But it just brought to mind all of the drama and bitchiness. All of the cliques and how so many girls just buckled under the pressure of trying to fit in."

"Yeah, but you never cared about fitting in," Danielle pointed out.

"You're right, but I—"

Chloe stopped there as something dawned on her. Actually, it was more like something slammed into her, a thought that hit her like a brick.

We haven't paid enough attention to the fact that the Lauren Hilyard's murder took place less than twenty-four hours after the high school reunion. We spoke with Tabby North and Kaitlin St. John about it, but that was about it. Instead of looking for people that presently have something against her, I wonder what we might find if we looked back twenty years or so to when Lauren was still in school. Even Brandie Scott claimed Lauren rubbed some people the wrong way back in high school …

In other words: did something take place at the reunion that might have re-sparked some old high school rivalries?

"You okay?" Danielle asked her.

"Yeah, why?"

"You sort of went blank there."

"Made a connection about the case I'm working. That being said … I hate to do it, but I'm going to have to leave for work the moment we get back to the apartment."

"That's fine. I apparently need to do some job searching. With Sam out of my life, I'm currently unemployed."

"Are you … okay? Money-wise, I mean?"

"Yeah, I've got some saved up. You don't need to worry about me, Chloe."

"I know." The conversation with Ziggler replayed in her head, the insinuation that she was trying to play the part of the mother role.

"So … the reunion? You want in? You're not going to make me go by myself, are you?"

"You know what? If I wrap this case … sure. I'll go. I could use some distraction from the men in my life, too."

"Ooh, do tell," Danielle teased.

"I don't think so. Not right now, anyway." She cast a grin her sister's way and added: "Maybe on the way to the reunion."

Back at the station, Chloe and Rhodes were hunkered over a small desk in one of the extra conference rooms. Printed versions of the case files were in front of them, as well as all of the notes Chloe and Moulton had taken during their first tour through Barnes Point. Chloe had put highlight marks on several of the names.

"I follow you loud and clear," Rhodes said. "But walk me through this one more time before we hit the road."

"The tight-knit community of women in Barnes Point clouded my judgment," Chloe said. "The women are still so close after high school—even *twenty years* after high school—that we approached the case from the present. That's what led us to suspects like Oscar Alvarez and Sebastian Fallen. But when Agent Moulton and I spoke with some of these women—Tabby North and Kaitlin St. John in particular—they went on and on about their high school days. It's why they were so excited about the reunion in the first place. I think something happened at that reunion. I think something was said or insinuated and someone had some very old feelings of hatred or resentment take control."

"If that's the case," Rhodes said, "it would be feelings someone has been holding onto for twenty years. Unexpressed emotions that might have some surging out all at once. That paints a profile of someone with violent tendencies pretty easily."

"Exactly." She then picked up her phone and scanned through her notes.

"Who are you calling?" Rhodes asked.

"I'm going to see if Tabby North and Kaitlin St. John are free for dinner."

Chapter Twenty Two

They met Tabby and Kaitlin at a locally owned and operated restaurant in the heart of Barnes Point. Called Robin's Bistro, it was very upscale—almost pretentiously so. The steaks were thirty bucks a pop and the martini menu, which was three pages long, offered nothing less than ten dollars.

When Chloe and Rhodes joined them at a table by the bar area, it seemed as if the local ladies had already started drinking. They each had a martini glass in hand, each of which was just about drained. Chloe wasted very little time on the introductions, feeling as if this was the moment she had been waiting for—that moment she had told Rhodes about earlier in the day: the knowledge that this trip to Barnes Point should damn well be the last.

"I know you were both close with Lauren, so the questions I have today might seem inappropriate. And they may be hard to answer."

"Well, if they're super personal, your best bet is going to be to speak with Claire Lovingston," Kaitlin said.

"I figured that," Chloe said. "But because she *was* so very close with her, I fear her intense friendship would affect her answers. I need truth and honesty for these questions. Even if it means speaking ill of a recent murder victim. Are you okay with that?"

Both women looked hesitant as they nodded. Tabby drained the rest of her martini and slid it to the side of the table, an indication that she wanted another one.

"You told me yesterday about how Lauren was well liked in school, but that some people liked her more out of jealousy than anything else. I want you to think back to high school. Is there *anything* you can remember that she did… something that might be considered mean or cruel?"

"Well, you know, it was different times back then. You could sort of tease people and it wasn't called bullying."

"Did Lauren do anything that might be considered bullying by today's standards?"

"Well," Kaitlin said. She paused here, maybe wondering if she could keep going. She already looked guilty and hadn't even said anything yet.

"It's okay," Rhodes assured her. "Even if it's a bad memory of Lauren, we're hoping it might help direct us towards some answers as to why she was killed."

"Well, like we said… when Jerry Hilyard snatched her up off the market, most of the guys in school couldn't believe it. Especially the jocks. Now… I don't know if Lauren ever cheated on Jerry in high school, but I know she had lots of chances. And I know this because there were a few times when she sort of ridiculed the guys that tried to steal her from Jerry."

"Ridiculed how?" Chloe asked.

"She'd spread rumors about them. Nothing too serious, you know? Stuff about bad breath or smelly feet or bad acne. I think she did one time say that Travis Norris had a small dick. That one stuck for a while, if I remember correctly."

"What about Jerry?" Chloe asked. "Did he ever get ribbed by other guys because they were jealous?"

"Not at all," Kaitlin said. "When Lauren started dating him, he was bumped up to something like god status within the school. He was suddenly extremely popular."

"Would you say that Lauren was a so-called mean girl?" Chloe asked.

"I don't know," Tabby said. "Again… as snobby as it sounds, we were all friends so if she did, we never noticed or saw it that way. If she *was* being mean to people, it wasn't anything like enormous or deplorable. Nothing that would have made me stop to think… wait, maybe I shouldn't be hanging around this girl."

"These guys she made fun of," Rhodes said. "Were any of them at the reunion?"

"Travis Norris was there," Tabby said, starting to connect some dots. "And I think there might have been at least one more."

"You mentioned her talking to Brandie Scott and how that seemed a little weird," Chloe said. "Was there *anyone* else that might have been there who spoke to Lauren that you felt just didn't fit?"

"No," Tabby said. "Not that I can think of…"

"Wait," Kaitlin said. "She *did* spend a lot of time with the DJ. Like, up by his little booth. I figured it was just to request songs or whatever, but she was up there for a while, especially as she drank more and more."

"This DJ… was he also a student when you were in school?"

"Yeah," Kaitlin said, her eyes wandering now as she tried to remember. "But I think he was like a class above us. He was a year or two older."

"Would he have known Lauren when he was in school?"

"Pretty sure," Tabby said. "Everyone knew Lauren… even the guys in the classes above us."

"You got a name for this DJ?"

"I do," Tabby said, reaching into her purse. She took out her wallet, flipping through a few credit cards and reminder slips before selecting a single card. It was a business card, simple and cheap. There was a picture of a vinyl record on it, with a header: *DJ Scott Lambast – all genres, all styles – call me for your next event!*

The bartender came over as Chloe pocketed the card. He took Tabby's glass for a refill and then eyed Chloe and Rhodes. "Anything for you ladies?" he asked.

"Thanks, but no," Chloe said. "We were just leaving."

And with that, they gave their thanks to the local women and headed back out into the night in search of a local DJ.

Scott Lambast answered his phone right away and, though he was preoccupied with a wedding band he was part of, offered to meet them at the band's practice space. It was located in the basement of the local rec hall. When Chloe and Rhodes arrived, the bass of the band was ringing through the first floor. Even before they walked downstairs, Chloe could recognize the bass lines of Bad Company's "Can't Get Enough of Your Love."

When they got downstairs, the music was almost overpowering, encased in the concrete basement. The moment they entered, though, a man playing one of the band's two guitars stopped right away—apparently Scott Lambast. As he unshouldered the guitar, he looked to the rest of the band and gave a quick "Be right back."

He met Chloe and Rhodes in the back of the basement. He looked a little out of sorts, as Chloe supposed anyone might, having received a call from the FBI about a recent murder in the area.

"You guys mind if we do this outside?" Scott asked. He led them out a small side door that led to a thin wooden walkway. A yard sat below, with basketball hoops and a horseshoe pit.

"DJ and a band," Rhodes said. "You must stay busy."

"Music is all I know and all I ever wanted to do. And in a place like Barnes Point, you have to keep yourself busy to make a living off of music. Now … you said on the phone that you had a question about Lauren Hilyard and the high school reunion, right?"

"That's right," Chloe said. "We met with some of her friends and one of them claimed they saw the two of you speaking a bit longer than it would take to request a song. Can you remember what you and Lauren might have talked about that night?"

"Oh, sure. Nothing too serious. We were just catching up. I was a year ahead of her class, but like just about every guy in that school, I had a thing for her for a while. I asked her about Jerry—teased her about him not coming."

"Did you find it odd that he didn't come with her?" Chloe asked.

"No way. Not Jerry. He was never one to do stuff like that. He hated dances and events of any kind. I'm pretty sure the only reason he ever went to a school dance back in the day is because he had the prettiest girl in school on his arm."

"So, back to Lauren," Rhodes said. "Was there anything at all the two of you discussed—maybe even just something she mentioned offhandedly—that seemed weird?"

"Nothing that I can think of."

"Did she seem to be in a good mood?" Chloe asked.

"She didn't at first. It was obvious that she did not want to be there. But I guess she had a few drinks and the music was doing its thing. By the time things got into full swing, she seemed to be enjoying herself."

"Thanks," Chloe said, feeling defeated all over again. This was going absolutely nowhere.

"If you don't mind my asking, what exactly are you looking for?" Scott asked.

"We don't know yet. Anything that might give us a clue as to whether or not something occurred Saturday night that might have resulted in Lauren being murdered."

"Well, I don't know if it will help, but yet another thing I do in addition to DJing is to provide these flashy kind of videos of the events I DJ. I do it by setting a camera up on top of my DJ booth. It's tedious because I go through all of the footage to find the highlights. I've barely started the project for the reunion, so the majority of the footage is still raw and uncut."

"If you'd let us see that footage, that would be a tremendous help," Chloe said. "And the sooner, the better."

"Of course," Scott said. He then looked back to his bandmates and shrugged. "I have to bounce, guys. You guys mind locking up?"

They agreed, and Scott walked with the agents out the back side door and around to the parking lot. As Chloe got into her car, she heard the band kick into Eric Clapton's "Wonderful Tonight."

Scott pulled out ahead of them, leading them to his home. Chloe glanced at her watch and saw that it was 8:41 and had a feeling that it was going to be a very long night.

Scott Lambast had a nice little recording studio set up in his basement. Chloe assumed his time and attention to music came easily because he was not married. The house, while nice and warm, had the feel of a man who had never been married, a man who enjoyed the life of a bachelor.

He sat down behind a desk that was decked out in a small control monitor that was hooked to several speakers, some of the wires snaking into the foam insulation of the small recording booth in front of the desk. Scott did not look at any of this, though; he swiveled his chair to look at the large desktop monitor on the other side of the desk.

"How many hours of footage are we talking about?" Rhodes asked.

"About five hours, I'd think. Usually, when things start to get chaotic and just sort of a drunken blur, I shut it off. It's rare to get anything that's showable in the highlights from my videos."

"How many of these have you done?" Chloe asked.

"This will be my ninth. I did the reunion last year as well."

"So you've done enough of these to maybe notice strange things?"

"I'll say," Scott said. "This includes a rather blatant but well-hidden sex act between a boyfriend and girlfriend at the high school's senior prom earlier this year. There's apparently a lot that can be done when the guy wears his pants a little loose. But… I digress. Yes, I have something of an eye for things that are out of place."

"If you have a few hours to spare, we'd appreciate it," Chloe said. "An extra set of eyes never hurts."

"I'll do what I can," Scott said. He pulled up the reunion footage and pressed play. He then got up and walked elsewhere in the basement, leaving Chloe and Rhodes to view the footage. The footage was only a single shot, but it had been mounted high enough to get just about the entire room—what looked like a nice-sized dance hall. The footage began before the music had started. Chloe watched as a few people started to file into the room, most of them heading to the small bar area that had been set up on the right side of the room.

Scott came back with two other chairs, simple folding lawn chairs that creaked when he opened them. He offered Chloe his seat while he and Rhodes hunkered down in the lawn chairs. Together, the three of them started to view the footage.

"I don't even see Lauren yet," Chloe remarked. "Can we fast forward a bit until she comes in?"

Scott bounced to action quickly. He set the footage to shoot forward at three times the normal speed. The footage blurred by in this fashion for several seconds until a group of three women could be seen entering from the bottom left of the screen. "There she is," Scott said.

"And that's Kaitlin and Tabby with her," Chloe said. The fact that she had spoken to these women about going to the reunion with Lauren and now seeing it on a screen in front of them was enjoyable in a strange way. It made Chloe feel that they were on the right track now.

"It's always odd to watch the parties from this vantage point, from up high," Scott said. "You can see these little clusters of activity, different conversations, different emotions."

Chloe saw what he meant right away. She could see Lauren Hilyard, clearly there against her will, sort of hunched over as she spoke to a few people that meandered over to her and her two friends. Not too far away from them, two men spoke closely, as if exchanging secrets.

They watched in silence, the only conversation occurring when Scott asked if he could get them anything to drink. They both accepted waters and continued to watch. As they did, Chloe noticed what everyone else had been saying; after a few drinks and once the party started to truly get going, Lauren seemed to loosen up. She would laugh on occasion and, as the night wore on, tended to move farther and farther away from Tabby and Kaitlin.

As they watched Lauren's movements, Chloe noticed another woman. She was standing alone not too far away from the bar. She remained by herself most of the time, only being interrupted whenever someone approached her to talk. The conversations were always short and the woman remained in place most of the time. While her posture was a little angled, it looked like she was looking in the direction of Lauren, Tabby, and Kaitlin.

"Who's that?" she asked, pointing to the screen.

"Not sure," Scott said. "Melanie something, I think. I noticed her a few times. Sort of pretty, but stayed to herself. She sort of stuck out—not really part of a bigger group, you know?"

Chloe eyed the woman a bit longer. She wondered if this woman had been the type who had pretended to intentionally be by herself in school but secretly wished to be part of a larger group. The woman's posture and the almost longing stares made Chloe feel bad for her.

She continued to watch the scene play out and was able to spot the moment where Lauren and Brandie Scott spoke to one another at the end of the bar. After a while, Lauren moved away from the bar and headed to the back of the room, where the bathrooms were located.

She disappeared from the screen for a moment as she stepped out of view, toward the women's bathroom. Chloe watched the doorway, noticing that a lone figure was starting to inch along the back wall. It was a man, standing by himself. He moved slowly, as if inching himself toward the restrooms in a way that made it clear he did not want to be noticed.

"See that?" Chloe asked, pointing to the screen. "This lurker?"

"I do," Rhodes said. "He looks sneaky."

"That's Jason Morton," Scott said. "He was always a little strange as far as I'm concerned. I never knew him personally, but there were plenty of alarming stories."

Chloe almost asked him what sort of stories he was talking about but then she saw Lauren appear back on the screen as she exited the restroom. She made it maybe two steps before the man who had been lurking against the wall—Jason Morton—stepped out in front of her. Lauren stopped and did not try to sidestep the man. She spoke to him and when she did, they stepped close to one another, as if exchanging secrets. Jason then took a step closer and for a single moment, they were so close it looked as if Lauren had her head on his shoulder.

But then, as soon as they came together in what looked like an intimate manner, Lauren was shoving him away. It was a hard shove, but not a very exaggerated one. Jason staggered back as Lauren walked away, nearly storming back toward the bar. There, she got a drink and headed back over to Tabby and Kaitlin.

"You know if there's a history between them?" Chloe asked.

"I'm not sure if there's any truth to it, but yeah… I think there might be. One of those sort of high school legends, you know?"

"About Lauren and Jason Morton?"

"Oh yeah. This, I think, was before she and Jerry became a thing. A girl who looked like Lauren but wasn't offering up sex got a certain reputation, you know? Cock tease. The Blue Ball Queen." He paused here, perhaps fully recognizing his company, when he added: "Pardon the crude expressions."

"It's okay," Chloe said. "Go on."

"Anyway, Lauren did get caught every now and then messing around with guys. Either on dates or, once or twice, at footballs games, behind the stands. But because she was so well liked and pretty, it was seen as this sort of alluring thing. She was considered desirable rather than something worse, you know? Rumor has it that at some point during high school, she let Jason Morton feel her up in the back seat of his car ... that she was about to go even further ... but that he couldn't get it up."

"But you say it's just a rumor?" Rhodes asked.

"Yeah. A weird one, too. Because the Lauren I remember from high school would not have messed around with Jason. But she sure wasn't above slinging insults at people."

"The version of Lauren Hilyard I'm getting from the people I've spoken with paints a different picture. I hear she wasn't necessarily mean, just non-inclusive."

Scott chuckled at this. "I'm not so sure about that. She called some guy a fat ass during lunch one day, loud enough for everyone to hear. Even offered him a second chair to accommodate his large butt. She'd constantly make fun of sweaty guys in gym class. There was this one story about a guy asking her out ... just randomly, you know. A brave kid, I guess. Rather than just saying she wasn't interested, she berated him in the hallway, embarrassing the hell out of him."

"I guess any friends she had wouldn't want to share that sort of thing," Chloe said. "Not wanting to speak ill of their dead friend."

"That, or the fact that they were just as bad sometimes," Scott said. "Anything not to seem different than their queen bee."

They were a little more than three hours into the video now. Chloe had gotten to her feet, pacing to keep her muscles from getting tight. Scott had put on a pot of coffee—also sitting in his studio space—and she was sipping from a cup. She now watched not only Lauren's movements but Jason Morton's as well. On a few occasions, he walked over to the exit doors and seemed to just float there. Maybe speaking to Lauren had irritated him enough for him to want to leave. Maybe he had been embarrassed all over again.

But then he slowly made his way back into the party. When he did, Lauren had made her way to the dance floor. She hugged to the outside of the dancing crowd, not doing much moving but remaining with a group of four or five friends. About halfway across the gym, standing near the back and pretending to engage in a group conversation with a few other people, Jason Morton was clearly visible. He was staring in Lauren's direction. In the footage, his face at something of a distance, it looked as if he were staring a hole directly through her.

Another half hour passed before anything of note happened again. Lauren and one of her friends walked over toward the bar. Jason, who had still been keeping tabs on Lauren, made a straight line toward the bar as well. He hurried his pace when he saw that she was about to get there before he did. When they crossed paths at the bar, Jason said something to her. He tried to get close to her again but Lauren stepped away. She responded to him in an animated way, speaking directly into his face and using exaggerated motions with her hands. Right away, a few people surrounding them started to laugh. Jason looked down to the ground, turned, and made a quick exit to the back of the room. He made his way to the exit doors and there was no hesitating this time; he hit them hard and left the reunion.

"Do you know if Jason Morton lives around here?" Chloe asked.

"Not in town, no. He lives in this little hole of town called Lovett. It's about half an hour outside of Barnes Point."

Chloe glanced to her watch. It was nearing one in the morning. She considered her options, wondering if they should wait until the morning. But her gut was telling her to move, to act on this right now.

"What can you tell me about him?" Chloe asked.

"There's not much to say, really. He's one of those guys that finished high school just to say he did it. He's worked a string of meaningless jobs since then. Clerk at a grocery store, cook at a burger place here in town, and, his most current job, inventory specialist at the Barnes Point Advance Auto Parts. There have been more in there, but those are just the ones I know for sure."

"He ever get in trouble with the law?" Rhodes asked.

"You know what?" Scott said, realization sinking into him. "I did hear some people talking about how he had been kicked out of a strip club in Richmond a few years back. Stayed in jail up there for a few days, I think. Locally, I don't know. He stays to himself. He was always like that, even in school. Which is why that rumor about him and Lauren Hilyard in the back of a car was so weird. Hell… maybe that's why it stuck."

"I don't suppose you know *where* he lives in Lovett, do you?"

"Sorry, no."

Rhodes followed Chloe and got to her feet. She let out a yawn and then looked almost admiringly at Chloe's cup of coffee.

"Mr. Lambast, thank you so much for your help."

"You want me to finish watching this to see if I notice anything else?"

"That would be a massive help," Chloe said. "Thank you for the offer."

She drained the rest of her cup of coffee, set the cup down on the desk, and then headed out of Scott's house.

"We going after him tonight?" Rhodes asked.

"I don't see the point. I say we go to the station, see if there are any records at all on Jason Morton, get his address, and meet him bright and early in the morning."

"Did you notice how easy it seemed?" Rhodes asked as they got into the car.

"How easy *what* seemed?"

"Well, that little altercation at the bar. Lauren was around people. She had an audience. And she gave them a show. And whatever she said got the response she was looking for. Sounds like the sort of person she was in high school, according to Scott. She slipped right back into that role a little too easily if you ask me."

Chloe only nodded, the thought striking her as profound. Perhaps Lauren had only fooled a few select people into thinking she had changed after high school. And if she had, surely it had only been for image management. And if that was the case, what had she been hiding about herself since graduating?

Chapter Twenty Three

Chloe pulled their car into Jason Morton's driveway at seven o'clock the next morning. He lived in a simple one-story house with a yard in serious need of some maintenance. It looked like the kind of house that had been in the town for decades, passed down by either family members or previous tenants who had gone elsewhere in search of greener pastures.

Rhodes, in the passenger seat, tossed the very thin file on Jason Morton to the back seat. Scott Lambast had not been wrong; Jason did have a very minor file at the Barnes Point PD. Three years ago, he had been brought in for questioning concerning a potential case of sexual misconduct at Barnes Point's rundown little bar, Nelly's. In a bit of a twist, another man who had been questioned about the incident had been Sebastian Fallen. In the end, neither man had been charged, though the notes in the file indicated that Jason's name had come up in a similar case a few years prior but the allegations had eventually been dropped.

His incident at a Richmond strip club was in the file as well. He'd apparently gotten handsy with a few of the dancers and after being called out for it, pushed one of the dancers. Security clocked him in the face and then escorted him out of the building. When he tried fighting security, the police had been called and he spent thirty-six hours in jail.

"None of this really screams *killer* to me," Rhodes said, nodding to the files she had just tossed into the back seat.

"No, but it spells … something," Chloe said.

They got out of the car and walked across a badly cracked sidewalk that led to the front door. Rhodes knocked on the door, the sound hollow and somehow loud in the quiet of the morning. There was a slight commotion from the other side and several seconds later, a muffled clicking as the door was unlocked from the inside.

A man's face peered out, tired and confused. A growth of thin beard outlined his face and his brown hair was in shambles. Chloe assumed he had just woken up.

"Who're you?" he asked.

"You're Jason Morton, correct?" Chloe asked.

"I am. Now, as I already asked, who are *you*?"

They pulled their IDs simultaneously, like some well-timed mechanism. "Agents Fine and Rhodes, with the FBI. We'd like to speak to you about Lauren Hilyard."

"Lauren Hilyard?" he asked, as if the name surprised him. "What the hell for?"

"We'd like to know what you two were talking about at the high school reunion last week."

Jason's eyes widened. He looked like someone had just read his mind or predicted his future. He'd clearly not expected them to know that he had spoken with Lauren at the reunion.

"Could we please come in, Mr. Morton?" Rhodes asked.

"No, I'd rather you didn't."

"I understand that," Chloe said. "But please know that I had a fellow in Barnes Point that refused to allow us into his home. He ended up in an interrogation room and we got what we needed anyway. So again … could we please enter your home?"

"Sure, I guess," he said. He stepped aside slowly, very uncomfortable as they passed by him. "I just woke up, though. And the place is a mess."

"I've seen far worse," Chloe said as they entered his house. The front door led them directly into a living room that smelled like burned bacon. The adjoining kitchen was in need of a thorough scrubbing but the place wasn't as bad as the exterior had led Chloe to believe.

"Mr. Morton, I'll save you the trouble," Chloe said. "We know you spoke to Mrs. Hilyard at least twice at the reunion. We know one of those discussions took place at the bar, right before you left very quickly. We also know that Mrs. Hilyard started a rumor about you in high school. So please be honest with us when you answer: what was said during those two conversations?"

Jason slowly sat down on his couch, frowning like a child forced to remember some particularly bad memory. "I'm not proud of it, but the first time, it started as just me saying hello and asking if we could put the past in the past. But it got sort of flirty pretty quickly. And I just asked her if she wanted to get out of there. But then she showed her true form … called me a name from high school that stuck because of her."

"Was the name a result of the rumor she spread about you?" Chloe asked.

"Yeah. They called me Limpy. Cute, huh?"

"Mr. Morton, was she ever overly cruel to you in high school?"

"Yeah, she was. She went above and beyond to insult me. Limpy … that stupid name still follows me around. If you know about the conversations at the reunion, I'm sure you know she shoved me. She called me Limpy then and everyone busted out laughing. Twenty years later and these people still haven't grown the hell up."

"Did you—"

Chloe's next question was interrupted by the ringing of Jason's phone—an actual landline. "Sorry," he said. "That's my supervisor. He's supposed to call me to let me know when I need to come in today. You mind?"

"That's perfectly fine," Chloe said.

Jason stepped away into the kitchen and answered the phone. He positioned himself around the corner of the kitchen that led into a hallway, the cord of the phone growing tight. Chloe listened in enough to make sure he was indeed speaking to his supervisor.

"Chloe," Rhodes said quietly.

Chloe looked to Rhodes and saw that she was nodding toward the small scarred coffee table in front of the couch. On the table, there were a few magazines—one the latest Sports Illustrated swimsuit edition—as well as the Barnes Point newspaper. Only a portion of it was showing, but halfway down the first page, Chloe saw enough of a smaller headline to gather what it said. She pulled the paper out and saw the headline, not the big story, but halfway down the first page.

Lauren Hilyard Murder Remains Unsolved, FBI on the Case.

Chloe didn't have time to truly look at the headline, though. When she pulled the paper out from under the magazines, she had loosened something else as well. It was a glossy Polaroid picture, featuring a young blonde woman—surely no older than eighteen, though that was a stretch. The girl was naked, lying on her back, her legs raised and parted while she did some self-exploration.

Chloe pushed the newspaper aside and found two similar pictures. The same girl was featured in each one. One of the pictures was focused on her naked breasts, the other on her exposed backside.

The girl was blonde and her face looked incredibly familiar.

The girl in the pictures was Lauren Hilyard… only much younger.

"What the hell are you doing?" Jason asked, now off of the phone and frozen in the kitchen.

Chloe drew her weapon and pointed it at Jason. She felt that it might be a little over the top and assumptive, but she was acting on pure instinct. It all seemed to add up, slowly but surely, toward a final answer.

"Mr. Morton, I need you to place your hands behind your head. You're under arrest for suspicion in the murder of Lauren Hilyard."

"Are you kidding me?" he said, his voice trembling. "Are you fu—"

"Now, Mr. Morton," Chloe said.

Jason Morton did as asked, his eyes darting back and forth as if looking for some way out of this. Rhodes hurried over to him and applied her handcuffs. He said nothing as Chloe holstered her sidearm and he was escorted out of his house by the two agents.

As Chloe and Rhodes led him down his front porch steps, they exchanged a look behind his back. It was a look of celebration, a look of *holy shit, that was kind of out of nowhere.* But Chloe was fine with that. She'd take a victory any way she could.

Besides, she knew all too well that normal-looking people were often the perfect disguise for heinous acts.

Chapter Twenty Four

Following Jason Morton's arrest, Sheriff Jenkins and a few of his officers visited his home. Within fifteen minutes, they found a shoebox filled with similar pictures. All of the pictures—more than thirty of them—were of Lauren Hilyard at the age of seventeen. The majority of them were either suggestive or straight-out explicit.

When Jenkins handed them over to Chloe, he did so with a bright red face. "They were right next to his bed," he said. "Juts right there, out in the open."

Chloe nodded, taking the box. She looked through it, but only briefly. She had seen enough to know what she needed. It seemed to be the bright red neon sign she had been looking for, an expression of guilt. Or maybe they had been motivation, some final push to summon up the nerve in Jason Morton to do what he had wanted to do ever since high school.

Of course, she could speculate and assume all day and get nothing. She carried the box of Polaroids into the interrogation room. Rhodes followed behind her, her eyes glued to Jason in a vile way. It made Chloe think that if given the chance, Rhodes might very well slice this man's testicles off.

Chloe managed to keep her cool, though. She approached the table, sat on the other side, and very slowly, very deliberately, dumped the pictures out of the box and onto the table.

"Sheriff Jenkins says these were right by your bed," Chloe said. "I'll skip the vulgarity of asking *why* they were there. What I want to know is how you have them. And why they'd be out in the open so soon after Lauren's murder."

Jason did everything he could to *not* look at the pictures. He looked back and forth between Chloe and Rhodes. "It's sick, okay? I know it. But it's not illegal, now is it?"

"What's sick?" Chloe asked.

"That name ... Limpy. I got it because Lauren told everyone about a problem I had. She and I ... we really did see each other for a while, but in secret. She was ashamed of me. There was some overlap when she met Jerry. We broke it off eventually, but ..."

"That still doesn't explain all of these pictures," Chloe said.

"Lauren made it clear to me before we did anything physical that she wasn't going to have sex with me. She said she'd do just about anything else, but not that. So imagine her surprise and my absolute horror when ... well, when I found out I had an issue. They didn't call it erectile dysfunction when I was young, but that's what it is, essentially."

"So you never had sex with Lauren?" Rhodes asked.

"No. And I think my problem ... I think that's why she stayed with me. She knew we could do all of this other stuff and it would never lead to sex. There were times when it almost happened ... times when I was almost working like I was supposed to. But no ... we never did. That's where the pictures come in. She let me do it. I think she got off on it. There were so many more than these. There were hundreds. But she asked for them back when we broke up. I kept some for myself."

"Even if I believed that story," Chloe said, "the timing does not sit well for you. We have you on camera, in a confrontation with Lauren Hilyard the night before she was killed. And then we find these in your home a week later."

"I swear ... it's just coincidence. I saw her at the reunion and it broke my fucking heart all over again. I pulled them out and just ..."

He stopped here and started to weep. But the tears and the choked back sobs were of anger. He balled up his fists and slammed them down on the table.

"That bitch ruined my life," he said. "Such a dumb thing ... such a mean and immature thing. It ruined me. I wanted to hurt her ..."

"Mr. Morton," Rhodes asked, "where were you on Sunday afternoon?"

"At home. Nursing a hangover. Getting those pictures out."

"You stayed at home all day?"

"No. I went out a bit after lunchtime."

"Where did you go?" Chloe asked.

Jason almost answered but seemed to understand where this was headed. A look of alarm crossed his face. Unable to look at the picture-covered table, he looked to the far wall instead.

"Where did you go?" Chloe asked again. "Mr. Morton… if you can provide your whereabouts and provide proof, you'd be free to go after some more questioning."

"Mr. Morton," Rhodes said, coming closer to the table now, "where did you go Sunday afternoon?"

He finally looked up at them and now the tears in his eyes were from more than just anger. He was broken. He was caught.

"Farmington Acres," he said.

And with that, he crumpled. He folded his arms on the table and laid his head down among the lurid pictures of the woman he seemed to have killed.

"He never made a confession."

Rhodes said this as they headed out of Barnes Point. She let the comment hang in the air, as if seeing if it sounded right.

"And I don't think he will," Chloe said. "Maybe at trial. But for now, he's still trying to hold on to high school. Trying to hold on to the dream woman that got away."

"Damn, that's sad," Rhodes said.

"If you really feel all that bad about it, we'll probably come back down in a few days if Morton still hasn't confessed. They can only hold him for four days without officially charging him."

"Oh, I don't feel bad for *him*. The whole thing just feels anti-climactic."

"I was thinking the same thing."

But the more time that passed—the closer they got to DC, leaving Barnes Point behind—the more certain she became that Jason Morton killed Lauren Hilyard. He murdered her because he had not been able to let go of the way in which she had hurt him in high school... and because she had chosen to continue to inflict those same wounds twenty years later. She had shattered an already broken heart and the result had been twenty years of pent-up rage and aggression coming out in a brutal murder.

Several minutes passed before either of them spoke again. It was Rhodes again and the question she asked took Chloe off guard.

"Were you and Moulton seeing one another?" she asked.

"Why do you ask?" Chloe asked, not seeing the point in flat out denying it.

"Because you're not talking about what happened. I broached the topic a few times and you shot it down each and every time. So, I was just wondering."

"Not officially," Chloe answered. "But all the same, it sucked to see him go through that."

Rhodes only nodded, apparently feeling that she had crossed some unspoken barrier. And that was fine with Chloe. As far as he was concerned, she, unlike Jason Morton, was just going to leave that hurt in the past and move on with her career—and her life.

Chapter Twenty Five

"You're coming to this reunion with me and you're going to like it."

Danielle was standing at the kitchen bar, setting out plates for the dinner she had made them. It was an eerie comment for Chloe to hear; she assumed Lauren Hilyard's friends had said something similar when she had tried to get out of going to her reunion. She'd left Barnes Point the day before but it still seemed to cling to her—the case, the town, the peculiar post–high school friendships.

"One of those things is doubtful and the other is *highly* doubtful," Chloe said.

"Consider it a celebration. You wrapped this case of yours and I've managed to somehow unhitch myself from an abusive man that hid his demons well. I don't intend to just sit around your apartment and bemoan our lives over wine all weekend."

"Then don't," Chloe said. "You go. You have fun."

"I'm not going without you," she said. "And you know . . . Jacob Koontz will probably be there. And according to Facebook, he's single."

"He got married straight out of college, Danielle."

"Ah, but, as you well know, sometimes those right-out-of-college relationships don't work. He's been divorced for about a year and a half now."

"Since when did you start Facebook stalking the people we went to high school with?"

"Since I started considering this high school reunion," Danielle said. "I want to go in with some sort of ammunition."

Chloe considered it for a moment and sat down on the couch, facing Danielle at the bar. "I've only been back there once, you know?"

"I do know. But we're not going to go traipsing down some messed up memory lane or visit any surviving relatives. It's just me and you, some people we went to high school with, and a whole lot of alcohol."

Chloe thought it over for a moment. Would it really be all that bad? What would she do if she stayed home tomorrow night? She'd probably sit alone, thinking of what she had potentially missed out on with Moulton. She'd rack her brain with reasons to doubt herself about the case, to convince herself that Jason Morton was not the killer despite the fact that all signs seemed to indicate that he was.

"I'll give you two hours," she said. "If it's an awkward snooze fest where people are doing nothing more than comparing jobs and spouses, we're leaving."

"I'll take it," Danielle said, grinning far too wide. "I don't get it. You were pretty cool in high school. In that quiet, unspoken way."

"That doesn't mean I ever want to revisit it," Chloe said.

"You think there's something wrong with me for *wanting* to go?" Danielle asked.

"No. You were always a social butterfly."

"And you were always the caterpillar wrapped up in the cocoon, refusing to come out and see all the color."

"If that weren't such a great analogy, I'd be pissed," Chloe said. "Shut up with it already. I said I'd go. What else do you want from me?"

Danielle smiled as she looked around the apartment and then back to Chloe. There was a weight to that stare, thick with unexpressed gratitude. "Nothing else," she said, all seriousness now. "You've done more than enough already."

"Good. Remember that when I'm dragging you by the arm to get the hell out of there."

Their hometown—or, rather, the only town Chloe could clearly remember growing up in after moving in with their grandparents—was a two-and-a-half-hour drive away from DC. When they entered into Pinecrest, Maryland, everything came rushing back to Chloe. It was terrifying for her to recall just how close she had come to marrying Steven and living here.

As she drove through town toward the high school, she passed right by the road that led to the subdivision she and Steven would have lived in. She wondered what had become of the house they had moved into. Had he sold it? Did he still own it? Even considering such things sent a chill down her spine.

After she parked and she and Danielle stepped out of the car, she felt a strange synchronicity sweep over her. Lauren Hilyard had been walking into her twenty-year reunion two weeks ago to the day. Looking to the building that was housing her own ten-year reunion made Chloe feel almost dizzy. It was being held at the Pinecrest Country Club, a building she had never stepped foot in while living in the town.

"You already look miserable," Danielle said as they stepped inside.

Chloe gave a fake smile as she opened the door to the country club and stepped inside. "No, no," she said sarcastically. "All smiles. I promise."

They approached a small kiosk just inside the doors. A man and a woman sat behind the desk, which held blank name tags and several markers. As they picked up the markers and started to fill them out, the man behind the kiosk made a little gasping sound and got to his feet.

"My God, it's the Fine sisters!" he said.

Somehow, Chloe had managed to push that unfortunate moniker out of her head. Once they had both started dating and word of Danielle's promiscuity started to circulate around the school, they had been labeled The Fine Sisters. Which was fine, seeing as how that was their last name—but it was the way in which *fine* was implied that had stuck. Fine, as in sexy or hot. Chloe had always resented it because she knew she had never been seen as hot when in high school. Not that she was aware of, anyway.

Chloe barely remembered the man, though Danielle was already wrapping him up in a big hug. Chloe stepped back and pretended to find something interesting in the hallway that led to the reunion's central hub just to avoid a similar embrace.

Danielle finally joined her, affixing her name tag to her low-cut shirt. Danielle had never been shy about showing off her assets and tonight was no exception. Chloe was happy for her, though; she looked cute tonight, and completely unaffected by recent events with Sam and their father.

"That was Malcolm something-or-another, right?" Chloe asked.

"Malcolm Price," she said. "He asked me out in tenth grade but I said no."

"Heart-breaker," Chloe said.

They walked into the large room that held the reunion. It was an enormous room, decorated to look like a rural lodge. Their high school banners were all over the place, as were balloons of navy and white, their high school colors. A DJ was set up in the far rear corner of the room, currently playing a Justin Timberlake song.

The next few moments passed exactly as Chloe had expected. She met several people she had gone to school with, a few she was actually delighted to see. She spoke with a woman who had been close friends with her through middle and high school; she'd gone to college in Alabama and had come home specifically for the reunion. It was the sort of commitment to high school memories that Chloe simply could not understand. Still, within her first hour, she and Danielle had somehow ended up splitting up. Danielle was talking to a few people she'd spent a lot of time with during her last few years of school (one of whim Chloe knew had once peddled cocaine and LSD through the school halls) while Chloe did her best to hold surface-level conversations with people who had been friends and, at best, passing acquaintances.

She checked her watch, fully intending to hold Danielle to her two-hour limit. When she saw that they had another twenty minutes left, she headed to the bar for her third drink of the night. She and Danielle had already reserved a room at a nearby hotel so if neither of them could drive, they were only a fifteen-minute cab ride from a bed to pass out in.

As she started on her drink—a poorly made rum and Coke—a hand fell on her shoulder. Her bureau instincts nearly had her grab the hand and wrench it around as she turned to face whoever was behind her. She pushed the urge down and simply turned around.

It was as if all of Danielle's teasing and prodding had manifested itself into reality. Standing behind her was Jacob Koontz—the first boy she had ever kissed, the first boy who had ever cupped her breast, the first boy she'd made cry when she eventually broke up with him. And in a cruel twist of fate, he somehow looked better than he had in school; his age showed, yes, but it had refined him somehow. In high school, he had the sort of face that could have starred on a family sitcom. Now, though, he had the sort of face that should have been on a *GQ* or *Men's Health* cover.

"Jacob," she said, very aware of the sizable grin spreading across her face.

"Hey, Chloe," he said. "I have to say … I did *not* expect you to show up at this thing."

"I hadn't planned on it. It all had to do with some nefarious dealings with my sister."

"Yeah, I saw Danielle when I came in. She made sure to point you out to me. She looks great." He smiled here, stepping a bit closer. "You do, too."

"Same to you."

Jacob stepped up to the bar and ordered a beer. As he waited for it, he turned back to her and grinned. "You know, I tried finding you on Facebook a couple of times but didn't have any luck."

"Yeah, I don't do Facebook. Too public. Too chatty."

"That's what I figured," he said. He then took his beer and raised it to her. "Good to see you," he said.

She clinked her glass against his bottle. "You, too."

"So what are you up to these days?" he asked. "I always assumed you'd end up doing something with law. Like an attorney or judge or something."

"Same ballpark, I guess," she said. "I'm with the FBI."

He laughed and then settled himself down quickly. "That's a laugh of utter shock," he said. "Not making fun. Because really … it makes sense. Are you like an agent?"

"Yes, I'm like an agent. How about you? What did you end up doing?"

"Well, I *was* a business owner until my divorce last year. My wife pretty much took the whole thing. So for the last few months, I've been a construction consultant … mainly for houses, but a few storefronts and things like that."

"Yeah, Danielle told me about the divorce. Sorry to hear it."

Jacob shrugged. "It was sort of doomed from the start, I suppose. Anyway ... so, with the bureau ... I guess you're living in DC?"

"Yeah. How about you?"

"Just outside of Baltimore."

And just like that, Chloe found herself slipping easily and naturally into conversation with a man who had nearly stolen her heart eleven years ago. That decade between then and now seemed like some huge chasm, though. It was hard to imagine her younger self talking to Jacob. But they had clicked in the sort of way that made both of them sure that they had been meant to be together, that they would last a very long time. She missed that naïve teenage love, but not the gullible person it had nearly made out of her.

They spoke at the bar for nearly twenty minutes, catching up and sharing their thoughts on current events, pop culture, and sharing high school memories—many of which involved their dating life. As they started to get truly comfortable, she saw Danielle walking across the floor, headed to the other side of the bar. She gave Chloe a sarcastic nod before glancing at a watch that was not on her wrist and then shrugging. Chloe rolled her eyes, but was unable to hold back her smile.

As she looked away from Danielle, she caught sight of a woman sitting by herself in a little lounge area across the room. Chloe could barely remember her from high school. She thought her name was Tasha or something like it. She looked quite uncomfortable, like she really didn't want to be there. It almost made Chloe feel guilty for having changed her tune so quickly.

"You okay?" Jacob asked. "You sort of spaced out there."

"Yeah, I'm good. It's just a lot, seeing all these people from high school and—"

Her name is Tasha Haskins, she thought suddenly. She never really fit in and never tried. And she's doing the same now. Watching everyone from afar, wondering what their lives are like. Maybe hers is the same. Maybe ... maybe you've seen someone just like her in the last few days ...

"Chloe?"

A thought dawned on her. It struggled to get out, wrestling through the haze of the three drinks she'd had so far.

"I'm good," she said, though she wasn't so sure she was. "Jacob, I can't believe this … but I think I have to go."

"Was it too much? Me just coming up and acting like ten years hadn't passed?"

"No, no … it's not that. It's a work thing and …"

She stopped here and grabbed a napkin from the edge of the bar. She borrowed a pen from the bartender and scribbled her number on the napkin. "Here's the proof I'm not just ditching you. Wait a few days and call me. I'd like to catch up."

"I would, too," Jacob said.

Chloe gave him a hug, her eyes already searching for Danielle in the crowd. She found her and broke the hug with one final goodbye to Jacob. It was harder to walk away from him than it should have been, especially with images of Moulton in the back of her head. She approached Danielle, who was currently awkwardly dancing with a few other women to a god-awful pop song that she *knew* Danielle hated.

"You look worried," Danielle said. "Is everything okay?"

"I don't know. Danielle, I just had a thought and … well, you're going to hate me for this but we need to go."

"It hasn't been two hours quite yet," Danielle said in a disappointed mocking tone.

"I know. I swear … Danielle, this is important. I think we might have gotten something wrong on the Barnes Point case and I need to get back to DC as fast as I can."

"Damn … you're for real, aren't you?"

"How much have you had to drink? Can you drive?"

"Two beers. Nothing strong yet. I can drive."

Chloe knew it was irresponsible, especially given her profession, but she didn't see where she had any other choice. "Thanks," she said. "Danielle, really … I owe you one."

Danielle said a few quick goodbyes and, to Chloe's delight, didn't seem to be too bothered to be leaving. In fact, she thought her sister looked a little excited to be driving her FBI agent sister back home so she could jump back on a case.

As Danielle pulled out of the parking lot, sipping on a water she'd taken from the bar before leaving, Chloe pulled out her cell phone. She called Rhodes first, feeling like a jerk to be making such a call at nine o'clock on a Saturday night. When Rhodes answered, she sounded slightly bored, yet glad to hear from Chloe.

"Sorry to bother you so late on a Saturday, but I think we might need to meet up. I think we might need to go back to Barnes Point."

"What the hell for?"

Chloe told her the thoughts that had gone parading through her head. Rhodes sounded convinced, almost in an excited sort of state by the time they ended the call. She then immediately made her next call, not expecting an answer, but hoping for the best. The call was answered on the third ring. When the person on the other end answered it, his voice was almost entirely drowned out by loud, blaring music.

"Scott? It's Agent Fine. From the sound of it, you're on the job."

"I am. What can I do for you?"

"Is there any way possible that we could meet up at your studio? I want to take another look at that video of the reunion."

"Give me an hour. I've got a backup I can bring in to relieve me."

Chloe gave her thanks and ended the call. She looked to the road, then to her sister.

"You sure you're sober?" Chloe asked.

"If I wasn't before, I am now. Hearing you on the phone like that, it's sort of exciting. I feel like a sidekick."

"That's exactly what you are. But as a sidekick, your partner is an FBI agent. That means you can speed it up a bit."

Danielle grinned and did as she was asked. The reunion nothing more than an afterthought in their heads, Danielle sped them back toward DC while Chloe looked back over the case, wondering how she and Rhodes had missed something so obvious.

Chapter Twenty Six

Scott Lambast seemed as if he felt very much like Danielle had felt; excited and eager to help out on the case in any way he could. By the time Chloe and Rhodes appeared at his house just shy of midnight, he had already settled down in his studio and pulled the footage up. He had paused it at the scene where Jason Morton could be seen lurking against the back wall, as if waiting for Lauren Hilyard to come back out.

"I figured this is where you'd want to pick it up," Scott said.

"A good thought," Chloe said, "but I need to go backwards a little bit."

Scott did as he was asked and cycled back through the footage. It took about twenty seconds for him to get to the spot she wanted. "Right there," she said, stepping forward and pointing at the screen—to the lonely woman at the end of the bar.

"You said her name was Melanie, right?" Rhodes asked.

"Yeah," Scott answered. "But I don't know about a last name. At the risk of sounding like a putz, I never really paid much attention to her in school."

Yeah, I bet no one ever did, Chloe thought.

Chloe watched Melanie for the next several minutes. She spent a lot of her time looking painfully in the direction of several different groups. But her eyes almost always drifted back to Lauren. Even when Lauren was separated from her group of primary friends like Tabby and Kaitlin, Melanie seemed to track her.

"Skip ahead a bit," Chloe said.

Scott fast forwarded the scene, Chloe keeping her eyes on Melanie. She stayed against that one side of the room, as if she were using the bar as a sort of base. She didn't drink that much; as far as Chloe could tell, she only had two drinks the entire time. When she finally did move away from the wall and started across the room, Chloe placed a hand on Scott's shoulder. "Stop it right there."

The screen went back to normal speed as Melanie seemed to be walking in the direction of Lauren and another woman. She got halfway across the room and came to a stop. She seemed to consider something for a moment before turning and walking to the back of the room toward the restroom. When she walked into the ladies' room, she stayed there for quite a while. Eight minutes passed by, most of which Scott fast-forwarded through, until she came back. When she reappeared, someone approached her and spoke with her briefly. But it was clear that Melanie was not interested.

Within a few minutes, she was back to stalking around the crowd. She blended in well; she did it in a way that suggested she had been doing it her whole life.

"Do you have the capabilities to print a screenshot of this out?" Chloe asked.

"The best I can do is get a screen grab and save it as a JPEG."

"That'll do."

As Scott worked at doing this, Rhodes and Chloe adjourned to the back of the studio. Rhodes took one final look back at the screen, where Scott had paused the video again.

"I know it seems like a stretch," Chloe said. "But it sort of fits, doesn't it? The girl that was never really seen by anyone in high school. Envious of the popular girl. Rhodes, did you see how intently she's staring at Lauren in that video?"

"I did. It *was* sort of creepy."

"We have to talk to her. And even if she does nothing more than give us more terrible stories about how Lauren Hilyard treated people in high school, I feel like someone that drawn to Lauren could either strengthen the case against Jason Morton or show the holes in it."

"But you don't think Jason did it anymore?"

"I don't know. The way he had those pictures ... it was pretty sad and perverted but there was nothing in them to suggest he wanted to see her hurt. He was objectifying her by looking back at those pictures, sure, but…"

"But a man that wanted her dead wouldn't be appreciating her body in such a way."

Chloe nodded. It had been the one thing that had not sat well with her since they had arrested Jason Morton. It had not seemed to fit with the profile she had been putting together in her head.

"I've got your picture printing out," Scott said. "But if you don't mind my asking, how are you even going to find her based off of this one picture?"

It was a good question, but Chloe already had a few ideas.

Nelly's was in high gear when Rhodes parked the car in the crowded parking lot. Even before they got out of the car, they could hear the bass of some shit-kicking country song coming from within the bar. They exchanged a slightly disgusted glance over the roof of the car as they headed inside.

Chloe sized up the room, a little taken aback at just how packed it was. She started to look around for people who looked to be between twenty-eight and thirty but found it harder than it should have been. She figured the best thing to do would be going to the expert. She walked directly to the bar and spotted the bartender who had been here when she and Rhodes had questioned Sebastian Fallen.

"Hey," the bartender said cautiously. "I'm not looking for another scene."

"We're not, either," Chloe said. "You know who Lauren Hilyard is?"

"Yeah. She was killed two weeks ago, right? Married to Jerry Hilyard. People still talk about how she was hot stuff in high school."

"That's right. Can you point out anyone in here that might have graduated in the same class as her?"

"Well hell… yeah, that's easy." He nodded directly behind them, to a small table where a man was sitting by himself. It was a man Chloe recognized—a man she had seen quite recently, in fact.

Jerry Hilyard looked like he might fall off of the chair he was sitting in. He had both hands wrapped around a mug of beer, looking down into it as if there might be tea leaves (or, in this case, hops leaves) to be read.

"How long has he been in here?" Rhodes asked.

"A while. Since at least nine. A few people have gone up to him to be polite. Offer their condolences and all. But he clearly just wants to be left alone, you know? He came in, ordered his first beer, and asked to keep an open tab ... and to make sure he never had an empty beer on his table until he left. I told him I could do that, but he'd need to leave me his keys. He did, and I have a cab company number ready to go."

"How many drinks in is he?"

The bartender shrugged. "I'm not sure. Eight? Maybe nine."

Chloe thanked the bartender and then slowly made her way over to Jerry. Rhodes followed behind, eliciting at least one catcall as she did so.

Chloe stopped at the table and took the open seat across from him. He looked up at her and it took a moment for him to recognize her. He nodded as if she had said something and then looked at his surroundings.

"Not my finest moment," he said. His words were slow, and he enunciated each one carefully. "I wanted to be out around people ... but all people want to do is tell me how sorry they are."

"Mr. Hilyard, are you okay?"

She had to raise her voice to be heard over the music. She hated herself a bit for recognizing the song. "Fast as You" by Dwight Yoakam.

"Sure," Jerry said. "Neither of my kids want to come home. Even after the funeral ... they wanted nothing to do with me. Lauren's parents think it's just too painful here right now for them. But they never asked how I was doing. Assholes are probably glad she's dead just so she can't be with me anymore."

Realizing that this could quickly devolve into a toxic bashing session, Chloe got straight to the point. She pitied the man but had to trust that the bartender with his keys would do the right thing when the time came.

"Mr. Hilyard, I want you to look at a picture for me and tell me if you know who it is. I believe she might have been in your graduating class."

She slid the picture over to him and he studied it hard—perhaps waiting for his vision to focus in on just the one version of the picture rather that then two or three hazy ones he was likely seeing.

"Yup. That's Melanie. Melanie Paschiutto." He then made a *pfff* sound with his lips and slapped at the picture. "Or, as everyone called her in school, Melanie Pa*shit*-o. I believe she had my lovely wife to thank for that little nickname. One of her fine contributions to high school."

"So Lauren knew her?" Chloe asked.

"Yeah, she did. Gave that poor girl hell in high school. You ever see that movie *Carrie*? The old one, not the new remade garbage. Carrie has her first period in the shower and the girls start chucking tampons at her. That's the sort of stuff Lauren did to her."

"Do you know why?"

"Other than being an evil bitch?" He frowned at this and choked back a sob. To make sure it stayed down, he gulped down some of his beer. It was getting close to empty, making him look over toward the bartender. "She wasn't like that when we got married. She got pregnant and I think she understood… started to regret being so fucking mean to everyone in school. I don't know… I think she still bashed people a bit during her little porch sessions with Claire or her tea and snacks with Tabby and Kaitlin."

"Do you know *why* Lauren was so mean to this woman?"

"Because she wasn't as pretty. She was odd. A little overweight. Acne. Hand-me-down clothes. It wasn't just Lauren. Everyone picked on her. Lauren was just sort of the ringleader."

And she chose to go to her high school reunion? Chloe thought. *What the hell for?*

But she was starting to think she knew exactly why she'd gone.

"Would you happen to know where she lives?" Chloe asked.

"Melanie? No. I don't think I've spoken a word to her since high school. I think she went to community college and stuck around here, but I never spoke to her after graduation. Hell… I doubt I spoke to her at all in high school."

"Well, thank you for your time," Chloe said. She got up from her chair and saw that Rhodes was looking at Jerry Hilyard as if the sight of him was breaking her heart. Chloe turned back to him and asked: "Can we give you a ride home?"

He thought about it for a moment and then shook his head. "No. I know I'm drunk and that's okay. It's the most I've felt... the most that wasn't sorrow or pain, that is... in two weeks. And it's nice." He smiled then, a smile that made Chloe want to weep. "It's numbing. Don't give a damn about anything. I just want to drink until I pass out and it all goes black."

He looked back down into his beer before draining it and showing the empty glass to the bartender. Chloe almost tried again but left him to it. On her way out, she passed by the bartender as he took Jerry his next beer.

"Be sure you take care of him," Chloe said.

The bartender only nodded, indicating that he'd basically accepted that duty the moment the poor man had walked in. It made Chloe feel a little bit better but she realized as they walked back out to the parking lot that although she felt she was definitely on to something here, the sight of Jerry Hilyard had affected her deeply.

It made her incredibly sad, but at the same time, more determined than ever to make sure she found his wife's killer.

Chapter Twenty Seven

It was three o'clock in the morning by the time Chloe and Rhodes had managed to get an address for one Melanie Paschiutto. The Barnes Point police department was poorly staffed at such an hour, most of the available manpower stationed on the town's many back roads to watch out for drunk drivers.

Rather than head out to speak with Melanie at such a ridiculous hour, they opted to get a room at a motel. Chloe fell asleep around 3:45, conking out the moment her head hit the bed. As was the nature of sleep, though, the final thought in her head as she drifted off followed her down and stuck to the darkness, not causing any dreams but keeping one thing in her subconscious, one thing to occupy her mind even as she slept.

It was a thought of Jacob Koontz, standing beside Kyle Moulton. It was her past, which was gone, and what she had thought might be her future, equally gone. And as that image drifted off into sleep with her, she could not help but wonder which one—the past or the future—might be more significant.

The alarm went off at seven o'clock. Chloe and Moulton worked well around one another as they dressed for the day. Hair and teeth brushed, somewhat energized by the three or so hours of sleep they'd had, they walked out into the morning. It was quiet and serene, Barnes Point offering a picture of its typical Sunday morning. Chloe wondered if Lauren Hilyard had experienced this on her last day alive or if she had slept through it, maybe snoozing off a few too many drinks.

As they got into the car, Chloe called Sheriff Jenkins to let him know where they were headed and some of the suspicions she had. Jenkins offered his help, stating that Jason Morton's refusal to give an admission as well as the lack of evidence was pointing to not only his release, but the eventuality of him no longer being considered the killer.

Chloe drove out to the edge of Barnes Point, taking a two-lane road that was perfectly bordered with trees that seemed to go on forever. Quaint little houses were tucked within the forest, barely visible from the road. About six miles into this repetitious scenery, they came to the address they'd found for Melanie Paschiutto the night before. There was a single car parked in the driveway. A swing set and a tattered old Little Tikes tricycle parked along the edge of the sidewalk indicated that there was at least one Paschiutto child.

They walked up to the front door, Chloe knocking lightly. Off in the distance, somewhere in the trees, birds were singing. She felt like they were in the middle of nowhere, the reality of Lauren Hilyard's death on the other side of the world.

A series of rapid footsteps came running toward the door. It opened slowly, revealing half of a small face. A little girl of about eight or so stared up at Chloe and Rhodes. When the girls realized she did not know either of these women, she stepped back and looked behind her.

"Is your mother home?" Chloe asked.

The girl nodded and the yelled: "Mom! Two ladies are at the door!"

With her announcement made, she ran back into the house, leaving the door open behind her. Within seconds, a woman appeared. She was fussing with an earring as she approached the doorway.

"Can I help you?" she asked, finally getting the ring into her ear.

"Are you Melanie Paschiutto?" Chloe asked.

"Yes, that's me." She eyed them both with skepticism. Chloe watched the woman's reaction, fairly certain that was a degree of distrust in her gaze.

"Do you have a moment to talk?" Chloe asked. She showed her ID, again looking at Melanie's reaction. She was showing very little, as if she was moderately disinterested in the entire exchange.

"FBI? What's going on?"

"We're investigating the murder of Lauren Hilyard," she said. Then, stretching the truth quite a bit, she added: "We're meeting up with everyone that attended the high school reunion two weeks ago, hoping to get some answers."

She thought she saw the slightest reaction in Melanie's expression. Alarm? Caution? For a moment, she looked like a woman who had kicked over an old log and discovered a snake.

"That's fine," she said. "But I'd rather be quick about it. My daughter and I are getting ready for church."

"Of course," Chloe said as Melanie invited them in. "Hopefully, it will only take a second."

Before Melanie had even closed the door behind them, she started talking. And she spoke quickly, making it clear that she was in a hurry and wanted them out of her house as soon as possible.

"So what kind of stuff are you looking for?" she asked.

"Well, we're just getting reports from everyone in attendance, trying to find out if there was anything they saw or heard that night that might lend a clue towards why someone might want Lauren murdered."

The three of them were standing in the foyer. Apparently, Melanie was not going to invite them inside. Chloe took in the layout of the house; living room to the right, small dining room off of that, a hallway directly ahead. Melanie's daughter was currently in that hallway, skipping into the bathroom at the end of it.

"I don't recall all that much," she said. "Lauren was … well, she was not particularly nice to me in high school. So honestly, I didn't pay much attention to her at the reunion."

Lie number one, Chloe thought.

"Was there a group you stayed with that night? Anyone you might have had a conversation with?"

"No. I sort of wandered from group to group. Lots of small conversations but nothing really meaningful."

Lie number two. Why would she be lying about such a thing?

"Ms. Paschiutto, what are your memories of Lauren Hilyard in high school? How would you define her?"

Melanie took a moment before she answered. As she did, her daughter started to hum a song behind her. She was brushing her teeth in the bathroom, keeping an eye on what was transpiring in the foyer.

"She was deplorable," Melanie said. She said it with venom in her voice, as if she were talking about some inhumane crime rather than another human being. "I daresay she was evil. Just mean to everyone that didn't fit within her little circle. She … she was the type of girl I avoided at all costs."

She said all of this with a weird look of pride on her face. But that look of caution remained on her face.

"Do you think she was so mean-spirited in high school that it might have given someone reason to kill her ten years later?" Chloe asked. "Perhaps over something sparked at the reunion?"

If she had looked like a woman who had discovered a snake under a log moments ago, she now looked as if that snake had struck out at her. Her eyes went wide for a moment and she actually took a step back. She quickly regained her composure, though. Still, that split second was all Chloe had been looking for.

"I don't know. It's hard to imagine that but … well, then again, she did some pretty vile things in school."

"Like what?"

Melanie thought for a moment and then shook her head. I'm really quite sorry," she said. "But we're already running behind. I like to get Aubrey to Sunday school right when it starts at eight thirty and we're already running a little behind."

"Sure, sure," Chloe said.

"Would you call us if you think of anything else?" Rhodes asked, handing Melanie one of her business cards.

"Of course," Melanie said, the relief on her face as clear as a vibrant painting.

"Mrs. Paschiutto, I do apologize," Chloe said. "I know this seems unprofessional, but do you think I could use your restroom?"

Still overcome with relief, Melanie thought nothing of it. "No problem," she said. "Right down the hallway there and … Aubrey! Can you hop out of there for a second so this nice lady can use the restroom?"

Aubrey did as instructed. She smiled at Chloe as she dutifully stepped out of the bathroom.

"Thanks so much," Chloe said.

As she started for the restroom, directly ahead in her line of sight, she hoped that Rhodes picked up on what she was doing. Within a few seconds, it was clear that she had. Rhodes started speaking softly to Melanie—small talk, about how nice and quiet it must be out here among all of the forest.

Chloe made it to the bathroom and turned to see that Rhodes had positioned herself so that Melanie's back was turned to Chloe. As for Aubrey, she had disappeared elsewhere in the house, heading toward the kitchen.

Chloe quickly ducked into the living room area. She looked around but found the place absolutely tidy and well kept. A bible and a devotional sat on the small coffee table and a stack of kids' movies sat in a neat stack on top of the old television. She hurried out of there and went back into the hallway. When she did, she nearly collided with Aubrey. The girl waved at her and when she did, Chloe waved back. It was clear the little girl wasn't much of a talker, so Chloe risked seeming rude. She walked right past her and into the first doorway she came to along the hall.

She walked into what was obviously Melanie's bedroom. It was not nearly as clean as the living room. There were dirty clothes strewn here and there and a few books scattered on the floor. She started for the nightstand to see if there was anything to find there. It was then, passing by the books, that she stopped.

She saw the cover of one of the books on the floor. It was tattered and had clearly been used quite a bit. It was a slim book with a glossy cover. The title read: **Barnes Point High School 2009-2010.**

Sure… there was a chance that it was left over from a nostalgic trip down memory lane from having attended the reunion. Still, it seemed ominous to Chloe. She picked it up from the floor and opened it up. The first thing she noticed was that hardly anyone had signed Melanie's yearbook. There were only a handful of autographs and messages in the inside cover and most of those were from teachers.

She quickly flipped through the book, finding the senior class. She located Lauren Hilyard's photo and was not at all surprised to find devil horns and inked fire coming off of her head. Over by the listing of her name, the word **bitch** had been scrawled. She flipped through the remainder of the book and saw Lauren again, posed with a boy under a picture labeled *Most Popular.* In the picture, Lauren's eyes had been X'ed over repeatedly, so much that there were little rips in the paper. The words **PRETTY IDIOT** were scrawled across her shirt in black marker.

As she reached the end of the book, something fell out of the back. It fluttered to the floor, landing at Chloe's feet. It was an envelope, unsealed, stuffed with newspaper clippings. Chloe looked through them and found four clippings. They were all from the local paper and all about Lauren's murder.

A chill crept down Chloe's spine as she looked to the floor and saw a few more books. There were a couple of hardback novels, but she also saw two more yearbooks, both from the previous years at Barnes Point High. She found Lauren's pictures in all of them. Like the senior yearbook, all of Lauren's pictures had been defaced. In the junior yearbook, every mention or picture of Lauren had been blocked out with a steady stream of the same word: *die, die, die, die, die ...*

She carried the books and newspaper clippings out of the bedroom and walked back down the hallway. Rhodes spotted her and Melanie's gaze followed. When she saw the yearbooks in her hand, Melanie's face went incredibly pale. For a moment, Chloe feared the woman was about to get sick.

"You went into my room," she said flatly.

"I did. And some of the things in these yearbooks ... they're not exactly becoming of a lady that is getting dressed for church."

"You invaded my privacy ..." Melanie said. Her eyes darted back and forth and her lips started to tremble as she tried to think of something else to say.

"Ms. Paschiutto ... we saw video footage of the reunion," Chloe said. "You stared down Lauren Hilyard almost the entire time. And based on information we've gathered recently, we understand that she practically victimized you in high school ... bullied you."

"She did. And… but…"

"It hurts to be left out," Chloe said. "It hurts even more when those that are leaving you out attack you for not being like them. It sucks to not be included… to be looked over and ignored, right?"

Melanie made a strange movement with her head then, as if she were trying to nod and shake it in a *no* gesture all at the same time. Tears started to pour from her eyes. Coupled with the angry sneer that slowly started to creep across her mouth, it was rather terrifying.

"Always looked over," she said in a hiss. "By Lauren Hilyard and her whore friends. By my own husband when he slept with every other woman in town and left me to raise this poor little girl on my own. A darling little girl that is suffering the same things I went through. Bullied and ignored. Some little shit put chocolate pudding on her cafeteria chair the other day. There's a little boy that pinches her and…"

"Ms. Paschiutto," Rhodes said slowly, calmly, "is there something you need to tell us?"

She started to breathe harder now, backing up against the wall. "It never ends," she said. "It stays in your head and it ruins your life and that bitch had the perfect life. Looks, money, a gorgeous husband that actually loved her, friends… and not a single regret about the menace she was in high school…"

Chloe felt herself tensing. Watching and listening to Melanie Paschiutto in that moment was like standing in front of a tea kettle, waiting for it to boil. Only she felt that something much worse than hot water would come out.

"Ms. Paschiutto, you can—"

"She deserved it! She deserved it and it felt… ah, God help me…"

She let out a wail as she pushed herself hard off of the wall. She came at Chloe quickly, flailing her arms as if she were being attacked by bees. She only got one swat in, trying to free the yearbooks from Chloe's hands. One of them fell to the floor but by the time she tried to swat again, Rhodes caught her flailing arm and pinned it behind her back.

Chloe stepped in to help but realized that Rhodes had it covered. When Melanie was pressed against the wall, she gave up. She sagged and started to weep as Rhodes applied the handcuffs.

A sound from behind her caused Chloe to turn. The little girl—Aubrey Paschiutto—was standing there, a hand over her mouth. It occurred to Chloe that the look on her face was more than one of bewilderment. Aubrey was recognizing something, making some connection that perhaps her little mind wasn't quite ready to handle.

"Did the prayers not work?" Aubrey asked. Her voice was tiny and constrained. She might have been on the verge of crying.

"What do you mean, sweetie?" Chloe asked.

"Don't you talk to her!" Melanie wailed. "Don't you *dare* ..."

"Mom said she'd done something ... something bad. A really bad sin. We prayed that God would forgive her. But ... you're here for her, so I think the prayers didn't work."

Chloe had no idea how to respond to her. She placed her hand on Aubrey's shoulder and led her into the kitchen, away from the sight of her mother in handcuffs.

"Was she bad?" Aubrey asked. "Was she right? She did a very bad thing?"

"Your mom made a very bad choice," Chloe said. She wanted to say something else but couldn't find the words to explain it to such a young girl.

Instead, she pulled out her cell phone and dialed up Sheriff Jenkins as Melanie Paschiutto continued to wail and scream from the foyer.

Chapter Twenty Eight

Everything after that happened in what felt like a whirlwind. Between finalizing things with Jenkins in Barnes Point and then making it back to DC, Chloe realized that she was both mentally and physically exhausted. The usual rush of adrenaline she felt after making a connection that closed a case wasn't there; it was replaced by uncertainty and a feeling that, even though she wrapped the case, she had somehow come out on the losing end.

Maybe it was having lost Moulton. Or maybe it was knowing that because of her so-called good work, she had left a daughter without a mother… something she knew far too much about.

Rhodes had volunteered to drive, apparently seeing the disconnected state Chloe was in. She nodded off for about ten minutes, waking up and not fully gathering where she was for a moment.

"You okay?" Rhodes asked her.

Chloe nodded. "Yeah. It's just this strange feeling of…"

Her phone rang, cutting her off. Before she grabbed it, she said a little prayer that it might be Moulton with some good news. But it was Johnson's name that was on the display. She almost ignored it but didn't see the point.

"Fine here."

"Agent Fine, I wanted you to know that I just got off of the phone with Sheriff Jenkins. It seems you left some things out of your informal debrief with me when you called earlier."

"I really don't think I did," she said. "I'll write it all up when I get home, but—"

"You're far too modest, Fine. Take the credit when it's due. He told me all about how you worked with a local DJ and video guy, looking through footage from the high school reunion. He also noted how you did this very late at night, rather than waiting. If he were single and a little younger, I'd daresay Jenkins might have a thing for you. He's over the moon about the way you handled yourself."

"Thank you, sir," Chloe said, suddenly not feeling quite as tired.

"Before you start the workday tomorrow, come by my office for a meeting with Garcia and me. We'd like to go over the case with you and talk about your future."

They set up a time for the meeting before Chloe ended the call. Rhodes looked over to her but said nothing. She, too, was tired. And if she was anything like Chloe, maybe she was also hung up on how they had nearly walked away from the case after taking in Jason Morton, so sure he had been the killer.

But even despite that corrected mistake, it was nothing compared to how Chloe was feeling about poor little Aubrey Paschiutto and how the outcome of this case would negatively impact her life.

"Chloe?"

Chloe opened her eyes, her heart pounding. Someone had said her name; someone was there with her. She sat up quickly, her breaths coming rapidly. Slowly, she began to understand that she had been having a dream. Nothing bad at all but certainly not a dream filled with rainbows and sunshine.

She looked toward the door to her bedroom and saw Danielle standing there. For a dizzying moment, Chloe thought she could also see Aubrey Paschiutto in the darkness. But it was just a play of shadows along the wall.

"Sorry to wake you," Danielle said. "But you sounded distressed. I know it was just a dream, but still … yikes. You sounded bad."

Chloe took a deep breath and let it out. She looked to her bedside table and saw that it was 5:35. "Did I wake you up?" Chloe asked.

"Not exactly. I haven't slept well for the last few days. Chloe … there's something on my mind and I think I need to share it with you."

"Now? At five thirty in the morning?"

"Yeah. I think so."

Chloe wiped the last remnants of the dream from her memory—a dream where Aubrey had been there every step of the way, walking right beside her as they took her mother into custody… as they showed Melanie the pictures of the Lauren Hilyard's murder scene. Of course, it had not happened like that. The Department of Social Services had come and sat with Aubrey until a next of kin could come and stay with her. It had been her uncle and as far as Chloe knew, she had remained with him in the three days that had passed since then.

"Okay," Chloe said. "Can you put the coffee on and give me a chance to get dressed?"

"Sure. But dress for a car ride. I'd like to take you somewhere if you don't mind."

"Danielle, what…"

But Danielle had already left the doorway and was headed elsewhere in the apartment. Chloe rolled out of bed and walked to the bathroom, where she threw some water in her face and brushed her teeth. While brushing, she tried to understand why those awkward fifteen minutes with Aubrey Paschiutto had affected her so much. Was it because they had arrested her mother in front of her? Was it because Melanie had insinuated that Aubrey had also been the victim of bullying even at an early age? Or was it because Aubrey had told them that her mother had confided in her, telling her that they needed to pray for forgiveness for the very thing she had done?

She wasn't sure. But she was very afraid that Aubrey's little face would be haunting her for a great deal of her life.

Chloe got dressed and walked out into the kitchen to the smell of brewing coffee. Danielle had also popped a few bagels into the toaster. She was spreading cream cheese on them as Chloe sat down at the bar.

"How far are we driving?" she asked.

"Not far. Reston."

"You want me with you to go back to your apartment?" Chloe asked.

"Something like that."

They gathered up their coffee and bagels and then headed out just twenty minutes after Chloe had gotten out of bed. They barely got ahead of Wednesday morning commuter traffic as they headed south into Virginia.

"That case really got to you, huh?" Danielle asked. She was driving, very focused on the road. She was tense, sitting upright as if awaiting some disaster.

"The case didn't. Just… the way it ended. Most cases don't end with the huge shootouts or chases like they show on TV They just… *happen.* And when it's over, you wonder what the big deal was about. But this time… this woman's daughter. The poor thing. I just don't even know how to process what her life will be like now."

What she didn't say but was thinking, was: *The poor girl was already being teased; it's only going to get worse as she gets older and kids find out that her mother snapped and brutally murdered someone.*

They arrived in front of Danielle's apartment just after seven. Chloe noticed that Danielle was looking around right away, perhaps for any sign of Sam. But the streets were mostly quiet, disrupted by only a few people heading out for work and an older woman walking her dog.

They made their way up to Danielle's apartment. The closer they got to it, the slower Danielle seemed to move.

"I don't think he'll show up again," Chloe said, easily recalling her encounter with Sam several days ago.

"I know. But… he was right here, at this door, hammering on it like he was going to kill me." She practically jabbed her key into the lock, as if stabbing it, and opened the door.

"So what do you need to get?" Chloe asked.

"Nothing. But I need to show you something. And I'll apologize beforehand. I should have showed it to you a long time ago. But… I'm ashamed to say that I just didn't want to."

"Okay, you know how to build up suspense…"

"Hold on."

She walked to her bedroom as Chloe sat down on the couch. She listened to Danielle moving around in the room, every movement made with great care. Whatever she was getting, she was not happy about it.

The tension in her posture during the drive, her build-up of small talk before getting it… she was nervous as hell.

She came back into the room with a book in her hand. It looked like a basic notebook, one of the cheap-looking standard sized ones with the black and white marbled print on the cover. Danielle sat down on the couch and handed the notebook over to Chloe.

"What's this?" Chloe asked.

Danielle sighed, unable to look Chloe in the eye when she answered. "It's Mom's journal."

For a second, Chloe felt as if someone had dropped a bomb rather than a book in her lap. She gripped it and picked it up, hesitant to open it. Of course, she was unable to help herself. She looked at the pages, all covered in her mother's slanted handwriting.

"How long have you had it?" Chloe asked.

"The entire time," Danielle said, wiping a tear away. "Remember when the police asked us later on if there was anything back at the house we needed? I told them to bring it to me. I knew where she kept it because I saw her putting it away one day…"

"You've had it since she died?" Chloe asked accusingly.

"I have. And like I said… I'm more sorry than you can imagine. I just… I needed something that belonged to her. And I didn't want to share it."

Honestly, Chloe knew she should be furious. But the moment in and of itself was heart-breaking. And besides that… she now had this huge piece of her mother within her reach. She thumbed through the pages and then looked at Danielle.

"And why are you showing me now?"

"When you started working towards trying to free Dad about a year ago, I almost showed it to you then. But I figured it would just make you mad. But now that he's out of prison and trying to step back into our lives like nothing happened, I thought you needed to see it."

Chloe opened it to the first page and started reading, scanning the page quickly. It felt like a private moment, and she was very aware of Danielle sitting directly beside her.

"Chloe, before you read it all, there's something you need to know. I know you never truly understood why I hate him so much. One of the reasons is easy enough to admit now that you have that journal in your hands. There was one night about a year before she died … I had a nightmare and snuck into their room. I was going to just crawl up in bed with them and nestle in, you know? But I got into the door and he was strangling her. They were standing up and he had this look in his eyes … this crazy look that, at the time, I thought made him look like a monster. And Mom's eyes were big and wide, too. She was terrified. But she saw me over his shoulder and Dad saw her looking that way. He saw me there and dropped her right away. To this day, I don't know what happened between them to make him snap like that. And neither of them pulled me to the side to talk about it. Not ever. They both just pretended that it never happened."

Chloe found herself wanting to argue against this … wanting to suggest that maybe she was still half asleep and had misunderstood what she had seen. But even in her head, Chloe realized how naïve that sounded. And the way Danielle was trembling as she told the story wasn't fake or rehearsed. It was tearing her apart to relive it.

More than that, it brought to mind the feeling of a memory that had tried to present itself earlier. An idea that there was something from their past that she was forgetting—some reason that their father had always treated Danielle different. Had it maybe been this event that had caused it?

"You said 'one of the reasons,'" Chloe said. "Are there more?"

Danielle nodded and pointed to the journal. "Yes. And they're all in there." She stood up and looked back toward her room. "I'm going to pack another bag or two for what I hope is just a temporary stay at your place. Read it. And maybe within a few pages, you'll understand even more why I never showed it to you."

Danielle walked back into her bedroom and closed the door. Chloe settled down with the notebook, her finger shaking as she opened it up again and started to read. Her mother's handwriting was very legible and neat. But that charming detail was quickly obliterated by the contents of the journal.

Within just a few lines, Chloe felt herself wanting to cry. A few more lines in, she wanted to visit her father and do to him what she had done to Sam several days ago—and maybe even worse.

It's not even sex to him anymore, but some way to control and punish me. He doesn't enjoy it unless he's hurting me.

I gained about seven pounds over the holidays and he's been calling me fat-ass for the last week. Says I look disgusting to him. Says my body has "gone to hell" ever since we had kids.

I don't think he meant to hit me the first time. I really do think he just lost control for a moment. But the second and third were intentional. I had to put a lot of makeup on this morning. Chloe even commented on it, asking if I forgot to blend it in.

Chloe was gripping the edges of the notebook tight, her teeth clenched together and her heart rampaging like a penned bull in her chest. But she could not stop reading.

I'm fairly certain he's cheating on me. He comes home smelling like perfume, but just barely ... like he's tried his best to wash it off. And when I try to sleep with him, he says he's too tired or that I'm not looking good and not turning him on. He's threatened to leave me if I don't lose weight. He's started to violently grab my breasts and the tiny little love handles I have, reminding me of how I used to look.

He hit me again today and I blacked out for a while. He apologized later and then went out. When he came back, he smelled like beer and that same perfume.

He strangled me tonight. We were arguing about money and how the girls are doing in school. I pushed up against him, arguing my point, and he slapped me in the face. Before I knew what had happened, he pushed me against the wall and strangled me. He said if I ever disrespected him again, he'd kill me. He said he had something better lined up, some better woman and some better life and all I needed to do was give him a reason to take me out of the picture.

She was only nine pages in by that point, but Chloe started to feel sick to her stomach. She tossed the book on Danielle's table and tried to stand. But her legs were wobbling. Her entire body felt out of balance as something inside of her snapped. Some foreign rage erupted a sob out of her that was part sorrow and part anger.

Slowly, Danielle opened the bedroom door and peered in at her. "You okay?"

"No," she said in a groan of rage. "Danielle… you should have showed me this sooner."

"I know. I'm sorry and—"

"I helped free him and… he…"

"I know," Danielle said.

Chloe finally managed to get to her feet. She picked the notebook back up and held it gently, as if it might be poisonous.

"I was wrong from the start," Chloe said. "My doubts… my hopes that he was a good man. Everything…"

It all settled into her head then. The logic and truth of it. A truth she had not only denied most of her life but one she had recently worked to falsify. As it settled on her, she spoke it into being, made herself listen to the words coming out of her own mouth.

"He did it," she said. Her tone was stern and confident and barbed with anger. "It was him all along. He killed our mother."

With that stark realization, another one came to her. This one helped to calm her, to even make her wonder if his freedom might play in her favor.

And now the bastard is out of prison. So if I go after him, he won't have the penal system or a jail cell to protect him.

Now Available!

SILENT NEIGHBOR
(A Chloe Fine Psychological Suspense Mystery—Book 4)

"A masterpiece of thriller and mystery. Blake Pierce did a magnificent job developing characters with a psychological side so well described that we feel inside their minds, follow their fears and cheer for their success. Full of twists, this book will keep you awake until the turn of the last page."

—Books and Movie Reviews, Roberto Mattos (re Once Gone)

SILENT NEIGHBOR (A Chloe Fine Mystery) is book #4 in a new psychological suspense series by bestselling author Blake Pierce, whose #1 bestseller Once Gone (Book #1) (a free download) has over 1,000 five-star reviews.

When a flashy, new neighbor flaunts her wealth in a suburban town, it isn't long before she's found murdered. Did her flaunting ways upset her envious neighbors?

Or was there a deeper secret to her husband's fortune?

FBI VICAP Special Agent Chloe Fine, 27, finds herself immersed in a small-town world of lies, cliques, gossip and betrayal as she tries to separate truth from lies.

But what is the real truth?

And can she solve it while also dealing with the release of her troubled father from jail, and the spiraling down of her troubled sister?

An emotionally wrought psychological suspense with layered characters, small-town ambiance and heart-pounding suspense, THE SILENT NEIGHBOR is book #4 in a riveting new series that will leave you turning pages late into the night.

Book #5 in the CHLOE FINE series is also now available!

SILENT NEIGHBOR
(A Chloe Fine Psychological Suspense Mystery—Book 4)

Did you know that I've written multiple novels in the mystery genre? If you haven't read all my series, click the image below to download a series starter!

Made in United States
Orlando, FL
18 February 2023

30104571R10355